THE FIREBLOOD'S CHOICE
By Kathe Todd

I0564583

Chapter 1: Anja

Bernadette and Andrion continued up the road, little more than a dirt track, as morning gave way to early afternoon. They had been trying to find the path to a mountaintop installation where, according to the broadside she had gotten from the Eorl of Westmarch, a dragon had taken up residence and was menacing the countryside. Above a hill that obscured the view ahead, around the next bend, Bernadette spotted black smoke rising. "Is there a town near here?" she asked Andrion. Nothing was showing on her magic map, though sometimes villages would not appear on it until you had either walked right into them or been sent on a quest to their locations.

"No, there's not much of *anything* up this way," Andrion replied. In his decade of roaming the province, he had been to most places that were worth visiting. As they continued up the road, they soon realized there *was* no town – only an isolated farmstead. Or what was left of it. A wheat field to their left smoldered, nothing but blackened stubble. The slightly charred carcass of a cow lay, partially eaten, in a paddock that had had its fence smashed to the ground on two sides. Most of the smoke was coming from a small house, now partially collapsed and open to the sky.

"This has to be the work of that dragon," Bernadette said quietly, her voice laced with suppressed anger. A Norseman, wood axe in his hand, lay crumpled face up on the front walk. His clothing and face were blackened. Picking her way gingerly inside the remains of the house, Bernadette looked around. The corpse of a Norsewoman lay face down on the floor, blackened like the man who had probably been her husband. And protruding from beneath a fallen roof beam, Bernadette could see a pair of pathetic little feet.

Fury filled her heart. A child, slaughtered with her family, and for what? A few mouthfuls of beef? But just then, she thought she detected some slight movement of those feet. "Andrion!" she cried, moving to the spot in an instant. "Help me!" He lent his prodigious strength, and between the two of them they were able to pull the beam away to reveal the still, pale form of a little girl no more than five years old. There was a purple weal across her forehead, and she remained unconscious. But it appeared that she was breathing slightly.

Bernadette knelt beside the tiny form, feeling for a pulse. There was one, though it was faint. Yanking her map out of her shirt, one arm wrapped around the child, she wished them all back to the Bathing Maiden. Andrion looked around, slightly disconcerted. Usually Berni gave him some warning before sending them hopping around the province.

Bernadette carried the little girl, cradling her tenderly in her arms, up across the deck and through the front doors to the main floor of the Maiden. Then she hurried up a short flight of stairs to one of the mezzanine's beds and laid the child down, carefully, before applying a healing spell to her patient. The girl's injuries seemed to melt away and her breathing became deeper and more regular, but she did not wake.

Bernadette peered at her anxiously. The child was pale of skin, with shoulder-length hair a slightly darker shade of auburn than Bernadette's own. Andrion stood at the foot of the bed, watching as Berni mothered the little girl. It filled him with a curious sense of longing. This side of his lover was rarely revealed, but it made him think of an impossible dream he sometimes entertained, that someday they might be married and have a family together. It was hard to imagine The Fireblood doing domestic chores, though!

As Bernadette sat there at the bedside holding the girl's hand and watching her, the little one's eyelids fluttered and she opened eyes that were a warm shade of brown – like Andrion's own. Should he and Berni ever have a daughter, he realized, she might look just like that. It was a riveting thought.

The girl blinked in confusion, then struggled into a sitting position, gazing owl-eyed at Bernadette. "Are you... are you my mother?" she asked tentatively. The blow to her head, or perhaps the trauma of the dragon attack, seemed to have erased her memory. Andrion realized now why Berni had waited until they had brought the girl here before healing her. What would it be like to awaken in the destroyed remains of your home, surrounded by the charred corpses of your loved ones?

Bernadette answered her thoughtfully. "No... I'm your Aunt Berni."

"Aunt Berni? ... Where's my mother?"

Bernadette changed the subject by asking a question: "What's your name, little one?" The girl's face took on a look of surprise, followed by consternation.

"I don't know." It was as Bernadette had feared. Not only had the memory of the recent cataclysmic events been erased from the girl's mind, she had lost her identity as well. But since she was now a homeless orphan, perhaps this was a blessing in disguise.

"If you don't mind," Bernadette told her, "I think I'll call you Anja."

The girl considered that for a moment. It sounded all right. "All right Aunt Berni, I can be Anja if you want." Bernadette spontaneously gathered the girl up in her arms and gave her a gentle hug, lightly kissing the top of her head.

"Good! Anja, this is the Bathing Maiden inn and it's going to be your home for a while. This man here is Uncle Andrion, and we have some other aunts and uncles for you to meet later. In the meantime, would you like something to eat?"

Anja took all of this in seriously, still trying to reconcile herself to the new information she was being given. And still missing the memories of her past, short as it had been. She felt as if she *should* have a mother and a father and a home that was not here, but all that was a blank – and in the way of young children, she was willing to let it pass. The idea of food drove all other considerations out of her mind.

Anja gave Bernadette a radiant smile and said, "Yes, please!" Bernadette took her by the hand and walked her down past the central bathing pool and over to the bar. She was glad that at the moment there were no long-donged naked men hanging around in it. The people of Agena in general were somewhat casual about nudity, but who knew what this girl's upbringing had been? She might well never have seen any adults in her life beyond her parents and the odd peddler or other traveler.

Bernadette boosted Anja up onto a stool at the bar, which the fire-haired youngster enjoyed quite a lot. It was fun to be perched up high like this, and even more fun to have "Uncle Lev" give her a roasted nut confection to eat. The Maiden didn't stock any milk, so she had a glass of water to wash it down with. Bernadette had some experience with kids, having a younger brother and sister at home in Auverne, and she asked Lev to get some goat's milk as soon as possible. It was supposed to be better for children than cow's milk.

While Anja ate her treat, Bernadette spoke quietly with Andrion. "We need to go kill that scaly son of a bitch dragon," she said. "I'll get Lifa to look after Anja and keep her entertained while we're figuring out what we're going to do about finding her a new home."

He looked thoughtful. "Yeah, I suppose it would be insane to just have her live here with us…"

She smiled. "Can you imagine the effect a five-year-old would have on the usual Maiden guests? No, she needs a nice home, in a town where there are other children, somebody to look after her all the time, and not quite so many naked adults running around."

"But, *Lifa?*" Andrion asked. Bernadette's mouth quirked.

"I know, she doesn't seem like the kind of person who will get along with children. But who else have we got? Erik? She's always been a dutiful body servant, and now she's just going to get a new duty. I'll give her some regular clothes so she won't be so intimidating." As Andrion stayed at the bar with Anja, Bernadette went and found some clothing in an appropriate size for the voluptuous body servant. She gave the dress and slippers to Lifa, and explained what she needed.

Bernadette was surprised at Lifa's reaction. She had expected the usual stiff, "As my warden commands" response, but Lifa's eyes actually sparkled and the faintest of smiles hovered about her lips as she followed Bernadette back to the common room and was introduced to Anja. "Hello Anja," she said. "I'm your Aunt Lifa, and I'll be staying with you while Aunt Berni and Uncle Andrion are gone. I'm sure we'll have lots of fun together. Would you like that?"

Anja examined her solemnly, then smiled and said, "You're pretty! Okay…" Bernadette and Andrion watched in bemused astonishment as a broad smile spread across Lifa's lovely features and she reached to give Anja a little hug.

Bernadette exchanged glances with Andrion and mouthed, "Who knew?" with a shrug and a smile. Before they departed on their expedition, Anja insisted on giving each of them a hug and a kiss.

"Bye bye!" she cried, as they took their leave.

Chapter 2: Seeking Home

Bernadette and Andrion had to fast-travel to the most recently-visited spot that appeared on the map, before resuming their search for a path leading up to the dragon's mountaintop lair. They passed the forlorn, ruined farmstead where Anja had been born, then continued on their way further along the trail. For a change some conversation was possible, as the wildlife of Iscandia was on a short vacation from its usual campaign of non-stop homicide.

"I think she's going to do fine with Lifa," Bernadette told Andrion. "Did you see that grin? That's the first time Lifa has cracked a smile since I've known her... though she *did* almost smile when I introduced her to Erik."

Andrion paused as he was walking beside her and said, surprised, "*You* introduced her to Erik?" She smiled at him, a bit ruefully.

"I didn't want him to get lonely while I was gone with you. And I saw he had an amulet like mine, so I figured he was used to... um, getting busy a lot."

They continued walking. Her train of thought leading her on, Bernadette asked Andrion "How come *you* don't have one of these amulets? Aren't they, like, standard issue for the Maiden guys or something?" Andrion's light tan skin didn't turn pink in quite the spectacular way that Berni's (or Erik's) did, but he still managed to color.

"I didn't usually do bed-warmer duty," he replied a little stiffly. "I was there more to make the customers feel at home, be available as a battle companion, stuff like that. We're not *obligated* to sleep with the customers unless we want to. When I told you that taking you to bed wasn't part of my job duties, I wasn't kidding. Of course if I hadn't seen that you had an amulet of your own, I could have gotten one before we..."

Now it was Bernadette's turn to pause. She spun to face Andrion and closed with him to give him an affectionate hug and a tender kiss, looking into his eyes with love. It had been months since her misunderstanding of that circumstance had nearly led to her cutting him loose, and it was only now that she fully realized that his hasty explanation at that time was true. Not that it mattered anymore.

Whatever he may have done as an employee of the Maiden before they met, he was hers now – body and soul.

They resumed walking. Changing the subject, Bernadette said "I'd like it if Anja could be in a family situation with brothers and sisters, and a real home. But for now, I think Lifa will make a good nanny until we can find a place for her to live permanently." Andrion wondered if he dared speak. But this seemed as if it might be the best opportunity he was going to get for a while.

"What if… You know, we could buy a house in Waterdon. There's one available, right near the main gates. Then maybe you and I could…"

She interrupted him. "Whoa, *whoa*! Don't get carried away, lover. I'm barely 23. I *would* like to settle down and raise kids someday, but I'm not through having adventures yet!" Seeing how crushed he looked, she took him in her arms again. The longer they were together, the easier she was finding it to tell him what was in her heart. "I love you, Andrion. As much as I've ever loved anyone, maybe more. But I still want to have some fun before I get tied down with a lot of responsibilities. Can you wait for me?" She peered into his face with an appeal that would have melted anyone's heart.

He held her at arm's length, gazing into her eyes with an intensity of love and joy that almost knocked her off her feet. "Whatever you want, Berni. As long as we can be together like this sometimes. But I'll hope for more, some day." It wasn't easy getting into a clinch in full armor, hung about with deadly weapons. But they managed it. After a deep and passionate kiss, they drew apart again.

Breaking the intensity of the mood, Bernadette said "let's go kill that damned dragon!" and set off up a likely-looking trail that appeared to lead toward the spot on the map where they hoped they could find the beast that had killed Anja's family.

In a little while the trail began climbing steeply, then broadened and swung past a short stone tower, before it funneled into a semicircular area backed by a Spell Wall. The dragon they'd been hunting was sitting atop the wall, hunched over it like a vulture awaiting the demise of a diseased cow. Bernadette and Andrion approached stealthily, then blasted it simultaneously with a surprise attack that sent it flapping off, roaring its anger and defiance.

Bernadette's latest bow was more powerful than ever. With that and the Dragonfall spell, which had proven to be well worth the trouble it had taken her to learn it, she was bad news for any *drache* that might be inclined to cause trouble for the human inhabitants of Iscandia. And though he had already had devastating skills in battle magic when they met, Andrion's time spent acting as Bernadette's companion and protector on her many adventures had improved those skills until he was a force to be reckoned with.

Suffice it to say, *this* murderous beast did not stay airborne long. Nor was it many moments after Bernadette's spell brought it down, before its flesh had vanished – and its soul had gone to feed her essential supply of mana.

As The Fireblood Bernadette was said to have the soul of a dragon. Musing on this, Andrion reflected that some of Berni's appetites *did* seem a bit draconian. But what drew him to her were her irrepressible energy, her human warmth, and her occasional vulnerability. Among other things…

He sometimes felt as if he simultaneously wanted to hold her and protect her, exult in battle at her side, make love to her until all the strength in his body was gone… and tell her to shut the hell up and let him get some sleep, when she would arise at dawn and begin prodding him to get up as well. Before her arrival, he'd been able to sleep as late as he wanted to almost all of the time. Now, he occasionally found himself getting up early even when she was not around.

Bernadette had her own perspective on her supposed draconian nature. She had to respect the *drachen*. They were ancient beings of immense power and intelligence, with knowledge no human still living held. Despite her sometimes impulsive nature she valued knowledge, and one of the things that drew her to Andrion was his love of scholarship and his fund of lore. But though there some few of the *drachen* whom she liked and valued as friends (notably Ehrgeizig, who had aided her in defeating Tarragin; and Sneyagflug, who had promised to come to her aid if called), most of them seemed inimical to human life and it was her mission, like that of the Guardians, to wipe them out or at least beat them back so that they were not a threat. Let them fly somewhere else, and she would be happy to leave them in peace.

After claiming this one's soul, Bernadette examined the items left behind on the ground beneath the bare skeleton. She had not yet encountered any new dragon spells in the months since she and Andrion had gathered all of them that were available at the Edelmied, the gem forge located in the upper levels of the subterranean ancient Norse stronghold Faastenberg. But she found a few spell stones among other loot – all of them ones she already carried within her. They were fabulously rare and extremely valuable, and had contributed considerably to her coffers in the months since Tarragin's defeat.

Bernadette turned smiling to Andrion. She had been considering what he'd said earlier, despite her rebuff, and had reached a decision. "I think you're right," she said. "We *should* buy that place in Waterdon. I've got gold coming out my ears now – we might as well spend some of it!" He smiled back at her, trying to hide the way in which her words caused his heart to soar. Did I just get my foot in the door? Was that the first pebble falling from the dam?

They fast-travelled straight to Wyrmshalla. When Berni seized on an idea, she would leap in with both feet. And in this case, it was all to the good. They found the local time to be somewhere around mid-afternoon. Bernadette had not yet completely figured out what to expect, when using her magic map. They marched right in through the front doors, she being currently in great favor throughout Iscandia – and here in Waterdon, especially.

Paolo Adelini, the balding and fastidious father of Bernadette's friend Alessia, was delighted to see her. She would like to purchase property in Waterdon? Excellent! A house was available now. Within a few minutes, Bernadette had purchased the small but conveniently-located Brightsgate Cottage, already furnished.

Chapter 3: And Finding It

Berni had been seized with the nesting instinct, it seemed to Andrion. This was a side of her he had not seen before, and one he had not so far discovered in himself. He had left Auverne some ten years previously and drifted around Iscandia like dandelion down, bouncing from one place to another with only his hunger for knowledge and the occasional liaison to pin him in any one spot for long. His two-year stint as an employee of the Bathing Maiden marked the longest time he had stayed put since leaving home all those years ago.

Andrion had been in love with other women a time or two, but none had ever reached down into his soul and laid claim to him as this one had. He regretted the difference in their ages, but still woke up every day delighted and disbelieving that this incredible young woman loved him and wanted to be with him. The fact that she also wanted to be with others, notably his friend Erik, was something he was willing to overlook.

After concluding their business with Paolo, Bernadette and Andrion made a beeline for their new acquisition. She felt that what was hers was theirs, as far as Andrion and Erik were concerned. They were her stalwart companions in all her enterprises, whether one or the other or both together, and she intended that they should all enjoy the spoils together, equally.

"Oh, this is cozy!" Bernadette exclaimed, delighted. Brightsgate Cottage was certainly not expansive, even by Waterdon standards. But it had a warm, homey glow that appealed to her in a way that ran deeper than she'd expected. Right inside the front door was a small round table with two chairs. Beyond that, a fire pit with a cooking spit took up most of the central floor area. Then there were a couple more comfortable chairs with a small table between them, and beyond those a larger table with benches, for eating. Storage cabinets and bookcases lined the walls. There was a little free space in one corner, but Bernadette had her own ideas for that.

Up a narrow staircase there was a loft area, with a small second bedroom off to the left and some loft furnishings. Circling around that area brought you to the master bedroom, a fairly spacious room with a double bed as well as plentiful storage for books, clothing, and other items. It even had another small table and chairs.

Bernadette stood in the doorway of that bedroom, taking it in for a moment. Though she had embraced the Maiden and its own master bedroom as her home, this was different. She was the Maiden's owner, yet it somehow belonged to the ages and the generations of firebloods who had owned it before her – and would, presumably, after she was gone. This house had existed before as well, true; but it was now all hers to do with as she would, to welcome in those she cared about most. No random strangers wandering through.

Bernadette turned to Andrion beside her. She gave him a look that immediately caused a stirring in his loins. "I think," she said almost shyly, "that this bed needs to be… inaugurated." He beamed at her.

"You are absolutely right, my love," he said. He reached for her and unfastened her armor. Tidily, proprietarily, she opened the chest at one side of the room and deposited her weapons and armor inside it. Then she helped him off with his and put it in the chest as well.

This felt so *right* to her. What is going on here, she wondered. It was as if one of the Great Secrets of the Universe had been revealed to her, or perhaps just one of the Great Truths about Bernadette Bouchard. Something deep within the human part of her soul was telling her she was home, and that this man by her side was one she wanted to share her life with for as long as they both drew breath. By the gods, she thought, taken aback. This is *it*. And I'm not *ready* for this to be it.

They were both now in their underwear, standing near the foot of the bed, and turned to clasp each other in their arms. The powerful emotions surging through Bernadette, both the realization that at some fundamental level all she wanted was a little house in Waterdon and Andrion at her side, along with her rejection of that as the period to the sentence of her life, had her feeling as if she were in a whirlwind. She loved him, she wanted him, she didn't know *what* she wanted! As ever, her personal motto of "don't worry about it right now" took hold – and she sank into his embrace with a surge of love that, at least for now, washed away her confusion.

It had been a couple of days since Andrion had last made love with Berni, and he was eager for that embrace. She was the most important thing in his life, now. No other woman had a prayer of attracting his attention, and the times when she was sleeping with Erik were times when he lay celibate, consoling himself with the knowledge that she loved him, that they would be together again before very much time had passed. Though the impact of Brightsgate Cottage had not hit him as hard emotionally as it had her, he had picked up *some* of what was going through her mind; and it spurred him to even more passion.

What Bernadette wanted right now above all else was to be engulfed in Andrion, here in the place she was already coming to think of as her new home – even though she was not actually planning to live here! How crazy was that? She didn't care. She washed over him like a warm wave; kissing, fondling, practically ripping his underclothes off in her eagerness to get skin-to-skin.

Andrion pulled her undershirt off over her head, claiming those marvelous breasts with his hands and his mouth. She had the most *perfect* breasts. They were so full, so shapely, so… irresistible. And he loved the way his hands and his mouth could bring those beguiling pink nipples to attention, inflaming her passions and taking her on the first steps toward what would, he knew, be an epic orgasm. His ability to carry his normally hard-headed lover beyond all power of rational thought was something he enjoyed immensely – even while he enjoyed their shared love of learning. It was as if their intellectual and physical/emotional bonds were residing in two different planes of existence.

Bernadette took her hands away from Andrion's body long enough to peel off her underdrawers and kick them away on the floor. The careful concern she'd shown with the neat placement of their armor and weapons was beyond her now. His hands, his lips set her on fire, and she could scarcely wait to feel that hard, throbbing cock within her. It pressed against her belly now, and she dragged him over toward the bed. Then falling onto it, she pulled him down on top of her and opened her legs like a flower to the sun, willing the hot rays of his searing passion to penetrate her to the core.

Andrion fell into her, this woman he loved, her warm depths opening to him while clasping him tight. Aah! It felt so good to be inside her, holding her close within his arms, his mouth on hers as his cock slid all the way in, then out and in again. Rising on his knees, he got a better angle and began moving more slowly, tantalizingly. His mind was a blaze of love and excitement, and beneath that a consciousness of his power over her – watching her face as he worked his magic with his cock.

Before long he began pumping faster, and soon Berni's face had gone pink, her head thrown back and her mouth in an "O," as her climax swept over her. This was always the crucial point for him. They were inextricably linked, and sometimes when she came he was unable to stop himself from coming along with her. But he wanted to give her more, wanted to send her to the moons, wanted to fuck her brains out. His male pride demanded it of him.

Bernadette had come to expect this, and it was one of the things she loved about him. He might not have the overwhelming, irresistible urgency that Erik sometimes brought to lovemaking; but he was always concerned about her and her pleasure. And with Andrion, she always felt that she was loved – not just the object of a particularly strong bout of lust. Now that she had come, she was feeling a little more in command; and she turned the tables on her lover. Using the surprising power of her muscular body, she flipped them over so she was now on top.

She looked down at him through slitted eyes. The look of love and ultimate pleasure in his warm brown eyes filled Bernadette with an answering love, and a determination to send *him* to the moons. She rode him for a while, letting her breasts bounce above him. She knew that he, like most men she'd met, found them fascinating. Then she pulled up off of him, his hard cock reddened and glistening with her juices, and knelt between his legs. She bent and, pressing on the outer sides of her breasts with her hands, engulfed his cock between them.

Oh! Andrion had not expected that. Berni's cool blue-gray eyes locked on his, her luscious mouth smiling at him with triumphant delight, and she enfolded him with those warm mounds of flesh. It was not the same as being within her cunt, not as hot and wet, but the excitement of watching and feeling the sensations as his cock thrust up between her bountiful breasts was an experience that was new to him. Then, breaking the gaze, she bent her neck to grasp the head of his cock as it emerged from between those globes of delight, immersing it in the warm fluids of her mouth!

Releasing her breasts, Bernadette bent to take Andrion inside her mouth – as fully as she was able to. She would never have been able to manage this with Erik – that man was simply too outsized for any human woman to take all the way in that way. If there was such a thing as Giant women, perhaps one of them would be able to suck Erik off as thoroughly as he deserved. These random thoughts, flitting through Bernadette's brain as she began giving Andrion the most thorough blow job she had yet attempted, led her to a mental picture of what Giant *men* must look like when aroused. Hah! Still, it added to her enthusiasm.

Gods, Berni was really going to work on him! She had teased and pleasured him with her mouth on many occasions, but Andrion had never had her using him in quite this way before. She looked so beautiful to him down there between his legs, her silken red hair glistening in the candlelight as her head bobbed, her hot, wet mouth taking him in far more deeply than he would have thought possible. The searing excitement of the situation took hold of him, and before he knew it he was rocketing toward a climax he was powerless to stop, his hands moving involuntarily to clutch her head as his cock strained upward, shooting his seed down her throat.

After Andrion's spasms finally ceased Bernadette looked up, a lazy smile painting her lips, as she swallowed and licked her lips. Then she climbed up his body to entwine herself in his arms, her head tucked under his chin. "I got you good," she murmured.

But Andrion was not entirely done with Berni. They talked quietly for a while, lying side by side on Brightsgate Cottage's master bed. Then, having gotten back some energy, he rolled her up again in his arms and made love to her long into the afternoon. By the time they had finished, utterly spent, it was still just light out. They were both feeling other hungers, so they got up and put on some robes before going downstairs. They had some foodstuffs in their packs, from which Andrion put together a meal of sorts for them. They ate from wooden plates, sitting before the fire.

Bernadette was in a pensive mood. She felt utterly relaxed and happy after being in Andrion's arms, coming over and over again. But as so often happened to her, especially if it was not bedtime when these frolics concluded, her brain had been kicked into gear once again and she was back to chewing over her problems and concerns. "I wonder," she mused aloud, "whether I really ought to go back to the Academy and see about developing a spell for hot baths." Andrion looked at her questioningly. "Back before we killed Tarragin, it occurred to me that a general lack of hot bathing pools like the one at the Maiden is Iscandia's biggest deficiency," she explained. "I sort of promised myself I would look into some way to make one appear by magic. And I really see that as a lack here. There's not even a privy chamber."

Other guys, she knew, would just smile at her foolishness. But Andrion was a mage, and a man who welcomed intellectual challenges. Wiping the last of the stew from his plate with the last hunk of bread, he chewed it thoughtfully. Then he spoke. "Hmm. The hot water wouldn't be much of a problem if you already had a tub of *cold* water. Fire spell, right? But conjuring the actual tub, and the water… My problem is, all my studies focused on battle spells. I knew I was going to need them when I got the hell out of Auverne. I don't even have your skills at healing, let alone conjuring."

"I haven't studied conjuring at all, either," Bernadette said. "Isn't that mostly just calling up creatures from the other planes? There ought to be some way to magically form a 'tub of hot water' object and just call it into being wherever and whenever you want it. Preferably, one that would *stay* hot even after you'd been soaking in it for a while."

"I don't know," he replied. "Maybe transformation is the right school. You could start with a cup of hot water as if you were making tea, and then transform it until it was big enough to sit and relax in."

Bernadette looked at him, her eyes alight with a combination of intrigue, affection, and amusement. "You may be onto something," she said. "Perhaps we really ought to pay the Academy another visit." She lapsed into contentment, enjoying the feeling of a full belly and the warmth of the fire. She sat silently, just staring into the flames, for a long while.

Andrion sat in equal contentment beside her, until a yawn sprang unbidden from his lips. He realized it had been a long day. "Bed, Berni?" he asked. She roused, having been close to dozing off herself.

"Leave the dishes for the morning, eh?" she asked. He nodded. He hadn't noticed any tendency on her part to demand that the place be shipshape before she could rest. Like as not, if somebody else didn't do the washing-up, it wouldn't get done.

They climbed the steps to Brightsgate Cottage's loft for the second time this day, taking turns at the chamber pot before slipping between the sheets. All passion now spent, they melted into one another's arms and drifted blissfully into sleep.

Chapter 4: Housewarming

Brightsgate Cottage's amber glass windows let in plenty of daylight, if no view of Waterdon beyond its walls. Bernadette awoke before much of that light had yet appeared, and was downstairs making tea when Andrion came down the steps, wearing casual clothing and scratching his head. "Where's that hot bath?" he asked her.

She sighed. "In our dreams, apparently..."

The two breakfasted on slightly stale pastries and some fresh apples, along with their cups of tea. Bernadette, too, was wearing "street clothes" – a simple but attractive dress, leather boots, and a short cloak with a soft cloth cap. There were no quests planned for the immediate future, at least not until they got Anja relocated.

After Andrion had washed the pot, plates, and cups from last night as well as this morning, they went on their way. Bernadette stopped by Valkyrie, right next door, to greet Alessia and chat with her for a few minutes. Then they fast-travelled back to the Maiden.

They arrived to a scene that halted them both in astonishment. As they opened the doors, they found Lifa, clad in her uncustomary housewife's garb, standing to one side of the common room clapping her hands, her eyes twinkling, as Anja, giggling and shrieking in delight, was carried around the room on the back of... Erik!

Well *here* was another surprise! Was *everyone* Bernadette knew secretly longing for the joys of parenthood? Erik was a giant, a happily effective killer. And a lover whose passion could sweep her away like a leaf on a gale, beyond coherent thought. But she knew what depths of sweetness, of tenderness he held. There resided within him a gentleness that touched her soul. And she had to admit that little Anja had melted her own heart, as well. So perhaps it was not such a surprise, after all.

Joy welling within her, Bernadette hurried forward, dropping her pack on the floor. Though she and Andrion still had no plans to live at Brightsgate Cottage, they had left quite a bit of their armor and weaponry behind in the trunk upstairs. It was a quick enough trip, when they needed to retrieve it. She swept to Erik's side, embracing him and Anja in a wide-spanning collective hug.

Erik's eyes, already twinkling at the fun he was having playing with little Anja, lit even more at the sight of his lover. She and Andrion had been away from the Maiden for a couple of days and as it happened he had not been there when they brought the child back with them. "Berni!" he exclaimed in his bass voice, folding her in a bear hug made slightly awkward by the presence of the little red-haired limpet clinging to his back.

"I see you've met Anja," she replied smiling. He grinned.

"She's taken over the place in your absence, I believe," he said. "She looks just like you. Is she your understudy?" Bernadette had swept in and carried off Erik's heart as well as Andrion's. Was Anja doing the same? It probably wouldn't be a bad thing, if so. Helpless little girls needed the love of as many people as they could claim, to protect them in a hard world.

Having greeted Aunt Berni, Anja wanted to return to the game at hand. "Come on, Uncle Erik! Ride me around again!"

"Sorry sugar," he replied with a grin. He reached back and grabbed her, lifting her over his head to swing her down, up again with a whoop, then gently back down to the floor. "I need to talk with Aunt Berni. Get Aunt Lifa to show you the pretty flowers out on the deck."

Once again Bernadette was thankful that Anja's amnesia had left her untroubled, once her injuries had been healed. Erik crouched down for the little girl to kiss him, then she ran off to Lifa. The once stony-faced body servant gave her a sweet, motherly smile and took her little hand, leading her out onto the Maiden's rear deck. It had a lovely view of the river and many planter boxes with chemial ingredients growing in them. Some of these *were* quite pretty.

Bernadette gave Erik a big, affectionate grin. "'Uncle Erik,' huh? Looks like she's got *you* wrapped around her little finger already."

He grinned back at her. "Like *you* don't? Give me a kiss!" She melted into his arms, giving him not only a deep kiss but a full-body hug as well. Somehow, she found the sight of Erik playing Daddy to be hot beyond belief. What *was* going on in her kinky little brain?

As much as Bernadette enjoyed making love with Andrion, her deepest connection with him was from the heart up to the top of her head. With Erik, it was from the heart down. They both had a piece of her heart, of which she had plenty to give; but just looking at Erik or being in the same room with him gave her a throb in the crotch and a warm feeling spreading up through her core. Little did she know, though she ought to have guessed, she had the same effect on him.

Throb aside, the morning was young and Bernadette had things to do yet today before playtime with Erik. She tucked that hot spark of sexual arousal into the back of her mind, like a treat she was saving for later. Pulling back from the embrace, she grinned at him again. "Guess what? We bought a house!"

"We?" Erik asked, puzzled.

"You and Andrion are my partners in crime," she assured him. "So if I spend a big wad of this cash you've helped me accumulate, it's for you and him as well as for me."

He smiled, pleased at the thought. He had everything he really needed right here – a comfortable bed, pleasant surroundings, plenty to eat and drink, and friends to hang out with. Not to mention, much of the time at least, his little fireblood lover to take him on adventures and light up his nights. But he knew Berni was irresistibly attracted to treasure, and if she wanted to include him in her purchases with the proceeds from that treasure he was happy to go along with it.

"Andrion and I killed the dragon that murdered Anja's parents yesterday," Bernadette told him, speaking more quietly. "Then I got to thinking that the Maiden really isn't the best place for a little girl to be living. The pools are a hazard, there are chillmarrow spiders and wolves and triceratops just a few steps off the deck, and there are no kids here for her to play with. So we went up to Wyrmshalla and bought Brightsgate Cottage."

"That's the little place next to Valkyrie, right?" Erik asked. He'd been patronizing that establishment, and selling his extra loot there, since coming to live at the Maiden a couple of years before. "It's pretty cute." Bernadette could tell that he thought the place too small, for a man of his proportions. And she had to admit it was. But then, she wasn't asking *him* to live there. As appealing as she had found it, she had other things in mind.

"I want to move Lifa in there with Anja," she told him. "It's convenient to everything. No hostile wildlife roaming the streets, and there are quite a few kids around."

Erik smiled. "Sounds like a good idea. You want me to help?"

"If you would," she smiled. She walked out the back doors to find Lifa and Anja. They had taken off their shoes and were sitting on the rim of the small soaking pool on the north side of the deck, talking quietly and kicking their feet in the water. Lifa had a hand to Anja's shoulder, ready to keep her from falling in.

"Lifa, Anja, good news! You're moving to Waterdon!" Bernadette declared. Lifa looked pleased, and immediately got up – taking Anja by the hand.

"What's Waterdon?" the child asked, addressing her question to Aunt Lifa.

"You'll like it, I promise. There's lots of places to go visit, and some children there you can play with. And we'll have our own little house to live in. You bought Brightsgate Cottage?" she asked, now speaking to Bernadette. The warden nodded. "I really like that house," she told both redheads.

Bernadette found it amazing how much more human Lifa had become since she had been introduced to Anja. It was as if the winter's ice had broken, and now sparkling water was flowing where before all had been cold and immobile. I ought to have brought home an orphan months ago, she thought whimsically. To Lifa, she said "I like it too. Andrion and I stayed there last night. But we want you and Anja to live there together. We might visit overnight or bring some other guests for you, but it will be your place. Yours and Anja's."

Lifa looked Bernadette in the eyes, her own filled with warm gratitude. And was that a suspicious moisture glinting in her eyes? Couldn't be. "Thank you so much, my warden," she said formally, her voice wavering slightly.

"Lifa? I know I'm your warden and that you have duties to me as my body servant. But do you think maybe you could call me Bernadette? I just don't feel very much like a warden."

Lifa actually smiled a little. "As you wish... Bernadette."

Coming right along, Bernadette thought. She led the pair back inside, and told Lifa "Please gather up anything you want to take with you. Whatever you and Anja need that you don't have, we'll buy in town. Erik and Andrion are going to help with the move." Lifa nodded her head and, still holding Anja's hand, went off with her to the spot on the sleeping loft where she usually bunked. She didn't have a lot, really – a few changes of underwear, some clothing, and the armor and weapons that had mostly been provided by Bernadette.

"Erik? Andrion?" Bernadette eyed her men, who'd been standing by watching her affectionately with the familiar "there goes Hurricane Berni" look in their eyes. "Can you pick up one of these beds from the mezzanine, please? I want to put it in that spare nook downstairs in the cottage so that if there are extra guests they'll have someplace to sleep." They exchanged a glance, shrugged, then headed off up the short flight of steps and hefted the single bed nearest to the bathing pool. Each of them took an end, and Bernadette stood there admiring their bulging muscles for a moment before scurrying off to open the doors for them.

In a fairly short space of time the little party was assembled in the road at the front of the building, and they were ready to leave for Waterdon. Bernadette made sure Andrion and Erik actually had their hands on the bed, and as she'd hoped the map fast-travelled all five humans along with their assorted luggage and furniture, depositing them on the main street of Waterdon just inside the gates. Alessia, out working at her forge, lifted her head and goggled at them as they lifted their burdens and proceeded the few dozen paces to the door of Brightsgate Cottage.

The men had to take the bed apart and lift it sideways to fit through the cottage's door. Then they set it up in the unfinished area off the dining room, and made it up again with its mattress and bedclothes. Next, they helped Lifa haul her collection of things up the narrow stairs. "You can take the master bedroom if you like, Lifa" Bernadette told her. "And Anja can have this little room for her own."

"I think that for now Anja will be sleeping with me," Lifa replied. "And I can move us into the little bedroom if you and…

uh… whoever, are visiting and want to stay the night." It appeared Lifa had not quite figured out what the story was with Bernadette and her two lovers.

"All right," Bernadette replied. "That will be fine."

After everything was in place and the move was completed Bernadette asked Lifa, "Do you have a list of things you'll need? We ought to go shopping." Lifa pondered. She had no money of her own, but accepted that her needs would be met by her warden.

"I'd like to go to Bernard's. And we could use some fresh meat and vegetables from the market. I think we can get some goat's milk there too."

"Oh! I almost forgot. I asked Lev to get some goat's milk for the Maiden," Bernadette exclaimed. "If he comes up with some, I'll drop it off."

Turning to the men, who were just standing there, Bernadette said "Why don't you two sit down and have an ale or two while we're out? There's a few bottles on the shelf. Hey Andrion, maybe you can use a frost spell on it!" Erik rolled his eyes, his face contorted in an expression of consternation.

"Oh, *no* mistress, not the ale! *Please* don't make us sit here drinking ale while you womenfolk have all the fun shopping!" Bernadette gave him a grin that showed a few too many teeth.

"Smart-arse!" she said. Then, turning to Lifa and Anja she continued "Ladies, shall we be off?"

The three of them left, and the two men seated themselves in the reasonably comfy chairs in front of the fire, each with a slightly chilled bottle of ale in hand and an ankle thrown up over the opposite knee. They turned to each other and grinned, then sighed contentedly. After downing around half of his ale in one long swallow, Andrion remarked to Erik, "*What* is our girl getting us into now? First we save the world, now we're rescuing orphans?"

"Wouldn't you?" Erik responded. "She is so damn *cute!*"

Andrion took another sip of his ale. "Who?" he asked then. "Berni, or Anja?" Erik took a long pull on his own ale, as if lost in thought.

"*Both* of them, of course. But you haven't spent much time with Anja yet. Just wait. I swear, it's as if she really is Berni Junior.

Minus the, ah, appetites of course. But she even *looks* just like
Berni." Another pause, considering. "And a bit like *you*, too, come to
think of it. Is there something you forgot to tell me?"

Andrion sighed, thinking "I wish." To Erik he said, "It *is* kind of
eerie, isn't it. When I first set eyes on her I thought 'that's my
daughter.' Mine and Berni's. But when I mentioned it to Berni, the
whole marriage-and-kids thing, she told me to back the hell off." He
sighed again ruefully, and took another drink of ale before
continuing, "I keep forgetting how young Berni is. Sometimes she
acts like she's *our* mother."

Erik was more pleased than he would admit at this confession
from Andrion. Even though he knew Berni loved him and wanted to
spend time with him, he could never quite shake the fear that
someday she might dump him to be exclusively with his friend. Both
Berni and Andrion had intellectual interests he didn't share.

Aloud, Erik said "Perish the thought! I assure you I have *never*
felt that way about my mother!" Andrion knew what he meant. Berni
might be a bit bossy from time to time, but she also had some kind of
near-magical ability to stiffen his dick – and presumably, Erik's as
well. He'd just as soon not delve into *those* details too much,
however. The conversation devolved into a discussion of Erik's early
life, growing up in Norcove. That frozen fishing village didn't have
much to offer a young lad, and like Andrion and Bernadette he'd
taken off as soon as he could get away.

Erik's parents still lived there, and he had an older sister —
married now with a couple of kids of her own – living in Coldstein.
He didn't visit with the family much. Andrion had known Erik for
more than two years, and he was surprised that he'd never learned
any of these details before. Admittedly the usual tendency among
Maiden employees was to talk shop, or politics, or discuss the quests
they'd been on and the many beautiful noblewomen they'd bedded.
Not that the two of *them* had discussed the noblewomen much –
Andrion mostly didn't do it, and Erik didn't talk about it.

As they were each finishing their second ales, the women
returned with their arms full of packages. They were chattering –
chattering! … and in high spirits. Anja in particular was beaming.
Not only had she acquired several new outfits to wear, and a new

doll, but she had met a nice girl a couple of years older than her, who was the daughter of one of the sellers in the marketplace.

Lifa now had several sets of non-armored clothing, and the excitement and pleasure she was feeling at the change in her circumstances had brought color to her cheeks and a sparkle to her eyes that made her look positively beautiful. Erik was a bit dazzled. If she had been like *this* that time he'd bedded her... But now, he was so besotted with Berni that other women had begun to lose their appeal. He still went with one, now and again, if Berni was gone for days and his horniness was getting out of hand. But it was scarcely any more exciting than jerking off. He no longer took any other woman to his bedroom in the basement, which he'd transformed into a sort of love nest for himself and Berni alone. If a Maiden guest wanted him, she'd better be prepared to get cozy on the loft.

Bernadette had sacks of food, a small cask of wine, and a bottle of goat's milk. She was also carrying a few bottles of water in her pack, and she poured two of these into a good-sized pot. "Andrion," she asked sweetly, "could you please chill this water with your frost spell?" He was pleased to do the honors, and the pot's bottom was soon covered in a thick layer of ice, the sides of it bitingly cold. Smiling her thanks, Bernadette placed the bottle of milk and several fresh bottles of mead into the pot, there to cool.

"We're having a feast in honor of Lifa and Anja's new home," Bernadette announced gaily, "and *I* am going to cook it!" She looked around at the faces of her friends for some reaction, then added "No, really, I am! I *know* how to cook..." Andrion and Erik broke into guffaws, and Lifa smiled but politely. She had less experience with Berni and her domestic skills – or apparent lack thereof. Bernadette joined the laughter, only pretending to be stung.

She knew as well as they did that she *very* seldom volunteered to do anything whatsoever in the kitchen and would be quite content to have all her meals prepared – and especially, cleaned up after – by others. As the eldest daughter in her household, these chores had fallen to her all too often and it was to escape these, as much as to find adventure and romance, that she had fled to Iscandia.

Bernadette was willing to make the occasional exception, however. She took out a slim stack of books she had bought at

Bernard's, tales that might be enjoyed by small children as well as adults, and placed them on one of the downstairs bookcases. After Lifa and Anja had returned from stowing their new possessions in the chests upstairs, she gave one of these to Lifa and suggested that they sit on the spare bed and read. The men could continue to sit in front of the fire, resuming their conversation, and she would take over the table for food preparation.

Producing a meal fancier than a pot of stew and some bread (purchased, not home-baked) was nearly impossible in the typical Iscandia kitchen. Bernadette had heard tell that in the kitchens of grand castles, like the eorl's palace in Sylvanian, there were immense ovens for the baking of pies, cakes, and breads. These kitchens held many spits and huge cauldrons, banks of tables where scullery maids by the score spent their hours chopping, all to keep the bellies of the high and mighty fed. Here, there was this table. Plus, a single pot suspended over the open fire, and a spit on which one could roast meats.

She'd bought a nice haunch of tender young goat from the meat seller in the marketplace, and made that her first priority. She chopped a lot of fresh garlic and herbs to season it with, then with Erik's help got it spitted. She tasked him, as he sat there relaxing by the fire, with turning the spit from time to time. No spit-dogs or spit-boys employed in *this* humble abode!

Given her limited cooking facilities, Bernadette's menu for this "feast" was really pretty simple. Aside from the roasted goat, she planned a one-pot ragout with potatoes, carrots, mushrooms, green beans, onions, and some herbs. She'd bought some fresh bread rolls as well. Almost no one in Iscandia baked their own bread at home. Plus, she had a good-sized paper packet of fresh pastries for dessert.

As Lifa read quietly to the rapt Anja, who it seemed had never before had any stories read to her, Bernadette sat using the tabletop as a cutting board, chopping up her vegetables. When she had them all in the pot, she added the herbs along with some water and a bit of the butter she had brought from the market. Then she put a lid on the pot and hung it on the hook. Now, all she needed to do was wait.

Hmm, but where? Lifa and Anja were such a tight little group on the bed, Bernadette didn't want to intrude there. Nor, listen to the story she'd heard countless times during her childhood. She was feeling very happy and pleased with herself, and Erik's presence was starting to remind her that it was *his* turn tonight. She was very much looking forward to some of the occasionally tender, frequently explosive loving he was wont to provide, and considered just sitting in his lap while waiting for the food to cook. But no, that would mess up the homey, casual mood. It might possibly break the chair, as well.

Instead, Bernadette pulled the small table out from its spot at the fireside, pushing it over against the wall. Then she borrowed a chair from the table near the door and parked it between Erik and Andrion, in front of the fire. She grabbed herself a tankard of wine before joining her two delectable lovers at the fireside. She'd brought along a towel to use as a potholder, and a wooden spoon with which to stir the ragout.

Erik gazed at her with a mixture of wonder and growing lust as she sat between them. He was as mindful as she was that tonight was his, to do all those things with her they both so very much enjoyed. He could hardly wait. But this was nice, too. He still couldn't get over the turn of recent events. First Berni and Andrion show up with an adorable orphan child. Then Lifa turns out to be the motherly type. Now, here was Berni buying stuff right and left before settling in to *cook* for them all. What next? Would she take up knitting? Reveal herself as the true heir to the throne of Iscandia? Anything seemed possible, and he was up for it all – as long as he continued to be a part of her life and a regular partner in her bed.

Berni gave him a meaningful glance, but the meaning wasn't clear until she said, in an undertone, "Erik! Don't forget to turn the spit!" He started, grinning sheepishly, and rotated the meat so it would cook evenly. Then his gaze went back to her, as she rose, towel and spoon in hand, to lift the lid on the cast iron pot and stir the contents. It smelled delicious! And she *looked* delicious bending over that pot, the velvety fabric of her dress snug through her slim waist and draping in folds over her firm yet divinely rounded rump. Other men might prefer a bit more plumpness, but Erik was a man of action and he appreciated a woman who could keep up with him. In point of fact he appreciated *this* woman, above all others.

Replacing the pot lid, Bernadette sat back down in her chair. Then she blew on the hot spoon until it had cooled a little before licking it off, all the while meeting his eyes with wicked promise. Oof! Erik's cock went rigid in an instant. It was going to be a long evening. He leaned forward to turn the spit again, hiding his erection. That meat smelled pretty damn good, too.

Anja was hungry before the food was ready, and Bernadette let her have an apple and some bread and butter. She didn't expect a five-year-old to appreciate the sort of meal she was preparing, but urged her to save some room for dessert. When the smells in the room were driving them all crazy, Bernadette got more towels so she and Erik could lift the spit and slide the now sizzling, medium-rare roast onto a platter to rest. Meanwhile the vegetable ragout was done to a turn, its separate flavors melding into one savory delight, and she took that off the fire as well.

Soon Bernadette and Lifa were raiding the dining room shelves for plates, and setting the long wooden table. Wine was poured for all save Anja, who had chilled goat's milk. Her warm brown eyes were alight with excitement, and she surprised Bernadette with a remarkably hearty appetite. She had seconds on meat, a goodly serving of the richly delicious vegetable stew, and some more bread and butter. *And* the better part of an entire pastry for dessert. Much as Andrion and Erik often wondered where Berni put all the food she usually consumed, Bernadette was amazed at the capacity of this small girl.

Toasts were made, the roasted meat was devoured almost to the bone, and the rolls and vegetable ragout were completely consumed. There was animated conversation and even hilarity around the table, as the group – an odd blend of friends, family, and relationships more difficult to define – celebrated the good fortune that they were here in this cozy home, enjoying good food, in good health, and with good prospects for the future. Anja faded as the evening wore on, and Erik carried her up the stairs to the master bed and tucked her in with a kiss.

Not too long after that, Bernadette rose somewhat unsteadily. "Don't worry about the washing-up," Lifa assured her.

"I would be delighted not to worry about that," she responded. Erik and Andrion exchanged a look. No surprises there. Bernadette gave Lifa a few hundred guilders. "Here's some money to cover groceries and such. We'll be checking in with you often, and if you need anything we're just a few minutes down the road, most of the time. If we're not home, Lev or whoever is doing innkeeper duty will see you have whatever you need." She gave Lifa a spontaneous hug, which the transformed body servant returned with a certain amount of hesitance. "Good night!"

Chapter 5: In the Basement

Bernadette, trailed by her two men, exited Brightsgate Cottage. Shortly thereafter they found themselves standing outside the Bathing Maiden. The evening had been delightful, and the cool evening air was already taking some of the wine fuzz from their brains. As the three entered the Maiden, Andrion turned to her and said "Berni, as the gods are my witness, may they strike me down if I ever again say a bad word about your cooking. That was fantastic!" He enfolded her in his arms, squeezing her tight, then bent to plant a less-than-chaste kiss on her lips.

She gazed up into his eyes, smiling. "See you in the morning!"

Berni and Erik went off, his massive arm around her shoulders, in the direction of the trap door behind the bar. Andrion watched them go, a bit of wistful longing clouding the overall mellowness of his mood. He had not been bullshitting her, the meal was truly wonderful. Why had he always assumed she couldn't cook? Ah well. There she went to be with Erik, and he had the large master bed all to himself tonight. Perhaps the memory of yesterday's activities and some help from his strong right hand would help to ease the pain.

Down in the basement, still bantering gaily and half-high on wine, Bernadette's anticipation of being in Erik's arms was approaching a peak. Whenever she was away from him for a while, the longing for him became so strong! Yet the same was true of Andrion. She needed *both* of them, and in the months they had all been together she had not yet come up with any solution to the conflict that worked better than the one they had arrived at back before defeating Tarragin – each of them taking turns to be with her.

As she stood beside the bed, Erik enfolded her in his powerful arms. Bernadette felt like a child, like the merest wisp within that embrace. He was so *huge*, her godlike young warrior! And so tender, so sweet, so sunny. He filled her heart with joy as he filled her loins with passionate longing. For a moment she just lost herself in him, surrounded by him, as he bent his head to drink her mouth in a hungry kiss.

In a few moments she broke from it, panting for breath. How he inflamed her! And then he said, in his deep rumbling voice, "Andrion wasn't lying. That dinner was *amazing*, Berni!" She rocked backward, clutching Erik's arms for support as she nearly fell over laughing. Just when things were getting intense! She leaned back into him, running her hand over the front of his trousers. That huge, insistent member was standing upright, rock hard beneath the fabric.

Bernadette lifted up Erik's shirt so that the tip of his cock, protruding from the waistband of the trousers, was exposed. She licked her thumb and forefinger and ran them over the top of it, pressing on the tumescent and velvety head and coaxing out a little clear, glistening fluid from the "eye" atop it. Gazing up into his luminous blue eyes, she said "Erik Johannessohn, I do *not* believe that it is my cooking that is currently on your mind."

He growled deep in his throat, and pressed closer to her. "You got me, Berni. You have well and truly got me…" He hooked his fingers into the top of her dress, never mind the lacings, and pulled it down to her waist. She lifted her arms free of the sleeves, and pressed her full breasts against his torso, savoring the contact of skin on skin as she continued to hold his shirt up out of the way. Then she looked up into his eyes again.

"Well," she said, "are you going to take that damned shirt off, or what?"

He blinked, then grinned and obliged, lifting the tails up over his head and skinning out of the voluminous garment in one sinuous motion. They stood now bare to the waist, his magnificently muscled golden torso pressed to her pale, slightly freckled one some eleven inches closer to the ground. She was at a good height, actually, to apply her mouth to his nipples – and she did so. She sucked at them gently, then tongued them until they stood at attention. Some distance below, his cock had discovered that it had not previously, after all, achieved full rigidity – and it now thrust upward another couple of inches beyond the waistband of his trousers.

Looking down, Bernadette unfastened the poor over-strained garment and let it slide down past his buttocks, allowing Erik's magnificent member to spring free. It towered before her, and she bent her knees to grasp it in both hands, applying her mouth to the head and licking up the salty juices that were oozing from it in anticipation.

Erik gasped and moaned slightly, more like a sigh, as she began licking him from scrotum to tip, squeezing the shaft in both hands. Once again, that mental image of an imagined Giant woman engulfing his entire erection in one mouthful sprang unbidden to Bernadette's mind, and she very nearly broke out laughing as she continued to tease him with her tongue and mouth. Oh, she loved sex play with Erik! It was always a joyful experience, even when it left her feeling as if she had been run over by an avalanche.

Before she could drive him over the edge, Erik seized her by the shoulders and lifted her gently up again to kiss her. Then he pushed the dress the rest of the way down, squeezing it past her hips to fall on the floor. As was usually the case with such garments, she was not wearing any underwear beneath it and now stood naked before him. He took her hand as she stepped gracefully out of the pool of fabric, then led her toward the bed. Along the way, his trousers also fell to the floor and were kicked aside.

"Have a seat, love," he said quietly. Bernadette sat on the edge of the bed, looking up at him. His angelic face looked down at her with love, his towering erection almost in her face. Then he knelt on the carpet beside the bed, and took her in his arms again. Her legs were spread wide to allow him to get closer, and that rigid cock was now pressed up against her sex, hot and pulsing. As he kissed her, squeezing her round breasts with his huge hands and thumbing her nipples into tingling excitement, Bernadette felt as if she might come on the spot – no penetration needed.

But Erik had more tricks up his sleeve. He bent now, resting his buttocks on his heels as he hugged her thighs with his arms and lowered his head to her quivering cunt. He began working his tongue within her folds, using his lips and fingers to inflame her still more. "Augh! Erik, yes!" she cried, lying back and pressing both hands on his golden head as he brought her quickly to the orgasm that had been building within her almost the entire time since they came down the ladder. She bucked and spasmed on the bed, thrusting her crotch into his face, as a gush of warm, slightly salty fluid flowed into his mouth and he drank it like the finest wine.

His manhood leapt still higher as she climaxed, eager for its own release. But as Erik got older, he was finding it easier to postpone that release – making it all the sweeter when it came at last. The orgasm might be the ultimate prize in this game of love, but getting there was more than half the fun. Now that his beloved had melted beneath the onslaught of his tongue, he was ready to take her with his cock. As Berni lay flat on the bed, panting, he crouched at the bedside and entered her, slowly and carefully.

Erik had never had trouble with Berni holding him, and wasn't expecting any now. But his wide experience with women of all stripes had taught him to use caution. Besides, there was a great deal of pleasure to be had pushing it in a little bit at a time, maybe pulling out a little, then going in a little bit more. Until, if he was lucky, it was *all* the way in, his full length enclosed in that hot, wet crevice. Berni certainly seemed to appreciate it.

Bernadette threw her legs up around Erik's hips, meeting his thrusts. That huge cock filled her so completely, hot and demanding. In what seemed like moments she was coming again, screaming his name; but he still managed to hold off. Was Erik getting more sophisticated with age? She had, at times, experienced him as an ingenious lover with remarkable restraint; but his usual style was one of unbridled passion combined with amazing physical strength and stamina.

She let her legs drop to the surface of the bed, clutching Erik tight with her arms, as she struggled to get her breath back after the latest mind-bending orgasm. Her vaginal spasms still gripping him like a fist, he stopped stroking for a few moments to let her recover. "Oh Erik, Erik…" she breathed. The things he did to her! Her eyes looked deep into his, her love shining naked within them. The wine still fuzzed her mind a little, and she felt as if it would soon be time for sleep. But she thought she knew how she could bring about a satisfactory conclusion for all concerned.

He looked at her expectantly, awaiting her command. "Let me up," Bernadette murmured. He obediently fell back, releasing her from the enormous weight of his body. His cock jutted above her, swollen and glistening. "Purple-headed love god" indeed! She tucked her legs up and scooted further up the bed, then turned around and got onto her hands and knees, crawling toward the headboard. She knelt there, her hands gripping the bedstead, legs slightly spread and her rounded rump thrust toward him, her swollen and soaking-wet cunt winking at him from between her thighs. Then she swiveled her head to look back at him over her shoulder, smiled beguilingly, and said "Come and get me, sweetheart!"

Now *there* was an invitation Erik was not likely to refuse. Berni's cunt a homing beacon, his cock fairly dragged him to the target like an excited hunting dog on a leash. In moments he was within her again, getting penetration to the fullest, the head of his engorged member bouncing off her cervix as he thrust faster and faster. His powerful hands gripped her buttocks, pulling himself to her as the searing passion that the evening's food and wine had deferred seized him at last. Bernadette took one hand off the bedstead and put it between her legs, massaging her clit in a fury as Erik exploded like a volcano within her, and she along with him.

Erik stayed kneeling behind her, still stroking, as his cock and her cunt pulsed in unison and a hot ocean of his seed filled her to the brim and dribbled out around the edges. Then he just bent his upper body over hers, clutching her to him, his arms wrapped around her torso and clasping her breasts, his mouth kissing her neck, her hair, her spine.

Both of them weak-kneed, they soon toppled over onto their sides and lay on the bed spooning, still joined, until their breathing had returned to normal and his cock, now completely spent, had softened and slipped from within her. They lay like that for a while longer, then Bernadette rotated in his arms and wrapped hers around his neck, kissing him deeply.

After that she tucked her head beneath his chin and contented herself with gently stroking his chest, occasionally applying a tender kiss to his collarbone or whatever patch of him (and there was so *much* of him) presented itself. She felt saturated with love, swimming in a sea of it, surrounded by it as Erik's strong arms surrounded her body. Her relaxation was so complete, it was not long before she began to drift off to sleep. Her last conscious thought was, "I don't ever want to give this up…"

Chapter 6: Packing to Leave

Bernadette awoke feeling warm and comfortable. She was curled up with her back to Erik, and he was wrapped around her. His stiff cock was a hot presence pressed between her buttocks. Mmm. And he was not asleep. As she stirred a little he gently brushed her hair aside and applied his lips tenderly to that sensitive spot where her neck joined the shoulder. She gasped slightly, a slow intake of breath, as the sensation ran like a streak of heat from there down through her core and her cunt spasmed involuntarily. His hands squeezed her breasts and his cock pressed still closer.

Making love in the morning was something she often avoided, frequently being more in the mood to leap out of bed and get started on whatever activities the day offered. She had a few of those in mind for today, but decided that this time, they could wait. Bernadette rotated within the circle of his arms and pressed herself against him, claiming his mouth in a deep soul kiss. His mouth, and hers, had tasted better once or twice; but it didn't matter. Her hand slipped down between them to squeeze that gigantic member. Then she threw a leg up over his hip and guided him inside her. Already her crevice was wet and ready for him.

Erik groaned softly with pleasure as his cock slipped home within her. "Oh Berni," he murmured, kissing her with renewed passion. He'd half expected to be turned away. That had certainly happened many times in the months since they had first become lovers. He began sliding slowly in and out, lying on his side. Then he rolled over atop her, supporting his weight on his knees as she spread her legs fully for him and wrapped them around his hips.

Now his strokes became faster, firmer, and her moans more urgent as she threw her head back, panting. As she came Erik's mind was ablaze, so close... but he held on. He wanted a little more. His cock throbbing within her as her spasms gripped him, he stopped stroking for a few moments to run his hands over her hair, kiss her face.

Bernadette opened her eyes to look at him above her, an expression of sleepy lust and warm affection suffusing his golden features. "Baby?" he murmured, and questioningly made a twisting gesture with one hand. Her eyes widened and she smiled.

"Oh yes," she murmured back. He pulled back to let her flip herself over onto her belly. Then she lifted herself up onto her knees, her ass thrust up toward him while her head was pillowed on her arms.

Erik's eyes lit. Berni loved to be fucked from behind, and he loved to do it – though he also enjoyed watching her face, kissing her lips while they made love. His quivering member thrust forward eagerly, finding its niche, juices running out the sides as it fitted tightly within her. He was immediately seized with a hot urgency. Months of familiarity had not drained her ability to produce this effect on him. He wanted to come inside her, he wanted to *climb* inside her, NOW! As he pumped furiously, the sensation arose as if a new sun had ignited at the point where their bodies met, and was growing with a white-hot intensity to obliterate both of them in a searing explosion that would leave nothing behind but some drifting ash.

Well, not quite. Both lovers were still quite firm and solid after the wave passed, collapsed on the bed on their sides, still joined. As the throbbing pulsations slowly subsided, Bernadette clutched Erik's hands to her chest, hugging him as he was hugging her. Whew! As he slipped out, she rotated in his arms for the second time this morning, pressing her sweaty body against his massive torso and applying sweet little kisses to his equally sweaty chest. "Ooohhh, Erik," she murmured. "I love you." He didn't reply, just enfolded her head in his arms and kissed her hair. She knew well enough how he felt.

In a little while, breathing returned to normal, she raised her head to look him in the eyes. "I'm going to Alfenstein later," she said. "Want to come along?" He smiled.

"Sure, why not?" he replied. He'd be happy to follow her anywhere, especially if there was a chance it might extend his turn in bed with her for another night. Bernadette kissed him lightly, then wriggled backwards out of the bed and put her feet on the floor. She grabbed the spare robe she kept here now, along with a few of her other things.

"Bath time," she said smiling, and headed for the ladder. Erik stood up, sniffing the air. Smells like sex in here, he thought. Not an unpleasant smell, but it might get a little rank after a few days away. He pulled the covers off the bed, and after donning his own robe he gathered the sheets in a wad and carried them upstairs with him. Drelos was on duty, and he asked him to see to the laundry. "Sure thing," the elf replied.

Idly scratching his belly, Erik headed for the pool. He found Berni soaking there, and was surprised to see that Andrion had joined her. Left to his own devices, his friend usually might sleep until late morning. But Berni seemed to be having her effect on him in more ways than one. She was holding his hand under the water and talking animatedly with him as Erik dropped his robe and joined them in the pool. "Hey," Erik greeted Andrion briefly.

"I was just telling Andrion about our trip to Alfenstein," Bernadette told Erik. "I think I'm getting close to having enough brownie points with the eorl that he might make me warden."

"Being warden is a great idea, Berni," Andrion told her. "Once you've gotten that honor, the city guards won't bother you anymore. Plus, you can buy property in the city. Ever thought about living in Alfenstein?" That intriguing city of stone, built by the dypalfar and located in Iscandia's far western march, was one Bernadette had only visited after Tarragin had been defeated. She'd been there several times since, enjoying its scenic locale and attractive architecture.

"I wouldn't mind having one of those houses," she said thoughtfully. "They are really spacious and nice inside. But I wouldn't want to live there all the time. *This* is my home, here with you guys and the rest of the Maiden crew. And close to Lifa and Anja in Waterdon." She pondered some more, then said, "But we've got plenty of money, now. I suppose if the eorl lets me buy a house in Alfenstein, I'll take him up on it. It'd make a nice base for us whenever we're out in Westmarch."

"Thanks, sweetie!" Bernadette concluded, making to give Andrion a hasty kiss before getting out of the bath. He forestalled her by reaching toward her to cup her face in his hands, and kissing her in a way that was thoughtful – and thorough.

On releasing her, he said quietly, "Don't be gone too long, love. I'll be waiting." A little thrill shot through Bernadette. Erik was a lot of fun, but Andrion was a serious lover. And he seriously had a hold on her heart.

Slightly shaken, Bernadette emerged from the pool and toweled off before putting on her robe. Erik had opted for a little wash-up instead of a full-on soak, and was now dressed in his light elven armor, anticipating their trip. She beckoned him over to their usual table and they sat munching on pastries washed down with hot tea, some fruit on the side. Their brief meal concluded, they returned to the basement to gather the rest of their things before leaving.

As was often the case, Bernadette had a little crafting she wanted to do before they took off. Erik was becoming ever more impressed with her level of expertise. There were smiths he'd been to here and there in Iscandia that couldn't produce a suit of armor, or a blade, any better than what she was turning out right here in their "bedroom."

"Look what I picked up a couple of trips ago," she told him, pulling a hunk of glistening black carapace out of the trunk where she stored her spares between quests, to work on at her leisure. "What is that? Mandimant?" Bernadette squinted slightly. "I hadn't thought of it, but it *does* look a bit like leukalfar gear. No, this is sablium! I found it in a chest way down near the bottom of some major barrow complex. But it's got magical properties. And I recently discovered that I can work on armor with enchantments on it."

As she spoke, she had the armor on the workbench. Hammering, punching, crimping, she worked it down to a size that would fit her. Then she surprised Erik by walking over to the bedroom area and peeling off her robe, draping it on the chest of drawers. He was well-sated by their activities of last night and again this morning, but he was always willing to appreciate a naked lady. Especially this one.

Next, she began wriggling into the armor she'd been working on. Erik's eyes widened. No underwear? As he observed the way the armor fit her, he realized no underwear would be possible without hanging way out beneath the armor in every direction. The gear looked like a sort of glistening, charcoal gray *bathing suit*. It had a chainmail bra that barely covered her bountiful breasts, some protection for the collarbone and upper arm areas, a bit of a gorget over the stomach, and a chainmail thong beneath a bottom section that wrapped around Berni's hips, the two pieces held together with a hinge at the front and lacings at the back. "Give me a hand with the laces?" she asked, backing up to him.

Erik stood there gaping at her. This was not armor, this was some kind of hard shiny sex fantasy brought to life! Beneath his elven armor (which, it occurred to him, was pretty sexy too) his cock was rising as he ran a hand caressingly over Berni's smoothly rounded hips before gathering the laces and tying the bottom section of the armor around her ass. Holy gods, she looked good enough to devour on the spot! How was he supposed to concentrate on killing aptrgangr with *this* vision before his eyes?

"It looks great!" he told her. "Now, hurry up and take it off because I want to fuck you right now." She snorted.

"I know, it's pretty over-the-top, isn't it? But a girl *does* like to feel pretty. The thing is, this stuff *works*!" She strutted over to the chest, vamping a bit, and pulled out an iron sword she hadn't ever gotten around to improving. It wasn't all that deadly a weapon. "Here" she said, handing it to him. "Go ahead and attack me."

Erik looked at her with an uncharacteristic expression of doubt and concern in his warm blue eyes. Their relationship was casual and fun, but underneath there was something deeper and he really *didn't* want to attack his beloved – not with any weapon sharper than the one between his legs. "Go ahead," she urged him. "I've got my healing spell all ready, so if you accidentally hurt me I can be perfect again in under a minute. But I need to prove my theory."

"Well, okay. But promise you won't get mad!" holding the dull sword in his huge hand with reluctance, he gave a half-hearted swing at her upper legs. If the armor didn't work as advertised, he'd just as soon not hit any vital organs. Where he swung the sword, he saw nothing but the smooth flesh of his lover's thighs. But the sound and the feel as it struck was like hitting ultra-hard wood. The sword bounced off with a loud "CLACK!"

Bernadette stood there smiling. "I didn't feel a thing!" she said, pleased. "Do it some more!" Emboldened, Erik began belaying the sword about her arms, shoulders, and midsection. He even stabbed it straight into her seemingly bare back, and each time there was a clacking sound and a sense of resistance as if he had just hit full sablium plate. There was no bleeding or bruising, nor did any marks appear on the armor. And Bernadette stood there, arms at her sides, smiling at him.

When he was convinced and had finally stopped hitting her with the sword, she grinned even wider and said, "Is that amazing, or what?"

"I don't get it," he said.

"Erik," she replied sagely, "we live in a world of magic. It's all around us. How can I nearly get an arm cut off and be perfectly fine a few seconds later? How can I move you, Andrion, Lifa, Anja and a double stack of luggage and furniture from here to Waterdon in the blink of an eye? I'll probably be an old granny by the time I've studied magic enough to understand how it all works, but for now let me just say that this sablium armor, and the elven armor I made for you and Andrion, has a magic to it. It's a little like a ward spell. You can see skin in a lot of areas, but those areas are still protected by the armor. Yet it's lighter, cooler, and more comfortable to wear than full plate."

Erik continued standing there, the iron sword hanging at his side, as he looked her up and down while digesting what she'd told him. Then he said, musingly, "Wow... Okay, I believe you. ...Can we fuck *now*?" He said this last with a little-boy mischievous grin that looked so ridiculous and adorable on his big, lofty face that Bernadette didn't know whether to leap into his arms or just burst out laughing. She settled for stepping closer and squeezing his free hand, standing on tiptoes to give him a kiss.

He wasn't entirely kidding about the fucking, and tossing the sword aside he grabbed her around the waist with both hands. He felt warm, supple flesh riding over firm muscle – in exactly the area where his sword had met hard resistance moments before. This was certainly very odd! He ran his strong fingers up her torso and inside the armor's bra top, brushing her nipples. It was all Berni, as far as his fingers were concerned. He bent to kiss her more deeply.

Bernadette pulled away from him, panting slightly. "Cut that *out*!" she said, smiling but outraged. "At this rate we'll be getting to Alfenstein a week from now. There'll be time for fun and games later dear, but for now we really need to be going." As if in direct contradiction to what she'd just told him, she then reached up under the skirt of his elven armor and squeezed his stiffened cock.

"Hey!" he growled, but smiled at her. Then he gave it up, and stepped away to gather a few things for his pack.

Chapter 7: Alfenstein

Bernadette and Erik climbed the basement's second ladder, which led directly to the Maiden's rear deck. From there it was the work of moments for Bernadette to carry them both to Alfenstein. They arrived inside the city's main gate in what looked like late morning, local time. They could have fast-traveled directly to the eorl's palace, a dark and crumbling dypalfar ruin called Dypendwelve; but Bernadette wanted to visit with a few of the townspeople on her way there.

She led them up the winding, intricate stone pathways, crossing and re-crossing the whitewater stream that cut its way through the center of town, and stopped at the forge of Dhyazh dan-Lugab. The middle-aged uruk woman had been one of the first people in Alfenstein Bernadette had befriended, during her first visit to the city not long after she, Andrion and Erik had killed Tarragin in Asengard and lived to tell about it.

They had traded weapons and armor on several occasions since. She greeted the smith formally. Uruks were, by and large, a formal people – tied to tradition. In Iscandia it was only rarely that they ventured outside their strongholds, as Dhyazh had done, and rarer still that they allowed outsiders within.

Bernadette spent some time negotiating with Dhyazh. She bought some items that were hard to come by, even for someone with the resources of the Bathing Maiden's basement; and sold her some of her surplus weapons and armor. Then she continued up the stairs to Magichemia, Alfenstein's chemia shop.

The proprietress, Clara, greeted her warmly. The old woman had named her shop aptly, as the art of chemia was truly a blending of magic and chemistry. Potions could do almost anything, from curing diseases and restoring health to sending one's enemies to an early grave. Clara had come to regard Bernadette as a valued customer.

Bernadette picked up a few of the harder-to-find ingredients from her, and sold off a double handful of potions she'd crafted that were not likely to be needed. In her quest to become good enough at chemia to produce the potions she really wanted, Bernadette had generated gallons of stamina poisons, potions that would temporarily boost carrying capacity, and other arcane substances she had no immediate use for.

Thanking Clara and moving on her way, Bernadette continued up a steep stone path beside rushing water to the steps that led to the doors of Dypendwelve. Erik followed behind. There had been a recent shakeup in the Reman administration that had resulted in a change of power here in Alfenstein. It was now Galdur Staerlin who sat the eorl's throne. Bernadette had met the previous eorl, Hjaermond, on a visit to the eorl's palace in Sylvanian. He was now living in the bowels of that stone edifice, in company with other former officials who had fallen from power as the result of the changes dictated by the empire.

Bernadette and Erik made their way up through the massive, mostly-ruinous dypalfar edifice that was Dypendwelve. It encompassed the eorl's palace, a storehouse of dypalfar artifacts maintained by the mage Miurlion, and a major dypalfar archaeological site. Bernadette couldn't really understand why the eorls of Alfenstein would choose to make such a place the seat of their power. It almost seemed as if they were mice, living inside the baseboards of a dwelling belonging to others. And there *were* others, she knew. Deep in the bowels of this place was a world of dypalfar automatons, leukalfar, and mandimants.

Arriving at the throne room, where Galdur Staerlin sat as eorl, Bernadette addressed herself to the steward sitting on a chair several feet down and to the eorl's left. "The dragon is dead, as you requested," she told him.

"Thank you. You have done a great service for the people of Westmarch," he replied, handing her a hundred guilders as a reward. Bernadette would happily have killed *that* particular dragon gratis.

"You have proven yourself to be a friend of Westmarch several times over," the steward told her, "and I am pleased on behalf of the eorl to award you the honorary office of warden. You are now authorized to purchase property within the city, and you are also granted this axe as a badge of your rank – and the services of a body servant at such time as you buy a house."

A body servant? That would be interesting. Lifa's loyalty had always been unquestioned – and if it was hard to penetrate the warden-body servant barrier in a quest for a deeper human connection, Bernadette at least appreciated that being provided with the services of a body servant was a singular honor. "I would like to purchase a house in the city," she told the steward.

He was most obliging, his usual stiff demeanor waxing positively cordial as he relieved her of some 13,000 guilders for the purchase of one Eastview , with all furnishings. Ouch. But really, they could afford it now. With the Maiden continuing to bring in profits in addition to providing Bernadette with free room and board, she had a steady income and almost no need to pay for anything. And her constantly-improving skills in smithing, chemia, and enchanting were turning her chance-found loot and ingredients into valuable treasure.

Getting some vague directions, in a fog of pleasure at the achievement of her goal, Bernadette wandered back out into the brilliant afternoon and began threading her way through the maze of Alfenstein looking for her new acquisition. Houses in Alfenstein were all packed together, no plots of land separating one from the other. Erik, as lost as she was, just followed behind her.

Finally they stumbled into the small market area just inside the main gates. Bernadette approached a pretty Afran woman, who with her husband and young daughter operated a stand selling the jewelry they crafted. As it happened, the woman knew the location of Eastview. Bernadette and her companion were directed to a steep, narrow, stone staircase off to the north side of the market. Then they were to take a left, followed by a sharper right up another flight of steps, which would then lead them up several turnings to the doors of their new residence.

Walking in through the intaglio dypalfar metal double doors, Bernadette was immediately impressed with the charm of the place. The entry hall soon opened out into a broad dining area, with rooms for chemia and enchanting off to the left and a wide hearth with some cozy chairs to the right. And, sitting at the table in the spacious dining room, was an enormous man clad head to toe in heavy armor.

Oh! Bernadette had not been sure whether all body servants were female, or what. Clearly, not. This one introduced himself as Bjorn One-Eye, and assured her that he was entirely at the service of his warden. She was quite taken aback. This guy was a serious hunk! Nearly as large and well-muscled as Erik, he was handsome save for an old injury that had blinded his right eye. She stifled the impulse to command him to strip on the spot, so she could admire those muscles in more detail and see whether the package came with a suitably sturdy cock.

Almost immediately, an idea came to her. Bernadette knew she was sometimes too impulsive, but this just felt so *right*! For the moment though, she asked Bjorn to prepare them some food while she and Erik explored the rest of the house. This place had cost only about half again as much as Brightsgate Cottage, but it seemed huge by comparison. Leaving the dining area they came to a broad living room/hall with another huge fireplace and cooking facilities. On either side of that was a spacious bedroom, the one on the left having a double bed while the one on the right, of a similar size, had only a single. The "servant's quarters," no doubt.

Still no hot baths, alas. But Bernadette had an idea that there would be plenty of room in which to install a decent-size bathing pool in the living area near the cooking hearth, if not elsewhere. She envisioned this place providing a more-than-adequate home away from home for her, Erik, and Andrion. Maybe the city even offered some night life! There was an inn just down a few flights of steps, near the main gates. While waiting for the meal, they peeled out of their armor and put on some casual clothing.

Bjorn came up with a better repast than she might have expected, served up on the large dining table that could have seated 8 or 10 with ease. There were salmon steaks, green beans, boiled potatoes with fresh butter, and plenty of fresh bread – all washed down with mead. Bernadette tried to draw Bjorn out, but Erik was more successful. They were fellow Norsemen, both big, bluff men of action; and they spoke a language Bernadette was not fluent in.

As the mead did its work, the evening became almost jolly. A hand on Erik's thigh, Bernadette did more observing than participating as the conversation swirled around the finer points of mayhem in Westmarch. Erik was enjoying himself, talking shop with a guy he had a lot in common with. He was a freebooter, with no one to call master (not counting this smallish woman whose quiet presence at his side loomed oh-so-large in his consciousness); and Bjorn had been oathbound to the march from an early age. But other than that, their paths in life had been similar. They were both adept at wreaking violence on all who were branded Enemy.

The hour was getting late when Bernadette began yawning, and suggested that they all turn in. Bjorn dealt with the washing-up, then retired to the small bed in the second bedroom. Bernadette and Erik, holding hands, headed for the master bed. They stood there at the foot of the bed, Erik enfolding her in a gentle hug as he towered above her. She pressed herself to him, loving the warmth and solidity of him, the scent that was uniquely Erik.

"I really *like* this place!" she said, backing off slightly to look up into his face. "Don't you?"

"It's great!" he replied enthusiastically. This spacious dypalfar-style residence was a lot more his size than the cute but overly-cozy Brightsgate Cottage. "I think we need to break in the bed, though" he suggested.

Eyes bright, she leered at him. "I believe that's obligatory," she replied.

He pulled his shirt off over his head, then reached down to untie the laces on her dress. This outfit was one he'd not seen before, and it took him a moment to figure out how to peel her out of it. Soon, though, his surprisingly nimble fingers were working the laces loose until he was able to push the dress off her shoulders. Meanwhile, she was doing the same for the laces on his trousers. Flushed with these simple accomplishments, the two stood confronting each other a few inches apart. Bernadette's breasts were spilling over the top of her dress, her nipples just peeking out; and the last couple of inches of Erik's cock protruded where his pants were opened at the top.

Bernadette stood there admiring him for a few moments. No matter how many times she got naked with this guy, she could still not get over how absolutely magnificent he was. She shrugged her dress the rest of the way off the upper part of her body, pulling her arms out of the sleeves, and cupped her breasts in her hands while gazing into Erik's eyes. "You like?" she asked, though it was a rhetorical question. She knew well how much he loved these appurtenances growing from her chest.

She stepped closer to him and gripped the waistband of his trousers, peeling them down toward his knees. His cock towered from the nest of light gold hair at his crotch, eager for whatever she might have in mind. Smiling, Bernadette bent her knees and, still holding her breasts, squeezed his rampant member between them. As she'd done for Andrion, she let him fuck her tits while she applied her mouth and tongue to the tip of his cock as it emerged above them. Erik's eyes lit and he grinned like a maniac at this unexpected move. He loved it when Berni came up with a new trick!

This was fun for Bernadette as it was for Erik, but it was starting to get to her back and legs. She rose to her full height again and beckoned him over to sit on the edge of the bed. His trousers slipped down to his ankles, nearly hobbling him; but it wasn't a long walk. Then she slid her dress the rest of the way off her body and kicked it aside, standing naked. She walked up to Erik, finding his face almost at a height with hers, and seized his mouth in a passionate kiss.

He reached out to grab her, his strong hands caressing her breasts, her torso, her hips as her tongue went into his mouth and she stroked his head and shoulders. Then she bent to grasp his quivering cock with one hand as, seating herself in his lap with her legs wrapped behind him on the bed, she lowered herself down and engulfed him.

Each of them gave a stifled cry as his cock pushed home. Ooh! Erik liked this. She had ridden him on a few occasions before, but never with him seated upright. He was able to grip her buttocks and bounce her up and down on his shaft without also having to support his own weight. Berni was soon screaming, her cries rising in pitch and volume. He pulled her all the way down on him and just held her in his strong arms as she spasmed, her vaginal walls clutching him in waves. Ah! That felt fantastic!

The evening of good food and drink, and the fact that they had made love this morning as well as the previous night had taken a little of the edge off of Erik's usually fiery lust, and as good as this felt he was able to delay his own orgasm. After holding Berni tenderly until her pulsations subsided, he lay back on the bed with her in his arms, then flipped them both over so that he was on top.

Now he knelt and began stroking gently in and out, sending waves of pleasure through both of them.

He rose on his arms above her, just watching her face. Her complexion was flushed, her luminous eyes gazing into his with love and complete surrender. Of all the women he had known in his short life, and there were a lot of them, this was the one he wanted over and over again, the one without whom he felt incomplete. Merging his body with hers was such bliss! He bent to kiss her, and as she took his tongue in her mouth it felt as if a link had been forged between his tongue and his cock, running through the center of his being like a burning cord. Suddenly he was seized by an excitement he could not suppress, and his strokes became harder and faster. Berni screamed again, and Erik gave a loud, drawn-out groan as her pulsing cunt milked him of his seed.

Bernadette dropped one leg down while still pinning Erik's magnificent member within her, letting them rotate to lie on their sides so she would still be able to breathe. They lay there enfolded in one another's arms, panting and grinning. "Oh Erik, what you do to me," she murmured.

"Me?" he replied in his bass rumble. "Look what you do to *me*! I can't be in the same room with you without getting a hard-on." She smiled at that. On one level they were fond friends; and on another, it seemed, there was an almost-supernatural lust connection between them.

Across the hall, Bjorn lay there in the darkness on his narrow bed, envy of Erik burning within him. It had been so long since he had a woman! A body servant's life was not his own to command, and if the eorl wanted to put him on guard duty for six months, alone, he was expected to be here keeping an eye on things – not out wandering the streets looking for female companionship. His new warden was beautiful, and she'd gotten to him in a big way. Not that he could imagine actually approaching her for sex. The social barrier was too great. Plus, obviously, she was taken. He grasped his stiffened member in his right hand and began pumping, reliving those cries of ecstasy in his mind as he sought some relief.

Chapter 8: Waterdon

In the morning, Bernadette woke entwined in Erik's arms. Snuggling seemed always to be required, here in Iscandia. The province never really warmed up. As her brain came awake and she oriented herself, she hugged him to her and planted very soft little kisses on his hands. What a man! Andrion might be the romantic lead in her personal story, but Erik was so crucial to her happiness that she could not envision being without him. Just being wrapped in his arms filled her with joy.

Thoughts of her plans for the day soon claimed her, and before Erik could get started on his usual morning campaign of inflaming her desire, she slipped from between the covers. He woke some time later, feeling a little chilled. Where was his beloved, forming a warm spot at his belly? He'd been dreaming of their latest encounter and his cock was rising; but she had fled.

Erik opened his eyes, finding himself sadly alone in the spacious master bed of Eastview . He sighed. If you could count on Berni for anything, it was early rising and short shrift to any ideas you might have of morning dalliance. Not that such dalliances hadn't *happened* on occasion, even in fact recently; but this absence was the norm. Now fully awake, he sat up in the bed and scratched himself sleepily. Might as well face the day…

Bernadette was definitely impressed to find Bjorn already up and dressed, and preparing breakfast for them all without having been asked to. This guy was not only a hunk, he was sharp! She gladly accepted a cup of hot tea, and sat at the dining table munching on a pastry. When she felt a little more together, she told him "We'll be taking you with us to Waterdon this morning."

"As my warden wishes," he replied stoically.

She felt a twinge of annoyance. This whole "body servant" thing seemed wrong to her. There'd been nothing like it where she'd grown up, and the idea that some arbitrary social distinction should cause a man like Bjorn (or, for that matter, a woman like Lifa) to treat her as if she was exalted beyond anything *they* could hope to achieve, was just ridiculous.

Fortified by her slight breakfast, Bernadette returned to the master bedroom to put on some clothes in place of her robe. She found Erik moving about, in the nude. Ooh, but no… "Good morning, lover," she purred, drifting to his side and taking him in her arms. "We're going back to Waterdon in a little while. Do you want to get some breakfast?"

Erik was still considering what to put on. "We're going straight back there? No fights along the way?"

Bernadette considered that thoughtfully. In Iscandia, you tended to assume that any journey upward of five minutes might very well lead to armed conflict. But in this case her plan was to fast-travel them from the little stone landing immediately outside Eastview to a spot just inside Waterdon's gates, a short walk from the front door of Brightsgate Cottage. "Casual clothes should be fine, love" she told him. Unable to resist, she gave him a squeeze that was a bit the other side of casual. Damn, but this man seemed to bring out her inner insatiable slut!

Erik appreciated the squeeze, but months of familiarity had attuned him to Berni's moods. He knew she was not really inviting him to sex, and he squeezed her back in a way that told her he'd be happy to take her up on any *real* invitation she should care to extend – later. It occurred to him, as he dug some trousers and a tunic out of his pack, that in the few months they had known each other he seemed to have… *matured* somewhat. The carefree existence of the past couple of years, since he came to be employed by the Bathing Maiden, was slipping behind him now. Berni was just a "kid," a couple of years younger than he was. But she'd taught him things he'd never have dreamed possible.

Erik came to the dining table in time to have a little of the hot tea and some bread and cheese, tucking an apple into a pocket for later. Not that "later" would be long, with Berni and her magic map. Such things were far from unknown in Iscandia, but she was the first person he'd known personally who possessed such an item. It certainly changed one's attitude toward time and distance.

Before they left Eastview, Bernadette made sure that Bjorn had packed with him everything he owned. She planned to uproot him utterly from the life he had known, this man half again her age. That she had the power to do so was implicitly accepted by all parties. She saw it as a lucky chance, an alignment of fate that made it possible for her to subvert the established order of things in ways that would enable her to achieve what *she* felt was justice.

A few moments after stepping onto the stone landing outside the doors of Eastview, the three of them found themselves standing just inside the gates of Waterdon, flanked by two of the city's many guards. Though it had been early morning in Alfenstein, it appeared that here dark was just falling. Another day lost?

As Bernadette oriented herself and began striding toward the door of Brightsgate Cottage, a dozen or two paces away, she found the guards on either side suddenly crying out in alarm. "Look out!" one shouted, and "Kill it!" the other cried. Barely visible in the dim evening light, a figure clad in dark leather and a black woolen cape was moving to attack the guards and Bernadette's party as well. She felt nigh on helpless. Her weapons, along with her armor, were in her pack. Erik, likewise, had no more than a dagger about his person. But Bjorn was still fully armed and armored.

She still had one weapon always at her command, and Bernadette cried "Kraf-Luft-Struung-Wund!" The sinister man in dark leathers was hurled through the air, landing a dozen yards up Waterdon's main street and tumbling to the ground, still for a heartbeat or two before getting back on his feet. Meanwhile the guards and Bjorn brought their weapons to bear, and in another few moments the man lay unmoving.

Bernadette approached the corpse, wanting answers. She had thought this area, the heart of Waterdon, to be a safe haven for Anja. "Those damned vampires!" one of the guards declaimed.

The other agreed, "Somebody needs to do something about them." Vampires? She hadn't realized they were that much of a threat, though she had to admit that they seemed to be coming to her attention more and more recently.

Vampires, which existed throughout Agena, mostly hid themselves away in secret places. They weren't known to seek their victims in the streets of places like Waterdon. Bernadette searched the body, and from the quality of his clothing this was surely a master vampire, one who had gathered around him a coven of followers and thralls. What he was doing here was anybody's guess.

"You blew him away, Fireblood," one of the guards told her. Likely there wasn't a citizen of Waterdon who didn't know her on sight, after her famous deeds of a few months ago. "You know," he went on, "You ought to think about joining the Daywatch Brigade. I'd join myself if I didn't have my duty to Waterdon and the eorl."

"Daywatch Brigade?" Bernadette asked. Why did that name sound familiar?

"They named it after the stronghold, I think," the guard replied. He gestured toward the north. "Its way up north, in a hidden valley west of Norcove. Fellow by the name of Malden is putting together a force to eradicate vampires, and they're rebuilding the old castle."

"I know the place," Erik put in. "I grew up in Norcove, and roamed that area when I was in my teens. The valley's something else, but the castle was pretty much a ruin the last time I saw it."

"Thanks," Bernadette said, "I'll think about it." She had her reservations about a campaign to eradicate vampires – after all, they'd been human once. Many were probably innocent victims, infected by the virus and transformed before they had realized they were ill. Yet still, if they were starting to come out of their hidden lairs to attack people on the streets, something would have to be done. She dug into her pack and got out a panacea potion, which would eradicate any infectious disease.

"Here, Bjorn," she said. "You'd better take this." Contact with the blood of vampires could turn you into one yourself, and while it was rumored that a cure was possible even after the symptoms had fully taken hold, it was supposedly both extremely involved and very expensive. Better safe than sorry!

Bernadette led her party to their original intended destination: the door of Brightsgate Cottage. They found Lifa standing before the fire, stirring the kettle while Anja sat at the table, drawing with charcoal on a scrap of paper. Anja looked up, her eyes alight in an instant. "Aunt Berni! Uncle Erik!" Bernadette swept the child up into her arms as the little red-haired whirlwind barreled into her. Then she handed Anja off to Erik, who lifted her high to enfold her in a bear-hug before letting her down again. The ceilings in Brightsgate Cottage were far too low to allow her to ride his shoulders.

Bernadette turned to Lifa. "How is everything?" she asked. Lifa smiled, pleased to see her warden and benefactor – the young woman she was just starting to think of as a friend.

"We're doing fine. But did you hear? There have been vampire attacks in the city." As a woman fully versed in the arts of killing, Lifa did not regard the threat as the average housewife might.

"Actually, we just met a master vampire as we were arriving here," Bernadette told her. "It was lucky we had Bjorn along." Lifa noticed for the first time that neither Bernadette nor Erik was wearing their usual battle garb – and that a tall, broad-shouldered warrior she had never seen before accompanied them.

He looked like a man worthy of respect, this fellow. A few years older than she was, and with the battle scars to prove his history. He carried himself erect, a true Norseman; and he had an air of seriousness that resonated with her. Though they had not yet spoken nor even been introduced, Lifa sensed already that this Bjorn was someone for whom duty was a vital component of his makeup – as it was for her.

Recovering her composure, Bernadette formally presented Bjorn to the household. "Bjorn One-Eye, this is Brightsgate Cottage, and this is Lifa – my Waterdon body servant. She is guardian to my ward, Anja."

The little girl, taking this all in with far less gravity than the adults were displaying, piped up at this juncture with a "Hi!" and a little wave. A hint of something akin to warmth flickered across Bjorn's features at that point. He wasn't sure what situation his warden was putting him into, but he was beginning to think he might like it. This Lifa was stunning! Her glistening dark hair and enormous dark blue eyes, coupled with her hourglass figure, put even his warden in the shade.

He said formally, "Pleased to meet you, Lifa. And Anja," bowing slightly to the red-haired gamin beaming up at him. He'd become used to a negative reaction when people saw his dead right eye; but this little girl didn't appear to be concerned by it.

"Are you a warrior, like Uncle Erik?" she asked. Before he could formulate an answer she continued, "Can I call you Uncle Bjorn?" Nonplussed, Bjorn just stood stiffly, a smile caught on his face as if it had been surprised there and was not sure whether to flee.

Bernadette stepped back, placing her hand on Erik's arm. She smiled, exchanging glances with him. This was pretty much exactly what she'd had in mind. "Bjorn," she said, "I'd like you to stay here in Brightsgate Cottage for a while. With these vampire attacks, I think Lifa could use some help protecting Anja. Or at least, with household chores and shopping and so forth. You can sleep in the spare bed over there," she gestured toward the bed Erik and Andrion had lugged from the Maiden. "… unless you and Lifa come to some other arrangement…" Was that too heavy-handed? Bernadette was new at this match-making stuff.

Lifa glanced at Bjorn, then at Bernadette with a look that hinted at resentment. Oh shit, too heavy-handed. But maybe the gaffe could be forgotten, in time. "Well, Erik and I will be off now" she said, a flush rising in her cheeks. Had this really been such a good idea? More kisses and hugs were exchanged with Anja, then the two of them backed out the door of Brightsgate Cottage and shortly thereafter materialized outside the Bathing Maiden.

Erik glanced at Bernadette as they made their way inside, a half-smile on his face. "So, Lifa and Bjorn eh? Are you sure about that?" Bernadette shook her head ruefully.

"It seemed like a good idea when we first got to Eastview and I realized I had a matched set of body servants. Now, I don't know. I don't think I can just push people around and have them do what I want them to do. But wouldn't it be great if they hit it off? It would be like Anja getting a mom *and* a dad, just like that." She snapped her fingers.

Chapter 9: Homecoming

Erik grinned at her, appreciating her motives if questioning her wisdom. "I guess we'll have to wait and see," he said noncommittally. As soon as they were fully inside the Maiden, Bernadette's eyes were moving around, searching for Andrion. Erik took note of this and knew what was on her mind. He'd accepted that he only held a part of his lover's heart, but it still gave him a little twinge of regret when her attention veered from him to his friend and rival. There were quite a few people in the Maiden, relaxing in the central bathing pool or having a meal at one of the tables on the mezzanine, but Andrion was not among them.

Giving Erik a kiss and a squeeze, Bernadette hastened up the stairs. She found Andrion sitting by himself at the table in the master bedroom area, sipping from a tankard of ale and looking thoughtful. A plate of food sat on the table in front of him. She called to him, "Andrion!" and rushed to him. His warm brown eyes lit at the sight of her, yet she sensed a cloud behind them. Something was troubling him. She fell into his arms, squeezing him to her as she pressed her mouth to his. "Is everything all right, darling?"

Andrion stood holding her, shaking off his melancholy with a will. She was here again, in his arms. But her days away had left him feeling as if the sun was never going to shine again. Was he losing his ability to remain satisfied with the arrangement that he, Berni, and Erik had come to a few months before?

He bore Erik no enmity. Who could dislike Erik? A stauncher ally or sunnier companion had never been born. Yet the uncertainty of Andrion's position, the never knowing when he got up in the morning if he would be with his beloved or merely missing her, while she was gone for an unknown period of days (or worse – here, but sleeping in another man's bed), was beginning to gnaw at the core of his being.

Berni was always honest with him, and Andrion felt he owed it to her to be honest in turn. But it was so painfully hard to articulate his feelings. What if she rejected them as an attempt to limit her freedom? What if she decided to throw off his clinging, needy love to go be young and carefree with Erik and whoever else caught her fancy? The ten-year difference in their ages meant they were at different points in their lives. With every passing year Andrion longed more for stability, for building a future – while Berni was just getting started, in the prime of enjoying her life without ties or responsibilities.

Bernadette was now holding Andrion's arms, looking up at his face as a series of emotions passed across it. This was serious! Whatever was bothering her lover, it seemed to be really tearing him up inside. And, after his recent revelations about his hopes for the future, she could only guess that her prolonged absence from his bed was at the root of it. "Andrion! I'm here now! I love you!"

He pulled himself away from the thoughts that were ravaging him, to look into her eyes with love. "I know," he murmured, and kissed her deeply. She received his kiss whole-heartedly, though the situation still troubled her. She loved Andrion more than she could express. That fidelity was not in her makeup, that she was irresistibly drawn to Erik, did not change that fact. After months of happy accommodation, she suddenly felt stabbed to the heart by the same conflict that had troubled her when she first realized that she loved and wanted them both.

But Bernadette's irrepressible nature soon reasserted itself. Pushing aside the intensity of her feelings, she let her excitement about the recent turn of events spill out to wash away the pall of heavy emotions. "Andrion!" she exclaimed, "I am now Warden of Westmarch!" He smiled at her, pleasure in her happiness easing his troubled mood. "Congratulations! So, you bought a house?"

"*We* bought a *wonderful* house!" she replied joyfully. "It's called Eastview, and it's not far from the Alfenstein main gates. It's like, *twice* the size of Brightsgate Cottage. *And*, it came with a body servant! A *male* body servant!"

Andrion cocked an eyebrow at her. "Oh?"

"Yes! His name is Bjorn One-Eye, he looks to be around your age but he's *super* grim and warlike, big like Erik. And we brought him back to Waterdon so I could give him to Lifa."

Andrion was a bit taken aback. "Um… Berni, you can't just move people around like you're playing with dolls." Ire flared in her eyes.

"I'll have you know I have *never* played with dolls." After a moment her anger subsided, however, and she appeared a little chastened. "I know, Lifa was mad at me too. But I think she'll get over it. She needs some help looking after Anja and I think both she and Bjorn were lonely, being body servants all by themselves. This way they'll both have some company, and if anything more comes of it all to the good." She considered some more before adding, "If Ormund can 'give' Lifa to me, I don't see why I can't 'give' Bjorn to her. She's beautiful, and Bjorn is a hunk even if he does look a little hard-bitten. They'd make a perfect couple."

Andrion shrugged. Once his little lover got rolling, there was no stopping her. What could he do but be swept along? Bernadette abruptly seated herself at the table and picked up a bread roll, taking a big bite and then washing it down with a little of Andrion's ale before continuing in a more serious vein. "Andrion, when we came into Waterdon a little while ago we were attacked by a master vampire right out in front of the door to Brightsgate Cottage. Everywhere I go people are talking about increasing vampire attacks, and I think it's time to do something about it."

She had some more bread and another sip of ale. Breakfast seemed to have been a long while ago. "I heard someone mention an organization that's forming, like the Brave Company or the Guardians, but specifically targeting vampires. They're recruiting at some fortress out west of Norcove, and I think we should join up. Assuming you want to come along with me?"

Andrion gave her his warmest smile. "I'll follow you anywhere, Berni. You know that. And fighting vampires seems like a worthy cause. What about Erik?"

Bernadette thought about it. Her two men in tandem were unstoppable. But just as she'd guessed when she first considered having both of them fighting at her side, the situation could be a logistical nightmare. She would barely be able to get an arrow in without risking hitting one or the other of them as they leapt into the fray. Of the two, she supposed Erik was the more effective killer. He accomplished by ferocity and main force in seconds what might take Andrion three or four times as long to achieve with battle magic. But

Andrion had more knowledge about the world and its dangers, and he and she made a better fighting team.

But of all the factors she was considering, the one that carried the argument for her was her relationship with Andrion. She'd gone off and left him for a couple of days, and returned to find him so sad at her absence that even her return had failed to completely lighten his mood. She needed to spend some time together with him, one on one, and reassure him that her love for him was as deep as his for her. Erik… well, she knew that Erik's once-casual feelings for her had gone deeper as well, and she would miss him. But she felt he was better-equipped emotionally to withstand a prolonged separation.

Andrion had seated himself beside her at the table and was watching her, waiting for an answer. Her decision made, she smiled at him and said "I think Erik should stay here. I'd like to have someone close at hand who cares about Anja and can help Lifa and Bjorn if they need anything. And who knows when we'll be back? This could take months." Elation flared in Andrion's heart. Yes! He might not wish Erik harm, but he wanted Berni for himself. He was coming to realize that more as the months went by. This anti-vampire crusade would be his chance to win her, if anything would.

He reached out to grab her hands, holding them firmly while looking into her eyes. "You and I should be more than a match for any den of vampires, love" he assured her. Noticing for the first time that she was eating his supper, he asked "Have you eaten yet?" An expression of puzzled concentration passed across Berni's face.

"Erik and I had breakfast in Alfenstein what seems like two or three hours ago. But I *am* hungry."

"How about we get a soak, and have Lev whip us up something for afterward?" he asked. He knew his beloved well, and the chance to climb into hot water was something she rarely passed up.

Bernadette smiled brilliantly at him, squeezing his hands then rising to her feet with a cheery "Okay!" She peeled out of her street clothes, much easier than getting out of armor. She enjoyed the excitement of questing in dangerous places, and was already looking forward to the project she was embarking on with Andrion. But a little peace and quiet now and again was enjoyable too.

As she was undressing, Andrion stood up again. Forgetting for the moment that he was planning to take a bath too, he just stood gazing at her. She stirred him to his soul, although he had to admit that his crotch appeared to be involved as well. Starting slightly as he remembered what he was supposed to be doing, he took off his shirt. By now Berni was standing there in the nude, rummaging through her pack for a robe, and he came up behind her to press himself against her bare skin. His trousers were soft, though what was contained within them was *not*.

He bent over her, wrapping his arms around her, inhaling her scent as his face pressed to her bare back. "Mmmm!" he said. Then, "Wanna screw first?" Bernadette snorted and stood upright suddenly enough to bash him in the nose; but he was ready for her and got out of the way. She rotated to face him, her eyes wide.

"Why Andrion," she said, surprise painting her features. "It's almost as if you could read my mind!" With that she stepped forward to fall into his arms, her breasts pressed to his bare chest as her hand wandered down to press and stroke the firm bulge straining his trousers.

Ooh, it was so hot! She felt a little guilty at leaving it all on its lonesome for so many days. Making love with Erik was Big Fun, but making love with Andrion had another dimension to it. Oh, how she wished it were possible to have *both* of them with no hurt feelings, but she realized that she was just going to have to face the facts. Andrion needed more of her than she had been willing to give him. Was she willing to give *him* up and tear his heart apart, just so she could have the freedom to hop from one bed to another for a few more years before settling down? She definitely *did* plan to settle down someday, have a family and a home and some continuity to her life. But not yet!

Still pressed against Andrion's chest, she sighed. She loved him so much! Maybe with him, a settled life wouldn't be so bad. And they could still have adventures together, perhaps. For a moment a vision appeared before her eyes, of a sprawling residence overlooking a sunny meadow with a sprightly river flowing at the bottom of it. Their children and Anja, along with Lifa and Bjorn's brood (she pictured two boys and a girl), laughed and played through the halls as she and Andrion returned, laden with loot, from another expedition during which the body servant couple had been watching the children. This fantasy seemed so utterly absurd, she found herself shaking with suppressed laughter.

"Berni?" Andrion asked. One moment she'd been about to get down and dirty on him, and the next she was lost in thought... and laughing?

"Nothing," she smiled. "Just a whacky thought. Let's see about *this*, shall we?" With that she seized the waistband of his trousers and pulled them down off of him. He could certainly have worn underdrawers with these, but seemed to prefer to go without them – and his fine, thick cock was standing at attention before her eyes.

She knelt on the carpet and took him in her mouth. Since she couldn't really do this successfully with Erik, she'd been honing all her cocksucking skills on Andrion; and she'd found that she quite liked it. That big, stiff, slightly salty member filling her mouth made her think of how it would feel in the other end, and the stimulation as her lips rubbed over it, her fingers tickling his scrotum as it tightened, conveyed his excitement to her like the electrical charge from a lightning spell.

Andrion gasped. Oh, yeah. He held her head gently as she worked on him. Damn, she was getting good at this! It had only been a short while ago she had first sucked him to orgasm, and now she seemed close to doing it again. Days without her had raised his libido to a sharp hunger within him. But no, no... can't come yet. He went from pulling in to pushing back on Berni's head, making her release him from her mouth and look up at him. Her eyes had gone softly focused. Evidently she was enjoying it as much as he was! But he still wanted to make her come.

"Slowly, my dear..." he murmured, giving her a hand so she could rise. Then he kicked off his trousers from where they lay puddled around his ankles, and led her to the bed. He beckoned her to sit down on the edge, then *he* knelt and began pleasuring her with his mouth. Ooh! Bernadette lay back to enjoy this, her legs spread wide. Andrion had a lot of talent in his tongue and lips, and he seemed to enjoy eating her as much as she did him. As ever, it took only a minute or two of this before the feeling rose in her, a little burst of pleasure in the area of her clit that radiated out to encompass her entire body. She cried out and pressed him to her as she came, then relaxed and lay there panting, smiling, as he kissed her inner thighs before beginning to work his way slowly up her body.

By the time they were face to face, his hard cock was slipping inside her still-throbbing, dripping cunt. Oh! That felt so good! As sometimes happened when they were together they moved as in a trance, riding the sensations of their bodies like a wave of warm silk while their spirits soared and twined. An endless instant later, the fire ignited within Bernadette and Andrion at once, spreading like a shockwave to engulf them in ripples of ecstasy. Andrion held her tightly, encased in her to his full length, gasping for breath. His warm brown eyes were alight with exultation, her cool sea-gray ones radiating love.

From the depression that had dragged him down before Berni's arrival, Andrion now felt on top of the world. She loved him, he *knew* she did! And she was willing to join with him in a long-term endeavor that would take her away from here, away from Erik, away from any other guys that might catch her eye. He understood that a woman with appetites like Berni's was a rarity, and that it shouldn't surprise him if she occasionally felt like dining on some less-usual fare.

He'd even be willing to grant her the occasional bit of outside activity, as long as her heart belonged to him and her children were his as well. Though now that he thought about it, why should *that* matter? He already loved Anja, no relation to either of them. He knew he would love any child that was a part of Berni, whether he had provided the seed to create it or not. It was loving and being together as a family, not sperm or egg, that made a father or a mother.

When their breathing had returned to normal, the two rose from the bed. Andrion donned his own robe and Bernadette completed the long-interrupted search for hers, which she put on. Then they walked down the stairs to the common room, holding hands, and slipped into the hot pool. They spotted Erik sitting at their usual table, a few paces from poolside. He too had evidently found breakfast either lacking or too long gone, and was working on a plate of food. Before climbing into the pool, Bernadette took Lev aside and asked him to deliver some more food to Erik's table. She could only hope some of it would still be left by the time they'd finished their soak.

Bernadette and Andrion joined a small throng of Maiden customers in the pool. Business seemed to be up, and she made a mental note to herself to check with Lev for her share of the profits. Her recent real estate purchases had left her purse a little on the flat side, and who knew what expenses might be involved in launching a general campaign against vampires? They sat there on a bench, holding hands and enjoying the hot water. Neither found much to say. After their blissful session of lovemaking they seemed to be floating, at peace with the world.

When the hot water had begun to carve wrinkles in the pads of their fingers they climbed out, stomachs rumbling. After toweling off and re-donning their robes they hastened to join Erik at the table. He'd finished eating, and was just sitting there taking in the ambience of the Maiden, enjoying himself after a satisfactory meal. He greeted them with a smile, and beckoned to the largely untouched plates of food that had arrived in their absence.

"Oh good, you left some for us!" Bernadette said teasingly. Erik grinned at her. "Eat up!" he said. She and Andrion fell to devouring the food with surprising hunger. He'd been about to eat dinner when she arrived, and she had been feeling a little peckish. For some reason, they were both now ravenous. When the gnawing in Bernadette's stomach had been reduced to a manageable level, she began filling Erik in on her current plan. "Andrion and I are going up toward Norcove, and joining up with that "Daywatch Brigade" group the guard told us about," she said.

Erik had an idea where this was heading. That lingering dread, which had grown at the back of his mind over the past few months, was coming to the fore. "You want me to come along?" he asked, though he feared what the answer would be. Berni touched his arm, even as she took a drink of her ale.

"I'd really like you to stay here, and keep an eye on Lifa and Anja," she told him. He felt as if protest was futile, but couldn't stop himself from making it anyway.

"Wasn't that why we brought Bjorn to stay at Brightsgate Cottage?" he asked.

Uh-oh, Bernadette thought. She had confidently expected Erik to accept whatever their relationship brought with a smile and a hearty "Oh well." Instead, it was beginning to look as though he was as unwilling to part with her as Andrion was. Now what? "Anja loves you," she told him. "She needs all the people she can get in her life who will be there for her. You can bring them supplies, come by for visits, make them feel like they have some support. I don't know whether Bjorn even likes kids. He certainly doesn't seem like a logical candidate for Dad of the Year."

"And *I* do?" Erik asked. Despite himself, despite the hurt he was feeling, he couldn't help smiling. Bernadette returned that smile. "Who *wouldn't* love you? Erik, you are marvelous! Anja adores you, and I am extremely fond of you myself! You'll be fine, and when the vampire threat is eliminated we'll all be back together again. Okay?" Her eyes were shining as she looked at him hopefully, and he was powerless to deny her. He had his own suspicions of the likely outcome of this prolonged adventure, but what could he do? He loved Berni, and he was going to love her whether she was his or not. A small fragment of his usual zest for life returned to him, as he considered that there were many joys to be found, if you had eyes to see.

Bernadette squeezed his hands and gave him one of those radiant smiles that came from the heart. She loved him, and she *willed* him to be all right, to be happy. She couldn't bear it if either of her men were lost in the sink of despair because she had decided to devote herself to the other. So that would *not* happen! She hoped.

The three of them finished eating their extended dinner, and sat talking and watching the passing parade as the life of the Maiden went on around them. "There seems to be lot more guests than usual," Bernadette remarked.

"They're all here for a glimpse of The Fireblood," Erik told her with a grin. She doubted that, since most people were not paying her any more attention than usual. It was not as if she was the most beautiful woman in the room, or anything.

But perhaps what he said had some truth in it. Her reputation had spread, and people with time on their hands might well seek out a brush with fame. They could go back home and say, "I went to the Bathing Maiden. Yeah, it's owned by the Fireblood. She was right there, eating dinner on the other side of the room. And I slept in one of the beds *she* slept in." Most of them wouldn't have recognized her if she'd gone up to them and squeezed their crotch.

As the hour grew late and the crowd thinned, the three friends parted ways – Erik to sleep (alone, apparently) in his basement bedroom while Bernadette and Andrion climbed the stairs to spend the night in the master bed. The afterglow from their recent time together left them still touching and stroking a lot, floating in a miasma of love that made it hard to focus on the world around them. When they had taken off their clothing and climbed between the sheets, Andrion took her in his arms and made love to her again, with the slow concentration that was possible now the edge had been taken off. It was a long while before they slept.

Chapter 10: Daywatch

For once, when Bernadette awoke Andrion was up as well. He felt alive with excitement at the prospect of embarking on this new adventure with her. Since the tumultuous events surrounding the Fireblood's defeat of the Soul-Devourer (with indispensable assistance from Erik and him), the three of them had looked on questing as a sort of sport or hobby. There were always nests of bandits to be cleared out, or they'd be sent looking for some missing artifact or another. They got great exercise, explored new places, and returned with all kinds of treasures. It was thanks to these activities (and Berni's growing skills in smithing and enchanting) that they had been able to purchase two nice homes in the span of a couple of days.

But nothing they had done was all that crucial. The population of Iscandia was not looking to them as saviors from some overwhelming peril anymore. Their service had not been forgotten, as yet; but it seemed as if the prevailing attitude was "what have you done for me lately?" Now, the increasing vampire incursions menaced everyone's safety. And they, he and his beloved, were going to do something about it. Whether they got the credit for it or not, it felt good just to be doing something so worthwhile. That he and Berni were doing it as a team made his happiness complete.

Bernadette was a bit surprised to find him rolling right out of bed with a smile on his lips when she sat up to put her feet on the floor, still yawning. Who is this man and what is he doing in my bed, she thought fondly. His cock was half-hard as he came around the foot of the bed to give her an affectionate squeeze before starting to get into some underdrawers. She decided not to encourage it. "Anxious to get moving?" she asked him. He grinned at her and nodded, his eyes sparkling. What a change from his troubled demeanor when she'd come home yesterday!

As usual before embarking on a major expedition, she took her companion down into the basement. Erik was already absent from his bed, which was neatly made. She hadn't noticed him on their way through the common room, and wondered where he'd gone. She went over their weapons and armor, improving and enchanting a few pieces for the fight ahead with an emphasis on weapons that might be particularly effective against vampires. Andrion hadn't yet gotten a good look at her new sablium armor, and he was as flabbergasted as Erik had been. "Ow!" he cried in mock pain. "It hurts to get a hard-on in this armor!" She shot him her best seductive smile and reached up under the armor's skirt to give him a squeeze. Gee, he wasn't kidding.

"My plan is to make all the bandits, vampires, and hostile mages weak with lust," she told him seriously. "As soon as I figure out what turns on aptrgangr, mandimants, and leukalfar, I'll be prepared for anything. Oh, and dragons… though now I think of it I don't know if there *are* any female dragons." Andrion just leered at her. Berni's … *tendencies* might sometimes be troublesome for him, but he *did* love that about her. She could stiffen him with her mere presence, even though he was no longer the randy young man who had first arrived in Iscandia a decade past.

Their armament complete, Bernadette led Andrion back up the ladder and stopped off for a consultation with Drelos, picking up some water and less-perishable foodstuffs for the trip. The whole time, she was scanning the room; and she finally spotted Erik, sitting at a table near the rear of the mezzanine. Stuffing the last of the supplies into her pack, she made a beeline for him.

Erik looked a bit thoughtful sitting there, drinking a mug of ale and working on a small plate of pastries. He brightened at the sight of her, though he could tell she was getting ready to tell him goodbye. He could only hope it wasn't forever. "You're off, then?" he asked diffidently.

"Vampires, beware!" Bernadette replied cheerily, trying to dispel the gloom. He looked her up and down in that ridiculously sexy armor, and just smiled a little. The force of whatever it was that drew her to Erik like a moth to a flame hit her squarely between the legs, radiating out from there in all directions to make her heart beat faster and her knees feel momentarily weak. She gave a nearly-imperceptible gasp.

"You take care of Anja and Lifa while we're gone," she admonished him in an effort to cover how much he had affected her. "And yourself, as well," she continued. Then practically hurling herself into his lap, she threw her arms around him to give him a hug and a passionate kiss before parting. Close to his ear, she murmured, "Goodbye, Erik. I'll miss you!"

He returned her hug and kiss with surprising force and murmured back, "I'll always love you."

That took her aback. Bernadette had always thought that her relationship with Erik was a cross between the love you felt for a good friend and an irresistible lust that drew her back to his bed time and time again even when she felt she should probably not be there. But over the months, it seemed to have developed into something more. A fine time to be learning that.

Breaking away, she stood to take her leave. Andrion put out a hand to Erik and said "Take care, buddy. We'll see you when we get back." Was there a look of triumph in his eyes? The Fireblood and her companion made their way to the doors of the Maiden then, and in a few moments they were standing just inside the gates of Waterdon.

Opening the door of Brightsgate Cottage after a knock and a "Come in!" Bernadette found a sweet domestic scene unfolding. Lifa was at the cooking stand stirring something in the pot, while Bjorn sat at the dining table across from Anja. They seemed to be playing some kind of game.

Anja looked up and squealed, "Aunt Berni!" as she jumped up from the wooden bench and ran to throw her arms around the woman who was the first person she could remember seeing in her life. Berni stooped to hug her back, then pursed her lips for a loud smooch. In a moment, the little red-haired whirlwind was off again. "Uncle Andrion!" she cried and he grinned broadly at her, scooping her up and tossing her in the air. Armored as he was, he couldn't exactly fold her to his breast; but he did bring her in for a kiss before setting her down again.

Bernadette's heart fairly melted. Anja was so lovable, and it gave her the greatest joy that others who she also loved felt the same way. Lifa had turned from stirring the pot and was looking on them all with a serene smile on her face, her eyes glowing with satisfaction. Bernadette expected their feelings were very similar at that moment. The little one was off and running again. "Come see!" she urged, leading Bernadette by the hand to the table where Bjorn sat, looking considerably less grim than the first time she had seen him. "Uncle Bjorn made us a game to play, look!"

Bernadette looked down, and saw that some brightly-painted rectangles of stiff paper were spread out on the table. Cards? She had heard of them, but had never seen any in Iscandia. "This was a game I saw in Remus," he told her in his deep voice. "There, they play it in taverns and bet money on the outcome. You can't buy cards in Iscandia, so while I was hanging around by myself in Alfenstein I got some paints and paper and made my own. See? There's two matching of every picture and you put them all face down, then turn up two at a time and try to remember where those pictures were. When you find a pair, you get to keep them." Looking at Anja in mock resentment he continued, "She's beaten me four times in a row."

Bernadette just goggled. The artwork on the cards was amazingly good, vivid pictures of everything from barnyard animals and more exotic beasts like dragons to human figures representing eorls, fine ladies, washerwomen, and so forth. "These are amazing!" she told Bjorn. "You actually *made* these yourself?" He looked a bit embarrassed. This was hardly the skill a fierce warrior, master of the longsword, was likely to brag about.

"It's just something I picked up. I've had a lot of time on my hands, while Eastview was vacant." He looked at Anja, and at Lifa, a slight smile playing across his lips. "Things have gotten a bit more interesting, now."

What unexpected facets people kept turning up with! The gigantic, lusty warrior Erik Johannessohn was playful and gentle. Stone-faced Lifa had just been waiting for a child to melt her heart. And doughty, scarred Bjorn, mighty fighter though he might be, was a talented artist. Bernadette wondered whimsically whether Andrion might suddenly demonstrate the ability to play the lute, or something equally unlikely. It all both amazed her and filled her with delight.

Recalling that she had brought gifts with her, Bernadette turned and opened her pack. She had brought a small stuffed toy for Anja along with the bottle of goat's milk Lev had procured, some pastries for everyone to enjoy, and for Lifa a pretty necklace. Lifa smiled and thanked her. For Bjorn, she proffered a ring. This simple silver ring was enchanted with fortified stamina in battle, though she suspected he scarcely needed it.

Thanks were given, then Bernadette announced "Andrion and I are going off to join that group that are banding together to fight vampires. After last night's attack, I think it's time we did something about them. I don't know how long we'll be gone, but Erik is staying at the Maiden and he'll be checking in with you often to see if there's anything you need. I think Waterdon is still pretty safe during the day, but you should be careful after dark."

Lifa might be beautiful, attired in a pretty dress and mellowed by her newly acquired status as foster mom; but she was still a swordswoman of no mean abilities. The look she gave Bernadette in response to this admonition left no doubt that any vampires wanting to harm Anja would have to come through *her*, and were not likely to make it to the other side. Bernadette gave her a fierce, approving smile, then turned it on Bjorn as he also indicated that nothing was going to get to their little girl while *he* was around.

Hugs and kisses, or at least hand-squeezes, were delivered all 'round. Then Bernadette and Andrion took their leave, and fast-traveled to Norcove. The two of them had been here together at the end of summer, searching for a fabled ceremonial spear reputed to be hidden in a nearby barrow. It had been pleasant enough then, its location near sea level surrounded on three sides by water making the climate more pleasant than in Coldstein – even though the latter city stood far south of here.

But winter was coming on now, and they found a light snow falling. Soon the harbor would be iced over, and the little town that served as capital for the sparsely-populated Seamarch would nearly grind to a halt. There was a copper mine a little east of town, and work there would continue. But the fisherfolk and sailors would dig in and huddle before their fires for the next few months.

"Did Erik mention his mother and father still live here?" Andrion asked, as they oriented themselves. They'd arrived in what appeared to be mid-afternoon, and needed to consider whether it would be better to put up in the inn here and set off in the morning.

Bernadette looked at him in astonishment. "Gods, no!" she cried. "Why didn't he mention that when we were up this way a few months ago?" Andrion shook his head, shrugging. Erik was so open, relaxed, and friendly, it was hard to imagine him having other than a good relationship with his family. But they had known each other for well over two years, and their conversation the other day was the first time he'd heard any of it.

"Maybe there was some bad blood between them," he offered. "Dad says 'Go ahead – throw away your wonderful opportunity to join the family fishing business and become a good-for-nothing adventurer. But don't ever darken our door again!' And so he doesn't…"

Bernadette couldn't believe it, but she couldn't offer a likelier explanation. She'd have to try to pry the story out of Erik next time they were together. Andrion went on, "He told me there's a sort of road, more like a cart track really, that runs along a few hundred yards inland from the coast heading west. If we stay on that, there'll be a mountain off to our south and a river flowing out into the North Sea. We turn there, and the river should take us right to Closevale."

The snowfall wasn't too bad, Bernadette judged. "Shall we just start walking, then?" she asked.

"Sure," Andrion replied, and instead of walking into town the pair turned west and soon picked up the beaten track that ran along near the sea. It was far enough inland to avoid disturbing the walruses that often rested along the rocky shore during the daytime.

The creatures were enormous, weighing more than a ton, and their twin tusks combined with that bulk could make them lethal if they decided you were intruding on their turf. They weren't easy to kill, either, with inches of blubber beneath a tough hide protecting their vital organs. Much better to stay out of their way!

They strode along making good time. There was not much snow on the track, and footing was good. Bernadette soon felt so warm from the exertion of walking with her heavy pack that she stopped for a moment and removed her fur cloak. It was made from the pelt of a single smilodon, the "snow cat" morph with its creamy and luxuriant white fur, and lined with light and water-resistant wool. She tucked into her pack, enjoying the feel of the cool air on her face. Andrion smiled at her, remembering the cat that had contributed that pelt.

The afternoon was wearing on toward evening, which comes soon at this latitude in late autumn. At least the snow had stopped. They had seen a few of the short-eared boreal hares, wearing brown and white as their winter coats began to come in, and once one of the little foxes that ate them; but the trip had been blessedly free of animal attacks so far.

A sturdy, well-worn wooden bridge around six feet wide stood across a small ravine ahead of them, leading on to the west. Bernadette stepped out onto the bridge and looked down. Below a small stream, perhaps 30 feet across, was bubbling and bouncing its way to the sea a quarter of a mile away, the water crystal clear – and steaming!

"Andrion, look at that!" she said, gesturing. He smiled.

"This must be where we turn," he said. They looked south, and spotted a faint trail running in that direction on the east side of the bridge. They soon set their feet on this new trail, wondering if there was a chance they could get to Daywatch before dark.

"Why is the water steaming?" Bernadette asked.

"It's warmer than the air," Andrion told her with a secretive grin." In answer to her questioning look, he said "I think you're going to be surprised when we get to Closevale, and I don't want to spoil it for you. Wait and see."

Her curiosity was piqued, but Bernadette stifled the urge to try to wheedle more information out of Andrion. She knew that he loved her, and if he teased her like this it was because he thought the eventual surprise would bring her joy. Let him have his fun.

The sun sank behind a mountain range off beyond the far side of the little stream, which had become narrower as they followed it toward its source in the mountains to the south. One peak in particular stood up above the rest, a little closer to them than the rest of the range. Its upper reaches were still lit, glowing orange in the sunset light.

"Is that a volcano, Andrion?" Bernadette asked, noting a wisp of smoke rising beyond the clouds gathered around the conical peak. He grinned at her. No flies on his beloved.

"Supposedly it's a dormant one," he admitted. "More so than Drakespire. There are ancient records of an eruption, mostly ash rather than lava, but I don't think it's actually blown its top since around the time the dypalfar vanished."

"Good to know," she replied with a smile. "And that's where we're going?"

"To a valley at its bottom," he said.

"I suppose this river must be fed by hot springs, then," Bernadette mused. "That explains the steaming." After another few paces she stopped and looked around them. There had been no trees near the coast, but they were now nearly ten miles inland and a few were starting to appear.

"I don't think we're going to make it to Closevale this evening," she said. "What do you say we walk up to the top of that little hill and pitch camp in among the pines?"

"Fine with me," Andrion replied. Being alone with Berni on their bold new adventure still had him simmering with happiness.

They'd brought extra bedrolls, knowing how cold it got in this part of Iscandia; and plenty of provisions, as well. After a hearty camp stew, augmented with one of those boreal hares Bernadette had nabbed for the pot as dusk was coming on, they pitched a tent and crawled inside it.

By now night had fallen, and though their campfire was close at hand it had gotten very cold. "This reminds me of that time in Alzhenten," Bernadette murmured into Andrion's chest as he held her close beneath the furs. They'd added her cloak as an extra blanket. "Your hands are warmer, now," he replied as softly. She could feel his hardness beneath the stretchy woolen underwear, and gave him a squeeze. Then she rotated, putting her back to him, and pulled down her bottoms.

In the morning Bernadette was up and heating water for tea over the rekindled fire, though Andrion still huddled in their bedrolls. She sighed to herself. It was too much to hope that he was going to change into a morning person, no matter how eager he was to be with her, she realized. She stepped over to the tent's opening and nudged him through the bedrolls with a toe. "Rise and shine, sleepyhead," she called fondly. "Let's get moving!"

The sun was well up by the time they were on the road again. The terrain was changing, rising gradually, and the little river had become narrower still and rushed quickly over stones in a bed no more than a few feet deep. Bernadette picked her way over to the water and squatted to put her hands in it.

"Whoo!" she exclaimed. "It *is* warm!" Unlike the hot spring they'd bathed in at Drakespire, this water seemed to have none of the sulfurous smell she associated with volcanoes. It was a little cooler than the water in the Maiden's inside bathing pool, crystal clear and seemingly not populated by any of the usual water life to be found in an ordinary stream. She washed her face and hands, enjoying the sensation. If they weren't in a hurry, she'd have liked to strip on the spot and go for a dip.

The day had dawned overcast, but the cloud cover was beginning to break up and visibility was good. The mountain, Vulfassdur, now towered above them as if it were so close they could reach out and touch it; and its slopes were heavily forested up to the timberline. It must stand nearly 14,000 feet high!

The trail, which wandered beside the sparkling stream, went up a little rise and Bernadette stopped to peer ahead, hands shading her eyes. Near the bottom of Vulfassdur, and over a bit to the right, there was a sort of blur close to the ground. "What do you suppose that is?" she asked Andrion. He stood beside her, peering ahead as she was doing.

"I think that must be the falls Erik told me about," he replied after staring for a minute. "That's good, it means we're almost to the trail that leads up and into Closevale." They picked up their pace, eager to reach their goal, and in another two hours were standing beside a broad, warm pool.

The little stream, smaller yet, fell down a cliff face for a distance of some one hundred feet before spreading out. Some past seismic event had blocked the water's escape beyond the waterfall, and the pool now emptied through a narrow crack between two boulders before plunging down a series of small cascades and resuming its progress toward the sea almost thirty miles away.

"Ooh, that pool looks so inviting!" Bernadette moaned. After hiking for most of the past two days and camping out, both of them were getting grubby. But now, she felt, just wasn't the time.

"Erik said there are some hot pools in the valley itself," Andrion told her. "I'm sure we'll be able to get a hot bath later, but I'm really anxious to make it Daywatch. Time to climb!"

He led the way as the path skirted the water's edge and went up the cliffside beside the waterfall in a series of switchbacks fit for a mountain goat. To make it still more interesting, windblown spray from the nearby falls coated the hikers, and the surface of the trail they were on, in a warm wet mist.

Huffing and puffing, both of them in good shape but heavily laden, they reached the top at last and stepped out into dryness and warm sunshine. Some twenty feet to their right the stream, running narrow, plunged over the cliff. And twenty feet in front of them, flanking the trail, were a pair of armored warriors. One of them was a burly uruk armed with a short bow, the other a gangly young Norseman who appeared to be close to Bernadette in age. He had a sword at his belt, but it was not drawn. It appeared that the two, obviously on guard duty, had been talking together to pass the time until the intruders had suddenly appeared at the top of the falls.

"Halt," the uruk sentry demanded shortly as Bernadette and Andrion approached. Even the ghastly-looking leukalfar couldn't compete with the uruks among the human races of Terris when it came to a forbidding demeanor. Hard to imagine that they were just as capable of interbreeding with the races of men as were the ljosalfar, nachtalfar, and sylvalfar.

Bernadette pasted a friendly smile on her face, though she didn't try to step any closer. "The Daywatch Brigade, I presume," she asked while holding out her hands to show that she was not threatening them with weapons. While the Norseman remained on his guard, feet apart and a hand on his sword hilt, the uruk (who was nearly as tall as Andrion, and wider) looked searchingly into each intruder's eyes and then relaxed.

"That's right," he replied gruffly. "I'm Borgrazh din-Zarb and this here" – with a jab of the thumb at the young Norseman, who was now smiling shyly – "is Uther High-Fane. I assume you're here to join up?" Bernadette's smile broadened, and she stuck out her hand.

"Pleased to meet you Borgrazh, Uther. I'm Bernadette Bouchard, Warden of Waterdon March and also Westmarch, and this is my companion Andrion Lamonte. We think it's time something was done about the vampire attacks, and we're here to help."

Uther's face took on a look of astonishment. "Bernadette Firemane? The Fireblood?" he gasped. Bernadette dropped her gaze, slightly embarrassed. She'd gotten used to being a local celebrity in the area around Waterdon, but she hadn't realized how far her fame had spread.

"That's me," she said ruefully. "Andrion was one of my companions that day in Asengard, when we slew the Soul-Devourer." The kid (Berni's age he might be, but he certainly seemed like a kid to her at the moment despite his height) gaped, struck speechless by the presence of these legendary beings. Even Andrion was a little embarrassed.

"Well anyhow," he said, trying to get past the awkward moment, "we're here. So where do we go to sign up?" Borgrazh gestured to the trail ahead.

"Most people come in from the south," he said, "and the castle's a lot closer to that end of the valley. You've got close to twenty more miles to go, but there's a good trail all the way. If you see steam coming out of the ground, don't walk on it – sometimes people or animals fall through and get scalded. And you'll need these…" He reached into a pocket and pulled out a couple of small metal disks. They were about an inch in diameter, of a silvery-looking metal, and embossed with a sunburst that had an open eye in the middle of it.

Bernadette and Andrion each accepted one of them. "Show those to any other sentries you meet," Borgrazh instructed them. "Since we put the word out for new recruits Malden's pretty concerned about vampires finding out about this place and coming to wipe us out before we get the fortifications repaired."

They thanked the sentry and went on their way. Twenty miles was a long walk, and they'd already had a pretty stiff hike today climbing that cliff face. But they hoped to make it to Daywatch, the "castle" as Borgrazh had called it, before dark.

Andrion had hoped Bernadette would be amazed and delighted by Closevale. But hearing Erik's description of the place had failed to prepare him for the reality. The two of them found themselves stopping to gaze around them in wonder; for here, not that far from icebound Norcove, was a little pocket of summer. Well, early autumn maybe. The valley was lush, the small stream that spilled over the falls at its north end joined by many little rivulets flowing down from the mountains on either side.

There were trees, flowers, and food crops growing here, fields of ripe wheat waving in the breeze. Vulfassdur loomed to their left, and perhaps ten miles off to their right other mountains formed the little valley's western wall. The midday sun beat down on them with surprising heat, and as hunger became an issue they stopped to have a little food – and shed some of their winter clothing.

There seemed to be no one within sight, so Bernadette and Andrion quickly peeled to the skin. His appreciative gaze had a trace of hunger in it; but they'd made love just the night before. With a sigh of regret that there wasn't more time, he got into his "regular" linen underwear and put his armor back on as she did the same.

After sitting on the grassy bank of the now-meandering stream for a while to eat some pemmican and drink from their water skins, the two pushed on. As they continued on the trail they saw much game – caribou, elk, and smaller deer, wild goats and sheep, rabbits and foxes. They heard wolves howling in the distance on the far side of the stream, but they were a long way off. What an idyllic place!

The castle, that ancient fortress known as Daywatch, came into sight long before they reached it. It appeared to be at least three stories high, a pile of granite that had been quarried from the mountains that ringed the valley. The valley floor was mostly level, but a low hill perhaps a hundred feet high had been chosen as the site of the stronghold. No doubt you could see from one end of the valley to the other from that top floor. The battlements looked ragged, glassless windows gaping like empty eye-sockets as the sun began to sink to the west.

Beyond the stronghold another mile or two the land sloped up gently and the valley's southern edge was blocked by the range that marched east and west across much of Iscandia's northern half. It was the same range that contained the Drakespire, though here they were hundreds of miles to the east of that fiery peak.

"There must be a pass between those mountains to the south," Andrion remarked as they beheld their destination. "Erik had only ever come in from the north, which makes sense if he was coming from Norcove."

"We'll have to leave the other way, so we'll know both entrances," Bernadette said thoughtfully. She was getting awfully tired of walking, and really looking forward to setting down her pack and having some supper.

The sun was disappearing over the western horizon as they wound their way around a wooden stockade to Daywatch's main approach. Bernadette and Andrion hadn't seen another living soul since leaving the sentries at the far end of the valley; but now as they approached the gate they found another pair eyeing them warily.

"Halt," commanded a grizzled Norse warrior dressed in mismatched steel and leather armor. He had an axe at his belt but was not brandishing it. His watch partner was an Afran woman in her thirties, short and broad, who had a serious expression and an air of competence. She somehow reminded Bernadette of Lifa, or at least of how Lifa might have been in another few years if Anja had not come along to lighten her outlook.

They introduced themselves, showed their tokens, and were admitted through the gate to the compound surrounding the castle itself. It had clearly been built to withstand assault by a large armed force, but the stockade fence looked newly-cut from the nearby pine forests. If a moat or tall stone wall had once surrounded the castle itself, these features had vanished over the centuries.

At the top of a short staircase was a pair of heavy iron doors, standing open. And beyond those, a good-sized entry hall was overlooked by a series of balconies. There had seemed to be no glass in this place, but looking up Bernadette and Andrion realized that three stories up was a skylight of sorts – a leaded glass dome that had astonishingly survived intact. It was glowing pink now, as the last of the daylight was about to depart.

A medium-sized young man with reddish brown hair, dressed in leather work clothes, came scurrying in from a side corridor and spotted them. "Hello!" he said, seemingly in a big hurry. "You must be new recruits!" He stuck out a hand. "Rene Augenois," he said, shaking hands with Andrion first. A fellow Galise!

After introductions had been made he said, "You must excuse me, I'm in the middle of a project and I need to get on with it. You'll need to speak with Malden, but I'll bet you'd probably like to eat first." He pointed to a corridor across the hall from the one he'd come in by. "Go down there, turn left at the tee intersection then take the first right. We're still getting set up, but there's a dining hall of sorts and you'll find stew and fresh bread. Just help yourselves. We don't have formal meals around here."

"Thank you, Rene," Bernadette said warmly. She liked this young man, who looked like he might be halfway in age between Erik and Andrion. She could imagine her younger brother, who'd been a gawky stripling when she'd left home a few months ago, looking like this in another twelve years. "And after we've eaten, where would we find Malden?"

He gestured to the hallway opposite the doors they'd come in by. "He's usually in his office during the evening. It's down that corridor, second door on the left. I'm sure he'll be pleased to see you've joined us!" With that he was off again, about his pressing business – out the front doors. He stopped and pushed them shut behind him, as it would soon be dark.

Andrion and Bernadette exchanged a look, then eagerly followed the instructions to the Daywatch Brigade's dining hall. It proved to be nothing fancy, but it was supplied with the essentials: there was a long wooden table with benches on either side, plates and cups and spoons, and a huge stone fireplace you could have roasted an ox in. An iron bar ran across it and there were two pots suspended from it, in which a rich-smelling venison stew with vegetables and barley was simmering. It smelled wonderful!

A platter sat in the center of the table, with a metal domed cover over it. As Bernadette sat down with her bowl of stew she lifted the lid and was pleased to discover, not the usual bread rolls but a country loaf rich with whole grains. She used the nearby knife to slice off a slab of it, putting it on a metal plate, and found that the small ceramic crock nearby contained freshly churned butter. Excellent!

The two sat eating their supper, going back to the pots for seconds after all the energy they'd burned the past couple of days.

Bernadette had a small smile on her face as she wiped the last little bit of the savory stew from her bowl with another slice of the nutty-tasting bread. "Ahhh!" she sighed. "Oh, I feel so much better!"

"Are you as excited as I am?" Andrion asked, putting paid to his last bite of stew. They had discovered cases of bottled ale sitting beside the fireplace, and had helped themselves to a couple each. She grinned at him.

"I know what you mean, love. This place has such an air of… purpose about it! It's clear they're just getting started, and there's a lot of work yet to be done before they'll be the kind of disciplined force that can really do something about the vampire threat. But it's fun, and kind of thrilling, to know that this thing is coming together and that we're a part of it!"

He reached across the table and squeezed her hand. They were still wearing their breastplates and greaves, but had shed their gauntlets for eating. "Boy, I'd like to set my pack down for the day," Bernadette remarked ruefully. "But we forgot to ask Rene where the dormitory is."

"There's a pantry over there," Andrion said pointing. "Why don't we just tuck them in there while we go looking for Malden? I'm sure he'll tell us where to sleep."

They did so, and a couple of minutes later found themselves at the door to stone chamber maybe twenty feet on a side. All that they'd seen of Daywatch so far, that is to say certain areas on the ground floor, seemed free of debris. But it was also, by and large, free of things like carpets, furniture, and wall hangings to add warmth to the cold stone. Fortunately, here in this snug little valley, the stone wasn't all *that* cold.

Bernadette spotted a man sitting behind a large wooden table that had books and papers spread out all over it, and guessed he must be the one they sought. She took a step into the room and rapped on the open door, getting his attention. His expression was stern, and he seemed a bit annoyed to have been interrupted in his work.

"What is it?" he asked sharply, not rising. From his appearance he was in his fifties, maybe of an age with Eorl Ormund of Waterdon. He was Afran, but there was probably some Norse or Galise in his ancestry too – his skin was a medium tan, his wavy hair cut short and turning from black to gray, his eyes a surprising gold color. He might have been handsome, were not his expression so cold.

"Sorry to disturb you," Bernadette said in a conciliatory fashion. Her diplomatic skills might be wanting, but she could make nice when she needed to – even with people who immediately set her teeth on edge, as this one was doing. "Are you Malden? We just got in from Waterdon a short while ago and Rene said that we could find you in your office. We're here to sign up for the Brigade."

Malden's stern expression relaxed, though he didn't exactly smile. "Ah," he said, "welcome to Daywatch then. I am Malden, the founder and organizer of this enterprise, and as I'm sure you can see I have a lot of work to do. What are your names?"

Bernadette had half expected recognition, after young Uther's reaction earlier today. But the introduction was met with a brief nod and the question, "And what it is that you two bring to the Daywatch Brigade? What are your skills?"

"I'm a competent swordsman, and a pretty good battle mage," Andrion replied modestly. In the months since he'd become Bernadette's battle companion his skills had advanced more than in years spent in lesser pursuits.

"Berni here is The Fireblood, of course," Andrion added. "and a damn fine archer as well." Malden cocked an eyebrow.

"That's an old legend, isn't it?" he asked in puzzlement. Gods, had this man been living under a rock for the past year? Bernadette wondered. Admittedly this place was a bit isolated, but if Uther had heard the news why hadn't his boss?

Andrion seemed a little offended. "Berni and I and our friend Erik went through a secret portal to Asengard a few months ago and slew the ancient dragon Tarragin, the one who was responsible for Iscandia's current dragon problem. Any of this ringing a bell?"

"Dragons?" the older man asked.

"If you haven't seen any, you're lucky," Bernadette told him. "I guess you've been busy and haven't noticed, but dragons began coming back to life at the beginning of last summer and they're all over the province now – killing people, stealing livestock, wreaking destruction just because they can."

Malden fixed his golden gaze on her for a moment, then shrugged. "Dragons are a new problem, and if as you say you killed the one who was bringing them back to life, they will eventually die out again. But vampires have been a threat to every decent human in Agena for thousands of years – sometimes even the *same individual vampires*, for thousands of years. Their reign of terror must end! I have devoted my life to fighting them, and now I finally have the means to eradicate them – from Iscandia, at least. Will you help me, or not?"

Bernadette and Andrion exchanged glances again. That was why they had come, was it not? "Yes," he said for both of them. "We are ready to join your fight."

"Excellent," Malden replied, showing his teeth in what might have been intended as a smile. "Soon we will bring the battle to the stinking vampires, but first we must finish the work of restoring this place to its status as a fortress. You can be sure that as the word spreads, we will find ourselves under attack. Report to my lieutenant, Grindmar, first thing tomorrow morning in the yard around the south end of the castle."

Evidently they had been dismissed. "Um, all right, we'll do that," Bernadette said. "But can you tell us where the dormitory is?"

"We don't have one yet," Malden replied. "That's only a tiny part of the work that remains to be done before we're ready to take on our foes." He gestured upward. "The second and third floors are essentially empty," he said. "Just throw down a bedroll and sleep wherever you like."

The two took their leave, returning to the entry hall. They'd spotted a stairway leading up while they were looking for the dining hall earlier. Andrion squeezed Bernadette's arm as soon as they were out of range of Malden's hearing. "I'm proud of you Berni," he said softly. "I half expected you to freeze that guy solid just to teach him some manners. What an asshole!"

She looked sideways at him and gave him a wry grin. "Indeed," she said, "but who knows what personal issues he has going on? Maybe his entire family was wiped out by vampires or something. Anyhow, the cause is just and I've already met some people here I *do* like. With any luck we can keep contact with our Mighty Leader to a minimum."

After retrieving their packs they found the staircase and climbed it. "Looks like sleeping here might not be much better than camping out for the time being," Bernadette remarked. Not only was there no furniture up here, the wall sconces held no torches and it was dark as pitch. Andrion cast another variation of his light spell, causing a cool white glow to emanate from the palm of his left hand. Holding it up, he lighted their way.

Finding a likely chamber they spread some fur bedrolls out on the stone, a couple beneath them for padding and another, opened out, to cover them as they removed their armor and tucked themselves in. It had been a long, tiring day; and in moments they had both fallen asleep.

Chapter 11: The Brigade

As it happened the chamber they had chosen in darkness the night before was open to an outdoor area on the second level of the fortress. Bernadette and Andrion found themselves snuggling together under the spread-out bedroll for warmth, and wishing for another one before morning. They woke to sunshine coming in through the door and the sound of birdsong in the fields around them Closevale was narrower at this end, with no more than five miles from Daywatch's western walls to the mountains enclosing it.

Bernadette felt marvelously restored by the night's rest, even if the bed had been far from soft; and her crotch throbbed as she ran her hands up her sleeping companion's firm torso. Andrion stirred drowsily. Morning already? He wriggled closer to Berni, his nose buried in her hair, and planted a kiss on her ear. She raised her head to him and returned the kiss, but on his lips. It was light at first, but delivered with more concentration as he woke enough to respond. Then she slipped her tongue into his mouth, as she reached down between them to grasp his rising member. He cupped her face in his hands, moaning slightly as he kissed her back.

Bernadette squeezed Andrion's cock rhythmically, and in moments it had gone from half-stiff to rock hard, the head plumping like a ripe plum. He transferred his hands from the sides of her head to her breasts, massaging them gently and thumbing the nipples to attention. She moaned, pulling away from the kiss to gasp a little. "Oh baby, yesss…" she murmured. They might have things to do and places to go this morning, but for once *this* thing took precedence over all others.

Mmm, she wanted to feel him inside her. But these stones, even padded with a double layer of bedrolls, were already starting to make her hip ache. What would they do to his knees? The morning sun had begun to take the chill off the room, and in the microclimate of this hidden valley it was not as cold, even, as in Waterdon. She threw the bedroll that was serving as a blanket off of them, and lay there just smiling lazily at him for a moment, taking in his tousled beauty. Since the first time she had set eyes on this man, the sight of him had filled her with desire and a quiet joy. Now that she loved him for what was inside as well as out, the effect was magnified.

With an effort Bernadette heaved herself up onto her feet, then took Andrion's hand and pulled him to stand facing her. She moved in close for a full-body hug, pinning his throbbing member between them. Then she stepped away a few paces, and said "C'mere, you." She walked over to the nearest wall and leaned against it, planting her hands on it a couple of feet apart. She stood with legs apart and rump thrust out behind her, then looked over her shoulder and said invitingly, "Well, come *on* then…"

Even after all these months Andrion never quite knew what to expect from Berni. Sometimes this was disconcerting, but usually it was a good thing – and this time he was quite pleased. He stepped close to her and caressed her hips and buttocks, then put two fingers in his mouth before inserting them into her cunt. It was nice and wet in there, so he took them back out and guided his cock into their place.

Oooh, yes! He began stroking in and out, slowly at first then faster and faster as she moaned and humped herself back to meet his thrusts. Both of them standing barefoot on the stone floor of the chamber was a little odd, but with no furniture in the room there was little choice and he didn't like the thought of what kneeling on that floor would do to his knees. He grasped her hips, thumbs digging slightly into her firm buttocks, pulling her to him on each stroke. They both knew this was not the time or place for a prolonged session of lovemaking, so he let himself go.

The sensations as Andrion's big, hard cock slid back and forth inside her soon drove Bernadette over the edge. She loved getting it from behind, and as she began to come and her cunt clamped down on him, he abandoned any efforts at control and just pumped his seed into her with a low groan. They stood there, knees flexed slightly as he bent over her, panting and gasping, for a moment or two. Then he pulled out, and streams of creamy cum ran down the insides of her thighs.

"Toss me a towel, will you love?" Bernadette asked. He did so, and she got herself cleaned up a bit before walking over to give him another hug and kiss. "Let's hope there's a bed in our future," she said ruefully. "I'd like to have another try at this soon." He gave her a smile that was half a leer. Then they both started looking around for their armor.

The two appeared in the dining hall, ready for business and only a little bit rumpled, as other members of the Daywatch Brigade were sitting down to a breakfast of sorts. There was fresh bread aplenty along with butter and jam, some apples and pears, and a pot of hot tea strong enough to peel paint. Expecting the possibility of another long day, they ate until sated.

They'd seated themselves beside Rene, and he was cheerfully willing to answer all their questions. Malden was not present. "He usually takes his meals in his room," the young Galise told them. "Not really much of a people person, is our captain." Bernadette raised an eyebrow at the understatement.

"He commanded us to report to somebody named Grindmar 'first thing,'" Andrion said as he slathered butter and jam on a slice of bread. "I hope he didn't expect us to be out there before breakfast." Rene grinned.

"Nah," he said, gesturing with the hand holding a partially-eaten pear, "that's Grindmar down at the end of the table. Nobody expects us to work on an empty stomach. He's kind of like our project foreman for now, though once we move into battle mode he'll be coordinating actions."

They eyed him with interest. He looked to be in his early forties, a somewhat grim-looking and hard-bitten Norseman. His sandy brown hair was beginning to thin in front and going gray, as was his short-cropped beard. He had an impressive-looking long white scar running from his left eyebrow to the corner of his jaw. "Is he..." Bernadette began delicately, wondering how to phrase this. Rene jumped in.

"He's the only person here who's worked with Malden in the past," he said quietly. "They knew each other back in the Conflict, but both of them mustered out of the imperial army after the truce. He's a toughie, but not really a bad guy. I think you'll enjoy working with him."

There were nearly a dozen people seated along the benches, eating and drinking and talking quietly together. "How many people all told are there in the Brigade?" Bernadette asked.

"Uh…" Rene did some calculating in his head. "Counting you two and Malden, there are nineteen. And I hope we'll soon be getting some more new recruits. We only decided to put the word out a month ago, and so far there's been a steady trickle. Just finding this place is enough of a challenge it tends to weed out people who aren't committed to the cause."

Bernadette washed her food down with a swallow of tea and chuckled. "And being committed is important, or they'd all pack up and leave as soon as they'd had a talk with Malden…" Rene chuckled in response.

"We all have our reasons for joining," he said. "I think most people are looking for some adventure, the chance to prove themselves as warriors – and the recent escalation of vampire attacks in cities is a cause for alarm."

They saw Grindmar get up from the table and decided they'd better do the same. There was a privy chamber off the passageway leading to the dining hall, with stalls opening onto a cesspit and basins with water for washing. The three of them made their morning ablutions, then Rene led the new recruits out the front doors and around to the southern end of the compound.

They found themselves standing in a broad area encompassed by the timber stockade fence. It was made up of logs from the nearby forests, sharpened on the ends and standing some twelve feet high. It certainly wouldn't keep out a determined military force, but would probably work well enough to hold off a small group of raiding vampires. Unless what Bernadette had read was true, and the blood-suckers could turn themselves into bats and fly.

There were some archery butts over against the western wall, and some dummies for sword practice as well. But for the most part, the area looked like a corporation yard. There were a couple of wheeled carts, stacks of cut lumber, carpentry tools and sawhorses, a smithy with a forge that looked like it had been constructed from the same stone used to build the castle. A huge pile of that same stone stood in one corner, many of the blocks broken.

Bernadette and Andrion stood beside Rene, looking around at their surroundings. Though the sun had not been up for two hours yet, the morning was already warming as if it were spring in

Waterdon, instead of nearly winter in the latitudes of Norcove. What an amazing place!

Everyone who had been at the breakfast table had joined them, but no one they hadn't seen before. There must be a couple of guards on the valley's southern entrance, a couple on the main gates, and two out twenty miles away at the post where they'd met Borgrazh and Uther (who were among the group now in the yard) yesterday, Bernadette realized. Presumably those posts must be manned 24 hours a day.

The burly Grindmar stood facing the dozen people who were milling around in the yard, chatting with each other, and cleared his throat. Silence immediately fell. "All right people, settle down," he said – cracking a cheerful grin that made his ugly face look almost cute. "I'm pleased to introduce you to our new recruits, who arrived yesterday."

The lieutenant waved Bernadette and Andrion forward, and shook their hands. "Welcome, Fireblood," he said softly. "The Daywatch Brigade is honored to have you." She colored a little. Grindmar raised his voice to address the small crowd. "This is Bernadette Firemane, The Fireblood. I'm sure you've all heard about her." He glanced over at Uther, who was beaming. My fan club, she thought. The kid had probably been telling everyone he knew about the celebrity in their midst.

Grindmar smiled at Bernadette's apparent discomfiture and winked. Then he went on, "And this is her companion Andrion Lamonte, whose battle spells are definitely going to come in handy once we start bringing the fight to the enemy." There was a little light applause, and grins all around as their new companions welcomed them into the ranks.

More quietly, addressing the two standing beside him instead of the whole group, the lieutenant asked "Your battle skills are beyond doubt. I'd heard of your exploits even before young Uther began trumpeting them. But we're in our building phase right now. Does any of you have skills in the area of carpentry, weaving, sewing, masonry, plumbing, or the like?"

The two were put on the spot. "I haven't really developed many skills in those areas," Andrion admitted. "I've been studying magic, and using it as an adventurer, for most of the past decade. But I'm strong and willing. If you need building supplies shuffled around, or cleanup work done, I can manage that."

"All right," Grindmar said with a nod. He gestured toward a tall, graying blonde Norsewoman with shoulders like a smith's, "report to Greta and she'll assign you some tasks. We usually break for a meal around noon, rest for an hour and then work until close to sunset. If you have some sturdy work clothing that'd probably be better than your armor for this kind of work. I usually tell everyone to keep a weapon to hand, but I guess you don't need one." He smiled again, and Andrion walked over to talk with Greta.

"And you, Fireblood? Have you talents more domestic than slaying ancient dragons and saving the world from destruction?" Grindmar asked with a wry smile. Bernadette grinned back at him.

"I can cook and sew a little," she said reluctantly. Only fair to mention it, though these were not her favorite activities. "I'm pretty good at smithing, probably about journey level now, and I know how to make a lot of useful potions if you've got ingredients." "Good, good," Grindmar said. "I'm sure we're going to be needing potions, but we need to acquire a chemia station first. There are a lot of herbs and what-not growing out in the valley, and if you can make up a list of what you'd need for panacea potion and some healing ones, we can buy some when we make the next supply run."

Bernadette glanced over at the nearby carts. They'd noticed a few horses pastured east of the compound's main gate when they came in yesterday. Sylvanian was the only city in this part of Iscandia big enough to offer much in the way of supplies, but even that would probably be a four-day round trip with a horse and cart – if you weren't just summarily robbed of your purchases by bandits along the road.

"I have something that might be even more helpful," she said, and Grindmar looked at her expectantly. She reached into the pouch at her waist and pulled out the map. "I can't say how much time will actually have passed while I'm gone," she said, "but with this I can guarantee that your supplies will get here in one piece."

Chapter 12: Building

During the next week Bernadette fast-traveled with the largest of the Daywatch Brigade's wagons and a couple of horses to pull it, back and forth to Sylvanian twice. Each round trip, including the time required as she drove the wagon around to suppliers to get loaded up, appeared to take close to 24 hours.

Andrion worked himself hard, finding that he enjoyed the sheer physical labor. He'd always kept himself in shape though his scholarly bent led to hours of inactivity, and the first couple of days he ached mightily by the end of the day. He was less than happy that Berni had ended up being drafted for supply runs, as it meant she was gone overnight and not in his arms. But he had new friends, all working together toward a goal, and he felt happy enough.

Rene, whose job as Grindmar's assistant seemed to involve pulling together the efforts of everyone else, led Andrion and Bernadette out toward the slopes of Vulfassdur on their fifth day as part of the crew. "It's a shame these pools aren't closer to the castle," he said apologetically. "As hard as everyone's working, we could all use a hot soak every evening. But the two-mile round trip makes that a little impractical."

Along a line where the slightly rolling valley floor joined the enormous mountain's lower slopes, was a chain of thermal pools similar to the ones they'd enjoyed at the Drakespire. The smallest, only a few feet across, was bubbling and Bernadette eyed it with concern. "Could you really boil eggs in there?" she asked, and Rene smiled. "It'd take a long time. The water's definitely hot enough to scald you, but it's not actually boiling. The bubbles are gases coming up from below."

Andrion nodded. He'd expected as much. Both he and Bernadette had abandoned their armor in favor of leather traveling clothes, which offered at least a little protection. Berni had her dragon spells and her bow slung over her back, in hopes of bringing down some game on this outing, but all he was carrying was a sack with some towels and changes of underwear. The thought of a hot bath was filling him with almost as much anticipation as it was his beloved – they'd both gotten spoiled, living at the Maiden.

The largest of the pools offered water that was considerably cooler than the smallest, diluted by snowmelt running down from Vulfassdur's peak. But it was still a bit warmer than the temperature of the water in the Maiden's hot pool, and it took some getting used to.

The three of them stripped off, and began easing down into the hot water with sighs of bliss. "Oh, that is so *good*!" Bernadette cried. Neither she nor Andrion had been able to do more than wash up their smelliest or dirtiest parts with soap and cold water from the basins in the privy chamber since arriving here. At least she'd been able to spend a comfortable night sleeping on a soft bed at the Dancing Rabbit during her trip to Sylvanian. Daywatch now had a first-floor chamber devoted to the production of potions, with a brand-new chemia station and a growing collection of ingredients neatly arrayed on shelves.

But here, she and Andrion were still sleeping atop fur sleeping pads in an unfurnished stone chamber on the second floor. The stiffness this had caused was leaching from their muscles as they soaked. Bernadette covertly checked Rene out. She was incorrigible, she knew it, but she just couldn't help herself. Even though a big part of her reason for joining the Daywatch Brigade had been to have her and Andrion together away from the Maiden, away from Erik, the presence of a good-looking naked man was always going to get her attention.

Eh, she liked Rene a lot but he was on the short and slender side for her taste. She was coming to think of him as more of an older brother, or at least a good friend on whom she had no carnal designs to speak of. Andrion ought to be enough man for anyone, yet whenever she thought of Erik she got a sharp pang of longing. She missed him so much – not just the amazing sex but his sweet and sunny disposition.

Their pleasant relaxation was interrupted by a roaring sound. Rene, who'd nearly been dozing off, looked up in alarm. He found Andrion and Bernadette already climbing out of the limestone-lined pool, and reaching for their towels. The roar had been unmistakable to *them* – a dragon had found its way to Closevale!

"What in all the hells is it?" Rene asked, paling though from the neck down he was pink from the hot water. "It's a dragon!" Bernadette cried, throwing on her clean underwear and her boots before picking up her bow. They could see the creature winging its way down the valley from the north. It flamed something on the ground, and a moment later stooped. It rose again with the smoking carcass of an elk clutched in its claws, flapping heavily, and continued on toward what looked like a nice high perch on which to eat its meal – Daywatch.

Berni was already a quarter mile down the trail heading home as Andrion and Rene gathered up the rest of their things and followed. It appeared that the dragon would be occupied for a while, devouring the elk as it perched atop Daywatch's crumbling top-floor battlements. The roof was built of stone, with crenellations all around it so that defenders could mass there and shoot down at anyone attacking while having a certain amount of protection.

Before they had covered the mile, though, it had finished its meal and was now investigating the nearby horse pasture as the gate guards called for help and began firing arrows at it. This was a big dragon, far smaller than Ehrgeizig or Sneyagflug but probably at least thirty feet from nose to tail. Evidently the elk was just an appetizer.

The horses were screaming in terror and scattering, and the dragon was attempting to incinerate them with its Holocaust spell while flying around at no more than twenty feet off the ground. It had not yet succeeded when a large force of the Brigade arrived and began shooting at it with arrows. Many of them bounced off the scaly blue-green hide, but a few were penetrating and the dragon was starting to get annoyed.

It was just getting ready to stoop on them when Bernadette arrived, gasping for breath. The proper speaking of a dragon spell required the right voice – not necessarily the same for one as for another. Fortunately with Dragonfall, great force was not needed. She only needed to be heard. "Alt-Wach-Sterb-Tot!" she cried, and a purple and green pulse exploded around the beast as it pulled up from its intended attack and clawed desperately at the air.

Over the months since learning that spell, Bernadette had used it several more times. She was coming to feel a little unhappy about killing dragons and absorbing their souls – they were after all unique, amazing, and sentient creatures. So she had not been seeking them out unless they were causing trouble to the human inhabitants of Iscandia. The dragon that had killed Anja's parents was only the sixth one she'd killed in four months. But she wasn't planning on letting this one get away! Once it had found this blessed valley, rich with game, it was never going to leave of its own accord and needed to be stopped right now before it killed anyone or ate any of their small horse herd.

The dragon seemed unable to keep itself aloft, and came crashing to the ground on the main trail in from the south. The brave defenders rushed it, ducking out of the way of fiery blasts and trying to get in arrow shots or sword blows while staying out of the way of the snapping jaws.

Bernadette, dressed only in her underwear (and all sweaty again, after that lovely bath too) was worried. None of these people had ever faced a dragon, and Andrion was still making his way here from the hot pools. She took a breath and spoke a spell, one that did *not* need to be heard to work its magic: "Zeht-Stran-Vig-Lang," she said quietly, and the sky went a strange color as time froze around her.

Nocking an arrow, Bernadette darted forward. She would have nearly a full minute of her own personal time in which to work, before she would become synchronized with the rest of the universe. In seconds she was beside the dragon. Its neck was stretched out, jaws open and about to snap on one of the defenders. She drew the bow and took careful aim on the creature's glowing red eye, driving the steel pointed- shaft through the eye and deep into its brain.

There was still time, and she went over to where the defender stood. He was rearing back, and might have evaded the jaws. But she wanted to make sure. She'd discovered that trying to manipulate any of her surroundings in a moment of frozen time was extremely difficult – but he was already off balance. She threw herself at him, pushing with all her weight, and he toppled over.

Just then the spell's effect ended and the world flashed back into color and motion. The dragon was dead as soon as time began to move, but its momentum carried the head forward another few inches before it came down, hard, not six inches from the feet of the fallen defender. He was staring at Bernadette, wide-eyed. "You…" he gasped, "Where'd you come from?" He began hauling himself back onto his feet, just as Bernadette's proximity to the dead dragon triggered the vanishment of its flesh.

She stood, swaying, as the power of the huge creature's mana and soul surged through her being. The crowd of Brigade members, nearly the entire complement save for Malden, was staring at her and gabbling in shocked amazement. Uther looked triumphant, the truth of his stories vindicated. Andrion, who'd just arrived with Rene bringing up the rear, looked relieved.

Bernadette suddenly realized she was standing there in her underwear, and hastened to grab her clothes from Andrion and start climbing into them. She felt a pang of bereavement for the lovely, relaxing bath she had *nearly* gotten to enjoy. The group was approaching the enormous skeleton now, fingering the bones as if expecting them to vanish as suddenly as had its flesh.

Bernadette worked her way in between the ribs and scooped out the little pile of treasure that had fallen to the ground. Marya, the plump and cheerful Afran woman who did most of the cooking, nudged her in the ribs. "And here I thought we'd be feasting on dragon steaks for the next month!" she said with a smile. "Does that always happen?"

Bernadette smiled back. "It's part of my heritage as The Fireblood," she explained. "I absorb all of the dragon's life energy, though I'm not sure why the flesh all vanishes too. Maybe it's because this dragon, and all the rest of them in this modern world except for the one who founded the Old Ones, *were* nothing but bones until a few months ago. They were given flesh and life by Tarragin, and I took it away again."

As she had come to expect, Bernadette found no spell stones left behind that she had not already absorbed. She felt sure that somewhere out there were some dragon spells – like the one Tarragin had used to rain fiery stones on them from the sky – that she had not yet acquired. But she guessed those would all be spells that even Ehrgeizig himself didn't know; so if she happened to find them it would be only by fortuitous chance. She was content enough with what she had.

Malden had been busy in his office, hatching his plans and marshaling his resources, and he not made his way outside to see what the commotion was until the fight was over. He came striding up, staring at the enormous skeleton lying in the road while nearly his entire force clustered around it.

Bernadette couldn't resist catching his eye, and gesturing toward the ex-dragon with a look that said, "See?" He scowled. "We need to get this thing out of the road," he said in a voice of command. "It'd probably be a good idea to break up the skeleton and carry the bones and scales over to the forge area," Bernadette suggested. "They make some really good heavy armor and two-handed weapons."

Seeing Malden's look of disapproval, she added "Or load them into the wagon, and I'll take them with me on my next supply run and sell them off. They're quite valuable." Malden nodded.

"We'll do that," he said. "Heavy armor is a liability for us, and we can certainly use the money." He seemed as if he were about to turn and go back inside the castle. But he put a hand on Bernadette's arm and looked down at her, meeting her eyes. "Thank you, Fireblood," he said gruffly. "Good job."

Chapter 13: Recruiting

The next day at breakfast, Bernadette and Andrion sat side by side eating scrambled eggs and bacon. A large flock of chickens had been added to Daywatch's compound, and it was hoped they'd soon be providing enough eggs and meat to supply the growing Brigade. Another two recruits had joined them in the past two days, wandering in separately from the south.

As the days went by more and more areas of the ground floor were becoming furnished. The workers had fitted out one of the larger rooms as a dormitory, though it was furnished mostly with cots rather than real beds. At least it meant sleeping up off the stone floor, and in a room with a large fireplace. But Bernadette and Andrion both found that sleeping on cots in a dormitory was not what they'd hoped for. Greta had promised Andrion that as soon as she finished with some of the other furnishings she was working on, she would build them a double bed and they could take over one of the chambers on the second floor that still had a door on it.

They kissed, and after a trip to the privy chamber they parted ways. Andrion was to be clearing rubble from atop the castle today, piling up stones so masons could use them for rebuilding the crumbling ramparts. Bernadette was preparing to get started cooking up some panacea and other useful potions when Malden found her and took her aside.

They sat at a small table that had been set up as a sort of desk, in a broad hallway across from the dining hall. "Apparently, I owe you an apology," Malden said. Bernadette nearly choked on her own spit. She'd never expected to hear those words coming from him, and waited for more.

"When Andrion told me you were The Fireblood and all that, I didn't really believe him," Malden went on. "I've been working here for months, originally with only Grindmar for help. We came here with the wagons loaded down with supplies last spring, and when rumors about dragons started filtering in with the recruits I discounted them as nothing but tall tales."

He looked at her apologetically. "Thanks for acknowledging that," Bernadette said graciously. "Andrion and I, and our friend Erik as well, really laid our lives on the line to stop the Soul-Devourer. It's nice to be appreciated." Malden looked uncomfortable.

Clearing his throat he went on, "In any case, I think maybe we need some help with weaponry. I know someone, a young woman I worked with around ten years back, who is one of the best weaponsmiths I've ever met."

Bernadette was a little perplexed. And what am I, chopped liver? But ten years back she herself had been a gawky girl of thirteen. It was quite possible there were smiths out there – older, more experienced smiths – who had skills and knowledge she had yet to master. So instead of getting her nose put out of joint she remained silent, waiting for the captain to explain why he was telling her this.

He went on, after an awkward silence. "Your showing up with that map of yours has been a godsend. I need you to go track down Diane and try to convince her to join us."

"Sure, I can do that," Bernadette said. "Any idea where she might be found?"

"You have your map on you?" he asked, and she pulled it out. He ran a finger over an area of Westmarch, some distance north of the main east-west road and beside a small river.

"She's Galise like you and your man," Malden said. "Diane LeBois. Smart as a whip, and good with anything mechanical. She's fascinated by the dypalfar and their machines, is always poking around their ruins looking for new devices. The last I heard, she was digging in what she thought might turn out to be the biggest dwelven ruin yet. It's somewhere around here, on the Gold River."

"I'll have a bit of a walk to reach there," Bernadette told him. The closest fast-travel point would probably be Floradel, where she and Andrion had started from when hunting for dragon spells in that ancient Norse ruin to the south. "Andrion's very interested in the dypalfar and their technology, too," she added. "Mind if I pull him off of rock-clearing duty and take him along?"

"That would be fine," Malden said. "I hope you're able to find Diane, and to… convince her to join us." Bernadette eyed him sharply.

"Is there some reason she might be unwilling to do so?" she asked. The older man looked uncomfortable again. "The last time we parted, it was on… difficult terms. I may have been a little undiplomatic…" he said quietly.

"Oh, no worries!" Bernadette said brightly. "I'll just tell her you're a changed man, and anxious to beg her forgiveness for your past transgressions. That ought to work, don't you think?"

Malden did not look amused, but admitted "I'll apologize to her if she thinks I need to. We really could use her expertise."

With a cheery wave, Bernadette galloped up the stairs to the roof. It was accessible only via a ladder leading up through a trap door, which had been designed with heavy iron bar closures on both top and bottom. Defenders, if overrun from within the castle itself, could make a last stand on the roof. Or conversely, they could keep invaders from coming in that way.

Andrion was straining under the weight of a hodful of broken stone that probably weighed a hundred pounds at least, carrying it across to the growing pile at one end of the roof, when she popped up through the trap door. He set his load down and ran a dusty arm over his sweaty forehead, grinning at her. The two of them were the only people up here, at the moment, and she leaped up to throw her legs around his hips and her arms around his neck, pressing her body to his and kissing him hard.

"Mmmf!" he said, kissing her back. A moment later she'd leapt down again and was grinning up at him.

"Break time!" she announced. "You and I are going on a mini-quest, searching for some woman Malden antagonized ten years ago. Doesn't that sound better than hauling stone?"

He grinned back. "The whole time I've been on this job I've spent wishing I'd apprenticed as a carpenter, or any skilled trade that doesn't involve working like a rented mule," he admitted.

"Oh love, your skills will be hugely valued as soon as we stop building and start fighting," she replied. "Anyhow, I'm proud of the way you've pitched in even if this probably wasn't what you signed up for. But now we have the opportunity to get away from all this for a while. If we work it right, maybe we'll even get the chance to sleep in an inn for a night. Wouldn't you like that?"

They went back downstairs together and Andrion washed the sweat and dust from his arms and face before getting into his armor.

Meanwhile Bernadette had donned her own, and they gathered up their weapons. She had a thought, and went to see Rene before leaving. It wouldn't really be playing hooky if they had an official errand to fulfill, would it?

As usual he was on the run, making sure that everybody was doing what they were supposed to in coordination with everybody else. He gave them a moment of his time though. Yesterday's dragon incident had made him realize that these new friends of his were important, valuable people.

"What's up?" he asked, and Bernadette waved her map at him.

"Malden's sending me off to find someone he wants me to recruit for the Brigade," she said. "I thought as long as I was going out I'd see if there's anything you need from the store. Nothing too big, mind – I'm not taking a wagon."

"We can always use more chemial ingredients," he said. "And we're getting low on ingots for the forge. It's a pity there're no mines around here." Ingots were heavy, but she and Andrion between them could manage a few.

"Sure, I'll bring you what I can," she promised, and he handed over a purse of gold. It wasn't entirely clear where Malden was getting his funding, but the Brigade seemed to have no shortage of money.

Stepping back a little to make sure that her emotional affinity with Rene didn't carry him along with them, Bernadette touched Floradel on the map and wished them there. Rene stood staring at the spot where his two friends had been, shaking his head.

They arrived on the main east-west road a little south of the small village. Instead of going on in, they turned west and took the road for around a mile before finding a trail heading north. The time was getting on for midafternoon, skies gray and a stiff cold breeze blowing. At least it wasn't raining, or snowing.

They strode along the trail staying alert, pleased to be alone together after nearly a full week of being surrounded by other people. Doing something as pleasant as walking in Iscandia's wilderness was a nice change from the chores that had occupied them at Daywatch, too. But they were both only too aware of the dangers here.

During the ten miles or so of trail between Floradel and the Gold river they were attacked twice, once by a particularly nasty humanoid creature all covered in gray skin, and again by a smilodon. After months in Iscandia Bernadette was becoming almost nonchalant about fighting off hostile wildlife. It was a given – if you were out walking around in Iscandia, things would come darting out of the bushes intent on killing you. And, presumably, eating you. With Andrion or Erik watching her back, though, they didn't stand a chance.

Where the road came down to the water there was a goodly waterfall off to the west. But directly in front of them the water formed a shallow, quiet pool and they had no trouble wading across. Climbing a low hill on the far side, they abruptly came to an area of low-lying dypalfar ruins with one small tower rising above them. And standing in the midst of these was an attractive, youngish-looking woman with dark auburn hair in a page-boy cut, dressed in steel-studded leather armor. This must be Diane LeBois.

She seemed a bit distracted, and as Bernadette and Andrion approached she looked up at them in confusion. "Diane?" Bernadette asked tentatively.

"I'm Dian LeBois," she admitted. "I don't believe we've met?" Bernadette smiled and held out a hand.

"Bernadette Bouchard, and this is my friend Andrion Lamonte," she replied.

"You heard there was a fellow Galise out here in the wilderness and decided to drop by with some decent red wine?" Diane suggested in amused tones.

"Good idea, I wish I'd thought of it," Bernadette replied with a grin. "We could go get some if you like. I think the inn in Alfenstein stocks some, and we could have a decent hot meal while we're at it."

Now the older woman was beginning to eye her with suspicion. "Ugh," she said, "do you realize how long it's been since I had a decent meal? Or slept in a bed?" She gestured toward her campsite, a tent pitched over beyond the dypalfar site with a little campfire ring in front of it. "But why are you *really* here?"

No use dissembling any longer, so Bernadette got right to the point: "Malden asked me to find you." Diane looked disbelieving.

"He *did*? Well isn't *that* something. After the last time we spoke, I gathered he thought my input was worse than useless. He said some very hurtful things to me before I left."

Diane couldn't be very much older than Andrion was, which would have made her young and impressionable a decade ago when she'd had her falling-out with Malden. Bernadette told her, "Malden can be prickly and ungracious, but he really is trying to stop vampires from ravaging Iscandia. And whatever he might have said ten years ago, what he told me when he sent me to look for you was that you were 'smart as a whip' and a wizard with dypalfar machinery. He really does value your skills."

"He said that? Really?" came Diane's reply. Bernadette was beginning to get the idea that she might have had a crush on the older man, who probably would have been twice her age back then.

"Are you aware that vampire attacks in population centers have increased dramatically?" Bernadette asked.

"I've been awfully busy with my archaeological work," the other woman admitted. "This hasn't panned out like I'd hoped it would, though. There was some kind of a cataclysm in the distant past, and the top part of the city collapsed in on itself. It's going to require a major investment of money to hire a crew to excavate the ruins down to what I'm sure will be one of the most significant dypalfar finds in Iscandia."

"I know what you mean," Bernadette told her. "Andrion and I went through the ancient dypalfar city of Alzhenten last summer, and were able to penetrate through a flooded tunnel into the lost Norse stronghold of Faastenberg. But the top couple of floors of that place had collapsed in an earthquake too, and even though we have the funds we haven't been able to get permission from the eorl to excavate the city's outside entrance."

As soon as the eorl of Icemarch had learned that there was an ancient Norse city containing a fabulously valuable treasure situated in his domain, he had demanded that anything found be shared with the march – and that government officials be involved in the dig. The project had been stalled for months.

"Faastenberg?" Diane gasped, suddenly deeply interested in their conversation. "I heard about that..." Then she realized what *else* she had heard about that. "You're the Fireblood!" she exclaimed. "You found the gem forge the ancient Norse heroes used to win the Uprising, and... Oh, we have *got* to sit down and talk! I'm dying to know what you found, in both cities!"

The hook was set. "We'd love to discuss that with you at length," Andrion promised. "And I'm very interested in your work with dypalfar technology as well. But we're committed to helping the Daywatch Brigade beat back the vampire incursions. I'm not much of a fan of Malden myself, but he's managed to assemble a pretty good team. Lots of good people, and we'd really like you to join us."

Diane gave it up. The chance to pick The Fireblood's brain on her discoveries in Faastenberg, and this astonishingly good-looking young man right around her own age appealing to her to join the team? How could she refuse? "All right," she said. "I'll come with you... Uh, where is it we're going?"

"Daywatch," Bernadette replied. "Up north not that far from Norcove."

"Oh, excellent!" Diane replied. "The stories of that place always fascinated me. The dypalfar have always been my passion, of course, but ancient Norse history is full of intriguing episodes as well. So much of what people imagine to be fanciful legends and myths actually happened! Is it true that the site of the fortress is a valley that's mysteriously much warmer than anywhere else in the region?"

"Not so mysteriously," Anders replied with a grin. "One wall of the valley is a dormant volcano, and there are hot springs down along its slopes. The heat is trapped by the mountains on the other side, and I'd be surprised if they even ever get snow. It's nice – you'll like it." She grinned at him.

"You already sold me. Let me break camp, and we can get started. It's going to be a long walk to Coverdale."

Now it was Bernadette's turn to grin. "Not so long as all that," she replied and brandished the map. "But let's stop by Alfenstein first. I have some shopping to do, and Andrion and I have a nice house there where we can stay." Diane gazed at her in frank astonishment.

Alfenstein wasn't all that far away, and they got there a little after dark. Andrion had not seen Eastview yet, and he was thrilled at the place's spacious rooms and architectural charm. They were able to heat water for washing and let Diane get cleaned up before they all walked the short distance to The Staerlin Inn.

Evidently the Staerlin family was a big deal in this city, and it was no wonder one of them had ended up being appointed eorl. Bernadette wondered at the Remans' heavy-handedness in summarily removing one ruler and replacing him with another. That seemed like exactly the sort of thing to get the Norse partisans riled up, rubbing it in their noses that it was the empire, not the local populace, that truly ran things in Iscandia.

They had a fairly decent dinner – grilled half chickens in a plum sauce, a grain pilaf, and some steamed kale with dried icefruit added to it for flavor and color. At this season, it was hard to get many fresh vegetables. And though the meat was white, not red, they washed it down with a couple of bottles of quite decent Jalais imported from Auverne. Of all the cities in Iscandia, this one was closest to the border and most likely to have good wine available.

Of course Diane had pried most of the story of the expedition to Faastenberg out of them by the time the meal was over, and the three of them were the best of friends as they made their way talking and laughing back to the door of Eastview.

Soon Diane had turned in, sleeping in the bed that had once belonged to Bjorn, and Bernadette led Andrion by the hand to the master bedroom. She had only slept one night in this bed, and she felt a pang of longing as she remembered her time in it with Erik. They'd been so busy lately, there'd been little time to think about home and the people there she missed. These included Lev and the rest of the Maiden's crew, Lifa and Anja. But of them all it was Erik whose image kept coming to her mind's eye. Had he given up on ever having her for his own, and gone on to find solace in other women's arms?

All these thoughts were passing through Bernadette's mind as she removed her clothing. She'd changed out of the armor into a winter dress and cloak before they had gone out for the evening, so it didn't take long. Andrion, naked to the waist, came up behind her and put his arms around her, squeezing her breasts and kissing her at the juncture of her neck and shoulder. A little thrill ran through her, and she rotated in his arms to seize his mouth in a hot kiss. There'd been a lot less time for making love than she'd hoped there would be on this anti-vampire crusade. Pushing thoughts of Erik out of her mind, Bernadette let herself fall into Andrion, sinking into his arms as into a delicious sea of pleasure and desire.

Chapter 14: Netherbane

Bernadette, Andrion, and Diane arrived near the main gates of Daywatch fairly late the following afternoon. They were laden with iron, steel, and dypalfar ingots from Dyazh's forge, a roll of hides bought from one of Alfenstein's general merchants, and as many ingredients for panacea and healing potions as Magichemia had been able to supply. Diane had volunteered to haul along several more bottles of the excellent Jalais in her own pack.

The three of them stood looking around them in the afternoon sunlight. In the two days Bernadette and Andrion had been gone, there were already changes. The dragon skeleton had been completely hauled away, and there was a sense of hustle and bustle as the members of the Brigade went about their assigned tasks.

Rene swept by, in high gear as usual, and greeted them Galise style with hugs and kisses on the cheek. His eyes lit at the sight of Diane. "Am I correct in guessing that you are the renowned Diane LeBois?" he asked, with a little bow. She looked amused.

"That's me," she said. He pumped her hand. "Rene Augenois," he said. "I'm sort of third in command around here, though that's going to change when blood starts getting spilled. I'm more of an administrative kind of guy," he added deprecatingly.

Charmed, Diane squeezed his hand. "Nice to meet you, Rene," she said. "I'm looking forward to working with you all."

"Malden and Grindmar have talked of nothing but you and your work since Berni and Andrion left to collect you," the young man assured her.

Diane blinked at him in astonishment. "Grindmar's here too?" she asked. The subject hadn't come up.

"Second in command, and my immediate boss," Rene assured her. "Excuse me, I must be off!" With that he vanished, and the three walked into the main entry hall.

"You know Grindmar?" Bernadette asked in a low voice as they came inside.

"He was one of the people working with Malden back when I was," she replied as quietly. "Even then, Malden was convinced that vampires were a threat that had to be eliminated. But he was having trouble getting the kind of support he needed. And considering his tendency to alienate those who tried to help him, that wasn't much of a surprise."

Their conversation stilled as they got inside and realized that Malden was standing near the rear of the space, not far from the corridor that led down to his office. He was in conversation with a man of around his own age, a portly Norseman with a few wisps of gray hair clinging to his mostly-bald scalp. He was dressed in dark red robes over the top of leather boots, and was wearing a baldric with a sword hung from it.

The three of them hesitated, wondering at the man's apparent agitation but not wanting to be obviously eavesdropping on his conversation with Malden. "Where have I seen that outfit before?" Bernadette murmured to Andrion.

"He's a member of the Netherbane Brotherhood," he replied. "They're an all-male order of warrior monks, who go around Iscandia trying to wipe out daimon worship. I don't know why one would be here. Vampires are a bit outside their usual purview."

Daimons, the more sentient among the residents of the planes of the Netherworld, were frequently beings with great magical powers. When they invaded the plane of Terris, they were often believed to be gods – and had been worshiped as such, here and there, for millennia. But these beings were often cruel and capricious at best – or monstrously evil at worst. Most civilized parts of the world had long since outlawed their worship.

The three edged forward slightly to hear the conversation. "Father Hjaalon laughed at me, Julianos," Malden said angrily. "You all laughed at me, said I was paranoid and that the vampires were no threat. And now you seek my protection? Why should I give it to you?"

The other man looked close to weeping. "Hjaalon is dead!" he cried in desperation. "They're all dead! Brother Stuhrdal and I were out, investigating a report of a cult of daimon worshipers near Karstein. We found some evidence of a blood ritual, and the signs of Haemion. But there was no one near. And when we returned to the chapter house, we found it half-burned and everyone…" he sobbed, "Slaughtered. Gruesomely, and with unmistakable vampire marks on them."

Malden looked shocked. His face pale and eyes wide with sympathy, he put a hand on the other man's shoulder. "I'm sorry, Julianos," he said sadly. "But I did try to tell them, did I not? The worshipers of Haemion are linked with vampirism. I'm not sure how, exactly, but there is a definite link."

The monk hung his head, eyes downcast and tears running down his cheeks. "You were right, Malden, and we were wrong." Then he seemed to get control of his emotions. Wiping away his tears on the sleeve of his robe, he looked the taller man in the eyes. "What are you about, here, if not to seek out vampires and destroy them? Stuhrdal and I followed the tracks of those who destroyed the chapter house to a cavern in the mountains not far beyond Karstein. All I'm asking for is some backup – can't you spare somebody to help us root out those fiends?"

"Where's Stuhrdal?" Malden asked. "He stayed behind in hiding, watching the cavern entrance to see who's going in and out, and try to get some idea of what we'll be up against. He's expecting me to return with reinforcements as soon as possible."

Malden sighed. They weren't ready, and there was so much yet to do! He dared not go out looking for trouble before Daywatch had been restored as a stronghold. Look how that dragon had nearly wrecked them! If it hadn't been for The Fireblood… He glanced toward the open doors and realized three figures were silhouetted against the light coming in from outside.

Andrion, Bernadette, and… "Diane, you came!" His face broke into the closest thing to a genuine smile the two Bathing Maiden residents had seen since they'd first met him.

"Hello, Malden," Diane said coolly, a little reluctant to approach. He strode forward, oblivious to her hesitation, and took her hands in his.

"I'm so glad you're here!" he said warmly.

"I didn't come here for you Malden," Diane said, extricating her fingers from his grasp.

"Bernadette and Andrion here convinced me that my skills were needed, and that you had gathered a worthy group of people committed to the cause of stopping the vampires. Just tell me where I can set up, and I'll get to work."

The captain seemed a bit taken aback at her rebuff, but thinking back to their last meeting he had to acknowledge that he was reaping what he had sown. "Fine, fine," he told his latest recruit. "The smithy is set up in the yard around to the south side of the complex, and if you go over there I think you'll find Grindmar there. He can help you get settled in." He looked fiercely into her eyes.

"And thank you, Diane, thank you. I really appreciate your coming."

Bernadette broke in at this juncture, stepping close to the monk. "Brother Julianos, is it?" she asked, looking at the old man assessingly. He appeared to have regained his composure. He nodded, looking at her questioningly. "I'm Bernadette Bouchard and my companion is Andrion Lamonte. If you'd like, we'll accompany you to take out that nest of vampires in the cavern. If as you say it's near Karstein, we could be there very shortly. I have Karstein on my map."

Chapter 15: Grisbarrow Crypt

Malden had raised objections, but Bernadette had overridden them. If she and Andrion could be spared for a couple of days to recruit Diane and do some shopping, they could bloody well be spared for a couple more to wreak vengeance on the vampire coven who had slaughtered everyone at the Netherbane chapter house. They dropped off their ingots and other items, wished Diane well, and were off as soon as they'd restocked their packs with weapons that might prove effective against the undead.

Karstein was just another of Iscandia's many little villages. It had a small inn, a general store, and an iron mine that provided a living for the two dozen or so inhabitants. As soon as the town appeared before them, snowy mountains forming a chill backdrop, Brother Julianos took the lead.

"I can't thank you enough for volunteering to help," he said. "Say, what's your connection with Malden?" Bernadette asked, curious. "Malden was once one of our order," the old man replied as they puffed up a steep mountain trail. She and Andrion exchanged glances. The captain, a member of an all-male monastic order?

Sensing their questions, Julianos went on. "He didn't last with us all that long. We're a celibate order, and a lot of men have trouble with that. We appreciated his help while he was with us. But he broke with our chapter's leader, Father Hjaalon. He was convinced that we needed to look more deeply into Haemion worship. We pursue all daimon worshipers, of course, but he was convinced that Haemion in particular had some connection with vampires."

"So you didn't believe him?" Bernadette prompted, stepping up her pace to walk beside him on the narrow trail. "The thing about Malden..." the monk hesitated, before going on. "He's always been obsessed with vampires, for as long as I've known him. As if they were the root of all evil, the only threat to decent people on the planet. We thought that his theory about Haemion was just part of that, something he'd convinced himself of because he was always seeing vampires behind every bush."

Julianos puffed, as the trail became steeper. At the top of the next rise he stopped for a moment and caught his breath. Then he said sadly, "Evidently we were wrong. And my brethren paid for it with their lives." Bernadette patted him on the arm.

"We'll root out those blood-sucking fiends," she promised him, and they continued on their way.

At last, around another turning of the trail, they came upon the broad opening to an ominous-looking cavern. There was no sign of Brother Stuhrdal, however. Perhaps he'd already gone inside? "Have you and your brother been inside this place?" Bernadette murmured to the monk beside her.

"No," he replied quietly. "It has an evil reputation locally. People in Karstein believe it's haunted. They call it Grisbarrow Crypt, though I hadn't heard that the ancient Norse ever buried their dead in such places."

"Me neither," she replied. Everywhere she'd seen dead – and undead – in Iscandia, they had been interred formally in carved stone catacombs. Perhaps this place predated the Norse? It was said that the eldalfar, ancestors of all the elven races, had settled in this region long before the coming of the races of men.

The three of them crept inside, and soon found the broad entryway shrinking to a narrow passageway before opening out again into what looked like a broad natural cavern with a small stream flowing through it. There were plenty of signs of human intrusion, however, including a small stone-built tower and a heavy iron grate barring entry to a passage leading out the rear.

No one was stirring in the dimly lit space, torches burning in sconces around the cave's perimeter and on either side of the barred exit. But there was evidence of a sharp conflict. Senses alert for danger, the three spread out to examine the corpses that were dotted here and there.

Bernadette turned over the face-down body of a tall man, who from his pointed fangs and pale complexion must be a vampire. He was dressed in tight-fitting black leather armor, and wore a curious-looking black metal badge with a red enameled circle in the center of it, another black circle within that like the pupil of an eye. She searched his pockets and found a couple of potion vials and some coins. A foot away from where he lay a sablium dagger had fallen to the stones, blood on the blade.

She pocketed the badge and went over to see what Andrion had found. He stood from where he'd been examining the corpse of a young Norsewoman. She didn't bear the marks of vampirism, but had also been carrying one of those badges. An arrow protruded from her chest. On the far side of the room there was a strangled cry from Brother Julianos. "Stuhrdal, no!" he wailed.

Andrion and Bernadette hurried over to him. He was on his knees, bent over the corpse of a man wearing the same dark-red robes. "Why, why couldn't you wait!" he sobbed. "We came as quickly as we could…" Bernadette put a sympathetic hand on the monk's shoulder, and he lifted his tear-streaked face. Before their eyes, grief was being transformed into anger.

"*Damn* those vile monsters!" Julianos grated. "May they be cursed to the darkest regions of hell!"

"We'll send them there," Bernadette promised. She handed over the badge she'd found, and the monk got to his feet.

"Haemion!" he said grimly. "Malden was right!"

"There's a dead young woman over there with an arrow sticking out of her, and she had one of those badges too," Andrion said.

"She was probably in thrall to the master vampire," Julianos replied. "I haven't studied them, but Malden has and he told me much during our time together in the brotherhood. Years after the infection has transformed its victim into a full vampire, and that vampire has fed on the blood of men, they acquire the ability to bend humans to their will – to turn them into willing allies, who will do their bidding without question. It is thus, so Malden says, that they are able to lure other humans to their lairs as prey."

Bernadette knew little about vampires beyond the folklore that was prevalent throughout Agena. They lived for centuries without aging, they couldn't go out in the daytime, they lived only on the blood of their victims, and so forth. It occurred to her that it might be nice to pick up some solid facts, if she and Andrion planned to set themselves up as vampire hunters.

Julianos straightened the body of the fallen Stuhrdal, and they went on their way. Taking the body away for burial would have to wait until after they'd cleaned out this den of Haemion worshipers – or vampires, or both. There was no sign of a lock or lever to lift the gate, but Andrion went up into the small tower and found the switch. This gate must have been manned in centuries past.

After the gate had lifted into the ceiling the trio continued on through the corridors of the crypt. They soon discovered that the vampires appeared to be necromancers as well – walking skeletons, wearing armor, patrolled the corridors. Brother Julianos proved to have battle magic at his command as well as a sword, and these undead sentries were reduced to scattered piles of bones as they made their way further along.

"How many were there at your chapter house?" Bernadette asked. They had been hunting through the labyrinthine crypt for nearly twenty minutes and had not found any more vampires beyond that one in the outer hall. Were they about to run into a whole army of them, lying in wait for the pitifully small force that had come to bring them to justice?

"Nine, including Father Hjaalon" Julianos replied quietly. "But I think it likely that the vampires came on them in the darkness while all slept behind what they imagined was the safety of locked doors. There need not have been all that many of them."

"I thought vampires couldn't come into your house unless you invited them in," she remarked. More folklore.

"That's a widely held belief," the monk replied. "But according to Malden, it's a false one. Sunlight and fire are truly a vampire's bane, but doors are no barrier to them."

"Even I have a spell that will work to open most locks," Andrion put in.

"And vampires may have centuries in which to perfect their magical arts," Julianos pointed out. "There may be only a handful here, but we still need to be prepared for one hell of a battle." They continued on.

They entered a room that was configured like a catacomb, walls lined with biers on which the dead might lie; but there were no corpses here. Or, more specifically, the bodies were not those of the honored dead. A woman who was clearly a vampire, dressed in black robes and armed with some kind of magical staff, lay on the floor amid the corpses of half a dozen chillmarrow spiders. They'd been seeing the gigantic arachnids' webs for some time now. The spiders loved to breed in dimly-lit caverns.

Andrion stooped to examine the corpse, coming up with another of those daimonic badges. "I don't think she was poisoned by the spiders," he remarked. "She has a knife wound in her throat."

"Malden claimed that the vampiric contagion renders the body immune to all poisons," the monk remarked. Andrion hefted the staff and aimed it at the far wall. As he focused his will through the enchanted stick, a blast of lightning flew out and sizzled where it hit.

"Not bad," he said, and tucked it into his pack.

Onward through the seemingly endless labyrinth, as Bernadette wondered just exactly what this place was. It did have some features that suggested a true crypt, a final resting place for the dead; but there other areas that just looked like a natural cavern and still others that were built up and furnished like living quarters. Whatever it had been in ages past, it had lately become the lair of the group of vampires and their cohorts who'd attacked the Netherbane chapter house.

In a small room off of a long passage, they found another dead vampire. He appeared to be a young man, but could be centuries old for all they knew. He, too, seemed to have been killed with a blade. His robe was slashed open at the front, drenched with blood, and none of them wanted to touch him. The room was full of books – some on shelves, many more thrown to the floor as if they'd been hastily searched and then tossed aside.

"Bernadette, do you by chance have any panacea potions with you?" Brother Julianos asked. Contact with vampire blood was very likely to result in infection. She smiled at him.

"I brought plenty," she said reassuringly. "You want one now?" He waved her off.

"Let's just not forget to take some when we leave," he replied, relieved.

The last of the walking skeletons had been defeated more than an hour ago, and this endless trudge through the dim stone labyrinth, finding only the dead, was beginning to get to Bernadette. *Come on, let's have a nice big fiery battle and toast our victory with some panacea potions, shall we?*

The corridor they were traversing opened out into a sort of gallery, with a waist high wall running along it and a stairway leading down at the far end. They could dimly hear voices, and Brother Julianos held up a hand for silence. They crept forward and peered over the barrier, to see a pair of figures they took to be vampires conversing on a stone terrace below them. Beyond that was a chasm, with some sort of platform standing up in the center of it.

The taller of the men said, "I don't care how long you've been searching, keep at it. We will not return without it, or Lord Karazin will have our heads." The other, evidently a subordinate, replied

"Yes, of course Szandor. But we're running out of places to search."

"I *know* it must be here somewhere. Keep looking."

Bernadette motioned to Andrion, and pointed to the shorter man who was starting to walk away to the right while Szandor stood, arms crossed, watching him go. They had worked together long enough now that they were nearly telepathic. As she drew her bow and took down Szandor with an arrow in the throat, his toady was blasted off of the terrace and into the abyss by twin bolts of lightning – smoking as he fell.

Brother Julianos turned to his companions with raised eyebrows. "Weren't you curious to find out what they were looking for?" he asked mildly. Bernadette grinned ruefully at him.

"Yes," she admitted, "but I thought we'd better take our chance to remove those two while they were unaware of our presence."

"You're probably right," the monk said with a shrug, and made his way toward the nearby stairs. They descended them to the terrace, and Andrion went over to see how deep the chasm was. Its bottom, and the vampire he'd sent there, were lost in darkness.

Meanwhile Bernadette went over for a closer examination of the late, unlamented Szandor. She'd shot him in the throat on purpose, and most of the blood was spread out in a pool around his head or soaking into his back. Gingerly, she went through the pockets in the front of his leather tunic. Another of those badges, some coins, some more unidentified vials of potion… and a scrap of paper which read "*Apoldros, King of Heaven* by Brother Zendris the Old."

She handed it to her lover. "Andrion, what do you make of this?" she asked. He was her go-to guy whenever she felt short on information. He looked it over.

"I'd assume it's the title a book they were looking for," he said thoughtfully. They all remembered the books scattered everywhere around the corpse of that male vampire. "But I have to say, an ancient religious book written by some long-dead monk seems a pretty unlikely item for a master vampire's reading list."

"I've never even *heard* of Apoldros," Bernadette admitted. "Who was he?"

"It's another name for Aderos," Andrion replied. "Besides being the creator god and head of the Agenan pantheon, he was worshiped as a sun god in ancient times. I suppose it's possible that Apoldros the sun god got conflated with Aderos at some point in history, but modern scholars think they're two names for the same god. You won't find any temples to Apoldros in Iscandia, though. That aspect of him has faded now that people understand more about the universe, I guess."

Classic Andrion, Bernadette sighed. His ability to wax pedantic in the midst of a violent struggle for survival had become one of his most endearing characteristics, in her view. "Well, whatever reason this guy's boss had for wanting the book, I suppose it would be a good idea if we find it first. Do you suppose those were the last of the minions?"

The three of them looked around. A narrow stone bridge crossed the chasm to that curious-looking circular stone platform that stood in the middle of it. It seemed to be the only place left to search. "Just keep alert," Julianos warned. "That might be the last of the vampires, but there may well be other things to fear in this place."

There seemed to be a few torches glowing around the perimeter of the platform, which somewhat resembled an enormous circular gazebo. They didn't throw out much light, and when they got closer they realized that the light was produced, not by burning oil and cloth wrapped around wood, but by glowing crystals encased in metal cages.

"Those remind me of the lights down in dypalfar ruins," Bernadette remarked as they stepped onto the platform. Andrion took a closer look.

"I don't think they're the same thing," he replied. "It's said that the ancient eldalfar used some kind of natural crystals, mined from the earth, that had the property of producing light indefinitely. I think that's what these are. You sure wouldn't want to try reading by them, but at least it's enough light to keep us from walking off the edge of the platform."

Now that they were closer, they could see that the platform's surface was incised with deep grooves, forming concentric rings. There were four rings, and at the very center stood a small plinth no more than four feet high. Bernadette moved toward the center, planning to examine the plinth, when she heard a voice that stopped her in her tracks.

"Hello, can I speak with you? Don't shoot!" Emerging from the dimness on the far side of the platform was a young woman. As she drew closer Bernadette revised her first impression. She was beautiful, and her face was unlined; but she was more ageless than truly young. And from her pale white skin and slightly glowing eyes, she was a vampire.

She was dressed in leather armor similar to that Szandor had been wearing, but she wore no badge of Haemion. "Are you with them?" Bernadette asked, jerking her thumb backward toward the body on the terrace. She was frankly astonished that this apparent foe would try to talk with them instead of just opening hostilities. What was her game?

The woman, who was slightly taller and a little slimmer than Bernadette, made a gesture toward the sablium dagger at her belt without touching it. "Actually," she said calmly, "I killed two of them before you got here." The three confronting her looked perplexed.

"Well, uh, thanks, I guess," Bernadette replied when it appeared no one else was going to speak. "But you and they seem to share a certain… characteristic, if you don't mind my mentioning it. Why did you kill them?" The woman's forehead furrowed.

"It's a really long story," she began, "and maybe someday I'll have time to tell it to you. But for now, let me summarize."

The three vampire hunters stood there feet apart and arms akimbo, listening as the woman launched into her tale. "My name is Nerissa von Hordenhaal," she began. "My family are minor nobility, and own an island not far off the northwest coast of Iscandia. We're... a very *old* family, though there have not been any new generations in quite a while. Anyhow, my father somehow dug up information he was convinced was a prophecy. It suggested that he, with the legendary Staff of Apoldros, would be able to permanently darken the sun so that vampires would be able to go out in the daytime without taking harm. He was sure that doing this would make him the champion of our kind, receiving the allegiance and thanks of every vampire on Terris."

"That book!" Bernadette gasped. "Does it tell where to find the Staff?" Nerissa nodded. "Since learning of the prophecy he had been searching for any information about the whereabouts of that legendary artifact, and he'd learned that a copy of the book naming its final resting place might be found here."

"So you were helping to search for it?" Bernadette asked. A look of annoyance crossed the vampire's pretty face and she sighed.

"I can see I'm not going to be able to cut a long story short," she said resignedly. "Please just remain still and let me finish, all right?"

"Sorry," Bernadette replied in a little-girl voice. Was this woman old enough to have acquired the ability to enthrall others?

Nerissa went on. "A bit of background, then. The contagion that causes vampirism was not native to this world. It was brought here, or perhaps brought into being, by the daimonic lord Haemion, thousands of years ago when he first came to this dimension from his native plane of the Netherworld."

Her audience remained mute. "Nearly every vampire in the world became one as the result of this contagion, which actually changes the cells of our bodies to grant us things like eternal youth and total immunity to poisons and all other infectious diseases. Not to mention the drawbacks like not being able to withstand sunlight, and the need to drink blood."

"Most vampires came to their vampirism unintentionally, therefore – transformed before they realized they had been infected. A cure is possible, but it is costly, painful, and time-consuming. The majority have accepted what they have become, and moved on – enjoying the benefits, if being inconvenienced by the drawbacks."

"Yet some have embraced their vampirism gladly, reveling in it and paying worship to Haemion, who is seen as the father of all vampires – our creator, in a way. And for those who come to Haemion seeking his favor, he has sometimes granted miracles. He transformed ordinary vampires, or those who were not yet vampires at all, into Netherblood vampires. These rarest of the kind have the ability to take the form of Haemion himself, or at least of a member of his daimonic species."

There were little gasps around the circle, but the listeners refrained from speaking. All three of them were learning things about vampires they'd never dreamed – and from the horse's mouth. "Centuries ago," Nerissa went on, "after my parents had been wed for some time and I had been born, they became so deeply involved in the worship of Haemion that he granted them this gift and they both became Netherblood vampires. It is hard for me to convey what an honor this was, for my father to be given such a gift. Haemion greatly prefers females, and he has not made another male Netherblood that we know of in the last several thousand years."

Bernadette's eyes were wide. How did Nerissa look so nearly normal, coming from such a background? "When I came of age, the ritual was performed and I, too, became a Netherblood vampire," the woman continued. "Centuries later Father discovered that so-called prophecy. It stated that a Netherblood vampire lord would be the one to darken the sun, and he knew it had to be him that was meant. And my mother and I are the only other two Netherbloods we know – there are no others of our acquaintance."

The others were beginning to jump ahead, seeing where this was going, but held their peace. "The prophecy said that Father could desecrate the Staff of Apoldros, filling its shaft with the blood of a Netherblood vampire. And additionally, the crystal atop the staff must be infused with the soul of the same vampire who had supplied the blood. A Netherblood must die, in order to corrupt the sun god's staff for the purposes of blotting out the sun."

There was a stunned silence, and after pausing for dramatic effect Nerissa continued. "My mother became convinced that Father meant to kill either me or her in order to perform the desecration ritual as soon as he got his hands on the staff, and she didn't want to wait around. She begged me to flee, then vanished herself. I've been in hiding for the past twenty years, avoiding any contact with my father or any of his supporters. But I decided I can't live like that anymore. What's the use in living forever, if you must spend all your time running and hiding? I learned that Father had at last found a real lead to the whereabouts of the staff, and I trailed his minions here."

"Are they the ones that slaughtered everyone at the Netherbane chapter house?" Brother Julianos asked.

"Yes," Nerissa replied, "I'm sure of it. They've been hiding in this cavern complex for days and sneaking out to feed at night, while I was staying out of their way and searching for the same book they were looking for. I saw them all go out in a group two nights ago, and heard them talking among themselves when they got back. As worshipers of Haemion, they regard the Brotherhood as the sheep regard the wolves. But these sheep have teeth, I'm afraid."

The monk nodded sadly. "So what have *you* been feeding on, this whole time?" Bernadette asked. Nerissa's story had the ring of truth, but that didn't mean they could trust her. She smiled and extracted a potion vial from an inside pocket, holding it up. It glimmered dark red in the bluish light.

"This potion has been known for millennia," she said. "It's not all that easy to make, nor are the ingredients easily obtained. But a drink of this will still the blood hunger for a day. And I can sustain my body on any food you can eat, if I have to."

"So what's your plan, Nerissa?" Bernadette asked. "If you can find the book your father's minions were looking for, what do you mean to do?" The other woman hesitated.

"I had thought to destroy the book," she said. "But who knows how many copies there are? There could be others, and if he finds one and learns the location of the staff we'll be right back where we started – only worse."

"But if your mother has vanished, and you stay out of his clutches, he won't be able to kill you in order to desecrate the staff, right?" Bernadette asked.

"Once Father has his hands on the staff, you can bet he'll find a Netherblood vampire to use on it. He might even talk Haemion into making one, just to be sacrificed for the cause."

"And you don't want to see the staff used for that purpose, even though it would benefit you?" Bernadette probed.

"I'm not convinced that if Father did succeed in his plan, that it would not bring about the end of the world," Nerissa explained. "It's not supposed to actually blot the sun out, but rather to change it permanently so that it no longer emits the rays that cause vampires to burst into flames and die with prolonged exposure. But suppose those rays are the same ones needed to sustain plant and animal life on Terris? What if we vampires are walking around happily in the daytime, and a few years later everything else has died and there's no more blood to drink? Kind of counter-productive."

"You or your mother mentioned this to your father?" Bernadette asked. It seemed like a pretty obvious concern.

"The great and mighty Lord Karazin von Hordenhaal cannot be bothered listening to the timid concerns of women," Nerissa replied bitterly. "He's so convinced that the prophecy foretells the ultimate rule of the vampires over everyone else on the planet that he completely discounts the possibility that anything could go wrong."

"Then we need to find that book, and use it to find the staff for ourselves," Bernadette said. "If we destroy the staff, then the prophecy is dead. I've had a little bit of experience with prophecy myself, you know – I'm The Fireblood." Now it was Nerissa's turn to look stunned.

"The one prophesied to stop the Soul-Devourer from bringing about the end of the world?" she asked. "Has that happened?"

"A few months ago," Bernadette confirmed. "I guess if you've been in hiding you wouldn't have heard the news, but dragons have returned to Iscandia. By the way I'm Bernadette, and these are my friends Andrion and Brother Julianos. Andrion and I, and our friend Erik, found a portal into Asengard and defeated the Soul-Devourer there, with some help from the embodied spirits of some ancient Norse heroes."

"Honored to meet you all," the vampire woman said. "And I like your idea, Bernadette. I was just about to resume my search for the book when those two minions of my father's showed up. And then *you* did. I think this platform is some kind of a puzzle box." Bernadette continued her interrupted progress for a closer look at the central plinth. It had a large red button on the top of it. Before anyone could suggest caution she put her hand down, pressing the button. A spike nearly a foot in length shot up through the center, piercing her hand.

"Ow, fuck!" Bernadette yelled, blood spurting. As she began applying a healing spell to mend the wound, things were going on with the plinth, and indeed with the entire platform. Eerie blue flames shot up through the grooves, not everywhere but only in some of the circles and in channels linking them. Bernadette, now that her hand was healed, realized that there were also pillars similar in size to the plinth sitting at some of the junctures where the circles and channels met.

"I have an idea about this," Nerissa said. If older equaled wiser, she ought to be the wisest of them – so Bernadette stood and watched as the vampire woman began shoving those pillars around – up and down the channels between rings. As each found its correct location, it spouted more of those blue flames from a bowl at its top.

In another few moments each pillar was in its right location, and the central circle descended into the floor – revealing a largish, rectangular stone pillar that rose to a height of four feet above the surface of the platform. Bernadette circled it, and finding a groove in one side she touched it. There was the sound of grinding stone, and the monolith descended again to reveal that it was hollow. And lying on a wooden platform within it was a medium-thick book. It looked to be in perfect condition, the engraved cover reading "*Apoldros, King of Heaven.*"

The four of them trooped back across the bridge to the terrace, where against one wall stood a wooden table and a couple of chairs. Soon they were poring over it. The book, apparently written by a brother of the Apoldrians, was sort of a biography of the sun god

Apoldros. It spoke of his origins, his attributes and powers, the forms of his worship, and the miracles that were attributed to him.

Bernadette thumbed through, and before many minutes had passed found a page titled "The Staff of Apoldros." There was an illustration, showing a staff made, not of the usual carved wood, but of metal. It was probably around an inch in diameter, the metal gold or at least golden in color, and a sturdy cage enclosing a perfect white crystal like an enormous cut diamond surmounted it.

"Father's 'prophecy' described it perfectly," Nerissa said, pointing. "That knurled ridge down at the bottom is supposed to be a screw cap for the shaft, which if filled with the blood of a Netherblood vampire would permanently desecrate the staff and corrupt its power." Bernadette was reading down the page. The staff had been given as a symbol of his office and the god's favor to the founder of the Apoldrian order, to be kept by the monks within their Grand Temple forever.

"It says here that the Apoldrians created a sort of holy precinct called the Eparchy, somewhere in northern Iscandia," Bernadette said, looking at Andrion. She and Nerissa had monopolized the book so that neither he nor Julianos could see the page they were reading. "Do you know where that is or was?"

"I read something about it once," Andrion admitted. "But I don't think it said where it was supposed to be. The book I read seemed to regard the Eparchy as a sort of olden-times fable, a place that could only be reached by the pure of heart after being shepherded through a magic portal by the keeper of the gate, or some such nonsense. I assumed it was just a fairy tale."

"I think we need to get back to Daywatch and tell Malden what we've found," Bernadette said.

"Daywatch?" Nerissa asked. "That place was in ruins before I was born. Is somebody living there again?"

"Oh yes," Bernadette replied, and then stopped dead. "Uh, the thing is, a guy named Malden has put together an organization dedicated to the eradication of vampires. There have been a lot more vampire attacks in the past few months, and he's rebuilding the old fortress to use as a stronghold for his 'Daywatch Brigade.' And we're members of it..."

Nerissa smiled wryly. "I'm guessing I wouldn't be welcome there. Is that what you're trying to say?" Bernadette dropped her gaze.

"Malden would probably want to kill you on the spot," she admitted.

"But I could be a help to him, don't you see?" the other woman replied. "I know everything there is to know about vampires, having been one for hundreds of years. And I know *why* there have been a lot more vampire attacks lately."

"Your father and his minions?" Bernadette guessed, and got a nod in reply.

"He's had everyone he could command out scouring the countryside looking for information about that book," Nerissa acknowledged. "And of course, vampires out searching still have to eat. When this bunch doesn't report back, he'll be sending another force to check on them. And the rest of his bands will keep searching. It's going to go on until we can find and destroy the staff."

Andrion had been letting Berni handle the interaction, seeing that the two women seemed to be hitting it off pretty well. But at this point he had a suggestion to make. "Nerissa, why don't you just turn this quest over to us? We found the ancient potion and dragon spell that let us defeat Tarragin, and I'm sure we can find that staff. You could just go back into hiding, and when we've succeeded in destroying the Staff of Apoldros we'll spread the word. You'll be safe from your father, then."

She gave him a look that said she appreciated the thought. But it wasn't going to happen. "I've had enough of hiding," Nerissa replied firmly. "I intend to be there when the staff is found, and to be sure that it's no longer a threat to the world. I've had a long life, and I'm not afraid to die if that's what it takes."

"All right then," Bernadette said. "If you're determined, we'll do our best to protect you from Malden. But you'd better be prepared for some hostility. I don't know what his history is, but he's kind of rabid on the subject of your kind."

"Oh I do," Julianos spoke up. "Sad story. Back before the Conflict, when he was just a young man, he had a girl and they were going to be married. But she caught the contagion and became a vampire. He was devastated and was going to do whatever it took to get her the cure. And she said 'No thanks.' She liked being a vampire, liked the idea of never growing old, and suggested he become one with her so they could live together down the centuries."

Bernadette's eyes were wide with horror, as she stared at the monk. Julianos looked back at her as if having trouble believing she couldn't guess what had happened next. "He killed her, of course."

Chapter 16: Mustering

They collected the rest of the bodies and threw them into the chasm, hoping that this lack of evidence might throw Lord Karazin's next searching party off the track. It had been late afternoon when Bernadette, Andrion, and Julianos had entered the cavern, but morning was well along as they emerged again.

"Excuse me," Nerissa said, stepping back inside. She took out a potion bottle, this one's contents a fluorescent yellow, and downed it.

"There's a potion for daylight exposure, too?" Bernadette asked, surprised.

"It keeps the sun from causing us to burst into flames and die, but doesn't completely eliminate the sensitivity to sunlight," the vampire woman explained. She dug a lightweight hooded cloak out of her pack and swathed herself from head to foot before stepping outside.

In moments of subjective time they found themselves standing in early afternoon sunshine at the bottom of the steps leading up into Daywatch. As usual in fine weather (and it had been fine, most of the time since Bernadette and Andrion had first come here) the doors stood wide open, and the place was aswarm with Brigade members about their work. The old fortress was really starting to come together, it seemed.

They made it in the front doors without speaking to anybody. No one was in sight in the entry hall, though there were signs that interior furnishings were continuing to accumulate. "Malden's probably in his office," Bernadette said, and led the way. Both Julianos and Nerissa looked around curiously.

They went down the hall and found their grim captain in his usual spot. He spent most of his daylight hours here, doing paperwork. Though he also spent some time in the yard practicing with weapons, keeping himself fit for battle. He looked up as the four of them stepped into the room.

"Glad to see you're all in one piece," Malden remarked gruffly. "I was afraid we'd seen the last of you when Julianos dragged you off." The captain had an oil lamp on his desk, but the room had no windows and wasn't particularly well lit. It took him a moment to realize that the cloaked fourth figure was far too short and slight to be Brother Stuhrdal.

Malden looked questioningly at Brother Julianos, and with a sigh he began his explanation. "I'm sorry," he said sadly. "Even though we got there as fast as humanly possible, it was already too late. Stuhrdal had gone inside for some reason, and he was dead when we found him." They had given the corpse a burial of sorts, laying it to rest in one of the crypt's interment chambers.

"Who's this, then?" Malden growled suspiciously, and Bernadette stepped forward.

"This is Nerissa von Hordenhaal," she said, blocking the captain's view. "She helped us kill the vampires that had destroyed the Netherbane chapter house and slaughtered its people, and she brought us some very important information about the vampire attacks. A powerful vampire lord named Karazin is at the root of them, and he's plotting to blot out the sun."

Malden jumped to his feet. "*What?!*" he cried. "Blot out the sun?" At this point Nerissa stepped around Bernadette and threw off her hood, her glowing eyes fixing Malden in a steely gaze.

"You... you're a stinking vampire!" He turned back to Bernadette, furious. "What the hell do you think you're doing, bringing this... *creature* here to our fortress? She has to be a spy!"

"I don't believe so," Bernadette replied calmly. "She told us what her father is doing, and helped us find the book his minions were searching for." She pulled the book out of her pack and flopped it onto the desk, open to the entry on the Staff of Apoldros. "That was supposed to be a weapon *against* vampires," Malden said, "if it even ever existed at all. Why would a vampire lord be looking for it?"

Some time later, after Nerissa had once again explained the prophecy and her family's role in it, Malden had calmed down. They could see the hatred seething behind his eyes, but it appeared he did not intend to drive a stake into the vampire woman's heart the moment she had left the protection of her friends.

"Diane's already starting to make some dypalfar weapons for us," Malden told them. "Maybe you could get her to give you some of them before you leave again. I'm assuming you intend to go searching for this Eparchy place?" Andrion nodded.

"The Mages' Academy at Eisenstag has the most complete research library I have ever seen," he said. "If we can't find something there, I don't know where else to look. And for the moment at least, we're one step ahead of Lord Karazin. We know where the staff's supposed to be, and he does not."

After talking with Malden and getting his permission for Nerissa to stay, the four of them walked out and went looking for Grindmar in the yard. The vampire woman pulled her hood up again, complaining about the glare. "Do you intend to come with us on our quest, Brother Julianos?" Bernadette asked.

"I think not," he replied tiredly. "I'll leave it to you young people. Likely I can make myself more useful working here. I have some of the skills of a builder."

Julianos had soon been directed to the barracks, which had now expanded to a second room full of cots. And Greta, who was busy nailing furniture together when they came up, happily dragged them off to their new bedroom. It wasn't much, but it was private and it was theirs. The wooden bed had a straw mattress, and there was a long table they could use to set their packs and gear on. No carpets, no other amenities. But it included a chamberpot!

In light of their recent adventures, and their intent to take off again soon on a quest of dire importance, Grindmar had given them the rest of the day off. "If you don't mind, I think I'd like to find a dark room and lie down until sundown," Nerissa told them. There were plenty of empty rooms on the second floor, and they found one with a door but no windows. She smilingly tossed a fur bedroll just like theirs down on the floor. "Thanks," she said. "I'll see you this evening."

"When was the last time we ate?" Bernadette asked Andrion. "Or slept?"

"I'm not sure," he replied tiredly. "Why don't we take a little nap?" They stripped to their underwear and, wrapped in each other's arms, drifted off to sleep.

Hours later, the sun moving well toward the western horizon, Bernadette and Andrion got up and found their way to the dining hall. Marya was in there, stirring a pot. "Glad to see you back, I missed you!" she said with a smile. "I won't have dinner ready for a few hours, but there's some bread and cold roast venison if you want it."

Fortified, the two walked out of the dining hall hand in hand. "Remember that bath we almost took?" Bernadette asked. She was starting to feel grubby beyond belief. Andrion's warm brown eyes lit.

"Excellent idea," he said. Half an hour later the two of them were stripped down and stepping into the hot pool.

Bernadette lay back with a sigh. "Please, Aderos and all the gods," she prayed, "grant me that there will be *no* dragons, bears, smilodons, mammoths, or cyclops coming our way in the next hour."

"Amen," Andrion replied. "And let me add, let there be none of our fellow Brigade members either." He leered at her, devouring her pink and nude body with his eyes.

She smiled back languorously at him. Then as he made a grab for her, she suddenly became an eel – flashing out of his grasp and kicking to the far side of the pool. It was no more than seven feet deep in the middle, both hot and cold streams upwelling from holes in the limestone bottom.

Andrion grinned at her, then relaxed near the water's edge where the pool was shallower, closing his eyes. Bernadette sighed. She'd been in the mood for some boisterous play. Erik was always up for that sort of thing, but Andrion was so much more mature. She took a couple of strokes back across the pool to lie beside him – and he struck like a snake, seizing her in his arms and pinning her to him as his rising cock pressed hot and hard against her warm belly.

"Mmmf!" she exclaimed as he engulfed her mouth with his, still holding tightly to her arms lest she wriggle out of his grasp. Then she melted into him, and he let her right arm go free. She reached down between their bodies, grasping his erection and giving it a firm squeeze.

"Ohhh," he moaned. "Berni, you drive me crazy!" She opened her legs to him and he surged inside her, filling her up with that big cock as the hot water surrounded them both. Oh, yes!

Nerissa chose not to join the group for dinner, and Bernadette wondered if they had anything she could – or would want to – eat. Or maybe she felt uncomfortable hanging around with a bunch of people who had signed up to kill people like her. They did what they could to try to pave the way for her joining them, talking up the help Nerissa had given them in the crypt, and the way in which she was risking her life to help them stop her father's insane and evil plan. Tired out, Bernadette and Andrion returned to their new bedroom not long after eating and were soon asleep.

Like most of the smaller rooms on the second floor, Bernadette and Andrion's bedroom had no windows. But her internal time sense told her it must be nearly time to get up. She'd found the straw mattress a little stiff, but putting their fur bedrolls over it had prevented it from pricking them. She'd slept pretty well, and it was now occurring to her that she and Andrion had shared this bed twice and had still not actually broken it in.

She sat up, looking at him where he lay sleeping with his back to her, his broad shoulders above the thin blanket they'd been given for covers. His face was so beautiful in repose! But at the back of her mind, an image of Erik's golden magnificence came to mind. Oh, she missed him!

Bernadette bent over and kissed Andrion tenderly on the ear. He stirred slightly, but didn't wake. Then she slipped back down below the covers and put her arm around his waist, seizing his cock where it lay half-hardened in front of him. *That* got his attention! He took her hand, then rolled over to face her and enfolded her in his arms. "Yesterday afternoon was fun," he murmured. "And it sure feels good to be clean. But I'd like to take my time before we have to run off and start sleeping under bushes again. Let me eat you."

They threw off the blanket and Bernadette lay back, hands behind her head and her knees up, as Andrion knelt between them and began licking, kissing, and sucking. Ooh! Her hands came down on his head as her hips thrust upward, and she moaned with pleasure as the sensations began to spread from her crotch through her torso.

"Yes, yes, YES!" she cried, and he tasted her salty juices on his tongue as she came hard. Making love with Berni in the morning was a rare treat. As Andrion raised up on his knees, grinning at her with his cock jutting, she sat up. "Mmm! Now me!" she said, and pounced on him with her mouth. He knelt there on the bed as she sucked on him, hands resting on her shoulders and watching with fascination as her rounded pink buttocks bobbed in the air up near the head of the bed. So close...

"Wait, love," Andrion said softly, as he felt himself about to explode. She took her mouth off his straining cock and looked up at him. "Let's..." he said, and gestured. They moved around on the bed so that she was kneeling before him with her head on the pillows, rump in the air, and he carefully slipped inside her. Oh, it was so hot and wet and tight in there!

He moved slowly within her at first, teasing strokes, until she had begun to moan and hump up against him. Then he began moving faster and faster, until there was no more control. As Bernadette screamed and quivered, Andrion plunged as deeply as he could inside her and filled her with a hot gush of cum. Ah!

Awhile later, dressed for traveling and with all of their gear packed up, Bernadette and Andrion were surprised to find Nerissa at the breakfast table. She smiled at them, hands cupped around a mug of Daywatch's fearsomely strong tea. "Did you get anything to eat?" Bernadette asked, concerned. Marya was working on a gigantic pot of porridge, and turned around.

"I've got a haunch of venison hanging down below," she said. "I could cut you a couple of steaks if you like."

"Thank you, that would be great," Nerissa said. As Bernadette and Andrion broke their fast on porridge and bread, the vampire woman daintily cut up two medium-thick slices of venison and devoured them raw and bloody.

She glanced up to notice her two friends watching her, and said "I told you I could live on any food you can eat," she reminded them. "I still have all the same organs I did before I became a vampire. But aside from the craving for blood, which the potion will relieve, I much prefer raw red meat over bread and vegetables. It seems more satisfying, somehow. And I *do* need to eat, or I'll lose energy and waste away."

"Oh, that reminds me," Bernadette said. She brought out a few potion vials and handed them over to Nerissa. "I got these off the bodies of some of the vampires we killed yesterday. Looks like mostly the daylight one. I suppose your father's minions wouldn't have wanted to deny themselves blood."

"Thank you," Nerissa said, and went on chewing. They had all nearly finished eating when Diane appeared, having evidently been up and working hours before they had risen.

"Oh good," she said briskly. "I wanted to make sure I caught you before you went off looking for that staff. I have something for you. Can you come out with me to the forge?"

They discovered that a corridor off the south side of the entry hall led out to a large space on that end of the building, with double doors leading into the yard. Diane handed Bernadette a curious-looking device, similar in size and shape to the kind of short bow the Reman riders were said to have used in their early days of empire building.

But this was made all of dypalfar metal. It had a broad channel at the spot where you might expect to nock an arrow, and a sort of lever mechanism with a ratchet. "It's called a crossbow," Diane explained. "The dypalfar, oddly enough, didn't tend to use them for their troops. They seemed to prefer swords and axes. But smaller versions of this are often found on their roller automatons. You may have seen one."

"Yes, I have!" Bernadette replied.

"They made much bigger ones as well, some with multiple bolts or long arrows like spears as weapons to defend their cities," Diane went on. "I've based this design on plans that I uncovered down at the bottom of a city out in Mountmarch. I made some modifications so it would be quicker and easier to cock." She demonstrated the movement, laid a metal bolt in the groove and then pulled the trigger. The bolt flew across the room too quickly to see, and buried itself in the archery target against the far wall with a loud "thwack!"

Bernadette took it to examine more closely. The gleaming dypalfar metal was certainly beautiful.

"People here tell me you're a pretty skilled archer, Bernadette," Diane said. "This weapon can't beat a regular bow, especially one like that elven-forged beauty of yours, for speed or accuracy. But within its range, it packs a much harder punch. Good for getting past heavy armor, or really tough foes. Might even penetrate dragon hide, who knows. And its biggest advantage is, it doesn't take months of training for someone to become effective using it."

"You've talked me into it, Diane," Bernadette said with a grin. "I'll take it. Do you have some bolts for me, too?" The dypalfar expert gleefully handed over a couple of drawstring sacks.

"These are solid steel," she said, gesturing with the brown bag. "And the ones in the gray bag are a hollow-point design with softer metal in the tip. When they hit, the tip deforms and it makes a bigger hole in your adversary. Very effective."

Andrion raised his eyebrows. A fellow scholar Diane LeBois might be, but it appeared she was a lethal lady as well. A woman after his own heart. Not that any other woman had a prayer of taking him away from Berni. The Fireblood had him – heart, mind, body, and soul.

After saying goodbye to various members of the team the three of them went out into the compound. The unrelenting sunshine had given way to gray skies and a light drizzle, which was probably snow a few dozen miles away in Norcove. "Not too bad," Nerissa remarked, peering up from within her cloak's hood. "Shall we go?"

Chapter 17: Hunting the Eparchy

Eisenstag was many miles to the east, but little further north. The party arrived in the quad at the Mages' Academy in the midst of a near blizzard, at a time that was impossible to determine without any sight of the sun. "So this is the famous Mages' Academy," Nerissa remarked. "I've heard about it for centuries, but I never actually visited it before."

They began walking inside, heading for the library. "Do you practice any magic, Nerissa?" Andrion asked. It was by no means required to attend an official school in order to become a competent mage.

"I have some battle skills, and some necromantic tricks," she said deprecatingly. "Nothing very fancy. And you?"

"Andrion can knock your socks off with his battle spells," Bernadette chimed in loyally. "Me, I mostly just do healing. But *I'm* the one registered here as a student, which allows us access to the books. Go figure!"

They went on inside, and there was Mhyrzon din-Tzrek at the desk. It seemed as if he never left his post. "Fireblood," he said in his usual gruff manner. "Still not attending classes?" Bernadette colored. She had really *meant* to come back here and study, but there had always been other things claiming her time – improving her skills at the smithy, raiding tombs for treasure, hot sex with Andrion. And Erik, sigh...

"I apologize, Mhyrzon," Bernadette said. She had her faults, but she was always ready to own up to them. "We're on another quest that's kind of important for Terris, and we need to do some more research." The elderly uruk eyed her skeptically.

"More dragons?" he asked.

"There still are plenty of dragons around," she admitted, "but that's not why we're here. There's a vampire lord searching for the Staff of Apoldros, and if he finds it he might actually be able to use it to blot out the sun. We need to find it before he does."

Mhyrzon raised an eyebrow and shrugged. "I don't know what I can offer you on the Staff of Apoldros," he said. "The Academy's collection includes many rare old books of history, and a lot on the subject of magic, but not much on religion."

133

He stepped out from behind the desk, nodding to Andrion and bypassing Nerissa as if he hadn't noticed she was there, and led them down into the stacks. High up on a shelf in one corner, some six feet off the ground, was a slim collection of around eight books – and most of them weren't all that thick. "Right there, that shelf," the librarian said, "is everything religion-related that we have. If you should come across any others in your travels, I'd be happy to buy them from you."

With that the uruk returned to his usual station, and Andrion handed the books down to Bernadette and Nerissa. They made their way over to the same table where, months before, he and his lover had found the recipe for the potion that had prevented Tarragin from escaping his doom.

As they all took seats, Andrion sighed. "Looks like this isn't going to take as long as I'd expected," he said. "Let's hope these actually have something to offer us. Berni, why don't you take these three." He shoved three volumes across to her. "Nerissa, you can search these two. And I'll take the rest. Does everybody have a notebook and pen?"

One of the books, as it turned out, was *Apoldros, King of Heaven.* "I suppose this copy is probably safe from my father," Nerissa remarked.

"If a troop of vampire minions came bursting in here and tried to make off with one of Mhyrzon's books, he'd probably blast them into the next march," Bernadette assured her. The librarian cared more for his books than most people did for their children.

Another of the books, one of the three Andrion had assigned to himself, turned out to be the one he had seen before: *Shrines of the Ancient World.* "This has some pretty solid historical data in it," He said as he thumbed through the pages. "Lots of information on the ancient pre-eldalfar shrines in Remus, and like that. But other chapters seem to be more like a report of legends, without any hard facts. Let's see…"

Andrion found the chapter on the Eparchy. "Founded in the first era after the Uprising, exact date unknown… The Apoldrians were a monastic order, utterly dedicated to the worship of Apoldros. They chose a northern site for their holy precinct, because it was there that

134

Apoldros shed his light for the longest. Pilgrims usually came in the summer, when the daylight hours were at their peak."

"Huh," said Bernadette. "Those old monks must have had a lot of time on their hands in the winter."

"Probably," Andrion nodded, and kept reading. "They built a network of shrines, with the first of them being deep within a nearly inaccessible cavern symbolizing the darkness of the human soul in the absence of Apoldros' light."

Nerissa rolled her eyes. She'd had centuries in which to conclude that worshiping the gods was so much nonsense. What had they ever done for her, or her people? Not noticing, Andrion read on. "In addition to the brothers of the order, who spent their time in prayer and meditation at the monastery where their Grand Temple was located, there were others called Protectors. They guarded the shrines, providing greeting and guidance to pilgrims. The first shrine, in the cavern, required that the Arch Protector, without whose permission none should pass, open the portal that led into the Eparchy itself."

"Sounds pretty straightforward," Bernadette said. "No reason they couldn't have a portal – after all, this place has one."

"I've read they also have them at this place's counterpart in Roma, the empire's capital," Andrion said. "But I have no idea what spells were used to produce them. From what I've read, all of the ones we know about that are still operating serve to transport the user no more than a few hundred yards, at most."

"Still," Bernadette went on, her usual optimism in full force. Was she not the famously lucky Fireblood, to whom good things always fell? "All we really need to do is find out where the cavern is. Then we just work our way down to the portal. I suppose the Apoldrians must have all died out thousands of years ago, but probably the portal still works. We just get it open, find their Grand Temple, and there the staff will be just like all those other fabulous ancient artifacts we've found. We smash it to smithereens or melt it down in a forge until it's nothing but slag, and Lord Karazin can go hang."

Andrion smiled slightly at his beloved. Sometimes she just seemed so *young*... But then her youthful enthusiasm was one of the things he loved about her. "I suppose we'd better keep searching through these books, then," he told the two women. "Sing out if you see any mention of that cavern."

Hours later, the eight books had been returned to their shelves. In only two of them, the two they had already seen, had there been any mention of the Staff, the Eparchy, or even Apoldros himself. They had hit a brick wall, and Andrion and Bernadette at least were fainting from hunger.

They fast-traveled to the Wavering Walrus in Eisenstag, and Nerissa sat and drank some red wine while her companions sated themselves on fish stew and bread. Fish held no appeal for her, and it wasn't as if she truly needed to eat every day.

"We've just read every single book the Academy had on the subject of religion, without finding a thing we didn't already know," Nerissa said. "I think maybe we've come to the wrong place." Andrion took another bite of his stew, thinking about what she'd said.

When his mouth was empty again he said, "Mhyrzon warned us they didn't have a lot. But who would have more? Some religious order?"

Iscandia boasted several religious orders, but they tended to be limited to one sex or the other, cloistered, and – except for the Netherbane Brotherhood – disinclined to have many dealings with the public. "What about the Pantheatos in Sylvanian?" Bernadette suggested. "They honor *all* the Agenan gods there, including Aderos. Mightn't they have a library specifically related to religious matters?"

Andrion and Nerissa smiled at her. "That sounds like a good idea," Nerissa said. "If you're finished eating, shall we go?" Bernadette considered. Clearly, their vampire friend didn't need as much rest as they did. And maybe she was eager to get to someplace where red meat would be on the menu. But Bernadette was tired, and she'd be willing to bet Andrion was more so.

"I think we should put up for the night here," she told them. "We'll get a fresh start in the morning."

Chapter 18: Let us Pray

They appeared before the gates in Sylvanian, to find that it was already well into the afternoon. Perhaps we should have come before bed, Bernadette thought. But then, they would have been arriving here in the morning feeling dead tired. And hungry again, she'd bet. They had eaten some bread and icefruit jam before leaving, and she already felt like it was time for lunch.

They hastened up the main street, heading for the Pantheatos. This tall and solid-looking building, with its tiled dome, stood on a promontory overlooking the river estuary – not far from the eorl's palace. It was far larger than any other place of worship in Iscandia, with living quarters and meditation rooms in addition to the large central cathedral. There was even a good-sized outdoor courtyard for group worship, weddings, and funerals.

They went in through the front doors of the main cathedral, which were open at all hours of the day or night. They were greeted by a pretty, youngish Norsewoman. "Welcome to the Pantheatos," she said sweetly. "I am Frieda, high priestess of the Six. If you wish a blessing, feel free to pray at any of the shrines."

"Thank you priestess," Bernadette replied with equal serenity. "We are in need of some information about the history of worship, specifically the worship of Aderos in his aspect as Apoldros, here in Iscandia."

Frieda looked perplexed. "My husband Engbard may be able to answer your questions," she said. "I will go and fetch him." She went down a staircase leading down from an alcove at one side of the central nave. Bernadette nodded her thanks, and strolled idly around looking at the shrines. The Six – Aderos, Marmira, Aryos, Daita, Beridan, and Agneta – had once been seven. But the worship of the god who was once a man, Dedrian, had been banned by the truce that ended the Elven Conflict twenty years earlier.

Engbard proved to be a middle-aged Norseman, brown of eye and hair (what was left of it). He wore a brown rough-spun robe belted with a woven cord, and affected a neatly-trimmed moustache and goatee that seemed at odds with his otherwise-simple appearance. "You seek information about the worship of Apoldros?" He asked.

"Specifically," Bernadette explained, "we're trying to learn the location of the portal to the Eparchy, where in ages past the Apoldrian monks had a Grand Temple and a network of shrines where pilgrims would come to worship." The priest looked blank. "How long ago was this, my child?" he asked.

"The Eparchy was founded something less than six thousand years ago," Andrion said. "We do not know how long it existed, or when it vanished. We've found no mention of it in any histories from more recent times. Actually, we were hoping that you might have some books here that we could search through, to see if we could find any references to it."

Engbard pondered the unusual request. Most who came here sought solace, spiritual guidance, the blessings of the gods. "We do maintain a small library," he admitted uncertainly. "But I doubt you will find what you seek therein. It is mostly books describing the gods themselves, their attributes, and the requirements that they lay on those of us who would live righteous lives. I only have one book that mentions Apoldros at all…"

"*Apoldros: King of Heaven*?" Bernadette asked, her heart sinking.

"Why, yes! How did you know?"

"Never mind," she said with a sigh. Turning to Andrion, she said, "So much for my brilliant idea. Where else do you suppose we could look – the Bards' Academy?"

"Oh," Engbard said, "I might still be able to help you. I would be happy to pray to Aderos for you. If he wishes, he may reveal to you the location of this portal, this Eparchy – assuming either still exists." Seriously?

"I'd be happy to make a donation to the church," Bernadette told him. Religion had never been a big part of her life, but there were few people in Aderos who would deny that the gods existed, and that they took an active part in the lives of their human worshipers.

Suddenly a thought came to her, one that had been flitting in and out of her mind for the past several days. "Father, could I seek a little spiritual guidance?" she asked.

"Certainly, my dear." The two of them stepped toward the rear of the cathedral, and spoke quietly together for a short time. Then Bernadette stepped away.

"Thank you, Engbard," she said. "We'll see you in the morning."

"What was that about?" Andrion asked, as the three of them made their way outside again. Sunset was coming on.

"Just a point of theology I wanted clarification on," Bernadette said. "Anyhow, he's going to pray to Aderos tonight, and if the god wants to answer his question he says it will come to him in a dream. We'll go to him tomorrow morning and learn whether it worked."

"And if not, I suppose the bards probably *are* our last resort," Andrion said. "They're required to learn all the old stories, as part of their job is to keep the traditions alive. But I'm afraid those old stories get embroidered a lot."

"What do you say we go down to the Rabbit and see what's on the fire?" Bernadette suggested. "I for one feel as if breakfast was a long while ago."

The three of them entered the inn as darkness was falling, and the surprisingly blond Reman innkeeper, Severus Octavus, bustled over to them. Nerissa cut through any confusion by immediately asking, "Do you have some beef steaks you haven't cooked yet?" He looked puzzled, but nodded. "Please bring those along with whatever my friends are having."

Severus murmured "at your service," and relayed their meal request to a serving girl. Then the trio seated themselves at a nearby table.

Their food arrived before long, tender cuts of beef grilled and served with green beans and boiled potatoes for Bernadette and Andrion, raw ones on a separate plate for Nerissa. They all dug in with good appetite, and it was some time before any conversation resumed. Severus came by their table to ask if everything had been satisfactory. His eyebrows rose a bit at the sight of Nerissa polishing off her bloody meat, but he remained discreet. "We'll need a couple of rooms," Bernadette told him. "And how about a bottle of red wine?"

None of them were all that sleepy, and they sat at their table drinking their wine and talking quietly. A pretty female bard entertained them with popular songs, accompanied by her lute. No one in the place seemed to have noticed that Nerissa was a vampire, though Severus certainly ought to have figured it out.

Bernadette had been dying to learn more about vampires, and she took advantage of the casual evening to sneak in a few more of her burning questions. "Is it true, Nerissa, that vampires can't have babies?" Nerissa looked a little annoyed at the question, but she gave a wry smile and answered it anyway.

"The effects of the contagion and the effects of the Netherblood transformation are essentially the same," she said with a touch of the schoolteacher in her voice. Andrion grinned.

"Our bodies cease to age from the day that the transformation is complete," Nerissa went on. "We breathe, our hearts beat, we eat and digest… and yes, we shit and piss just like everyone else. But vampire women don't ovulate, and vampire men do not produce sperm in their semen. We still have a sex drive, but it becomes… altered, somewhat. If we want to produce 'children' the usual method is to supply a non-vampire with our own blood to drink. They will catch the contagion from it, but in a way that forges a connection between the drinker and the donor."

Whoa, Bernadette thought. She was almost sorry she'd asked. But her burning desire to know drove her on. "What about the enthrallment? Can all vampires bend others to their will?" Nerissa flinched a little. This was a sore subject for her.

"Those who have fed on the blood of humans, over time, gain the ability to enthrall them," she admitted. "I have this ability. But I choose not to use it. It is now repellent to me."

End of discussion. Andrion changed the subject, and when they'd finished the wine Severus led them upstairs to their rooms. He put Andrion and Bernadette in the room on the right – the very room where she and Erik had stayed, several months ago, after her escapade at the Ljosalfar Consulate.

The memory of that night, and the following morning, sent a sharp surge of lust through Bernadette along with a twinge of regret. Even though she was trying hard to devote herself to being with

Andrion, was considering giving up her carefree life to make one with him alone, she couldn't help missing Erik. The idea of never making love with him again filled her with a sense of unbearable loss.

As soon as the door had closed behind Severus, leaving them alone at last, Bernadette lunged for Andrion. He was standing at the foot of the bed and was knocked backwards, letting himself fall flat on the bed with his legs hanging over the end and Bernadette sitting on him. He grinned at her and raised the upper part of his body to pull her down for a tender kiss. Then he remarked casually, "Don't you think it might be a good idea to take off our armor, love?"

She bent down to clash the hard sablium of her armor's upper section against the equally hard metal of his elven gear. Banging a couple of times she smiled back at him and said, "Looks like you're right…" Reluctantly, she rolled off of him to sit at the side of the bed. He sat up and helped her with her buckles, pulling the top part of the armor off her leaving her nude to the waist, her full breasts bobbing appealingly.

She stood up then and Andrion, still sitting on the bed, knelt to help her unlace the sablium plate that constituted the armor's main lower piece. There was also a sort of chain mail thong bikini bottom, and her firm but rounded buttocks were exposed. The sight of them made him anxious to remove his *own* armor, because the hard-on he was getting was really kind of painful. Parting the plate, he gave her butt cheeks a firm squeeze and ran his hand down between them to caress her sex. Then he hastily stood up and began (with some assistance from Bernadette) to get his own armor off in a hurry.

In moments their hardware had hit the floor and been kicked aside, and they stood naked a couple of feet apart – each drinking in the sight of the other. As much as she loved having sex with Andrion, or necking with him, or having long and interesting conversations with him; sometimes Bernadette thought she could just spend hours *looking* at him. Perhaps her vision was colored by love and attraction, but she still thought he was one of the most beautiful men she had ever seen.

She broke her spellbound gaze to step closer to him, putting her arms around his neck and pressing her body to his. His cock pressed against her belly, warmer by far than the rest of his skin and pulsing slightly with eagerness. It seemed to her that it had a mind of its own, sometimes – as in fact, it also seemed to its owner. What was *on* that mind most of the time, he had noticed, was this lovely lass who was now squeezing so close to him a flea could not have gotten between them.

He bent his head to kiss her deeply, his tongue in her mouth and his hands roaming her body. They stroked down her back and seized handfuls of her buttocks, pulling her still closer. Oh, Berni! As he pulled away a little he saw her eyes were alight with desire. No other woman he had met took such deep pleasure in love as she did, or inflamed him so much.

Putting his hands on her slender waist, he guided her over to the bed. "Sit down," he murmured, panting slightly. "I want to eat you." It had been a couple of days since their bath, and her sex was a little musky. Andrion didn't mind at all. She tasted like Berni, like feminine arousal, like home. She had not menstruated since he had known her, apparently the result of the amulet she wore that protected her from pregnancy and venereal diseases. It had a different effect on men, though he wasn't sure what it was. Erik, who wore one all the time, certainly didn't seem to suffer any curtailment of his sex life as a result.

These clinical thoughts, passing through Andrion's mind as he pleasured his beloved with his lips and tongue, did not detract from his own arousal in the least. That second mind residing in the swollen head of his cock didn't give a rat's ass what the mechanism of Berni's amulet might be, or even if she wore one. Hell, *its* agenda was probably to convince her to take it off, so it could get busy impregnating her with a little brother for Anja.

At the other end of things, Bernadette was as usual floating in a cloud of delicious sensation as Andrion's mouth worked its magic at her fork. Lying back, humping her crotch into his face and stroking his hair with her eyes closed, she let herself ride that wave, up-up-up until she burst in a prolonged moan of ecstasy, wetting his mouth with a flood of slightly salty juices. As she climaxed she threw her eyes open, staring up at the dimly lit ceiling above the bed, sparkling lights exploding inside her head. Aaah!

If she thought about it, it seemed slightly unfair to Bernadette that *she* got to come over and over again, but Andrion (or Erik, or any of the many other lovers she had known) had to wait awhile before they could repeat. But on the other hand, that was just the way Nature worked. Why fight it? Lifting herself up on her elbows, she looked down at her beloved as he raised his eyes to hers, a satisfied smile on his face. He loved to make her come, and she found that one of his most endearing qualities.

Come here, she beckoned silently, her lips curving in bliss. Andrion stood from his crouching position then climbed onto the bed, straddling her, before walking himself up on his hands to join her. His face was wet with saliva and her juices, and he stopped halfway up to blot it off a bit between her breasts, turning his head from side to side to nuzzle them. Then he began working his way up from there, planting hot kisses on her bare skin: her breastbone, her collarbone, the neck where it joined the shoulder (ooh!). He ran his tongue up her neck from there to her chin, arriving at last at her mouth and engulfing it in a deep kiss.

He had still not entered her with his cock, which was quivering with eagerness. Now he began working it back and forth in her sopping wet furrow, pressing it to her and rubbing against her clit. This was delicious agony for him as it was for her, but he kept at it until she was crying out again, so close to coming that the moment he rammed it home she screamed and bucked, spasming upward to meet his thrust as if she had been struck by lightning.

Andrion closed his eyes, the feelings as Berni's cunt clenched around his cock almost too much to bear. But he just managed to hold on. He wanted more, wanted this to go on forever. In the back of his mind he knew that wasn't possible, but he knew it *could* last a little longer, at least. He gave Berni a moment to recover and fully enjoy her orgasm, stroking slowly and gently and kissing her fervently until her spasms had subsided. Then he began using deeper, firmer strokes, penetrating her to the fullest. Augh, it felt so *good*!

Andrion had done this to her on many and many an occasion, and Bernadette loved it every time. It was almost magical, the way he could draw her to a screaming peak of sensation, let her rest a bit, then do it again and again. If Erik did this on a regular basis she'd have been worn to a nubbin, but somehow with Andrion she had the ability to pour herself fully into the experience taking nothing but pleasure, unbelievable pleasure, and suffering no harm.

They made love face to face for a time, then by unspoken agreement pulled apart long enough for Bernadette to get on her hands and knees facing the head of the bed – so Andrion could enter her from behind. In this position her irresistible ass beckoned to him, and the feelings as he thrust deeply inside soon sent her tumbling over the edge once again. This time, she sensed his urgency as he reached his own climax at last, and it heightened her excitement as they groaned in unison and he pumped his load into her. His strokes continued for another few seconds until every drop had been expelled. Then he bent down to wrap her with his body as they both knelt, panting.

The two of them, still locked together, fell sideways onto the bed with their heads resting on the pillows. Andrion squeezed Bernadette tight, kissing her shoulder. "Oh, darling…" she murmured breathlessly. After all this time, the experience of making love with him was still mind-bending and left her feeling as if she had been transported to some other plane of existence. She hugged his arms to her as he was hugging her from behind, her mind still fragmented by lust and love.

After he had softened and slipped from within her, Bernadette rotated in his arms and planted a deep kiss on his lips, her hands cradling his head. "I love you," she said softly, "so *much*…" He lay there, still trying to bring his *own* mind back into focus. It appeared to have wandered off while Mind #2 was having so much fun.

Kissing her back, then hugging her to him tightly and gently kissing her forehead, he replied as softly "Berni, you are everything to me." Promise you will never leave me, his mind continued. But his mouth prudently left it at that.

In the morning they were all up early, drinking tea considerably weaker than that served by the Daywatch Brigade. Nerissa eschewed food, taking another of the potions that would ward off her blood hunger – and one to shield her from the effects of sunlight. Bernadette fretted about her new friend. Did she have an adequate supply of potions? As much as she was coming to like the vampire woman, she couldn't help feeling a little uneasy around her.

They made their way through a light drizzle to the Pantheatos, and found Engbard on duty in the central cathedral. "Good morning to you, Fireblood," he said. She hadn't mentioned that – had Aderos tipped him off? The gods worked in mysterious ways, Bernadette mused.

"Good morning, Father," she replied courteously. He was beaming at her, at all of them, and she had hopes that his news was good. It was.

"Divine Aderos has answered my prayers!" he said jubilantly. Bernadette supposed that for one who sought the gods as a calling in life, having those divine beings actually respond to one's overtures must be the pinnacle of personal fulfillment. "Do you have a map?" he went on, and she pulled it out of her pack.

Engbard placed his hand on a spot almost exactly central in Iscandia, on the southern slopes of the mountain range that cut across most of the province from east to west. "Aderos spoke to me in my dreams," the priest said, "and told me that the pathway to what you seek will be found within Nightvoid Cavern. As he spoke, the three of them watched an arrow appear. Yes!

Bernadette through her arms around the startled priest and gave him a hug. "Thank you, Father!" she cried. "You may have saved the world from destruction!" He smiled avuncularly at her.

"Aderos has pointed the way," he said. "Saving the world will be up to you, but I don't doubt you can handle it."

After Andrion and Nerissa had also thanked the priest – with handclasps, not hugs – they turned to go. Then Bernadette, bringing up the rear, stepped back. She had almost forgotten! "Father," she murmured, looking into his eyes hopefully. "About that other thing... did you get an answer?"

He smiled warmly and nodded his head. "The answer," he said, "is yes."

Chapter 19: Nightvoid Cavern

In the street outside the Pantheatos, her heart singing with excitement, Bernadette studied the map. The marker for Nightvoid Cavern seemed to be pulsating slightly, but she could not take them there... yet. Her nearest fast-travel point appeared to be the cave wherein they'd maimed the chymera for the sake of the Destroyer of Magic potion, several months back. But somehow, she didn't think they wanted to go there.

Instead, she took them to one of the ancient Norse burial places where she, Andrion, and Lifa had visited so soon after Bernadette's arrival in Iscandia – back when she had barely begun to understand her Fireblood nature. No skeletons now patrolled the place, and they walked past it looking for a trail up into the foothills to the northeast.

They found one and began following it, and within an hour or so the party were entering yet another dark and dismal cavern. The mountains of Iscandia were honeycombed with such – and when men and elves had not found natural caves, they had dug their own.

This one was if anything darker than most, and Bernadette found herself wishing for the power of night vision some races were said to have. Fortunately for all of them there seemed to be no enemies here but chillmarrow spiders, and their glowing eyes betrayed them as they scuttled through the passages. After an indeterminate time spent wandering thus, killing several spiders, the party found themselves standing at the edge of a deep, circular chasm. It was too dark to see much, but it seemed to go down a long way and there might possibly be a pool of water at the bottom.

An extremely rickety-looking wooden plank bridge spanned it, and on the far side Bernadette could see a table with a lantern and a pickaxe resting on it. "Andrion, can you put one of your light globes over there?" she asked. He obligingly hurled a globe of the type that would stick itself to whatever surface it first touched, shedding a coruscating white light that revealed the ledge was a dead end.

"I don't trust that bridge," Bernadette told her companions. "Let's see if we can find another way down." She wasn't sure why, but she was convinced in her mind that the portal they sought – or whatever it was Aderos said was their goal – would be down at the bottom of this black pit.

"I have excellent night vision," Nerissa pointed out. "Why don't you let me take the lead?" Oh, of course. Vampires' eyes glowed slightly, and with their sensitivity to sunlight they were forced to be creatures of the night. It stood to reason they could see better in darkness than did ordinary humans.

"Sure," Bernadette replied. "Just don't leave us behind."

Following Nerissa's back with Andrion bringing up the rear, Bernadette found herself feeling less anxious. The vampire woman's spellcraft proved to be strong, not surprising if she'd had centuries in which to develop her skills and supply of magical force. She blasted chillmarrow spiders to flaming ruin, briefly lighting up the narrow tunnels as she sought a path for them down, down. The tunnels crisscrossed and wandered, but Nerissa managed to avoid getting them lost.

Finally they found themselves standing on a dimly-lit subterranean shore, beside a broad lake that stretched off into the darkness. What light there was, Bernadette realized, was emanating from plants that were growing here and there. She'd seen luminescent fungi before, but these appeared to be flowering plants. How weird, she thought, wondering what they could possibly use for pollinators. Their leaves were white, not green, the flowers glowing blue and pink, and she harvested a few. Who knew what uses they might have in chemia?

Far down the cavern from where they'd entered it they could see the glow of a different sort of light. Might there be human beings here? Gripping her bow, Bernadette murmured to her companions, "We ought to go investigate that." The three waded into the water, finding it only a few inches deep, and climbed a rise on the far side.

As they came nearer, they saw a human-looking figure performing some sort of obeisance before a sunburst-topped pillar. Beside it stood a structure like a gazebo, glowing in the warm yellow light of a pair of torch stands. "What's that?" Nerissa asked sharply. "I can feel some kind of power from it…"

Bernadette and her companions went closer still, and the figure spoke to them: "Come forward. You have nothing to fear here." He appeared to be elven, slender of build yet shorter than most, with extremely pale skin and white hair. His unlined face suggested that his hair color was the result of heritage rather than age.

When they stood before him, he said "I am Arch Protector Duraenis. Welcome to the Great Eparchy of Apoldros." Bernadette's heart beat faster as she realized that they had managed to find exactly the place they needed to go – and it was still manned!

"This cave is a temple to Apoldros?" she asked him.

"Apoldros, Aderos…" he replied. "So many names for the sovereign of the white elves."

Bernadette exchanged a brief glance with Andrion. His eyes were alive with excitement. The white elves were supposed to have been extinct for millennia, the leukalfar their degenerate descendants. "White elves?" she asked him. "You're a leukalfar?"

"I prefer white elf," he said. "The name 'leukalfar' has come to mean something negative." She could certainly understand that. This slim but muscular elf had two good eyes and bore little more resemblance to the leukalfar she had met than she did herself.

He went on, "Those twisted creatures you call leukalfar, I call the changelings." Digesting that, Bernadette moved on to more pressing matters.

"We are here seeking the Staff of Apoldros," she told Duraenis.

"Of course," he replied. "I should have known that the first people to appear here in more than a thousand years would not be pilgrims." After a brief pause he continued, "The staff you seek was kept within our Great Temple, deep within the Eparchy. It is probably still there, but it will not be easy for you to acquire."

The white elf sighed. He'd been stationed here, alone, for a thousand years waiting to welcome pilgrims who never came? Bernadette thought. Glancing around, she saw that there was a campsite nearby, with a fire pit and a bed of sorts. What a life!

"A thousand years ago, more or less," Duraenis explained, "The changelings who had been living in the areas around the Eparchy since their dypalfar masters had left them behind rose up and attacked the Great Temple in force. They slaughtered everyone, and so far as I know they have occupied it since then. My brother Signis – my brother in blood as well as in the order of the Apoldrians – was then Archon of the order. I assume that he was killed along with the rest."

"Didn't you fight back?" Bernadette asked. From what she had seen of the "changelings," they lacked much in the way of organization and their weaponry was primitive.

"The Eparchy was a place of peaceful worship," the Arch Protector explained. "There was but a small group of protectors, and we were no match for the changelings' sheer numbers. Those of us who were not on duty at the shrines fell with the rest, and we who were… stayed at our posts. I began turning away pilgrims who came, telling them that the Great Temple was no more. And then, after a generation of men, there were no more pilgrims."

"We must find the staff," Bernadette told him. "Let us through, and we will try to cleanse your Great Temple of the changelings."

"What do you mean to do with the staff, anyway?" the monk asked her. She thought fast. Whether he let them through might depend on how she answered. But she didn't want to lie.

"We mean to destroy it," she admitted, "to prevent its falling into the hands of an evil vampire lord. He wants to desecrate it with vampire blood, and use it as a weapon to blot out the sun."

Duraenis eyed her thoughtfully. "You cannot destroy the Staff of Apoldros," he said. "It is a thing of our god, created by his hand, and indestructible. It might, though, be possible for this vampire lord to use it as you say. If you can obtain the staff and bring it to me, I can call on Apoldros to bless it so that it can be used instead as a weapon against he who sought to corrupt it."

Bernadette looked around at her companions. Andrion and Nerissa exchanged glances, then both looked at her and nodded. Clean out an exceptionally large nest of leukalfar in exchange for a weapon to defeat Lord Karazin and his vile plans? Sure!

"We'll do it," Bernadette told the ageless monk. "Just open the portal for us and we'll go straight to your Great Temple and clean it out. If you can find some more monks to join your order, you can open up for business again."

Duraenis shook his head. "You will not be able to go straight to the Great Temple, for without the tokens of the Shrine Protectors you will be unable to pass its gates," he explained. "The portal I will open for you will transport you to the Passage of Darkness. From there you must make your way into the Eparchy itself, a region of mountains and canyons wherein you will find four shrines. Each of them is manned by one of my brethren, my fellow protectors whom I have not seen in all the long years since the invasion of the Great Temple."

"How do you know they're even alive?" Bernadette asked. "Wouldn't the changelings have wiped them out after they'd taken out everyone at the temple?"

"I know," the monk replied. "Each of the shrines is warded by Apoldros, and by stepping inside his shrine the Protector would be safe from all harm. Additionally, the five shrines – including this one – are linked. We five can communicate with each other psychically while meditating within them."

"So we have to get tokens from your brother Protectors?" Bernadette asked.

"That is correct," Duraenis replied. "In times past, and for thousands of years, pilgrims would come to worship Apoldros. As they visited each shrine, they would meditate within on the virtues presented – each different. When they had received enlightenment, the Protector would give them a token and they would continue on. When at last they reached the gates leading to the Great Temple, they would deposit the tokens in the receptacle and the gates would be opened to them. The gates, like the shrines, are warded by our god and cannot be breached by any mortal force. Yet somehow the changelings found their way inside. This has troubled me for centuries."

Duraenis stepped forward to the pillar where he had been praying when they came in. He remained standing, performing some silent ritual that involved a lot of intricate hand gestures. Suddenly the pillar shimmered out of existence, and the circular stone pad on which it sat became a coruscating pool of blue-glowing energy.

"I will leave the portal open for you, so that you may return to me with the staff," the monk told them.

"What should we expect on the other side?" Bernadette asked.

"Many things haunted the Passage of Darkness even when pilgrims came here often," he replied. "The changelings and their creatures, poisonous plants, and other things unseen, all intended to be a test of the faith and endurance of the pilgrims. Be careful."

"Mightn't the changelings come here through the portal while it's open then?" she asked, concerned.

"A good point," Duraenis said. He reached into a pocket of his robe and pulled out three small golden metal disks. Each was embossed with a sunburst and enameled in black. They seemed to glow faintly in the dim light of the cavern. "Each of you, carry one of these with you," he said passing them out. "The portal will be set to admit only one carrying my token."

They thanked him and stepped leerily into the portal. It was a curious sensation, stepping forward as if to the shore of the underground lake, and one's next step carrying one a little way down a nearly pitch-black tunnel, lit only by a few of those glowing plants. They had come to the Passage of Darkness!

Chapter 20: The Eparchy

It wasn't much different, actually, from what they had come through earlier. Rather than some magic portal, they might simply have turned a bend in the underground labyrinth they'd been traversing before meeting Duraenis. "That was strange, but not unpleasant," Nerissa remarked.

A thousand enemies could be lurking in that darkness, and Nerissa took the lead again. But Bernadette's anxiety was getting the better of her, having to rely on the vampire woman to warn her of danger – and then not being able to see what was attacking her until they were standing nose to nose.

She hadn't learned that spell for having one's palm glow, but she had learned one of the variations of the light globe spell: the one that caused a glowing orb to appear a few feet above one's head and follow along like a puppy on a leash. She sent one up, and it floated no more than three feet above her head – along the tunnel's low ceiling. After a minute, it winked back out of existence leaving her blinder than before. She just didn't have the strength of magic to cast such a spell and have it last. A pity she hadn't found any dragon spells for such a purpose!

"Let me, love," Andrion said, and held out his left hand. The light from his palm was both softer and steadier than the globe had been, and while Bernadette's view directly ahead was enshadowed, she could at least see well to either side.

They had not gone very far along the corridor they'd begun in, when they came across an oddly familiar-looking organic object lying along one side of the corridor. It was oblong and armored in overlapping chitinous plates, looking like a mandimant but gray rather than black or red and lacking a head or legs. "What's this, Andrion?" Bernadette asked. He plunged the sword he was wearing on his hip into it, the hard sablium slicing through the chitin like cheese, and a gush of yellow ichor squirted out.

"Aha, thought so!" he said. "I've read about them, but hadn't actually seen any before. That was a mandimant pupa. They live for years growing ever bigger, shedding their carapaces. You remember the little ones we saw in Alzhenten?" Bernadette shuddered. The swarm of voracious little creatures might have reduced her and Andrion to bones in minutes, if he hadn't fried them with a fire spell.

"Uh huh…"

"They eventually become huge, then form these hard pupae. When they emerge, they are flying adults that mate, lay eggs, and then die. Most of the mandimant's lifespan, years of it, is spent as a larva."

"Fascinating," Nerissa remarked in a voice with a slight edge of sarcasm. "Shall we continue?"

"Keep an eye out for the adults," Andrion warned her. "They look like four-legged, two-winged flying wasps the size of eagles. No mouthparts, because they don't eat after they come out of their pupae. But they have a venomous stinger six inches long."

"Will do," the vampire woman replied shortly, and moved on ahead of them.

After traversing the dark passageways for another few minutes, they began to encounter leukalfar sentries. They patrolled the darkness usually one or two at a time, and it wasn't that hard for the three intruders to bring them down. Whenever they spotted any more of the mandimant pupae Andrion destroyed them with his sword. At last they came to a section of corridor with a couple of chains hanging from the ceiling.

Bernadette gingerly pulled one of the chains, causing a section of wall to rumble out of their way. Good, no traps. Proceeding cautiously, they soon came into an area that was as strange as any they'd seen. The caverns had opened out, and were illuminated by giant glowing mushrooms the size of small trees. Eerie glows lit the ceiling too, either from glowing ores or smaller luminescent fungi. It was alien, and beautiful. But it kind of gave Bernadette the creeps.

She discovered the hard way that an unfamiliar flower she attempted to pluck was poisonous just to breathe near. But they found little else to threaten them, and she began to relax. Pools of water were here and there, and they began to see some unfamiliar wildlife. One animal was clearly a predator, and Bernadette performed a preemptive strike on it with her bow.

They all clustered around the corpse. "Have you ever seen anything like this?" Bernadette asked Andrion. He shook his head, his eyes agleam. Not counting her, few things got him more excited than the opportunity to learn something new. He bent to study it.

"It looks a lot like a smilodon," he said, examining the two enormous fangs and sharp claws, "though its fur is a lot shorter and it's a little smaller. But the main difference is these markings."

The markings were beautiful, rows of pale-colored spots against a background that, in this light at least, looked to be a medium shade of brown. They walked on, and in a while came to the corpse of a deer-like animal that had presumably been killed by the cat. It, too, resembled more familiar forms of Iscandia but was smaller and also had that pattern of spots and stripes running through its coat.

After going around a few more bends they saw actual daylight ahead, and emerged into a mist-shrouded valley that was surrounded on all sides by rocks. Tall mountains loomed in the distance. There were also some ruined stone structures in the further distance, and they could see a few of those oddly-marked deer grazing further down the valley.

"This is amazing," Nerissa said with a touch of awe in her voice. "It's almost like another plane of existence." Perhaps, despite her vampiric nature, she was finding it as much of a relief as Bernadette did to leave the dark caverns behind. Bernadette locked eyes with Andrion and she knew that he, too, was glad to be out in the open air. She checked her map, and saw that they were indeed, as the book had claimed, far to the north of Iscandia.

Arches beckoned ahead, marking a clear path. But around halfway down the small valley's length there were other paths going up hillsides to the left and right. Better to do a little exploring before following the one most clearly marked. Taking the lead again now that she could see, Bernadette led them to the north up a slope, and after reaching its summit and winding down amidst trees, bushes, and snowdrifts, they found another shrine.

A heavy snow was falling as Bernadette approached the Protector manning it. "Welcome," he said. "I have communicated with my brother Duraenis, and he has told me of your quest. This is the Shrine of Vision, and I am Brother Edurnis. I know you came not to worship our god but to free His temple from the invaders. But should you seek enlightenment, you may meditate within the shrine."

Like the one presided over by Duraenis, this was a white stone building standing maybe twelve feet high, with a hexagonal base fifteen feet across. Inside, the visitors could see a pillar with a golden sunburst floating in midair above it. "Thank you, Brother Edurnis," Bernadette said respectfully. "But our mission is urgent. Could you just give us your token, so we can be on our way?"

"Very well," he replied with a trace of sadness. Imagine having a job to perform and nobody to perform it for, as you waited out the centuries!

He handed a single sunburst token to Bernadette. It was identical to the ones the Arch Protector had given to all of them, save that the enamel was white. "We only need one?" she asked him, and he nodded.

"When you have the four tokens from me and my brethren at the shrines within the Eparchy, and have reached the gates leading to the Great Temple, deposit them in the container beside the gates and they will open to admit all of you."

Thanking him, the travelers went on their way. Andrion and Bernadette took a moment to get cloaks out of their packs and put them on over their armor, keeping the snow out of their faces. Nerissa was already wearing hers, of course. They returned down the hillside and this time Bernadette bowed to inevitability and took the path that led through the arches. They found a mountain pass infested with chillmarrow spiders, and the three of them were forced into furious action for a few moments until all of them were dead.

After passing the spiders they found themselves in a river valley. As they approached the shore Bernadette looked right and left, and spotted another shrine sitting beside the river's banks to the south of them. They hurried down there. This stop on their journey proved to be the Shrine of Knowledge, manned by Brother Artidel. All three of the white elves they had seen so far – after no one had seen any in time beyond mind – were similar enough in appearance to seem like brothers in truth or at least first cousins. Each was ghostly pale, with ice blue eyes and that fine, silvery white hair.

After receiving Artidel's token, Bernadette stepped out and looked around. Across the partially frozen river in the valley below them, she could see a path winding up the opposite bank that looked promising. Before crossing, though, she reached into her pack for some bread and cheese and handed some to Andrion as well, along with some water to wash it down with. This stage of their anti-vampire campaign, alas, looked as if it were turning into another one of those marathons with no sex, little food, and sleep only a remote possibility.

Bernadette was acutely aware of how dangerous that could be. Well, not the no-sex part. Even as good as Andrion looked in that armor, being half-starved and nearly exhausted had a way of keeping her lusts to a manageable level. But they were all, with the possible exception of Nerissa (whose powers she still did not fully understand), losing their edge as time went on without rest and proper food. This could mean the difference between them defeating their enemies or the other way around.

The three proceeded up the hill, and at its top they found themselves looking at a broad frozen lake, the water from it spilling out in a broad waterfall at the center of its northern edge. At the far end, Bernadette thought she could see the next shrine.

Not trusting the ice, Bernadette led them along the rocky southern shore. She didn't need to add hypothermia or drowning to the list of perils they faced. They picked their way to shore without any mishaps and walked up the path to the next shrine. This, the Protector – Brother Ferandis – told Bernadette, was the Shrine of Determination. He, too, had been informed of their quest and after a brief conversation Bernadette pocketed his token and the three moved on. Three down, only one more to go! On leaving this shrine, they climbed a snowy hill to the west and soon found themselves in a sort of outdoor labyrinth – complete with leukalfar and mandimants.

This was something outside of Bernadette's experience. Leukalfar and mandimants were creatures of the dark, denizens of the deep places where dypalfar had once lived – or so she had believed. She had never seen either of them dwelling above ground, but here they were. A network of canyons seemed to be filled with leukalfar dwellings, almost... villages. Most of the yurts looked as if the inhabitants had just stepped out on an errand. Not that there weren't plenty of living inhabitants, but they surprised none in the act of daily living. All they encountered were what appeared to be sentries, all of them creeping silently along on the alert for intruders.

Exploring each bridge and walkway searching for the path to the final shrine, Bernadette found surprising amounts of treasure in the huts and on the bodies of their fallen attackers. Gold and gems weren't much in evidence, but valuable weapons and armor abounded. How could these isolated people amass such wealth, and what did they do with it? Did they somehow trade with others, perhaps leukalfar from neighboring bands?

After the third or fourth time she and her party had encountered and killed leukalfar guardians, Bernadette sighed. She'd been half-hoping they would find a leukalfar rookery, a village where these descendants of the white elves might be caught acting... human. Raising babies, chattering around a fire, carrying out the activities of ordinary life. They found places where leukalfar were apparently doing chemia, crafting the poisons they used on their weaponry. Places where that weaponry was created. Food caches, cookfires, hides ready for tanning. But if this sprawling network of canyons was a village, it was a village without life beyond guards.

And she and her party were lost. Supposed to be the Mighty Leader, Bernadette realized that she had no idea whether she had been up this particular ramp, over that stone bridge before. Were they travelling in circles? She was too tired to think, and a glance at Andrion told her that he was carrying on by main force of will. There were circles under his eyes, and his expression was haggard. Enough!

Chapter 21: Recharging

They came to a leukalfar yurt standing by itself on an icy promontory sometime after dusk. They had killed the local guardians, and Bernadette decided that they must take the risk that more would come in the night. Perhaps Nerissa, with her vampiric powers, could stay awake and stand guard? Whatever, she and Andrion *must* take a break or they might spend the rest of their (short) lives wandering here.

"We have to stop and get some rest," Bernadette told her companions. She got no arguments, though she could tell that Nerissa was suppressing impatience. It was only reasonable, Bernadette supposed, for her to bear the frailties of her mortal friends without understanding them. Nerissa had been as human as they were once, but that time was far in the past.

The hut offered a fire pit, and after a bit of work with her fire spell (inadequate in combat, but good enough for these purposes) Bernadette had a merry blaze going and they were able to sit down and take some of the chill off. There was also a raw leg of goat in a leather storage jar, nearly frozen, which she affixed to a spit. Time for something a little more substantial than bread and cheese!

The meat took a while to cook. Bernadette reduced the cooking time by slicing off some raw steaks with her dagger before spitting it, which she gave to Nerissa. The vampire woman thanked her, but set the steaks on a platter close to the fire to thaw a little and approach the temperature of living flesh before sinking her teeth into it.

Bernadette and Andrion removed their armor and put on their wooly underwear, the brief intervening nudity bearable this close to the fire and of no concern to Nerissa. Then they sat on a couple of bedrolls snuggled together for warmth, her fur cloak thrown over the two of them. Their closeness gave comfort, but both of them were so tired that there was no spark of sexual desire in their contact.

Bernadette found herself yawning, the warmth of the fire urging her to just drift off to sleep snuggled beneath Andrion's arm. But the smell of the cooking meat was doing a pretty good job of fighting that impulse, as her stomach rumbled fiercely. It seemed like days since they'd had a hot meal. Not that this was much of one – some sizzling-hot meat dripping savory juices, with more of the stale bread from their packs to sop them up. They washed it down with water.

Nerissa devoured her now-warmed and bloody but still raw goat leg steaks with more enthusiasm than they'd expected. Bernadette felt glad they'd been able to provide them to her, all things considered. When she and Andrion had eaten their fill of the cooked goat meat they sat back for a while, gazing into the fire with sleepy contentment. "Nerissa, are you able to keep watch while we sleep?" Bernadette asked. She couldn't just doze off without making sure they'd be safe.

"Certainly," her vampire friend replied. "We don't really need to sleep, though we... rest at times. I think I had enough rest at Daywatch, and again at that inn in Sylvanian, to last me for a week. Go ahead and get some sleep."

Thanking her with a sleepy smile, Bernadette turned to Andrion and cupped his face in her hands. "Good night, love" she murmured, kissing him. Making sure she had weapons near at hand, she lay down on the bedroll. Andrion curled up beside her, cupping her with his body, and pulled the cloak over them as a blanket. He pushed her hair aside and kissed the back of her neck, sending a little thrill through her despite her exhaustion.

"Good night," he said softly.

They slept like logs through the night, untroubled by enemy incursions. As the first light of dawn came through the opening of the yurt Bernadette's eyes fluttered open. The fire had mostly died down and it was beginning to get a little chilly in here. But Andrion was a warm, solid presence at her back, one arm thrown over her. She took his hand in hers and brought it to her lips to kiss. A powerful wave of love surged through her. Alas, though, their current set of problems had not vanished in the night.

Building up her resolve, Bernadette slipped from beneath the warm fur and decided to put her armor on over the top of her long underwear. It looked funny as hell, true; but it was warm and didn't involve stripping down to bare skin. Finding a bit more wood she built up the fire. Nerissa, seemingly untroubled by the cold, was keeping watch at the yurt's entrance. As she heard Bernadette stirring she turned and smiled. "Sleep well?" she asked. Bernadette smiled at her.

"Yes, thanks. All quiet out there?"

"Not a peep," the vampire woman replied.

They'd left quite a bit of the goat meat on the bones last night before sleeping, and Bernadette put it back on the fire to cook a little more. Then she gnawed some of the hot, succulent meat off the bone. Nudging Andrion with her foot, she said "Andrion! Sorry but it's time to get up." He flinched and groaned, but soon acknowledged the necessity and sat up. He looked her up and down in her peculiar outfit, blinking slightly at the daylight coming in through the doorway.

After apparently considering his remarks for a moment he said, "Well, *that's* a new look…" Bernadette smiled at him fetchingly and spun around.

"Do you like it? I do believe it will be all the rage in Coldstein this season…" He grinned at her.

"How can I argue with that?" he asked, and put his own armor on over the top of his wooly underwear.

"We're a matched set!" she crowed, stepping close for a kiss. "Would you like a little goat?" she offered, extending the greasy leg bone.

He took it from her and bit off a few chunks. Both of them now had grease all over their hands, and were licking their fingers. Nerissa watched the pair with a certain amount of amusement. Wiping her hands on a spare linen undershirt from her pack, Bernadette turned businesslike. "I guess we'd better get going," she said. Her companions agreed, and in a few minutes the three of them were outside the yurt and looking around.

Chapter 22: The Great Temple

Bernadette felt much, much better after a hot meal or two and a night's sleep. To complete her joy, the snow that had been falling since they arrived here had decided to hold off for a while and visibility was greatly improved in the early morning light. She took out the map and looked at it. It had duly provided markers for each of the shrines they had visited, and there was an arrow pointing the way to the next one; but the map was two dimensional and this system of canyons and caverns was not. Just because you knew in what direction something lay, did not mean you could get there.

Nothing for it but to continue along the string of leukalfar dwellings that ran up the canyon, interspersed with stone bridges and ramps made of mandimant chitin. They spotted more of the mandimant pupae, and then found themselves attacked by a pair of the flying mandimant adults! As it had for the nymphs they'd encountered months before, Andrion's firebolt spell proved highly effective. In order to fly, the adults had exoskeletons that were far thinner than they had been during their long lives as larvae. They were fragile and easy enough to kill.

Andrion and Bernadette lingered for a few minutes examining the singed corpses. On the chance that the stingers and their attached venom sacs might have some use in chemia, she extracted them carefully with tongs and put them into a sealed metal jar – one of the ones they'd made for their ingredient-hunting expedition months before.

The walkways sometimes ran along the canyon floor, at other times climbed to the heights. They found a frost troll penned near one summit, which had killed several of the leukalfar who had confined it. Leukalfar guards were infrequent, but had to be dealt with as they continued on their way.

They halted for another brief rest and a makeshift meal at around midday, judging from the position of the sun. Ahead, it looked as though the canyon they were traversing was coming to a dead end. Then Bernadette spotted a narrow opening, rimmed with icicles and dripping icy water, off to one side. A path led into it, so she stepped within. All her senses were on the alert, and she spotted some leukalfar guarding the place before they had gone very far inside.

Any guard she saw, who did not also see her, did not have long to live.

This didn't seem like the usual cavern. The ceilings were high and there was a lot of light, with water running somewhere down near the bottom. Snowy ledges occasionally connected by chitin bridges were their pathways, and there were yurts scattered here and there. They worked their way down toward the bottom, the three of them a match for any leukalfar attackers; and finally emerged into a narrow section of canyon. Proceeding down it to the end, they found a tunnel that climbed upward – with a shrine visible in the near distance when they emerged from it. Hooray!

This time, it was Brother Mendalis welcoming them to the Shrine of Eternal Light. He was far shorter than any of his brethren they had met so far, seeming not that different in stature and build from the leukalfar. But he had the same pale blue eyes, and they had a bit of a twinkle in them as he said, "The gates leading to the Great Temple are down that path, and not more than two miles from here. May Apoldros guide your steps and lend strength to you against your foes."

"Thank you, brother," Bernadette told him sincerely as she pocketed the final token. Its enamel was a pale blue. They set off along the trail feeling exultant to be approaching their goal at last, though there was a trace of anxiety as well. What would they encounter when they reached their goal? She supposed that they would likely find the temple buildings taken over by the leukalfar, raising their mandimants and building their chitin yurts within its mighty halls just as they had done in the dwellings of the dypalfar. Had Duraenis made reference to the dypalfar having been the changelings' "masters"? What had he meant?

Snow was falling once again as they rounded a bend and beheld a tall, castle-like stone structure on the far side of a bridge ahead of them. The bridge spanned a chasm that, when they got close enough to look down into it, seemed to be sheer-sided and hundreds of feet deep. It split the earth beyond the range of sight in either direction.

A pair of iron pillars flanked the entry to the bridge, rising an impossible forty feet high with a pair of barred gates the same height between them. The construction should have collapsed under its own weight ages ago, Bernadette thought. This must be evidence of the divine warding the Arch Protector had spoken of. On the left-hand post a small cylindrical container was mounted, and she pulled out the four tokens she'd received and placed them inside, closing the lid afterward.

There was a sort of humming sound in the air, the iron gates vibrating. Then, with the gentlest of clicks, they opened inward. Bernadette peeked inside the cylinder, and the tokens were gone. Magic! They walked across the bridge, through a series of pointed stone arches reminiscent of others they'd found here and there during their tour of the shrines. Ahead, their shape was echoed in the building's architecture.

After crossing the bridge the three climbed a broad flight of steps and entered a front courtyard, getting a look at the Great Temple close up. A heroic-sized statue stood in a central position. "That's a statue of Apoldros," Andrion remarked. "I believe this same statue was pictured in the *King of Heaven* book."

"Either that or the statue's based on the standard representation of the god," Bernadette replied. She wondered if any of the gods actually looked as they were pictured, or if these were just anthropomorphic interpretations of a divinity humans could not truly comprehend. Deep thoughts, for her.

This seemed to be the main entrance, two enormous doors of golden metal similar in construction though not in design to ones they'd seen in dypalfar ruins. An enormous sunburst glowed above them. So far at least, there'd been no exterior signs of a leukalfar occupation. "This is it," Bernadette told her "troops." "Get ready for a fight."

Bernadette gripped her bow in one hand and tried the door. It opened. The three of them stepped inside and stood dumbfounded – and shivering. Outside, blizzard conditions reigned. In this cavernous hall, it was much colder. While still thankful there were no mirrors around, Bernadette was very glad as well that she was wearing her wooly underwear. All around the room figures stood like statues, caught in action poses and encased in ice. They included various classes of leukalfar as well as mandimants. She knew these were no statues, though. "These leukalfar are… they're frozen in the ice,"

Nerissa said. Just so they don't suddenly thaw out, Bernadette thought.

Some of them held valuable items, and Bernadette was unable to resist relieving a few of them of these treasures they'd no longer be needing. She plucked an amulet from the frozen fingers of what looked to be a leukalfar mage. It remained motionless. "These have to be some of the forces that invaded the temple and slaughtered the monks," Nerissa said. "I wonder how long they've been like this."

After searching the main chamber, which Bernadette guessed must have been the central chapel when this place had been run by the Apoldrians, they began exploring other rooms leading off of it. They hadn't found the staff they sought, and had seen none of the usual signs of a place of worship, either.

In a chamber two halls over from the chapel, Bernadette spotted one leukalfar-sicle with a particularly valuable weapon, and took it off of him. Whereupon he thawed in a heartbeat and began attacking them. Oh, shit! To her astonishment he lunged right past her to attack Nerissa and Andrion, though. So she just put a couple of arrows into his back and he burst into glimmering pieces as if he'd been carved from ice. That wasn't so hard, Bernadette mused. Certainly not enough of a problem to keep her from gleaning any other valuables these once-and-possibly-future enemies might have on them.

In the next room a lone frozen leukalfar stood in a circle with half a dozen frozen mandimants, as if he were about to conduct them in a sing-along. Bernadette relieved him of a necklace worth nearly a thousand guilders. At which not only he, but his enormous arthropod companions as well, all came to life at once! She hadn't expected that, and soon found herself backed up against a pillar while three of the angry mandimants attacked her in concert. She hurled them back with Gale, then put arrows into them before they could get close again. But by the time all their enemies lay in re-frozen chunks on the stone floor she was gasping for breath and in pain. A few moments of her healing spell put it right again.

Moving on from that room, the trio came to an opening that led into another ice cave. This one, more like a tunnel, soon took them through to an opening. Beyond it they could see another part of the building, hung with icicles more than the height of a man. Jumping down from a ledge, Bernadette found herself in a narrow corridor. It was blocked to her right, so she followed it down to the left. Andrion and Nerissa were right behind her.

At the far end of the corridor they entered another cavernous chamber, this one still stranger than any they had previously seen. Enormous knives of ice (or stone?) jutted up at angles from the floor like spears placed to halt a cavalry charge – if the horses were 20 feet tall. The room was thronged with more of the frozen leukalfar and mandimants, and snow seemed to have drifted through an opening in the roof to turn the floor at the far end of the room into a slope.

Leerily, Bernadette led her companions further into the room. They found a staircase rising, blocked at the top by more of those spikes. And beyond those, a pale white elf sat rigidly on a carven stone throne, seemingly staring at them. They'd found human skeletons aplenty as they searched the temple complex for the staff. But this monk, while unmoving, was fully fleshed. Was he frozen, like the mysteriously undead-seeming invaders?

Then he spoke. "Did you really come here expecting to claim the Staff of Apoldros?" he asked, in a voice that was grating and dripping with scorn.

"Who are you?" Bernadette gasped in shock.

"Archon Signis, at your service," the robed figure said, rising. His tone was not a friendly one.

"Your brother Duraenis believes you dead!" she said. "He's been mourning you for the past thousand years. Why didn't you contact him to tell him you were all right?"

"Ah yes, dear Duraenis," Signis said sarcastically. "So noble, so dedicated. For a thousand years he has watched and waited alone… and for what?" This guy was really giving Bernadette the creeps, but she couldn't just stand there and say nothing.

"He's been waiting for someone like me to come along and cleanse the Great Temple, so that Apoldros' Eparchy can become a center or learning and devotion again, I think," she said quietly but loud enough to be heard by the monk thirty feet away. He had not sat down again, but he was not stepping out from behind his barrier either.

"And what the hell have *you* been doing all that time?" Bernadette asked angrily. "Sitting around on your frozen throne with nobody to talk to but a bunch of frozen changelings and their pets? I don't see how your life has been any more productive."

"Ah, but you're wrong," Signis replied. "I've been waiting all this time for my prophecy to bear fruit, to bring me a Netherblood that will let me fulfill it."

"You?!" Nerissa snarled. "*You're* the one who created that 'prophecy' and put it out into the world?"

"Exactly, my dear," the elf replied. "I can sense your true nature. I had hope that one whose blood and soul were needed for the blinding of the sun would come seeking the staff, drawn or driven by the prophecy I had sent out into the world. I had hoped that it would not take so much time, but then what is time for one such as me?" Considering there were five other white elves in the world who were all presumably thousands of years old, Bernadette supposed he had a point. Or did he mean something else?

Signis drew forth a vial from his robe, four inches long and purple in color – a vial intended to capture the magical essence from a human soul! The ordinary white glass vials were incapable of holding such. A brilliant beam of white light flew from the hand that held the vial, emerging as a purple ray that flew across the room and struck Nerissa in the forehead.

"He's cast a binding on you, Nerissa!" Andrion warned. If she died anytime in the next five minutes, her mana and her soul would be captured by that vial, where it could be used in enchanting – presumably, to enchant the Staff of Apoldros. But where *was* that staff?

Aware of her danger, Nerissa hurled a bolt of lightning at the white elf monk. It splashed harmlessly off of an invisible barrier that surrounded him, where he stood before the throne. Bernadette tried an arrow from her bow, but to no more effect. "And now," Signis said with satisfaction, "It is time for you all to die!"

With a wave of his hand he commanded a group of the frozen leukalfar to spring into life and begin attacking them. Bernadette immediately darted up the snowbank near the back of the room, hidden in the shadows. From there she was able to pick off her targets with her bow as they engaged with her companions. In short order their revived foes were nothing but a collection of scattered ice chunks.

Signis was apparently not dismayed by their fast work in dispatching his minions. "An impressive display," he grated, "but a wasted effort. You delay nothing but your own deaths!" He gestured again, and another half dozen of the gelid guardians came alive. Bernadette and her companions redoubled their efforts. Andrion conjured a fire demon, whose fireballs were particularly effective against their icy foes. The number of them remaining was dwindling.

A tinge of desperation creeping into his voice, Signis said "This has gone on long enough." He hurled the last of his frozen forces against them – and one by one the creatures were shot, flamed, crushed, and scattered. Didn't know who you were up against, eh Signis? Bernadette thought with cold satisfaction. Now they just needed to figure out how to get at *him*.

"No!" he cried angrily. "I won't let you ruin centuries of preparations... Death first!" Signis cast some unknown spell, and Bernadette realized that the roof of the chamber, all too close above her head, was now rumbling and falling down around her ears. Shortly thereafter, she realized nothing at all. When she regained consciousness she found Andrion bending over her, feeling her brow.

"I'm all right," she murmured, struggling to sit up.

Nerissa was standing close by, and above her Bernadette could see that the room they'd been in was now open to the sky. How had they all managed to survive that? Signis had evidently fled his throne, and Nerissa was urging her to rejoin the battle. Shaking her head to clear it and gulping down a health potion, Bernadette tried to focus on her words. "He's up there, on the balcony," Nerissa was saying. "Come on!"

Nerissa was already on the move, and Bernadette followed her. They crossed a rubble-strewn courtyard and she noticed there was an un-manned shrine in the middle of it, flanked by two staircases leading up to a curving stone balcony. Bernadette climbed the staircase on the left to join Nerissa where she was confronting the deranged archon.

"Enough, Signis!" Nerissa demanded. "Give us the staff!" The man stood crouched slightly, evidently injured; but still convinced of his superiority.

"How dare you," he ranted. "I was the Archon of Apoldros, girl. I had the ears of a god!"

"So what happened to you?" Nerissa asked. "Why have you done this?" Signis regarded this pronouncement with scorn.

"Duraenis and his fellow Protectors all thought the changelings attacked on their own," he said. "Did they never wonder how they passed the gates? Who let them in, who directed their every move? Look into my eyes, Nerissa. You tell me what I am."

Nerissa took a step backward, astonishment on her face. "You're a vampire! But... Apoldros should have protected you, should have cured you..."

The snow elf spoke bitterly: "I was infected by one of my own initiates, and my god turned his back on me. I took my revenge on His holy order, those of them I could reach. And I set my net, put my plan in place, to destroy the rest of His creation." Bernadette was staggered. This twisted soul had been pleased that he'd drawn a Netherblood vampire here so he could desecrate the staff and put out the sun himself. But his plan would have worked just as well if Lord Karazin had gotten his hands on it, instead.

The Archon, now standing upright, gave an evil smile and said triumphantly, "Soon I will have your blood and soul, Netherblood, and the prophecy will be fulfilled!" Rage blazed in Nerissa's orange-glowing eyes, and she closed with Signis to lift him off the ground. Whoa, Bernadette thought. The slender woman, no larger than she was, had picked up the burly-looking white elf by the upper part of his robe as if he were a small child.

"My soul is my own," she said, controlled fury in her voice, "And I'll be keeping my blood as well!" Lifting him higher she went on, "Let's see if *your* blood has any power to it!" With that she hurled Signis back against the stone balustrade, and shot a magical firebolt at him.

Bernadette drew her bow and Andrion began shooting lightning bolts after calling his fire demon. Things got chaotic as Signis summoned a gigantic frost demon, and Bernadette was very busy for a few moments sending it back where it came from. By the time her attention was free, Nerissa was struggling with the Archon further along the balcony, and she had to move to the left to get a clear shot. As Andrion hurled ice spikes into him, she got in one good shot and the white elf fell to the stones, dead. Better late than never, Bernadette thought a bit ruefully. She made sure that Andrion and Nerissa were all right.

The three of them went down the stairs for a closer look at that shrine. As Bernadette had hoped, the Staff of Apoldros (exactly as pictured in the book) floated in midair above a pillar similar to the ones in the other shrines. She hesitantly reached out a hand and seized it, feeling a slight tingle but no ill effects. It came away, and she held it out to her companions.

"It's so beautiful!" Nerissa said in hushed tones. It was that. The snow had stopped falling but the skies were still leaden and the gem surmounting the staff looked dull, somehow. Had the ages dimmed its power? The book had said it would deliver the force of Apoldros' light when used in the same way that ordinary magic staffs were used: point and will. But hadn't Duraenis said something about needing to perform a ritual over it, first?

It seemed to be getting darker. Probably, sunset was coming on. Bernadette was cold and hungry and tired, and she felt sure Andrion was as well – though Nerissa looked about the same as usual. "Mission accomplished, sort of," she announced. "But I think we should see about finding a place to eat and sleep for tonight. In the morning, I have an idea about how we can clear the rest of the frozen invaders out of here. We did promise Duraenis we would 'cleanse' this place.

Chapter 23: The Next Step

This had been a monastery, after all, a place where the monks lived and worked as well as worshiped. They soon found a wing with small dormitory rooms, four beds to the room and with a fireplace in each. The frozen antagonists seemed only to have been gathered in a few of the main central areas, with the rest of the sprawling complex empty.

After breaking up one of the beds with the wood axe he carried in his pack, Andrion laid a fire and set it ablaze with his powerful fire spell. Bernadette grinned at him, admiring his skill. They were able to heat some water for tea, washing down pemmican. Nerissa contented herself with drinking some of the tea, and taking another of her potions. By the time they lay down to sleep, the chill was off the room nicely.

In the morning, the bold adventurers set forth to comb the entire temple complex for enemies – frozen or otherwise. Along the way they came away with quite a few bits of small loot, lifted from the leukalfar who had invaded the place a millennium before.

Bernadette used her Holocaust dragon spell to obliterate the frozen invaders. It was probably twice as hot as any ordinary fire spell, and at close range it mowed them down and melted them into sludge. The few that managed to animate before being destroyed were swiftly taken down by Andrion and Nerissa.

Rather than undertake the two-mile walk back to the Shrine of Eternal Light, they fast-traveled to it using Bernadette's map. "Good morning Brother Mendalis," she said cheerfully.

"You're alive!" he said with a certain amount of surprise. "What found you, at the Great Temple?"

"Archon Signis was not killed as you had thought," Bernadette explained. "He had been turned into a vampire, and I think he lost his mind. He was the one who commanded the changelings to attack the temple, and who let them in through the gates."

"I think the hunger may have affected his mind," Nerissa said thoughtfully. "Unless he was reviving his frozen troops to drink of their blood from time to time, he must have run out of potions a long time ago."

"Anyhow," Bernadette went on. "Signis is now dead, and all of the remaining attackers who were inside the temple have been eliminated. The place will need some repairs and some sweeping up, but it should be ready for your order to set up shop again. I assume you five wouldn't have kept manning your shrines for all these centuries unless you had hoped to someday re-open for business?"

"Indeed, you speak true," Mendalis said. "Let me communicate with Arch Protector Duraenis and learn what he would have us do." The white elf entered the shrine and knelt before the pillar with its glowing sunburst for several minutes, as the rest of them huddled in their cloaks wishing they could get in out of the snow. Clearly, winter was *not* the time to visit the scenic Eparchy.

Finally Mendalis rose to his feet again and came back outside. He was beaming, the huge smile seeming out of place on his elvish face. "Arch Protector Duraenis intends to close the portal and come through to us here at this shrine, where he will take over as Archon and begin the work of setting the Great Temple to rights!" He said excitedly. "This has not happened in eons!"

There was a shimmer behind the Protector, and suddenly the figure of Arch Protector Duraenis appeared inside the shrine. "I didn't know you could use the shrines like that," Bernadette said. It would have saved them a hell of a hike!

"Only one of the Protectors can do so," Duraenis said as he strode out before them. "And none has done so in a very long time. I myself had not left my post since before the attack of the changelings."

"Who will guard the portal, then?" Bernadette asked. The monk turned to his colleague.

"Mendalis, you are hereby appointed acting Arch Protector. Go through to Nightvoid Cavern and take up your post." The smaller monk embraced his brother, then went to do his bidding. In moments he had disappeared.

"Mendalis told you of Signis?" Bernadette asked, and the new Archon nodded sadly.

"If only he had shared his plight with us, instead of striking out!" he said miserably. "We surely could have brought about a way for him to be cured, perhaps if all of us had beseeched Apoldros together." He shook his head and sighed. "Signis was ever proud, willful, and quick to anger. And he has brought ruin to the Eparchy. But now it may rise again."

He stood considering for a moment, then added, "Deep inside, it brings me joy that the changelings weren't to blame for what happened here."

"Why is that?" Bernadette asked.

"Because," Duraenis explained, "that means there's still hope that they might one day shed their hatred and come to worship Apoldros once again. It's been a long time since I felt such hope, and it's been long overdue. My thanks, to all of you."

"You said that you could perform a ritual that would enable us to turn the Staff of Apoldros into a weapon against the vampire lord who meant to desecrate it as part of the plan hatched by your brother?" Bernadette reminded him.

"Oh yes, certainly," he said. She handed the staff to him and he turned to the shrine, holding the staff out gem first as if he were planning to thrust it at someone standing on the far side of the pillar. Again, he intoned something they could not hear and the sunburst floating above the pillar burst into radiance as bright as the real sun – which, they had reason to believe, was floating somewhere up above this place's persistent overcast.

The Archon handed the staff back to Bernadette. "Use it as you would an ordinary staff, and it will bring forth Apoldros' holy light to destroy your enemies," he said. "You can bring it back here if you need to recharge it, for ordinary magical essences will not work. And it still could be desecrated, so don't let it fall into the wrong hands."

"Thank you, Archon," she said humbly. From a near-penniless immigrant a few months ago she had come a long, long, way.

"You're welcome," he told her. "I don't know when we may speak again. If you have any questions before you leave, I suggest you ask them." Oh, Bernadette thought. In that case, did anyone pack a lunch? We'll be here until Terris' rotation grinds to a halt, if not later. Especially if I encourage Andrion to participate.

Aloud, she asked "Who were your people, the white elves?"

"We were once a wealthy and prosperous society, living throughout Darkreach and parts of Iscandia," he replied. "Yet we were less numerous than our kin, the other descendants of the eldalfar. And unfortunately, we were constantly at war with the Norsemen who claimed this land as their ancestral home. They outnumbered us greatly, and when it seemed we were faced with extinction we turned to our cousins, the deep-dwelling dypalfar, for help."

"Surprisingly," he went on, "they agreed to help, sheltering us from attack in their underground cities patrolled by the automatons they built with their arts. But in return for this privilege, we must pay a terrible price... the blinding of our race." Bernadette was stunned, scarcely believing what she'd heard. Why on Terris would the dypalfar demand such a thing of "allies" – and considering that the leukalfar if eyeless were anything but blind, what was the point?

"You and your fellow Protectors remained unchanged," she pointed out. "Surely some others of your race survived as well?"

"The Apoldrians were a celibate, all-male order," Duraenis explained. "Here in our hidden holy precinct, our Eparchy, we were safe from the Norsemen and from the dwelves as well. Others, those in our communities, either took the dypalfar's bargain or were exterminated by the Norsemen."

"And those who took the bargain?" Bernadette asked. "How did they become as they are?"

"I've often asked myself the very same question," the Archon replied. "The blinding of my race was supposedly accomplished with a toxin. Apparently its effects mutated them somehow, turned them into the sad and twisted beings they've become." So, he was as ignorant of the details of leukalfar existence as anyone Bernadette had yet met.

It seemed likely that Andrion was right, when he'd told her all those months ago that *she* might end up becoming the world authority on the subject of the leukalfar and their lifestyle. Clearly they were sentient beings, but so savage – their culture completely unknown to the rest of the world. Until someone from outside their race could learn to speak with them and be admitted to their circles, she doubted any more would be learned. And that was not a task she hankered for, just at the moment.

173

The conference with Duraenis was over, it seemed. Bernadette knew Andrion would have liked to stay there indefinitely pumping him for any scraps of information he could furnish – she half would, herself. But they had achieved what they had come here for, and it was time for them to go. They were not finished with Lord Karazin, indeed the fight against him had barely begun; yet there was a personal matter that had been nagging at her for days, one she must take care of before it drove her insane.

"I think you know what we have to do now," Bernadette said to Nerissa.

She looked a little unhappy, but replied, "We have to face my father, have to stop him once and for all. If we don't, he'll keep trying to get the staff, and my blood, until he succeeds in carrying out Signis' plan."

"He'll have to die," Bernadette pointed out. The vampire woman nodded, a little sadly.

"I've been thinking about this for a long time," she said. "It's not easy. But I don't think we have much of a choice. This has to end now."

"I hope Malden's finally ready for some action," Bernadette replied. "We're going to need all the help we can get."

Nerissa argued, "Fighting vampires is supposedly his whole purpose in life. Surely he'll jump at the chance to go after the most prominent vampire lord in Iscandia, once he learns we have a god-given weapon on our side."

"You're right," Bernadette told her. "But first we need to take a little break and pick up some more help. We're going home."

Chapter 24: Taking a Break

Bernadette pulled out her magic map. In moments the three of them were standing outside the Bathing Maiden. Fortunately for Nerissa, the sky was overcast and a light rain was falling. "You own this?" Nerissa asked.

"All mine," Bernadette replied with a pleased smile as they made their way inside. "It's sort of a perk for being The Fireblood."

"You really have to give me all the details of that story," Nerissa said.

"It's a long one," Bernadette told her, "which I'll tell you soon. But first, are you up for a hot bath?" She gestured toward the central pool.

Nerissa's orange-glowing eyes widened. "That's full of hot water?" she asked, disbelieving.

"Indeed it is," her friend assured her. "And I plan to be sitting in it sometime in the next three minutes."

"Sounds like a fine idea," Nerissa agreed. "Is there someplace I can put my things?" Bernadette led her up the stairs and told her to take any bed, as she and Andrion continued to the master bedroom. It had been unused in their absence, and seemed a little… forlorn.

Being back here in her beloved Maiden filled Bernadette with a whirl of feelings. She was delighted to be home, and she was really looking forward to that hot water. And to seeing Erik, whom she'd been missing more and more as the days went on. She felt that Andrion was the first and foremost love of her life; but the idea of parting with Erik forever filled her with deep sadness. How could she possibly give him up? She had a plan, a half-assed plan, but she didn't see how it could possibly work. Oh, maybe I'll get killed while I'm trying to defeat Lord Karazin, she thought whimsically, and then I won't have to deal with it. She put it out of her mind for the moment.

Bernadette and Andrion dumped their belongings and armor and put on robes, carrying another one with them as they walked back down the gallery toward the stairs. Bernadette handed the robe to Nerissa, who was somewhat shyly peeling out of her tight leather armor. "Don't worry," Bernadette told her, "nudity is pretty common here and nobody pays much attention to it."

175

"If you say so," the vampire woman replied with a tense smile. I have to remember how little she's had in the way of normal social contact, Bernadette thought as they went back downstairs and slipped into the hot pool.

Aahhh! That was *so* wonderful! What could possibly be better than sitting in hot water up to your chin after days in armor, fighting frozen creatures? Nerissa, as she was getting over her embarrassment about stripping down in front of everyone, seemed to be enjoying it too. Seemingly there was no conflict between vampirism and hot baths.

"So you were telling me about what you had to do as The Fireblood?" Nerissa asked conversationally, as she and Bernadette sat side by side enjoying their hot soak.

"Ah, yes…" Bernadette launched into the Condensed Version of her tale, starting with her arrival in Iscandia from Auverne and the fight with Tarragin at Plainview; her discovery of her fireblood status and dealings with the Old Ones; and how she, Andrion, and Erik had eventually traveled through a portal to Asengard and defeated Tarragin once and for all with help from three heroes of legend.

Nerissa just sat there soaking in the hot water, and soaking up Bernadette's tale – her mouth half-open in amazement. Even an immortal vampire of indeterminate age could be impressed. When Bernadette wound down she said, "Absolutely amazing. I had no idea the world was even in peril. Thanks for saving it." She wasn't entirely joking.

Bernadette smiled at her. Just then, glancing up, she saw the front doors open and Erik come through them, dressed in casual clothing. Her face lit up like a beacon and she jumped to her feet, her full breasts bouncing and sending water drops flying in all directions. "Erik!" Erik had just finished walking back to the Maiden after a trip to Waterdon, and Berni was the last person he expected to see. He stood there just inside the door, gaping at her as a delighted grin came over his handsome face, momentarily speechless. He was already getting stiff.

Erik wasn't the only one astonished. Traveling with the pair, Nerissa had realized that Bernadette and Andrion were more than just battle companions. She had assumed they were married, or at least lovers. But the look on Bernadette's face as this unfamiliar blond giant walked in had her rethinking her assumptions. Recovering his composure Erik walked around to the rear side of the pool and Bernadette, still standing, reached up to give him a hug and a warm kiss.

"Berni, you're here…" he seemed stunned.

"We stopped by for a bath!" she replied gaily. "Care to join us?" Erik's face colored. He and Berni shared this problem, their fair complexions like a red-glowing beacon whenever some strong emotion passed through. Being this close to Berni, and her all naked and pink and glad to see him… An area of his anatomy a bit south of his belt was *very* glad to see her as well, and there was no way he was stripping naked and getting into the pool with all these people around. Someday, he thought dreamily, he'd like to get her in the pool at two in the morning when nobody else was around… That thought didn't help the situation any.

"Um, I just had a bath earlier," he said. "Why don't you get out and join me for some supper?" He looked at Andrion and the woman he presumed was their companion, including them in the invitation. Now *she* was something else. Lithe and beautiful in a dark sort of way, she seemed young and old at the same time. But her orange-glowing eyes gave him pause. She must be all right if his friends were hanging out with her, but she still made him a little uneasy.

The three had soon climbed out of the pool and toweled off before slipping on their robes, refreshed by the hot soak. Bernadette headed straight for Erik, throwing her arms around him in a full-body hug and kissing him passionately, glowing with wellbeing and elation. Nerissa stole a glance at Andrion to see if she could figure out what was going on here. He was looking at his (Girlfriend? Friend with benefits?) with a touch of resignation showing in his eyes, but a slight smile on his lips.

Nerissa gave an internal shrug. Whatever was going on with her new friends, it was apparently complicated and she'd just have to wait for Bernadette to explain, should she choose to do so. Meanwhile, she glanced around the Maiden a little. There were certainly a lot of good-looking men around here. None of them vampires, of course. Her people definitely tended to keep to themselves. One of the parts of life she had missed while she was in hiding was sex, and since she'd been out in the world again there had been little enough time to think or do anything about it. But the hunger, the mental hunger at least, was growing.

The problem was, sexual desire and blood hunger were linked in her kind. A vampire would not be likely to achieve orgasm unless they were feeding on blood while engaging in sex; and the potions she'd been drinking daily for many years suppressed both urges. Many vampires she knew would simply enthrall a mortal, have their way with them sexually, and over a period of weeks drain them until they were too weak to live. If they liked them enough, they might convert them to vampires. If not, the thralls died.

Such was not for her. Nerissa had a moral outlook, gotten from her mother, that made such behavior repugnant. She had enjoyed sex with other vampires in the past and once or twice found a mortal lover who was willing. But such relationships were eventually doomed, unless the mortal wanted to become a vampire. A few liaisons, then she would have to break it off before the blood loss became too serious. She sighed. Better just keep taking potions, she supposed.

Meanwhile the party had seated themselves at a table overlooking the common room, and Bernadette had motioned Lev over. "Welcome back, Fireblood," he said respectfully.

"Knock it off, Lev," she replied with mock annoyance. "It's *Bernadette*, thank you very much, and could you just bring us three servings of whatever's on the stove. And some of whatever red meat you have that's raw? Oh yes, and some mead, and a bottle of red wine?" Lev was grinning at her, ticking her order off in his head. He had a prodigious memory, and made one hell of an innkeeper. At the mention of raw meat he eyed Nerissa surreptitiously, but said nothing.

As Lev scurried off to fulfill Bernadette's request she turned to Erik and said "Erik, I'd like you to meet our new friend Nerissa. We met her after we got involved with the Daywatch Brigade. Nerissa, Erik is the man I told you about, who helped me and Andrion defeat the Soul-Devourer. Erik, Nerissa is a vampire. But she's on our side." She waited for some reaction, but Erik gave only the slightest start, a hint of puzzlement in his gaze. Good old unflappable Erik.

Bernadette went on to explain how Nerissa was helping them in their fight to stop her own father's plan to extinguish the sun, and as their food arrived and they all started eating both she and Andrion related the tale of their adventures to date. Nerissa seemed a little reticent, as she sat there delicately eating some raw leg of goat with knife and fork, sipping red wine; but she added something now and again as she had deeper knowledge to contribute.

After they'd covered everything there was to tell of their doings since they'd left the Maiden a couple of weeks ago, Erik had his own story to relate. He'd been walking into Waterdon most days, finding the road mostly pretty quiet and safe. He brought supplies to Lifa and Bjorn, played games with Anja and kept an eye on her while one or both of the body servants went on errands around town. He'd been enjoying himself, actually, and with a sly smile he told Berni, "I think you're going to be pleased with the way things are working out at Brightsgate Cottage."

Bernadette's eyes widened. "Do you mean...?"

"You'll just have to see for yourself," he teased her. "You *are* planning to visit before you go off hunting vampires?"

"Oh yes, absolutely," she replied. It was getting a little late for a visit now, but maybe they could go there first thing in the morning on their way back to Daywatch. She squeezed Erik's enormous hand where it rested at his side, and then ran her finger up the palm. He flinched slightly and looked her in the eyes. The naked desire there took him by surprise.

Lev had turned the bar over to Drelos, removing his apron (which both Bernadette and Nerissa thought made him a lot more attractive), and picked up his lute. He began regaling the Maiden visitors with a few Iscandia standards. He wasn't exactly a top-quality bard, but he'd do until one came along. As they sat there finishing their meal and enjoying the music, a handsome, slightly familiar-looking sylvalfar man came by the table. "Do you mind if I join you for a moment?"

"Do I know you?" Bernadette asked him. She thought it a little odd that one of the Maiden guests would intrude at the owner's table. Months in Iscandia had begun to erode her natural trusting nature.

"Maervon, at your service," he said with a slight bow. He was tall and graceful, his tilted almond eyes a deep amber brown, brown hair streaked with blond. Almost an elven version of Andrion. "We have met briefly in the past. I usually visit here a few times a year, in the course of my business. I'm a timber buyer for Imperial Trading."

Throughout this exchange, though Maervon was supposedly talking to Bernadette, he was looking at Nerissa. Aha, Bernadette thought. Our Vampire Mistress has captured herself a new thrall. Well, not really. At least, Nerissa had said she didn't do that. And had seemed pretty offended that she'd mentioned it, too! But Bernadette's inborn desire to see everybody she cared about happily hooked up with a love partner was bubbling up within her. The elf must know what he was getting into. Nerissa's looks were unmistakable to anybody with eyes to see. Was she likewise interested?

Nerissa sensed the elf's interest, and she was intrigued by it. He'd spotted her across the room, and been drawn to her like a moth to the flame. Was he ready for all that entailed? As Bernadette motioned Maervon to pull up a chair and he sat close beside her, Nerissa turned to him and fixed his warm brown eyes with her glowing orange ones. No point in beating around the bush. "I'm a vampire," she told him quietly, showing her fangs.

"I know, I know!" he replied eagerly. Then seeming a little ashamed of himself he added, "I can't help it. I am drawn to your kind, for whatever reason. And you, my lady, are the most beautiful vampire I have ever seen."

"You have been with other vampire women?" Nerissa's sharp question was to the point. She had to know that he understood what he'd be getting into. This would likely be the briefest of liaisons, but her hunger for it was already growing. She refused to use her vampiric power of enthrallment, however. The human "kind" – Norsemen, Remans, Galise, Afrans, and the various sorts of elves, harbored all sorts of sexual kinks. Being the object of some man's "perversion" made her feel a little odd. She'd prefer to have sex within the context of a relationship, but with mortals that could not be. Oh hell. She was hungry, she was horny, why not?

"You want to be my bed-warmer?" she asked him. He nodded eagerly. "And my dessert?" she said, showing those fangs again.

"Oh yes," he murmured so softly the others at the table were unlikely to hear.

"Thank you for supper," Nerissa said, standing up and nodding to Bernadette. "Nice to meet you, Erik. I think Maervon and I are going to go… talk about something. See you in the morning." With that, she left the table. Her eager elf was right behind her.

After the pair had walked away out of hearing Bernadette said "I'd wondered about that. She's so beautiful, and she just spent the last twenty years hiding from everybody she knows. Then since we met up with her she decided to throw her lot in with the people who are trying to exterminate her kind. And we've been running around ever since." Andrion had something to contribute, an odd bit of lore he'd picked up during his years in Iscandia.

"Supposedly," he said, "vampires having sex need to feed on blood while they're doing it."

Bernadette looked at him in alarm. "Does that mean Nerissa's going to kill that elf?" He put a hand on her arm in reassurance.

"No, I think it'll be all right. She definitely doesn't seem to be as far gone in evil as her father and his minions, and it's quite possible for a vampire to feed on a mortal without killing them. She just needs to use a little restraint."

"Oh," Bernadette replied, relieved. "I'm sure it'll be fine then." After a moment's thought she added, "I guess it's not likely to end up a big romance, though, huh?"

"More like a quick hookup," Andrion informed her. "When vampires get involved with mortals long term, the mortals either die or have to become vampires themselves." Bernadette sighed. She had continued to hold Erik's hand, and now the moment had arrived. Taking Andrion's hand in her other one, she looked into his eyes.

"I need to talk about some things with Erik, so we're going to go downstairs for a while. I'll see you later."

We *are*, thought Erik? This was news to him, and he wasn't sure if it was good or bad. Andrion, hoping that what Berni was planning involved telling Erik that she was going to be with Andrion exclusively now, wasn't too concerned. He gave her a kiss. "See you in a while, love," he said. She kissed him back, and squeezed his hand before she and Erik arose and made their way over to the bar, and the trap door behind it leading to the basement.

Chapter 25: The Choice

After Bernadette and Erik had descended the ladder, she jumped into his arms, throwing her arms around his neck and her legs around his hips and planting a big kiss on his lips. So far, so good, he thought, pulling her tightly to him and kissing her deeply in response. This went on for a while, and his poor cock (which had finally subsided about the time the food arrived) came right back up, ever hopeful.

Finally breaking the kiss, Bernadette leaned in. She couldn't stand it any longer, and it was time to lay it on the line. Resting her forehead against Erik's she said, breathlessly, "Erik! I want to marry you!" Erik was poleaxed. Berni wants to *what??!* In a million years he had never thought he would hear her say these words. Andrion was the older and wiser one, the stable one, the guy who wanted to settle down. She had in effect dumped *him* to go questing with Andrion for an indeterminate length of time, and he'd been convinced that his worst fears had been realized and she was never coming back, never going to share his bed again.

As casual as Erik's attitude toward sex and love had been throughout his young life, that thought was like a wound that was too deep to heal. He had been nursing that pain the entire time she was gone. And now, she said she wanted to *marry* him? He caught his breath, holding her even closer, and said, "Berni? ... What about Andrion?"

"Oh," she said, sending him even deeper into confusion, "I want to marry *him*, too."

Erik stepped over to the bed and deposited his erstwhile lover on its surface, then knelt at the side of it so he could look into her eyes. Bernadette looked back at his, the hurt and confusion showing in their sky-blue depths, and felt a stab of pain. She was doing it wrong again! Taking a breath, she began trying to explain. "Erik, I love you. And I love Andrion. I can't bear to part with either of you. I have *tried*, really tried, to act like a normal woman and just choose one or the other. And I can't. I'm willing to give up all other men, but I can't give up *you*. And I can't give up *him*, either. Can you understand?"

Erik gazed into her eyes, the plangent appeal there along with the love and desire he had seen so many times before, and his heart melted. "Oh Berni, you drive me crazy. I love you, and I'm willing to marry you. Even if you're also married to Andrion. *I* love him too. But how are you planning to pull this off?"

An expression of joy transformed her face, as she beamed at him and brought him in for a tender kiss. "When we were in Sylvanian trying to find out the location of the Eparchy, we asked the priest there, Engbard, to pray to Aderos for guidance as to how we could go there. And I asked him to also find out from the god, while he was at it, if I could marry two men at the same time. I kind of explained what my problem was. He didn't give me any details, but he said the answer was yes."

Erik took this in with a certain amount of skepticism. He had never heard of such a thing. But even if it were possible, how was she going to convince Andrion to go along with the arrangement? His friend was a lot older, and a lot more conservative. Would Berni's plan be like a punch in the gut to him? He kept his reservations to himself, however. What mattered, above all, was that Berni loved *him* enough to want him as a permanent part of her life! Before he met her, he would never have imagined that such a thing could mean so much to him. Women with marriage on their minds were a hazard to be avoided, not a goal to be sought. But she had stolen his heart, and now he didn't want to live without her.

Pushing his advantage, he took her in his arms and kissed her passionately as his fingers trailed down to unfasten the robe's tied belt and reach within to squeeze a breast. Between him and Berni there was some kind of magical sexual connection, which seemed to blaze from a spark to a raging forest fire in an instant; and as he gently tweaked her nipple he felt the thrill that ran through her as if it had passed through his own body. His cock throbbed, aching to be inside her.

"Oh, Erik…" she breathed, reaching for him. In moments he had pulled off his clothes and stood naked and rampant before her. Her robe discarded, Bernadette gazed up at him. His magnificent physique, his angelic face, and that huge, stiff cock were so compelling she got short of breath just looking at him. She felt so relieved to have confessed her desires to him, and to have had them accepted. There was still that little matter of discussing the situation with Andrion… and defeating the evil vampires, of course. But she felt sure that all would work out for the best. Was it youthful innocence, or the power of The Fireblood that made her feel that way?

She grabbed him by the hips and pulled him closer, his gigantic member thrust almost into her face. Taking it in both hands, she began squeezing and stroking it as she licked and sucked the head and ran her tongue up and down the shaft. Erik moaned slightly, resting his hands on her silken hair as she did her best to pleasure him this way. Since reaching adulthood he had not yet met a woman who could take him completely inside her mouth, but Berni didn't do a bad job of trying.

When the sensations were beginning to carry him away Erik pulled back, crouching to put his tongue in her mouth. Then he stooped lower, kneeling now, and took first one breast, then another in his hands as he suckled them and brought the nipples to erection. Pushing Berni gently back to lie flat on the bed, he began tonguing her slit, sucking at her clit within its swollen hood and running his tongue deep inside her.

It didn't take much of that before Bernadette was panting, thrusting her pelvis upward to meet Erik's mouth as he brought her rushing toward climax. She pressed his head down as she spasmed, throwing her head back to cry out as the wave of ecstasy spilled over her. Then, panting, she reached to pull at his massive shoulders, dragging him up until his face was on a level with hers and his quivering, rock-hard cock was slipping inside her.

The feelings as Berni's hot, slippery cunt engulfed him were so intense that for a moment Erik just gasped for air. Then, locking his mouth on hers, he began pumping in and out, driving all the way into her with each stroke. She broke from the kiss so she could breathe through her mouth, panting and moaning as the friction of his driving cock began taking her over the edge again. Erik had not been celibate during her absence, expecting that he might never hold her in his arms again; but now here she was – and the excitement of that, the utter delight of it, was filling his mind with white light. There was no holding back.

The two of them thundered to climax, then collapsed as if they had been flattened by an oxcart. Bernadette rolled Erik over so she was lying above him, his cock still clasped within her as the spasms of her orgasm gripped him and the last drops of his seed were squeezed out. As he softened and began to slip out, she continued to lie atop him, his massive chest like a mattress on which she might take a little nap. She kissed his chest, tongued his nipples, stroked his arms as her head was tucked below his chin.

When their breathing had returned to normal she wriggled up his body a little and looked into his eyes. His expression of blissful contentment filled her with happiness. She planted a few sweet kisses on his face, then rolled over so that she was tucked beneath his arm, her head resting on his shoulder. They continued like this for some time, not speaking. Finally Bernadette heaved a soft sigh and said quietly, "Erik, I think I'm going to spend the night upstairs." He bent to kiss the top of her head, his question unspoken.

"I still have to sell my plan to Andrion. I'm not sure how he's going to like the idea." After another minute she added, "He loves *you* too, I know he does. But his attitudes are a little… conventional. So I need to work on him some more. Okay?" Sitting up slightly, Erik gathered her in his arms and kissed her firmly.

"Don't worry, Berni," he told her smiling. "Don't you always come out on top?"

"Sure I do," she acknowledged with a grin. "And I want to bring you along with us when we go to take down Lord Karazin. But there are some things I need to get straight with both of you. You know how you guys get when all three of us are questing together." Erik felt a little hurt at that.

"You didn't mind having us with you when we killed Tarragin," he pointed out.

"That was a special case," she replied, "and I couldn't have done it without you. But whenever both of you are along on a quest, I feel paralyzed because I can't shoot without hitting one of you. You're always jumping into my shot."

Erik digested that for a moment in silence. He had to admit, when he and Andrion were working together with Berni there was a tendency for them to get a little… overly enthusiastic. Each of them was so determined to protect their beloved that they didn't really give her a chance to add her own contribution to the battle. And much as he and Andrion wanted to protect her, it would be insane not to admit that she was a formidable warrior in her own right. Her skills, especially in archery, had become amazing over the months since they'd met.

Squeezing her to him and kissing the side of her head he said, "You have a point. I hereby promise to be constantly aware of you when I'm charging into battle. OK?"

"I'm going to hold you to that promise," she said. Then, giving him an enthusiastic kiss, she rose from the bed. Cleaning herself up with a towel from the bedside, she put her robe back on. Turning to Erik again as he lay there watching her, she said "We'll probably be getting breakfast early and then going up to Waterdon to visit with the Brightsgate Cottage crew before heading off to Daywatch. You won't *believe* the changes in that place. See you then?"

"I'll be ready," he replied equably, a sunny smile wreathing his lips.

Bernadette waved at him and was soon up the ladder to the Maiden above. Andrion was no longer at the table, so she took a quick dip in the pool to wash away any stickiness that might have resulted from her recent romp. She didn't feel guilty about being with Erik, exactly, but it just seemed more… polite, somehow, not to be shoving it into Andrion's face by showing up reeking of another man's seed.

Toweling off, Bernadette donned her robe for the fourth time this evening and went up the stairs. She chose the side of the gallery opposite to the one they'd ensconced Nerissa in. Whatever she might be getting up to with her elf, Bernadette would prefer not to intrude. She arrived at the master bedroom and found Andrion still up, sitting at the table sipping some mead and reading a book.

She stole up on him and enfolded his head in her arms, kissing the top of it. He roused from his concentration to smile up at her, then rotated in his chair to hug her around the hips. He buried his face in her midsection, pushing aside the fabric of the robe to kiss her in the general vicinity of her navel. Ooh. "You waited up for me," she said with quiet delight.

"Not sleepy yet," he replied, standing and drawing her into the circle of his arms. She sensed that he was reclaiming her, after her visit with Erik.

Gathering her courage, speaking to his chest, Bernadette told him, "I asked Erik to marry me." Andrion stiffened momentarily, then hugged her even tighter.

"You what?" he asked softly.

"*And* I told him I want to marry *you*," she added, lifting her head to look him in the eyes. A complex parade of emotions seemed to pass through them as he gazed at her. Curiously, he appeared to be a lot more focused on her second remark than he had been on the first.

"You really want to marry me?" he asked, naked longing in his voice. Bernadette threw her arms around him, squeezing him tight. Then she stepped back a little to look into his eyes again.

"Yes, I do," she said softly. "And I want to go on adventures with you, and I want to have your babies, and I want Erik to be part of our family. I need him, and I need you." Andrion looked down at her, her gray eyes almost purple in the dimly lit bedroom. And he realized that she was being completely honest with him. What she had to say was not what he longed to hear, not entirely. But maybe it was close enough.

"Yes, Berni! Yes! All right, I *will* marry you – and if you want Erik to be part of our marriage that will be all right. As long as we are together." He hugged her tight. In another moment he added, "Uh, how were you thinking that was going to work, exactly?" "You remember my 'spiritual advice' from Engbard? According to him, me marrying two men at once is all right with Aderos, at least."

He took it all in then said lightly, "Considering both of our families are in Auverne and Erik's is in Norcove, I suppose it's not going to be much of a wedding."

Bernadette laughed out loud, hugging him tight. Her joy was so great, she thought she might burst. Everything was going to be all right! Oh, provided she *didn't* get killed trying to defeat Lord Karazin, of course. After a moment she told him, "I asked Erik to come along with us for this last part of the mission. But when the three of us are questing together and run into an adversary, trying to keep from shooting you two is really difficult. He's promised that he's going to stay aware of me and my lines of fire, and I want you to do the same."

Andrion considered that for a moment, and had to admit that there was truth to what she said. He'd gotten carried away a couple of times himself when the three of them were questing, and taken an arrow shot by his beloved as a consequence. When it was just the two of them, their almost-telepathic bond seemed to prevent such mishaps. He held up a hand, palm forward. "I hereby swear to stay aware of you and not get in the way," he said. "Maybe I'll just stay at your side and fire lightning bolts, avoid the hand-to-hand stuff." She grinned at him.

"So, tomorrow we're off to visit at Brightsgate Cottage and then heading for Daywatch?" he asked.

"That's the plan," Bernadette said. She was still floating on Cloud Nine, scarcely daring to believe that her harebrained plan seemed to be working out exactly as she'd hoped. She had the feeling there were still a few... details to be sorted out. But her future suddenly looked brighter than it had since she had first realized that Andrion wanted more from their relationship than she had been giving him.

Andrion shrugged out of his robe and tossed it aside. His cock was standing upright, ready for her. This might not be the complete triumph he had hoped for, but it was more than he'd expected and he was feeling nearly as joyful as she was. She shed her own robe as she rose to meet him, pressing close to embrace him and tilt her face up for a kiss.

Bernadette's recent session with Erik had been exciting, satisfying, wonderful. But her passion was inflamed again as she melted into the arms of this man she loved so much it took her breath away. Leaning into him, pushing him gently before her, she guided him backwards to the bed and he sat down on it. As he sat there on the edge she knelt and took his cock in her mouth, sucking him in deeply and tonguing the head as it slipped inside. Andrion gasped.

After working him over for a while, she beckoned him further up the bed, until he was sitting near the head of it with his cock standing straight up like a torch. Then she crawled up the bed after him, her eyes alight with desire and a wicked mischief. Resting her hands on his shoulders and bending in to kiss him deeply, she came the rest of the way up and straddled him, slipping down over him to engulf his cock in her hot, slippery depths.

Andrion gasped a second time, and shuddered as she slid all the way down on his shaft. Clutching her buttocks, he gave her a boost as she bounced up and down on him. Oh, yeeeesss! Her breasts brushing against his chest, her face held an expression of exalted bliss as she rose and fell. His grip on her ass tightened as the sensations began to overwhelm him. No, wait! Not yet! But there was no stopping it. The feeling rose within him like a tidal wave surging to shore, and he couldn't do anything but ride it until it crashed on the beach, washing away everything before it. As he gave up his seed in a groan of ecstasy, Berni was screaming at the top of her lungs, vibrating atop him.

Both of them sat there gasping for breath afterward, like fish cast up on the shore by that tidal wave – and about as weak. Bernadette fell over Andrion cradling his head in her arms. He wrapped his around her back, pulling her to him as she continued to encase his softening member within her. "I love you so much," she said softly to him. "We'll have beautiful babies…"

By the gods! That remark electrified him. He wanted Berni's babies almost as much as he wanted Berni, but... "Not yet, though, right?" he asked.

She smiled down at him, her eyes widening. "Oh, no! Not until we're through with Lord Karazin, at least! And we've still got to find a place where we all can live. Once I take off my amulet it will probably be a month or more before I can conceive a child." Selene had been quite clear about the details when presenting Bernadette with that amulet all those years ago. Though worn around the neck, its power was very specific to her genital area. It had halted her monthly cycles as a side effect of preventing conception, something she had not minded in the least. She had a moment of regret that moving into the next phase of her life would be going back to that messy necessity; but really it seemed a small price to pay for the joy she anticipated.

Chapter 26: Announcements

Bright and early the next morning, Bernadette awoke with bliss still simmering gently within her. She was wrapped in Andrion's arms and content with life. She would save the world from the vampire threat, claim both the men she loved so dearly, and they'd all live happily ever after.

Below this layer of elation, a less-optimistic particle of her mind whispered that the world had ways of smothering the best-laid plans; and even when you got what you wanted, there was no guarantee of happiness. She told it to shut up and let her enjoy the moment. If things didn't always work out, happiness could still be found if you knew how to look for it.

Extricating herself from Andrion's embrace and sitting up, she bent to kiss him on the side of his face. "Time to be moving, love!" she chirped at him; and for once he didn't groan or get a firmer grip on the covers. His eyes opened and he melted her with that warm, loving gaze before he, too, sat up and stretched. They helped each other into armor, gathered their packs, and swung by Nerissa's bed on their way to the stairs. They found her elf lying in the bed looking a bit the worse for wear but with an expression of satisfied exhaustion on his face, snoring lightly. Nerissa was up and getting into her own armor, looking more relaxed than she had since they'd met her.

In the dim light of the sleeping loft, her eyes seemed to be glowing more than usual. "Did you sleep well?" Bernadette asked her prosaically, with only a trace of an undercurrent.

"Wonderfully," Nerissa replied with a slight smile.

"We're going to get some breakfast, then pay a visit in Waterdon before we go back to Daywatch," Bernadette informed her. "Oh, and I've asked Erik to join us. He's an amazing fighter, and should be a real asset when it's time to storm the castle."

"I'd just like some tea," the vampire woman said with a shrug.

Downstairs, they found Erik occupying the same table they'd had dinner at the night before. He looked freshly bathed beneath his nicely polished armor, and gave Bernadette a huge smile as she and her small party appeared. "The pastries are still warm!" he exclaimed. "Dig in!" Wonderful! As often as not, it seemed,

Bernadette found herself eating whatever was around for breakfast – usually cold, stale, or generally unappetizing. Yet here were pastries still steaming slightly, giving off a delightful aroma, and plenty of delicious hot tea to wash them down with. There were fresh apples, as well.

As they seated themselves at Erik's table the two mortals dug in, Nerissa sipping hot tea. Erik caught Bernadette's eye with a questioning look, which he then directed at Andrion. Washing down a mouthful of pastry, she broke into a broad grin. Then she grabbed one of their hands in each of hers and said to both of them, "Congratulations, we're engaged!" Both Erik and Andrion smiled at this. Then Andrion reached across Berni to shake Erik's hand.

"Brother," he said briefly, and Erik echoed him. They smiled into each other's eyes.

Meanwhile Nerissa, drinking her tea, looked at the trio and wondered what had just happened. Was Bernadette announcing her engagement to Andrion, or to Erik? Or to *both* of them? She felt sure that if she waited awhile, all would be revealed. If still no better understood. Among her people, marriage was uncommon and usually for money or social position. When you were going to live forever, barring violence, a marriage made for love was not likely to stand the test of time.

When their breakfast was concluded, Bernadette got up and went to the bar, her companions trailing behind. She got Lev to give her some supplies for their journey, and picked up her share of the Maiden profits – several thousand guilders. Then she led them out the inn's front doors.

The morning was partly sunny, and Bernadette could tell it was bothering Nerissa. She'd been planning to enjoy the morning sunshine and get a little exercise walking into town, but changed her mind and fast-traveled them there instead. Then they walked the few short paces from the gates of Waterdon to the door of Brightsgate Cottage, and knocked.

It was still pretty early, and no businesses were open as yet. There was no answer to her first knock, and Bernadette wondered where the occupants could be. They couldn't be out shopping... She knocked again, then heard footsteps coming down the steps inside and the door was shortly pulled open by Lifa. She was wearing a robe and slippers, her hair disheveled and her eyes looking still soft-focused from sleep. Her face lit up when she saw who it was, and motioned them inside.

A deep, rumbling voice came from upstairs. "Who is it, Lifi?"

"It's Bernadette, with Erik and Andrion," Lifa called back up.

"I'll be right down" came the voice of Bjorn, and he soon appeared, tightening a belt over a tunic and wearing trousers – no armor. He also looked a bit mussed as he descended the stairs, having clearly just gotten out of bed… but *which* bed? Bernadette thought she knew, and her eyes were shining with delight.

Bernadette made introductions, and the two body servants greeted Nerissa without showing any sign that they recognized what she was. Bjorn touched Lifa's arm gently and said, "I'll put the kettle on."

She nodded in thanks, and called up the stairs again, "Anja! Aunt Berni is here!"

"Coming!" the little voice piped up, and shortly the door to the small second bedroom opened and Anja, wearing a flowered nightgown, came down to greet them. That answered *that* question.

After hugs and kisses had been exchanged, Bernadette produced a bag of warm pastries she'd brought from the Maiden. Bjorn made tea, and the four who were soon to be traveling drank some of that but left the food to the three Brightsgate Cottage residents. Anja was especially delighted – like most little ones, she loved anything sweet.

As she sat stuffing a warm sugar roll in her mouth with happy smacking noises, Bernadette talked quietly with Lifa and Bjorn. "How have things been around here while I was gone?" she asked.

"It's been pretty quiet. No more vampire attacks at all," Lifa replied. Dragons still posed a threat, Bernadette supposed, but fewer of them were being seen in cities since Tarragin's demise. "Erik's been a huge help," Lifa added. "He's been coming by every day to bring us supplies and play with Anja. I think that man's going to make a great daddy someday."

Bernadette beamed at her. "I have some good news, but I'm not sure how to explain it. Andrion and I are getting married. And I'm marrying Erik too!" Lifa was a bit taken aback. Like most people of her class, she was pretty conservative in her views and she had never heard of such a thing in Iscandia. People in exotic foreign parts might marry more than one spouse, usually a man with multiple wives – or so she had heard. But not around here!

"Um… congratulations," she said politely. Bjorn had been taking this in with a certain amount of interest. He had initially assumed that Erik and Berni were a couple, and now learning that she was planning to marry both him and Andrion made him mentally shake his head. He was sure her plans would only lead to trouble, but he had something else on his mind.

"My warden, uh, Bernadette… There's something I would like to ask you before you go. Now that Lifa and I are living here together with Anja we've… uh, decided that we would like to… uh, if we can have your permission…"

Lifa gave Bjorn a fond glance, and cut to the chase. "What my dear bear is trying to say, Bernadette, is that he and I would like to be married. To each other," she clarified, just to be on the safe side. Bernadette gave her a brilliant smile, hugely pleased that her plan had worked out just as she'd hoped.

"That's wonderful! I'm so happy for you!" She thought a moment and added, "Could the wedding wait until after we've finished with the vampire problem? I'd like to stand you to a proper wedding at the Temple of Marmira in Lakedon, but we're going to be too busy to do that for a while."

Lifa returned her smile. It was the most joyful expression Bernadette had seen on her face to date, though certainly her smiles had been more frequent since Anja came along. "Thank you! That would be wonderful. We shouldn't have any trouble waiting, though I half wish we could come along and fight with you."

"You're fighting here," Bernadette told them. "Keeping Anja safe is my top priority."

There were more hugs and kisses before they left, and Anja (her face now sticky) remarked to Nerissa, "You have pretty eyes. I like how they glow."

"Thank you," the vampire woman replied gravely, and gave the little gamin a kiss on the cheek before turning to leave. The four of them fast-traveled from the street outside Brightsgate Cottage, and soon found themselves standing outside the main doors of Daywatch.

Chapter 27: Reconnaissance

Another sunny day in Closevale, and from the position of the sun it was early afternoon. Erik gaped, amazed at the changes that had taken place since he'd visited this once-ruin in his teens. "Wow," he said softly. "This Malden guy seems to have brought some good people on board."

"Let's hope they'll prove to be as good at fighting as they are at building," Bernadette remarked as she led them inside. They almost literally ran into Rene, as he came hurrying through.

"Andrion, Bernadette, you're back!" he said cheerfully. "How did it go? Did you find the staff?"

"I have it right here in my pack," Bernadette gestured. The thing was sticking out a few feet over her head.

"You'll be looking for Malden, then," the young Galise said. As usual, he was in a tearing hurry to be someplace. "You'll find him out in the south yard, conferring with Diane. 'Scuse me, I have to run!"

Erik grinned at his retreating back. "Friend of yours?" he asked Andrion.

"Rene Augenois," he said with an answering grin. "Very energetic young man, but he's a good guy. We'll get a chance to talk with him later, I'm sure. Come on, might as well meet Malden."

They hung a left and went down to the south end of the building and out the doors there. They found Malden and Diane standing together at a drafting table. She was gesticulating at some plans and he was looking unhappy about something. The perfect time to change the subject!

The two looked up as the party of four trooped in. Malden gave Nerissa a sour look, but gazed up at Erik in wonder. In full armor, the young Norseman was the very image of a powerful warrior hero out of legends – just the sort of fellow you might like to recruit to your cause.

Bernadette pulled the Staff of Apoldros from her pack and held it before her. "We got it!" she said, beaming. The captain reached to take it from her and she pulled it back a little. "Careful, not a good idea to handle it too much. This was infused with the power of

197

Apoldros' light by the head of his priesthood up in the Eparchy, and I'd just as soon save its charge for when we're facing Lord Karazin."

He seemed a little unhappy, but had to acknowledge it was her that had found the staff and was entitled to be the one wielding it. "But you got it, that's the important thing," he said with a near-smile. "That vampire scum Karazin won't be getting his hands on it now, so the sun is safe."

"That's sort-of why we're here, Malden," Bernadette said. "Nerissa and I both believe that now is the time to hit Karazin and his minions – and hit them hard. She's going to lead us to Castle Hordenhaal and help us get in there so we can take them out before they even realize we're after them. If we wait too long to strike, they may get word that we've found the staff and be building their forces to oppose us. Wouldn't you agree?"

The older man was put on the spot. "I don't know, I... I'm not sure we're ready for this. So much of our effort has been put into restoring the fortress, we haven't really had time for full battle drills."

"I tell you what," Bernadette replied. "I think that Nerissa and I, and my partners Erik and Andrion, should make our way to Hordenhaal and check the place out. That will put it on my map, so that I can fast-travel our entire assault force directly to the island."

"That's a good idea," Malden replied. He hadn't even begun thinking about logistics, but this slip of a girl (okay, slip of a world-famous, fireblood, savior-of-the-world girl) was way ahead of him.

Bernadette went on, "That's going to take a couple of days, so you can get your forces marshaled. I'd suggest not bringing anybody who personally doesn't feel they're ready to participate in a full frontal assault. You have some people like Rene and Marya whose skills are valuable in a support capacity but shouldn't necessarily be in combat – at least not until they've had more training. Agreed?"

Malden felt as if he'd been run over by a speeding wagon. Andrion and Erik were grinning at each other, that "there goes Hurricane Berni" look in their eyes once again. When their beloved got on a roll, there was no stopping her. After clearing his throat, the captain said "That... that seems appropriate. I'll put Grindmar on the project of getting everyone ready. Um, when will you be back?"

Bernadette pulled out her map, setting it atop the plan (which appeared to be another crossbow design) and scanning Iscandia's northwest coast. "Could you point out Hordenhaal, Nerissa?" she asked. The vampire woman, stepping carefully around Malden, came to stand beside her and put a slim finger on a small island sitting no more than a mile from shore, not far from a headland. As she did so, an arrow appeared.

"Hmm," Bernadette mused. There wasn't much of anything in that remote and chilly corner of the province. Her closest fast-travel point, it seemed, was Drakespire Cave. She grinned over at her two men, watching her work with expressions of fond amusement. "It looks like it's back to Drakespire for us," she said cheerfully. "Do you think it'll be full of bandits again?"

Dragons and the walking undead stayed killed, but prime bandit lairs always seemed to acquire new tenants. And of course, Bernadette just loved killing bandits because they were murderous scum who deserved to die – and they usually had really great loot. Even as wealthy as she'd become now, the lure of glittering treasure never failed to draw her.

"Maybe we can sneak around them," Andrion suggested with a twinkle in his eye.

"Or maybe not," Erik added with an evil grin, his hand caressing the handle of his axe. Nerissa, Malden, and Diane just stood looking at them, and Bernadette eventually realized she hadn't answered the captain's question yet.

She looked him in the eye and said, "I think three days from today should be enough time for us to go and come back. I'll try to get some idea on the return trip how long it will actually take to fast-travel there. It would be best if our force could arrive in broad daylight."

"Very well then, Fireblood," Malden said. "We will be ready to take the battle to Lord Karazin three days hence." The party were rested, fed, and well-supplied. There seemed to be no reason for them to delay leaving, so Bernadette led them out a little further into the yard. Moments of subjective time later, they found themselves standing just down the slope from the entrance to Drakespire Cave, as evening was coming on.

Bernadette had had a pretty good idea of what they would find when they got there, and in the few seconds the fast-traveling took in subjective time she had tucked the map away and drawn her bow. The short, stocky, and heavily-armed Reman woman standing watch outside the cave's entrance was too shocked to react to the sudden appearance of four intruders before she lay bleeding on the stone pathway, an arrow sunk to its fletchings in her breastbone.

Bernadette put a finger to her lips, warning her companions to silence as she quickly rifled the corpse. Both Andrion and Erik were mindful of the trouble they'd nearly gotten into last time they were here, having failed to check the surrounding area for stray bandits before assuming that the ones they'd killed inside were the entire gang. They scouted out several hundred yards from the cave opening, including down along the banks of a nearby creek. But there were no others to be found.

Now their fireblood leader began stalking silently down the passageway, her fellows at her heels. The time was right for the evening meal, and they found half a dozen bandits inside the first large chamber – sitting at a long wooden table spooning up bowls of stew. Andrion and Erik held back while Bernadette lined up her shot, before any of the bandits realized they had company.

She chose her target with care – taking the tallest and most heavily-armored of the crew, sitting on the far side of the table, with an arrow to the throat. Bowls flew to shatter on the stone floor as the rest of the outlaw band scrambled to their feet, reaching for weapons. Most had set them aside, as it's awkward to sit and eat with a sword at your side or a bow behind your back. Though they outnumbered the intruders, they fell one by one without ever laying a finger on the ones who had invaded their hideout.

Bernadette slung her bow behind her back, a look of mixed satisfaction and disgust on her face. "Well, *that's* a mess, " she said.

"We'll take care of it, love," Erik said with a grin. After searching for valuables he hefted a body under each arm and vanished down the tunnel. He reemerged, sweating, a few minutes later.

Meanwhile Bernadette and Andrion had been stripping the rest of the corpses. She looked up at Erik as he returned, a question in her eyes. "Dumped them in the lava crack," he said with a grin. "Gimme a hand with the rest of these, will you Andrion?"

While the rest of the bandits' bodies were being disposed of, Bernadette and Nerissa explored the main cavern and then the smaller one beyond. "Your crew are very… effective," the vampire woman remarked with a wry grin.

"That's my boys," Bernadette sighed.

"And you're actually planning to marry *both* of them? Ye gods…" Her friend just smiled.

They added water and additional provisions to the remains of the bandits' stew in the pot over the cookfire, and spent the night sleeping in comfort within the warm central cavern. Laden with gold, jewelry, and weapons from the late outlaws' cache, the party set out on foot for the coast some seven miles away. This stretch of Iscandia's coastline was rugged and forlorn, with no major towns or even much in the way of farming. A stiff, icy onshore breeze had them raising the hoods on their cloaks as they set off north up the road that ran half a mile inland from the cliffs.

High overhead a dragon circled, roaring out its defiance of any who might challenge its territory. Bernadette tensed, ready for a battle; but it stooped on something – probably an elk – at least a mile to their south and she relaxed. Dragons could be very aggressive, but they were also smart enough to realize that a man alone or a wandering elk was easier prey than a party of armed warriors.

They walked through the morning, seeing lots of deer and elk grazing on the windswept coastal plateau but little else stirring. When stomachs began to growl the four just sat down in the grass at the side of the road and ate trail food from their packs. As usual, Nerissa had nothing. Bernadette wondered idly what would pass as trail food for a vampire – the odd raw squirrel, perhaps?

As they continued north the land fell away and the road came down to skirt the pebbly beach of a broad, roughly semicircular bay. The sky was overcast but no rain or snow was falling, and visibility was good. They'd been seeing the occasional small rocky island to their west for the past couple of hours, and now Nerissa halted and pointed out to sea.

"That's it, out there to the west," she said. A pile of stone was just visible on a rocky island, bigger than most, on the far side of a narrow strait. "We used to keep a boat on the beach here to get back and forth." Bernadette checked her map, and sure enough the arrow for Hordenhaal was right across from where they were standing.

The four peered around, seeing no boats on the strand. Of course, one could hardly just leave a boat pulled up a few yards from the water – it would be washed away the first time there was a good storm. "Let's spread out and search the bay," Bernadette suggested. The bay was more than a mile from north to south, and on either end of it the cliffs rose to a modest twenty feet while a small creek cut through the center of the beach on its way out to sea.

"Found it!" Erik bellowed from where he'd been searching to the north. They joined him there, and found a wooden dory some sixteen feet long, pulled up close to the cliff and secured with a lock and chain to a steel eye-bolt embedded in the cliff face. Erik stepped close to the cliff and heaved on the chain, his massive muscles standing out as he strained on the bolt. With a crack the bolt was wrenched from the stone, and he tossed the chain into the boat before picking up the bow end. The others stared at him for a moment, then seized the boat by stern and sides to lift it and carry it down to where the small waves crashed onto the stony beach.

There was a single pair of oars lying in the boat's bottom, and Erik soon had those slipped into the oarlocks. When everyone was seated to his satisfaction, he began pulling strongly for the nearby island. "Used to do this a lot when I was a kid," he remarked with a grin. "It brings back memories."

"Head a little to the south," Nerissa directed from a seat facing the rower. "We want to avoid pulling up in front of the castle, where the guards are."

"Your father has guards out in the daytime?" Bernadette asked, sitting beside her vampire friend and enjoying the play of Erik's muscles as he worked the oars. What a magnificent specimen he was!

"Father has a lot of thralls at the castle," Nerissa explained. "Non-vampires have many advantages, being able to thrive on common foods like bread and potatoes, and having no problem going out in the daytime. Maybe as many as half the castle staff are thralls." Bernadette frowned.

"If we succeed in killing your father, will that break the enthrallment?" she asked. She hated the thought of killing people just because they'd fallen victim to a vampire lord's control.

"If you could take a thrall captive and hold them for a period of several days, it's likely that the imprinted loyalty to the vampire who enthralled them would ebb and they might eventually return to their normal selves," Nerissa explained. "But in a battle situation, they'll fight you to the death. I don't think we'll be able to save many of them, I'm afraid."

Following Nerissa's direction, Erik rowed the dory into a small inlet on the south side of the island. Stone jetties flanked it on either side, and he hopped out to steady the boat as the rest of them climbed out. He pulled the chain and its attached eyebolt out and draped it on the stone, which probably should be enough to anchor the small craft in this quiet backwater.

"You really know your boats, Erik," Bernadette remarked. He grinned at her and shrugged. She was burning to quiz him about his family and early life, but this didn't seem to be the time. Nerissa nudged her and put a finger to her lips, pointing to the nearby castle. In the gray afternoon light they could just see walking skeletons patrolling the walls. Not all the non-vampire guards here were human thralls, she realized. Good to know.

"It looks like your father has his fortress well-guarded," Bernadette remarked in an undertone. So far, the intruders seemed not to have been spotted by the undead sentries.

"Those were human victims set to walking centuries ago," Nerissa replied softly. "They will not leave their posts, if we attack from the other side."

The four of them crept along close to the castle walls. It was not truly a fortress, less so than was Daywatch; but it was an enormous three-story stone building covering more than an acre of land. They could see a wooden door high up at the top of staircases leading up from the little harbor, but no other openings on this side. In places, the stone seemed to have collapsed forming little alcoves amid the ruins.

"Did your family build this place?" Bernadette asked. "Oh no," Nerissa replied. "We've occupied it for a few hundred years, but it's far older than that. It was abandoned when my parents came here, with me as a small child. That was after Mother and Father had been granted the Netherblood gift. They brought along thralls and some of their vampiric "children" as well. It was mostly thralls, and Mother, who raised me until I was old enough to participate in the ritual."

Bernadette looked at her friend, owl-eyed. She hadn't expected Nerissa to part with so much personal information in answer to a casual question. "The ritual?" she asked hesitantly.

"I'd rather not talk about it," her friend said with a shudder. They walked on.

The castle was built facing the land to the east, with broad stone steps leading up from the shore. There seemed to be no one about. "Where are the front door guards?" Bernadette murmured, peering up the steps.

"You see the stone archway?" Nerissa asked, pointing. "There's an alcove behind it. Two guards are posted on the front doors, and they stay in the alcove. That way they're out of the wind, and have some shelter if somebody comes in shooting."

"If two of us can creep up without being spotted, we should be able to take them out without raising an alarm," Erik opined. He might not be all that deep a thinker, but he was highly experienced in battle situations. Nerissa shook her head.

"I can take care of them," she said. "Did you notice the statuary?" Flanking the staircase, two on either side, were grotesque-looking statues around eight feet tall. They appeared to depict some form of demon or perhaps daimon – the distinction being the degree of sentience.

"Those aren't statues," Nerissa went on. "They're demonic guardians from one of the planes of the Netherworld. They've been bound to serve Father, and will come to life and attack if any intruder comes within their range. They should ignore me, as I'm sure Father would be delighted to see my return. Likewise, the door guards will either recognize me as the prodigal daughter or at least as a vampire. After I take out the guards, the rest of the force should attack with an eye to eliminating the stone demons as quickly and quietly as possible."

"If one of them comes to life, will they all do it?" Bernadette asked, a plan beginning to form in her brain.

"No, their awareness of threat is only triggered by an intruder stepping within six feet," Nerissa replied. "But as the stairs are only ten feet wide, going up them in the middle would trigger the demons on both sides."

"I think I know how we can deal with them," Bernadette said. "Probably any plans for once we're inside the castle should be discussed with Malden, Grindmar, and the rest of the Daywatch Brigade. Shall we head back there now?" The sun was a bright spot in the cloud cover, and from its height above the sea to their west it was approaching four in the afternoon. In seconds, the beach in front of Castle Hordenhaal was empty of life.

Chapter 28: Mustering for Battle

It was dark when the party of four materialized outside Daywatch, the doors closed. A couple of the Brigade were stationed outside them, fully armed and armored. It appeared that Malden had gotten them onto a war footing at last. "Ahead of schedule, Fireblood," the man on the left said. Bernadette didn't recall his name, but he looked to be a grim fighter.

His partner, Greta, greeted her with a smile and unlocked the doors to let them aside. "Everybody but those on watch are probably still in the dining hall," she told them. "I could certainly eat," Erik remarked as he followed Bernadette and Andrion off to the right and down the corridors to the dining hall. Another table seemed to have been added since they were last here, and the room was full of people – many of them wearing armor. There must be nearly thirty fighters now!

There was a chorus of greetings as the four of them came inside, and took seats along the far end of the second table. Marya, who'd been eating her own supper, came up and told Nerissa, "We butchered an elk yesterday. Can I get you some raw steaks?"

"Thank you, Marya!" the vampire woman said warmly. That a member of this crew dedicated to exterminating her kind should make such a thoughtful gesture filled her with a curious and unfamiliar sensation of... belonging?

Shortly the Afran woman had brought bowls of venison stew and a fresh loaf of barley bread to the new arrivals, along with Nerissa's raw steaks and a pot of butter. Everyone else was finished eating, just lingering at table to talk excitedly among themselves about the coming fight. "Does anyone know the time?" Bernadette asked, as she slathered butter on a thick slice of the hearty bread.

A clock, evidently a recent acquisition, stood atop the massive stone mantelpiece. "It's nine o'clock," Marya said, glancing up at it as she set about doing the post-dinner cleanup. "That's a five-hour difference from when we left," Bernadette mused around a mouthful of bread and butter, "but it's probably an hour earlier at the coast because they're so much further west of us. I don't know..." Math was not her strong suit, and few people paid much attention to clocks in their world.

Swallowing and washing down the mouthful with a slug of sour red wine, Bernadette concluded "If we leave here by midmorning, we should arrive at Castle Hordenhaal with plenty of daylight left to spare." There were murmurs of agreement from her companions as they dug into their repast.

By the time the travelers had eaten, others had moved away from the table and some of them had sought their beds. Malden, Grindmar, and Rene lingered behind, anxious to speak with them. "We've configured one of the ground-floor chambers as a sort of war room," Grindmar said. "Please follow me."

The seven of them made their way further north, in the same wing where the dining hall was located, and into another windowless chamber. None of the ground-floor rooms in Daywatch had more than arrow slits for light and ventilation. A large wooden table similar to the dining table they'd just left behind sat in the middle of the room, and on it a map – a non-magical map – of Iscandia, along with parts of Auverne, Remus, and Darkreach, was spread.

Nerissa stepped forward with a stick of charcoal and drew a circle around the island Hordenhaal sat on. Then she asked, "Do you have a blank sheet of paper?" A smaller table sat in a corner, with rolls of paper and other supplies on it. Nerissa unrolled the sheet of nubbly, hand-made paper on the table beside the map and began to sketch on it.

They discussed the entry, Nerissa's plan to take out the door guards, and Bernadette's plan to deal with the stone demons. Erik grinned when he learned the role she'd planned for him in that. Meanwhile Nerissa had begun sketching the interior of Hordenhaal. "A great deal of the castle is at least partially ruinous," she told them. "When I left twenty years ago Father had around thirty people sharing it with him – a dozen or so thralls for performing domestic chores and obtaining supplies, and the rest vampires he and Mother had created, or the vampire children of those."

It sounded as if they might be closely matched in numbers. But wasn't a single vampire more fearsome in battle than an ordinary human? "I can't say, Nerissa went on, "whether the numbers have increased since then. But Father has been actively seeking information about the whereabouts of the Staff of Apoldros, so it's likely at least half a dozen of his minions will be out in the field searching and not there at the castle."

There were nods all around. So far, the leadership did not appear to be cowed by the task at hand. Nerissa continued sketching from memory. As that ruinous pile of stone had been her home for centuries, she certainly ought to know it well. "Down these two staircases from the entry hall is the dining hall. I think the original occupants of Hordenhaal probably used it as a ballroom – it's huge. Off of that we have the kitchens, some work rooms, and up the stairs is the grand gallery where my family keeps trophies of their exploits…" From her expression, those trophies were something she'd rather not discuss with present company.

"You said your people don't sleep, but rather rest," Bernadette said. "If we're there in mid-afternoon, will we find most people resting?"

"It's hard to say for certain," Nerissa replied. "Indoors, we may be active at any time of the day or night depending on what's going on. All of my father's minions are bonded to him, having been made vampires by drinking his blood. So they, all the vampires at the castle, are a little more closely knit than most. We don't tend to be very gregarious, normally."

"Looks like we're going to have to take care of everybody outside at the front, let ourselves in through the doors, and then play it by ear," Bernadette said, and Nerissa nodded.

"I wish I could be more specific, but I haven't dared to set foot in that place in twenty years. Everything may have changed. But once we're inside, I'll be able to direct people to sleeping chambers and so forth. It's the best I can do."

"How do we even know we can trust you?" Malden snarled, eyeing the vampire woman with naked hostility. "You could be leading us all into a trap, food and thralls for your monstrous father and his friends." Nerissa seemed taken aback, but Bernadette stepped up to defend her friend.

"You're wrong about her, Malden," she said firmly. "She's risked everything to help us, and could easily have snatched the staff away from us after we retrieved it. I saw her pick up a large man, well elf, and throw him across a balcony. She's had plenty of opportunities to do me and Andrion in, and instead she helped us to our goal and is helping us now, working against her own father. I trust her, and so should you."

Nerissa looked at Bernadette with an expression of melting gratitude, her eyes glowing more than usual. You couldn't get that kind of friendship from a fellow vampire... "Thanks, Berni," she said. "But that reminds me. The thralls are no stronger or more agile than any other mortals, but vampires possess superhuman strength. You want to avoid closing with them as much as possible. Those crossbows of Diane's, especially with the hollow-tipped bolts, would be a good weapon to use."

"She's drafted the rest of our smiths into churning them out since you left," Grindmar said. "There are not enough for everyone, but we'll have quite a few. I'll make sure those who don't already have a bow of some other long-range weapon are armed with them."

"Good," Nerissa said. "Also, if you have any silver swords, that would be the best weapon to use at close range. But forget about poisoning your weapons – poison doesn't affect us."

Malden still looked a little unsure, his suspicion of Nerissa and her motives not completely allayed. But clearly, others he trusted believed she was all right – so he should set aside his reservations. Even so, he'd be watching her with an eagle eye for any signs of treachery... "I think we've planned as best we can for tonight, and should be up early tomorrow," he said. "Let's all get some rest, and in the morning we'll rally our troops."

Bernadette had last spent the night with Andrion, and would have loved to spend tonight with Erik. But now that the three of them were pledged to live and love together, she didn't really want to kick either of them out in order to be with the other. Instead, she said "I think I'm going to sack out on one of the cots in the barracks," and set off in the direction of the nearest dormitory. Andrion and Erik exchanged a look, shrugged, and followed her.

Chapter 29: Lord Karazin's Bane

Marya had outdone herself, rising in the wee hours of the morning to bake enough bread that everyone in Daywatch could have their fill of the still-warm, hearty loaves along with masses of butter and pots of peach jam. For protein, she sliced a gigantic smoked ham for those who wanted to make a sandwich between slabs of the bread. And for Nerissa, some more raw venison.

Everyone ate lightly, too anxious about the forthcoming battle to want to stuff themselves. At Bernadette's advice, knowing how map travel could leave one hungry just an hour or two after eating, everyone brought along food in their packs along with weapons, ammunition, and cloaks against the icy cold that had much of Iscandia in its grip at this time of year.

After eating and kitting up they all (minus half a dozen who had opted to guard the fortress in their absence) gathered in the yard south of the castle. Grindmar addressed them first, announcing loudly and in clear, simple terms what they would be doing. He'd selected a handful of sergeants from among the more promising recruits, and each of these was put in charge of a squad.

But Malden was determined to address the troops before they departed. "For too long we've allowed these vampires to poison the night and kill our people! Now, we finally have the means to strike back!" He continued, "We now have the Staff of Apoldros. The gods themselves have favored us and we must answer with action!"

Bernadette hoped he was right about that. She hoped that her plan for the staff's first use, after they'd gotten inside the castle, would be a success. But she hadn't wanted to waste any of its limited energy experimenting. What if she used up whatever power Duraenis – or perhaps, his god Apoldros at the monk's behest - had infused it with, right before she *really* needed it to take down the Netherblood vampire lord?

Bernadette's attention refocused on Malden as he went on, "The time has come to finally put an end to Karazin and his unholy prophecy! We will march on their lair and destroy those wretched abominations so they can no longer corrupt our world!" Murmurs of approval went up from the Daywatch Brigade gathered around their leader.

Well, the troops had been fired up. Time to get on with it. "Everybody gather around me," Bernadette said. There were thirty-one people in the group counting herself, and she had never tried to transport so many with the map before. Now would be a really crappy time to learn this wasn't going to work, she thought, as she embraced every one of them with her mind and wished them all to Hordenhaal.

A light snow was falling, and behind them waves crashed on the shingle shore. It worked! Malden and his command structure gestured for silence, and there were no murmurs of astonishment – bless them. Many of these people had probably never experienced being transported by map before, and it could be quite disorienting. Greta, old soldier that she was, pulled a slab of bread out of her pack and began gnawing on it as she looked around at the castle and its surroundings with interest.

Putting a finger to her lips, reminding everyone to remain silent, Nerissa pulled her hood up over her head and began walking up the center of the staircase. The stone demons remained statues, ignoring her as she walked between them. This one belonged here, they knew.

Nerissa reached the sheltered alcove in front of the doors, finding the two door guards huddling together on the left side of it and sharing a mug of hot cider. Their enthrallment gave them absolute loyalty to Lord Karazin and his household, but it didn't turn them into inhuman automatons. They had the same needs and desires they'd had before being enthralled.

The older one recognized her as she pulled down the hood of the cloak to reveal her face. "Lady Nerissa!" he cried. He had known this seemingly young woman since he was a very young man himself, and in all that time she had not changed in the least.

She turned to him, a look of sadness in her orange-glowing eyes. "Hello Johan," she said. Suddenly her hands shot out from beneath the cloak, seizing each man by the throat and lifting them high, pressing them against the stone walls as they choked and thrashed. When the thrashing had stopped, she dropped them to the floor of the alcove and they lay still.

Nerissa stepped out from the alcove and gave a thumb's up signal, and Bernadette, Andrion, and Erik went into action. As the blond Norseman moved back some eight feet beyond the right side of the stairway until he was opposite the first of the stone demons, his companions hugged the stone railing – approaching the demon after Erik was in position. The railing was waist high, the demon perched on a flat-topped stone pillar built into it.

As they came within the triggering range, the stone demon crackled into life – its stone carapace shattering and falling away. Bernadette cried out "Eiz-Nehm-Bild-Stalz!" and the creature went rigid again – not stone this time, but a block of solid ice. Immediately, Andrion added his strength to Bernadette's as the two heaved the creature off of its pillar to crash on the stones below the stairway.

The thing's left arm and webbed wing broke off as it hit, and Erik was on it like a ferret pouncing on a mouse – wielding his sablium war hammer. The black metal was harder and stronger if lighter than steel, and in the hands of the powerful Norse warrior the temporarily-frozen demon had soon been reduced to shards. As it thawed, the pieces became stone again.

The Daywatch Brigade had been watching this operation with their hearts in their throats, and it took all the efforts of the commanding officers to keep them from breaking out in a cheer as the monster was destroyed. Andrion, Bernadette, and Erik repeated the procedure with the second demon on the right side, then relocated carefully to the left side – staying out of range until it was time. The delay while each stone demon was broken up gave Bernadette enough time recharge her spell stone. She was finding that as she used particular dragon spells more, it seemed to require less time to recharge the stones. Or perhaps it was just that her overall supply of mana was growing?

Now the entire troop surged quietly up the steps, following Bernadette and Andrion as they went up to meet Nerissa at the door. Erik was behind them, but came up alongside Bernadette as they waited for Nerissa to get the door open. "Johan had the key in his pocket," she murmured to her companions as she turned it in the lock.

Once all of them had come inside, moving as quietly as possible, Nerissa motioned to them to wait while she crept silently down the hall to the balcony overlooking the dining hall. She reasoned that, should the room be occupied and she be spotted, her presence would not cause alarm. Oh, and it was. Seemingly the routine had changed, for there were at least a dozen people sitting at tables in the hall below. They were feasting on the corpses of what appeared to be human victims, and paying more attention to their food than to their surroundings. She didn't see her father among them.

Tense, Nerissa crept quietly back to where the Brigade was waiting – Bernadette, Andrion, and Erik in the forefront with Malden and Grindmar close at hand. "Twelve in the hall," she murmured to them. "Are you ready to try it?" Bernadette nodded, pale in the dimly lit hallway. Grindmar motioned for the archers to come forward: six of them, three with longbows and three with the specially-made crossbows.

"Nerissa, you need to get completely out of sight for this," Bernadette warned. The vampire woman nodded and slipped back out the front door, leaving it ajar so she could hear what was happening. To the archers, The Fireblood said, "Get into position on the stairs, but keep low below the railing so you won't be seen. On my signal, close your eyes tight. Then as soon as you hear me say, 'go,' get up and start shooting!"

They all nodded silent assent, and followed Bernadette as she crept down the hallway to the balcony overlooking the dining hall. A stone balustrade some four feet high fronted the balcony and formed a railing for the outer side of the staircases on either side of it, and the seven crouched low as they approached.

Bernadette had her bow strung, but it was the Staff of Apoldros that she held as, seeing her troops in place, she stood up and peered over the balustrade to the room below. There were six tables in the room, arrayed in a U configuration so that the lord of the manor could sit at the head with his minions on either side. The two tables forming the head were empty, but there were eight people seated along the right leg and another four on the left – all immersed in their gory meal.

She gave the hand signal to the archers on either side, and they obediently squeezed their eyes shut. Then, pointing the diamond tip of the staff down into the room, she closed her own eyes and poured her will into the staff. Blast them to dust, she urged the divine weapon. Her eyelids went red for an instant, and there were shrieks from below.

"Now!" Bernadette screamed, and as she tucked the staff into the scabbard she'd cobbled up for it and pulled her bow, the archers began riddling the occupants of the dining hall below with arrows and crossbow quarrels. Those vampires nearest to the actinic blast had been set ablaze, their clothing on fire and their faces blackened. It would have taken minutes of constant exposure for the concentrated sunlight to kill them, but they were hurt and hurt bad.

The rest of the Brigade, Andrion and Erik in the forefront, came galloping forward to plunge down the stairs and mop up, as Bernadette and the rest of the archers held their fire. Eight of the injured vampires had fallen to the enfilade, and the remaining four were too dazed and damaged to put up much of a fight as they were swarmed under by two dozen fired-up foes.

Soon all was quiet again. "These were all vampires," Nerissa said, trying not to see their faces. They may have become sunk in evil, but they were people she had known for most of her long, long life. "I have an idea of how we might be able to avoid having to kill all the thralls," she went on. "As I'm Netherblood, and close kin to the lord who enthralled them, I may be able to override Father's enthrallment with one of my own. Then I can question them about who is here, and where. We really need to know before we start searching the castle."

Bernadette looked at her friend anxiously. "Oh, Nerissa… you should not!" The vampire woman gritted her teeth.

"I know I swore I would never use that power, and I have not done so in hundreds of years," she said sadly. "But this will save lives! I have to do it." She began moving off in the direction of the castle's kitchen. Killing Johan had hurt, far more than she had expected it to. She couldn't bear to see the rest of the mortal servants she'd known for years destroyed, just because of something her father had done to them.

Nerissa walked into the kitchen, and found the cook and two helpers at work on a meal for the rest of the thralls. Though vampires ruled here, a castle required many hands to run it. And vampires were little inclined to put their hands to ordinary everyday tasks. "Helga, so good to see you!" she said, addressing the plump cook. The last time she'd seen this woman, she'd been a young scullery maid newly enthralled and brought from the mainland. The current kitchen helpers looked too young to have been here before the mistress and daughter of Castle Hordenhaal had gone missing.

The woman straightened up, dusting flour from her apron, and gaped at Nerissa in disbelief. "Lady Nerissa? Is that really you?"

"Yes, it's really me," the vampire said, embracing the cook slightly. "I've returned. And who do we have here?" she asked. It was necessary to make physical contact and speak the subject's name to achieve enthrallment.

"This's Berta and Genevieve," Helga said. "They're good girls, very loyal to the master." As were they all, Nerissa thought bitterly. Karazin von Hordenhaal deserved loyalty from no one, but took it as his right. Moments later she had stolen that loyalty for herself, and the three women looked at her expectantly, eager to fulfill her commands.

"How many people are in the castle now?" Nerissa asked, and it was Helga who answered.

"Let me see. For servants, counting us and the men on the front door, there's sixteen. Most of 'em are working around the castle now, cleaning and dusting and the like, but they'll all be gathered here for supper in another couple of hours."

"Good, good," Nerissa said. "And as for the lords, Father and his people?"

"Eight of them are off on some errand or other," Berta said calmly. "Don't know what, but they've been gone a good long while." Huh, four of those were ones we killed in that crypt near Karstein, Nerissa thought. That left another four out wandering loose... "T'other nineteen are about, here and there, like usual. You must've met the ones as were having dinner in the hall when you came in. And the master's at his devotions up in the chapel, I believe. He said he'd be down for supper late."

"Thank you Helga, Berta, and Genevieve. Listen carefully. I have come here tonight with some people – regular people – not the lord folk. If you see anybody you don't know, be courteous to them and help them in whatever way they request. Do not attack or harm anyone, and if any of the other servants come here tell them to do the same. Do you understand?"

"Yes, ma'am," they chorused, and Nerissa returned to the dining hall.

The Brigade were pacing around anxiously, on the alert for trouble, and several people flinched as she returned. "There are more people than I'd hoped," Nerissa told them. "Another eleven enthralled servants are wandering around the castle, performing domestic chores. They're likely to start showing up here in the next couple of hours for their supper in the kitchen, and if they see the carnage here they're going to go on the alert."

"Let's get these bodies cleared out," Erik suggested. He and around half of the Brigade jumped to the task, hauling the dead vampires up the stairs and out the front door. They dumped the bodies over the edges of the stairway on either side, out of the way and soon to be covered with snow – considering the way it was coming down.

"Everybody take a panacea potion," Grindmar commanded when the body-disposal squad had returned. The chances of *not* catching the vampire contagion after handling the blood-stained body of a vampire were slight, but the potion would stop that contagion in its tracks.

Nerissa continued her tale, relieved. At the best of times the dining hall was splashed with blood, and it was unlikely the servants would notice that there was more of it than usual. "As for vampires, there are another seven that we haven't found yet plus my father. And I think I know where to find him. We should concentrate on the vampires, as they are a lot more dangerous than the thralls. All right?"

Malden eyed the young-seeming vampire woman musingly. His hatred of the vampire kind was deep-seated, and it was hard to put it aside. But so far Nerissa had been a valiant ally. Was it time for him to revise his thinking? They fanned out in small groups to search the rest of the ground-floor rooms. One group surprised a maid who was dusting, and were able to subdue the unarmed woman until Nerissa could be brought to enthrall her and send her off to join the others in the kitchen.

Bernadette entered a room with some crafting tables in it and heard a muffled voice saying, "Is someone there? I thought I heard..." Followed by Erik and Andrion, she tracked the sound of the voice to a closed room. Flinging open the door Bernadette stepped inside, and was immediately attacked by a red-armored vampire. She hurled him across the room with a spell, then put a couple of arrows into him for good measure before Andrion and Erik rushed in to finish him with blades.

They returned to the dining hall, to learn that all the rest of the rooms on this floor had proven to be empty. As a group, the Daywatch Brigade mounted the main staircase leading to the second floor. "The rooms for resting are all along this corridor, on both sides," Nerissa told her companions. There were six rooms, and six remaining vampires not counting Lord Karazin. Would they find one in each room?

So far, they had not lost a single Brigade member, and Malden wanted to keep it that way. He had Grindmar divide up them into groups of five, each standing station outside a door. If a fight in one of the rooms brought vampires out of the others, they would be met with an overwhelming force.

On Malden's signal, each of the six doors was opened at once. None was locked. Bernadette, leading the team that included Erik and Andrion as well as two others, crept silently into the room and cast a light spell. As the globe floated up to the ceiling, it became clear that nobody was in this room with its six small beds.

As they came back out there was a crashing sound, and two Brigade members came hurtling backwards out of a room at the end of the hall with lightning wreathing them like gossamer cloaks. Of course, it stood to reason that vampires would acquire skills with magic, having all those centuries in which to study and practice.

The next room down on this side had been empty as well, but the room across the hall from it was apparently the site of a pitched battle. Bernadette hurried over and poked her head in. Two Brigade members lay slumped against the far wall, and a vampire man and woman, completely naked, stood back to back as the other three members of that five-person team tried to get at them with swords. Stupid!

"Everybody close your eyes!" Bernadette yelled, and whipped out the Staff of Apoldros. Once again the world went bright behind her closed lids, and the vampires gave an agonized scream. As the two huddled, blistered and smoking from the close-range blast of sunlight, the attackers leaped forward to run them through. Being careful to avoid the blood, she hurried across the room to see to the two downed men.

They had merely been stunned, she was relieved to see. No healing spell was going to bring someone back from a broken neck. Moments later the fallen men were on their feet, and meanwhile Erik and Andrion had run down the hall to help with the other three rooms where resting vampires were found. As Bernadette and the rest of the group emerged from the room, one of the men she'd just revived told her, "We found them two fucking! And sucking, like – but not the way you might expect!" He seemed to think this was just the sort of information a young woman like herself might be eager to hear.

Two of the remaining three rooms had contained a single vampire each, and the third had held another pair – but these had merely been resting and had put up a hell of a fight when the Daywatch fighters had burst in on them. Andrion had been the one to set the vampire mage's robe on fire with a doubled-up burst of firebolts, halting his attacks as four crossbows drew a bead and brought him down at last.

That was the last of the vampires, thank Aderos! Or, maybe Apoldros… Not counting the Big Cheese himself, whom Bernadette was *not* very eagerly looking forward to meeting. "Everyone who came in contact with blood, take another panacea potion," Grindmar commanded. In Bernadette's absence, another budding chemiast had followed the instructions she'd left and prepared dozens of vials of the stuff.

"What now, Nerissa?" Bernadette asked. "Do we chase down those thralls and try to get them into our camp, or go after your father first?" The vampire woman considered. "I think we'll better go after Father now," she said. "The thralls should be rounding themselves up in the kitchen for their supper in a little more than an hour from now.

And if we succeed in killing Father, his death will make it all that much easier for me to break their enthrallment."

And if we *don't* succeed, Bernadette thought, it probably won't matter because we'll all be dead. Stifling a shudder, she said "All right. Do we all mob your father at once, or what?"

"I think I'd better confront him alone, first," Nerissa replied. "Maybe you, Erik, and Andrion can follow along close behind to lend me some support, but everyone else should hang back unless it looks like a melee is called for. I don't want any more people than necessary getting hurt."

Bernadette considered this statement, and decided to take it in the way it was probably meant: that she, Erik and Andrion were the Brigade's most skilled and effective fighters, and less likely to fall than the rest. She refused to believe that Nerissa thought them expendable.

Nerissa led them up another flight of stairs leading off a corridor to the south, and down another corridor to a pair of ornate black metal doors. The figures worked in them were disturbing to look at. "This is the family… chapel, I guess you'd call it. It's where we worshiped Haemion, and where I underwent the ritual to transform me into a Netherblood. Everyone here, some of the thralls excepted, was expected to pay regular worship to Lord Haemion, and Father often comes here to meditate."

Bernadette had a horrible thought. "Um, is this daimonic lord likely to put in a personal appearance when we burst in and start attacking his darling boy?" Nerissa smiled bitterly at the thought.

"Not likely," she said. Traveling between this plane and the plane of the Netherworld where Haemion rules others of his kind requires a great deal of energy. To bring him here usually requires a blood sacrifice, the entire blood supply of half a dozen adult humans, say. Plus a virgin girl waiting to be dedicated to him as an additional lure…" She shuddered.

Oog, Bernadette thought. I'm sorry I asked. "We'll be right behind you," was all she said, and hung back as Nerissa walked forward and opened the chapel doors. A dark figure in a black cloak with a scarlet lining knelt before a blood-stained altar at the far end of the room, and as she stepped down the aisle Bernadette, Erik, and Andrion crept in behind her as quietly as possible.

Though no one had made a sound, the vampire lord seemed to sense their presence. He stood, a tightly-muscled but slender man nearly Erik's height with coldly handsome features and glossy black hair. Bright red candles burned in tall candlesticks on either side of the altar, and in sconces around the room, casting flickering shadows.

"Nerissa, my darling. You have returned." Lord Karazin looked around the room with an eagle gaze, eyes glowing orange. "But where is your bitch of a mother? Did she not come with you?"

"I have no idea where Mother has gone," Nerissa told him. "You drove her away, as you drove me. All over some prophecy that was nothing but a sham, a trick – and described an act that would probably bring about the death of you, me, and everyone else on Terris."

"Nonsense!" the vampire lord thundered, seeming somehow to grow taller. "I will find that staff, and I will infuse it with your blood and soul. When we can walk in the day as we do in the night, our people will rule the world! And *I* will be their overlord – for all eternity! I will be as a god!"

"If you think to have my blood for your insane purposes, Father," Nerissa said with steel in her voice, "you will have to come and take it!" With that, casting her cloak aside, the woman before them transformed into a creature seven feet tall, dark red of skin, with long pointed ears and a three-foot tail tipped with spikes like those of a dragon. She had long, leathery wings sprouting from her shoulders. Actually, she rather resembled the overall shape of those ill-fated stone demons out front, but considerably more slender. She had breasts, but they were small – almost unnoticeable.

The room was a hundred feet end to end, forty feet wide, and the ceiling rose fifty feet above the center aisle leading to the altar. As Nerissa flapped her wings and lifted off the ground, firing twin streams of lightning, Lord Karazin transformed into a similar, but correspondingly larger and more powerful, version of the same daimonic creature – the male of the species.

"Get him!" Bernadette cried, and Andrion began shooting fire bolts at the flying vampire lord as she and Erik drew their fire-damage bows. For such an enormous flying creature in a relatively small space, Lord Karazin was proving surprisingly agile and hard to draw a bead on. But when he went on the attack, she was able to get an arrow into him and Erik another.

They were hurting him! The daimons of the Netherworld were not truly gods, just long-lived flesh-and-blood creatures with powers that were not common to the ordinary humans of Terris. In this form Lord Karazin was certainly pretty damn scary, but other than being able to fly he wasn't necessarily any more effective than he had been as a man.

As Bernadette was thinking this, a sizzling bolt of lightning flew past her to crash into one of the chapel's ceiling supports, and all of the hair on her head and arms stood up. Yeow! She dodged out of the way, running along the outer edge of a row of stone benches, and stepped out into the aisle for another shot at the flying monster.

Karazin was bleeding from half a dozen arrow strikes now, and there was a blackened and blistered scorch mark across his belly where Andrion had struck him with fire. Suddenly Bernadette flung herself to the side again as the flying vampire came down the aisle at speed, twelve feet in the air. But he was not chasing her – he was making for the altar!

He touched down, his bare feet on the bloody surface, and a shimmering field seemed to envelop him. Bernadette, still standing near, fired an arrow at point-blank range – and it bounced off! Shit, he was drawing power from that altar somehow and it was enabling him to shield himself from attack... and his wounds were healing too! Lord Haemion might not be able to be here in person, but seemingly he'd provided his protégé with one hell of an advantage.

In desperation, Bernadette pulled out the staff while still holding the bow in her other hand. She pointed it at Lord Karazin from a distance of no more than six feet. "Nerissa! Hide!" she shrieked, and turned to see her friend diving for the far corner of the room. The soundless actinic blast dazzled Bernadette's closed eyes as she willed the staff to release its power.

"Aaauuugh!" the vampire lord howled, writhing in agony. The sunlight had passed right through his shield just as room light did, which Bernadette had hoped would be the case. Otherwise he wouldn't have been visible behind it, right? Lucky guess. Lord Karazin was blistered over the entire side of his body that had been hit by the light, in a half crouch as he screamed his pain and rage.

"Shoot now, Erik!" Bernadette shouted, as she stood off to one side and drew her own bow. "Thwip! Thwip!" With a meaty double smack, two arrows appeared in the vampire lord's chest. Erik's bow was nearly a foot longer and had twice the pull of hers, and though he was much further away both buried themselves almost to the fletchings – a couple of inches apart.

His shrieks subsiding into a burbling moan, Lord Karazin seemed to dissolve before their eyes, collapsing into a red ruin on the altar top. The repellant goo slopped over the edges and began dripping to the floor. Bernadette turned her eyes away, her gorge rising. The man was even more disgusting in death than he'd been in life!

At the far end of the room she saw Nerissa flutter to the floor and transform back into her human form. Somehow, the leather armor she was wearing was back in place though she'd appeared to be unclothed as a daimon. Malden, Grindmar, and the rest of the crew came in, weapons at their sides, gazing in horror at the altar.

"Well, now that's done," Malden said, grim satisfaction in his voice. He seemed relieved that their trust in Nerissa had not been misplaced. He turned to Nerissa, seeming to regard her as human for possibly the first time since they'd met. "I… I suppose this is difficult for you," he said haltingly."

As if trying to put him at his ease Nerissa replied, "No. My father had become a monster, as dangerous to his own kind as he was to the rest of the world. He had to be put out of his misery." But despite her harsh words, there was an edge of sorrow in her voice.

Shaking herself and getting a grip on her emotions, Nerissa said "It would be good if everyone in the Brigade could stay out of the way until the enthralled servants come through the dining hall on their way into dinner," she said. "As many of them were enthralled to my father, they may have sensed his death or at least gotten the feeling that something was wrong. I need to be down there to meet them, to take control and assure that they don't attack us. Later on they can be freed, I hope."

The Daywatch Brigade occupied the three vampire resting rooms that had contained no occupants earlier, and were free of bloody corpses now. They closed and barred the doors behind themselves, and then sat around on the beds – eating food and drinking water from their packs, talking among themselves. The emotional reactions to the raid ran the gamut from excited jubilation to traumatic shock. Most had experienced combat and lived to tell of it, but few had taken on such foes before.

In another hour Nerissa came upstairs and began knocking on doors. "It's all right," she called, "You can all come out now." They filed out into the corridor and went down the stairs to the blood-spattered dining hall, seeing no one. "I've replaced my father's enthrallment on the servants with my own," their hostess explained. "They've all been told that it was time for father and his minions to go, and that this was good and proper. After they've had their supper, they will go to their quarters as usual. And in the morning, they will begin cleaning this place out."

"What will you do now?" Bernadette asked Nerissa.

"I'm not sure," she replied. "I need to search for my mother, see if I can figure out where she fled to. She's the rightful mistress of Hordenhaal, and I feel sure she will rule more kindly here than my father did. Theirs was an arranged marriage, and though she went along with my father's wishes for a long time I don't think she ever really forgave him for putting her – and me – through Haemion's Netherblood ritual."

"After that," Nerissa went on, "I think I'll think I'll return to Daywatch. They ought to see the benefits of having a vampire on their side, now." Bernadette squeezed her friend's hand.

"I'm going to be busy for a few weeks, planning two weddings. But I trust the Daywatch Brigade can get along without me now. They certainly proved themselves capable today, and they'll have the Staff of Apoldros as a part of their arsenal."

The grim Daywatch leader came up to them, and formally took Nerissa's hand. "You have proven yourself worthy of our trust," he said sincerely. "And you have earned my thanks." To Bernadette he added, "The Daywatch Brigade will dedicate itself to keep the staff safe, making sure that prophecy will never come to pass. You, too, have my thanks." He nodded to Andrion and Erik, saying "And you as well." Erik was grinning, that boyish look of evil glee he sometimes had when he'd just successfully turned his enemies into paste.

As Malden went off Bernadette turned to Nerissa again. "Nerissa, have you ever considered taking the cure, becoming fully human again? If you want to do it, I'll support you all the way." The vampire woman looked from Bernadette to Andrion and Erik, and back again.

"I'll think about it," she said. "But I'm going to have to talk to someone in Normarsh. Could you give me a ride?"

Chapter 30: Triumphant

They took Malden, and the rest of the Daywatch Brigade, back to their hidden fortress – arriving in the early part of the night. Bernadette had explained to him that she was not sure she'd be able to join them again – not with all that she had on her plate. But if they needed to recharge the Staff of Apoldros, they should send a messenger to her at the Bathing Maiden in Waterdon and she would see it done.

Nerissa promised to return in a few weeks, after she'd taken care of her personal business, and the four of them – Bernadette, Andrion, Erik, and Nerissa – set off again via map for Normarsh. That damp place was not all that far, geographically, from Closevale and Daywatch, and it appeared they'd arrived sometime past midnight.

"I'll be perfectly fine," Nerissa told them. "I know my way around these parts well and I *am* a creature of the night – at least for now!" Bernadette and the men each hugged her, then vanished as they were whisked away by map to the Bathing Maiden. The sun had not long ago climbed over the eastern horizon. Bernadette's heart swelled with joy at the sight of home appearing before her eyes. "Last one in's a shri!" she said cheerily to her companions, and headed for the front door.

Soon the three of them were soaking in the tub. They talked about their recent quest, then conversation moved to the future. "So," Erik remarked with a twinkle, "I guess Lifa and Bjorn will be getting married soon?" Bernadette smiled at the thought.

"Let's go see them after we've had some rest," she said. "I need to talk about a few things with them, and there are some preparations I want to make before the wedding."

Andrion eyed her sidelong. "What about *our* wedding?" he asked. He still wasn't completely convinced it was going to happen. Would Berni continue to elude them both without making a commitment? She looked thoughtful.

"I still haven't figured out exactly how we're going to do that," she admitted. "And aside from that issue, I want us to have our own place together. I love it here in the Maiden, but this is more like a public trust than our personal property – and there are always strangers wandering through. But I don't want to move too far away from Waterdon. I like this area, and I want to be close to Anja while she's growing up. Maybe you guys could look around while I'm running my errands and see if there are any places available? I've got all that loot I just polished up ready to sell, and that should bring a fair amount of gold…"

Erik and Andrion exchanged a glance over Berni's head as she was momentarily abstracted, thinking about her plans. Both of them were getting some ideas. They hoped their family would be growing, so a house in town was a bad idea – no room for expansion. But there was a lot of open space in the countryside near the Maiden, and a couple of farms that, perhaps, might come on the market if the price were right.

After a pleasant soak they got out, and dispersed to their sleeping areas. It had been nearly 48 hours of actual time since any of them had slept, and Bernadette and Andrion fell into the master bed without even a half-hearted suggestion that they would make love first.

Some hours later Bernadette awoke refreshed. The excitement of all the plans she had to put into motion was making it hard for her to stay asleep, and she was already fully dressed – in light leather armor and with a dagger at her belt – by the time Andrion awoke. "Are you coming?" she asked. He threw the covers off and gave a couple of tugs to his cock, peering down at it as if it were something he hadn't seen before. "Apparently not," he said in a tone of disappointment.

Bernadette snorted. "Come on, you, let's go!" She left him to get into his clothes and headed downstairs. Erik was in the common room, dressed in soft, casual clothing and unarmed. Looking her over with mild surprise he said, "Are we expecting a battle of some sort?"

"I thought it would be enjoyable to walk into town, since the weather's so nice," Bernadette replied.

"I've been walking back and forth for weeks, and it's been perfectly safe," Erik said smiling, "but if anybody attacks us I'll just rip them apart with my bare hands." She rolled her eyes at him. He was joking, but she didn't doubt he could and would do it.

Andrion soon joined them, and they gathered up some supplies and food items from Lev before setting out. "I want to throw a little celebratory dinner at Brightsgate Cottage this evening," Bernadette told her men as they started. "I feel like this is the start of a new and better life for all of us."

"Good idea," Erik said. Then he added, "Can I cook it?" Bernadette halted her stride and turned to stare at him.

"I beg your pardon," she told him. "It sounded as if you just asked to cook us all dinner."

Erik gave her a grin that was half cherub, half formidable warrior – both of which he was, when you came down to it. "I never mentioned I like to cook?" he asked as if surprised. Andrion, too, was looking at him in disbelief. During the years the two had spent together as employees of the Maiden, all of their meals had been provided for them. Bernadette had that feeling again, as if she had stepped into some unexpected alternate universe where everyone she knew was harboring hidden talents.

"You realize the facilities at Brightsgate Cottage are pretty limited, right?" Bernadette asked him, trying to take a more businesslike approach. "And do you have a menu in mind?"

"I think I can come up with something we'll like from what we're carrying right now. And if I need anything else I can run up to the market and buy some more supplies."

She resumed walking, saying offhandedly, "I'll leave it up to you, then. And thanks."

They passed Stormstrife Farm across the road from the Maiden, and a little further up the road Coldburn Farm, a narrow twenty acres with a small farmhouse and mill tower. Crossing the river on a stone bridge they turned east and passed the Bees' Brew Meadery, before crossing again and passing the stables. Bernadette had once thought it might be a good idea to keep some horses here; but as her travels in Iscandia had marked more and more locations for her on her map, it had no longer seemed worthwhile. Horses took effort and expense to keep, and she was not a very good rider in any case. Plow horses belonging to her farm-dwelling childhood playmates in the region around Pied-de-Puce were the only ones she'd ever had much contact with.

As they passed Waterdon's main gates, the guards welcomed Erik heartily. He *did* mention he'd been coming here a lot. Inside, Bernadette spotted Alessia working at her forge, and greeted her.

"We just got back from killing the vampire lord that was threatening Iscandia," she told her.

"I hope that means we won't be getting any more vampire attacks," the smith replied.

"Me too," Bernadette said, "but there are still vampires around. Let me know if you see any. Oh, and say hi to Wolaf." With that, they continued to the front door of Brightsgate Cottage.

Bernadette knocked, and the door was opened shortly by Bjorn. He was wearing trousers and a leather jerkin, and looking more relaxed than ever. Clearly, family life was agreeing with him. Bernadette gave him a slight hug and a kiss on the cheek, then she and her companions came inside the little house. Lifa was folding some wash on the dining table, and Anja was "helping" her.

They looked up, expressions of delight on their faces. "Aunt Berni!" Anja squealed, and rushed to be picked up and kissed. "You've grown!" Bernadette exclaimed, a warm squishy wave of affection washing over her along with a hint of regret that she'd missed even a couple of weeks of the child's life. Anja looked pleased at this pronouncement. What child doesn't long to grow up, even as the grownups are wishing they could return to childhood?

Bernadette passed her squirming fire-haired armful to Andrion, and turned to greet Lifa. The woman's eyes were shining as she stood and extended her hands to squeeze those of her warden and friend. "I'm so glad you've returned safely!" she said. "Did you… uh, succeed?"

Bernadette smiled broadly at her. "Yes. We bearded the evil vampire lord in his den, and killed him and his minions. We had a lot of help from Nerissa and the Daywatch Brigade, fortunately."

Lifa felt a twinge of wistfulness as she heard of these bold deeds. She was a superbly trained and competent fighter, and as much as she loved Anja and her new life here in Brightsgate Cottage, there were times when she missed the excitement and satisfaction of armed combat in the cause of Good. But now, she was starting to think there might be another reason for her stay away from danger.

Andrion had now passed Anja to "Uncle Erik," whom the little girl adored. It was he who came to see her almost every day, bringing her treats and playing games with her or taking her around the town to play in the fountains or socialize with some of the other children in town. He gave her a kiss, then seated her in the crook of one massive arm so she could participate as he and Andrion began telling Bjorn about their recent exploits. Bjorn, too, while happy to hear about the fight, was a little regretful he hadn't been there participating.

Lifa and Bernadette sat side by side on the table's outside bench. "So," Lifa said, broaching the subject delicately, "now that you're finished with your anti-vampire campaign, when do you think we might be able to have the wedding?" Bernadette grinned.

"Eager for it, are you? I need to talk with you about some details and I have some business to take care of first, but I think we could be ready in, say, three weeks' time? Will that be okay?" Lifa felt a little bad about pushing her warden on the matter, after all that Bernadette had done for her; but if she was right, it would best to get married as quickly as possible.

"Three weeks will be all right," she said. "Will you be able to fast-travel us to Lakedon?"

Bernadette hadn't even considered the possibility that she might not. "I was actually able to transport thirty-one people during our raid on Lord Karazin," she said confidently. "Your wedding party should be no trouble at all." At this point Anja, who was finding the men's talk less than entrancing, wriggled down from her perch on Erik to run over and join her and Lifa where they sat talking.

"Aunt Berni, I can read now!" the little girl announced.

"Really? That's wonderful!" Bernadette told her, glancing at Lifa. Lifa beamed, the warm smile of a proud mother.

"Bjorn made her an A-B-C book, and she's memorized it, I think. But it's a start. Anja, why don't you get your book and read it for Aunt Berni?"

"Okay!" chimed the exuberant youngster, and ran to the "spare bedroom." The nook with the extra bed in it had become the family's library, a quiet corner in which to read.

Anja returned in a moment lugging a book about a foot square, with thin boards for covers. The boards and the pages within them had been pierced with holes, then bound with strips of rawhide. "Bjorn is amazingly handy," Lifa remarked. "We picked up a few tools from Bernard's and he's set up a sort of work area out behind the house. He's been building all kinds of things." Bernadette glanced around and realized there was now a painted wooden rocking horse standing over in the corner near the spare bed.

Anja squeezed in between Berni and the woman she was coming to think of as "Mama," and rested the book on her lap. The first page showed a remarkably lifelike painting of an apple. "A is for apple," the gamin pronounced sagely. Then she flipped the page over. "B is for Boy," she said, then added "That's Lars. Sometimes Bjorn takes me to play with him." Bernadette was certainly impressed, not only at the bright child's leap toward literacy but at the beautiful artwork in the book. Bjorn might be a hell of a fighter but his talents were being wasted if he did nothing but wield an axe all day.

They sat there listening and admiring the pictures as Anja "read" all the way through to "Z is for Zombie" – which she then told Bernadette was another name for aptrgangr. Where in heaven's name had this small child learned anything about aptrgangr? Lifa, sensing her unspoken question, explained, "I told her about them. Bjorn and I can keep her entertained for hours with tales of our adventures. And, I made friends with Garimund while I was living up at Wyrmshalla. He lets me borrow books from the castle library."

The "reading" session concluded, Bernadette smilingly thanked her young ward, giving her an affectionate squeeze and a kiss on the forehead. Then she resumed her discussion with Lifa. "I need to know how many people I will need to move around," she explained. "I think we'll have a big party at the Maiden after the wedding, so I'll need to gather anybody you want to be at the ceremony in Lakedon at the Maiden, then move you and us and whoever else back to the Maiden afterward for the party."

Lifa considered thoughtfully. She could hardly believe this was happening. When she'd pledged her service to Ormund, she had expected to lead a life of service to the march, and probably give it up while still a young woman in some conflict or another, fighting to defend the life of her warden – whoever that might turn out to be. Now, a completely different future was opening up before her, though her obligations to the march had not ceased. As long as her warden wanted her to live at Brightsgate Cottage and look after Anja, that was her duty as well as her delight.

But the life she had chosen for herself after her parents had died had not led to her forming a lot of close friendships. She looked back on the last few years, before Anja – and later, Bjorn – had opened her heart; and she could not relate to the person she had been. I was so *serious* then, she thought. She didn't realize how serious she *still* was, though the focus of her seriousness had changed. Whatever Lifa set herself to, she put all her soul into it. But now, it was paying her back in warmth and joy and feelings she had never before experienced.

"I have a few friends at the Maiden, and I've made some friends around town since we've been living here in Brightsgate Cottage," Lifa said, "… I would love to have them come to the party afterward. But as far as Lakedon is concerned, the only person I really think should be there is Eorl Ormund. He holds my oath, and I think he should be present at the wedding. I don't have any family."

"You do now," Bernadette told her, squeezing her hand. Lifa looked a bit flustered. "I'll see if I can get the eorl to join us," she promised. "And please give me a list of any other people you want at the party, and I'll make sure they get invitations." Bernadette just sat there for a moment, her arm around Anja – who was taking all of this in with a certain amount of interest. What little girl isn't interested in weddings? Well, that's sorted, she thought. She still needed to pose a similar set of questions to Bjorn. Would he want Eorl Galdur to attend?

Realizing that the afternoon was getting on, Bernadette turned to Lifa once again. "I thought we might have a little celebration here tonight, in honor of the fact that we've defeated the evil vampire lord and also because of your forthcoming nuptials. Is that okay?"

"I didn't really have any plans," Lifa assured her.

"Good! I hope… I have to warn you, Erik has said that he will be cooking for us." Lifa smiled at her broadly, an expression Bernadette had seldom seen on her face before.

"Oh!" she said. "Well *that* will be all right then."

Bernadette gave her a questioning look. "You didn't know Erik likes to cook?" Lifa asked her, somewhat surprised. "While you and

Andrion and Nerissa were off questing, he was here with food a couple of nights a week. He said he never got the chance to cook at the Maiden…"

"Well I'll be dipped in dragon shit," Bernadette muttered profanely – then glanced to see whether Anja had noticed. Anja was turning the pages of the book in her lap, her lips moving slightly as she went through them again, and Bernadette had some faint hope that her expletive had not been heard. If she was about to start spending more time around children, she was going to have to get a grip on her tongue.

Looking over to the men, Bernadette realized they were still shooting the breeze about their martial exploits, recent and otherwise. Get a bunch of warriors together in a room, and the talk about killing and maiming could go on for hours. Not that she didn't get positive enjoyment out of defeating enemies, and could certainly enjoy discussing techniques or rehashing past battles. But there *were* other topics of conversation in this wide world.

Raising her voice a bit to be heard over their masculine banter Bernadette said, "Hey, Erik! Do you suppose it's time to get started cooking?"

He broke his attention off from the discussions that had been occupying him, Andrion, and Bjorn to say, "Hmm. I suppose it is. Excuse me, gentlemen…" They'd dropped their sacks of supplies on the floor when they came in and had then become distracted by conversation. Now he gathered up all they'd brought with them and carried it over to the table saying "Excuse me, ladies… and Berni." She gave him a mock glare.

Erik dropped the provisions on the table and began spreading them out to rummage through them. "I wish this place was big enough for a real kitchen," he remarked as he began assembling his ingredients and seasonings. Bernadette was intrigued. She, too, enjoyed cooking but was often put off it by the pathetic facilities available in most Iscandia homes.

"Need some help chopping?" she asked, wanting to get some more insights into this latest unexpected facet of her beloved golden warrior.

"Sure," he replied. Lifa and Anja got up to give them room, drifting over to hang out with Andrion and Bjorn. Bernadette noticed that Lifa slipped beneath Bjorn's arm as if she belonged there, Anja snuggling up against her leg. Erik produced a large cast iron pot with a wire bale handle, suitable for hanging on a hook above the fire. The central fire pit that occupied such a large part of Brightsgate Cottage's main living area was capable of holding two or three such hooks in addition to a three-foot spit for roasting meats.

"I'd like three or four onions, half a dozen carrots, and a couple of apples chopped up about like this," he said, holding up one of his huge hands and indicating a size equal to about half the smallest joint of his pinky finger. "Those should go in this bowl. Then in the kettle I want more carrots and onions, but about twice as big. And a couple of cabbages, cut up into one-inch pieces, along with about 4 potatoes the same size. Got it?"

Bernadette goggled at him for a moment, hardly believing she'd been sleeping with this man for the past several months without having ever actually met him. Having also fallen in love with him and promised to marry him, she welcomed this new and unlooked-for aspect of his personality as just another reason for that love. And, having many years' experience as a scullery maid of sorts (what else are eldest daughters for, after all?) she got right to work on the chopping.

Meanwhile, Erik produced three dead chickens from one of the sacks they'd brought. Huh, she hadn't noticed those. With a pot of water he'd gotten Andrion to heat for him in a hurry, he soon had their feathers off and back into the sack, along with the heads, feet, and innards he'd neatly removed with a razor-sharp knife. Anybody in the habit of decapitating aptrgangr or gutting bandits had better not be squeamish about poultry, and Bernadette observed all this with a clinical interest.

As he was finishing with the chickens, she had filled the bowl with the chopped veggies as requested. Erik added some salt and a few chopped herbs, then began filling the late chickens' body cavities with the mixture from the bowl. After that he wrapped them up in some twine, and spitted them before placing them over the fire to roast. Bernadette was impressed, and also felt a little… cheated, somehow. Why hadn't he ever offered to cook for *her* in all these months?

After the chickens were sizzling over the fire, Erik hung the pot in which she'd put the other veggies over it as well, with a good quantity of water added along with salt and more herbs. After that, the two of them were able to relax, sipping some chilled ale (Andrion had become quite adept at applying his frost spells to the chilling of beverages, thus making him a popular fellow at any gathering) and relaxing as they waited for the food to cook.

Bernadette made a move on Bjorn, dragging him away from the conversation of Erik and Andrion to ask him about his guest list for the wedding. He seemed lost in thought for a while, considering. Like Lifa, he was without family and had spent most of his adult life in service to the march. But the eorl to whom he had originally given his oaths had been supplanted as a result of the political shake-up some months back. Eorl Galdur had taken over those oaths along with the rest of Westmarch, but it was not to him that Bjorn truly felt loyalty.

"Can you find Eorl Hjaermond for me?" he asked. Bernadette knew *just* where to find him. The hapless ex-eorl now whiled away his hours in the basement at the eorl's palace in Sylvanian, with others who had suffered a similar fall. She had chanced upon them while fulfilling a quest several weeks ago. "I'm sure he'd be delighted to attend," she told Bjorn. "And if there's anyone here in Waterdon you'd like to invite to the party at the Maiden, just give me their names."

Bjorn gave her a shy look. Getting up in the faces of Insurgents or standing off bandits, this man knew no fear. Put him into a social situation with women, and suddenly he was tongue-tied. Yet he'd somehow managed to win over Lifa, a woman Erik had failed to get through to. Bernadette could only assume the two of them had a bond forged by the similar paths they had taken in life. She gave him a reassuring smile and said, "Just ask Lifa to give me a list with all the names on it, within the next week or so, okay?" He smiled back at her with only a bit of discomfort showing and said, "Sure."

The chickens were sizzling before long, and done sooner than Bernadette had expected. They'd each (Anja excepted, of course) had a couple of ales and were beginning to feel pretty mellow. Erik slid the chickens off the spit and then used a razor-sharp kitchen knife (*not* a dagger, she noticed – where had he gotten such a thing?) to carve them up into quarters after spooning the now-steaming chopped veggies out of their centers.

That went into a bowl, the chicken quarters onto a large platter. The contents of the large pot, now cooked to bits, were pureed as Erik used his famously amazing arm strength to beat in a quantity of fresh cream with a Galise whisk, a tool Bernadette had not seen since coming to Iscandia. Meanwhile the bread rolls, fresh earlier today, were toasting on a curious-looking square grill mounted on four straight legs. Erik had set it into the fire as he took the pot off.

Bernadette was fascinated by all of this. Erik used some techniques she wasn't familiar with, and the results looked intriguing. As a woman of prodigious appetites in all things, she was eagerly looking forward to the taste test. And for almost the first time since they'd met, she was looking at this magnificent man with an eye to picking his brain instead of just trying to fuck his brains out.

Rousing herself from her reverie, Bernadette got on the ball and set the table as it appeared it was time for them to eat. The five adults and one small child fairly crowded the dining area as they gathered for the feast. Erik started them with steaming bowls of the savory cream soup, then presented the chicken with veggies and bread rolls on the side. They washed it down with a pale chilled wine from Auverne. How in all the hells had Erik managed *that*? Anja happily drank freshly squeezed apple juice, and as usual polished off far more food than Bernadette would have thought possible. With an appetite like that, Bernadette half expected her to be looking Bjorn in the eye in another few years.

The conversation was animated as they ate, and Anja was a happy participant. With no brothers or sisters she was the only non-adult in her family, and she seemed to accept that socializing with adults was what she was supposed to do. Since every adult there loved her and was willing to indulge her, she was included as a member of the group and her contributions were taken as seriously as anybody else's. In fact, they all found what she had to say delightful.

A five-year-old's perspective on the world is always worth listening to.

Still, as the evening wore on she began to tire. The energy of small children is concentrated, able to sweep adults off their feet; but that little package cannot have the reserves for a sustained effort. Her stamina abandoned her, and Bjorn hugged her to him as he noticed her flagging. "About ready for bed, Ani?" he asked. Many children would have resisted, but Anja seemed to have a good sense of herself.

"I'm sleepy," Anja replied. "Will you read to me?"

"Say goodnight to your Aunt Berni and your uncles first," he told her. She got down from the bench and went around bestowing hugs and kisses. Then Bjorn had her select a book from the shelves near the spare bed before scooping her up to carry her to her bedroom on the floor above.

The four remaining continued their conversation, and Bjorn rejoined them in a few minutes. Bernadette noticed how peaceful his expression was. She felt a profound sense of happiness that her efforts had brought this family together. She loved Anja and wanted always to be a part of her life, but she knew that Lifa and Bjorn had truly become the girl's parents.

The celebration wound down and Bernadette reminded Lifa that a list of the local people she and Bjorn would like to have invited to the forthcoming party should be given to Erik or dropped off at the Maiden within the next week, if she was not yet back from her planned errands. Then she, Erik and Andrion made their farewells, stepped outside the door, and fast-travelled back to the Maiden.

Chapter 31: An Interlude

As they walked in the door, Bernadette took a breath. She was floating pleasantly on a combination of ale, wine, and jubilation at the successful conclusion of their quest – and the promise of joy in the future. This did not seem to be the time to tell one man, "See you in the morning" while going off for hot sex with the other. She looked from Andrion to Erik and back again. "What do you think, guys? Threesome?"

She had not made love with the two of them at once since early in the days when she'd first realized that, as much as she was smitten with Andrion, she loved and wanted Erik as well. One-on-one gave more opportunities for losing yourself in the loved one, jumping into a river current that could sweep you both along to explosions of ecstasy. But making love with both of them together was exciting – and it meant that neither would be completely left out or relegated to "sloppy seconds."

Erik and Andrion met each other's gaze above her head, and they were of an accord: go for it! The new understanding among the two of them and their beloved seemed to have cemented their friendship more firmly, somehow. They were now brothers, bonded by their battles together and by the love they both felt for Berni. And watching her take it from both ends at once was an experience not to be missed.

So, in agreement, the three of them climbed the stairs to the sleeping loft and proceeded down the western gallery to the master suite. Bernadette's excitement was rising as she began removing her leather armor. Andrion soon peeled out of his vest, and he and Erik began taking off other articles of clothing. Shortly they were all standing there in their underclothes, and Bernadette stepped close to Andrion to lift up his shirt. She bent to lick his navel, and as she did so Erik pulled her underdrawers down and ran his hands over her buttocks.

Ooh! Encouraging Andrion to pull his undershirt up over his head she turned her attention to his drawers, pulling them down to his knees and exposing his rampant cock. Grabbing double handfuls of his muscular butt cheeks, Bernadette bore down on him. She'd been perfecting her technique on him and him alone, and she was now able to gobble Andrion almost down to the root – though it did tend to choke her a bit. She wondered if there were some way to suppress the gag reflex and take him *all* the way in.

Behind her, meanwhile, Erik had removed his own underclothing. He pulled her undershirt up over her head, only momentarily inconveniencing her as she bent her mouth and hands to pleasuring Andrion. Wrapping himself around her from behind, he squeezed her breasts with his hands as his pulsing cock nestled in her backside like a sausage in a roll. Even as Bernadette devoted most of her attention to taking Andrion inside her mouth, the feel of that hot, hard member pressing against her filled her with excitement.

Bernadette wriggled a bit and her drawers slid down from her knees to the floor, whereupon she stepped out of them with one leg and used the other to kick them to the side. Now she was able to spread her legs wider apart, giving her a better height for sucking Andrion's cock as well as an opening for Erik – if he was picking up on her signals.

Oh, he was. Putting two fingers inside her to assure that she was wet and ready to receive him, he guided his throbbing member into her vestibule and began working it further inside, a little bit at a time. With each thrust it went deeper, until he was buried to his full length within her. Electrified by the sensation as his huge cock filled her, Bernadette gulped and gobbled Andrion with even more enthusiasm, taking him in deeper than she had ever managed before. But as Erik began pumping into her faster, she had to ease off on Andrion for a while so she could breathe. The panting as she approached orgasm required more air than she could get through her nose.

She still managed to suck down on him hard about every other breath, not wanting to short-change him on the action. Besides, the presence of his thick, insistent cock in her mouth, the slight saltiness of the fluids she was extracting from him, filled her with even more urgency. In moments she was coming, standing up, in a way she wouldn't have thought possible. Oh, by the gods!

Andrion and Erik both managed to hold on through Berni's climax, though it was a close thing. Her excitement was contagious – and for Erik, his cock encased within her and feeling her spasms, it was almost too much to bear. The fact they were both standing helped a bit. It takes a certain amount of attention to stay on your feet.

Andrion reached down to hold her shoulders, helping her to support her weight as she shuddered and screamed around her meaty mouthful. Then he raised her up, gently, and kissed her passionately. Behind her, Erik pulled out and wrapped her about in a tight hug, his arms encircling Andrion as well. Then the three stepped apart a bit. "How about the bed?" Erik suggested, gasping for breath.

Bernadette recovered enough awareness to consider this proposal, and it seemed like a good idea. The three of them fell down on the coverlet for a moment. Then Andrion bent and began working his way down from her navel to her sex, pleasuring her with his mouth, while Erik kissed her thrillingly and fondled her breasts, tweaking her nipples to erectness as he stimulated her lips, her ears, her neck with his mouth and tongue.

Swamped by the sensations, Bernadette kept one hand on Andrion's head while the other gripped Erik's cock and she erupted in another orgasm that seemed to go on for minutes. Andrion smiled up at her as she vibrated, screaming. When she had settled down from that he suggested, with gestures, that she kneel on the bed in front of him. Then he entered her from behind as Erik, standing at the bedside, received the benefit of her mouth, tongue, and spare hand.

The three of them moved in rhythm, both men now feeling that it was time to let go. Bernadette sensed their surrender, and she put some extra effort into bringing them in. She had had two unbelievable trips to the stratosphere, and it was time for them to join her. Agh, if only she could take Erik all the way inside her mouth. As the sensations from her cunt mounted, Andrion's more than ample ramrod plowing her enthusiastically, she made a huge effort and stretched her mouth wider than ever before. Erik's cock filled her, pushing down past her teeth – past her tonsils, it felt like.

Glug! Her cunt spasmed one more time as Andrion pushed deep, deep inside her, shooting his wad. And at the same time, Erik's hot seed began spurting down her throat. Nearly choking, she swallowed convulsively and it almost felt as if she was going to have cum running out her nose. Good grief! Bernadette gasped for air, her knees feeling weak. There was a lot of that going around, as Andrion behind her and Erik at the front sagged, gasping and panting.

The three of them collapsed in a heap on the bed. Erik still couldn't quite believe what had just happened, and he was concerned. "Are you all right, Berni?" he asked. She gulped a couple more times, her chest heaving (fascinating to watch). Then she smiled at him, eyes somewhat glazed, and drew up to him to give him a passionate kiss. With her tongue pushing into his mouth he got a faint taste of his own spoog; but clearly she was okay.

Breaking away from the kiss, Bernadette fell back on the bed with her men on either side. She felt utterly drained, even though filled up to overflowing at the same time. And more than a little bit sticky, she realized. But she lacked the energy to get up and take a bath. "Andrion?" she said somewhat plaintively after she had recovered enough breath to speak. He bent to her attentively. "Could you hand me a damp towel? I don't think I can walk…"

Andrion rolled out of bed and poured some water into the basin on the chest of drawers, then dipped one of the Maiden's ubiquitous towels in it. He brought it back to the bed, and began giving Berni a sponge bath. He started at her face and neck and worked his way down, sure that once he hit the crotch he'd be needing a new towel. Bernadette sighed, lay back and just enjoyed it. As Andrion ministered to her, Erik rolled on his side and stroked her face, applying gentle kisses to her chin, neck, and shoulder.

The "bath" completed, Bernadette smiled and asked Andrion for a drink of water. He poured one from the ewer beside the basin into a tankard he found on the table. She thanked him, then scooted up into a sitting position to drink. Ah, that was better. "I think," she said sleepily, "that it's beddy-bye time now." Erik smiled and kissed her deeply.

"You sleep here, love," he told her. "I think I'd like to spread out in my bed downstairs." Her eyes opened wider briefly, sharp awareness mingling with love as she looked at him.

Then she drew him close for a hug and kiss before saying "Good night, love. See you in the morning."

Andrion bid Erik good night and the hulking Norseman gathered his clothing and put it back on before going down the stairs, headed for the basement sleeping area he had claimed for his own. True enough, this bed was a tight fit for the three of them. Erik was enormous, Andrion merely large; but add the two of them to Berni and you were going to need a bigger bed. Berni's thoughts appeared to be running in a similar vein, as she remarked "After we're married, I'd like us to have a really huge bed. And a bedroom for each of us, for when we just want to sleep."

That was a radical thought. Andrion had never seen a bed bigger than the one they were about to sleep in. But they were rich. They could have a bed built to whatever specifications they wanted. Make it big enough for the whole family, why not? He smiled to himself at the mental image of himself and Berni, packed into a gigantic bed with Erik and three or four kids.

Lying down beside his beloved, Andrion snuggled her into his arms and kissed her fervently. "I can't wait," he told her. Then they blew out the candles, and in a few more minutes they were both fast asleep.

Chapter 32: Projects

Bernadette came to consciousness snuggled tightly against Andrion's chest, his breath lightly blowing her hair as he snored gently. The temperature must have fallen overnight. She nuzzled in closer, squeezing him with her free arm and planting a warm kiss on his nipple. She felt his cock stir as she did so, and looked up to find him fully awake, eyes open and looking at her with warm affection and warmer lust. "Good morning love," she murmured quietly.

He stroked her face, pushing her hair back out of her eyes. "You're starting to change me, you know?" he remarked in a low voice. She looked at him questioningly. "Before I met you, I had a really hard time getting out of bed in the morning. Since I was a kid, I would sleep until noon if you let me. But sleeping with you is making me more of a morning person, or something…" She smiled, hugely pleased. Those who have never had any trouble rising early usually assume that those who do are that way due to some character flaw.

He bent his head slightly to give her a deep kiss, then asked "What are your plans for the day?"

"I've got to run some errands around Iscandia," she told him. "I shouldn't need any help, so you and Erik are free to stay here. Maybe you guys could check on local real estate like I asked?"

He nodded thoughtfully, saying "Good idea." In the meantime, his member was standing firm against her belly and her slit was getting moist from its proximity. She undulated beneath the covers, giving a little pelvic thrust and lifting a leg so that his shaft slipped into the groove and rubbed against her clit.

"Ooh," he gasped, gazing into her eyes. "You wanna?..." She nodded, her eyes glowing with love and desire. Then she yanked the covers off of them, giving her room to throw her leg up over his hip as she guided his throbbing erection inside. As he pushed all the way into her, she threw her head back and moaned. They made love lying on their sides for a while, then rolled over with him on top, so he could get some leverage. She spread her legs wide and bounced on the bed, meeting each of his thrusts with one of her own. He kissed her neck and collarbone as she threw her head back, keening as she rose toward her climax.

When Berni popped, Andrion did too. Despite his claim of newfound morning alertness he was still pretty sleepy, and she had taken him by surprise with this unexpected morning session. He couldn't count the number of times they'd made love since they'd met; but wouldn't have much trouble counting the times that had occurred immediately after waking. Probably wouldn't need both hands. He supposed it was just as well he'd come so soon. He doubted Berni was looking for anything beyond a little "goodbye kiss" before going off on her errands – certainly not a marathon fuck-fest.

After a brief rest, they both got up. Bernadette put on a robe and headed for the bathing pool, and Andrion followed her. They found Erik downstairs, sitting at their usual table and eating some breakfast. After a soak, Bernadette got out and went over to him, still wearing her robe, to give him a hug and a kiss – and steal a few morsels off his plate. He didn't even try to stop her.

Bernadette soon excused herself and went off to get dressed, putting on her leather armor and making sure she had plenty of weapons and potions in her pack. Then she slapped her forehead. Before she went anywhere, she needed to do some smithing. With the Maiden's well-stocked basement shelves, she could have set up in competition with Alessia if she'd had a mind to. First, though, she stopped off at the table again and ate some breakfast with Erik and Andrion before going downstairs. The two of them had been engaged in an animated discussion when she came over, but the talk seemed to be about the weather while she was there eating.

Bernadette went behind the bar and through the trap door, climbing down the ladder into the basement. As she arrived at the bottom, she looked at Erik's bed and a little shudder ran through her – centered on her crotch. She had enjoyed some of the hottest, most mind-blowing sex of her life down here, and not always on the bed. She shook herself. She'd been most thoroughly laid last night by *both* her studly hunks; and again, if more gently, this morning with Andrion. If she couldn't manage to survive a day or two without a dick inside her, it would be a sad state of affairs.

She wanted to ensure that the guys had plenty of money to work with in case they found a suitable property to buy. Eastview, which they already owned, would be nice, but it didn't have any room for expansion and more to the point it was in Alfenstein. Not the kind of place she wanted to be bringing up children, assuming they eventually had some. So, she set to work with a vengeance at the forge.

With freshly improved items and a big stack of things she and the others had picked up on quests, Bernadette filled her pack to overflowing and left the rest of it sitting in a couple of chests in the basement. Then she staggered back up the ladder to the Maiden's main floor. She went to the bar and asked Lev for some food. As she was wolfing down a bowl of vegetable soup and some fresh bread rolls, Andrion and Erik came in the front doors together. They were dressed in street clothes.

She waved to them and they came over, observing her bulging pack on the floor beside the bar and the fact that she looked ready to set off on a quest of some sort. "We just talked with Astrid across the road," Andrion told her. "She doesn't think the Stormstrife clan would be willing to sell. Apparently the farm is quite a money-maker for them." Bernadette pricked up her ears at that. Stormstrife Farm was directly across from the Maiden and would have a lot of advantages as far as its location went, as well as plenty of space for expansion. Too bad it wasn't for sale.

Finishing her stew, Bernadette told them "I left a big pile of arms and armor downstairs for you guys to sell while I'm gone. I'm counting on you to drive a hard bargain, Andrion!" she smiled, letting him know she wasn't entirely serious. "I'm taking a pack-full with me to Alfenstein, to sell to Dhyazh. I have a *ton* of errands to run, so I might be gone a few days. But don't worry about me." Despite her admonition both Erik and Andrion looked concerned. They respected her skills as a warrior and she had saved *their* asses in battle as often as they had hers; but they were used to guarding her back and hated to let her run off on her own.

Erik put a massive arm around her for a squeeze and said gruffly, "Stay out of trouble, you." She stood on tiptoe to give him a deep kiss.

"I promise," she said sweetly. Then she kissed Andrion as well before shouldering her pack and going out the door. They waved goodbye to her, both of them looking a little worried.

"She'll be all right," Andrion assured his friend. "Hell, she could probably kick *us* up one side of the street and down the other." Erik nodded.

Chapter 33: Staerlin

Bernadette arrived just inside the gates of Alfenstein and found to her dismay that it was nine in the evening, too late to visit either Dhyazh or the eorl. Well, wasn't this just why she had bought a house here? She took a sharp right then a left, heading up a steep staircase to a street on an upper level. A couple more turns and three more flights of steps brought her to the handsome dypalfar metal doors of Eastview, the key for which was in her pack.

Bernadette let herself in, went up the ramp to the main dining area and dropped her pack on the table. It was past suppertime here but she had only just finished eating lunch and wasn't very hungry. Nor did she feel particularly sleepy. The place seemed cavernous, empty – without Bjorn, Erik, or Andrion to share it with. She took a book from a shelf (the place had come with many such) and sat reading it for a while in a comfortable chair by the fire. Then, restless, she got up and carried her pack to the bedroom. She dumped it out and put the arms and armor she'd brought to sell in the trunk at the foot of the bed.

Then she peeled out of her leather armor and put on some town clothes. The nearby inn, where she had enjoyed a meal and a long talk with Andrion and Diane a couple of weeks ago, might offer a little entertainment and fellowship before it was time to go to sleep. Bernadette took along a little minor weaponry just to be on the safe side. The political situation in Alfenstein was uneasy, with a hidden faction of Insurgent supporters pitted against the ruling Staerlin family. Now that Galdur Staerlin was eorl, their apparent domination of the city was complete. But even with the streets well-patrolled by guards, she thought it wise to take precautions.

The inn was, of course, the Staerlin Inn. It was owned by the Staerlin clan, Bernadette was informed by the rather grumpy innkeeper. Karl and his wife Freya ran the place, but rather than trying to make visitors welcome they seemed to spend most of their time sniping at one another and airing their dirty laundry for the benefit of anyone who happened to be within earshot. Put off, Bernadette ordered a bottle of wine and a glass, along with a little bread and cheese to keep her from getting too drunk, and took her refreshments over to sit by the fire.

Despite the unwelcoming innkeepers the inn itself was spacious and attractive. And the area behind the U-shaped bar, a group of chairs around a cheery fire, was inviting. Bernadette seated herself by the hearth, setting her plate and bottle down then pouring herself a glass of wine and sitting back to enjoy the music being delivered by a bard over on the far side of the room.

Across from her sat a young Norseman who, from the armor he was dressed in, was most likely a mercenary. He was kind of hunky, though she was a bit put off by his war paint or tattoo or whatever that red design was splashed across his face. People didn't go in for such things in Auverne, and she much preferred men with unadorned faces. As Bernadette took her seat the young warrior looked up with sharp interest, a gleam in his eye. Uh oh.

She smiled back at him slightly, then raised her glass before taking a drink. She was here for some company, right? "Hi, I'm Wolfang," he said with a slight Norse accent. "I'm available for hire, if you're in need of some protection. Just 500 guilders and I'll follow you anywhere." Oh, she thought. And here I assumed he was overcome by my beauty. Perhaps if he'd seen her in her sablium armor...

Bernadette replied, "I'm... uh, *Warden* Bernadette – The Fireblood." Might as well establish my credentials, she thought. She really was an important and famous person in Iscandia, was she not? Warden of two holds, savior of the world? And a 23-year-old with limited social skills, as well – but who's counting? Wolfang looked impressed.

"The Fireblood? Really?" Bernadette felt relieved. After her recent experience with Malden, she'd begun to wonder whether her reputation in Iscandia was all it was supposed to be. Sure, people in Waterdon thought she was great. Erik and Andrion and her friends at the Maiden thought she was great, too. But was she a household name throughout the province? At least Wolfang definitely seemed to have heard of her.

Bernadette smiled self-deprecatingly. "That's me," she said, adding "I've had a very busy year."

"By the gods, I should say so!" Wolfang exclaimed, moving across the fire to take the seat beside her. Evidently in mercenary circles, at least, she was something of a celebrity. How cool! Wolfang reached out and shook her hand. "I'm very honored to meet you," he said with astounding sincerity. At closer glance, Bernadette could see he was not very much older than she was. Perhaps younger than Erik, even.

The bard continued running through the Iscandia standards as the night wore on, and inn customers came and went. Wolfang pumped Bernadette for tales of the adventures that had led to Tarragin's downfall, apparently thrilled to have this opportunity to spend time with her. Had not the Maiden been so close to Waterdon, in between there and the Old Ones' mountain home, she might have ended up traveling here and hiring Wolfang, and *he* would have become part of the story – and most likely the one sharing her bed, she realized. He really was cute, if in some ways a bit like those farm boys she had come to Iscandia to escape.

The two of them had shared her bottle of wine, and Bernadette had ordered a second one that they'd also drunk together. She'd eaten her bread and cheese and followed that with the last of the evening's stew as the hour was getting late; so she was well-lubricated but still (mostly) had her wits about her. Wolfang seemed to have loosened up a lot since they'd first met, but was clear of eye and steady of hand so he was holding his wine without any difficulties. Likely, he was a good man in a fight.

When the bard finished for the night and went home, Bernadette realized that she and Wolfang (and the yawning Karl) were the only people left in the room. Even Freya had gone to bed. Time she was off home, to get some sleep before running her errands! "I've really enjoyed talking with you, Wolfang," she said rising. "But I've got business in the morning and I need to get some sleep." He eyed her boldly, stepping close and looking into her eyes. His were brown, not dissimilar to Andrion's.

"I have a room here at the inn," he said softly. "Would you like to join me?"

Bernadette was taken aback. The attraction was there. She'd been feeling it all night. The woman she had been half a year ago would have happily jumped into the sack with Wolfang, and if that had worked out she might have turned it into an ongoing thing. But now, suddenly, she realized that her mind, her heart, and even her wayward and perpetually-horny cunt had evidently been wrapped up, completely claimed, by the two men who had become an essential part of her life; and she really had no desire whatsoever to take Wolfang up on his offer. She had turned into a different person.

Bernadette smiled at him, putting a hand on his shoulder. Then she reached up and gave Wolfang a kiss on the cheek. "Thank you for the offer," she said quietly, "but I'm… otherwise engaged." He immediately got shy and shamefaced, embarrassed that he had had the temerity to proposition a woman as important as The Fireblood. "It's all right!" she said, sensing his thoughts. "I wish you every success." She held out her hand and squeezed his, then made her way out of the inn and up the stairs to "home." The streets were nearly deserted.

Lying in Eastview's master bed naked and alone, her mind somewhat fogged by wine, Bernadette spread her legs and put her right hand down between them. In her other hand she cupped her left breast, squeezing it and tweaking a nipple as she brought herself to orgasm. The images playing in her head were of the night before, sandwiched between Andrion and Erik and loving every minute of it.

Chapter 34: Meanwhile, Back at the Ranch

Andrion and Erik were sitting at their usual table in the Maiden, a couple of chilled ales to hand and some salty potato chips in a bowl between them. This was a recent invention, apparently, as someone had almost by accident discovered that if you sliced potatoes thinly enough and cooked them in hot fat, they would crisp up into something that most people would keep eating compulsively – especially if you sprinkled on plenty of salt. The ale made you crave the chips, and the salt in the chips made you crave ale; a vicious – and delicious – circle.

They weren't paying a lot of attention to the food and drink, however. The two were co-conspirators, and they were deep in the midst of a plot. "I checked with Ogden at the Clan House and he is completely adamant," Andrion informed Erik. "That farm is the Clan's major income source and they have no desire to sell it. And there are so many of them. If he died, we'd just be dealing with another and they all have the same attitude."

"Damn," Erik replied. They'd both seized on Stormstrife Farm as the ideal location for their family home, so close to the family business (i.e. the Bathing Maiden) that you could stroll across the road in your robe to use the bathing pool.

Both of them loved Berni deeply, enough to put up with the unconventional arrangement she had proposed – that she would marry them both. But as they joined forces, they were coming to realize that being married to Berni would offer them huge advantages. She was The Fireblood, warden of two holds. She was rich and famous as well. Marrying her wasn't just the realization of their personal dreams of love – it was a good career move. So they'd gone from a reluctant acceptance of what appeared to be the only terms that would let them keep the woman they both loved, to active and eager participants in the plan. And part of that plan was, she was not going to know what they were doing until after the wedding.

Admittedly, what they were doing was pretty much what she had *asked* them to do. But they planned to do it in a way that would completely blow her mind, that would be better than her wildest dreams – and she would not find out about it until they carried her off after the ceremony. That was the theory, anyway. In practice, they were discovering a few flaws. Starting with the apparent non-availability of the place they had both decided was the perfect choice.

Erik took another handful of the delightfully crispy chips and washed it down with a hearty gulp of ale. Ah, what a combination! Meanwhile, his mind was roaming. "Well, if we can't get Stormstrife, what about Coldburn?" Andrion also ate a few chips and drank some ale, as he considered Erik's suggestion.

"It's not as big, and not as well situated," he mused. "But it's pretty close. Let's walk down there and see what we can find out."

The pair, wearing trousers and shirts and very lightly armed, finished their ales and exited the Maiden's front doors to take a left turn off the porch and follow the road up in the direction of Waterdon. At Coldburn Farm, they stood assessing the place. It wasn't bad – close to the river and the stream that joined it, and centrally located between Waterdon Stables and the Maiden. Bram, a sour-faced middle-aged fellow they'd met casually on trips to town over the past couple of years, was out weeding a cabbage patch as they approached.

"Ho, Bram!" Erik boomed. The man rose from his labor and stood eyeing the two of them suspiciously.

"Hello… uh, Erik, is it?" he replied uncertainly.

Waxing hearty Erik said "Right you are! And you remember my friend, Andrion?"

"Oh aye," came the reply. "Can I do anything for you? Because as you can see I've got work to do…" My, what a friendly fellow. Erik might have expected anybody in the midst of weeding cabbages to be eager for the excuse to down tools.

Andrion took over at this point. Having a few years on Erik, he tended to become the spokesman when Berni was not around. "We were just admiring the farm, Bram," he said jovially. "And we were wondering, might you be the owner?" Defying expectation, Bram's eye waxed even more jaundiced.

"Might, and I might not," he replied grumpily. Then relenting, he went on "It's Safar you'll be looking for. Afran fellow, up at Waterdon. Too mighty by far to be coming around *these* parts." He spat. Clearly, Safar was not held in high regard by his tenant farmer.

Erik and Andrion exchanged looks. "Thanks, Bram" Andrion said, then the two walked back down to the road for a consultation. "You know Safar?" Erik asked in an undertone.

"We've met," Andrion replied. "The guy's a complete asshole, near as I can tell. Really full of himself. But I think if we're going to go talk to him, we ought to have cash in hand. Let's go back to the Maiden and get Berni's stash. Then we can sell it in town before we look up Safar."

"Good idea," Erik said. The two turned and walked back the way they'd come.

They stopped off at Stormstrife farm and hired the use of a farm cart and a horse for the trip. Berni had been accumulating a *lot* of weapons and armor over the past months, in the process of developing her smithing skills. She no longer really had any need to go questing, as with a steady supply of raw materials she was now capable of turning out top quality goods right there at her own forge in the basement. If she hadn't already been The Fireblood, she could have had one hell of a career as a smith – perhaps even become more famous in that occupation than that Edmaar Snowhair guy who worked the Godsforge for the Brave Company up behind Ynglingar.

Erik and Andrion left the horse tied to one of the Maiden's front porch posts while they hauled the cart around to the rear deck. Then Erik went down the ladder from the porch's trap door and handed items up to Andrion, who loaded them on the cart until they'd cleaned out the amazing cache of weapons, armor, and other items of value their beloved had left them to sell. Puffing a bit as he came up the ladder after the last load, Erik goggled at the contents of the cart. "Where did she *get* all this stuff?" he asked his friend. Andrion had been travelling with Berni a lot more in recent weeks than he had.

"Here and there," Andrion replied. "We picked up quite a lot during our travels. Plus I think she made a lot of it. She's been working on improving her skills, and that generates a lot of armor. I think Berni just really enjoys making things, even if she doesn't know what to do with them after she's made them." Erik nodded. He'd noticed that about her.

It took the combined efforts of both of them to wheel the overloaded cart back around to the front of the Maiden and out into the road. Then they unhitched the horse from the porch and got him into the traces, happy to turn the job of pulling the cart over to him. Erik and Andrion strolled along beside the cart, Andrion keeping a hand on the horse's headstall, as they made their leisurely progress down the road and up the hill into the city.

It was only late morning, and they had a busy day ahead of them. Erik popped in at Brightsgate Cottage to say hi while Andrion was negotiating with Alessia and Wolaf. The woman smith was amazed at the quality of goods that her friend Bernadette was turning out. In a way, she felt as if she were the younger woman's mentor, having been one of the first to give her the opportunity to try her hand at the forge after Bernadette had first arrived in Iscandia. The collection of arms and armor was worth far more than the amount of coin they had available: but Andrion struck a deal with them. They would take it all now, and pay him in installments over the next couple of weeks. And in the meantime, Andrion had over 10,000 guilders in his pocket.

He stopped by next door with a hug for Anja and greetings for Bjorn. Lifa was out, visiting up at Wyrmshalla Bjorn said. Snagging Erik, Andrion returned to the now much-lighter cart and they continued on their way up the street. Not all the items Berni had left them were goods that Valkyrie would sell, so their next stop was Bernard's. The shopkeeper was his usual obnoxious self. As a fellow Galise, Andrion had done his best to warm up to the man; but it was just impossible.

The bargaining session began. In addition to numerous gems and items of jewelry, some of which Berni had made herself (her sessions at the forge could produce quite decent-looking circlets, necklaces, and rings as well as heavy armor and deadly weapons), they had mage robes, regular clothing, and a surprisingly large collection of dragon bone and scales that she'd been hoarding since her earliest days as a dragon-killer. So far as any of them knew the stuff was only useful for making armor or weapons; but having never found any examples from which to learn the crafting of those, Berni had now decided to sell off some of her surplus.

Bernard was delighted to acquire whatever they had to sell, and when Andrion was finished dealing with him he was 7,500 guilders to the good and the Galise merchant was cleaned out of cash. He didn't try offering an installment plan, here. They could sell more to Bernard another day, when his coffers had been replenished.

Their final stop was The Potent Potion, next door to Bernard's. Andrion greeted Adele warmly, having been a customer of hers occasionally since first coming to the area. The middle-aged woman brightened up the moment he came in. Such a nice young man. Such a nice, fantastically handsome young man. And ooh, his blond friend was pretty cute too. Adele was a Reman and no fool, but she couldn't help being affected by the presence of two such gorgeous specimens of masculinity in her shop. It did not take Andrion long to sell off the bulk of Berni's unneeded potions and ingredients – draining Adele's cash supply and enriching their coffers by a further 7,000+ guilders.

The horse was now looking considerably happier than it had when they started out, and the cart considerably emptier. Andrion and Erik split up the remaining contents between them, stuffing them into packs. Then Erik spotted Anja's friend Lars darting around the marketplace and paid him five guilders (a princely sum) to keep an eye on their borrowed horse and cart while they went looking for Safar.

Chapter 35: Safar

The man was usually to be found roaming Waterdon's marketplace, Andrion knew. And it didn't take long before they spotted him descending the steps that led up toward the city's residential district. A trim, dark-skinned man dressed in rich clothing, he was unmistakable. Andrion had dressed in clothing that was respectable if not opulent. He was beginning to wish he'd put on the outfit Berni had gotten him for the time when they'd gone up to talk Eorl Ormund into letting them trap the dragon Sneyagflug in his palace.

Erik trailing behind, Andrion approached Safar as he stepped down onto the market square. "Safar!" he called. "Might we have a word with you?" The Afran gentleman peered down his nose at them, not recognizing Andrion. "Andrion Lamonte," he said, proffering a hand that was pointedly ignored. "We've met before. My associate Erik Johannessohn and I are agents for Warden Bernadette, The Fireblood."

Safar's eyes lit with recognition. In Waterdon, at least, no citizen had failed to take note of Berni's exploits. "Oh yes, Mister Lamonte" the landowner replied stiffly. "How may I help you?"

"I wonder," Andrion said smoothly, gesturing toward the door of the nearby Flying Horseman, "if you would care to join us for some lunch? We have a business proposition we would like to discuss with you."

Safar seemed to be quite amenable to this suggestion. Anybody offering to pay was not to be dismissed. Erik nodded to him, looming slightly. He often found that his huge size had a salutary effect when trying to convince people to go along with his wishes – not that he'd ever been a bully or anything close to it. In this instance though, he sensed that he'd been cast in the role of the ominous enforcer. He wished momentarily he were darker of aspect and perhaps possessed of an eye patch or at least a few facial scars.

The three of them crossed the market plaza and entered the inn, where they were greeted by Britta. Everyone who had spent much time in Waterdon knew Britta, and she knew them. She was forever talking of selling the Horseman and retiring from the innkeeping business; but somehow she seemed to hold on, year after year.

Andrion took a table for the three of them over in the far corner of the room, then went back to the bar and quietly asked Britta to give them some bottles of mead and whatever was cooking in the kitchen. She smiled at him and accepted his gold, before handing over the mead. "The food will be right out," she promised. Andrion returned to the table carrying the mead. Over the past few weeks he'd become accustomed to having his bottled drinks chilled, and was regretful that these were at room temperature. But applying a frost spell directly to a bottle could have unfortunate effects, so he just carried them over and rejoined his companions.

Handing the drinks around Andrion said, "Our food will be here shortly."

Ungraciously, Safar demanded "I would really like to know what it is you want. You realize that I'm an important man. I'm often called upon to advise the eorl on political matters. My input is invaluable, of course. But this is all probably a bit over your head," he added, taking a swig of his mead.

Andrion and Erik exchanged a brief look. What an asshole, indeed. Politely, Andrion said "Ah yes, Eorl Ormund. My fiancée and I – that would be Bernadette – convinced Ormund to allow us to use Wyrmshalla to trap a dragon. That resulted in our being able to travel to Asengard and defeat the Soul-Devourer. I'm sure you must have heard about it?"

Erik was impressed. His friend Andrion had many abilities and was one hell of a smart guy, but he had never personally witnessed this facility with political manipulation. Safar was taken aback. For once, he had the feeling that he was in the presence of personages who might, just possibly, approach his own lofty importance. "Perhaps," he said hesitantly, "we'll discuss it after we have our lunch…"

The food arrived, and it was nothing fancy. You had to go far into the dining rooms of the high and mighty in Iscandia to come up with a meal that went beyond the basics. The three of them tucked into their bowls of stew with bread rolls, washing it all down with mead and making polite conversation. Andrion was a bit surprised, actually, that Safar was capable of such. Every time the two had met in the past the man had treated everyone around him as if they were something he'd just scraped off the soles of his boots.

The bowls were emptied and the last sheen of savory stew wiped from them with the last of the bread. The three took swallows of their mead to wash it down, and then assessed one another across the table. Safar was the first to speak. "Well then," he said, burping politely and patting his mouth with a linen handkerchief he'd produced from his waistcoat pocket, "how may I assist you gentlemen?"

Andrion, who had been devoting his attention to the excellent stew for the moment, bore in once again on his objective. "Erik and I have been speaking with your tenant Bram out at Coldburn Farm," he said. He tried to affect an air of hauteur similar to Safar's, but found it a bit hard to pull off. "As it happens, that property is in very close in proximity to ours, the Bathing Maiden." He glanced at Safar and saw recognition. "I'm sure you've been there? It's the premier inn in Iscandia, some think…"

"Ah yes," Safar said. "Of course…" In actuality he had never set foot in the place. His wife Halima had heard stories, and there would never be an end to it if she learned he had been spotted in such a notorious den of iniquity.

"As I was saying," Andrion went on, "we learned from Bram that you are the owner of Coldburn, and we are interested in acquiring it. We are thinking of expanding our interests in the vicinity of the Maiden." He hoped he'd struck the right tone.

Safar frowned, appalled at the suggestion. While he had other holdings, Coldburn Farm (which he rarely actually visited) provided him with income as well as a sense of being an important landowner in his adopted land. He hoped never to have to return to the stinking desert of Zahar that had given him birth, and anything that might erode his status here in Iscandia was to be regarded as a threat. "Coldburn Farm," he said stiffly, "is not for sale. It's a very successful business, as you can see." He gestured to his rich garb. "Thank you for the meal, gentlemen," he said rising. And stalked out of the inn.

Erik and Andrion looked at each other in consternation. "I thought that was going pretty well," Erik said.

"Shit," Andrion muttered under his breath. Then he looked at Erik and said, "So did I. What did I do wrong?" The two of them sat there finishing their bottles of room-temperature mead.

After a minute or so Erik had a thought. "Have you met Safar's wife, Halima? She spends a lot of time up at the temple of Agneta."

Andrion, still slowly swallowing the last of his mead, looked electrified by Erik's remark. "I *have* met the lady in question," he said, a wicked smile coming over his features. "What do you say we go have a chat with her?" Erik returned his smile in kind. Once again, it appeared that they were both thinking the same thing. Leaving a tip on the table for Britta, the pair exited the Flying Horseman and climbed the steps toward the fountains. On its left, they entered the doors of the Temple of Agneta, goddess of endings.

As they'd hoped they found the dusky Halima within, performing her daily duties at the temple. She was a priestess and healer, an odd occupation from what they knew of her personality. Both Erik and Andrion had encountered her out and about in Waterdon over the past two years, and she made no secret of her contempt for her husband and his haughty airs.

She greeted them coolly, and asked "How may I help you? Do you have wounded for us to tend?" Agneta was both the goddess of aging and death, and that of rebirth and regeneration.

Andrion smiled winningly (he hoped) and said, "No, we're fine. Halima, I'm Andrion Lamonte and this is Erik Johannessohn. I believe we've met a few times?" Halima nodded, and Andrion continued, "The reason we're here is that we'd like to talk to you about your husband Safar." The woman's dark features took on an expression of scorn. If those two had married for love, clearly that bloom had withered over the years.

"Is there somewhere we can talk privately?" Andrion asked her, and she motioned them over to a quiet recess in one corner of the temple.

"So, what about Safar?" Halima asked. "That man acts like he's married to himself."

"We just met with him," Andrion told her. "We were prepared to offer him a large sum of money for Coldburn Farm, but he refused to discuss the matter with us."

The woman's eyes gleamed. "*How* large a sum of money?" she asked.

Halima cared nothing for the farm. She and Safar had a comfortable lifestyle here in town and she had her work at the temple. But the idea of puncturing Safar's ego and reaping a large amount of gold at the same time definitely appealed to her. How she had come to loath the man!

Andrion hesitated. He was pretty sure that Halima was not in a position to sell the farm to them herself, and he'd planned to start with a low offer and then bargain the price up. The nearly 25,000 guilders they were lugging around was five times what he and Berni had paid for Brightsgate Cottage, and should have been more than enough to buy the smallish farm.

But now he needed to name a figure that would encourage Halima to work against her husband's wishes and assist them. "I was going to offer 20,000," he told her, trying to sound confident. "Of course if necessary, I'm prepared to go higher. We're negotiating the purchase on the behalf of The Fireblood," he added.

Halima's opinion of men in general was none too high. It seemed to her that all they cared about was war and politics – and they treated their women like cattle. But The Fireblood was a different story. *There* was a woman she could admire, and if these men were her agents she would be happy to do them a favor.

"If you're associated with The Fireblood you must have some influence with the eorl, yes?" she asked. Andrion considered. Certainly, Eorl Ormund welcomed them courteously when they visited at Wyrmshalla, and he was deeply indebted to Berni. Everybody on the planet was indebted to Berni, whether they knew it or not. On learning of her destiny she had not quailed or faltered, but had stepped right up and put her life on the line to stop the Soul-Devourer.

"I think you could say that Ormund will listen to us when we speak," he replied. "What's your idea?"

"Safar won't listen to me," Halima said. "But he spends half his time with his lips pressed to the eorl's backside. If you can get Ormund to tell Safar to sell to you, he'll do it in a heartbeat."

Andrion smiled warmly at Halima, causing her to slightly revise her opinion of the male sex. There was something about that smile…
"Thank you, Halima!" he said, and the two took their leave.

Chapter 36: Influence

Outside in the plaza near the fountains Erik and Andrion conferred. "If we buy Coldburn it's going to need a lot of work, and we haven't got a lot of time," Erik pointed out.

"I'm afraid you're right," Andrion told him. "I'd like to get the horse and cart back and change into some fancier clothes, but the day's getting on. We don't want to catch Ormund at supper."

Thus agreed, the pair mounted the steps leading up to Wyrmshalla, admiring the view. As they came in they met Lifa leaving, a pile of books in her hands. She greeted them warmly, and Andrion decided to bring her in on their conspiracy. "Don't say a word to Berni, okay?" he warned.

Smiling mysteriously, she said, "My lips are sealed." Then she continued on her way back home as the men walked through the hall and toward the dais where Ormund lounged on his throne.

Ormund sat up straighter as they approached him. He knew them well as the boon companions of the Fireblood, who had travelled with her to Asengard and assisted in destroying Tarragin. As Andrion appeared to be the spokesman of this small delegation, it was he that the eorl greeted with. "A fine day to you."

"And the same to you, my eorl" Andrion responded politely.

"And how may I help you?" Ormund continued. Despite the fact that any citizen of Waterdon could walk up to him and get a moment of his time without an appointment, the eorl usually made a point of how busy he was.

"We've come to ask a favor sir," Andrion told him, "on behalf of The Fireblood." Ormund looked slightly irritated but he nodded.

"I certainly owe her a favor or two," he admitted. "What is it that you need?"

"It's a matter regarding one of your citizens from Zahar," Andrion said formally. "A certain Safar. I'm sure you know of him? He claims to be your frequent adviser…"

Ormund snorted in disgust. "That lickspittle! What about him?" Andrion considered how best to frame his request before continuing.

"The Fireblood is desirous of obtaining Coldburn Farm, near her inn a short way outside the city," he explained. "We approached Safar, who is the farm's owner, but he refused to consider our offer.

261

He said the property is not for sale. We were wondering if you might be able to convince him to change his mind?"

Smiling grimly, the eorl replied, "I do believe that if I told him to leap off the balcony out back, he'd do so without a moment's hesitation. I don't think I should have any trouble convincing him to entertain your offer. I assume you're prepared to pay fair market value?"

"Certainly," Andrion replied. "The Fireblood always pays for what she receives." He thought it would be impolitic to mention that her current fat coffers were in large part due to a long campaign of raiding tombs and pillaging bandit lairs.

"Consider it done, then" Ormund said, smiling more warmly. "Will there be anything else? I do have a march to run."

"Thank you sir, that's all we needed" said Andrion. He and Erik nodded respectfully and then took their leave. They collected their horse and cart in the market square, thanking Lars for his trouble. The boy seemed to love horses, and had been sitting on their beast's back and stroking its neck when they arrived.

They led the creature back up toward the gates, the empty cart rattling on the cobblestones, and returned down the road toward home. As they were passing the meadery, Erik had a thought. "Hey," he said brightly. "Here we are going right past the meadery with a horse and cart, and large sacks of gold. Why don't we pick up some supplies for the Maiden?" Andrion grinned at him.

"Erik, you're a genius," he said fondly. They went inside and soon negotiated the purchase of several cases of the amber-colored honey beer, which Bees' Brew employees loaded into the cart for them.

Erik and Andrion were quite pleased with the idea, though the horse was less enthusiastic. After arriving at the Maiden they enlisted the help of Fenris, Lev, and Drelos in unloading. Then Erik led the horse back across the road and returned it and the cart to Astrid, who thanked him for bringing it back so promptly. She asked him if he'd like to come in for some tea, an invitation he politely declined. From the look in her eyes, tea was not the only thing on her mind.

Erik found Andrion taking a bath when he came in, washing off the dust of the trip to and from Waterdon. Not a bad idea, so he joined him. Then they got out and dressed in clean clothing, and wandered around the Maiden for a while. Andrion went out on the deck and practiced his battle spells on the target dummies for some time, and Erik went down into his basement lair to do some smithing. He'd been watching Berni work, and he had a project of his own that he hoped to develop the skill for. He'd made arms and armor from iron and steel, and was not bad at it. But now he was working with gold and gems, and found it took a lot of care and attention.

The two of them met for supper at their favorite table, and after eating sat enjoying the usual evening entertainment at the Maiden. Lev sang and played his lute, people got up and danced to the music, and there was a parade of good-looking women going into the bathing pool. These two might be committed to spending their lives with one woman, but that didn't mean they didn't still like to *look*. Both of them were missing Berni, though, and they turned in relatively early.

In the morning Erik lay in bed for a while, thinking of Berni and absently stroking his hardened cock. "Come back soon, love!" he sent a thought into the ether. He was a young man with a powerful libido, and going a couple of days without release was creating a "hard"-ship. He sighed. The Maiden was crawling with beautiful women, many of them disporting naked in the pools and away from home, looking for some fun. But now that he had made a commitment to marry Berni, he didn't want to bed any other women. He'd made no promises, nor had she; but somehow that seemed to be part of their understanding.

He sighed, then took care of himself before getting up and dressed. As he was eating some delicious warm pastries for breakfast, washed down with hot tea, Andrion came down from the loft looking like he'd slept under a haystack. "Hey brother!" he called. "What happened to you? You look a bit… rumpled." Andrion grinned at him sleepily.

"Give me some of that tea and a few minutes to wake up," he pleaded. "This getting-up-with-the-chickens thing is new to me." Erik grinned in turn and signaled to Drelos, who was on the bar this morning, to bring some more tea and treats.

As the two were nearly finished breaking their fast, sitting there with a good view of the pool and the front doors, whom should they see walking in but Safar. He seemed to be dressed in even more outrageous finery than usual, and was looking around goggle-eyed at the graceful architecture of the inn and the two gorgeous young women who were relaxing naked in the pool. As one of them made eye contact, he quickly looked away. Then he spotted Erik and Andrion and came over to their table, eyeing the women sidelong as he crossed the central hall.

When he arrived at their table he seemed taken aback. Erik, the supposed muscle in yesterday's conference, looked presentable enough; but Andrion, the well-bred spokesman, was sitting there with hair uncombed wearing clothes that looked as if he might have dug them out of the drawer last, after everything else in the room had failed the smell test. Which was, in fact, approximately the case. Still, Safar had been given what he took to be his orders; and he forged ahead.

"Good morning, Mister Lamonte" he said stiffly. Andrion, caught unawares, scrambled to recover the situation.

"Ah Safar, so good to see you. You must excuse my appearance. As you can see, things here at the Maiden can get a little… exciting. And I had a very late night." Safar took another look at the women in the pool. And he's The Fireblood's fiancé, he thought. The dog! Safar only *wished* he could get away with behavior like that.

Andrion was somewhat surprised to find that, apparently, his disheveled appearance and the explanation for it had *raised* him in Safar's estimation rather than the reverse. The man, self-important as he was, seemed eager to get to the point. "The reason I've come today," he began as Erik gestured to a chair and he seated himself at their table, "is that I've been thinking and have decided that I might, after all, be willing to consider an offer on Coldburn Farm. For the good of the march, of course, and as a personal favor to Warden Bernadette…"

It worked! Andrion thought, while schooling his face to blank indifference. "Oh?" he replied, eyeing Safar coldly. "After your refusal yesterday, we have of course been considering *other* properties…" Safar looked confused. Did they want the farm or not?

Erik sat there looking like 250 pounds of dumb Norse muscle, ready to pound anybody that caused problems to his boss. Safar didn't want to get in trouble with the earl, and he wasn't much interested in crossing these two either now he had learned they were, as it seemed, high up in the earl's favor.

"I'd be willing to accept a reasonable offer for the property," he said graciously. "I think thirty thousand should be adequate."
Andrion turned a gaze on him that would have frozen a snow cat.

"Thirty thousand? Are you insane? I was thinking more along the lines of ten. The land doesn't amount to much and the house is tiny." Safar cringed. He had as much as been directed by his earl to sell the place to these agents of Warden Bernadette for whatever they offered, but it was a major part of his holdings in Iscandia. He couldn't possibly be expected to let it go for such a pittance!

Trying not to reveal the duress under which he was negotiating, Safar tried a counter-offer. "Don't be ridiculous!" he cried. "Land this close to the city walls is almost unavailable at any price, and this land has been tilled and enriched for generations. The house may be small, but it is sturdy and well-built. And the place has provided me with a generous income, as it will you. I could not possibly let it go for less than twenty-five thousand."

A glint in his brown eyes was the only hint of the triumph in Andrion's heart as he pushed ahead. He had every intention of delivering fair market value to Safar and Halima in exchange for their property; but he and Erik would also need money to start on the remodeling that would be required to turn Coldburn Farm into the country estate of Berni's dreams. If it were to be done swiftly, they'd need to hire a horde of workers.

The negotiations went on. Erik leaned back in his chair and sipped his cold tea, glaring menacingly at Safar the while as his friend and the Afran wannabe-patrician went back and forth. When a deal was finally struck, Erik was pleasantly surprised. Safar had at last rolled over for 18,750 guilders – far less than they'd been prepared to pay. He hoped Halima wouldn't be too disappointed, and expected that likely any disappointment she did feel would be directed at her sorry spouse for failing to make a better deal. Poor Safar was clearly doomed.

Chapter 37: Men of Property

Andrion excused himself and went back upstairs to put on a more appropriate outfit, clean his teeth and comb his hair. He returned downstairs a few minutes later looking much more like an Important Citizen, and with the cash in hand. The three of them made the trek back to Waterdon and up to Wyrmshalla, where they dealt with Paolo Adelini (a friend of Erik and Andrion, as he was the father of Berni's friend Alessia).

The balding Reman witnessed the exchange and signed the official documents, transferring the deed to Coldburn Farm to Bernadette, in joint tenancy with Erik and Andrion. The laws of Waterdon permitted married couples to own property together so that if one died the other was automatically the sole owner. In this case, Paolo had never seen an arrangement quite like the one Andrion tried to explain to him; but he went along with it – as his eorl was clearly throwing his support their way.

They both shook hands with Safar, the man flinching as Erik's bear paw squeezed his hand tight. Then Bernadette's two fiancés waved "thanks" to Ormund as they exited Wyrmshalla and proceeded down the steps. They stopped in at Brightsgate Cottage briefly to tell Lifa and Bjorn the news. Bjorn had now also been brought into their conspiracy, and he was eager to help. He accompanied them as they continued on their way out of town, keen to visit their new acquisition. "You're an amazing artist, Bjorn," Erik told him. "Have you ever done any architectural drawings?"

Bjorn frowned slightly as they walked along. "I've drawn pictures of buildings," he said. "But I haven't done the kind of drawings that builders use with all of the measurements exact, so that the workers know where to place the foundations, how big to make the walls, how long to make the floor joists and the rafters and so forth. That takes special skills."

"Floor joists? Rafters? You're ahead of us, then" said Andrion. "Let's just go take a look, and maybe we can put our heads together so you can draw the house as we want to see it when it's done. Then we can hire somebody who can put in all the details. We need to move fast, if we're going to get it all done in time. I have the feeling Berni's going to come back from her trip with a wedding date."

Bjorn grinned at him. "That I can do, if you tell me what you want to see." The three of them continued on down the road past the meadery and over the bridge, to find themselves at Coldburn Farm. As usual at this hour of the late morning, Bram was out working the fields and forking some hay into the paddock for the farm's lone cow.

"Ho, Bram!" Andrion called. The sour man turned as they approached with a look that implied irritation at once again being interrupted at his chores.

"I thought you ought to know," Andrion said, unable to keep a grin from spreading, "that Safar is no longer your landlord. This farm is now the property of Warden Bernadette, along with me and my associate Erik," he added – gesturing at Erik and brandishing the deed.

Bram looked nonplussed, then said "Does this mean you'll be throwing me out, then?" Uh oh. Andrion hadn't really considered this aspect of the transaction. "Because," Bram continued, "I'd be really glad to get the hell out of here. I've got a daughter down Deepwald way, keeps telling me I should move in with them and help look after the little nippers. Seems like a lot less work than all this. But I've had responsibilities, like, to Safar. Couldn't just leave."

He looked at them appealingly, and Andrion smiled at him. "Do you think you could stay on for a few weeks, Bram? We'll be needing to make some major additions to the house before we're ready to move in here.

"Oh, that'll be alright," he replied with the first smile either of them had seen on his face during the time they had known him. "Belike, you'll be needing some help with that construction? I've got some skills that way, and I can put you onto some mates of mine. They really know the craft, and they'll fix you up a treat."

"Excellent!" Andrion exclaimed. "We've got plenty of gold for you *and* your mates, if you can do the job right. Do you mind if we look around?"

"Step right in," Bram said, leading them to the front door. The house was, as Safar had said, sturdily built. And the room on the other side of the door was good-sized. A fire pit similar to the one at Brightsgate Cottage occupied the middle of it, with a spit for hanging pots and another for roasting meats suspended above it. But that room was almost the entire cottage.

Off to the left there was a narrow bedroom with a single bed, and a small alcove gave off the main living area for a pantry. But that was it. The place made Brightsgate Cottage look like a palace, and Andrion was almost thinking Safar might have gotten the better of their deal. On the other hand, there *was* all that land.

"Go ahead with what you were doing, Bram," Andrion suggested. The man went back to his farm chores as Andrion and his two companions seated themselves on a bench that ran down one side of the room's dining table. There was another good-sized table over against the wall to the left of the entry door, but no chairs. It appeared the farmhouse had been set up for a lone tenant, not a growing farm family.

Andrion had a roll of paper in his pack, and he pulled it out. With a slim stick charred in the fire, he began sketching on the paper. "Here's the existing house," he said, drawing a series of small rectangles off toward one edge. "I think we're going to need three or four bedrooms and a large nursery, a dining hall, a good-sized bathroom, a real kitchen, a space for chemia and enchanting, and some outdoor areas for relaxing and enjoying the views of the river. Does that seem about right to you, Erik?"

Erik looked at him, a bit taken aback. "Uh, Andrion... how many kids are we planning to have? Why so many bedrooms?" he asked.

"That'll be up to Berni and the gods, I suppose," Andrion replied. "But three of those bedrooms are for you, me, and Berni. I think we should each have our own space. We can't all sleep together all the time, but I think one of those bedrooms – probably Berni's – ought to be big enough so we *can*. With a custom-made bed. The extra bedroom could be the one that's here now, so we can have a servant living in. We're rich, don't forget!"

Erik mulled that over for a while, and from the look on his face he was liking the idea. Yeah, they *were* rich. Even Iscandia's wealthiest citizens had a lifestyle not that much different from that of the average merchant, but then *they* might just be lacking in imagination. "What about a bathing pool?" he asked. "I'm assuming

Berni can walk down the road to the use the smithing facilities at the Maiden, but she's not going to be trotting over there naked. We'll need some kind of a hot bath here."

"I have some ideas, about that," Andrion said. "I've heard about places where they have cisterns on the roof, or up on a tower, to catch the rainwater. Then they pipe the water down to the house and it just comes out of a sort of valve in the kitchen or the bathroom. I don't think we'd have room for a bathing pool the size of the one at the Maiden, but we could make one big enough for two or three people. And there are a lot of ways we could heat the water."

"And a privy, right?" Erik asked. Usually privies were closets that deposited wastes a goodly distance down, into a pit of some kind. The smell was pretty obnoxious, especially in summer. Using chamberpots allowed you to carry the wastes further afield; but that involved a lot of unpleasant labor.

"I have another idea," Andrion told him. "There's a system where you use a sort of porcelain chair and your wastes are carried away by water to a tank underground. All contained, so there's no smell. Then the wastes break down in the tank and the remnants are gradually distributed through perforated pipes and soak into the soil, enriching it. We could plant cabbages over the top!"

"*Nice* cabbages?" Erik asked skeptically.

"No smell, I swear! After your stuff has decomposed for a while it's a good fertilizer!" Andrion insisted.

"Sounds like a good idea, then," Erik agreed. As they'd been talking Bjorn's lone eye had lit up with inspiration. He seized the charcoal stick from Andrion and began sketching on the paper, working out from the current floor plan. "I think it would be better to stay on one level," he said as he worked. "I don't think you want to support a second story on top of this house, and you've got plenty of room to spread out." He continued mapping out the house Andrion had described.

"You could run a porch all along the east side here," Bjorn said, pointing. "You'll have views of the sunrise over the mountains, the river, and the Maiden. Then each of the three main bedrooms would give out onto the porch, where you could just hang out and relax – also, easy access from one bedroom to another…" he glanced at them. He was still a bit unsure about the moral implications of his friends' three-way relationship with his warden, but he'd concluded it was not his part to judge them. They were clearly good people.

"This room we're sitting in could be split up into kitchen and dining," Bjorn continued. "That little bedroom off to the side could be for the servant or whoever. And then on the west side of the three new bedrooms, you'll have a hall with your bathroom and a big crafting area giving off of it, and the nursery running crosswise to cap the addition. What do you think?"

All three men were excited. What could be finer, really, then envisioning something and having the ability to turn it into reality? Andrion looked thoughtful. "What about a library-slash-schoolroom?" he said. Erik and Bjorn regarded him blankly. They were not scholars, as he was. "Well, maybe later," he said ruefully. If they did end up with a pack of kids, they would certainly be needing a place in which to educate them. Despite the high literacy rate in Iscandia, there were no public schools.

Having come up with a working sketch, the three of them walked back out of the cottage and found Bram. "We have an idea what we want," Andrion told him. "Is any of your builder friends able to produce architectural plans?"

"No problem," the man replied. "Tell you what – you're down at the Maiden, right?" Andrion nodded. "I'll go talk to Hegmar up in town, and I'll have him come down and meet you there later on today. All right?"

"That would be great," Andrion said. "Here, let me give you some money so you can get things started." He slipped Bram a hundred guilders, with which he seemed well pleased.

"Well!" he exclaimed. "I'll just be off then. See you later!" With that he took his tools over to a shed built onto the side of the cottage, and legged it off in the direction of Waterdon.

"Looks like we're underway, then" Andrion said with a grin at his companions. "Bjorn, care to come down to the Maiden for some lunch?" Bjorn considered. Inn food and an ale or two with his friends was very appealing, but he had a family life now that meant a lot to him.

"Another time," he said regretfully. "Lifi and Ani will be expecting me." Erik and Andrion exchanged glances, then smiled and bid him farewell as he, too, began walking toward Waterdon.

"Is that what we have to look forward to?" Erik asked with a smile, as he and his friend turned their footsteps toward the Maiden.

"Yes," Andrion said contentedly, "I believe it is."

Chapter 38: Warden of Westmarch

Bernadette came to consciousness and stretched beneath the covers in Eastview's large bed. And stretched... No, as far as she threw her arms and legs, there was no warm, solid man sharing it with her. She squeezed her eyes shut and threw out her lower lip, pouting for the benefit of no one whatsoever. Over the past few months she'd rarely had to sleep by herself, and had grown quite accustomed to snuggling with one or both of her lovers during Iscandia's usually-chilly nights. This sucked!

Well, nothing for it but to hurry about her business, the sooner to get back to their arms. As she crawled out of bed and put on an outfit that was considerably fancier than her usual garb, Bernadette wondered how her men were doing on their own. Erik especially, she guessed, would be missing her. His libido seemed to be turned up a few notches above that of most men she'd met, and she wondered if he'd be sleeping by himself. She didn't really mind if he boinked the odd Maiden visitor. Those women were passing through all the time, and none of them were a threat to her relationship with Erik.

She'd placed a small mirror atop the chest of drawers and tried to check her appearance in it. She couldn't really get the full picture, but judged she looked acceptable enough. Her stomach was growling, so she looked around for some food to eat. Nobody had been living here in weeks, though, and there was nothing resembling breakfast to be had.

Sighing, Bernadette shouldered her pack and walked out into early morning light in Alfenstein, the Elven City. The day looked like it would be a fine one, sunshine mixed with puffy clouds and a light breeze. Alfenstein really was nice to look at, even if a little inconvenient to navigate in if you didn't know it well. As many times as she'd been here, she still occasionally got lost.

In the market area near the main gates Bernadette found a meat seller, but a raw haunch of goat or beef roast didn't seem like quite the thing; so she returned to the Staerlin Inn. It was a little early to find Dhyazh at her forge or Eorl Galdur on his throne, so she had time for some tea and whatever food the inn might have to offer.

She found Karl's wife, the sour-looking and oft-complaining Freya, tending the bar. Bernadette smiled at her and asked cheerfully, "What's on the menu?"

The woman looked at her as if she'd made an indecent suggestion, then grudgingly replied, "I've got some fresh bread came in this morning, and some fruit. And there's tea brewing."

"That will do nicely," Bernadette beamed, pretending she was being treated courteously. She handed over more coins than were asked for, and Freya's attitude improved a little.

Bernadette took her food and drink over to the fire, and sat eating it. The bread really was pretty good, though she wished it were possible to get some other kinds of fruit here. Maybe some nice crisp pears, or some plums in season? As she was eating, Wolfang appeared. "Good morning!" he said, his embarrassment of the night before seeming to have faded. She greeted him in turn, and shared some of her tea with him as they sat chatting while she finished her meal.

When nothing but crumbs remained, Bernadette stood up brushing off her skirts. "I must be off then," she told Wolfang. "I've got to go do some business with Dhyazh, and then I'm up to Dypendwelve to ask a favor of the eorl."

Wolfang looked a little nonplussed. "Good luck with that," he said. "Galdur Staerlin's not as easy to get along with as old Hjaermond was."

"Yes," Bernadette replied wryly. "I've met him before. He made me Warden of Westmarch, though. That ought to be good for something." A little of Wolfang's shyness returned, as he recalled what a lofty personage he was addressing – even if she *did* just look like an attractive young woman.

"You're right," he mumbled. "Take care!"

Bernadette bid Wolfang farewell, and wound her way up the confusing labyrinth of streets and bridges, crossing Alfenstein's central stream a couple of times on the way to her friend Dhyazh's forge. She greeted the slender uruk woman formally but with a smile, and they chatted a little bit.

After their conversation, Bernadette unslung her pack and the bargaining session began. "You made these yourself?" Dhyazh asked, looking mildly surprised. "They are excellent."

"Some I made from ingots, some I improved from the condition they were in when I acquired them," Bernadette replied matter-of-factly. Inside, she was beaming at Dhyazh's approval. When they'd first met, her own skills had been barely above apprentice level – and now an actual uruk smith was saying her work was "excellent"!

They haggled for a while, and Bernadette got good market value for her pieces. The ones she'd enchanted, often earlier versions of enchanted weapons that had been supplanted in her arsenal as her skills increased, fetched even more and she left with a fat sack of gold in exchange for them. Bidding Dhyazh farewell, she walked up a couple of flights of stairs to Magichemia for a brief chat with Clara. She'd left all her surplus potions and ingredients with Andrion and Erik, wanting to leave them plenty to turn into gold in case they found a suitable property for sale while she was gone. But she bought a few of the ingredients on offer. She'd not had much time for gathering her own lately; and she could certainly afford to buy them now.

From there it was only a short walk up three or four more flights of stairs to the doors of Dypendwelve. Guards standing there in the morning sunshine greeted her respectfully, as much because of her refined appearance as from recognizing her as a warden. She nodded to them calmly, adopting an aloof air, and strolled in through the doors.

As many times as Bernadette had been to Dypendwelve, she could not shake the feeling she was walking into the ruins of a building just destroyed by an earthquake; or perhaps an archaeological dig. Why by all the gods did not the Staerlin Clan use some of their vast resources to fix the place up? There was no shortage of stone, and at least the passageway between the doors and the throne room could have been turned into a walled corridor. Eh, perhaps the "Dypalfar Ruin" look appealed to the Alfensteinians' sense of aesthetics.

Climbing to the throne room, Bernadette greeted the eorl and curtsied to him. They exchanged a few pleasantries, then she broached the subject of her request. The eorls of Iscandia were much more used to making requests of their citizenry than fulfilling ones made by them, and he was none too happy. But after half an hour of negotiation and the application of some gold, Bernadette got what she had come for; and when she left the keep she had a signed writ in her pocket.

Bernadette returned to Eastview, admiring the views along the way, and gathered up her things. She changed back into leather armor and slung a bow over her back before stepping out onto the house's porch to consider her next move. She needed to go to Lakedon and arrange for the wedding to be performed, but she thought it likely she had better go to Sylvanian first. Some of her plans might take a while to reach fruition, and time was short.

Chapter 39: Plans

Erik and Andrion sat eating cold sliced beef with bread and cheese. They had some potato chips on the side and washed the food down with chilled ale, a satisfying repast. Neither of them knew Bram's friend Hegmar on sight, but as he had not appeared by the time they'd finished their leisurely lunch Andrion volunteered to keep an eye on the door. He knew Erik had some project going in the basement, though he didn't know what it was.

Andrion fetched a book from one of the shelves on the mezzanine and sat reading it. It was one of the many volumes of *Tales of the Nachtalfar*, being a collection of night elf folklore. He was more often to be found reading books of genuine lore or practical how-to manuals, and this stuff was definitely in the fairy-tale camp; but it was enjoyable enough without being so engrossing he would fail to keep an eye out for Hegmar.

He'd finished that book and started the next volume before the door opened to reveal a rather short and weedy-looking middle-aged Norseman with thinning brown hair. He was clutching a roll of paper in his hand and peering around expectantly. This must be the man! Andrion walked over to him where he stood on the landing just inside the doors and said, "Hegmar?"

"Aye," the man replied. "And you might be Andrion?"

"So glad you could make it," Andrion told him, shepherding him across the common room to the table he, Erik, and Berni most often used when dining or just relaxing in the Maiden. There were a few people soaking in the pool, and Hegmar leered appreciatively at a couple of the younger women. "Heard about this place," he said with a smirk. "Cor, they weren't kidding!"

"Please have a seat and I'll just go fetch my associate," Andrion said. Their lunch dishes had long since been cleared and the table was clean and ready for their conference with the builder. "Can I get you anything from the bar?" he asked before turning to leave.

"A nice bottle of mead, perhaps?" The little man's grin got wider. "That'd be most kind of ye," he said, pulling at the front of his soft cloth cap in a gesture of respect.

Andrion opened the trap door behind the bar then knelt on the floor and stuck his head a little way into the opening. "Erik! You down here?"

"Yeah," came the bass reply.

"Hegmar's here!" Andrion shouted, then waited until he heard "Oh! I'll be right up," before getting back on his feet. He snagged three bottles of mead out of the washtub they were using for a cooler and added three from the nearby case to replace them. Then, after assessing the state of the ice, he applied a frost spell to the tub until the melt water had gone solid again.

Striding back to the table he proffered one of the meads to Hegmar, setting the other two on the table and taking a seat. "Erik should be here in a moment." Indeed, as he glanced over toward the bar he saw his friend's blond head and massive shoulders rising up behind it like a breaching golden whale. Erik closed the trap behind him and, spotting the bottles sitting on their table, came right over to join them.

Hegmar was dumfounded as he took the bottle Andrion had handed him. "This's *cold*!" he said in astonishment.

"Try it, I think you'll like it" Andrion assured him, popping the cork on his own bottle and taking a satisfying swig. Erik, too, eagerly uncapped his own. Hegmar shrugged and did the same. Mead was mead, he supposed, and this was the familiar Bees' Brew mead from the brewery he'd passed on his way over here from town.

Steeling himself, Hegmar took a hesitant sip. Those who knew him well would have been surprised to see him *sip* anything, let alone Bees' Brew mead. He let it wash down his throat, clean and refreshing. Hey, this *was* good! Very quickly, he took a couple of swigs and exhaled sharply in satisfaction. "How'd you *do* that?" he asked. "Get it cold, like?"

Erik smiled at him. "Andrion is a powerful mage," he told the little builder. Seeing the man's alarm he added, "He just used his magic on some water to make ice, that's all. The ice keeps the mead cold. We chill all our mead and ale here now, and it's getting very popular." Hegmar blinked at him.

Then, shrugging, he downed most of the rest of his bottle of mead and said, "I'm a convert. Now, you wanted to look at some drawings?"

Erik and Andrion exchanged glances. "Bram gave you our rough sketch, right? And you've seen the farm house. We thought we'd just discuss hiring you to make some drawings that the construction crew can work from."

"Oh aye," Hegmar said, with a sly smile. "But happens I'm good at my trade. And your sketch was none too bad. Might I ask who made it?"

"That was our friend Bjorn, who lives at Brightsgate Cottage. He's got a knack for drawing and painting, but he said he'd never done any architectural drawings," Andrion explained.

"He's got a knack for that as well then, I think," pronounced Hegmar sagely. "I'd consider taking him on as an assistant, if he's not otherwise engaged." Andrion considered thoughtfully. Bjorn was a warrior, and of course he was sworn as a servant of Westmarch on semi-permanent assignment to Berni. But he might be needing a trade that would keep him closer to home after he was wed.

"I'll mention it to him," Andrion concluded. "Can we see what you've got?" Hegmar spread out his roll of paper, which proved to be Bjorn's drawing rolled inside of one he had made. Bjorn had captured everything they had discussed with a detailed floor plan, notes in a careful and legible hand delineating the special features of the piped water system, the planned waste disposal system, the kitchen, and so forth. Hegmar had taken this concept and transformed it into something that looked like it was ready to slide off the page and become reality before their eyes. With skillful strokes of pen and brush (and straightedge, Andrion guessed), Hegmar had produced views of the transformed house as seen from the road to the east, from the south, and from the north.

Both he and Erik were gazing avidly at Hegmar's drawings, the dreams they nurtured for their future together with Berni somehow made manifest on that roll of paper. "This is amazing, Hegmar!" Andrion exclaimed.

"What *he* said," Erik added.

"Now this isn't final, you understand," Hegmar said. He seemed to go from being a scurrying rat of a man to a consummate professional in the blink of an eye.

"If you approve what I've got here, I'll get a surveying crew out to the site tomorrow morning. I hear you're in a hurry, like. We'll take all the measurements and I'll do a materials list and order what we'll need for the building. Then we can get a crew out maybe later that same day to start grading and digging for foundations and that septic system you want. That's going to add quite a bit to the cost, though, you realize?" The man's folksy accent seemed to come and go; but Andrion and Erik were starting to think they'd put the job into the right hands.

"Do you need some kind of a deposit?" Andrion asked. He realized that the final cost of their planned renovations was likely to be sky-high, but there would be no way for Hegmar to provide them with an estimate until after the list of materials had been determined, at the earliest. He knew Berni had tens of thousands in gold stashed, but he didn't see any way they could ask her for the money without blowing the surprise. Well, they had several more thousands coming in from Valkyrie in the next week or so. He could only hope it would be enough. "Five thousand guilders will get me started," Hegmar said. He seemed to regard the money as secondary to his excitement with the project at hand.

"You'll notice," Hegmar went on, gesturing to his elevation drawings, "that I've got the cistern up at the top of a new building on the upper slope of the property. You'll get more height and more water pressure that way, and you can use the inside of the tower for storage, drying herbs, whatever you want. That means a bit more pipe getting into the house, but you don't have to mess up the architectural lines by putting in a flat roof in the middle of the place to hold the cistern. Lots less risk of roof leaks inside the house that way, too."

Andrion was impressed, and sold. Clearly this Hegmar, however dubious he might seem as a person, really knew his stuff. And he was prepared to work quickly, giving them half a chance to meet their as-yet somewhat nebulous schedule. Still carrying some of their haul from yesterday, he pulled out his purse and deposited five thousand guilders on the table before them. "We'll need some kind of written contract, I think" he said, not yet shoving the money across the table.

"Right with you guv'nor," Hegmar said, reverting to his sometimes accent. He pulled another roll of paper out of his pack. On it, in his own neat penmanship, was laid out a clear and simple contract. He would provide the drawings and the building crew, and acquire the materials necessary for the work. The work to be performed was listed in detail. A full estimate of the total to be paid would be delivered after the materials list had been determined and costed. In addition to the deposit, a further payment would be due at the stage where walls were rising, with the remaining amount due on completion to the satisfaction of the contracting parties. Adjustments to the total might be made if the customers decided they wanted any changes to the original plan.

Hegmar had just gone up several notches in Andrion's estimation, and he could see from Erik's expression that he too was impressed. Erik had more experience than he did in hands-on craftsmanship, really, and he made sure that they had both studied the contract before signing it and paying over the deposit. Hegmar shook hands with them both and thanked them, saying he expected he would see them tomorrow up at the farm. As he went out, he made sure to ogle the naked ladies in the bathing pool.

After the little man had exited the Maiden, Andrion turned to Erik. "I think," he said, "that Bram has found us the Real Deal."

"I'll drink to that," Erik responded. "You want one?" Andrion smiled and nodded, and soon the two of them were sipping a couple of deliciously chilled bottles of mead. Their discussion ran on well into the afternoon.

Chapter 40: The Exiles

Bernadette fast-travelled to Sylvanian, only to find that once again she had arrived after dark. Curse you, magic map, she railed mentally. Without the map she'd have probably spent most of the past few months in Iscandia travelling across country while being attacked by smilodons, bears, and creatures less wholesome. Assuming she survived that long. Or maybe she and everybody on the planet would be dead, she having failed in her quest as Fireblood or perhaps never having even realized she *was* Fireblood. Tarragin would have brought about the end of the world, and neither she nor anyone else would have been in a position to curse the annoying time distortions that fast-travelling brought with it.

"Forgive me, magic map" she murmured facetiously as she considered her next move. Clearly it was too late for some of her intended errands, but perhaps she could still get a few things done before what was apparently going to be another bedtime a few subjective hours after she had gotten out of bed. Though she had to admit, she felt far more tired and hungry than should have been possible if only those short hours had truly elapsed since breakfast.

She walked up the city's long main street and past the wall that separated the commercial area near the gates from the residential district that led from there to the eorl's palace. The area also included the Bards' Academy and the Hall of the Dead, as well as the homes of some of Sylvanian's most prominent citizens.

Bernadette approached the eorl's palace, her goal. The guards at the front doors of the palace greeted Bernadette courteously enough. Even in her leathers, she was familiar as a friend of the march, one who had provided valuable services and was a friend of their eorl. She, in company with one or another of her lovers, had performed several services at the behest of Eorl Bergen, earning his gratitude but not an invitation to be made Warden of Mountmarch. Considering the position of warden could potentially carry responsibilities with it, perhaps that was just as well.

But it was not Bergen Bernadette had come here seeking. After entering the hall, she went not up either of the curving twin staircases leading to the throne room, but off to the left. There, a set of stairs went down into the basement. Within that dismal space she found a ragtag band of Iscandia's dispossessed elite and their retainers, sitting down to a modest meal at a long table in one corner of the room.

As she approached the group, Bernadette was surprised to be invited to join them at the table. Since her stomach had no more idea of what time it was than her head did, she happily took a place – squeezing in next to Eorl Hjaermond. As they broke bread together, he remarked "You're The Fireblood, aren't you?

"Yes," she admitted.

"I thought so," the old man replied, offering a hand. They continued their meal, Bernadette fairly astonished at the appetite that had reared its head the moment she tasted food. What, she'd had a nice stroll up to Dypendwelve and back, followed by a somewhat shorter one from the gates of Sylvanian to the eorl's palace. How did this translate into a hunger that felt as if she'd spent the last eight hours fighting her way past legions of aptrgangr? I hope I don't get fat, she thought.

As the meal concluded, Bernadette turned to Hjaermond and said, "I have some good news for you, and an invitation. Can we go somewhere more private?" Hjaermond looked at her questioningly, then stood and gestured toward a corner of the large stone-lined room in which they sat. They found a couple of chairs and sat, away from most of the room's inhabitants.

"I'm sure you will remember your sworn man Bjorn One-Eye?" Bernadette asked. The old man's eyes went far away for a moment.

"Young Bjorn," he said, recalling times before he had been deposed. Then his eyes cleared and he pierced Bernadette with a look that demanded more information. "Yes?" he prompted.

"I've been made Warden of Westmarch by your successor," she said, hoping to gloss over too much mention of the man the Remans had placed on Hjaermond's throne. "He assigned me Bjorn's services, and I took him with me to Waterdon, where I am also warden."

Hjaermond nodded. He was more than a little in awe of this young woman. After all that she had achieved in defeating Tarragin, he was not at all surprised that she was warden of more than one hold. If anything, he was surprised she was not yet warden of *all* of them. Bernadette continued, formally, "He and my Waterdon body servant Lifa wish to wed, which I have approved. And he has requested that you be present for the wedding."

Tears glistened in the old man's eyes, but did not fall. He was touched beyond speaking that Bjorn should wish him, now a useless relic, to bear witness to the happiest event of his life. Getting a grip on himself, he answered the earnest young woman who was watching him so intently, hope in her eyes. "Of course," he said softly. "Of course I would be honored to attend. But where, and when? These days," he gestured around the cheerless basement room, "I have so few resources."

An instant resolve flared up in Bernadette. Though the imperial decision to reconfigure the rulership of some of Iscandia's marches had had nothing to do with her, the old man's plight struck her to the heart. "You'll come with me and stay at the Bathing Maiden until it's time to go to the wedding," she told him.

"I must take Selden with me," he protested.

"Selden?" she asked.

"He's my uncle, and was my steward when I was eorl," Hjaermond explained.

"Of course," she responded reassuringly. "That will be no problem. I will come and get you both and we'll fast-travel to the Maiden tomorrow sometime. Will that be all right?"

Hjaermond smiled at her wryly. "Believe me, I'll be here. I have nowhere else to go. Selden and I will await your return." Bernadette stood up and squeezed Hjaermond's hands, giving him a warm smile that quite melted the old fellow's heart. She skated by on her youth, her beauty, and her reputation far more than she realized. But in this case it was her kindness and concern that had won her another friend.

Bernadette climbed the stairs to the entry hall of the eorl's palace, still in the grip of bittersweet emotions. She had to admit, she liked Hjaermond as a person better than she liked Galdur, who was a typical member of his family and too grasping by half. And she felt they'd reached a satisfactory conclusion to their discussion, her mission fulfilled. The old man and his even-older uncle would likely enjoy their stay at the Bathing Maiden.

It was too late, Bernadette decided, to approach Engbard for details of the dream granted to him by Aderos in answer to his prayers. But he had definitely seemed positive – jubilant, even – and she hoped for the best. Tomorrow she would rise early and go talk with the priest at the Pantheatos.

Chapter 41: The Work Begins

Andrion woke in the Maiden's master bed and reached sleepily for Berni, before coming awake enough to realize she was not there – and he didn't know when she'd be back. She'd often enough been sleeping elsewhere during their time together, but this was the first time in weeks that he actually had no idea where she was. She'd said Alfenstein, but where was she going from there? As much as he missed her, and missed making love with her, he hoped she would stay away a little longer. He and Erik had a lot of work to see to, if they were to prepare their surprise.

The thought of that project galvanized him, and he jumped right out of bed. This time, mindful of his embarrassment yesterday, he took the time to wash up and neatly comb his shoulder-length hair before going downstairs. Maybe I should let it grow and tie it back, he thought. That might be less work. Andrion found Erik up and eating breakfast at their usual table, though he could see from the color of the light coming in through the Maiden's bottle glass windows that it was pretty early in the morning.

He pulled up a chair and grinned at his friend. "Anxious to get started?" he asked. Erik smiled back at him around a mouthful of pastry.

Then, washing it down with a mug of hot tea, he said "I can't wait. Not that we're actually doing the work, but I think one or the other of us needs to be there from the start and make sure it's being done right."

"You know more about that kind of thing than I do," Andrion told him, biting into his own pastry.

Erik glanced at him. Hum, he'd never considered that he might know more about *anything* than his older and more erudite friend did. But their life experiences had not been the same. It stood to reason that, though Andrion might hold a much larger and wider store of knowledge in that brain of his, Erik could have more expertise in one or two areas. He'd worked with his hands often, while Andrion had been studying magic and poring over musty old tomes.

"I have the feeling it might be a good idea to have Bjorn join us, too" Erik said after swallowing another bite and washing it down with some hot, sweet tea. "I think he's done enough building to have at least some idea of what he's seeing when somebody else is doing the job." Andrion continued chewing and nodded.

When his mouth was free again he said, "Why don't you and I go into Waterdon this morning and talk with him? We can drop off a few supplies and say hi to Anja, and check at Valkyrie to find out how soon we might get the rest of our money. I really hope we'll have enough to cover Hegmar's needs without asking Berni for more. That could get awkward."

Erik smiled, nodding. "Sounds like a good idea. We've hardly ever asked her for cash. She's likely to get suspicious if she returns from her errands and the first thing we have to say is 'Honey, give us some money.'"

Andrion, finished now with the couple of pastries and mug of tea which were all he really wanted at this hour, mused "There's some ingots and magical essence vials down in the basement. We could sell those to Bernard, or maybe Garimund would pay us for the vials. Or we could just ask Lev to give us some gold."

"You're right," Erik said, looking relieved. "We should have more than enough to finish the project without bringing it to Berni's attention. Are you ready to go?"

Erik stood and Andrion followed, brushing crumbs off his trousers as he rose. They stopped off at the bar to pick up some supplies. As Berni's fiancés, they were both lauded by their fellow Maiden employees (Fenris in particular was sorry it had not been *him* who'd claimed the beautiful Fireblood's heart) and treated as if they were her proxies in her absence. So there was no problem taking anything they wanted without paying for it, or issuing orders.

They found the weather on the raw side this morning, with rain threatening and a stiff breeze making them wish they'd brought along cloaks. But walking soon warmed them. As Andrion and Erik approached Coldburn Farm they saw Hegmar outside it with a couple of helpers. He had a pair of curious-looking instruments mounted on tripods, and coils of twine knotted at intervals, with which he and his crew appeared to be taking measurements. This looked promising. Andrion greeted him, and said "We're going into town but we'll be back in the next hour or two. Can we confer with you then?"

Hegmar, focused on what he was doing, broke his concentration long enough to give them a lopsided grin and say "A'right. See you…" before returning to the task at hand.

As the two friends continued up the road to town their discussion mostly revolved around Hegmar. There was something about the man personally that made him seem questionable, somehow – but from what they've seen of him on the job he knew his shit. Getting in the main gates of Waterdon by around 9, Andrion and Erik made straight for the door of Brightsgate Cottage. Co-owners of the house in theory, if not in actual law, they still respected the privacy of the occupants and knocked. Then they waited for admittance.

It was Bjorn who opened the door to them, greeting them with a broad grin. "Good morning!" he said heartily, seeming to be in as good a mood as ever they'd seen him. He ushered them inside the cottage, where they found Lifa standing at the fire stirring a pot of wheat porridge while Anya sat at the table reading her alphabet book. Clearly, Bjorn had captured her imagination with that.

"Have you eaten?" Bjorn asked them.

"Thanks," Erik said. "We ate before leaving the Maiden."

"Well, have some tea then," their host said, gesturing toward a tall pewter pot sitting atop an iron trivet on the table. They thanked him, and helped themselves to a couple of steaming mugs as the rest of the family tucked into bowls of the porridge, lightly sweetened with honey and swimming in butter and milk.

Erik, whose breakfast had been cut somewhat short by his eagerness to leave this morning (and whose appetite had been further stimulated by the walk here) looked at that porridge a little regretfully. But he felt it best to hold his peace. You can't just pop in on somebody cooking for the family and expect them to magically stretch the meal to feed extra mouths.

As the family ate, Erik and Andrion began telling their co-conspirators about developments in the project – also obtaining Lifa's collusion in their plan to take Bjorn with them as part of the "oversight committee" to make sure that the work was done as they wanted. About halfway through this, it abruptly occurred to Andrion that Anja was sitting there, eating her breakfast and taking all this in.

What "news" might she happily share with Berni on their next meeting?

"Anja," he said, making sure the little one was paying attention to him. "Do you know what we're talking about?" The girl looked a little unsure.

"You're making a house?" she asked hesitantly.

"That's right," he told her. "We're making a special house where Aunt Berni and I and Erik are going to live, and you and Lifa and Bjorn will come and visit there whenever you want. But we want to make it a special surprise for Aunt Berni. Do you understand?"

The youngster's warm brown eyes lit up. "Oh! I *love* surprises!" Andrion grinned at her.

"So do I, and so does Aunt Berni. But in order to make the surprise, we need to do everything in secret. That means that you *can't tell* anything you know about the surprise when Aunt Berni comes to visit. And you shouldn't tell her that you know there's a secret, either, or she will get suspicious. Do you think you can do that?"

Anja gave him a coy look that was somehow much older than her five years, and batted her eyes at him innocently. "*What* secret?" she said.

The four adults in the room looked at Anja in surprise. Just how bright *was* this child, and what did it portend for the future? Andrion had a feeling it would all come back to haunt them when she hit adolescence; but for the moment it appeared their secret was safe. After Bjorn had finished his breakfast (and washed up his bowl, spoon, mug, and the cooking pot as well, his friends noted), he kissed Lifa and Anja goodbye. "I'll be down at Coldburn Farm most of the day," he told them. "You can send a runner if you need anything."

"We'll be fine," Lifa told him somewhat coolly. "Do you want me to pack you a lunch?" Bjorn glanced at the other men in the room.

"We'll get lunch at the Maiden," Andrion told him.

Their schedule for the day thus arranged, the three still-impressive but increasingly domesticated warriors left the cottage. They found Alessia outside Valkyrie just resting with her back against a post. "'Morning Alessia," Andrion greeted her. "I was wondering whether you had any more gold for us?"

She smiled at him. "Yes, quite a few of those pieces you placed with us have already been sold. Bernadette does good work." She produced a sack of gold and counted out another 3,000 guilders. "That leaves us owing you, let me see, 7,000 guilders, right?" Andrion nodded. Alessia had him sign a receipt, and they went on their way.

By the time the three men had gotten back to Coldburn Farm, it appeared that Hegmar and his crew had finished their measurements of the existing small farmhouse and were now laying out the new wing. Twine was affixed to small iron stakes, marking out the boundaries of the structure and the interior walls of each room. Andrion, Erik, and Bjorn were captivated. It was as if their mental vision was being transformed into reality before their eyes. Admittedly a sketchy reality; but here on the actual building site it was possible to visualize the additions much more fully than when they were just making marks on paper.

Andrion introduced Bjorn to Hegmar, who shook his hand and reiterated his offer to take Bjorn on as an assistant. Bjorn nodded at him rather gravely, but informed him that he was oath-bound to serve Westmarch and not free to take on any permanent assignments without the express command of his warden – and ultimately, his eorl. Should his service to Bernadette terminate for some reason – such as her death, a falling-out with the eorl, or her simply no longer claiming his services, his duty would revert to Alfenstein.

The little builder eyed him appraisingly, "'S a pity," he declared, then shortly got back to showing them around the site. "Here's your new wing," he said gesturing at a rectangle somewhat wider than the original house and joined to it at the northern end. "We've got your craft room on the west side, along with the bathroom and the 'privy'. The hall leads down the middle. On the east side, there's your bigger bedroom with smaller ones on either side, with the porch running along the east side of those and a door out to it from each of the bedrooms. And your nursery runs across the width of the wing at the northern end of the hall."

Hegmar gestured to where his crew were even now delineating a square maybe 20 feet on a side, somewhat to the west and north of the original house . "They're laying out your water tower now," he said. "I've got the bathroom and privy right next to the original structure, so the water can serve those rooms and the kitchen with the minimum amount of piping. Now that waste system, it'll have drain pipes running underground west of the annex to the tank over here…" more gestures, to an area that was currently marked with what looked like powdered chalk, "and the water from the kitchen and the bath will drain there too. Then your drain field goes down the slope toward the road."

The discussions went on for some time, Bernadette's three adherents becoming more and more impressed with the way Hegmar was handling things. For the first time since they'd hatched this scheme, Andrion was starting to think they might actually pull it off. They paced around the site, making sure that the dimensions of the rooms seemed right. The only thing the design seemed to lack was a single large room where the entire family could relax together; but in warm weather, at least, the roofed veranda would meet that need. And they could always add more rooms as needed over the years.

Andrion had a thought, and asked Hegmar, "Can you get some decent sized clear windows?" Large areas of plate glass were unheard-of in Iscandia, but the farm's picturesque setting called for windows you could actually look out of. Hegmar shook his head. "I've got nobody can make glass you can see through, to speak of. But your friend said you're a wizard?"

Andrion nodded. "What I can do, see, is frame the windows in and make shutters for them. All tight and secure, come night or bad weather. Then in fine weather, you just open up the shutters and there's your view. And mayhap, you can figure out some way to make a sheet of glass that could go in there so you can see out but not get the wind and the bugs? You do it, and everybody in Iscandia's going to want that. You and me, we could set up in partnership, like. What d'you think?" Hegmar smiled what Andrion assumed was intended to be winningly. He smiled back.

"Sounds like a good idea, Hegmar," Andrion said. "You frame those window openings and cover them with shutters we can close and lock from the inside, for now." He and his cohorts continued walking around the place, their minds alight with inspiration and anticipation. They could hardly wait to see this actually take shape. As morning wore on into afternoon Hegmar's crew took a lunch break, downing tools to plop down beside the house and produce bread, cheese, apples and ale which they consumed with enthusiasm.

"Are we good, then?" Hegmar asked them. The lines of the addition, as delineated by the twine, appeared to be properly placed, square and true. There were still a few details of construction to be worked out but it appeared that the "map" was in order and work could proceed.

Andrion and Erik, after a glance at each other, said in unison "I think so." Hegmar produced yet another piece of rolled paper from inside his cloak and they all trooped inside the house. He spread the paper on the table near the door and Andrion and Erik were required to sign off on it.

"I need your okay before I get started on the digging," he explained. "I'll have another crew with shovels out here after lunch. Then tomorrow I should have the final construction drawings done, and I'll be giving you the final estimate after I cost the materials. We should be starting to rise above ground level in another few days." Erik and Andrion gulped, and signed. They *needed* this to proceed in a hurry, but the fact that it was doing just that left them feeling as though they wanted to pull back and reconsider. Being men of action though, they stifled their misgivings and forged ahead.

Leaving Hegmar to eat his own lunch and send for his digging crew, the three strolled on down the road a short distance to the Bathing Maiden. Bjorn had not been here before, and he was fairly dazzled at the handsome, well-built inn with its upper story and several pools. Particularly, of course, the hot pool in the common room. Early afternoon was a slow time for the pool, though, and no naked people of either gender were to be found therein.

Bjorn bent to put his hand in the water and his good eye lit. "You're planning something like this for the house?" he asked Andrion. In the minds of the three conspirators, their project had become "The House."

291

"Smaller," Andrion demurred. "Maybe a third this size, but deep enough you can get wet up to your armpits. I still haven't worked out the water system, though. A tub this deep holds a lot of water, and if we're relying on our cistern for filling it we can't be draining it every day. It rains here a lot, but not *that* much – and we know Berni's going to want to bathe every day."

They all headed for the "Owner's Table," as they were coming to think of it, and Erik motioned Lev over. "What's on the fire?" he asked.

Lev smiled. "How about some fresh-caught salmon? Pulled them out of the river an hour ago. And there's bread and some grilled leeks…"

"Sounds good," Erik told him. "And some chilled ales all 'round?" Lev nodded, and soon returned with three bottles of the best.

As the three men enjoyed their frosty bottles of ale and waited for the food to arrive, they resumed their discussion. "The hot pool over there and the warm one out on the deck operate with some kind of dypalfar mechanism that keeps the water circulating, filtering and purifying it somehow while maintaining the temperature," Andrion explained. He went on, "While Berni and I were chasing The Staff of Apoldros we met some actual white elves, the race that was corrupted into the leukalfar by the dypalfar."

Bjorn had gotten some of this tale after they'd returned from their vampire-killing expedition; but he hadn't heard all the details and his eyebrows raised as Andrion continued. "From what that Duraenis guy said the dypalfar were a bunch of bastards. But it's too bad there aren't still a few of them around. Or better yet, some really comprehensive technical manuals explaining how their machines work – along with a Dypalfar-to-Common Speech dictionary." He sighed.

Their salmon steaks and leeks arrived, sizzling from the grill and looking juicy and delicious. They were accompanied by more chilled ale and a plate of bread rolls, and for the time being the three men abandoned talk for food. Lev had used some kind of herbs on the salmon, that lent it a piquant and delicious tang. When appetites had been blunted, conversation resumed – with frequent pauses as they continued to work their way through the rest of their repast.

"Andrion," Erik said, "I don't think we need all three of us out there at the site this afternoon. They're just digging holes, after all. Why don't you put your mind to the hot water issue this afternoon, while Bjorn and I go back up there and oversee the work? I know I'm eager to see every detail of how they do it, in case I want to do it myself someday. How about you, Bjorn?"

The somewhat grim-looking warrior smiled and nodded. "I'm thinking that some of the improvements that are being made to the house might be applied to Brightsgate Cottage," he speculated.

Andrion thought that a fine idea. His mind had leapt to the challenge of the puzzle before it like a trout to a tempting fly, and he was already chewing over half a dozen possible solutions. He had a few ideas about the glass, too, but those would require some experimentation. The three finished their meal and, burping gently from the bubbles in the ale, split into two groups. Erik and Bjorn left by the front door and went down the road to Coldburn, while Andrion went upstairs and changed into some lightweight armor. What he planned to do would require some protection.

Chapter 42: The Pantheatos

Bernadette woke with the dawn in her room at the Dancing Rabbit. She had been given a small room across the hall from the one where she and Erik had had their exciting tryst months before, and as she came to consciousness she was not sure whether she was sorry or glad not to have spent the night in that same room. Every time she came here to spend the night she found herself recalling that other night, and on this occasion she had nobody with her to relieve the resulting tension. The ability Erik had demonstrated since she'd first set eyes on him, to send her pulse racing and her cunt throbbing, apparently applied even in his absence.

She dedicated a little solo orgasm to the memory of that night before getting out of bed. Damn, she was really starting to get horny. But there were still many tasks to perform, and not much time to do them all. Bernadette considered, and realized that she'd promised Hjaermond she would take him and Selden back to the Maiden until it was time for Bjorn and Lifa's wedding. That would certainly put her in range of the men she was craving.

Feeling buoyed at the thought, she washed her face and hands in the room's basin and used a damp towel to perform a perfunctory cleaning of her limbs, armpits, breasts, and crotch. It wasn't just her hot studs she was missing – the Maiden's hot bathing pool beckoned to her like the vision of an oasis in the mind of a man dying of thirst in the wastes of Zahar.

Dressing once again in her "warden" garb, Bernadette sashayed out the front doors of the Rabbit with a wave to the proprietor, and no thought whatsoever of breakfast. She'd pick something up later. But first, she had to confer with Engbard at Sylvanian's Pantheatos. Was it only a week or so ago she had last seen him? So much had happened since then!

Bernadette made her way to the temple's main entrance and went inside. She was met by Frieda, the priestess she had seen here on her previous visit. "Welcome daughter," the Norse woman told her sweetly. "If you wish a blessing, feel free to pray at any of the shrines."

"Thank you priestess," she replied with equal serenity. "I would have words with Engbard."

Frieda bowed slightly. "My husband is yet below," she said, gesturing toward a staircase leading down from an alcove at one side of the central nave. "You can go down and speak with him if you like." Bernadette nodded her thanks, and headed in the direction the woman had indicated.

The public areas were grand-looking, but as she descended the stairs she found living quarters as humble as those in any farmhouse. Engbard greeted her with a twinkle in his eye. "So, you have returned," he said. "How went your quest for the Eparchy and the Staff of Apoldros?"

"We found quite a surprise there, Father," Bernadette told him. Would you believe it, there are five living members of the original order of Apoldrians still living there, tending their shrines? And they're white elves – unchanged leukalfar, as they were before their betrayal by the dypalfar!"

"Astounding," Engbard replied. "Such religious devotion, to outlast the millennia. And does this mean that the original race of white elves might be reborn?"

"Not unless we can locate an all-female white elf religious order someplace and talk both groups into giving up their vows of celibacy, I fear," Bernadette replied wryly. A stray thought came to her. Might the original white elf strain be bred back by a mating between one of those monks and a female of the changelings? Somehow, she couldn't quite see it happening. In any case, the elven races bred at a fraction of the rate the rest of humanity did.

"If I can get some time off from the Pantheatos someday, I would greatly like to make a pilgrimage to the Eparchy," Engbard said.

"They're working on restoring it now," she told him. "Maybe in a few years they'll be open for business again. But it's not an easy place to get to."

"Well, enough about that," the priest said. "Our father Aderos smiles on you, it would seem. He spoke to me in my dream and told me that your two loves could be bound to you in matrimony, under the auspices of the Pantheatos. Are they in accord with this?"

Bernadette flashed him a brilliant smile, her heart in her eyes. "I asked them, and they both said yes! We're going to be married, and soon!"

Engbard smiled kindly at her. "You would like to have the ceremony in the courtyard?" he asked. The Pantheatos' outdoor area, with its altar and benches, was perfect for weddings provided the weather held fair. But with express permission from the father of creation, how could it not?

"Yes!" Bernadette cried, her mind already racing toward plans. She had doubted that her wedding would be more than some surreptitious and left-handed affair involving her and her two grooms, with a priest on the side and maybe a witness or two. Might they actually do it up in style?

"And when would you like to hold the wedding?" Engbard asked, bringing Bernadette up short. How could she specify a date? Had Erik and Andrion found a home for them? She really wanted to start her married life with them in their own place, private and away from the constant traffic of the Maiden. But what if it took months for them to find the right place? Now that she had learned her dreams could be a reality, she didn't want to wait that long.

Bernadette demurred for a moment, calculating. The wedding between Lifa and Bjorn was now something like three weeks away, and she still had to arrange for that to take place at the Temple of Marmira in Lakedon. After that wedding there was the party at the Maiden, and she wanted some time after that to decompress and finalize arrangements for her own wedding. "Would five weeks' time be all right?" she asked, followed by "Oh, what day is it?"

Engbard looked at her questioningly. "It's the first of Sunreturn," he said, adding "Happy New Year." Bernadette was pretty sure it had been the 30th of Longnight when she left on her trip to Alfenstein. Year-end celebrations didn't amount to much here in Iscandia, and she'd scarcely noticed the date. That meant she'd lost two days, and given that she'd slept a night in Alfenstein and another here, that wasn't unreasonable.

"Could we set the date for, say, Maritag the 10th of Fevrous?" she asked, calculating quickly.

The priest turned to a book sitting on a nearby table and leafed through it. It appeared to be some kind of diary or appointment book, with a page for each day. "Will early afternoon work for you?" he asked, "perhaps one in the afternoon?" This was all really happening! Suppressing a surge of excitement/anxiety, Bernadette told him that would be fine. "Let's see," Engbard said. "You are Bernadette, The Fireblood of course. Do you have a surname?"

Bernadette replied "Bouchard. Bernadette Bouchard." He produced a quill and inkwell and marked her down in the space allotted to one in the afternoon on the date in question.

"Your grooms' names?" he requested.

"Andrion Lamonte and Erik Johannessohn," Bernadette said proudly. The sense that her dreams were within her grasp was beginning to sink in, and with it a sense of huge power. If she could do this, she could do anything!

"Duly noted," Engbard said, his pen scratching for another moment. "Please contact me at least a week in advance with any special requests regarding the ceremony, and we'll expect to see the wedding party here by 11 in the morning on the day." He squeezed her hands, amused at this famously powerful young woman's air of triumph mixed with perplexity. He loved being an agent of the gods.

Bernadette's face lit. "Thank you, Engbard. Thank you! I'll be in touch." With that she turned and walked back up the stairs, her head fairly spinning. She had done it, it was really going to happen! Though not, she soon realized, without a lot more work. Leaving the Pantheatos, she walked back down the street in the direction of Sylvanian's main gates. Along the way, she was scanning the people on the street to the left and right of her. Before long, she'd spotted a young woman who looked just about right.

Approaching her, Bernadette said "Excuse me. My name is Bernadette, and I was wondering if you could do me a favor. I'll pay you fifty guilders if you'll come with me to The Golden Thread for a few minutes." The buxom, fresh-faced girl eyed her suspiciously for a moment, then seemed to conclude that this strange woman accosting her did not present a threat.

"Why not?" she smiled, accepting the coins Bernadette pressed into her hand, and falling into step with her as they continued to the establishment in question. "By the way, she added, "my name is Saalma."

So far as Bernadette knew, The Golden Thread was the only shop in the whole of Iscandia devoted solely to selling clothing. Throughout the province, those who did not have the skill or inclination to sew their own clothing, but who also had the coin, could hire a seamstress who worked out of her home. But here in Sylvanian, the haughty ljosalfar sisters Senalie and Miralie ran an establishment that catered to the sartorial needs of Iscandia's elite.

Inside the shop, Senalie greeted her pleasantly enough. Though neither of the sisters (nor any ljosalfar Bernadette had yet met, actually) was what you'd call warm and friendly, Bernadette was recognized as a well-heeled customer. "I have a special commission for you," she told the elf woman. I need a wedding dress, and I need to pick it up by the 12th. It should be beautiful, the finest materials you have, I think ivory satin and lace. And this young lady Saalma is my fitting model." An eyebrow cocked, Senalie looked the girl up and down.

"I'll need you to strip down to your underwear," she said brusquely.

"Right here?" Saalma asked, taken aback.

"Certainly not," the ljosalfar woman replied. "If you will all step through to the fitting room?"

Senalie gestured them into the rear of the shop, where a curtained alcove protected the customers' privacy. Saalma felt a little uneasy about this but hey, it was all women here and fifty guilders was fifty guilders. Besides, she was taken by the romantic nature of the request. Some lucky woman, presumably built like her, was going to receive a beautiful dress to be married in. So, she removed her dress and stood still, legs slightly apart, as Senalie took her measurements.

"I will need her here for another fitting after the dress is cut and sewn," Senalie stated. "And I can't guarantee a perfect fit on your bride, assuming this girl is not she."

"It's to be a surprise," Bernadette explained, "so I can't bring the bride in. But I'll give it to her far enough before the wedding that I can bring it, and her, back here for a final fitting if need be. Will that work?" Senalie looked annoyed, but on the other hand Bernadette was one of her wealthiest and most famous clients so she supposed she could humor her request.

Making an effort, she pasted a smile on her face and said, "That will be fine. I'll complete the dress and you can pick it up as early as the 10th, if you like. I'll need a hundred-guilder deposit." Wow, Bernadette thought. A full suit of off-the-rack fine clothing such as she'd worn on her trip to Wyrmshalla only cost around half that to buy. But on the other hand, this was a very special occasion. And she had no shortage of funds, especially after her transaction with Dhyazh.

"Certainly," Bernadette told Senalie. "If you're finished with Saalma, we should let her go on her way." The ljosalfar seamstress nodded, and Saalma slipped back into her clothing, giving Bernadette a toothy grin and a word of thanks before returning to the errands she'd been running earlier. "I have another commission for you as well," Bernadette said. "There's a little more time on this – The wedding will be here in Sylvanian on the 10th of next month. Mine!" she broke into a self-satisfied grin, and Senalie couldn't help smiling as well – this time in genuine pleasure.

"Well," Senalie said, "Who's the lucky man? Is it that hunky Norseman you've been traveling with? Or the cute Galise?" Bernadette had run into Senalie a few times over the past few months, sometimes with one and sometimes the other of her lovers, acting as questing companions.

She gave Senalie a wicked smile and said, "Both of them." The Elf woman blinked, then looked thoughtful.

"That should prove... interesting," she commented.

Bernadette pressed on to the details. She had given this some thought and she had her own ideas for the design of her gown. She was no artist, at least not in the same league with Bjorn, but she had produced a sketch that conveyed the general idea. "I want it in rainbow jewel tones," she explained, "layered and draped with hidden clasps to hold the layer pieces in place. I'll probably need to come here on the morning of the day and have you put it on me, then I can throw a cloak over it and walk up to the Pantheatos. Will you be available that day?"

"Certainly," Senalie assured her. She and her sister rarely took a full day off. She was intrigued by this very original concept for a gown that worked like a puzzle, and looking forward to creating it. "Let's get your measurements, then, shall we?" Bernadette stripped off her fine apparel and stood while she was measured and prodded. When that was done, Senalie said "I'll need a further hundred-guilder deposit for this one, as well. And I would really like to work up a final drawing, in color, of what the dress will look like before I actually start cutting and sewing. Maybe you could okay that when you come to pick up the other dress."

"That's a good idea!" Bernadette said, pleased. This was turning out to be such fun! "May I put my clothes back on now?"

"In just a couple of minutes. Would you please stand there as if you were at the altar?" Bernadette considered what pose that might be, based on the few weddings she'd attended in her life. Several of the girls she'd grown up with had married young, but those were simple village affairs with dresses sewn by their mothers. She settled on standing there with her weight balanced evenly, feet slightly apart, and her hands held before her as if she were clutching a bouquet.

Meanwhile, Senalie had returned with a sheet of fine paper mounted on a board, and a stick of something that looked like it was made out of dull steel. It came to a point at one end, and Bernadette quickly saw that it was a drawing implement of some kind. It left fine, light gray marks on the paper. In a surprisingly short time Senalie had done a full-body portrait of Bernadette standing there in her underwear. Her arms, neck and face were well delineated, but her legs and body were just some faint outlines.

"Will you be wearing your hair up?" Senalie asked. Huh, Bernadette hadn't even thought of it. She'd given so little time in her life for these "girly" things like hairstyles, usually either letting it hang long and straight as it did now, or tying it back with a cord to get it out of her face. But why not wear it piled up on her head? This was a once-in-a-lifetime occasion, and she was sure she could get one of the women at the Maiden to help her with it before coming here on the day of the wedding.

"Yes, I think I will," she responded finally to the question. With a few more strokes, Senalie shaped a mass of hair atop Bernadette's head in the drawing, her graceful neck exposed.

"Okay, you can get dressed now" Senalie told Bernadette. After slipping back into her clothes she eagerly approached to get a look at the drawing. Wow, Senalie was as good as or better than Bjorn was! Sketchy body aside, the woman in the drawing was clearly Bernadette – or how she would look with her hair up. She made a mental note to try that style next time she wanted to impress somebody with her high-class refinement. It was certainly a lot more elegant-looking. "I'll use your sketch and this drawing as the basis for my final drawing, showing what the dress will look like on you. I think you're going to like it!" Senalie said, breaking momentarily from her usual snooty ljosalfar reserve.

Thanking Senalie warmly, Bernadette paid her the two hundred guilders as requested and took her leave. Standing in the street outside the shop, her heart soaring at the thought of her forthcoming wedding, she was brought up short when her stomach announced in no uncertain terms that it was about to divorce her on grounds of non-support. Well, she needed to sit down and gather her thoughts, in any case. She stepped across the road to the Dancing Rabbit, where she ordered some stew and bread at the bar and then took a seat at a small table.

Bernadette washed her food down with water, not usually her first choice but she wanted to keep an absolutely clear head. She was beginning to feel like a carnival juggler with a dozen plates spinning in the air, and more due to go up at any moment. While shoveling food into her mouth in a manner at odds with her ladylike attire, she opened her small journal to the current page and looked it over. Wishing she had a drawing stick like the one Senalie had used (note to self: find and buy!), she pulled out quill and ink and began updating her to-do list.

Good grief, there were old quests in here from before she and Andrion had joined the Daywatch Brigade. At the moment, her enthusiasm for slaughtering a blameless giant in exchange for a few hundred guilders had dropped to near zero. Nor did she want to risk her ass eliminating bandits or rooting out Insurgents. Let some other adventurers have the fun – and the gold – for now.

Flipping to a fresh page she wrote down dates. The date she was to pick up Lifa's dress, the date of her wedding. Pick up Hjaermond and Selden, that would probably be the first thing she did after lunch. She needed to discuss some things with Eorl Ormund back in Waterdon, but felt that should wait until after she'd gone to Lakedon to set a date and time for Lifa and Bjorn's wedding.

Was she forgetting anything? She'd put finding a place for herself and the guys to live into their hands, and as much love as she felt for them along with respect for their abilities, she had no idea whether this was a task they would be up to handling. Hell, she wasn't sure it was a task *she* was up to handling. She'd bought two properties in her life, both within the past few weeks, and in each case she merely took the only thing that was offered. The Maiden had been handed to her on a platter, and she liked it a lot – except for its air of being a public place.

Finishing her meal, Bernadette blew on the page to dry the ink before closing the book and tucking it back in her pouch. Time to walk up to the eorl's palace and collect the former Eorl of Alfenstein.

Chapter 43: Experimentation

Suitably garbed, Andrion borrowed a heavy steel bucket from Lev and, armed and with a battle spell at the ready, carried it down the stairs leading off the Maiden's rear deck to the shore of the river less than a quarter of a mile down the hill. Despite its proximity to Waterdon the area around the Maiden could be wild and dangerous. Sometimes they had wolves or ogres coming right up onto the decks. It was the reason that Fenris could usually be found patrolling the area around the building, armed to the teeth.

Luckily, Andrion encountered nothing worse on his way to the waterside than a couple of enormous crackclaws, which he blasted to oblivion from a safe distance with his lightning spell. As he'd hoped, he found a wash of clean, fine-sand beach on a stretch of the river where it bent away to the east. Brushing away leaves and twigs, he filled the bucket about half full with the sand before returning to the Maiden.

Andrion let himself into the basement through the trap door on the rear deck. He had never actually worked with glass before, though he had some understanding of the principles involved. He set the bucket of sand into the forge fires and fed them, pumping the bellows to bring the heat up. Then he applied his most intense fire spell to the bucket's contents.

Soon the bucket was glowing, and the sand within it was beginning to show signs of melting. But Andrion couldn't maintain the fire spell – his magical energy kept running out. Berni had given him several items of clothing and jewelry that she'd enchanted to raise his overall magical energy level and improve the rate at which it replenished itself. He went back upstairs, leaving the bucket in the forge, and returned in a few minutes prepared to give that sand the burning of its life.

With this magical enhancement, he was now able to make the heat soar. But as the sand formed into a blob of glass within the bucket, the bucket itself melted through – leaking the thick, molten glass into the forge fire. Shit! Andrion was beginning to wonder just how crazy he was. Did he really think he could do something no glassmaker in Agena had yet achieved?

Time for a little study. Leaving his mess behind, he climbed the ladder to the trap door behind the bar and began rummaging through the bookshelves that were scattered here and there throughout the Maiden. No tomes on making glass. Indeed, few enough books on any technical subject. He knew just where, if anywhere, such books might be found – the library of the Academy at Eisenstag was the most extensive he had ever seen. And its uruk librarian, Mhyrzon din-Tzrek, was an acquaintance of his. But without Berni around to take him there with her magic map, getting there in a reasonable amount of time was an impossibility.

Reluctantly, Andrion concluded that the issue of large panes of clear plate glass would have to wait until he had more understanding of basic glassmaking. He still had some ideas of how it could be done, but just being able to create glass from sand would be required before he got into any fancy techniques. He was tempted, after this rebuff, just to grab a snack and go down to Coldburn to gawk at the work crew and hang out with his friends; but he restrained himself.

Getting an ale from the bar and a roll of paper, Andrion sat at the table in the master suite, where things were quieter in the afternoon, sketching ideas for a hot water system. You could, he supposed, split the flow from the tower-mounted cistern into two pipes, with one of them going to a device that would heat the water and then to specially dedicated valves that dispensed only hot water while others, not connected to the device, would dispense only water at whatever temperature it came in at from the cistern. In high summer, that would probably be fairly warm.

Hmm, you could create a sort of hot water reservoir. But for the water to stay hot, it would either need continuous energy applied to it or massive amounts of insulation to keep it hot once it had been brought to the desired temperature. Oh, how he wished for a dypalfar engineer whispering in his ear! Andrion considered some other ways that hot water could be produced. If you ran water through a series of copper tubes such as were used to produce spirits, you could apply heat to the coils and the water would be instantly heated as it made its way through them. But how would you trigger the heat?

Andrion was still at his drawing board hours later, still wracking his brain for viable ideas, when Erik returned to the Maiden. He'd parted company with Bjorn as they left Coldburn Farm, Hegmar and his work crew accompanying Bjorn back to town. Erik looked around for Andrion but found no sign of him. He wasn't down in the basement, though he noticed there was a strange-looking mass of twisted metal and glass in the embers of the forge fire.

Shrugging, Erik got a bottle of chilled mead from Drelos, who'd taken over from Lev at the bar. Along with it he got a bowl of potato chips. The popularity of these was spreading. Upstairs, Andrion pushed himself away from the table and sighed. He had not yet hit on the glowing inspiration that was going to solve the problem once and for all, and he needed a break. When he came downstairs he spotted Erik, and snagged a bottle of mead from the bar before joining him and helping himself to Erik's chips.

"So, how goes it?" Erik asked him.

Andrion sighed. "Still working on it, I'm afraid. I don't think I'm going to be able to do the glass thing for months or years yet. But I should be able to pull off the hot water. Just haven't worked out the best way to do it yet."

Erik smiled at him. "You'll figure it out, if anybody can. Boy, wait'll you see the job site!"

Andrion perked up at this. "Yeah?"

Erik continued, "That Hegmar really knows what he's doing. He had guys with shovels swarming all over the place, digging out the basement and the foundations and excavating the pit for the waste system. Bjorn and I really picked up a few things. I guess tomorrow we'll find out what the bite is, and how soon the place will be done. But at the rate he's working, we might be living there in a month!"

"Let's hope Berni doesn't decide we're getting married in a week then," Andrion said, swallowing a mouthful of chips and washing it down with a swig of mead.

Chapter 44: Home Again

It was at this moment that the Maiden's front doors opened and Bernadette walked in, dressed as an upper-class woman and accompanied by a regal-looking older Norseman – and another who looked positively ancient. Erik's eyes lit up. Oh, he had missed her! "Berni!" he shouted enthusiastically. Both he and Andrion noticed, as she came out of the shadow of the sleeping loft and into the center of the common room, that their beloved seemed to be glowing with happiness. *This* was a good sign…

"Erik! Andrion!" Bernadette cried in response, a huge smile lighting up her face like a beacon. She broke from the side of her two elderly companions to rush to the table where her two loves sat, eagerly awaiting her arrival. She stood between them and threw an arm around each one's head, squeezing their faces and planting kisses on their hair. Then, recalling herself, she turned to the gentlemen who were still making their way toward the table.

"Erik Johannessohn, Andrion Lamonte, may I present Hjaermond, formerly Eorl of Alfenstein, and his uncle Selden. They'll be staying here at the Maiden so I can take them with us to Bjorn and Lifa's wedding." Erik and Andrion stood in respect. Neither of them had ever met Hjaermond while he was eorl, but all they'd heard of him suggested he was a fair and honorable man.

After hands had been shaken all 'round Andrion asked, "Are you gentlemen tired? Would you like food or drink, or perhaps a rest?"

Selden, who looked eighty if he was a day, spoke up, squinting around at the room and its inhabitants. "It seems like it was just lunchtime, but it's getting dark outside!"

Bernadette put a reassuring hand on his arm. "It's just the fast-travelling, Selden," she told him. "Sometimes it can be… surprising." The old man seemed to recall. Someone in his position must have zipped around the continent via fast-travel often enough in his life. He subsided.

"Perhaps you would like to soak in a hot bath?" Bernadette asked. She was eager to turn her guests loose and get next to her men.

"That's a hot pool?" Hjaermond asked, gesturing.

"Yes!" She replied. "It's wonderfully relaxing. And nobody here pays any attention to nudity."

Hjaermond eyed her wryly, his gaze pointedly going to the pool where a buff young man and a couple of attractive women were enjoying the waters. "I can see that," he remarked.

"Let me find you two some beds," Bernadette urged. You can put down your packs, and then we'll get you some robes and you can have a nice soak before supper."

Hjaermond nodded. "Come on, Uncle. Let's go see what the rest of this place is like." Selden was still looking around him with a certain amount of confusion, though Bernadette noticed his eye kept returning to the women in the pool.

She led the two elder Norsemen up the stairs to the sleeping loft, and found them an alcove with a couple of single beds and some nightstands and chests of drawers. She helped them get settled, and produced a couple of the Maiden robes out of one of the chests of drawers. These were laundered regularly and scattered around the Maiden for the use of the guests, one size fits most.

"Well," she said, extricating herself. "Enjoy your stay. Food and drink are available just about every hour of the day or night at the bar, the pool is always hot, and you'll find plenty of towels at poolside. We usually have some entertainment in the evenings. And Waterdon is just a short walk up the road from here. I expect that we'll all be going to Lakedon for Bjorn's wedding in about two weeks' time. If you need anything, please check with whoever is dressed as an innkeeper."

Hjaermond, amused at her obvious eagerness to be free of them, nodded graciously and smiled. "Thank you Bernadette, I appreciate your hospitality. We'll see you later, I'm sure." Bernadette smiled at him in turn and darted back down to the common room, fairly bursting with her news. Erik and Andrion, who'd been sitting there waiting for her return, saw her streak down the stairs and approach them comet-like, radiating joy like a spring sunrise.

She hurled herself into Erik's lap, only to bend and enfold Andrion's head and shoulders in her arms, giving him a deep kiss. Feeling slightly cheated, Erik squeezed her buttocks beneath the soft fabric of her dress and then wrapped his arms around her in a bear hug, and pushing her hair to one side, kissed her neck. Realizing there was no way she could hug up both her men at the same time, Bernadette popped back up out of Erik's lap and pulled a chair over to sit between them.

"We are getting *married*…!" she squealed. Oh, that explained it. Andrion and Erik failed to completely share her excitement at the news, but they warmed with enjoyment of her enthusiasm. And what had they been doing, these past few days, but work toward making a home where they would all live together after that blessed event?

Andrion was quicker off the mark. "That's *great,* love!" he exclaimed, grabbing her for a hug and a kiss.

Erik, thinking about their project, added "Um, when's the day?" "The 10th of next month!" she exclaimed. "In the courtyard of the Pantheatos in Sylvanian! We can have a *real* wedding!" Both men did their best impressions of suppressed enthusiasm. What was it with women and their love of weddings? If you were lucky, a wedding was a brief but meaningful ceremony followed by a great party. But the marriage that followed it would go on, with any luck, for hundreds of times longer. Why all that focus on the preliminaries?

Being men who loved Bernadette, as well as men who were not completely stupid, they kept these thoughts to themselves. "That gives us a little over five weeks," Andrion remarked.

"Oh!" Bernadette exclaimed, her eyes going wide. "Did you have any luck finding us a place to buy?"

"We're still looking," he said. "There's not all that much real estate on the market around Waterdon, so I think we're going to have to find a place and put pressure on the owners to sell."

Bernadette considered this. She'd been afraid that would be the case. In the world of Iscandia, families held onto their property for hundreds of years and all of the really good places had been snapped up generations ago. Not that there weren't thousands of square miles of empty land ready to be homesteaded; but she didn't think she and her family-to-be were up for fighting off hostile wildlife and bandits on a daily basis.

"Let me give you some more money," Bernadette said, reaching into her pack and pulling out a fat sack of gold. "Did you get a good price for the stuff I left?" she added, as she scooped gold coins out onto the tabletop. Andrion and Erik were staring at the growing pile of gold, trying not to grin like idiots. Seemingly there would be no need for subterfuge to get the extra gold they expected they would need to cover Hegmar's bill when he submitted it.

"We turned most of it over to Alessia and Wolaf," Andrion told her. "They didn't have enough cash on hand, but Alessia really wanted it all. She says your work is getting so good she's afraid you'll put her out of business. Anyway, we worked a deal with them where they'll pay us the rest as the money comes in. Probably in another two or three weeks." Bernadette practically purred at hearing of Alessia's assessment of her work. She had no real desire to set up as a full-time smith, but she did love working with her hands and it filled her with pride that her friend, whose skills she admired, should account her an equal.

Grinning at Andrion and Erik in turn, Bernadette continued counting out gold until it was fairly spilling off the edges of the table. "How much do you think we'll need?" she asked. She had more than fifty thousand guilders stashed here and there, and could double it in a month if she needed to, the way things were going. As she'd promised them they would be, back after they'd defeated Tarragin, they were rich – and the sky was the limit.

Erik and Andrion, in turn, just watched with wonder as the pile got larger. "That's about twenty-five thousand guilders," Bernadette told them. "Do you think that will be enough?" Considering that the most prestigious available house in Sylvanian was going for that much, she certainly hoped it would be enough for a small country manor of some sort here in the Waterdon area. As much as she liked Waterdon, it was not a bustling center of trade and political activity like Sylvanian. It wasn't even a seaport.

Erik got up and went over to the bar to confer with Drelos, returning in a moment with a sack that had recently held apples. The sweet scent of them rose up as he held the mouth open near the edge of the table, and Andrion scooped the glittering coins into it. There was something slightly hypnotic about running your hands through all that gold. "With this, we should definitely be able to convince somebody to sell," Andrion promised Bernadette.

She beamed at them. Despite Bernadette's enthusiasm for plunder and treasure in general, money really meant very little to her. As long as she had her home and her lovers and enough food to eat, there was little enough use for the stuff. Except for occasions such as this one, and what could be better than to wave the magic golden wand and make all her dreams come true? She hoped.

Erik scooped the last few coins into the sack and pulled the drawstring, tucking it up against one of the table's legs. He smiled broadly at Berni, the import of her news just beginning to get to him. "We're getting married!" He wrapped her in a hug and planted a deep, enthusiastic kiss on her lips. As he did so, she reached down between them and stroked his erection where it pressed against the front of his trousers. Oh, she knew him too well!

Erik broke away from the kiss, looking deep into her blue-gray eyes with his sky-blue ones. He saw joy, and love, and wicked desire. But a little decorum here in the middle of the common room might be in order. They'd been snacking and thinking about supper before Berni came in with her entourage. "Are you hungry?" he asked. The wicked desire in her gaze increased fourfold as she looked him up and down, her eyes lingering on that bulge in his pants.

Bernadette loved them both, loved them deeply. But there was no getting around it that, when it came to sexual arousal, Erik held the upper hand. She had tried to analyze it but had failed to come up with any answers. Whatever that connection was, it completely bypassed the rational functions of the mind and went straight for the crotch. Tonight, after days apart, she wanted each of them – but she wanted them separately. The threesome thing was fun and exciting, but it didn't allow for the level of concentration that one-on-one did.

She decided to hold off a little longer on a decision as to who would come first, and have some supper. It had been at least a few hours, she thought, since her delayed breakfast/early lunch at the Rabbit. Bernadette motioned to Drelos, who came right over and welcomed her back. They ordered food and drink all around, and sat talking as they waited for their meals to arrive.

Bernadette chattered enthusiastically about her trip, not revealing the reason for her visit to Galdur Staerlin(a secret she meant to hold tight until she'd successfully accomplished the separate parts involved), but telling them about Engbard, the "favor of Aderos," and the dress she planned to surprise Lifa with. She glossed over her own dress, as this was in some ways intended as a surprise for them.

The food arrived and the three of them tucked into it with their usual enthusiasm. There were no picky eaters to be found in this group. Andrion and Erik were short on conversation, as the Big News that was boiling within them was a secret they were keeping from Berni. They wanted to present her with Coldburn Farm (got to change that name, definitely) as the house of their dreams, not a work in progress. So, they exclaimed and asked questions, letting her dominate the talk as they finished their meal.

Chapter 45: Taking Turns

While she'd been enthusiastically relating her tale to her lovers, another part of Bernadette's mind had been considering all the options and had concluded that what she really, really needed to do first was take a hot bath. So, blotting her mouth demurely with a napkin, she rose and squeezed her men's shoulders before excusing herself and heading upstairs. They were perhaps a little disappointed, but certainly not surprised.

"Think we ought to join her?" Andrion asked. Erik would love to join Berni in the pool – provided nobody else (possible exception: Andrion) was around. But after days of deprivation, there was no way he was getting into the pool naked with her and maybe half the customers in the Maiden, at the start of a busy evening. He'd be flying his flagpole for the world to see, and maidens had been known to faint at the sight.

"Why don't you?" Erik suggested. He had hopes, yea expectations, that Berni would be coming to his bed before the evening was out. But he felt Andrion ought to have a turn as well. The two of them sharing one woman was a challenge, definitely. But it kept things interesting. And what a woman! She was worth whatever it took.

Andrion smiled at him and gave his arm a quick pat before turning and dashing up the stairs. He wanted to catch Berni before she came back down. He found her in the bedroom, trying to figure out how to put away her fine garb without getting it all wrinkled. Bernadette turned at his approach, giving him a welcoming smile with a hint of heat in it.

"What we need in here," she said, "is some kind of a cabinet that's tall enough to hold a full length dress. With maybe a rod running across it near the top, and some kind of small rack with a hook sticking out of it so you could drape your clothes on the rack and then hang it on the rod. Then the weight of the fabric would pull the wrinkles out, and the doors of the cabinet would help keep out the moths. Maybe you could even make it out of cedar wood."

Andrion stood transfixed. What an idea! He suddenly wanted to run into town and tell Hegmar to add it to his plans. Though he envisioned these cabinets, lined with cedar wood, being built into the walls of the bedrooms and big enough that you could step inside them. But... At the moment, his body had a few other items at the top of the priorities list. He stepped to Berni's side where she stood in her underwear and gently took the dress out of her hands, laying it on the bed. Then he took her in her arms.

Kissing her deeply on the lips, he then broke away from her mouth to bury his face in the space between her neck and shoulder, his arms reaching down to clasp her to him and squeeze her buttocks. "I have missed you..." he murmured. Heat rose in Bernadette as she squeezed him back. Oh, Andrion... She could feel his cock, hard and insistent, pressing on her body through the several layers of cloth that separated them. Her recent mission had been busy but not strenuous – she was hardly even grubby. Surely, the bath could wait awhile.

Bernadette reached up to kiss Andrion's neck, running her tongue along it and pushing aside the hair to take an earlobe between her lips, gently sucking it. He gasped. "As I see it," she said thoughtfully, "the problem here is that we're both wearing way too many clothes. Especially you..."

He grinned at her. "How can I argue with that?" He stepped back and pulled his shirt off over his head, tossing it onto the top of the dresser. After due consideration he carefully picked up her fine dress and draped it there.

Meanwhile, Bernadette had pulled off her undershirt and was now wriggling out of her drawers to stand naked before him. Ah! She slipped her fingers into the waistband of his trousers and began pulling them off of him, slowly. Oh, he was not wearing any underdrawers. Naughty boy. She stopped a little way down, the waist squeezing him midway down the buttocks and the top few inches of his erection protruding in front. She bent to lick it, taking the head in her mouth and sucking out drops of slightly salty fluid. He *had* missed her, oh yes.

Crouching, Bernadette pulled Andrion's trousers the rest of the way down to the floor and he stepped out of them. Then she pressed on his flat, muscular belly until he had backed up to the bed and sat down upon it, putting him at a level where she could kneel before him and take him fully in her mouth. He was in agony. That felt so *good*! And he did *not* want to shoot his load like a kid. He wanted to make love to her until she was screaming.

Pushing Berni gently away, Andrion lifted her by the arms and beckoned her onto the bed beside him. "You're driving me wild," he told her quietly. "Let's take it a little slower." She understood, and came into his arms again for a deep kiss. Her hunger for him was urgent, but she too could postpone the fulfillment of her desires. They sat side by side on the bed, kissing and stroking, enjoying the sensation of skin on skin. She squeezed his cock but then moved her hands elsewhere: pressing, tickling, just barely touching. The feelings were wonderful to Andrion, but the urgent desire to pop his rocks had receded.

Andrion eased Bernadette down on the bed and she spread her legs for him, inviting him to worship at her gates with his lips and tongue. Oh, yes! They both enjoyed this, he because of the power he had to give her bliss, she because – well, because it felt blissfully wonderful. He soon had her gasping and moaning, escalating until she exploded in a powerful orgasm. She'd enjoyed a couple of these by herself while she'd been gone, but this was much *much* better.

With the flood of warm juices in his mouth, Andrion knew his beloved was ready to receive him. And he was oh, so ready to be there! His cock throbbing with eagerness, he mounted her and pushed his way inside. So hot, so tight, so right! Pumping in and out of her with powerful strokes, her legs clasped around him to meet him on each stroke, he thrust his tongue into her mouth. Then, in between gasps, he moaned "Berni! I love you…"

"I love you too Andrion," she responded moaning "We'll be together forever!" The thrusts came faster, and she lifted her legs to rest her ankles on his shoulders. "Yes! Yes! Yes!"

The two of them exploded in ecstasy, then collapsed in a puddle of love and stickiness on the bed. Recovering awareness in a moment, Andrion rolled over on his side. Berni had dropped her legs off his shoulders already, and she now let the bottom one lie straight, the other thrown up over his hip, so she could continue to hold him inside of her while she smothered his face with kisses. "It's been too long, my love," she murmured. "And I have to leave again soon. But I won't be gone so long this time, I promise."

Andrion wrapped her in his arms, squeezing her as if he planned
never to let her go, kissing the top of your head. "It's all right, dear,"
he said softly. "Soon we'll all be together and nothing can pull us
apart." He hoped it was true. They lay there for a while longer,
having little to say, just soaking up the warmth and wonderfulness of
being together.

But eventually the heightened stickiness factor drove Bernadette
to sit up and say, "Hmm, I thought I was going to take a bath… ?"

Andrion smiled at her fondly. "I could use one too, I believe.
Shall we?" They arose from the bed and put on robes, returning
downstairs. Erik was still sitting at the table where they'd dined,
sipping a mead and enjoying the ambience of an evening at the
Maiden. He waved to them cheerfully. They tossed their robes aside
and sank into the hot water with sighs of pleasure.

Erik came over and sat at poolside to chat with them, cross-
legged on the tile. His proximity to the naked Berni had his cock
stiffening, pressed down along one leg of his trousers. He hoped this
wasn't too obvious, but she spotted it soon enough. A couple of soul-
shaking orgasms with Andrion had not dulled her hunger for Erik.
She splashed him playfully, soaking his clothing. He backed away in
a hurry and gazed down in dismay. "Look what you did!" he said in
mock fury. "Now I'm going to have to go downstairs and change."

"Wait," Bernadette told him, squeezing Andrion's hand and
giving him a kiss before lifting herself up out of the water. "I'll come
with you." Erik grinned at her in a way not unlike that in which a
smilodon might grin at a fawn it had found standing alone in the
forest.

"Oh you will, will you?" Toweling off, she returned his leer with
one of her own.

"I must make amends for my transgression," she said meekly.
Erik wanted to grab a couple of handfuls of flesh and take her right
there, but he restrained himself.

"Come along then," he said sternly, and she followed him,
wrapped in her robe, to the trap door behind the bar.

Erik hit the floor first, Bernadette right behind him. With a
jubilant whoop, she threw herself onto him, wrapping her arms
around his neck and her legs around his hips, grinding her pelvis into

his hard-on beneath the snug-fitting trousers. Her cunt was still slightly wet from the bath, but then so were his pants. She planted a deep kiss on his lips, then pulled back a little to gaze into his eyes, her pupils dilated with arousal and the dim light of the basement.

"You can't imagine how long I've been waiting to do this!" she panted, grinning. Erik reached his hands up under the robe to seize her buttocks, exactly as he'd wanted to do moments before, and bounced her up and down a little, squeezing her tight to him. Mmm, that felt really good. He kissed her back, first on the mouth and then on the neck and shoulder, burrowing down to push the cloth of the robe aside.

"Erik," Bernadette murmured breathlessly in his ear, "why are you still wearing all this clothing?" Oh, good point. Erik walked over toward the bed wearing her like an apron, and she released her grip on him. Still clutching her buttocks, he lifted her up and forward a bit in a gentle arc to bounce on the bed, lying on her back. Then he began doing a fast strip. If somebody had told him he was not allowed to exit the burning building until he was naked, he could probably not have done it any faster.

In seconds, it seemed, Erik's dampened clothing was lying on the floor at the foot of the bed and he stood looking down at her, his rampant member swollen and purple-headed, the golden perfection of his smooth-skinned, muscular body on display, blue eyes drinking Bernadette in as she lay on the bed with her fiery hair spread out around her head like a halo – even as she was savoring her view of him.

In another moment he said, "Now, where were we?" and reached to scoop her up once again. Oh, yes. Bernadette pressed Erik's engorged cock between her slit and his belly as she locked herself onto his body. He could easily support her weight, and she rubbed against him as they kissed passionately. Her clit swollen and throbbing as well, juices making her vulva slippery, she humped herself up a little more and then slipped down over him, ensheathing him from root to tip. Then, holding tight to her ass, he began sliding her up and down the shaft.

Erik recalled another occasion when they'd made love standing up like this, there in the bandit encampment near Forestville. At that time she'd screamed his name so loudly he'd thought it might possibly wake the bandits they'd just killed, and she'd taken him right off with her. He'd noticed that combat seemed to tweak up Berni's sex drive. Now, there'd been no blood shed; but it had been days since they'd been together and their eagerness for one another was having almost the same effect.

"Erik, oh gods Erik, yesss…" Bernadette moaned, her entire consciousness eclipsed by the sensation as she was pressed against him, his powerful body supporting hers while that enormous cock filled her completely. Slip, slide, pound… the elastic and cushiony tip of his love-lance bounced off her cervix each time she came down, and she soon found a fire rising to engulf her as her vaginal muscles clenched down hard on him in a rippling motion. "Yes! Yes!"

Erik held on, but just barely. Standing up helped a little with this, as it took some of his attention just to stay upright supporting both his weight and Berni's. But his teeth were clenched, and his cock felt as if it were swollen to twice its usual (already magnificent) size and lit up like a beacon with the heat of their joining. He gasped and panted, changing his grip to hold Berni around the waist as her legs dropped nerveless from their grip on him, keeping her from slipping off of him.

Flexing his knees, he eased her down onto the bed and the two of them, still joined, gradually slid up it until Bernadette's head was resting on a pillow. Then they rolled so they were lying on their sides, face to face, and continued making love at a slower pace. This allowed for plenty of kissing and stroking, which inflamed them both anew; and before long Erik's strokes were coming faster and harder again and she knew he wanted to let go. "Do me from behind, Erik," she murmured. The power and force of him behind her, like a rutting bull, filled her with excitement. He was happy to oblige.

Erik pulled out of her, his massive golden scepter reddened and glistening, and Bernadette rose onto her knees with her hands resting on the headboard, her rump thrust out to receive him as he pushed it back inside. After its brief absence, its return sent a thrill through her that almost tripped her over into another orgasm on the spot. But the best was yet to come. He knelt behind her, pumping deep inside, faster and faster until they both exploded. Ah!

Almost immediately Erik rolled back over onto his side, pulling Berni with him as his still-throbbing cock was gripped within her. He cuddled her to him, squeezing her, stroking her hair, applying kisses to her shoulder and neck. It was so good to have her in his arms! After he had slipped out she turned around to throw her own arms around his massive torso, kissing his slightly salty chest. Then he rolled over onto his back, resting his head on the pillow, and she pillowed hers on his shoulder – lying on her side with a hand across his chest.

They lay there in the afterglow for a while, then Bernadette broke the silence. "It's good to be home, love."

He bent his head to kiss her forehead. "It's good to *have* you home. But I suppose you have to leave soon?" She sighed, snuggling closer.

"I really need to go to Lakedon and get a firm date for Lifa and Bjorn's wedding," she said. "But I can come right back from that. Then I have some more business to do in Waterdon, after which I'll be home for a few days before I have to go back to Sylvanian to pick up Lifa's dress. I *hope* it'll fit her and we won't have to take another trip to Sylvanian before the wedding."

While Berni was laying out her projects and plans, Erik was mulling over his own. The work at Coldburn seemed to be proceeding at a lightning pace from what he knew of such things, and they now had all the cash they could want to hasten it along. But could he and Andrion, working together with Bjorn, have their dream home habitable by the 10th of next month? Well, he supposed it would still be a happy wedding surprise for her even if all they had to show her was a construction site. But he really, really wanted it to be perfect for her. She was his perfect woman, and she deserved the best.

He squeezed her up in the crook of the arm she was resting on. "So, you're leaving for Lakedon tomorrow. Want to sleep here tonight?" Bernadette had spent her previous night at the Maiden with Andrion upstairs, so that seemed appropriate. She loved sleeping with both her men, but she had to admit to herself that Erik was a little more compatible with her sleep schedule. He didn't groan and hide under the covers when she wanted to get up and moving at a reasonable hour.

She tilted her head up and kissed him. "Sure, that'll be fine." After another moment she said, "It's a bit early to be going to sleep, though. Want to go up and jump in the pool?" She'd just come from the pool a while ago, but both of them were now pretty sticky again.

Bernadette got up and retrieved her robe, while Erik hung his damp, discarded clothing on hooks before pulling his own robe down and donning it. Then the two of them climbed the ladder to the trap door, and rejoined the evening Maiden life in full swing. Andrion had gotten up and put on some clothes, and was now occupying their usual table with a flagon of something in his hand. He smiled and saluted them with his stein as they came in, and they waved back before climbing back into the pool. It was almost as though the lovemaking session with Erik had just been a sort of interlude in the middle of her bath.

They didn't stay in too long. The Maiden was busy tonight, and others were waiting for their turn in the hot water. Bernadette and Erik got out and wrapped up in their robes, then joined Andrion at their table. Without the privilege of proprietorship, they might have been hard put to find a table to sit at. She spotted Hjaermond and Selden coming down the stairs a little while later, looking around for someplace to sit. She invited them over to join them at their table. After all, they were here at her invitation.

Learning they hadn't eaten yet, she beckoned Lev over and ordered them some food from the kitchen. Come to think of it, though it hadn't been that many hours since she ate supper herself, Bernadette was feeling hungry again for some reason. Two vigorous sessions of sex with her fiancés wouldn't have done that, would it? She settled for a bowl of the new potato chips that were becoming so popular. It was easy to see why. They didn't have that much flavor of their own, but the crunchiness and the salt seemed addictive. Andrion had been drinking wine, but they all switched to chilled ale.

Hjaermond and Selden appeared to be enjoying themselves immensely. They ate their food with gusto and exclaimed at the chilled ale. They sampled the potato chips, which met with their approval, and ogled the naked women in the bathing pool discreetly. Part of the "clothing optional" theory was that polite people didn't stare at naked people, pretending rather that skin was as valid a getup as any other sort of garb. In practice, if covert glances were arrows some of the better-looking people of either sex hanging around in the pool would be looking like porcupines. And the pool tended to be a place where many liaisons started. Bernadette herself had first met Andrion in those very waters, and look where that had led.

The five of them talked long into the evening, Hjaermond and his aged uncle regaling the youngsters with tales of adventure and battle in Westmarch in the days before Andrion, Erik, and Bernadette had even been born. In turn, they shared some of their own adventures. The tale of Tarragin's defeat in Asengard was a crowd-pleaser, though there were already some in Iscandia who believed it to be nothing but a fanciful tale for children. Bernadette supposed, somewhat sadly, that by the time they were all dusty bones the people of the province would think she and her heroic companions had been only a legend, made-up characters in a story.

The older men's energy began to flag, and they smilingly thanked their hostess before tottering up the stairs to bed. Yawning and stretching, Bernadette realized she had better be getting to sleep soon too, if she wanted an early start on her trip to Lakedon in the morning. She moved from her chair to Andrion's lap, throwing her arms around him for a deep goodnight kiss. "I'm sleeping downstairs tonight, and off to Lakedon in the morning. I hope you'll be up before I leave..." He kissed her back, with feeling.

"I'll meet you for breakfast," he promised.

Hand in hand, Bernadette and Erik returned to the trap door and climbed down the ladder for the second time this evening. Erik was already thinking of another go-round, but she was really sleepy. Very much fast-travelling in a short period of time and you wound up with your body having no idea what time it really was. After dropping her robe again, Bernadette pressed herself against Erik, kissing him lingeringly and not without heat. But the effect was spoiled when she burst into an enormous yawn. His cock was halfway up, but Erik knew it would be better if his beloved got her sleep, so he didn't press the issue. There was always a chance in the morning...

Chapter 46: The Temple of Marmira

Erik woke before Bernadette did and pulled her into his arms. Before she had a chance to protest he was making love to her, slowly and with concentration. So she lay back and enjoyed it. Toward the end, she enjoyed it quite a lot. But when it was over, she was soon out of bed. Sticky yet again, sigh. She put on her robe and climbed the stairs, Erik following behind her, and the two of them got into the pool for a brief wash. Then Erik returned to the basement, and she headed for the steps to the sleeping loft. Her clothing and gear were in the master bedroom upstairs.

As she approached the stairs, Bernadette was somewhat surprised to see Hjaermond and Selden coming down them dressed in Maiden robes, soft slippers on their feet. They wished her a good morning, beaming as they set off to partake of the hot waters while nobody else was in there. She smiled back, tickled, and continued on her way to the bedroom. She expected to find Andrion asleep and likely wanting sex as soon as he woke up – which she was determined *not* to give in to. She'd like to visit the Temple of Marmira clean from her bath, not covered in sweat and spoog; and she'd already had three baths in the past 16 hours or so.

Instead, she was surprised to find her beloved up and putting the finishing touches on his attire. His face lit up as she came in, and he drew her into his arms for a kiss. "Good morning, my love," he said cheerfully. Perhaps she really *was* changing him! She hung her robe on a hook and then had to fend Andrion off as she tried to get dressed. He did indeed want sex, but as he was already up and dressed it wasn't too hard to talk him out of it.

After some consideration of her plans for the day Bernadette decided on an outfit that combined fine fabrics and a fashionable cut with freedom of movement, and brought along her weapons. She expected to fast-travel from outside the Maiden to the gates of Lakedon and didn't anticipate combat along the way; but Lakedon was full of thieves and robbers, and dragons had been known to attack even in the middle of cities sometimes.

The two of them went down the stairs together and met Erik for breakfast at their usual table. Anticipating them, he'd had Lev bring plenty of food. There was a large pot of hot tea, slices of bread toasted and smeared with butter, a platter of scrambled eggs with cheese, and some fresh apples. Bernadette's eyes lit as she saw the spread, and she dug in with enthusiasm. Nothing like getting well-fucked of a morning to improve one's appetite for breakfast!

Her stomach comfortably full and her prospects bright, Bernadette felt happiness bubbling within her. She had a mountain of work to do before everything would fall into place, but her optimism was soaring and she dismissed the difficulties with her usual savoir faire. Everything would work out fine, she was sure of it. Andrion and Erik seemed to be simmering with anticipation, looking forward to their wedding she supposed. Oh! That reminded her, she had one more surprise to prepare. She thought she could take care of that in Lakedon, as well.

No point in delaying. Bernadette stood up and her men stood with her. She hugged Erik to her, reaching up for a kiss. Then she did the same for Andrion. "See you before long," she told them. "I hope I'll be back by tonight, or tomorrow at the latest." "Take care, Berni," Erik said, and Andrion added "See you soon, love." Stepping out the front doors she pulled her map out and wished herself to Lakedon.

In her whole, far-from-lengthy life, Bernadette had never paid much attention to time. Morning was when the sun came up, noontime found it straight overhead, and dinnertime was usually when it had set. The seasons changed, but what day it was wasn't of much consequence. Yet there *were* such things as clocks here in Iscandia, and calendars as well. Priests had their rites linked to special days of the year and were more attuned to these matters than most people.

Now, with a tight schedule to keep, she suddenly felt the need to know what day it was, and what time on that day. And she needed to start figuring out exactly what was going on in the outside world during the few seconds of subjective time that passed when she fast-traveled using the magic map. It wouldn't do for them to show up a day late for the wedding, and a day early would be kind of a problem as well. So, having learned that she'd left the Waterdon area at around nine in the morning of the 2nd Sunreturn, Bernadette immediately set about learning what time and date they were keeping here in Lakedon.

She could tell from the dim light that it was certainly no longer morning. It appeared to be some time in the evening. She expected that if anyone besides the priests at the Temple of Marmira would have a timepiece, it would be the people at the inn; so she turned her steps toward the Smiling Salmon. Bernadette was greeted pleasantly enough by Zendna, the saurion woman behind the bar.

Zendna told her that it was about nine p.m. on the second day of Sunreturn. So, the "few seconds" of travel had taken up twelve hours of time. Bernadette considered that as Lakedon was far to the east of Waterdon, local time might be later than time at home – meaning that it might *not* have actually taken twelve hours to get here. But the end result was the same. It was too late in the evening for her to go to talk with Yusuf, the Priest of Marmira who arranged traditional weddings. And far too late to conduct her other business as well.

Rats! What seemed like a few minutes ago she'd been keyed up with excitement, eager to push on with the list of things she must do. And now it was bedtime in Lakedon and Bernadette was not in the least bit tired or sleepy. Well, there was no help for it. She rented a room from Zendna and dropped off her pack, then returned to the common room and ordered an ale.

Before long she was approached by a slim but muscular young man, little taller than herself and dressed in mage robes. From his look he was a Reman, with straight black hair pulled back in a ponytail, and sharp brown eyes flanking a hawk nose. He had an air of cocky arrogance that Bernadette found appealing, somehow.

"Do you mind if I sit?" he asked, gesturing to the empty chair beside her. She smiled slightly and nodded that he was welcome to join her if he wished. She needed some company to while away a few hours until she was sleepy enough to go to bed. The thought that there were more things to do in bed than sleep crossed her mind, and she wadded it up into a little ball and sent it shooting across the room into the nearest tankard.

The Reman held out a hand, and introduced himself as Rubio Dimaris. "It seems you're traveling alone," he said. "For a modest fee, I'll bring my formidable arcane powers to bear against your foes. What do you say?" Bernadette eyed him skeptically.

"Arcane powers?" she asked demurely.

"I am a master battle mage," he replied confidently.

Inside, Bernadette smirked. Andrion could chew this guy up and spit him out, both physically and magically, she was sure. Still, there was no point in being rude. "Thanks," she said, "but I'm actually covered on that front. I just sent my battle mage on an errand and he'll back in a day or so, so I don't need any more help. But can I buy you a drink?"

Rubio's eyes glinted in the dim candlelight, and he gave her a slightly vulpine smile. "Why thank you," he said. Argani-Zhe, Zendna's husband, brought a couple more ales over to the table and the two of them spent the next several hours sipping ale and regaling each other with possibly true tales. He seemed disinclined to believe Bernadette's boldly stated claim that she was The Fireblood, not that he came right out and accused her of being a liar. But she could tell from his sarcastic quips that he doubted much of what she told him. Now that she thought about it, a lot of what she and her companions had done *did* seem like a fairy tale.

For his part, Rubio related his exploits as a sellsword (sellspell?) in Iscandia. He'd acted as a hired companion for dozens of adventurers, he said, and had raided many famous tombs. Aptrgangr, bandits, and even dragons had fallen to his skill in battle. Bernadette judged him to be about Erik's age or a little bit older, certainly not as old as Andrion. He would have to have started learning battle magic in his cradle and begun his adventuring at about the onset of puberty to have had half the adventures he claimed, but she was entertained and didn't call him on it.

Bernadette's good spirits were restored by the ale and the company, and it was getting awfully late before she realized that she was half tipsy and finally, tired enough to try for a few hours of sleep. She stood and, extending her hand to Rubio, said "It's been a pleasure to meet you. Perhaps if I'm in need of an extra mage on some future quest I'll look you up. Is this your home base?" she asked, looking around the room.

"I'm here most of the time, if I'm not on a job," he admitted. He looked a little disappointed. Perhaps he'd thought she might be going to invite him to her bed, after plying him with liquor all evening. Sorry!

Bernadette went upstairs to the small room and made sure to latch the door before stripping off her clothes and lying down to sleep. This was Lakedon, after all. She woke in the morning with a bit of a headache and dry mouth, so she took a drink of water from the nightstand and used her healing spell until she felt fully restored. After she had dressed and gathered up her things, she descended the stairs intending to get some breakfast before going to the temple. But who should she see in the common room but Yusuf!

He was a good-looking, youthful Afran swathed in his monk's robes from head to foot, and he greeted her with a blessing from his goddess. "Yusuf!" she said happily, "You're just the person I was looking for. I'm Bernadette, The Fireblood. Might you remember our prior meeting?" She had encountered him wandering the streets of Lakedon while she was here on a quest some months back, and had asked him about the work of the temple. She'd introduced herself then, though she'd had no need of his services, and had given him the small donation he requested.

"The Fireblood! Certainly, I remember. All of Iscandia owes you a great debt. Is there some way I can be of service?"

"I'm here to arrange a wedding," Bernadette told him. Yusuf looked pleased and a little excited.

"Your own?" he asked hopefully. She smiled at him ruefully.

"I'm afraid not," she said. "This is for some friends of mine."

"Let's go to the temple and discuss it then, shall we?" The two of them exited the inn and walked the short distance across the central marketplace and over the canal to the steps leading up to the temple.

Yusuf produced a book similar to the one Engbard had had, along with a quill and a bottle of ink. "When were you wanting to hold the ceremony?" he asked her.

"I was thinking of the seventeenth of Sunreturn, two weeks from today," she said.

"And at what time?" Oh, that was a poser – now that she knew about the twelve-hour fast-travel gap. With the ceremony here and the party at the Maiden, they'd be leaving Waterdon in the evening in order to make it to a morning wedding and then going back to find it now the following evening – and everybody would likely be too tired to enjoy the party after not having slept. Maybe it would be better, Bernadette realized, to have the party the day *after* the wedding. She was hoping for fine weather and food on the deck.

"Let's say nine in the morning," Bernadette told Yusuf.

He jotted it down in the book on the appropriate page. "And the name of the couple being wed?"

"Bjorn and Lifa. Enter the house name Steadfast. That's the name they will have when they are joined."

Yusuf raised an eyebrow at this, but recorded it as given. "We'll see you then, by nine on the morning of the seventeenth." She gave him another donation before leaving, then scurried over to the marketplace. Business there was now in full swing, and she was glad not to spot Hamish in the crowd.

Bernadette approached Daaralie Irilion, the sylvalfar jeweler who sold her wares daily in Lakedon's central plaza. "How may I help you, miss?" she asked. "Hello, Daaralie," she said. "I don't know if you remember me. I'm Bernadette, The Fireblood. I found some gems for you a few months ago. "Of course I remember," the wood elf replied in her lilting tones. "Your service will not be forgotten."

"You make a lot of the jewelry you sell, right?" Bernadette asked her, and she nodded. "I have a commission for you, two men's rings in gold, and I need to be able to pick them up on the seventeenth." She handed a colored sketch across the counter. "You see, the outside bands are to be of yellow and bronze gold, and the center one of red." Gold could be alloyed with other metals to produce any colors from silvery white to deepest bronze. "Each ring will be three separate parts, but they will mesh and click together to form one ring of three colors."

Daaralie's tip-tilted brown eyes looked from the paper to her face, intrigued. "This is an interesting design. I have never seen anything quite like it before." The gears were turning in her head, and she was already working out how she would construct the rings. "It should be no problem to have these ready for you on the seventeenth. Do you have the sizes?"

Bernadette had made rings for Andrion and Erik before and knew their sizes by heart. She had developed some facility with jewelry, but made only the simplest of popular designs. For these, she wanted a master jeweler – and she had noticed, when she had delivered the requested gems, that Daaralie had made some beautiful pieces.

Giving the elf a smile and a hefty deposit, Bernadette was about to leave when she remembered one more thing. "Do you have any simple rings with the Blessing of Marmira enchantment?" she asked the sylvalfar woman. "Certainly," the jeweler replied, displaying a tray of rings that were simple bands, the most common wedding rings in Iscandia.

Bernadette selected an inexpensive silver one and paid her for it. Then she pulled out her map and vanished from the market square, reappearing outside the Maiden in darkness. She hurried inside to check with Lev and learned that it was around nine p.m. on the third. So, the east-west dislocation had not made any difference. The trip took about twelve hours each way. How very odd!

Chapter 47: Return of the Prodigal

Andrion was in the common room sitting at their table with Hjaermond and Selden. The two old men certainly seemed to be getting into the swing of things. Coming in the front door, Bernadette walked over to join them. Andrion's face lit at the sight of her. He gave her a hug and kiss, then she pulled up a chair and seated herself at the table. She signaled Drelos, and asked him to bring a bottle of wine and some glasses, along with some bread and cheese, to the table. It seemed like she ought to be having breakfast, but she thought she'd better try to align herself with local time.

"How'd it go in Lakedon?" he asked her, squeezing her hand. "Everything's fine," she told him, smiling. "Lifa and Bjorn's wedding is scheduled for the morning of the seventeenth. Oh!" she added, remembering the news she had to impart. All the months she'd been running around Iscandia with the magic map, and it had only very recently occurred to her to actually pinpoint the amount of time that was consumed in a journey that seemed to last seconds. Of course, there had never been any deadlines before. "I've been gone almost two days, right" Andrion nodded. "You left yesterday morning." "Okay, I got to Lakedon too late to talk to Yusuf yesterday. I found out it takes almost exactly twelve hours to fast-travel there from here."

Andrion looked thoughtful. Despite his years in Iscandia he'd never had access to a magic map until he met Bernadette. He, like she, had thought that the time differences were random and had never thought to do any measuring either. "So," Bernadette was continuing, "I had to put up at the Smiling Salmon overnight, and then I met Yusuf in the morning and made my arrangements. Not counting the time I was at the inn, it seems like I've hardly been gone from here any time at all. But I've lost a whole day. And I feel more tired and hungry than I should, too." At that the bread and cheese arrived, and she was silent for a few minutes as she ripped into it.

Once her immediate hunger had been appeased, Bernadette told Andrion "I think the best way to work it is we'll gather the wedding party here at the Maiden fairly early in the evening on the sixteenth, and fast-travel to Lakedon arriving early in the morning on the seventeenth. Then after the wedding, we'll all go back home and it will be evening again. We'll have the party starting around mid-afternoon on the eighteenth, and on into the night." Andrion raised an eyebrow. It sounded complicated, but Berni seemed to have matters well in hand. She'd always been a pretty good organizer.

"Where's Erik?" Bernadette asked, after a look around the area had failed to reveal him.

Andrion smiled slightly. "Oh, he's down in the basement working on some project of his. I don't know what it is, but it seems to be taking him a long time. I'm sure he'll be up soon. He hasn't had supper yet, unless he brought some food down there with him." Bernadette nodded, wondering just what Erik was up to. Likely it was going to be a surprise, so she'd best not pry and spoil it.

They sat conversing quietly and enjoying the music, and before long Erik did appear. He was startled and delighted to find Berni sitting with Andrion and their guests, and trotted over to enfold her in a bear hug – lifting her part of the way out of her seat. "I was just thinking about you!" he proclaimed in his bass voice.

"I'm glad to see you, too!" Bernadette said enthusiastically, hugging him back. Erik seldom failed to fill her with joy (not to mention lust) just by his presence.

This evening though, her lust seemed a little muted. Was it the time distortion? You could count "one one thousand, two one thousand, three one thousand…" and reach a fairly accurate tally of the time that seemed to pass while you were fast-traveling. And you could check the time and date at the start and end points of your journey and learn how much time had passed in the outside world between your departure from one place and arrival in the other. But what sense did your body make of this? Was it splitting the difference? Your mind might tell you you'd arisen after a good night's sleep, eaten breakfast, and gotten on the Magic Map Express all within the past hour. So why would you feel tired and hungry when you arrived?

More research needed, Bernadette concluded. If anybody cared enough to do it. Though she had a love of finding out new information, her interest was more focused on practical applications of that learning. Andrion, on the other hand, pursued knowledge for its own sake. And that sure came in handy, now and again. She loved him for it (among his many other delectable and/or useful attributes).

There were now five of them packed around the table, and Bernadette was beginning to wonder if it might be a good idea to have a bigger table built for them. Especially since her plans for the next few weeks involved inviting still more guests to the Maiden. Then, the front doors opened and a familiar-looking woman came in. It… it was Nerissa! But she looked different, more vibrant. She quickly spotted them across the room and came over to the table.

"There you are," she said. "I'm… I'm back." Bernadette was gazing at her friend in delighted wonder. Her eyes, no longer glowing bright orange, were a deep blue. And her complexion seemed to glow with an inner warmth that had been missing before.

Seizing Nerissa's hands, she asked "You're not a vampire anymore?"

"All clean," Nerissa assured her with a self-deprecating smile. "I feel like I can breathe again, for the first time since I was turned." Bernadette grinned at her, happiness welling up inside.

"The world is alive," Nerissa continued, "and so am I, again."

"That's wonderful!" Bernadette said enthusiastically, rising from her chair to enfold the no-longer-vampire woman in a warm embrace. "Come and sit! I'm going to go get us some more table." She gestured Nerissa to take her chair, and went off for a consultation with Drelos.

After she explained what she wanted, he said "There's a small table back in the kitchen area you can borrow, and a spare chair." The two of them carried these items back up to the mezzanine and with a bit of shuffling, added the extra small table to their larger one to make one big enough for the six people now in their party.

While she'd been gone Andrion (who, with Bernadette, had spent a considerable amount of time questing with the former vampire) and Erik were congratulating Nerissa and welcoming her back to the land of the living. When Bernadette had re-seated herself, she introduced her friend to Hjaermond and Selden.

Nerissa was somewhat reticent to discuss the details of her life as a vampire or the recent killing of her father, nor did she want to provide any details about the process that had been involved in curing her of her vampirism; so Bernadette steered the conversation onto other topics. The older men were quite delighted to be introduced to this beautiful and apparently young woman, never guessing that she'd been old before they were born.

Nerissa took some wine, bread, and cheese when it was offered, eating and drinking with relish. "I can't tell you how good it is just to eat simple, wholesome food," she said. Awhile later, though, she remarked "It's been a long journey from Normarsh, and I would really love a hot bath. Would anybody care to join me? Erik and the older men declined, but Bernadette and Andrion said they wouldn't mind a soak.

The three of them went upstairs and Bernadette, with a bit of difficulty, found Nerissa a bed. She was going to have to talk to Lev and Drelos and ask them to stop taking overnight guests for a while, to make room for any additional guests she might invite in the weeks leading up to the weddings. In the bedroom, she and Andrion stripped down and of course he enfolded her in a tight embrace as soon as the two of them were naked. His cock was on the rise, and a spark of arousal was beginning to flicker within her.

She kissed him warmly, feeling that spark ignite to a steady, cheerful flame. Oh, yes. She ran her hands over the smooth skin of his back and buttocks, squeezing him to her and feeling that hardness pressed against her belly, the tip moist. But... "I'll spend the night here with you, love. I can hardly wait. But I think we should go downstairs now and have that bath. Don't you?" Bernadette asked, and Andrion could hardly argue. His erection soon began to subside and they threw on their robes and joined Nerissa on the trip back down to the bathing pool. It even behaved itself as they were soaking, in the company of several other Maiden guests. The place seemed to be getting more popular all the time.

The trio conversed lightly among themselves and with the others in the pool, and Bernadette was taken by the way Nerissa's forthright humor now seemed to have come alive – just as she had. She positively sparkled, talking animatedly and flirting with several of the men in the pool. She no longer had to limit her liaisons to men who were willing to give blood as part of the deal, Bernadette realized – and if something deeper than a lust connection came of it, she was free to pursue a long-term relationship. What a difference!

Bernadette noted that Nerissa was not wearing an amulet like she and most of the Maiden's employees wore, however. She made a note to get her one as soon as possible. As a vampire Nerissa had had no worries about being impregnated or catching a disease. It would be tragic if, so soon into her new-found freedom, she found herself caught with an unplanned pregnancy or something worse.

Above them, Erik was relaxing at their extended table and swapping stories with Hjaermond and Selden. After a few minutes in the pool Bernadette excused herself, rose, and after toweling off put on her robe and walked over to join them. Andrion, enjoying the company in the pool, stayed behind. As Bernadette approached the table the two old men smiled at her appreciatively. They might not be able to *do* much with a naked lady the likes of the Fireblood, but they were old – not dead.

Erik grinned as she slipped in beside him and put a hand on her knee, giving it a squeeze. She smiled up at him and squeezed his enormous bicep in response. Then she murmured in his ear, "Erik. Do you happen to know where I could get another amulet?" she gestured by pulling her own out from where it lay on her collarbone and waving it at him. He raised an eyebrow questioningly, then seemed to put it together.

"For Nerissa?" he asked, equally quietly. She nodded.

He considered for a moment. At one time the Maiden's management had maintained a collection of these, but over the years they had been parceled out. "How about if I give her mine?" he suggested. Bernadette studied him, startled. "I'm only sleeping with you," he pointed out, "and you've still got yours. So what do we have to worry about?" She just looked at him, her eyes glowing with love. This was probably the most touching gesture this sweet, sweet man had ever made, and it moved her to her soul.

Bernadette threw her arms around his neck and locked her lips on his for a deep kiss. "Thank you, Erik! I can't tell you how much this means to me!" He looked a little shy.

"Well… you could *show* me," he said, leering slightly to show he wasn't entirely serious. Oh, damn. She'd already promised to spend the night with Andrion.

"I'm… otherwise engaged, tonight," she said, nodding toward the pool. Then her eyes lit with inspiration. "But I'll make it up to you in the morning, I promise!" Erik removed his amulet and handed it to her, feeling as if the gesture was far more momentous than he was letting on. He'd been wearing it continuously for years, and now… he didn't need it anymore.

"I'll hold you to that," he said, squeezing her tight.

At about this juncture Andrion and Nerissa had reached the point in their soak where they must either exit the water or be consigned to prune-hood, and they came walking up the few steps toward the table, glowing from the hot water. Bernadette motioned to Nerissa to come and sit beside her. "Feel better now?" she asked.

"Oh, yes!" her friend responded. "I've got to see whether we can set something like this up at Daywatch. Andrion, did I hear you mention that the pool is kept hot and clean by some kind of dypalfar mechanism in the basement?"

"That's right," he replied. "I wish I understood how it works." Oh, how he wished. In the time Berni had been gone he'd been putting in long hours at the drawing board, racking his brain for ways in which they could have hot running water in their new home at Coldburn. In his spare time, he'd been racking it to come up with a better name for the farm. That could wait. But now they had a deadline for their wedding, and a lot of other things happening in the meantime, he needed to come up with answers before construction got too far along.

"I'll bet Diane LeBois could help you with that," Nerissa remarked casually. "She's probably Iscandia's foremost expert on dypalfar technology, though that old mage out in Alfenstein knows quite a bit about it as well. Will you be coming out our way anytime soon?" Andrion looked at her questioningly.

"Our?" Nerissa took his meaning.

"Yes, I'm still planning to rejoin the Daywatch Brigade. Now that I'm cured of the infection, I think I can be even more useful to them. Even Malden is starting to respect me. I just wanted to come here and see you all again, but I'll be on my way there tomorrow. It's quite a walk."

Andrion digested this for a moment, inspiration starting to bloom. "I *would* like to return to Daywatch," he said. "There are a few pieces of unfinished business I'd like to take care of there, as well as finding out if Diane can develop something like the pool's systems for the Daywatch Brigade. Those volcanic hot pools are just too far away for convenience. But Berni's in the middle of planning two weddings. She can't take the time to go down there with us." Turning to Berni, he asked "Darling, is there a chance you might be able to loan me the map for a few days?"

Bernadette considered. She had at least a full day's worth of business to transact here in Waterdon, and didn't really have to go anywhere else for another five days or so. She'd never lent the map out before, but there was nothing she would deny Andrion. Besides, she was curious to see how it would function for him. She guessed it would offer him fast-travel to any point that it had previously taken him to, when he was traveling with her. Would it also offer him other points, places he had been to himself on foot, before they met? "That should work all right, just so you're back here by the ninth so I can get to Sylvanian and pick up Lifa's dress," she told him. "It's upstairs in the trunk. I'll leave it for you when I go into town tomorrow morning."

Andrion gave Bernadette his most melting smile and reached around Nerissa to squeeze her hand. Then to Nerissa he said, "Well, that's taken care of. I'll fast-travel you back to Daywatch tomorrow morning." Nerissa grinned at him, the first time he had seen this particular expression on her lovely features. It made her look a lot more... approachable.

"*Thank* you Bernadette, Andrion! That will save my poor feet a long trip. And probably, the bandits between here and there will be happy not to have met me – though they know it not."

The evening was wearing on and the party broke up, heading for their beds. Hjaermond and Selden were the first to leave. When they had departed Bernadette, sidetracked from her original objective of some hours before, recalled her intentions and slipped the amulet to

Nerissa. "This is a gift for you," she told her friend. Nerissa looked touched.

She glanced down at Bernadette's chest and said, "It's just like yours."

Bernadette nodded. "You know what it's for?"

Nerissa's face lighted with a secret smile. "I have a pretty good idea," she replied. "Thank you," she added sincerely, bending her head to hang the amulet around her neck. "I haven't ever needed one, because of the way I was turned, and to tell you the truth it hadn't really occurred to me that I was going to need one now. I have a lot of lost time to make up for." She cast her eyes around the room in an exaggerated leer. Bernadette laughed. "Well, maybe I'll wait until I get back to Daywatch before I start making up for lost time," Nerissa finished. "There are some good-looking new recruits."

"Don't do anything I wouldn't do," Bernadette told her smiling. "Well, I'm for bed. How about you, Andrion?" He smiled and stood up eagerly to join her. He had not forgotten her promise. Erik was sorry to see them go, but looked forward to Berni's "making it up to him" in the morning. He and Nerissa sat there for a while after the other two had left, chatting quietly. Mmm, Erik is *really* hunky, Nerissa thought. And such a sweetie, too. Pity he's taken. Well, she'd be back at Daywatch tomorrow, amidst a growing cadre of unattached men. I'd like to jump that Malden and fuck his brains out, see if it sweetens him up any, she mused wickedly.

Erik stood up, giving Nerissa's hands a squeeze. "I'm glad you decided to make the change," he said. "I'm sure you're going to enjoy your new life. It's a lot sweeter, I think, when there's a limited supply of it." With that he took his leave, heading for the basement. Nerissa sat drinking a last glass of wine and looking around the Maiden for a few minutes more, then went up the stairs to bed.

In the master bedroom, Bernadette and Andrion hung their robes on hooks and stood looking at each other, clean and naked. And in the latter case, rampant. Andrion might have a little more control over such things than did his younger friend Erik, but Berni's nude presence – especially after a couple of days away – had him standing at attention. She smiled at him, looking with love into his beautiful face. Then her gaze ran down, and her smile grew broader. Mmm.

Bernadette approached him and squeezed in tight for a hug and kiss. "Where were we?" she asked, as if either of them might have forgotten. Stepping back a little and putting her hands on his hips, pushing Andrion back toward the bed, she said "That looks good enough to eat. I think it's time for some dessert." He got up onto the bed, lying with his head on the pillows, and Bernadette knelt between his legs to seize his swollen cock in her mouth. He'd noticed she seemed to be enjoying this more and more of late – and possibly getting too damn good at it, as well.

Andrion scooted back down the bed a little, his feet hanging off the end, and reached for Berni's hips. "C'mere, you," he said, and pulled her around so she now had her crotch in his face. This allowed him to pleasure her with his mouth while she did the same for him, and helped keep him from shooting quite so fast as the incredible sensations of her sucking and licking him became more and more insistent.

They stayed like this for a while, moaning over their respective mouthfuls. Andrion found that from this direction he had to develop a somewhat different technique, but he soon had it down – judging from Berni's reactions. Abruptly she lifted up off of him, releasing his quivering member from her mouth and pulling her dripping cunt from his face. Then she performed a sort of crouching pirouette and straddled him, sinking down on his shaft all the way to the root. Oh!

Next, Bernadette began grinding on top of him, pubic bone to pubic bone, moving in circular motions that felt really amazing. Her head thrown back, her face bright pink spreading down over her shoulders and chest, her mouth open in an "O," she cried out and her cunt clasped him harder in rippling spasms as she came. Andrion watched her avidly, loving every minute of it, but still holding off his own climax.

In another few moments Bernadette fell forward onto his chest, kissing him deeply, and beginning to move up and down with her knees, riding on his slippery shaft. Ohhh, yes, that felt very good too. Andrion was close now, so close, and he wanted to regain control of the speed; so pulling her close to him he rolled over in the bed, putting her on the bottom now, and knelt so he could thrust into her – somewhat slowly at first, teasing a little, then faster and faster until he was pounding into her like a pile-driver. She came once again, screaming, as he let out a long groan and, toes curling, exploded deep inside her.

They rolled onto their sides, gasping and panting, mouths locked in sloppy kisses, their minds ablaze. When the white heat of orgasm had faded they still lay, snuggled together and grinning like maniacs. "Oh, Andrion," Bernadette breathed. "I love you so much…" Awhile later she added, "I think tomorrow will be the first time *you've* gone somewhere without *me* since we met. I'm going to miss you." Andrion smiled and kissed the top of her head.

"A man's gotta do what a man's gotta do," he said self-importantly. She smiled into his chest. She had the feeling that, just as with Erik, Andrion had something up his sleeve. Well, she had her own little secrets she was saving as well. She stifled her curiosity, content to wait for the surprise.

After lying there murmuring about nothing much, the two of them got up and did a little cleanup with water and a towel, before climbing back into bed to fall asleep, wrapped in each other's arms.

Chapter 48: Erik's Reward

Fairly early in the morning Bernadette woke and got a drink of water from the bedside pitcher. Andrion stirred, missing her, then opened his melting brown eyes to gaze at her as she stood there in the nude. Reaching for her robe, she smiled down at him and spoke quietly: "I'm going to go catch a quick bath and then have a talk with Erik. I've left the map here on top of the chest of drawers." He smiled and answered as quietly, "I don't think we need to be leaving for Daywatch just yet. I believe I'll catch a little more sleep." She bent to kiss him, then headed downstairs as he rolled over, covers up around his chin.

Bernadette made her bath a short one. She'd taken one only a few hours ago, but wanted to be clean, fresh, and glowing when she gave Erik his morning treat. On the way to the trap door she smelled pastries. "So soon?" she asked Drelos, and learned that he now had a woman getting up at four in the morning to do baking in the large oven that had recently been installed in the kitchen. All of the extra inn business was making it hard to get enough fresh bread and pastries delivered. And this way, the baked goods were *really* fresh.

They smelled so wonderful Bernadette got a tray of them to take downstairs with her, along with a pot of herbal tea and a couple of thick mugs. She'd once heard someone jokingly remark that the way for a woman to please a man was to show up naked and bring mead; but at this hour Erik was just going to have to settle for breakfast. The naked part would soon be achieved.

Bernadette found her golden giant sleeping face down in the bed, looking more golden still in the candlelight. She laid the tray down on the chest of drawers, wondering if the delightful smells might penetrate Erik's consciousness. So far, there was no sign they had done so. He had only a thin sheet draped over him. Somebody his size could conserve body heat a lot better than she could, another reason she loved sleeping with him on chilly nights.

Bernadette slipped her fingers beneath the sheet's top hem and began pulling it down, all the way down past the end of the bed. Erik's feet hung over the end – the standard beds of Iscandia were not built with him in mind. His breathing remained steady and deep, with no sign that she had disturbed him. She stood there for a moment, just admiring his massively muscled backside. The bulging trapezius muscles, the well-defined lats, and oh those glutes.

She reached out her hands and settled her fingers like eiderdown at the top of his buttocks, stroking down them like butterfly kisses. Erik twitched slightly and uttered a muffled grunt, but subsided once again. Her eyes lit with mischief, Bernadette next reached down below his butt, to tickle his scrotum where it lay just peeking out between his legs. Like a lightning strike, Erik suddenly whirled to face her, his hand snaking out to grasp her wrist!

Bernadette jumped, but couldn't go anywhere with Erik pinning her. He was grinning at her, and she observed that his massive cock was standing straight up. "You caught me," she said with a rueful smile. He nodded, and continuing to hold her wrist he guided the hand attached to it… down onto his erection, whereupon he released her and gave her a meaningful look.

Bernadette continued what she'd been doing, which was stroking him gently on his sensitive parts. But now she was no longer trying to keep from waking him, she begun to rub harder and squeeze as well. As his cock grew still longer and thicker and the head began to purple, she brought her mouth to bear. She had actually managed to take Erik all the way inside her mouth once, but it had damn near choked her and she hoped he'd be willing to settle for a little oral and manual stimulation instead.

As she was working on him his nose twitched. "Is that freshly baked pastries I smell?" he asked disbelievingly. She looked up at him, both hands squeezing now, and gestured with her head toward the tray. His eyes lit up. "I've got to have me some of that. But first, I want some of *this*," he said, pointing at her. "Come sit on my face." Her eyes widened slightly, but his wish was her command.

As Erik slid down the bed a little Bernadette climbed up it until she was straddling his head with her legs. He gripped her by the buttocks to keep her weight off his chest and neck, and began running his hot, wet tongue deeply into her slit. Like every part of Erik, his tongue was a bit longer and thicker than average. Hell, she'd seen some guys whose *dicks* weren't as big as that tongue. Fortunately, not from such a close vantage point as this.

She'd come down here with the intention of servicing Erik, paying him back for the favor with the amulet. But soon Bernadette found herself riding his face, bouncing and moaning, until a tingle arose in her clit and shot up through her midsection all the way to the top of her head. She knelt there quivering for a few moments, screaming out her release. Erik looked up at her, a self-satisfied grin plastered on his face. Sometimes, she thought, her men got almost as much enjoyment out of making her come as they did coming themselves. Now that she considered it, it was among their most endearing qualities.

All those muscles weren't just for show. Erik had amazing strength, and he used some of it now to slide Bernadette down his body so he could sit up. Her ankles were now up on his shoulders, and he gently lowered her onto his rigid member. Then bending his knees, he continued on over so she was now lying with her head hanging off the edge of the bed, in danger of falling save that he held her.

Bernadette was young and limber, and bent almost double as Erik pounded into her she found that the position opened her wide to his thrusts. His excitement rising, he pushed in harder and faster, until she had to slip her ankles down. He moved his arms out of the way, one at a time, so she could lock her legs around his hips and meet him stroke for stroke. She found herself coming again and again, but still he held on, somewhat to her surprise. Except that by now, she wasn't forming many conscious thoughts.

As she lay there puddled on the bed after her latest orgasm, head still hanging off the edge, Erik put his hand beneath her head and rocked back on his knees, lifting her to cradle in his arms. She hadn't even kissed him yet this morning, but she did so now. He scooted them a little further back toward the head of the bed, then gently pulled Bernadette off of his erection and encouraged her with hand gestures to rotate until she was kneeling with her back to him. Then he entered her again.

And now, it started all over again. Slow, gentle strokes. Coming almost all the way back out, rubbing the head around the rim of her vulva, then popping back inside. Short strokes, longer ones, gliding, coming faster, now faster and deeper and harder and OH! The two of them fell full length on the bed, Erik's cock and Bernadette's cunt throbbing in unison, as he filled her with his semen. As the pulsations subsided, he quickly rolled them to the side – sensitive of her need to breathe.

Erik hugged Bernadette from behind, his massive arms wrapped tight around her and his short beard tickling her ear. "Thank you for bringing me breakfast," he rumbled softly. She just squeezed his arms tighter around her and gave a contented sigh. When she thought of all the sexual frustrations of her younger days, this seemed like heaven. She knew that inevitably as they all grew older and children came along their sex lives would change, but there would be other joys to compensate. For now, this was bliss and she intended to savor it to the fullest.

After some minutes of quiet snuggling the two both began to think about those pastries, cooling on the chest. No point in letting them get too cold! Erik handed Bernadette her robe and a towel for some clean-up, then put on his own robe and brought the tray over to set on the bed. It was likely time to change the sheets, in any case. What matter a few crumbs?

Bernadette sat cross-legged on the mattress, a pastry in one hand and a mug of still-warm tea in the other. Having gotten fucked to a fare-thee-well only a few minutes after waking this morning, she was having a little trouble marshaling her thoughts. "Let's see," she said, her mouth half full of sweet goodness, "Andrion and Nerissa are taking the map to go to Daywatch. I guess that means I'm going to have to walk into Waterdon this morning. I need to tell Lifa and Bjorn when their wedding day is, and get the list of people we're supposed to invite to the party. And then I have to talk to Eorl Ormund."

Erik halted, frozen – having just stuffed a pastry into his mouth and being about to reach for another. Uh oh, he thought. She walks past Coldburn and the first thing that happens is she gets curious and goes to ask somebody what's going on. Maybe she even runs into Bjorn there, which is probably a dead giveaway. Then she goes up to see Ormund, and the first thing out of his mouth is, 'How are you enjoying your new farm?'

"I'll come with you!" he told Berni enthusiastically. "I've got some business in town, too."

Bernadette was surprised and pleased. She'd love to have Erik's company anytime, really, and not just in bed. "Great, sweetie!" she said, reaching out a sticky free hand to squeeze his. "Let's finish our breakfast and get dressed. Then we probably ought to see Andrion and Nerissa off before we leave."

"Sounds good," he said, tucking one more roll into his mouth before washing it down with a draught of tea and then dusting his lap off before reaching for the ewer to pour some water for hand-washing.

Bernadette used the basin too before kissing Erik and saying, "See you in the common room." She found Andrion and Nerissa fully dressed and sitting at their table when she came out from behind the bar. They were partaking of a hearty breakfast, and waved cheerfully to her as she came through heading for the stairs. Freed of her blood hunger, Nerissa seemed to be acquiring a sweet tooth. She was munching on pastries and apples.

Chapter 49: Excursions

Upstairs, Bernadette gave herself a sponge bath before putting on her clothes. She wanted something that bespoke authority for talking with Ormund, but also offered a bit of protection in case they were ambushed by hostile wildlife on the way into town. Even within the shadow of Waterdon's walls, one could sometimes find peril in broad daylight. She added a finely wrought leather breastplate to an ensemble of soft wool with fur and velvet accents. Then she looked over the contents of her pack.

From the way it was nearly empty, it was high time to do some more smithing – and selling. Her enchanting skills could still use some work. And, stuck at home for a few days, without the map, seemed like the perfect time to improve them. For now, though, she just took her bow and arrows plus a well-honed sablium dagger for protection. Everybody carried a dagger for cutting meat, and polite society didn't look askance at one whether you carried the most basic iron dagger that would have trouble dealing with a haunch of goat, or a gleaming glass one enchanted to turn your enemies into glowing pink slime.

Hmm, Bernadette mused as she assembled her outfit. That "glowing pink slime" enchantment would be a nice one to learn. I wonder where I could get that? She laughed to herself. As fantastic as the world and its many magics was, it could not outstrip her imagination. For *some* reason, she just seemed to be in an awfully good mood this morning.

Returning back downstairs fully dressed and ready to go, Bernadette found Andrion and Nerissa finished with their meal and standing up as Erik, having deposited his breakfast tray at the bar, was walking across the room to join them. The four of them strolled out the Maiden's front doors and stood on the porch conferring. "Do you have everything you need?" Bernadette asked Andrion somewhat anxiously. He was wearing his armor and appeared to be carrying all his usual weapons. "Potions, money?" He smiled at her reassuringly.

"It's all covered, Mom." Ouch. Evidently she had not really come to terms with his going off and leaving her. He was a grown man ten years her senior and a proven warrior. Get a grip, Berni.

343

She smiled ruefully at him and stepped up to give him a kiss and the sort of hug one wearing street clothing gives to someone in full armor. Turning to Nerissa, she said "Would you like to come to the wedding parties? We're having them both here at the Maiden. There will be one on the eighteenth for Bjorn and Lifa, and another one the eleventh of next month for us. In fact, I'd like to invite everybody in the Daywatch crew to that one. But they'd have to make their own way here. Maybe you could all walk into Norcove and take a wagon to Waterdon?"

"Whether anyone wants to come with me or not, I will definitely be here for your party on the eleventh," Nerissa promised. "I think that in some ways, the love you three share is a large part of what convinced me to become human again. I want that kind of love." Bernadette felt tears threatening as Nerissa's words touched her to the soul.

"Don't worry," she told her friend. "You'll find it. There's probably not an unattached straight man in Iscandia who wouldn't leap at the chance to be with you."

"Thanks," Nerissa said wryly, a little smile quirking her lips. It wasn't just a matter of finding somebody to jump into bed with you, after all. But that was certainly a start...

"Andrion," Bernadette said, suddenly remembering her curiosity when the subject had come up last night. "Stand over there and pull out the map." Looking puzzled, he walked down onto the road and did so. "What cities do you see?" she called to him. He'd looked at the map over Berni's shoulder many times in their months of traveling together, and what he saw now looked pretty familiar.

"It looks about the same," he called back.

"Can you think of any places you've visited without the map, and see if they're showing?" Andrion considered for a moment. He'd been to most places in Iscandia over the past decade, including some that were not on *any* map. Oh, wait. There was a giant camp not that far from Norcove, he recalled now. What was the name? It had been four or five years ago, when he'd been wandering as a solo adventurer, that the Eorl of Seamarch had offered a bounty for killing the giant at... Two Trees Crossing, that was it! It was out in the frozen waste some hours south of the "city" of Norcove. He'd dispatched the giant, a feat facilitated by scrambling up a pine tree out of reach of the angry fellow's massive club, and claimed the bounty.

Andrion searched the map area south of Norcove, but there was no sign of the encampment. He turned and walked back to where Berni, Erik, and Nerissa awaited him. "I went to a place a few years ago that's not showing on the map," he said. "I think that means that this map will only take the person in possession of it to places that they have visited *while* they had possession. Since I was part of your party, as far as the map was concerned, I count and it'll take me – and whoever is 'with' me – to all the places we went together, including some I only visited when you took me there using the map. But if we were to walk into Waterdon and hand this map to one of the guards at the gate, I don't think it would take him anywhere. Not even any places he'd been to before he got the map."

He realized at this point that his audience's eyes were taking on a glazed look. Rats. "Let's just say, it should take me and Nerissa to Daywatch. But Berni, I think you and Erik should stay way back or you might end up coming along with us."

"Why don't you and Nerissa walk up the road a few dozen paces? Erik and I will stay here on the porch," Bernadette suggested. She had followed Andrion's explanation, more or less, but it had only raised more questions. She suspected the "science" of magic maps might well take years of study.

She and Erik stood as the other two descended the steps and began walking up the road. "Goodbye! See you soon!" Bernadette called, once again gripped by a feeling of painful separation as she watched Andrion walk away. She'd left *him* plenty of times, for days at a time. What was her problem? When Andrion and Nerissa had reached a point in the road a hundred or so feet from the Maiden, he stepped close to his female companion, mentally encompassing her as a part of his "group" or whatever it was, touched Daywatch on the map and wished them there.

Bernadette and Erik watched Andrion and Nerissa waver slightly in the morning air, then vanish from view. She turned to her companion, smiling. "It worked! Well, shall we be off?" The two of them strode off in the direction their recent companions had taken, and before long they were abreast of Coldburn Farm. "Oh my!" Bernadette exclaimed, staring open-mouthed at the horde of workers swarming around the place. Massive amounts of stone for the basement and foundations had now been delivered, Hegmar's final estimate having been approved and a further deposit made by the conspirators.

"Oh that," Erik remarked nonchalantly. "Seems the owner, Safar, has decided to expand the place. He thinks he'll make more money if he gets more people living there." Bernadette looked a little puzzled, but readily accepted Erik's explanation. After all, he had been around the area a lot more than she had of late. More often than not even when she was in the area, she would fast-travel into town and never go past this little farm.

"I thought it was just one old man living here?" she asked.

"New tenants coming," Erik explained. "More hands, more crops. That's what I heard, anyway."

They resumed walking up the road, soon leaving both the farm and the discussion behind. Inside the gates of Waterdon, Bernadette greeted her friend Alessia with a wave of the hand and made for the door of Brightsgate Cottage. "I'll hook up with you later," Erik told her. "I've got some business to take care of." Bernadette looked at him nonplussed. Erik usually visited with the family at Brightsgate Cottage on an almost daily basis, and she was surprised he would pass up the opportunity to be there when she gave them the news that their wedding was definitely on the schedule.

"All right then," she told him. "I'll probably be heading up to see Ormund at Wyrmshalla within the hour."

"I'll meet you up there," he promised, hastening off up the road. What *was* he up to? Bernadette wondered. Well, time would likely tell. She continued on to rap at the cottage door, which was shortly opened by Anja. The girl seemed to have grown a little since the last time she was here, if such a thing were possible. She was wearing a pretty dress and had her long auburn hair in two ponytails, held high on either side of her head with pink ribbons.

Bernadette grinned at her. She was so adorable! Personally, pink ribbons were not her thing; and she was hard put to imagine they were Lifa's either. But they looked awfully cute on a five-year-old, and she didn't doubt Anja would grow out of them in time. Anja's face lit up, and she hurtled through the door to hug Bernadette around the middle, crying "Aunt Berni!"

A moment later, with that ferret-like speed that seemed to characterize all her movements, Anja had stepped back to admire Bernadette's raiment. She'd often seen her in more businesslike garb, but seemed to approve of this outfit. "You look very pretty and important!" she declared.

"Thank you Anja," Bernadette replied sincerely. "May I come in?"

Remembering her manners, which her foster parents had been trying to teach her, Anja curtsied and stepped aside, saying "Please!" and gesturing to the interior of the small home.

Lifa was in the kitchen area, washing dishes with lye soap in a wooden tub. "Bernadette!" she exclaimed, "you're back!"

"Yes," Bernadette responded, swelling with pleasure, "and I have good news. Is Bjorn around?"

For some reason this question seemed to catch the other woman off guard, and she appeared to miss a beat before saying, "Oh, he's off working on a project. He'll probably be gone all day." She gave Anja a look, which Anja returned with an expression as of someone unjustly accused of malfeasance.

Bernadette was disappointed. She'd envisioned telling the couple together. Well, Bjorn was a man – and men can't be expected to sit around the house all day. "You'll have to give him the news for me, then," she told Lifa. "Your wedding will be in the temple of Marmira in Lakedon at nine o'clock in the morning on the seventeenth of this month. We'll all be gathered together at the Bathing Maiden no later than seven o'clock on the evening of the sixteenth, and will fast-travel to Lakedon from there. We expect to arrive in Lakedon a couple of hours before the ceremony. After the wedding, we'll fast-travel back to Waterdon. I can drop you three off back here to spend the night. Then the following day, we'll have the big party at the Maiden starting around two in the afternoon."

Lifa was just standing there, a soap-dripping pot in her hands, looking at her raptly. "Well?" Bernadette prompted, "What do you think?" Lifa glanced down at her hands, dropping the pot back down into the washtub.

Then a radiant smile spread across her features as she gazed at her benefactress and said, "Bernadette! This is wonderful! I can hardly believe it's happening…" Anja, too, seemed delighted by the news.

"You can be the flower girl," Bernadette promised her. "I'll give you some flowers to carry and you'll walk down to the altar ahead of Aunt Lifa and Uncle Bjorn. You drop the flowers one by one on the floor in the aisle. And then you come stand by me and Uncle Andrion and Uncle Erik while the priest says the wedding words."

Anja was goggle-eyed at the prospect. "Oh, and you'll wear your prettiest dress, too." Lifa smiled at that. Even she, destined to become a swordmaiden and bondswoman to the march, had liked pretty dresses when she was that age. Of course, that was before she'd been orphaned. She wished she had a prettier one to wear for her wedding, but really any of the clothes she'd acquired since starting this new chapter of her life were prettier than what she'd owned before.

"Now that we have the date," Bernadette was continuing, "I need to have that list so I can send out invitations to everyone for the party. I'll be formally asking Eorl Ormund to the wedding in person, of course." She considered for a moment, then decided surprise was not called for and said, "I already have ex-Eorl Hjaermond and his former steward, Selden, staying with us at the Maiden. So you can tell Bjorn I have his request covered." Lifa smiled, pleased at this news. She knew it had troubled Bjorn to have his bond summarily handed over from one eorl to another.

She went over to a nearby bookcase and pulled down a roll of paper, on which she'd written the names and locations of the people she and Bjorn wanted to have invited to their wedding celebration. Bernadette scanned it quickly. The list wasn't all that long, but of course it didn't include any of the Maiden employees who would be there in any case, all of whom Lifa had come to know during her months as a resident of the place.

Everyone was in the local area, and there should be no problems getting them to the Maiden. The place was becoming so popular, any local that hadn't been there yet was either scheming on an excuse to go or pretending they'd already been. Bernadette wondered idly whether, at this rate, she might end up getting more prestige points for being the inn's proprietor than she did for being the savior of the planet. Now *that* would be typical…

Bernadette lingered talking with Lifa and Anja for a few minutes more. Meanwhile, as soon as Erik had left her he had headed up the nearest staircase at a trot, and (puffing a bit; there hadn't been enough of either questing or athletic sex to keep him in peak condition of late) reached the doors of Wyrmshalla within a minute or two of the time he and Berni had come in through the front gates.

Smoothing his clothing and catching his breath for a moment, Erik then strolled through those doors as if he owned the place. He might lack the polish and panache Andrion could bring to bear when confronting the nobility, but he had his own sort of gravitas. Plus, people generally liked him. In fact, Eorl Ormund liked him. A fine example of a young Norseman, he thought as he saw Erik approaching the dais. Today as it happened was a slow day for march business, and the older man welcomed the chance for a little converse with this jovial young fellow who was, it seemed, of some importance to The Fireblood.

"A good day to you," he said as Erik approached.

Erik bowed respectfully and said, "The same to you, sir."

"So, how is Coldburn farm working out for you?" Ormund wanted to know. "I'm assuming the purchase was satisfactory?"

Erik gave him one of his famous blue-eyed, boyish grins sure to disarm anybody and said "Thank you, sir. Safar was most accommodating to us. We've purchased the property and are now employing a large crew of local residents to extend the house." He wavered at this point from his bluff, forthright manner and admitted almost shyly, "That's what I wanted to talk to you about…"

Under Ormund's penetrating inquisition the whole story came out: Bernadette's betrothal to them both, their desire to surprise her on their wedding day with her dream house, the problems they were having keeping the project a secret now that she was here and spending several days in the area before their friends' wedding. Ormund cocked an eyebrow at the revelation of The Fireblood's own

349

unusual wedding plans. This sort of thing was just not done, in his experience. But on the other hand, she *was* The Fireblood. That she wanted to bow to convention enough to be formally married was something, at least. And he found the whole situation with her two fiancés' efforts to surprise her charming.

"So," the Eorl said, summing up, "she's coming here in a few minutes to talk with me. And you'd like me *not* to mention that I'm aware of any real estate transactions involving you two?"

Erik smiled, relief painting his features that he'd managed to get the point across. "That's it exactly! Er, if you're all right with that...?"

Ormund smiled broadly. "Of *course* I'm all right with it!" he said. "We men have got to stick together, right?"

Erik nodded, feeling a bit like a kid despite his size. "Thank you, sir!"

The eorl having nothing else to occupy his time for the moment, he and Erik engaged in a casual discussion almost as equals. Ormund might be a hereditary aristocrat with the running of an entire march as his responsibility, while Erik was just a young Norse sellsword from a tiny town in the far north; but his forthcoming marriage alliance with The Fireblood, however unconventional, had elevated his status in Iscandia society. Erik accepted this as equably as he did most things in life, and chatted amiably with the older man until Bernadette appeared.

She strode up to the area below the dais and gave him a smile, squeezing his hand. "I'm sorry you missed Anja," she told him. "You should have seen her face when I told her she was going to be the flower girl at the wedding."

Erik smiled beatifically back at her, and said "Well, my business is concluded. I think I'll leave you to your own business and go pop in on Lifa and Anja. Shall I meet you at Brightsgate Cottage for the walk back to the Maiden?"

"That would be fine," Bernadette said, squeezing his hand again.

Erik nodded respectfully to Ormund and said, "Good talking with you, my eorl." Then he took his leave. As he walked back down the hall she followed him with her eyes, wondering how he happened to be talking with Ormund. The eorl had certainly met both him and

Andrion on the occasion of the trapping of Sneyagflug, before they'd killed Tarragin. But she didn't realize they were on speaking terms.

Turning back to Ormund, Bernadette looked him in the eyes. The old man's blue eyes were twinkling and he appeared to be actively anticipating whatever she might have to say." What *was* going on? "Ah, Fireblood!" Ormund said warmly, a trace of amusement in his tone. "In what way may I assist you?" Bernadette cocked an eyebrow at him.

Then, following her usual policy of simply plunging ahead in the face of puzzling evidence, she said "I bear good tidings, my eorl." Mentally she thought of him as 'Ormund,' but she maintained a modicum of respect for his rank and for the man who held it.

To her delight and astonishment, he replied with "Please, Fireblood, I think that you might call me Ormund. And may I call you Bernadette?"

Almost thunderstruck at this turn, she smiled at him and said, "All right… Ormund." It certainly helps, sometimes, to be a good-looking woman in your early twenties.

For almost the first time since she and her companions had defeated the Soul-Devourer, Bernadette felt as if the respect she was due was coming to her at last. Why should she *not* move among the circles of the elite, on a first-name basis with eorls and other nobles? She had poured out her life's blood for her adopted province, and everyone in it owed her recognition, at the least. She smiled secretly to herself and continued, "My news concerns the body servant Lifa, whose services you assigned me when you first made me warden."

Both of them seemed lost for a moment in memories of that day. It had happened in the aftermath of the first dragon attack near Waterdon, the day she had first discovered she was fireblood. Ormund looked thoughtful. "I remember Lifa well. She gave her oaths to me and the march when she was scarcely more than a girl. Has she given satisfactory service?" he asked.

Bernadette smiled at him. "Satisfactory, and more than satisfactory," she said. "I now also have in my service one Bjorn, a body servant of Alfenstein, and the two of them are to be wed." By Iscandia law, you might marry when and whom you would. But if

351

you were pledged to the hold, there was no guarantee that you would not be forced to leave your spouse's side if your sworn duty called.

Ormund's lined face lit in a smile of pleasure. "Lifa, to be wed… how wonderful! I confess, I never thought I would see the day. She's such a serious young thing. Beautiful, to be sure, but…"

Bernadette returned his smile. "Things have changed quite a bit for Lifa in the past few weeks," she told him. "In any case, the wedding is to be held at the Temple of Marmira in Lakedon at nine in the morning on the seventeenth of this month. Lifa hopes that you will be there to see her wed. As I'm sure you know, she has no surviving family."

The old man looked touched. He'd felt sorry for the fierce, beautiful young orphan woman who had come to offer her service. How remarkable that her life could have taken this turn! Looking up at Bernadette, he said "Of course, I will be there." He called to Paolo, who was standing off to the side of the dais being unobtrusive, and said "Please make a note in my calendar. I think that we'll take a fast coach on the fifteenth. That should put us in Lakedon in plenty of time for the ceremony. And arrange some suitable wedding present, if you will." Paolo nodded, pulling out an appointment book and making notations.

Bernadette's smile deepened as little as she said to the eorl, "As for the matter of wedding presents, Ormund, there are some other matters I would like to discuss with you. And I think Paolo will need to be involved, as well." She stepped closer to the dais and began speaking softly.

Chapter 50: Return to Daywatch

After the usual few moments of disorienting darkness, Andrion and Nerissa found Daywatch shimmering into existence before them, their feet planted on the dirt path leading to the front steps. It worked! He found himself exulting at the realization. Despite all his calm and rational assessments, a tiny part of his mind had whispered that it might not work at all – or would go horribly wrong. From the darkness surrounding them, it was definitely past eight.

Was their belief in some logical correlation between actual geographical distances and the "real time" taken up by fast-travelling accurate? Though time was not officially controlled throughout the province, most people who had clocks or cared about them would set them to twelve noon when the shadow of a stick driven straight into the ground was at its shortest. That ought to mean that here, further to the west, it would only have been eight or maybe even seven when he and Nerissa had left Waterdon at nine this morning.

The problem fascinated Andrion, now that it had been brought to his attention. He'd always brushed it aside in the past, having only begun to use a magic map after he became embroiled with Berni and her destiny as The Fireblood. They'd been running all over Iscandia as fast as they could, with the time and date of their arrival of little concern compared with what they had to do when they got there.

So, Nerissa following, he eagerly led the way up to the doors of the fortress. They needed to get inside as quickly as possible and take a look at the clock on the mantle in the dining hall. They found a few people still sitting at table, and Marya engaged in her customary chores of cleaning up the cooking pots, plates, and cutlery. She might not be out with the Brigade taking down vampires, but hers were the efforts that kept everyone well fed and fit for battle.

"Andrion!" the well-fed, dark-skinned woman said with a flash of white teeth. "There's still another couple of bowlfuls of stew if you want it, but I was just about to clear up for the evening."

He smiled at her and said "Sure, I'll take it off your hands. What's the time?" She looked up at the clock. Winding it every morning was one of her duties, and she was proud to be one of the few people in the province with such a modern marvel in her hands.

"It's a bit past nine," she said. "Erik didn't come with you?"

"He's keeping Berni company back in Waterdon," Andrion told her.

Just then his companion joined them, saying "Hello, Marya." The woman turned from her work and then did a double take.

"Nerissa?!" Nerissa smiled sweetly at her. "You're…" Marya sputtered, "you're… not a v…?"

"I took the cure!" Nerissa crowed. "Bernadette gave me the idea, and I decided to go for it. I'm a new woman now, and I'm here to help the Daywatch Brigade in its work."

They took the last of the remaining stew and joined some of the other Brigade members at the table. One of the youngest recruits, a Norseman of perhaps nineteen years but strapping and muscular – looking like a more compact version of what Erik must have been six years previously – gaped at her in wonder.

Nerissa held his gaze with her limpid blue eyes and he seemed to shudder a little. He'd always thought her exotic and attractive, but like most of the other women here she was too much older than him and generally out of his league. Now she was different, more vibrant and less scary – but still, completely out of his league. He sighed softly.

Nerissa smiled at him. He was young and healthy and not bad looking, but there were limits. There wasn't a man living in Iscandia she could hook up with and escape the charge of robbing the cradle; but it made sense for her to seek men who had a few years on them, at least.

As he filled his mouth with the savory stew, Andrion mused. Seemingly the trip here had taken twelve hours, the same as Berni had said was required to travel between Waterdon and Lakedon. But as the crow flies, the distance to Daywatch was much less. Unless… Perhaps, the elapsed time was based on how long it would actually take you to walk? There were good roads leading to Lakedon, but one had to climb mountains and worm one's way through hidden passes to reach here.

Marya finished her washing-up and came over to sit with them. "So, Andrion," what brings you back to us?"

"Well," he explained, "I really came here to drop Nerissa off and consult with Diane. I suppose she's gone to bed already?"

"A little while ago," Marya confirmed. "She spends most of her days at the forge, translating ancient dypalfar designs into weapons we can use in our campaign. But she's an early riser. She'll probably be up in another seven hours, if you want to wait. Me, I was just about to hit the sack. You're welcome to a cot, if you'd prefer."

Andrion considered. His mind was telling him it had not been three hours since he rose from a good night's sleep, wrapped in Berni's arms. His body seemed to be trying to convince him that it was bedtime. He decided to accept the latter set of information, since he didn't really know what he would do to pass the time until Diane was up and about in any case. "I'll take you up on that cot," he told the young woman. "What about you, Nerissa?"

"I feel as if I could use a nap too," she said, yawning. The pair bid Marya a good night and made their way through the corridors to the barracks area.

In the second of the dormitory rooms that had been set up, where there were still a few empty cots, Andrion dropped his pack beside the one he'd been offered and peeled off his armor, sliding onto the taut leather and pulling the thin blanket up to cover himself. In surprisingly little time, he found himself dropping off to sleep.

In the morning Andrion woke as those around him began to stir. He spotted Diane already getting into her leathers, and hurried to put his armor back on. She'd left the room by the time he finished (while Nerissa, he noticed, slumbered on), but he found her again in the dining hall, drinking tea. "Andrion!" she said cheerfully, "I thought I spotted you. Where's Bernadette?"

Andrion gave her a winning smile. "Good morning, Diane. Bernadette's back in Waterdon, making arrangements for our wedding." The Galise woman's eyebrows raised at this news.

"You and she are getting married, huh? Congratulations."

His smiled deepened as he corrected her: "Berni and I and *Erik* are getting married… It's a long story, but apparently we have the approval of the gods. We're all standing up together at the Pantheatos in Sylvanian next month."

Diane seemed a little taken aback by Andrion's statement, but in a moment recalled her manners. "Well, I wish you three all the best," she said. "What you did has gone a long way toward making Iscandia safe from vampires."

He grinned, having more startling news to share. "Wait'll you to talk with Nerissa! I brought her back with me last night and she's still sleeping, but she's taken the cure. She's no longer a vampire!" Diane's eyes widened even more and she sat there, momentarily at a loss for words.

Finally she blurted, "Andrion! That is wonderful news! Oh, I *do* like Nerissa. I'm so glad she decided to live again." She took another sip of her tea, considering the ramifications. In another moment she added, "I can't wait until Malden finds out. *That* ought to set him back on his heels. He was so hostile when she first came to us, but everything she said she would do she did without flinching, even helping to bring down her own family. I think he's been feeling bad about some of the things he said to her. And now, he won't even have vampirism to hold against her."

Diane's bright and active mind, similar in bent to Bernadette's or Andrion's own, continued to work as she took a bite of the bread and cheese set before her and washed it down with another swallow of hot tea. "Oh!" she burst out suddenly, "Nerissa can be a sort of missionary for us! We won't necessarily have to slaughter every vampire we meet, not if she can talk some of them into taking the cure as she did. We might even wipe out vampirism in Iscandia, between curing the ones who are willing and killing the ones who aren't."

Andrion smiled, and helped himself to some bread and cheese from a plate on the table, also finding a mug of tea. Many of the thoughts Diane was having had also passed through his head, since Nerissa's return. When Diane had run down and his mouth was no longer full, he said "Diane, bringing Nerissa here is only part of the reason I came. I need to consult with you about dypalfar mechanisms." Diane's face lit with instant enthusiasm at this news. She was used to being regarded as something of a nutcase, since her fascination with the dypalfar and their technology was not universal.

After the two had finished eating their breakfasts, Andrion explained in detail what he needed from Diane. "The Bathing Maiden, where I've lived for the past couple of years, has a large hot bathing pool set into the floor in the central common room. It's kept at a uniform temperature, the water level stays at the same height, and the water is always sparkling clean no matter how many people are bathing in there. And believe me, some of them *really* needed a bath."

Diane looked intrigued. There was many a time she'd like a nice hot bath herself, but the walk to the hot springs here, and the short winter daylight, made it hard to get out there. Indoors, hot baths involved kettles and washtubs – and a lot of prep time. Andrion went on, "That's all being taken care of by an installation of dypalfar machinery in the basement down below the pool. I've been down there and looked at it a couple of times, and it's just spinning away there on its own the same as the ancient machinery in a dozen dypalfar ruins I've visited. But I have no idea how it works."

"And you're just curious?" Diane asked, prompting Andrion for more details. "Erik and I are preparing a surprise for Berni, for after the wedding," he explained. "We don't want to live at the Maiden – there's no privacy to speak of. And it's not the kind of place for raising children, either. But we want to stay close to the area, and as there no suitable places on the market we bought an old farm nearby and are doing a massive remodel of the house. Berni doesn't know anything about this."

Diane's eyes were twinkling with amusement, now. How romantic! Her happiness for her three Daywatch colleagues was only slightly shadowed by the wistful thought that it had been a long time since there'd been any romance in *her* life. She had her work, and it occupied most of her attention. But just occasionally, a little loving would be nice. Maybe it was time for her to start looking around a bit.

"So, we're trying to make sure the house has every creature comfort," Andrion continued. "I designed the water and sewer systems, sort of, but we want to have water coming down by pipes from the cistern running hot in the kitchen when we need it to, and a good-sized tub or small pool in the bathroom that's kept hot and clean just like at the Maiden. And I'm completely stumped on how to do that. I'm hoping maybe you know what sort of dypalfar technology is being used, and how we can adapt it to our new home."

Diane smiled broadly at him, excited. Applying her large fund of specialized knowledge to a challenging project on behalf of friends sounded like *exactly* the sort of thing she needed to shake up her routine. In the time since the Daywatch Brigade had brought down Lord Karazin, she'd been spending almost all of her time either at the forge, making enhanced crossbows and experimenting with different types of bolts; or researching ancient texts, looking for clues as to the whereabouts of more dypalfar technology to borrow or adapt.

"I'd be delighted to help you, Andrion!" she said. "I'm going to have to look at the machinery in the Bathing Maiden basement, of course, before I know exactly what we're dealing with; but I have a few ideas. It'll take me awhile to gather up everything I want to take with me. Are we going to fast-travel?"

Andrion nodded, saying "Berni lent me her map for the trip down here. It took us just about twelve hours to get here, so if we can leave by six this evening we'll get to the Maiden at a decent hour tomorrow morning. I promised Berni I'd get the map back to her pretty soon, as she has some more wedding errands to run. It's not just us who are getting married. Berni's body servants Bjorn and Lifa are tying the knot over in Lakedon in another couple of weeks."

That settled, the two parted ways. Diane scurried off to discuss her plans with Malden and the other smiths who were making arms and armor for the Daywatch Brigade, to show her assistants how to make the crossbows she was working on now, and to gather not only a supply of clothing and weapons for herself, but a collection of tools and dypalfar devices she thought might be helpful. She also brought along a couple of her ancient tomes, in case one of them might point the way to something she didn't realize she needed until after she'd been to the Maiden.

For his part, Andrion was at loose ends. He got his pack ready to go, then wandered around chatting with various Daywatch Brigade members. Walking through an anteroom, he came upon Malden in conversation with Nerissa. The handsome if stern and aged Afran seemed rapt, looking intently into her no-longer-glowing eyes. Nerissa seemed to be emitting a sort of come-hither vibe. Surely she could not be trying to seduce Malden, after all the viciously unkind things he had said about her in the past?

Walking on without interrupting their conversation, Andrion wondered: did any of the purported vampire powers persist after the cure? Clearly her eyes now appeared normal and she was not bothered by sunlight, seemed to revel in it in fact. But might she still possess physical strength greater than normal, or have the power to enthrall others? But he believed her when she'd told them she would not use that power except at the direst need. Otherwise, she would surely have used it to dial down Malden's hostility. He'd been damn close to killing her on the spot.

Andrion climbed the stairs past the room where he and Berni had had their exciting liaison some weeks ago, to walk out on the parapet and admire the view. The castle's setting was a pretty one, certainly. Back downstairs, he went down to the archery butts for some crossbow practice, and walked around the outer walls. Then, feeling peckish, he went back inside and found Diane eating lunch.

Marya had laid out platters of cold sliced beef, loaves of bread, and winter pears, and Andrion made himself a sandwich. Between mouthfuls, Andrion asked Diane "How's it going?" Though not leaving until six was his own suggestion, and it made the most sense, he couldn't help being anxious to go. Work on the house was proceeding with lightning speed, and he and Erik needed to present Hegmar with their "hot water system" before it got too far along. Other concerns niggled at him too. He hadn't felt half as anxious preparing to go up against the Soul-Devourer as he did now, contemplating their wedding.

Diane smiled at him, sensing some of what was bothering him. She was anxious too, could hardly wait to see this marvelous hot water device; but it made no sense for them to arrive late at night, and plenty of sense to make sure she'd brought along everything she could think of that might help their project. After all, as the shortest possible distance between Daywatch and this Bathing Maiden Andrion was taking her to was a 24-hour round trip, it paid to double-check.

"I'm well along in my preparations," Diane assured Andrion. "I wish I had more dypalfar ingots, though. It's hard to get supplies out here."

"No worries there," he replied. "We keep a well-stocked crafting shop in the Maiden's basement. There's usually a couple of dozen of every kind of ingot, and almost anything else you could want." Really? She thought. This Maiden sounded more and more like it was worth a visit. She'd chatted briefly with Nerissa during the later part of the morning and *she* seemed to think it was the best inn in Iscandia. Maybe on the whole continent of Agena, even.

After lunch, Diane went back to gathering her supplies and Andrion wandered into the living areas upstairs, where he found a small library. He was soon engrossed in a book on the dypalfar he hadn't seen before, and sat reading for hours. When he finally came up for air, he sensed that it must be getting close to time to leave. Reluctantly, he re-shelved the book and went downstairs looking for Diane.

As he walked toward the stairs, he encountered Nerissa and Malden coming out of Malden's chambers. She looked like the cat that had gotten the cream, and he looked... bemused. His usual stern and intense demeanor had been replaced with an expression of mildly surprised pleasure. Andrion felt a bit poleaxed himself. *What* was that woman up to? He supposed she might be feeling some urges, and she'd gotten that amulet from Berni; but why pick the cranky old Afran when there were all these friendly young men around? Well, far be it from him to judge the love lives of others...

Chapter 51: Plans Afoot

When Erik left Berni's side in Ormund's throne room he did not immediately exit the hall. Instead, after her attention had been engaged by the eorl, he walked over past the long dining table and into the alcove where Garimund had his magical laboratory set up. There were chemia and enchanting stations, with many ingredients and magical essence vials scattered in among the books on the long central table.

The two of them were close in age, despite Garimund's lofty position as court mage to the eorl; and despite their differing interests they had become friends over the years Erik had spent in the area – more so now that he was friends with Lifa, who had also known Garimund while she was living in Wyrmshalla.

"Greetings, O Mighty Wizard," Erik murmured in Garimund's ear as the young mage was bent over the enchanting table, deep in concentration. Erik's own mental associations with enchanting tables had, in recent months, been substantially altered by his activities with Berni. He thought with a touch of pity that Garimund would likely never get to experience anything like that. As far as he knew, the man was a virgin.

Garimund jumped half a foot, then smiled ruefully as he realized his enormous young friend was looming above him. "Erik, don't *do* that! I might have turned you into a toad!"

Erik smiled back at him. "That'd be one *big* toad," he remarked genially. "So, have you heard? We're getting married!"

"We?" the young wizard asked. He knew that Erik was romantically involved with The Fireblood, had been there when he and Andrion, that Galise mage, had flown off on dragonback with her a few months ago. But he'd gotten the impression that was sort of a casual thing.

"Me and Berni… and Andrion, of course!" Erik replied, intending to blow Garimund's mind and meeting with fair success. Garimund looked as though he thought he had misheard him.

"You and Andrion are *both* marrying The Fireblood?" Erik nodded, grinning. He was taking more satisfaction than he'd expected in ruffling the feathers of society with the revelation of their unconventional arrangement.

"Well…" Garimund gulped, not wishing to appear behind the times, "Congratulations. When's the joyful day?"

"The tenth of next month, in Sylvanian," his burly friend replied. "You'll be invited to the party out at the Maiden on the eleventh, so don't forget to mark the date." Garimund looked pleased at this news. Like most Waterdon residents who didn't get out much, he'd heard wild stories of night life at the Maiden and was itching to see for himself.

"There's something I'm hoping you can help me with, though," Erik continued. "Do you know the Blessing of Marmira enchantment?" Garimund considered. There wasn't that much call for this particular spell. It certainly wasn't all that useful; but it *was* the enchantment traditionally cast on wedding rings.

"I haven't learned it, but I have an old wedding ring in my possession. If you'll pay me for the ring, I can destroy it and learn the enchantment. I assume you've got some ring you want enchanted?"

"It's not finished yet," Erik told him. "But I'm getting close. I could bring it up here sometime in the next couple of weeks, and you could put the enchantment on then. How much do you want for the ring?" Garimund was still feeling a little taken aback. His friend Erik, a veritably godlike warrior who had (to hear some tell it) laid half the women in the Waterdon area, packing it in to be with one woman forever – and that woman shared with another man? It hardly bore thinking about, but apparently it was true. On the other hand, he had to admit that The Fireblood was one hell of a woman. She'd figured prominently in some of his one-handed orgasms.

The young wizard stammered, brought back from his fantasies, to say "Uh? Oh, ten guilders will be plenty." Erik pulled out a small coin purse and handed over the requested amount. These days, he had no shortage of money. And he was determined to spend it as needed.

"Thanks, Gar. I've got to run, get some more errands done before Berni's finished talking with the eorl. But I'll see you when I get the ring finished. Take care!" With that, he hastened down the steps and left the building.

Erik trotted down the several flights of stairs he'd trotted up, earlier. If he wasn't going to be doing much questing, he mused, perhaps he should just come here and run up and down the stairs for a few hours each day. A guy his size needed to stay in shape, or he'd be looking like a two-legged walrus in no time.

Erik reached the bottom of the stairs near the gates, and went in to talk with Wolaf. "Good to see you, friend," the equally hulking dark-haired Norseman said as he walked into the shop. Wolaf was one of the few people Erik had met who could look him levelly in the eye... and possibly, throw him across the room. Erik ascertained that Valkyrie had now sold the rest of the consigned weapons, and collected the remaining money due. That left them with enough gold to cover the full amount of Hegmar's final estimate, and thousands left over in case of cost overruns. Considering Andrion had yet to come up the plans for the hot water system, there likely would be some of those. But no worries!

As Erik was preparing to leave, Wolaf said "You know, Alessia and I were talking about the things you've been bringing us. She's really impressed with the quality, and she's wondering if you'd like to go into some kind of a partnership. You bring us all your output, we sell it, and you'd get your cut of the sales of your own goods, plus a percentage of the profits on everything else we sell. What do you think?"

Erik considered. That seemed like a better idea than opening up their own store out at the Maiden, or at the farm. People were used to seeking out Valkyrie when they needed arms or armor, and it was centrally located near the front gates of one of the province's foremost cities. But he didn't know whether Berni really wanted to go into business making and selling armor. At the least, he was fairly sure she hadn't time to embark on a new business venture for the next few weeks.

"Bernadette's our armorer," Erik told Wolaf. "I'll bring it up to her, and she might be interested. But at the moment, she's a little too busy to be doing much smithing. We're getting married, you know." Wolaf grinned at him.

"I hadn't heard!" he boomed. Before he could get any farther, Erik explained the unusual circumstances. They didn't seem to faze

Wolaf in the least, and he was delighted to learn that he and Alessia were invited to the big celebration at the Maiden on the day after the wedding. As a hard-working married couple, they seldom had a chance to party.

"See you soon, then," Erik said and left the shop, heading next door. He, Lifa, and Anja were playing Bjorn's card game when Bernadette returned from her conference with the eorl, bearing signed and sealed documents hidden in her pouch and an air of triumph. There were times when power and prestige were so *handy*. She and Erik had nowhere particularly important to go, all their errands in town now concluded (though Bernadette had no inkling of what Erik's had been, and he was equally ignorant of hers). So they settled in to enjoy some family time with the little fire-haired darling who had helped to bring them all closer together.

Lifa laid on some snacks as the afternoon wore on. Bernadette and Erik had skipped lunch, but they had plenty of bread and cheese and freshly fried potatoes to tide them over until the supper Lifa had promised them. Lifa had even come up with a new and surprising variation on the potato chips that had only recently swept to popularity: instead of cutting the potatoes into thin slices, she cut them into elongated chunks the diameter of a woman's pinky finger and as long as the potato.

After dropping them into the hot fat until they were bubbling and golden, Lifa fished them out with a slotted spoon and set them to drain on a rack above a platter. They could be eaten now, but if you waited until they cooled and then put them back into the kettle of boiling tallow for another few minutes they emerged golden brown and delightfully crispy. A sprinkling of salt completed the process.

They all enjoyed several servings of these as the afternoon wore on to evening, washed down by ale that was regrettably little cooler than room temperature. Bjorn had dug a sort of cellar beneath the cottage where root vegetables and other items could be kept far cooler than the outside air; but they'd all become a bit spoiled by Andrion's trick with the frost spell and the drinks cooler.

"These are sensational, Lifa!" Bernadette exclaimed as she grabbed a handful of the deliciously crispy potato fingers. "We've got to start serving these at the Maiden." "It takes a little longer than the chips," Lifa said. "But it's handy that you can pre-cook them and then let them cool and keep them around for hours until just before eating – then give them the second cooking so they get all hot and crisp." Indeed. The chips came out of the kettle crispy and stayed that way, all moisture having been driven from the potato slices by the hot oil. But there was no way you could keep them fresh, and if not eaten immediately they soon lost a lot of their savor.

As evening came on Bjorn appeared, perspiring a bit. He'd been perspiring all day, in fact – acting as a member of the construction crew as much as an overseer. He'd refined and expanded on the architectural drawings, and was gaining an education in all aspects of house-building daily. After years during which he'd learned little or nothing save what he could teach himself, this project had expanded his horizons until he felt like his understanding was growing at an exponential rate.

In his artist's mind he envisioned it as a blossom opening to the sun, drinking in knowledge and becoming larger and more beautiful with each passing day. Just as his heart was also expanding, welcoming in Lifi and Ani and the people he had come to think of as friends – even if Bernadette was technically his boss. In short, life was good – and looked to be getting still better in the near future. He was delighted to come home to his beloved and their daughter and find Erik and Bernadette there, too.

On the other hand, Bernadette's presence created the need to dissemble. She was not supposed to know about the farm, the house, or the surprise that Erik and Andrion were preparing for her. And Bjorn was not accustomed to deception. Bernadette approached him and threw her arms around him, for which he was also not prepared. She was so emotional, this young mistress of his. No more skilled at deception than he was himself, really – whatever she felt in her heart was there on her face for all to see, nor would she make apologies for it.

Bjorn's feelings toward Bernadette were a curious amalgam of admiration for her as an attractive young woman (though she couldn't, in his opinion, hold a candle to his Lifi), respect for her as both his warden and a person who had performed legendary feats, and the protective love a brother might feel for his wayward little sister. It was the middle attitude that came to the fore when she asked him casually, "So what's this big project that's keeping you out all day?"

Yet, he didn't even really have to lie. "I met a local builder who needed some temporary help on a construction project. He likes my ability with drawing, and I'm sort of learning the trade."

"That's wonderful, Bjorn! So good to learn new skills… Say, are you working on that farm out by the Maiden?" she guessed with alarming accuracy. Bjorn froze for a moment.

"Uh, that's right, I …" he began to stammer out, wracking his brain for a suitable lie; but Bernadette rode right over him blithely.

"Erik and I saw that this morning on the way into town!" she said enthusiastically. "He told me how Safar is hoping to grow more crops with a larger farm crew. It seems like a good idea." She patted his arm encouragingly, proud that he was taking the initiative to expand his abilities. That he was technically supposed to be hanging around Brightsgate Cottage at her beck and call, ready to carry out any orders she might have for him, was something they'd both ignored.

"Well, good… uh, good. Are you staying for supper?" Bjorn asked, hoping to change the subject.

"Yes we are," Bernadette replied with a sly smile. "And I have some news for you…" She told him of the forthcoming wedding and the plans surrounding it – including the information, which she hadn't yet told anyone, that Eorl Ormund had agreed to be there. Bjorn fairly glowed with happiness on hearing the news. There was still the issue of his responsibilities to Westmarch; but as long as he was in Bernadette's service, at least, she was the boss – and she, clearly, wished him and his bride-to-be nothing but happiness and prosperity.

Lifa served them all venison steaks in a red wine and mushroom sauce, with a boiled grain pilaf that was cooked in venison broth and seasoned with herbs, tiny chunks of carrots and shreds of cabbage mixed in. It was amazingly good, and Bernadette was once again astounded at the unexpected talents of those around her. After supper, Erik and Bjorn volunteered to do the washing-up and

Bernadette accompanied Lifa and Anja upstairs to tuck the girl into bed and read stories to her before she went to sleep.

This gave the men a chance to confer. With Berni hanging around the Maiden while Andrion was at Daywatch, Erik was not able to spend the bulk of his days at the project site. He spoke quietly to Bjorn, handing him a scrubbed plate to be rinsed and dried. "How's it going? I barely managed to convince Berni of that story about Safar when we walked past this morning."

Bjorn smiled wryly at him. "It would have been nice to have some warning!"

"Sorry," Erik replied. "She's been running around so much with that map of hers I haven't been keeping up with her plans. Then last night after supper Andrion asked her for the use of the map so he could take Nerissa back to Daywatch."

"Nerissa?" Bjorn asked, surprised.

"Yeah, she's back – and she's not a vampire now. She got cured. I get the feeling she's going to be breaking some hearts pretty soon… But anyhow, I don't think that was the real reason Andrion went to Daywatch. I think he's hoping he can pick up some clues to the dypalfar technology we need for the house's hot water system. But how much time have we got before Hegmar needs it in place?"

The washing, rinsing and drying went on. "Don't worry about that," Bjorn told him. "I've made sure that the design includes plenty of room for whatever system is going to heat the water coming in from the cistern, and we're leaving space below the tub for *that* system too. If you recall, we decided to excavate a full basement, and there'll be steps down to a good-sized entry door. We should be able to finish the entire addition right up to the roofs and then start doing the interior work, leaving the hot water systems for last."

Erik was seriously impressed at the air of expertise Bjorn had acquired in just a few days on the job. And a little envious, as well. He enjoyed acquiring new skills too, but he was falling behind in learning about house-building while working to distract Berni and keep her away from the project. He sighed, and set to work scrubbing the stewpot, up to mid-forearm in hot soapy water. As he worked at this, a thought came to him about *how* he was going to keep Berni distracted, and he immediately cheered up.

The men were just finishing up their chore as the women came quietly downstairs. Bernadette felt a sensation of bliss. She had just had a delicious meal that she had not had to cook, and then somebody else had cleaned up after it while she engaged in the onerous task of lulling an adorable five-year-old to sleep. Sometimes, it was hard to imagine life could get any better. And then she recalled that she and Erik were on their own tonight; and it did.

These thoughts on both their minds, Bernadette and Erik cut the convivial evening a little shorter than they might otherwise have done. Who knew, perhaps Lifa and Bjorn might be feeling a little celebratory at the news of their impending nuptials, and wishing for some privacy. They soon said their goodbyes, and set off on foot out the gates of Waterdon and down the road toward the Maiden.

Night had fallen some time past, but it was fairly warm for this time of year. Waterdon never seemed to get all that cold, considering it was little further south than the miserable environs of Coldstein. Bernadette had had a few glasses of wine with supper, but other factors were at work on her as well and her mood was soaring. After they'd left the stables behind and were alone together on the moonlit road, she whirled around and launched herself into Erik's arms. "Oh, Erik! I'm so happy!"

She planted a big kiss on him before letting herself drop to the ground again. He grinned at her, white teeth glistening faintly in the moonlight. If she was happy, so was he. And if moonlight is the natural element of lovers, the planet of Terris was made for such as them. What a sight, when all three moons were in the sky! As they continued on their way home, the question of the real estate search came up again. "We've been all around the city," Erik told her. "I'm beginning to think that the best thing might be to buy some land and build a house on it."

"Hmm, that's not a bad idea," Bernadette said.

She'd hoped to go straight from their wedding to a home of their own, one without a parade of strangers wandering through it. But aren't good things worth waiting for? If they started with land they could design their own home, make it everything they wanted. After all, they were rich. All of Bernadette's thinking on the subject had been geared toward the idea of compromising her hopes and dreams with the limited reality of what was available in the Waterdon area. Not that ideal homes were really available anywhere. She liked Eastview quite a lot, and would always have a warm place in her heart for Brightsgate Cottage; but neither of them was the house in which she wanted to raise her children.

The more she thought about it, the more appeal the land idea had. So what if they had to wait a few months to achieve their goal? Their lives at the Maiden were certainly comfortable enough, and what was wrong with continuing in that way a little longer while engaging in the fun project of finding their land, then designing and building the home they all wanted on it? Bernadette was sure Andrion and Erik would have their own ideas to add, and as it would be home to all of them it was only reasonable they should all get to contribute to its design.

All this time they'd been walking, and after completing this train of thought joy bubbled up in Bernadette once more. She was so in love – with Erik, with Andrion, with the Maiden and the friends she was making here in Iscandia, with the idea of a home and family that only weeks before she'd rejected as a death sentence for her freedom. Now, she realized, part of being free was freedom to choose the responsibilities you *wanted*, the ones that would reward you in ways that no carefree, knockabout life could ever do.

Yes! She wanted Andrion's babies, and Erik's, and a life filled with meaning. Everything was going to be all right, was going to be wonderful. But evidently, she'd better keep her amulet on for a while yet. Once again, Bernadette halted her progress to dance in the road ahead of Erik and leap into his arms. "You're a genius!" she declared, clinging to him like a limpet and kissing him deeply. Surprised and delighted, he was perfectly happy to accept genius status in exchange for his small suggestion – the more so because it so marvelously obfuscated the secret plan he and Andrion were hatching.

He gathered her into his powerful arms and kissed her thoroughly in return. His cock was achingly hard beneath his trousers, Berni's magical ability in full force. I love her so much! Erik realized with surprise. It wasn't just the sexual element, though that was certainly a component. Her kind heart, her sincerity, her

369

bravery, her wit and beauty – they all called to him and made him hers as no other woman had been able to do. She had him by the heart, and he was glad.

The two of them were ill-suited by size for walking the rest of the way to the Bathing Maiden necking like a couple of love-struck teenagers; but they gave it their best shot. Along the way there was giggling, fancy footwork, stumbling and occasional bouts of very heavy breathing. How fortunate no bandits or hungry smilodons were prowling the moonlit night!

By the time they finally made it back to the Maiden, Bernadette and Erik found themselves surprisingly warm for a night in the middle of winter. "I have an idea," she murmured in his ear, which brought him to instant alertness. When Berni got an idea, he'd learned, it was almost guaranteed to be something he was going to like. Instead of going inside the Maiden, they walked around the deck's north side to the back. The moons were setting, and already the rear deck and its two pools were dipping into shadow.

The larger pool set into the Bathing Maiden's deck was intended for swimming, in warm weather to cool off or as exercise for hardier souls at other times of the year. Its waters were approximately at the same temperature as those of the Brightwater, flowing along down at the bottom of the slope to the east. Those were fed in part from the snows atop the Hochstein, so now in the first week of the new year the larger pool had sat unused for some time.

The smaller pool, however… It was not hot, like the water in the bathing pool inside. But it was definitely warm, a lot warmer than the air temperature on this night in Sunreturn. To the slightly overheated pair returning from Waterdon, it felt perfectly wonderful. And there was absolutely no one around. Fenris patrolled the grounds during the daytime, but there wasn't much for him to see or guard against at night; so he was probably inside having supper or relaxing in the hot pool. Bernadette and Erik were alone.

Like two kids engaged in some delicious mischief they stripped off their clothing, dropping it at poolside, and slipped into the warm water. "Ooh!" Bernadette exclaimed, diving under and then popping back up blowing, like a breaching walrus. "This is wonderful!" Erik sank into the water, sliding all the way down to the bottom where he held his breath, looking up at her, before his buoyancy dragged him to the surface again. This pool was of a similar size to the one inside, and having it all to themselves meant they could really move around a little and play.

The situation had reminded Erik of an oft-cherished fantasy of his, and he was pursuing it. In a few moments he had pinned Berni against the bench that ran along the pool's east side, and his hands were running all over her naked body. She struggled a little, but not for long. Her breasts bobbed on the surface between them as he squeezed her close, hands massaging her buttocks as his stiff cock jutted, pressing against her abdomen. Erik's mouth engulfed hers, tongue down her throat, excitement roaring in his veins.

Being in the water took away most of their weight, making things possible that normally would not be. It was almost like flying. Bernadette flexed her body and wriggled out of Erik's grasp like a fish, darting away to the bottom of the pool and then surfacing, a wide grin on her face, at the far end. Water plastered her hair down into red snakes draping her shoulders and breasts. His eyes shining with delight and strong desire, Erik rumbled "I'll get you!" This put Bernadette in mind of the fun they'd had in that icy pool east of Forestville, back before the push to defeat Tarragin. She'd been tempted then to let Erik catch her and have his way with her, but time concerns had gotten in the way. Now, they had all the time in the world.

As before, Bernadette was too quick for him to catch in open water. But in the relatively narrow confines of the pool, Erik was able to corner her – smothering her with hot kisses and driving her insane. The urge to give in to him fought against the desire to prolong the fun of the chase – and she led him around and around until he was beginning to get a little winded. Finally, she took pity on him. From across the pool, she beckoned: "Sit down." Catching his breath, he smiled and did as he was bidden. His member still thrust up rigid in his lap, quivering with eagerness to sheath itself inside her.

Bernadette dived beneath the water and swam across to him, then holding her breath began working over his cock with hands and tongue. The water was sweet, and almost body temperature. Before long, of course, she had to come up to breathe. Huh, she thought. Should have taken a potion of water-breathing before we got started here. Ah well, another time... She surged up from beneath the surface, shooting up to throw her arms around Erik's neck, as he seized her buttocks and slipped her down on top of him, engulfing that eager erection. OH yes...

As Erik began fucking her at last, neither he nor she had to put out more than the tiniest bit of effort for maximum movement. It was like making love floating in air. Was this how dragons did it? Bernadette wondered. Actually so far as she knew there *were* no female dragons. Did they all just spontaneously arise, transformed from volcanic lava or something? Speaking of volcanic...

The prolonged, rising excitement of the chase culminating at last in their near-weightless joining had both of them gasping, moaning, and screaming as the sensation where cock met cunt burgeoned into an unstoppable wave of passion. The surface of the water was hurled violently about as Erik pounded into Bernadette with increasing fury, splashing their faces. They scarcely noticed. Before very long he pulled her all the way down onto him as his cock pulsed and spasmed, shooting inside her clutching depths.

Bernadette wrapped her arms tight around Erik's neck, kissing his wet cheek, then seeking his mouth to merge herself more fully with him. Wow! This was something she'd never tried before, and the effect had been soul-shaking. Now, though, she was wondering about the water. She didn't fully understand how the pool's cleaning system worked, but it seemed likely they might shortly be swimming in diluted jiz – as soon as they came apart.

Pulling away from the kiss, Bernadette murmured in Erik's ear. "Can you lift us out of the water before you slip out?"

Taking her meaning, he replied "I think so. Just let me get..." he grunted, grasping her buttocks and standing up, as she held tight to his neck and wrapped her legs around his hips, "a grip." Holding her tightly, mindful of how slippery she was, he walked carefully up the pool steps and to the deck above, stepping a few feet away from the water before releasing her.

Bernadette slipped to the deck's surface, Erik's cock popping free and hot semen running down her inner thighs to mix with the water clinging to them. "Hang on a second," Erik said, digging into a small chest atop the deck at poolside. There was a supply of the ubiquitous Maiden towels within, and he handed her one. Smiling up at him, she took it and began wiping down her limbs and crotch. Meanwhile, he took another to blot the slippery mix of fluids from his sagging member.

When both of them had cleaned up a bit they tossed the towels to the deck and stepped together to embrace again. "By the gods, Berni," Erik murmured softly as he held her close. "Do you know how long I've wanted to do that?" She smiled up at him, a wicked smile barely visible in the dim light.

"As long as *I* have?" she asked. They were loving the feel of skin on skin, but now they were wet from head to foot and the evening was wearing on, it began to occur to them that it *was* the middle of winter.

With an involuntary shiver, Bernadette said "I think it's time to put clothes back on." Erik hugged her a little tighter, then let her go. They both used more towels to dry off, then slipped back into the clothing they'd discarded so hastily on their arrival. "Well," she remarked, "might as well go inside and join the crowd." Hand in hand, they walked in through the back doors of the Maiden and headed for their usual table.

Chapter 52: The Secrets of the Dypalfar

Andrion and Diane materialized outside the Bathing Maiden as the first rays of dawn were spreading from behind the mountains to the east. They'd left Daywatch in early evening, and while the trip had seemed to take no more than a few seconds they were both feeling a bit tired. It had been more than 24 hours of actual time since they'd arisen from their cots in the fortress to the east of Lakedon.

Despite that tiredness, they were both eager to examine the dypalfar mechanism that kept the Maiden's bathing pools clean and at the proper temperature. Andrion had glanced at it once before, but had no idea what he was looking at. With Diane's expert help, he hoped it might be possible to find or build something similar for the hot pool he and Erik wanted to incorporate into the home they would share with Berni.

Figuring nobody but Drelos (and his kitchen help) would be up and about yet and seeing no need to disturb him, Andrion led Diane around the north side of the building to the hatch set into the rear deck, near the warm bathing pool. They went down the ladder and found themselves standing in the basement. At the far end, Andrion could see Erik curled up asleep – presumably with Berni. Oh crap, he hadn't considered that.

Gesturing toward the bed and putting a finger to his lips, Andrion made sure Diane knew that they must be absolutely quiet. He walked silently to the door leading to the Well of Truth's chamber and they went inside. Then he gently closed it again. Now, they could speak softly without being heard. He led her through the second set of doors, to the chamber where the Maiden's spirit guardian resided in a pool of blue light. The light flared slightly, but the Well recognized him as the beloved of The Fireblood and let him pass without comment.

On the left side of the chamber, Andrion pressed the wall in two areas and there was a faint "click." Then a section of the wall swung inward, leading to a short stone-lined corridor. Dypalfar lamps glowed on either side, providing cool illumination. "Fenris showed me this a couple of years ago," Andrion murmured softly. "I was curious as to how the pool stayed hot and clean, but after looking at the mechanism I wasn't any the wiser."

Ahead of them was a stone wall, the outer side of the hot pool. To the right another chamber opened up, and as they approached it they could hear a faint whirring, almost like the susurrus of a breeze blowing through a forest. Andrion beckoned, and there was the dypalfar device. "This is the quietest dypalfar machine I've ever seen," he told Diane. "When you're questing down in the ruins sometimes the noise of the machinery is so deafening you can't hear the leukalfar sneaking up on you until they're trying to stick you with a sword."

Diane rolled her eyes and nodded. She'd spent plenty of time in dypalfar ruins herself, and the hazards of those places – leukalfar, mandimants, and hostile automatons – were all too familiar. Two large and gleaming dypalfar metal pipes ran between the machine and the wall on the side where the hot pool was, with another four pipes running down from the machine into the stone floor. "Are there three pools?" Diane asked, her mind already ticking along like a dypalfar device itself.

Andrion nodded, adding "The one on the other side of the wall is inside the Maiden's common room, and it's kept hot. There's another about the same size set into the deck, which is kept at about body temperature, and a big one for swimming in, also in the deck, that's not heated at all." Diane, her eyes drinking in the overall design and its details, nodded distractedly.

Slinging the pack she carried to the floor with a sigh of relief, Diane crouched and began rummaging through it until she'd produced a roll of soft leather a little more than a foot in length and perhaps four inches in diameter. Laying it on the floor, she untied the cord that held it and rolled the leather out to reveal a set of small, gleaming tools the likes of which Andrion had never seen before. He crouched on his haunches to get a better look at them.

Diane glanced up smiling and said quietly, "Aren't they amazing? They're probably the most sensational dypalfar find I've ever come across. This is the actual tool kit the dypalfar mechanics used for working on their devices." Andrion just stared at them, awed. As beautiful as they were, he had no idea what you could use

them for. He was beginning to wish he'd paid less attention to
history and ancient lore in his studies, and more to practical matters
like building and crafting.

Diane walked around to the far side of the gently humming
machine, and working with a couple of the tools from the kit she had
soon somehow removed a panel from the side. "Aha, I see!" she said,
peering into the depths. Oh good, Andrion thought, because I sure as
hell don't. "You said the water level is maintained automatically?"
Diane asked.

"That's right," he said. "If the outside pools get a lot of
evaporation or a heavy rainfall, somehow the level always stays
about the same. And sometimes people will splash out some of the
water from the inside pool. But it always comes right back up."

"There's a well on the property?" she asked next. "Right off the
south side of the building, near the kitchen" Andrion confirmed.
Diane continued poking and prodding, reaching a small tool in to lift
something then dropping it back down again.

After a while she said, "All right, I think I can see how we can
duplicate this in small scale for Bernadette's hot bath in your new
home. It'll be much simpler than this, since the water supply for
keeping the level right can be gravity fed. And you'll only need one
unit, maintaining one temperature. Plus there should be a lot less
purification needed if it's just you and your immediate family using
the tub. But we're going to need to pick up some specialized items.
What do you say we get something to eat, and I can dig through the
books I brought and get an idea of where to find them."

Diane refitted the panel, then she and Andrion sneaked quietly
back out through the doors to the basement. They found, however,
that while they'd been investigating the machinery the occupants of
the bed had arisen and departed. The two conspirators went out
through the trap door to the deck and walked around to enter the
Maiden through the front doors, finding a few people beginning to
stir now. They spotted Bernadette and Erik breakfasting at their usual
table, and walked over to join them.

Bernadette's eyes lit at the sight of Andrion's face, and she
jumped up to throw her arms around him and give him a big kiss.
"You're back!" she crowed unnecessarily. He'd been gone for nearly

three days, and while she and Erik had found plenty to keep themselves busy – by day and by night – in his absence, they'd missed him. Motioning them to sit, Bernadette greeted Diane warmly. During their brief association she'd come to like the woman, even if her obsession with dypalfar technology tended to give her a distracted air at times.

"So," she said to Diane. "I see Andrion dragged you back here with him."

"Yes," Diane replied. "Nerissa's very eager to come up with something similar to the bathing pools you have here for Daywatch, what with the hot springs being so far from the fortress, and I had some ideas about how your heating and purification system might work but I needed to look at it for myself. I thought I might enjoy a little vacation from Daywatch, in any case. I've been up to my eyeballs in advanced crossbow designs since I got there."

"How long did the trip take, Andrion?" Bernadette asked next.

"Right around twelve hours," he replied. Bernadette sat idly munching a pastry and doing calculations in her head.

"I have to go pick up something in Sylvanian on the tenth," she told them. "And I'm pretty sure that's about an eleven-hour trip so I'll probably want to leave sometime on the ninth. Then I should be back late on the tenth. But it'd probably be best for you to wait until after I get back from that trip before you try to take Diane home. Will that give you enough time for your investigations, Diane?"

"I hope to study the system and figure out what's needed, then see about obtaining the parts. I think that'll take at least four or five days, so that ought to work out pretty well." With that she relocated to a nearby empty table and dropped some books she'd been carrying on its surface. "If you'll excuse me, I have a little research to do. Oh, and could I have some of that tea?" Amused, Bernadette handed her a cup as well as a plate with a couple of bread rolls on it. Sticky sweet buns might not be the best thing around ancient tomes of dypalfar lore.

After Diane had relocated, Andrion scooted in close to Berni and planted a kiss on her cheek. "Everything going all right?" he asked.

"Wonderfully!" she responded happily.

"Oh!" Erik spoke up in his bass rumble, "one thing that happened while you were gone was that Berni and I decided it might be better for us to give up on buying the perfect house in the Waterdon area and start looking for some land to build on instead. She's okay with continuing to live here for a few months after the wedding." Were the hint any heavier, it might have punched a hole in the floorboards and come to rest in the basement.

Andrion smiled at him, and said "That's a good idea, Erik. I'm fine with waiting, too." He gave Berni a squeeze.

Washing down her pastry with some tea and licking her sticky fingers, Bernadette continued catching Andrion up on the news. "I went up to Wyrmshalla a couple of days ago and got Ormund to agree to come to Bjorn and Lifa's wedding. He's even getting there under his own power so that's one less person I have to worry about transporting. And I told them the news – they were thrilled about it. Let's see…" Another couple of bites of food and another swallow of tea went down before the next bit of news came up.

"So yesterday, I had some free time and I spent most of the morning and early afternoon crafting. Erik even gave me a hand. He's actually getting pretty good, you know? We hauled everything we made down to Valkyrie in the afternoon and I talked with Alessia and Wolaf. Turns out they want to do a partnership with us! So I can just knock out a few pieces of enchanted arms and armor every week, and they'll take all my output and pay us as it's sold. Plus we'll get a percentage from everything else they sell too!"

Andrion smiled at this news. He had the feeling that their days as freebooting adventurers might be drawing to a close, and it was good to know that the family would have another source of income besides the Maiden. Between Berni's outstanding skills at the smithy and her growing facility with enchanting, she could probably work a couple of days a week and bring in all the gold anybody could need. For that matter, the farm should be a source of income for them too. Safar had certainly regarded it as a profitable business.

The three of them sat eating and talking desultorily for a while longer. At the nearby table, Diane sat up abruptly with a barely audible gasp. It got Andrion's attention, and she gave him a meaningful look. She'd found something! Pulling a scrap of paper out of a pocket, she marked her place in *Dypalfar Questions* (Andrion didn't see which volume it was), and said "Do you think I could have a look at your water system, now?"

"Sure," Andrion replied, giving Berni a kiss before standing up. "This way – there's a trapdoor down in the basement behind the bar."

He led Diane across the room and they climbed down the ladder. They went in the doors again, making a pretense that this was their first examination of the system. Actually, it was just a good excuse to confer in private. "I've discovered a reference to the type of dypalfar devices we need to assemble our water system," Diane told him. "And I think I know where we can find what we need. There's a dypalfar ruin that looks to be no more than about a day's travel from here, called Bzaltham. We should be able to walk there and back in about the time we have before Bernadette returns from her trip to Sylvanian."

Andrion mused. One more big adventure? Diane had seemed to acquit herself adequately during their storming of Castle Hordenhaal, and she was a wizard with weaponry – which suggested a martial bent. But were the two of them up to fighting off a horde of hostile leukalfar while hauling who knows how many pounds of dypalfar devices around with them? A third team member might be in order.

"I think it might be a good idea to get Erik to come with us," he told her. "He's one hell of a fighter, plus he can carry a whole lot."

"That would be fine," Diane said. She wouldn't mind spending a little more time in the company of that golden icon of manly perfection. What straight woman wouldn't? Even if he *was* pledged to another, it didn't hurt to *look*.

When they had been down in the basement long enough to simulate the initial inspection that had already occurred, the two returned upstairs. Berni had gone someplace leaving Erik alone at the table, giving them the perfect opportunity to fill him in on their scheme. He had some more news to impart, as well. "Yesterday while Berni was hammering out details with Alessia and Wolaf, I went over to Arngeld's place to see about getting him to build us a new 'Owner's Table' for the Maiden. You recall how we were talking about needing a bigger table here?" He gestured at the surface where they sat.

Andrion nodded. "Anyway," Erik went on, "You also remember the really big bed we were talking about?" Andrion's eyes lit, while Diane looked blank. "I discussed it with him, and he figures he can build it in pieces and then assemble it inside the bedroom. We won't have to worry about fitting it through doors. So I ordered it! It's going to be seven-and-a-half-feet long and ten feet wide. He's got his wife and a couple of their daughters working on the mattress and bedding, too. It's going to be the only thing of its kind in Iscandia!"

Andrion gave his friend a toothy grin and slapped him on the shoulder. "Genius, Erik! I can't wait to see it. And sleep in it with you and Berni."

Erik grinned back, then said "Was there something you and Diane wanted to talk about?" Oh, right! Andrion and Diane in concert filled Erik in on the status of their investigations into the mechanisms keeping the bathing pool hot and clean, and the need for an expedition to Bzaltham in search of components. "I heard that place was infested with bandits," Erik remarked. "At least the outer parts of it. They usually won't go in too far, because of the leukalfar and automatons. Do you want me to come along?"

Both Diane and Andrion grinned at him. "Exactly what I was about to suggest," Andrion said. Then, after a moment's thought, he added, "What's going on with the house?" It had only just occurred to him that Erik was supposed to be acting as their liaison with Hegmar while the work proceeded.

"It's doing fine," Erik assured him. "I had to take a few days off from going down there because of being here alone with Berni, but Bjorn has been handling things beautifully. He's turning into a builder before our eyes. According to him, they're well underway with the stone understory and foundations, and they've started on the cistern tower."

Catching a sudden look of concern in Andrion's eyes, Erik added "Don't worry. Bjorn says they're leaving you plenty of space for the kitchen hot water system and access through the foundation for whatever kind of system you're going to set up for the bathing pool." Relief suffused his friend's features. "I hope your confidence that I *will* be setting up hot water systems is justified. Until I hit on getting Diane to reverse-engineer the Maiden system, I was stumped."

"Did you say something about hot water for the kitchen?" Diane asked.

"Oh yes, we're hoping to have some of the water that's piped into the house run through a set of coils that will be heated, so you can open a valve in the kitchen and get hot water for washing dishes or clothes."

"You should have mentioned that," she chided. "It's no problem, we can do that with some of the same components that are used in the hot pool system. But I'll need to add a couple of items to my list." She pulled out a piece of parchment, already heavily annotated, and scrawled a few additional items at the bottom with a curious-looking implement.

"What's that you're writing with?" Andrion asked.

"It's another dypalfar invention," Diane said with apparent pride suitably clothed in modesty. "It's cunningly carved out of dypalfar metal with tolerances so exact that you can drop ink in here at the bottom – she gestured to a carved finial on the opposite end from the pen's nib – using a pipette, and carry it around upside-down in a pocket without it leaking. When you're ready to write with it, you just shake it up a little and then hold it with the nib down to write. Only a little ink at a time can flow out of the metal tip. If you leave it too long without writing or use the wrong kind of ink it can get clogged, but a little soak in a cup of hot water will get it working again."

This was fabulous! Carrying around feather quills and ink pots was such a nuisance he'd given up keeping a journal years ago. Andrion suddenly had the sense that his life was slipping away from him. All the fabulous adventures he had had, the things he had seen and learned and done, had gone unrecorded – at least by him. Bernadette was already complaining that their deeds of a few months ago were fading into garbled legend. He had to get one of these pens, or perhaps get a jeweler to make one, and start writing everything down for posterity. At the very least, the children he hoped he and Berni (and Erik) would have someday would want to read these tales.

Andrion jerked his mind back to the business at hand at this point, and said "It's agreed, then. Berni will just have to do without us for a few days, and Bjorn can handle things out at the house. It's about a full day's journey to Bzaltham and back, so if we're going to go there and find what we need and be back here by the 11th to take Diane back to Daywatch, we're going to need to leave as soon as possible." The two at the table with him nodded, but he was already considering additional problems.

"Diane and I woke up what seems like a few hours ago but was really early yesterday morning. I think we both need to get some sleep as soon as possible, so we can't just leave immediately. Do you think we could set out around mid-afternoon, maybe, and at least get some miles down the road before it gets too dark to travel? Then maybe you, Erik, could pop up the road and let Bjorn know what's going on while Diane and I take naps."

Erik looked at them both, and nodded. "And while you guys are asleep I'll gather up some supplies for the trip," he said. "Diane, what do you have in the way of weapons and armor?" She looked a bit surprised. Practical considerations were not always foremost in her thinking.

"Just what I've got on," she said, gesturing at the studded leather armor she was wearing. "And I've got a couple of our best crossbows plus plenty of the regular and hollow-tipped bolts." That armor wasn't bad, actually. And those crossbows packed a bigger wallop than even some of the most expensive regular bows.

"Sounds good enough," he said. "Why don't you go find a bed, upstairs?"

Andrion stood and said, "I'll show you the way," guiding her by the elbow to point Diane in the direction of the stairs to the sleeping loft. Sleeping in the middle of the day while the life of the Maiden went on around you could be a bit of a trick, but you could pull it off if you were tired enough. He and the Galise woman climbed the stairs, and he directed her down to the shadowy recesses of the eastern sleeping gallery where a spare bed was available. She thanked him, and shortly lay down fully clothed to rest. One advantage of leather armor, it was comfortable enough to sleep in.

Andrion continued on to the master bedroom, and found Bernadette in there pawing through the chest and throwing clothing onto the bed. Evidently she and her wardrobe were having a serious discussion. He came up behind her as she stood there, arms crossed, glaring at the garments spread across the bed, and wrapped his arms around her tightly while he pressed his lips to her neck. The unexpected sensation made her jump, but she leaned into it a moment later.

Bernadette and Erik had been having a high old time alone together in the Maiden, their lovemaking rattling the roof and going on late into the evening. They'd even done it on the smithing bench in between bouts of crafting, and given the chemia table a try. It wasn't as capacious as the enchanting table. Sex with Erik was solid-gold bliss, no denying it. But she had still missed Andrion. She was marrying them both for the simple reason that she could not bear to part with either of them. It was certainly fortunate that the two were fast friends.

Bernadette rotated in Andrion's arms, her wardrobe dilemmas put on hold, as she melted into him for a deep kiss. He thought it fair to explain to her, however, that he would soon be leaving. "Diane found a place where she thinks she can find the components she needs for a hot water system," he told her. "And it's too dangerous for her to go alone, so Erik and I are going with her." Bernadette was taken aback.

"Uh? Should I go too?" she asked. She wasn't used to being left out of quests, but she was really too busy to go on any expeditions right now.

Andrion drew her closer still, kissing her hair. "It's an easy walk," he told her confidently. "With Erik along, we'll just knock off the opposition, make away with the goods, and be back here in a couple of days. By the time you get back from your trip to Sylvanian, we'll all be back here. And then I can borrow the map again to run Diane home."

Bernadette's brows knit. She was not happy at the idea of her bridegrooms running off to fight leukalfar and who-knows-what-else without her. But she needed to trust her men. Time and again they'd proven their abilities, and she really had no reason to fear for their safety. Besides, it was a noble thing for them to volunteer to help the Daywatch Brigade, and they should be supported. She herself might be willing to spend more time with that organization, helping in their anti-vampire campaign, if hot baths were to be made available inside headquarters.

"When are you leaving?" Bernadette asked him, without a trace of argument. Gods, how he loved her! Give or take a few early morning conflicts, she was the perfect woman.

"In order to get there and back in plenty of time, I think we'll head out this afternoon. But I really need to take a nap first."

It was still early morning, and he and Diane should be able to get in several hours of sleep before leaving. "Oh," Bernadette said, beginning to pluck the clothes from the bed and toss them back into the chest. "Not without a little nooky first, I think." She seized him by the shirt front and dragged him to her, practically climbing him as she writhed against him. His cock immediately stood straight up.

Well, maybe he wasn't all *that* tired after all. It had been a few hours, or maybe a few days, since Andrion had last had Berni in his arms. And he knew he couldn't go off and leave her for half a week without taking this opportunity to make love with her again. In the brief moments during which these thoughts had crossed his mind, she had peeled out of the stretchy dress she was wearing and was already standing naked before him. Now she began working on his armor. In another few moments he too was naked, the armor tossed negligently to the floor.

Bernadette gazed up at him. Andrion, her first true love, the sometimes-exasperating man who had become as essential to her as breathing. So beautiful, so desirable, so strong and intelligent, such a *good* man. Her desire for him was mounting as they stood there, nearly touching, then fell together in a passionate embrace. In moments they had dropped onto the bed and he entered her, no slow buildup this time. For once, his aspect as a careful, thoughtful lover was cast aside and there was nothing between them but naked desire and deep, deep love.

They plunged together into a spiraling wave of pleasure, carrying them upward until it seemed as though they must burst through the Maiden's wooden roof and up into the sky, exploding in a fountain of sparks like a pyromancer's display. In mere minutes Bernadette had extracted every drop of seed from Andrion and left him gasping for breath, wrapped tight by her arms and legs, his mind a blaze of white fire.

When his breathing had slowed to the point where speech was possible, Andrion gasped "By the gods, Berni!" She grinned into his chest, still gripping him tightly with arms, legs, and cunt. In another few minutes he slipped from her grasp, though, and rolled onto his back. Bernadette nuzzled into his shoulder and lay there resting against him. She'd gotten up early this morning, a couple of hours ago, after having made love with Erik for an hour or more the night before. But she wanted more skin time with Andrion, before he and Erik vanished on their quest. So she closed her eyes and let herself drift off to sleep in his arms.

Chapter 53: To Bzaltham

Bernadette wasn't good at sleeping while the sun shone. Down in the depths of an aptrgangr-infested barrow, she would sleep when she was tired and wake when her internal clock told her it was time to do so. Here in the Maiden, though there were no windows on the upper story, her internal clock kept telling her time was a'wasting. It didn't matter that she had no particularly pressing items on her schedule. So, after coming back to consciousness two or three times she abandoned the effort and snuggled in a little closer to Andrion, kissing his neck.

"It might be time to get up, love," she murmured in his ear. He stirred, struggling for consciousness. As disrupted as his own internal clock had become from a fast-travelling round trip to Daywatch, he'd have happily slept another several hours. But he needed to get moving! So, with a supreme effort, he shook off the cobwebs and dragged his mind kicking and screaming back to full awareness of his surroundings. Oh, they included a naked Berni. How delightful. He turned on his side and wrapped his arms around her, pulling her tight for a kiss. Mmm.

Bernadette kissed him back, with enthusiasm but no agenda. It seemed to her that if he and the rest of his team were planning to leave on a walking tour of the lands to the east and north, they might want to get moving. Andrion appeared to be ramping up for another round of lovemaking, but she reluctantly forestalled him. "Don't you want to leave for this dypalfar ruin of yours?" she asked. He squeezed her tight and sighed.

"Yes," he said. In another moment he added "Hold my place for me, okay?" She smiled.

Andrion rolled out of the bed and began gathering up his gear. Bernadette got up and helped him into his armor. In a minute or two, he was shouldering his pack and she was back in the dress she'd cast aside earlier. The whole wardrobe project could wait. Seemingly, she was about to be completely on her own for a few days and should have all the time she wanted to catch up on projects.

They walked through the eastern gallery and found Diane sitting up and putting on her own gear. Good. Telling her they'd see her downstairs shortly, Andrion and Bernadette continued to the stairs and went down into the common room. Erik was sitting there at their usual table, fully armored and looking the tiniest bit impatient. "Are we all set?" Andrion asked him, and he nodded with a smile. Outside the context of battle, it was hard to catch Erik Johannessohn without a ready smile. "Diane's on her way down," Andrion added. "Does anybody have the time?"

"According to Lev, it's almost 2:30," Erik said.

At this juncture Diane hurried down the stairs and joined them, looking slightly flustered. "Is there anything to eat?" she asked. Andrion hadn't considered that in his concern to get moving, but he realized it had been several genuine, real-time hours since they last ate and his stomach had a thing or two to say on the subject.

"I'm on it," Erik replied, pulling a couple of bundles out of his pack. He handed one to each of his traveling companions.

Peeling away the wrappers, which appeared to be a sort of paper impregnated with beeswax, Andrion found a familiar-looking bread roll. But it had been cut down the middle, and slices of cooked beef and cheese laid between the halves. There was some kind of a savory sauce, as well, though Andrion couldn't put a finger on what it was. Sinking his teeth into an enormous bite, he chewed and declared "This is great, Erik! Where'd you get this?"

"It's an invention of Lev's," Erik said. "He's always got travelers wanting food for the road. Look," he added, pulling out an additional waxed paper packet for each of them, "potato chips."

Thus able to walk and eat, the three companions made their way toward the Maiden's front doors. In the road outside, Bernadette hugged and kissed her men and squeezed Diane's hands, wishing them luck in their quest. Then she stood and watched them stride down the road, two of them still munching. After no more than a hundred feet, they cut east off the road and headed across country. Her heart was in her throat as she watched them go. She was left behind. Was this what it would be like when she was heavy with child, or nursing little ones?

Andrion took the lead as the three of them set off across the slightly rolling plain, aiming for the mountains piled up to their left – across the valley of the Brightwater from Throat of the World. They had some decent maps with them, but unfortunately these were of the non-magical sort. Still, they could get some idea of where they were and where they wanted to go. He spotted a likely looking trail leading up the slope and into what appeared to be a snowy mountain pass heading north.

They soon found themselves looking at snow-covered peaks dotted with enormous pines, but between the crags the terrain remained gentle enough for passage. Andrion led his companions up over a snow-covered saddle, and on the far side they could see the land sloping down again. A little further along they found themselves gazing down a steep, rocky, slope at what was clearly a dypalfar tower.

"I think that's it," Diane said, checking the paperwork about her person. Andrion couldn't believe it. He'd expected to be traveling on into the night, but from the angle of the sun it was still not much later than five in the afternoon.

"Are you sure?" he asked her. Iscandia was riddled with dypalfar ruins, after all. Perhaps they'd stumbled over one that wasn't marked on their maps.

"I'll be able to tell for sure after we get down there," she said, beckoning toward a series of walkways and staircases flanking the tower.

The three of them picked their way down the steep slope, hopping from boulder to boulder until they'd landed on one of the snow-covered walkways. After that, Diane pulled out the book she'd been studying earlier and scanned it. "I'm almost certain this it is," she said firmly. "Let's find the entrance." The place seemed to be deserted, and in a short while they came to the entrance to a dypalfar lift. It was locked from the inside, though. They began picking their way along the rooftops, looking for a way down.

Below them and to the right, Andrion could see a skin tent. As he and his companions hopped down onto the plaza it was pitched on, a bandit sentry looked around puzzled. Clearly, he'd been on guard duty without any intruders for far too long. Before he could muster a response to the sudden appearance of enemies, Diane had sunk a steel bolt into his breastbone and he fell limply to the stairs below.

They were now on the alert for additional sentries, but encountered only one more bandit as they approached the large, central doors leading into the ruin. He didn't even get a shot off before they'd sent him to oblivion. Inside, the doors gave upon a broad, low-vaulted stone hall with heavy, carven stone pillars on either side. A large, circular dypalfar metal medallion in the courtyard at the bottom of the ramp suggested a trap of some sort, which they easily avoided.

Instead of walking through the central doors, Andrion led them down a corridor to the left. There they found a sleeping area, and a heavily armored uruk taking a nap on a fur sleeping pad. Again, Diane was quick with her crossbow. Andrion was beginning to realize that perhaps he needn't have worried about the dypalfar expert's ability to take care of herself.

Turning a corner, the three stalked silently onward. A spitted shri occupied one corner, and ahead of them their path ran through gleaming dypalfar metal gates and down another stone ramp. Near the bottom of it, they suddenly found themselves attacked on three sides by more members of the bandit gang. Neither Erik nor Andrion had much respect for bandits. Overall they tended to be dimwitted, deficient in battle skills, and poorly equipped. These were no exception, and it was scarcely moments before the three were no longer a threat.

"This is about what I expected," Erik said quietly. "I'd heard there was a band here."

"Not a very competent one," Andrion remarked. The trio crept on around a couple more corners, and found a central chamber that looked like it was probably the bandits' main campsite. A man garbed like a leader was sitting in a chair facing the fire while a subordinate talked to him from across the hearth and another stood to one side. Before Andrion could even start hurling bolts of destruction, Diane drew a bead with her deadly crossbow and took the leader down with a single shot. Then as Erik and Andrion charged in, she picked off the guy on the far side of the fire.

Looks like I'm just here in an advisory capacity, Andrion thought. It occurred to him that there might have been a time or two, while he and Erik were accompanying Berni, when she'd had the same thought. No wonder she'd been so fierce before they set off for Castle Hordenhaal! Andrion searched the bodies, checking for anything useful like maps or keys, and pocketed some gold. The bandits certainly weren't going to be needing it.

As yet they'd found little in the way of the dypalfar artifacts they were seeking. Andrion cast a glance to the left and saw slatted dypalfar metal gates ahead on the floor they were standing on, and a second set on a floor above. Enormous dypalfar metal pipes, more than the thickness of a man, ran across the ceiling. "I think we need to go in there," Diane gestured, "but it's probably not necessary to open those gates ahead of us." Andrion realized that the locked gates before them gave on a chamber that was easily accessible from another set of gates, already open, to the left.

They found a staircase leading up to the second floor, and Diane was riveted by the sight of a pair of weapons emplacements. These, all of dypalfar metal, looked like a pair of gigantic quadruple crossbows positioned on either side of the sort of lever one often saw operating dypalfar lifts. The weapons were pointed down toward the floor below, and Diane ran to examine them. Then she pulled the lever, and watched enormous dypalfar bolts shoot out, eight at a time, to rake the unpopulated area they had recently left behind.

"It's a good thing these weren't manned against us," she remarked half-aloud. A cache of the bolts was lying against the wall behind them, and she tucked one into her pack. Weapons like these would be hugely useful for defending a castle, such as Daywatch. A little further along, as if the guard had officially been handed over from the bandits, the three began to encounter dypalfar automatons. Most in this area seemed to be the larger size bugs, about as big as a really large chillmarrow spider and similar in shape.

Diane's improved crossbow with its superior bolts proved to be deadly to the dypalfar mechs, Andrion noted. Berni had had a lot trouble taking them down with her arrows, and her spells had been almost completely ineffective against them; but the crossbow was sending each one flying in a shower of sparks. He made a note to tell Berni about this. She had one of these crossbows herself, and could perhaps enchant one for extra damage. Much better than a regular bow, it seemed, where dypalfar automatons were concerned.

Diane bent to examine the scattered remains, and stood triumphantly with an openwork metal globe in her hands. A red gem of some sort glowed in the center, and though the automaton that had housed it had ceased functioning, an inner cage was still spinning beneath the outer housing. "A full size power cell!" she told her companions triumphantly. "I hadn't expected to find one in the remains of a spider. You usually have to destroy a robon to obtain one. We could use three more of these, or as many as we can carry if there are more to be had. This is what makes the bigger machines move."

They continued through the maze of corridors and came to a stone ramp flanked by staircases, with a groove running the length of it down the center. As soon as they approached a shaft erupted from the groove and began spinning, unfurling two long blades that sliced through the air at about waist height as the device twirled its way from one end of the groove to the other and back again.

Andrion had seen these in dypalfar ruins before, as had Diane, and they waited their chance, climbing the stairs and pressing themselves against the walls while the whirling blades of death went past, then charging fast up to the top before they returned. Erik, with his bulk, was not so fortunate. A blade clipped him, knocking him momentarily to his knees, and then got him again as he stood up. Cursing, he darted out of the way of it and then dashed to the top of the steps, limping.

He stood there at the top with them, panting and looking annoyed. "You're supposed to *duck,* Erik," Andrion explained.

"Shut up and hand me a healing potion," his friend growled. He'd scarcely had time to down the potion, swiftly recovering from his slight injuries, when the three were attacked by a smallish dypalfar robon. Snarling, Erik swung his axe high and nearly took its head off. The thin sheet metal of the automaton's carapace was no match for the solid, heavy steel of that enormous weapon.

They took a moment to recover while Diane searched the deactivated mech. It was nearly intact save for the smashed head, and she used some of the tools in her kit to dismantle it. This yielded another power cell and a large vial of magical essence, plus some useful cogs and levers. As she collected the pieces, she was already envisioning how they would fit together. They might need to fabricate some parts, but she was becoming increasingly confident that they'd succeed in making the hot water system Andrion wanted. Hell, they might set up a factory and put them into production. Every wealthy family in Iscandia would want one of these units in their home.

Ahead, the three had to negotiate another trap in which a gas jet stood on one side of a narrow passage while a piston on the opposite side would push the unwary traveler into the flames. This time, they all made it safely past. Erik was learning fast. They passed through several more rooms, finding additional materials for the project: cogs, gears, levers, and dypalfar lubricating oil. The last had been pressed into use by modern men as a chemial ingredient, mostly used for poisons; but it was a key component in the ability of dypalfar machinery to keep working millennia after its creators had vanished. It was probably the best lubricant the world had ever seen.

Eventually they reached a dead end with only one exit: a lift that stood before them, beckoning them who-knows-where. Andrion looked around at his companions, particularly Diane, seeking a consensus. She nodded at him, so he pulled the lever. They shortly found themselves confronting a dimly-lit corridor with double doors at the end of it, which opened onto another ramp like the one they'd climbed earlier. A rock fall had left it partially ruinous though, and the blade trap stood at a drunken angle above the groove, no longer a threat to anyone. They vaulted an enormous pipe lying in their path and climbed the ramp.

Now, for the first time since they'd entered this ruin, they began to encounter leukalfar. Their yurts, fashioned from the chitin of mandimant larvae, were scattered here and there throughout the cavernous rooms they traversed. The "changelings" themselves, apparently so lacking in social cooperation that they were most often to be found alone, posed little challenge to the three well-armed and well-organized humans. Andrion, Diane, and Erik picked them off as they found them, searching the corpses in case they might have picked up anything useful down here.

They followed the corridors through various bends, looking around at the gigantic dypalfar structures that surrounded them. Only

Diane had any idea what these constructions had been used for, and she was less focused on them than on finding the precise components she needed for the project at hand. At one point, though, she spotted a section of pipe that looked to be the right diameter for their needs.

She'd already concluded that they were going to have to fabricate pipe for their purposes. From the descriptions Andrion and Erik had provided of the house's water system, they would already be having a considerable length of copper pipe made to conduct water from the cistern atop its tower to the house, as well as terra cotta or possibly cast iron drain pipe leading to the sewer system. But for the hot pool, Diane wanted pipe crafted from dypalfar metal, in the same diameters as she was looking at here. She needed a small section to take with them, so the fabricator would have something to copy.

"Andrion," she asked, "how hot is that battle magic of yours?"

"Pretty hot," he responded, puzzled. "If I cast lightning and fire together I can melt right through armor."

Diane smiled broadly at him. "Perfect," she said. "Could you see if you can cut about a one-foot section of this pipe, please?" She'd put an ear to it and heard no sound of anything passing through, nor had they seen any further gas jets after the one they'd passed all that time ago. Still, she encouraged Andrion to stand well back when applying the magic to the pipe, while she and Erik stood still further off.

Andrion had never done anything like this before. He'd become a little more adept at focusing his battle magic in the process of refining his drink-cooling abilities, but this was the first time he'd ever tried to make a narrow cut in something instead of just blowing it to smithereens. As he attempted it, though, he realized that the spell was obedient to him. Much as he could focus it on a particular target, picking a bandit off of a distant lookout post, he could direct the width of the blast; and by narrowing it, caused the intensity to rise exponentially.

After an initial false start that left the section of pipe with a large chunk missing (and confirmed, to everyone's relief, that nothing was flowing through it), Andrion concentrated his mind and began producing a bolt of mixed fire and lightning like a glowing bar no more than half an inch across, that cut through the dypalfar metal like a knife through… not butter. More like venison from a particularly tough old stag. But still… The brilliant light generated by this beam of destructive energy caused all of them to squint and turn their heads aside, even at this distance.

In his years of practicing battle magic Andrion's supply of magical energy had increased enormously. The armor and other items Berni had enchanted for him increased it even more, and sped the rate at which it replenished itself. He was pleased and somewhat astonished to find that, despite the high intensity of the flows he was producing, he was able to cut all the way through the diameter of the pipe without running out. The cut was a little ragged, due to his having been unable to really see what he was doing.

Diane and Erik were alternately turning away in pain at the brilliant light and peeking back to watch in awed fascination. When the cut went all the way through, they suddenly remembered to breathe and then grinned at Andrion. "Holy crap, that was amazing!" Erik boomed.

Andrion grinned back. "It was, kind of, wasn't it?" Though use of his magical energy did not take away from his stamina, he still felt like he needed to take a short break. In another minute he was ready to begin again, cutting the pipe a foot or so from the site of the first cut.

This time the process went faster, as Andrion's confidence grew. Molten dypalfar metal dripped in a glowing stream like candle wax to the stone floor, and in a minute or less the entire section of pipe separated and fell with a clang. Diane reached for it, but Andrion grabbed her wrist. "It's hot!" he reminded her. "Wait a second." He switched to a more broadly focused frost spell and in moments the pipe section was slightly below ambient temperature. Diane tucked it into her pack with a smile and a word of thanks.

A little further along the trio came to an area where four short pillars, each surmounted by a glowing blue pushbutton, offered a minor challenge to passersby. Andrion immediately wished Berni were here. Her facility with this sort of puzzle was nothing short of magical. He tried to guess which button to press and ended up getting toasted by flames, which he swiftly evaded by jumping out of the way.

Several more attempts eventually led to a gate across the corridor to their left being opened; whereupon Diane insisted on going back to the pillars and spending several minutes dismantling two of them with her tool kit so she could steal the button modules. As the gate was now open, Andrion supposed, the loss of the buttons wouldn't hurt anything.

After Diane had all she wanted from the area, they proceeded down the now-opened corridor. Ahead, another set of gates barred passage to an area screened off by a slatted fence of dypalfar metal. They proved to be unlocked, however. As they came in, a pair of the large mech bugs converged on them. Diane shattered one with a bolt from her crossbow, while Andrion halted the other with a bolt of lightning before Erik knocked it skittering into the wall in pieces with a blow from his axe.

Diane rifled the remains and came up with another power cell. Only one more to go, plus whatever else she needed. Andrion was beginning to feel pretty tired, and he wondered how long they'd been down here. When you were questing in the sunless depths of dungeons or dypalfar ruins, on constant alert against attack, it was easy to lose all track of time until you were ready to drop.

In a pen off to the left side of the entryway a couple of enormous mandimant larvae were chittering agitatedly. There were no leukalfar in sight, however. Diane seemed to find the creatures offensive, and leaned in through a low opening to shoot at them with her crossbow until both had ceased moving. After that Andrion picked the lock on the gate to the pen and they went in to see if there was anything there worth taking. They found no dypalfar artifacts, but he carried off some mandimant chitin for Berni.

On the far side of the room a tall shimmering plate of dypalfar metal stood up against the wall, with a pool of water in front of it. Gears were making tortured thumping noises, jerking back and forth but not spinning. Diane approached a short pillar standing at the top of a set of steps leading to the pool, and pressed the button set in its top. But nothing happened.

Looking around, she assessed the state of the machinery in the room. Then she spotted a long metal strut caught in a set of gears near at hand. Reaching up, she grasped the strut and freed it. Now these gears were spinning; but the thumping continued. Andrion and Erik stood watching as she made a circuit of the room, closely examining each set of gears. As she did so, they realized there were leukalfar yurts in the room's far corners. They had to dispatch several of the creatures as Diane continued searching for faults in the room's mechanisms.

Letting the men handle the hostiles, Diane focused her attention on the gears. Around the room, she found gears that had been intentionally jammed with pieces of scrap metal. She had now freed three sets of gears, and had examined every set in the room but found no more obstructions. Yet the thumping continued. Wait…

Peering down through the crystalline waters of the pool, Diane realized there were more gears down there, at the bottom of one of the structures that flanked the short staircase. "Erik?" she asked. Why get all wet when there was a nice young warrior near to hand with nothing to occupy him?

"Yeah?" he responded in his rumbling bass. "Think you could swim down there and see if anything is stuck in those gears?" she gestured.

He grinned at her. "Sure, no problem." He peeled off his armor, causing Diane to bite her lip as his magnificent physique and finely-formed, hefty manhood were fully revealed. Definitely, she thought, it might be time to start looking for some male companionship. Erik dove into the pool with scarcely a splash despite his size, and in another moment surfaced with a broad smile, waving a hunk of dypalfar scrap metal. "Got it!" The thumping had ceased, and now all the gears seemed to be turning smoothly.

Erik boosted himself back out of the pool in a shower of droplets and rummaged in his pack for a towel. After drying himself off he got back into his armor. Diane stood, trying not to stare at him, until he was dressed again. Rrrowl. Then she tried the button again, and the sheet of dypalfar metal on the far wall, hinged at the bottom, dropped toward them to form a bridge across the pool.

This also revealed a passageway behind it, which was blocked by an enormous dypalfar robon. Oh, crap! The three sprang into action. Diane's crossbow bolts, so effective against the smaller mech spiders, were considerably less so against this much larger contraption with its correspondingly thicker carapace. She shot twice, then staggered back as Erik charged in, axe swinging, and Andrion shot a focused beam of combined fire and lightning to cut a swath inches deep across the thing's head.

With a groan of tortured metal, the robon collapsed to the walkway. Leery of heat, Diane approached it and began breaking into its interior compartments with her tool set. She was pleased to find another power cell, the last one she needed. The three skirted the wreckage and continued down a corridor behind it, where a wall-mounted lever caused a set of bars to drop into the floor.

Beyond it was a medium-sized room with massive, carved stone pillars holding up the ceiling on either side of a smallish, waist-high roofed cage of dypalfar metal bars. A frisson of recognition passed though Andrion as they approached it, and he grinned. When packing for this trip, he had dug the dypalfar attunement sphere they'd found when down in Alzhenten out of the chest in the master bedroom where Berni had tossed it. He'd just had a feeling it might come in handy.

The room was uninhabited, by either mechs or leukalfar, and he decided this might be a good time to take a break. "Is anybody besides me tired and hungry?" he asked, and got murmurs of agreement from Diane and Erik. They tossed some bed rolls down on the stone floor and sat on them, and Erik pulled more of the wrapped meat and cheese rolls from his pack. Hours of travel had not improved them, but washed down with bottles of water they were edible; and hunger supplied savor enough.

After their meal, Andrion and Diane lay down while Erik stood the first watch. In a couple of hours Diane arose and let Erik catch some sleep; then Andrion took a watch. All remained quiet. When everyone had had enough rest they breakfasted on dried beef and apples, washed down with more water, before continuing on their way.

Andrion pulled the dypalfar sphere from his pack and approached the metal cage. "You brought one of those!" Diane said in pleased astonishment. "It didn't even occur to me."

"You've got one, too?" Andrion asked, as he nestled the device in the socket designed to hold it and keyed it to activate. "I found one years ago, and it's come in handy more than once," she replied. "But I was focused on other things for this trip. I should have known I'd forget something."

"No worries," Andrion replied as the stone surrounding the cage sank down into the floor to form a spiral staircase. He retrieved the sphere and stuck it back in his pack.

At the bottom, double doors gave on another stone corridor. Diane halted their progress at that juncture and spent a long time dismantling components of the mechanism that had opened the stairway. Andrion and Erik sat on the steps and watched her, talking idly as they waited for her to finish.

Chapter 54: Into the Depths

They started moving again, through the doors, and Andrion had an immediate sense of déjà vu. The space was dark, and huge – but it looked a lot like that section of tunnel near the end of the Passage of Darkness, as he, Berni, and Nerissa had been traveling to the Eparchy. Diane turned to him, looking thrilled, and said "This is Undernight, isn't it?"

Andrion looked at her questioningly. "Undernight? Berni and I saw something similar to this when we were looking for the Eparchy, but it was much smaller."

"It was an ancient underground stronghold of the dypalfar," she explained. "Supposedly this huge cavern system linked several of the cities that are scattered around Iscandia on the surface above. This must be what was meant in the book, but I didn't understand that it would lead us here. Amazing!"

"So what is it we're looking for here?" Andrion asked.

"I just need a few special light globes and we should be able to go home," Diane replied.

"Any idea where we might find those?" he asked, gesturing around at the sprawling underground complex dimly lit by glowing minerals and gigantic luminous mushrooms that grew like trees here and there.

"Most likely, they would be in an area where water is being handled. Like a pumphouse, perhaps. So if we look for water going into a building, that will probably be the spot."

"All right then," he replied, "lead the way." Diane made a beeline for a river that ran through the area. They walked along the shore, passing a building with an enormous golden globe atop it. Some of the buildings here were massive, but it was hard to make out details in the dim, strangely-colored light.

Diane walked along with her eyes glued to the opposite shore, relying on her two companions to alert her – or defend her – if any hostiles showed up. Shortly she spotted exactly what she was looking for – an inlet of the river that ran into the bowels of a massive building on the far shore. Stripping down with enemies lurking in the dark seemed like a bad idea, so they waded in fully armored. The water wasn't deep enough for swimming.

The men's glistening elven armor actually fared much better for the dip than Diane's leathers did. Her armor was water-resistant and supple, and could even be washed; but for the moment it clung clammily to her legs like the embrace of an undead lover. Shudder. Inside the tunnel, Diane saw just what she was looking for, and it drove thoughts of discomfort from her mind. A double row of green-glowing lights ran down the center of the tunnel, perhaps three to four feet above their heads.

If only I hadn't left my ladder in my other pack, Diane thought with dismay. Hmm, Erik was pretty darn tall and his arms were long. "Erik, can you reach those lights?" He stood on tiptoe and stretched upward, but his fingertips were inches short of brushing them.

"Nope. But I could lift *you* up to them," he replied with a grin.

"Good idea!" she said, pulling out her tool kit and gathering a couple of implements she thought she would need.

Erik crouched on the floor and Diane stepped over his broad back, draping her legs over his shoulders and leaning forward over his head as he gathered his legs under him and stepped, crouching at first, back into the water. There the tubular tunnel was taller and he could stand up. Diane now had to duck a little in order to keep from cracking her head on the ceiling, and her damp crotch was pressed up against the back of his neck while her thighs gripped the sides of his head. Erik found himself stiffening a little at this, though he had no real desire for Diane. It reminded him, though, of some times when Berni's thighs had gripped him – from the other direction.

For her part Diane was so excited by her dypalfar tech find and so absorbed in claiming these treasures, that she scarcely gave a thought to her intimate juxtaposition with Erik. Now maybe if she'd been facing the other way around… She soon found she was able to pry the bezel apart – removing a protective glass lens that served to concentrate the light and extracting an object shaped roughly like a chicken's egg that was twice the size, cool to the touch, and glowing green. Like the power cells, it seemed to tap energy from some other plane of existence. After holding one in her hand for a minute her skin began to smart, and her eyes were also burning from looking into it.

"Andrion, catch!" she said, carefully handing the light globe down to him. "Better wrap it in a towel," Diane warned him. "The rays are harmful up close." She tucked the bezel and its glass lens into her pack. Then she asked Erik to take a step forward, so she could get another. She thought that for a house system the size of the one Andrion had talked about they would only need two, but here were two dozen. She didn't think they could take them all, but she certainly intended to take as many as they could reasonably carry.

In the end it was Diane's neck rather than Erik's shoulders that gave out, and she stopped and asked to be let down after collecting eight of the globes. As near as she could tell, these were identical to the ones in the system at the Maiden – and their harmful effects at close range seemed to be a sign that they could be used for the same purpose.

After getting back onto the ground and rolling her head around to ease the crick that had formed while she'd worked scrunched against the ceiling, Diane smiled at Erik and stepped close to give him a slight embrace, reaching up to apply a peck to his cheek. "Thank you, mighty steed!" she said jauntily. Now that the work was done, she felt elated at their success. Erik grinned down at her and gave a slight bow. Andrion, who'd had nothing to do but catch and stash the globes as they came down, seemed anxious to leave.

Despite her feeling of triumph, Diane realized her eyes were burning and tearing and her hands felt as if they'd been held too close to the fire for too long a time. "Do you have another of those healing potions, Andrion?" she asked. He smiled and produced one of the more potent variety.

"Your eyes look like you've been drinking brandy for a few hours," he told her with some concern. She nodded and gulped the potion down, soon feeling its powers erase her hurts – including the residual aching in her neck and shoulders.

"Thanks," she said sincerely. "Do you suppose there are some lifts up to the surface around here? We're ready to go."

Andrion beamed at her. "I haven't noticed any," he said. "But it stands to reason there should be some. We should be looking for a fairly small, square building that reaches up to the ceiling."

The three waded back across the river, leaving the plundered pumphouse behind, and continued on down the banks of the stream for a while. Before long Andrion spotted what he was looking for, and beckoned his companions to follow him. He was feeling vastly relieved that they had been wandering around in this dark, spooky place for what seemed to be the better part of two hours and had not been attacked by anything whatsoever. Almost miraculous!

They opened the front door and stood on the platform, then pulled the lever. When the lift came to a stop they found themselves dazzled by late afternoon sunshine glinting off a snowy hilltop, seen through the golden bars of the cage surrounding the lift's upper entrance. A lever in a corner soon unlatched the gate, through which one could now return down the lift to Undernight in the future – should it suddenly begin to seem appealing as a vacation spot, say.

The hilltop didn't offer a lot of features, not even a path. But to the south, which Andrion identified with his inborn sense of direction (along with the fact that the sun seemed to be setting to their right as they faced it) they could see what was unmistakably the peak of the Hochstein, gleaming golden in the late sunlight. For all he knew, the entrance to Bzaltham where they'd come in might be a few miles beyond the slope ahead of them.

Best not to linger. It would be okay to camp for a night before they made their way back to the Maiden, but it would be preferable not to do so in six feet of snow. So, once again assuming the role of Mighty Leader, Andrion led his team off up the snowy slope to the south. The terrain, unfortunately, was not cooperative. The mountainous regions of Iscandia seldom were. You'd be moving right along on a path that was almost ready to graduate to trail status, and the next thing you knew you were standing at the top of a hundred-foot cliff.

Thus there were many detours, and meanwhile the sun sank steadily toward the western horizon. If Bzaltham were near they managed to miss it completely, instead coming out of the mountains near an underground bandit lair to the southwest of Coldstein. By now it was full dark, and their breakfast seemed to have been eons ago. Three sorry bandits were standing watch in an encampment outside the entrance to the cave, so they killed them (one apiece;

share and share alike) and then appropriated their campsite for the night.

There was even a haunch of goat roasting on a spit, and some potatoes that they baked in a cast iron pot thrust into the coals. After their last couple of meals of trail food, this was a feast; and Diane stoked the celebratory atmosphere by producing a bottle of red wine from her pack. She and Erik were so happy to be out of Undernight and near the road that led to the Maiden that they failed to take the opportunity to rag Andrion for his inept Native Guide act. It appeared that the walk that had taken them three or four hours coming might be a day and a half going back – but they had hot food in their bellies, a wealth of dypalfar artifacts in their packs, and a reasonable amount of shelter for the night.

After eating they rehashed their adventure, and Diane tried to explain how the components she had gathered were going to fit together to form the hot water systems for the house Andrion, Erik, and Bernadette would be living in as a married triple. Erik enjoyed making things with his hands, but technical explanations went past him. And Andrion's scholarly bent ran more to history and lore than mechanical engineering. So, she soon realized her audience was not following her and gave it up. They all curled up in their bedrolls, reasonably sure that the bandits would have no reason to reinforce their outside crew in the night.

They woke in the morning and had cold sliced goat and some hot tea to wash it down with, and more apples from their packs. A couple of hours' walk took them to the road beside the river that gave Coldstein its seaport status, and they crossed it near a lumber mill. Now they had a fairly direct road to take them almost all the way back to the Maiden. They would have to cross the river once again before reaching it, though.

They found themselves approaching a bandit lair near sunset. It was the same roadside tower Andrion and Bernadette had cleaned out months ago, and it now had new tenants. They decided to go ahead and deal with the bandits. Andrion and Erik were such deadly fighters that the average bandit gang had no hope against them – and with Diane's lethal crossbow added to that, the motley crew manning the fortress didn't stand a chance.

After kicking the bodies aside and looting the corpses, the three made themselves a tidy supper from the bandits' stores and drew lots for the available beds. Erik lucked into the double bed where Andrion and Berni had spent a hot night early in their relationship.

The next morning they breakfasted on stale bread toasted over an open fire and slathered with butter that was a bit past its peak. They washed it down with hot tea before getting onto the road, eager to return to the Maiden. Not far from home the trio encountered another group of bandits of a sort, a small troop of Reman soldiers who'd apparently taken to waylaying travelers on the road and demanding gold in exchange for passage.

Andrion, who had met the commander of the imperial garrison at Sylvanian, could imagine what that stern Reman officer would do with these scum if he knew of them; and he decided to take that task on himself since Vadrian wasn't here. With the able assistance of Erik and Diane the soldiers-turned-robbers were soon dispatched, and the trio found the bodies of several travelers nearby. The bastards had been murderers as well as thieves, and good riddance.

The Maiden beckoned to them across the water as mid-afternoon approached. But by mutual agreement they decided to add some minutes to their journey by taking the road down to the bridges and coming in by land. None of them wanted to arrive in soaking-wet armor. It was with a sigh of relief that Andrion at last led his footsore band to the Maiden's front doors and headed inside.

Chapter 55: Bernadette on Her Own

After seeing the party off on the road outside the Maiden, Bernadette walked back inside. As much as she was already missing Andrion and Erik, this rare opportunity for time to herself seemed like a treasure trove, and she felt unable to decide what to spend it on first. After some consideration, she returned to the master bedroom and resumed going through her wardrobe.

I need more *nice* clothes, she thought. As a person of some prominence in Iscandia, especially locally, she was beginning to sense that that the catch-as-catch-can casualness that had marked her garb for so many years was no longer in keeping with her public image.

She had some wonderful armor now, and Senalie in Sylvanian was making her a wedding dress that would be the talk of the province; but as she spent less and less time prowling dungeons or slaying dragons, she needed clothing that expressed both her individual tastes and her position as a person who was rich, famous, and influential. Let's not forget fabulously beautiful, she chided herself. Keeping a grip on the size of her head was just *one* of her problems.

It was a pity there was not a clothing shop closer to home. Perhaps she could design some everyday clothes for herself that did not exactly resemble the everyday clothing of every other wealthy woman in Waterdon. But did she have the time, and the skill, to sew them herself? Most commoners of course made their own clothing, and simple enough clothing it was. Perhaps she needed to pay a call at Wyrmshalla and discuss the matter with some of the ladies of the court. They must know someone in the area whose skill with a needle was beyond the ordinary.

That decision reached, Bernadette threw most of the clothes back in the trunk and tucked some others into her pack, to sell at Bernard's on her next trip to town. Which would be soon, she realized – she still needed to get Lifa and Bjorn's invitations to the wedding party on the eighteenth delivered, and there was less than two weeks to go before the event. Yesterday evening, after their return from Waterdon and the forging of the partnership with

Valkyrie, she'd pressed Erik into service with her penning copies of the party invitation.

Bernadette had seen books everywhere in Iscandia – often multiple, and identical, copies of the same title. Somewhere, these books were created. But nowhere had she learned how or where that happened. They might have hatched from eggs, for all the information she had. So, to produce the 16 party invitations she and Erik had had to pen the same text by hand, 16 times. She was pleased to learn that, as unlikely as it might seem, Erik proved to have a clear, attractive hand with a quill pen. What a treasure he was!

When the invitation copies had been written, the evening was wearing late and she'd stacked them up on the table in the master suite, having other amusements in mind. Had she known both Erik and Andrion would be slipping from her grasp the very next day, she might have skipped the invitations entirely. Ah, well. Now she brought a candle over from a nightstand to sit on the table as she folded each invitation, and sealed it with a blob of wax into which she pressed her Fireblood signet.

Bernadette didn't have a lot of occasions to produce official Fireblood correspondence, but it had occurred to her some months back that it might be useful to be able to do so; so she had designed a signet for herself and had it crafted by the family of jewelers who did business near the front gates of Alfenstein during one of her early visits there. Preferring to wear as few rings as possible, she had the seal mounted on a handle and kept it in a drawer when not in use.

Now to address them. She pulled out a fresh quill and Lifa's list, which thoughtfully included not only the names but the locations of the invitees. Designations such as "Second house on the right side of the Temple of Agneta, Midton, Waterdon," were as much address as you ever got in Iscandia if your house didn't actually have a name. Bernadette had heard that in Remus the imperial government had established a mail service. That would be a little impractical in this broad and sparsely-populated province, she feared.

By the time she had finished preparing the invitations for delivery it was suppertime, and Bernadette decided to wait until tomorrow to see about delivering them. She broke bread with Hjaermond and Selden at her usual table. The old men weren't bad companions, but she was beginning to wonder if she'd adopted them for life. They were enjoying themselves so much at the Maiden that it would seem heartless to dump them back off in the basement of the eorl's palace in Sylvanian, after Bjorn and Lifa's wedding.

After eating Bernadette went back upstairs and put on a robe, heading for a soak in the hot pool. She was going to miss having this so close to hand when they moved to their own house – unless maybe they could somehow figure out how to build one of their own. Rather than socialize with the other people in the pool, she lay back in the hot water and spent a few minutes fantasizing about her dream home. Then, relaxed yet energized, she returned upstairs and put on her smithing outfit. She had enchanted a circlet, armor, gloves, boots, ring and necklace with the permanent spell that would enhance the wearer's skills in making or improving arms and armor. The set of garments elevated her already-fine skills to master level.

She'd mostly been doing production work just to earn some money lately, making a few pieces from scratch and improving others that had come into her hands. Now Bernadette took the time to try some experimentation. A daimonic bow had fallen into her possession, more powerful for its draw weight than any she had previously owned, and she now set about trying to copy it.

She'd been studying some tomes on the subject, and learned that they were made of sablium but magically enhanced by the fusion of a Netherworld daimon's blood into the metal. The design was unique, and only this combination of Terris' most desirable metal and the blood of a sentient being from another plane of existence had the degree of strength and flexibility to properly make use of it. The exact technique was difficult, but by the end of the evening she was looking at two daimonic bows and could not tell one from the other.

Feeling immensely pleased, Bernadette disrobed and slipped into the basement's bed all by herself. This was the first time she had ever slept here alone, and she missed Erik's presence enormously. She lay right in the center of it with her arms and legs outstretched, staring up at the ceiling, and sighed deeply. Then she curled up into a ball, lying on her side, and went to sleep.

Chapter 56: A Blur of Motion

Came the dawn, Bernadette was up with the chickens. Not that the Maiden had any chickens. Maybe we ought to fence off the side yard and keep a flock, she mused, as she slipped on a robe and climbed the ladder to the floor above. With as much business as the Maiden was doing these days, they needed more and more foodstuffs. The ovens that had been added to the kitchen were a help, but they could use expanded cooking facilities as well. Preparing the food for the two forthcoming parties was going to be a challenge.

She slipped into the hot pool, which she had to herself at this hour. Even as her body relaxed and enjoyed the water her mind was churning with ideas, to-do lists, and a thousand concerns. She really didn't want to forget anything, but there was so much to do! Bread and pastries were already baking in the kitchen, the delicious smells causing her stomach to growl and remind her she was just lying here in hot water when she should be eating breakfast and getting to work on the day's projects.

After toweling off Bernadette went upstairs and put on some appropriate clothing. She was going for a fusion between practicality and dressiness, as the trip on foot to Waterdon was never guaranteed to be free of peril, but she also expected to be stopping in at Wyrmshalla. She didn't want the society matrons to write her off as one of *those* women, when she asked them for the name of their seamstress.

So, Bernadette put on an ankle-length velvet skirt with soft, agile leather boots below and a silken blouse with mutton-chop sleeves above. Over the blouse she wore an elven metal cuirass of her own design, more delicately and decoratively worked than normal elven armor so that it resembled jewelry rather than the protective garment it actually was. She'd even set it with a few gemstones, rubies of course. Her work with jewelry was still pretty basic. She was able to turn out rings, necklaces, and circlets of the standard Iscandia designs, but for finer stuff she turned to professionals.

The cuirass was enchanted with enhanced health, stamina, and magical energy. Bernadette let her long auburn hair flow down around her shoulders, pinning it back from her face with a gold circlet she'd made. She was likely never going to approach Andrion in her skills as a battle mage, but thus garbed and with her lethally enchanted dagger at her belt (not to mention her dragon spells), she should be more than a match for anything that might accost her between here and the city gates. Unless it was a dragon, of course – in which case, her plan was to run like hell.

Thus garbed, Bernadette tucked the party invitations into the decoratively worked leather pouch she carried when her full pack was not needed. It didn't have nearly the carrying capacity, but she had need to carry only the invitations and some gold, along with the small collection of clothing she wanted to sell. She descended the stairs, looking regal, and made her way to the Owner's Table, as they'd now begun calling it, where a small pot of hot tea and a plate of warm pastries soon appeared. Drelos was awfully good at his job.

The Maiden guests and residents were beginning to stir now, but the two elderly members of Alfenstein's former ruling family had not yet put in an appearance. Bernadette ate her breakfast with a certain amount of dispatch, anxious both to get moving and to avoid being delayed by falling into conversation with them. They'd taken her invitation to stay at the Maiden whole-heartedly, and seemed now to believe that she was here for no other reason than to entertain them and see to their every need.

Lev was up and wandering around though he hadn't gone on duty yet. She grabbed him and Drelos for a brief consultation. "We need to have a conference about the party here on the eighteenth, and also the one next month. Can we all get together here this afternoon after I get back from town?"

"You're the boss," they both assured her. Neither of them ever left the Maiden if they could avoid it. Departing with a smile and a wave, Bernadette set off out the inn's front doors into a winter morning bright with promise.

It was amazing, Bernadette mused, as she began walking down the road to the south, what an equable climate Waterdon had. Sure, it rained here frequently. That led to plentiful crops and no shortage of water for those who collected it in cisterns or dug wells – which never needed to be all that deep. But it almost never snowed, the wind was seldom more than a gentle breeze, and there were never the oppressively leaden skies or thick fogs that plagued some other regions. At the moment, here at the end of the first week in the new year, a deep blue sky was dotted with cumulonimbus clouds that suggested little threat of precipitation. A perfectly lovely day for a walk, even if she did have the map back again.

She soon came up on Coldburn Farm, and was impressed at the speed with which the work there was progressing. Already the stonework for the foundations was done, and a tower some twenty feet on a side was rising behind the house. She spotted Bjorn standing amid the construction workers looking supervisory, a sheaf of drawings in his hand, and gave him a friendly wave as she went on past.

This led her to musing about their own home, again, and she ran through in her mind the areas where land might be available. There was a bandit den in a shallow cave tucked down below the city walls over on the west side. Perhaps they could get Ormund to cede them the land after they cleaned out the bandits (again; she and Erik had killed them all several months ago, but like all such places it had soon found new tenants), and turn the cave into the house's root cellar – then build out from there.

Hmm, not a totally bad idea. It was a bit far from either the city gates or the Maiden, but both could be reached by fast-travelling in seconds. And the view out over the plains to the west, if not as attractive as the river view on the east, was not unpleasant. Lost in thought, Bernadette had continued her progress up the road from the river, moving across Waterdon's southern overlook; and was taken completely by surprise when a shri popped up to attack her.

As usual, her first response was the Gale spell. It was the first she had fully learned, and one of the most useful in her repertoire. The hapless creature flew through the air, tumbling, to land in bushes some thirty feet away. Meanwhile she cast a lightning battle spell, and blasted it to oblivion. Damn! That'll teach you to be mooning while you're supposed to be keeping a lookout, she told herself with annoyance. The creature had left several dirty scratches on her lovely velvet skirt. She brushed at it as best she could with her hands, wishing there were healing spells for dealing with property damage.

Bernadette came in through the gates in Waterdon and waved to Alessia, who was already out working at her forge. Then she continued on up the road to the central marketplace. As she'd hoped, Anja's young friend Lars was hanging around. She had the general idea that he was the son of one of the stall holders. He appeared to be around eight, a handsome lad with dark brown hair and blue eyes. Most people throughout Agena learned to read and write, usually taught at home as there were no schools established for children. Bernadette hoped Lars was one of them.

"Hello, Lars," she said. He smiled uncertainly at her.

"You're The Fireblood, right?" he asked bluntly. "Erik and Andrion's friend? And Anja's?"

"That's right," she said, giving him what she hoped was a motherly smile. Anja had opened up a whole new world to her, but Bernadette didn't really think she had this motherhood thing down yet. "Lars, I was hoping you could help me with something. Can you read?"

He sneered, an expression that looked out of place on his cute, boyish features. "Of *course* I can read," he replied. "I'm not a baby!"

"I'm sure you're not!" Bernadette replied, anxious to get back into his good graces. "I have some letters here," she said, proffering the ribbon-tied bundle of invitations, "that need to be delivered to some people here in Waterdon." She untied the ribbon and sorted through, removing three of them from the stack. Those, she would deliver herself. "I was hoping that you might be able to help me with delivering these. Do you know any of these people?" She handed him the remaining stack.

In part, she was testing whether Lars' claim to be able to read was justified. He went through the folded, addressed missives, studying what was written on each of them in Bernadette's neat calligraphy. His lips moved slightly as he read each one, then nodded and tucked the folded paper to the bottom of the stack. In a couple of minutes he had the bulk of the stack in one hand and three or four in another. "These," he said, waving the larger stack, "are all people I know. These others I don't know but I can take it where it says."

Bernadette's face lit with pleasure. "Excellent!" she said. "I'll give you ten guilders if you can deliver all of these to their recipients and meet me back here in three hours' time. And I'll buy you lunch. Deal?" Lars' eyes were wide. Ten guilders was a fortune! And lunch, too?!

"It's a deal!" he cried, then dashed off. His agile mind was already planning his route. Waterdon wasn't that big a city, but what if some of the people were not at home?

Bernadette smiled as the lad vanished. She had reason to believe he could be trusted. In a town the size of this one, almost anyone who had stayed here for long came to know almost everyone else. Reputation was everything, and you didn't screw people and expect to be able to survive for long. Plus, Anja had vouched for him.

She noted that Bernard's was now open for business, and stepped across the way to enter the shop. Dealing with Bernard was as pleasant as immersing oneself in a mixture of honey and cow dung; but the man provided a service and he wasn't horrible to look at. Bernadette sold off her extra clothing and acquired some raw materials for future projects. Then she went next door to spend some time bartering with Adele. She endured the wizened Reman woman's usual claims to have detected some hideous pestilence infesting her person, bought an enchanter's potion superior to the ones she was currently able to create, and purchased a few ingredients she needed. Her recent activities hadn't given her many opportunities for harvesting.

This business concluded, Bernadette returned down Waterdon's main street and knocked at the door of Brightsgate Cottage. Lifa answered the door, and greeted her with a smile. With Bjorn going off to work each morning, she found herself short of adult company sometimes. Though really Anja was so adorable, it was hard to complain; and they always had the opportunity to walk about in the business district, where she could chat with the stall holders while Anja played with their children.

"Your wedding party invitations are being delivered as we speak," Bernadette said with satisfaction. Hiring Lars to do the legwork had been a great idea. Now she was free to simply hang out with Lifa and Anja until lunchtime. Well, nearly lunchtime. She had another project she needed to deal with while she was here; but that could wait for a while.

Lifa had finished tidying up after breakfast and the cottage was clean. She made some tea and she and Bernadette sat chatting, while Anja played at their feet or joined the conversation at her whim. A couple of hours flew by and Bernadette took her leave, saying "I'm off on some errands soon, so I probably won't see you for a few days." There were hugs and kisses, then she stepped out the door and walked a good twenty paces over to Valkyrie.

Alessia, in between armor pieces, was leaning up against a post that supported the building's porch roof. She greeted Bernadette, her newly established business partner, with a smile. Bernadette smiled back at her, then said "I have an odd project for you. I think this is something you and Wolaf can handle better than I can." Motioning toward the crafting bench, she walked over and pulled a sheet of paper out of her pouch and spread it on the gray metal surface.

It was a drawing she'd made. She was not nearly as good at this sort of thing as Bjorn was, but was capable of sketching something that, heavily annotated with dimensional details, might serve to tell a craftsperson what was wanted. It pictured an iron table mounted on six three-foot steel legs, each with a small round foot on the end to increase stability. The flat iron tabletop surface was perforated with small round holes, and wrapping around it was an iron skirting some six inches tall, forming a sort of box that sat on the legs. A small lip ran around the top edge of the skirting, set on the inside and perhaps half an inch down from the top. And resting on that lip was a series of four iron grates, each of them three feet (the depth of the table) by two feet (one-quarter of the table's length).

Bernadette and Alessia studied the drawings for quite some time, Bernadette answering questions and explaining the purpose of this or that design element. It was clear to Alessia, who had visited the Maiden and seen Bernadette's smithy there, that something this size could never be crafted there. There'd be no way to get it out of the basement. But here at her open-air forge, there'd be no problem. Making something like this was little different from crafting armor or weapons, and the iron would be cheap.

"This shouldn't be too difficult," Alessia told her friend. "How soon do you need it?" Today was the seventh.

"I'd like to have it ready by the fifteenth," Bernadette told her. "And I'll need Wolaf to help with moving it. I should be able to fast-travel it back to the Maiden from here, but it's probably going to take three or four people to move it around to the deck in back."

"And you're going to cook on this?" Alessia confirmed, still wrestling with the concept.

"Sure," Bernadette told her. "Just think of it as a long, shallow firepit on legs with a lot of cooking grates on top."

Alessia pondered that for a while. "We should easily have it ready by the fifteenth," she said. "Will you be bringing us any more arms and armor in the meantime?" Bernadette smiled slyly.

"Are you interested in some daimonic pieces?" she asked. Alessia's eyes widened. "Daimonic? You've got daimonic?"

"I made myself a daimonic bow last night," Bernadette replied. "And I've got plenty of sablium ingots and a small supply of daimon's blood. A lot of the weird creatures that have attacked me over the past few months had it, and I didn't know what to do with it until now."

"That'll be great!" Alessia said. "We have a few really wealthy clients who are always looking for top quality." She stood for a moment, gazing inward, then smiled brilliantly at her friend. "You know," she said, "I think we're *all* going to be rich!"

The sun, playing peek-a-boo with the fluffy clouds above, looked to be approaching high noon; so Bernadette walked back up the street to the market square. Lars was not in sight, but in a minute or two she spotted him sprinting down the stairs from the direction of the fountains on the level above. He was panting a bit as he saw her and hurried to her side. "Done!" he cried, smiling. Bernadette smiled back at him.

"I'm very impressed, Lars. Here is your gold." She pulled a 10-guilder piece from her pouch. "And what would you like for lunch?" she asked.

He looked at her slyly, wondering how far her offer extended. After all, an offer of lunch might be no more than a bread roll and a slice of cheese. "The Flying Horseman has some venison stew," he suggested hesitantly. "And they've got potato chips!" he added with enthusiasm. Aha. Bernadette was not surprised to learn that this dish, first created in the Maiden's kitchen, was beginning to spread to other establishments. They were so addictive!

"Sounds fine," Bernadette told him. She let the boy lead her up the stairs to the Horseman's front door and they went inside to sit on stools at the bar. She greeted Britta, who as usual was talking of how she hoped to sell out and retire from the innkeeping business, and ordered two bowls of stew along with two servings of potato chips, with water to wash it down with for both of them. The day was young, and she needed to keep her wits about her.

They ate mostly in silence, punctuated by the crunching of the slightly greasy but delicious chips. Lars' appetite seemed to be in fine condition after his morning of dashing all over Waterdon. Bernadette did manage to learn that his father ran the game stall in the market, that his mother had died when he was born, and that he was usually at loose ends during the day. He went hunting with his father some days, but mostly spent his time hanging around the business district looking for paying work or (so she inferred) a little mischief.

Thanking Lars again for his excellent delivery service, Bernadette left the inn and mounted the steps heading for Wyrmshalla. As usual, she was greeted with great courtesy by the guards. They were a rough lot, but they could admire someone who'd performed such feats as she had. Many of the court residents were sitting at table having a midday meal, but she found Garimund crouched over his enchanting table in the room to the east of the main hall.

He jumped as he suddenly became aware of her silent presence behind him. "Fireblood!" he stammered, his face (what she could see of it inside his wizard's hood) reddening. Having the object of your nighttime fantasies appear at your elbow can be disconcerting. Bernadette gave Garimund a reassuring smile.

"Bernadette, please. How are you, Garimund?"

"Oh, I'm fine... uh, can I help you with something?" He was mindful of the need not to blab about Erik's request.

Bernadette proffered the invitation with his name on it. "It's your invitation to Lifa's wedding party," she told him. He smiled.

There was *another* woman who'd occasioned some nocturnal throbbing.

"I heard she was getting hitched," he said. "Didn't think I would ever see the day. She used to be so solemn…" Wow, he realized, that was two parties he was being invited to in less than a month. At this rate, he might actually acquire a social life. But what he really wanted, above all else, was to get laid. Maybe there'd be some unattached women at the party. "Thanks!" he grinned at her, then said, "Got to get back to work…"

Bernadette took her leave and went in search of Lifa's other invitees. Each of them was delighted to receive the invitation, the more so as it was hand-delivered by The Fireblood herself. Lifa's friends in the palace were not the sort of people to have their clothing tailored by others, though; so she still had to do a little schmoozing with the ladies of the court. She invited herself into a group of them still seated at the table, and was welcomed.

They ooh'd and aah'd at her outfit, admiring the cuirass. It was martial-looking and feminine at the same time, and richly ornamented enough to appeal to their sense of snobbery. After chatting for a while, Bernadette came away with the name of one Gerde Snowhair, part of that sprawling clan of Norse chauvinists, who had become the dressmaker for several of Waterdon's wealthier matrons.

Ooh, I'm gonna be a wealthy matron, Bernadette thought as she trotted down the stairs. She wasn't ready to go see Gerde yet, and the afternoon was young. She decided to go back to the Maiden and practice her smithing, see if she could make some more daimonic pieces. Plus, she needed to do some sketches of clothing she wanted made. To speed things along, she used the map for her return trip.

Chapter 57: Trimming the List

Bernadette returned to work at the smithy. When she tired of this work, she made yet another costume change into a comfortable stretchy dress she liked to wear around the Maiden, then recalled that it was time to meet with Lev and Drelos to discuss the forthcoming party arrangements. She returned to the common room and beckoned them back into the kitchen area, where they could speak without interruptions. Drelos motioned a lovely young elf woman, who had recently been hired to help around the inn, to take over the bar for him while they consulted.

"Here's the story then," Bernadette began, laying out details for them so that food could be ordered, staff arranged, and so forth. "I've ordered up a special cooking table from Valkyrie. It's supposed to be ready by the fifteenth, and I'll need a couple of strong men to help with moving it. Erik should be back here by then… Anyway, it's about eight feet wide by three feet deep and the plan is to set it out on the deck to grill meats for the party. We'll have to see how the weather's looking. If there's a chance it might rain we'll need to rig a tent or canopy over it. I expect it to become a regular part of the Maiden's kitchen equipment. You'll build a big hardwood fire in the middle of it and when it's getting down toward coals spread them out, then lay the cooking grids over the top. You should be able to cook enough meat for fifty people at a time on it."

The two innkeepers looked suitably impressed. Their Fireblood employer was really shaking the place up. She went on, "I expect we may have as many as thirty to forty guests, not counting people who are usually here at the Maiden anyway. We'll need lots and lots of chilled ale, so maybe we should have a couple of large barrels with ice in them. I think that if you put water into a broad baking pan and apply a frost spell, it should freeze very quickly. Then you can break the ice into bits, and pour it out into the barrel. Put in some bottles, repeat the whole procedure, and so forth. Does that sound like a plan?"

Drelos spoke up. "I have a minor frost spell," he said. "but I could use a stronger one – and more magical energy." Bernadette thought that over.

"I'll see if I can buy you a spellbook for a more powerful frost spell," she promised. "And I can enchant you some accessories that will increase both your basic magical energy store and your regeneration rate. I'd really like to have somebody besides Andrion who can chill drinks in a hurry!"

He nodded his thanks. Being able to chill drinks was turning into something of a marketable job skill. He'd been doing it for the Maiden since Andrion had first shown him the technique, and was already getting better at it. Meanwhile, Bernadette was marshaling her thoughts. "Let's see… The party will start at two in the afternoon and continue on into the evening, so some people will probably come early and leave early while others will be hanging on late. We'd better have a lot of mead and wine in addition to the ale, plenty of chilled drinking water, and maybe some apple cider. We'll need tons of potato chips, and maybe some of those fried potato fingers I told you about."

Lev had a comment at this point. "I was wondering if you could get something fabricated for me," he said. "Fishing the potato pieces out with a spoon is very slow going, and it's not going to work if we're feeding a crowd. What I need is a couple of wire baskets, probably dypalfar metal or copper, that are shaped to fit down inside a large pot and have a handle sticking out of the top. The mesh should be small enough so potato fingers won't fall through it." "Hmm," Bernadette responded. "I can probably make something like that myself, if you let me have one of the pots you want to use."

The consultation continued for another hour, as the three of them discussed all of the food, drinks, tables, chairs and other considerations needed for handling an event this big. Bernadette left it with another two pages of notes, and each of the men had his own to-do list as well. She joined Hjaermond and Selden at her table for supper as usual, and after eating she went upstairs and put on a robe. She took a fairly brief bath, once again too wrapped up in her concerns to be properly sociable.

After the bath Bernadette retired to the master bedroom with a glass of wine, to sit updating her journal and sketching some outfits she'd like to own. It was a rare treat to have so much time to herself, but she missed her men. And she was beginning to get horny. How many more nights would she have to sleep alone, anyhow?

She'd started keeping a journal several months back, and its pages were filled with tiny writing as she'd tried to make the most of each page. I'm surprised I can even read it now, she thought, scanning back over some of her earlier adventures. She had not recorded any details of her romantic encounters, of course, but even reading phrases like "Spent night with Andrion, love again in a.m. Wow" were enough to give her a warmish feeling in her crotch. Oh, hell.

Instead, she flipped to the back of the book and her timetable/to-do list. How satisfying to check the invitations to Lifa and Bjorn's party off the list. Unfortunately, the list had now grown by another several inches. Tomorrow she would need to leave for Sylvanian, where she had to pick up Lifa's dress and okay Senalie's final drawing for her own. She wasn't sure how long the fast-traveling would take, so she wanted to err on the side of caution even if it meant spending another night in the Dancing Rabbit. The name aside, she'd become rather fond of that establishment.

When she'd recorded every last thing she could think of to do in the next few weeks, Bernadette yawned and stretched. Time to get to bed. Stripping naked, quite safe from nocturnal attacks and pleasantly warm, she lay there in the darkness thinking of the man who usually shared this bed with her. His smooth caramel-colored skin, his melting brown eyes, his rock-hard cock… Oops. She began thinking about their brief and red-hot encounter right before he'd left, and rubbed the area around her clit with her right hand while the other massaged her left breast, tweaking the nipple. She soon gave a soft cry, as wetness flooded her. Oh Andrion, hurry back!

Another lonely morning. Well, not lonely, really – but the lack of a strong male body in the bed with her left Bernadette feeling a bit bereft. She had lots to do and there was no fun to be had here; so she was soon up and dressed in her smithing gear. She breakfasted while wearing it, a light meal of bread and cheese washed down with hot tea. Then it was down to the basement, with one of Drelos' largest cast iron pots in hand, for some more experimentation.

Bernadette had a goodly collection of dypalfar items she'd salvaged from ruins during her many quests over the past few months. They didn't fetch all that much compared with arms or armor, and it had always been her intention to smelt them into ingots for making armor. But the Maiden's shelves had kept ahead of her needs, so far. Now she began rummaging through it. She had a dim memory, a visual impression… yes, there it was!

From the look of the piece, it was part of a broken dypalfar mech of some kind. And it was completely wrapped in stiff dypalfar metal wire. She unwound it and found that there was quite a lot of it. It seemed to hold whatever shape you bent it into, though changing it to a new shape was not that easy. Setting the pot on the workbench (triggering another memory of a time down here with Erik that sent a hot shiver through her), Bernadette began using a pair of heavy nippers, a pair of pliers, and a wooden hammer to lay strands of the wire down into the pot, forming it into a convex cage. She kept it up off the bottom a bit with a thin piece of ceramic tile, and formed it so that there was a little space between the wire and the pot all the way around.

When she had all of the pieces laid in one direction, she laid a similar number of pieces in crosswise. Then she bent some pieces into circles of descending sizes, the biggest fitting the top of the basket, with a loop of wire off one side of it for the handle, and three others going down to the bottom. This would all have to be joined, somehow. She carried the pot with its wire assemblage over to the forge and let the pot sit in the coals. The thinner wire was soon hot and glowing. Then she stoked up the smelter and put in some of her smaller dypalfar scrap.

At the forge, Bernadette hammered out a long thin bar of steel as if for a short sword, but circular in cross-section. She flattened one end and then punched it into the shape of a tiny ladle. Then, using two pairs of tongs, she lifted the glowing pot off the forge fire and carried it over to the smelter. Dipping her impromptu implement into the molten metal filling the ceramic bar mold, she began dabbing all of the places where one piece of wire met another with droplets of the molten metal. Gravity had its own ideas about this, and before she had finished soldering all the joints there were dribs and drabs of dypalfar metal all over the inside of the pot and the wire cage had adhered to the tile on the bottom in several places.

Bernadette used a pair of triple-layer leather gloves to lift the wire cage out of the pot. The tile came up with it. She set it on the workbench, and while waiting for it to cool some more she took a well-sharpened steel dagger to a stick of firewood, carving it into a smooth wooden handle. A hand drill put a hole into it, which she was then able to force down over the double wire handle of the basket. By now it was cool enough to touch, and she went to work with cold chisel and other finishing tools to break it loose from the tile and clean up some of the rougher areas.

Oh, what time was it? She really needed to be leaving soon. The basket she'd crafted was pretty rough looking, but she thought it might do the job Lev was looking for. And dypalfar metal had the advantage of being extremely tough and impervious to oxidation. Examples of it lying in dank ruins for millennia still looked good as new.

Bernadette took a few minutes more to chip the spilled dypalfar metal out of the pot. The seasoned cast iron had not readily clung to the spills, in any case. Then she carried pot and basket back up the ladder and presented it to Lev with a grin. "What do you think?" she asked. He looked astonished.

"Wow. I suppose I'd better wash it in hot soapy water before I try it out. Are you staying for lunch?"

"I suppose I can," she said. I'm going to go get packed up for traveling, and then I'll grab a bite before I leave. You're going to make potato chips?" She knew those were faster to cook than the fingers were. He nodded, and hurried off to get the new basket washed and dried. He took extra time with a soft towel, knowing that any residual moisture could be explosive when it hit the hot fat.

He had another pot identical to the example pot sitting on the fire full of hot tallow, something they kept around the Maiden kitchen nearly all the time now. He set the basket in and observed that it tipped slightly. Hmm, that was a design consideration he hadn't thought of. Since he'd never seen or heard of such a thing as a frying basket before, he hadn't expected to have his invention tested so soon – and found wanting. Experimentally, he took a slender-handled spoon and balanced it on the far edge of the pot from the basket's handle, slipping below the top ring and keeping the basket level.

So far, so good. Now, with the lightning knife strokes of long practice, he began chopping clean, dry potatoes into thin slices, dropping them by handfuls into the hot fat and stirring them with a fork to make sure they didn't stick together. When he judged there were as many in the pot as it could handle, he resumed stirring occasionally until all of the potato slices were cooked through, golden brown and crispy. Then he lifted the basket by the handle, causing the spoon to fall off the far side of the pot. What it really needed, of course, was a smaller protrusion similar to the handle to suspend the far side of the basket from the edge of the pot.

Now Lev was standing there holding the very hot wire basket full of very hot freshly cooked potato chips, over the very hot pot full of boiling fat. Hmm. With the old hand technique, you would just spoon the chips out a few at a time and set them on a wire rack over a platter, where the excess fat would run off of them and could later be poured from the platter back into the pot. But what if you could just use the basket to drain the fat directly back to the pot?

He was very thankful Bernadette had thought to put a wood insulator on the basket's handle, but even so standing this close to the hot pot was becoming increasingly uncomfortable. He went ahead and dumped the large basket of chips onto the usual drain rack setup, where it mounded up. This was easily four times the number of chips they would normally try to cook at one time. His mind was already at work designing some kind of hooks that could be clipped onto the pot so the basket could sit above the hot oil draining all by itself.

Bernadette came down the stairs with her pack to find Lev grinning at her, and approaching with grilled meat sliced thin and laid between two halves of a toasted bread roll, with melted cheese on top. Accompanying that was a mound of the still-hot, lightly salted chips. They were crispier and more evenly cooked than had usually been the case. A chilled ale completed the presentation.

She beamed up at him. "Wow! I take it it worked?" He smiled back.

"There are a few things I didn't think about when I told you what I wanted. But this will do fine for now, and after you get back we'll talk about improvements to be made. I think the Mark II will be even better. And thanks!" He bustled off, having a busy lunchtime crowd to deal with. Bernadette sank her teeth into the delicious combination of warm sliced meat, melting cheese, and crusty bread. At the rate the food around here is improving, she thought, I'll be as big as a house. I'm going to need more exercise!

Finishing her delicious meal, alone with her thoughts, Bernadette washed the last crumbs down with the last swallow of ale and blotted her mouth with a napkin. She stopped by the bar to thank Lev again for the excellent food. "I'll be back in a day or two," she promised. "What's the time, please?" "He checked the clock they kept behind the bar.

"It's 1:15 p.m.," he told her. She strolled out the Maiden's front doors and pulled out her map, touched the symbol that represented Sylvanian, and wished herself to be there.

Chapter 58: The Boys are Back in Town

As Andrion, Erik, and Diane stepped into the Maiden they found the place bustling. It seemed to grow more popular with each passing month, as word of it reached the far corners of Iscandia. Likely the inn's several innovations, including the hot bathing pool and the recent invention of potato chips, were part of the draw. All three of them, the men especially, were fairly ravenous by now. Breakfast had been scanty and many hours in the past.

They found Lev manning the bar, engaged in some washing-up now that the crowd had begun to thin. Despite the Maiden's location on the fringes of the Waterdon trading area, they were starting to see a surge of locals coming here just for lunch. This included some of the workers from the nearby Coldburn Farm project, who were swelling the ranks still more.

"Welcome back!" Lev greeted them, adding "You missed Bernadette by about an hour and a half. She's off to Sylvanian." Both Erik and Andrion were a little disappointed, though they'd expected that would be the case. Much as they missed her and lusted after her, it was probably for the best. Her absence meant they could pursue their efforts to prepare their magnificent surprise without constant deception.

"Ah well," Andrion said casually. "What have you got to eat?" Lev gave a smile of secret satisfaction, an unusual expression for the calm and matter-of-fact innkeep.

"I have just the thing. Here, have some cold ales," he said proffering three frosty bottles across the bar, "and go sit at your table. I'll have lunch for you in about fifteen minutes." Andrion took an appreciative swig from his ale.

"Seems like Drelos is keeping up with chilling the drinks," he remarked.

"He's getting better at it all the time," Lev replied.

The three made their way to their table, setting their packs on the floor carefully. All of them were carrying valuable dypalfar devices they had gone to a lot of trouble to acquire. They enjoyed their chilled drinks, talking about the recent expedition, until Lev arrived at the table with an enormous tray on which three more chilled ales and three plates of food were resting.

Aha, more of the bread, meat, and cheese combinations. Except these were freshly prepared, not wrapped in waxed paper, and seemed to be hot, the cheese melted. Erik's eyes were focused on the food with a degree of concentration usually reserved for the thighs of his beloved. Lev rested the heavy tray on the table and began passing the plates and bottles around. No utensils were needed, but he had brought some napkins.

Erik sank his teeth into the hot sandwich. Damn, that was *good*! Then he took a small handful of the side dish. "Hey, these potato fingers are really delicious!" Lev smiled.

"I asked Bernadette to make me a sort of wire basket for cooking them in, and she came through like a champ. Wait'll you taste the chips!" He left them to their food, and went back to the bar.

As they devoured their delayed midday meal, the three talked about their immediate plans. Now that they had all the pieces, Diane needed to finalize her design for the water system and start constructing it. Andrion was to help her with that, and see that the space reserved for it at the house was adequate for their needs. Erik was anxious to finish the ring he intended to slip onto Berni's finger at the wedding – and equally anxious to be back at the farm, participating in the construction project.

As he had throughout their expedition, Andrion assumed the role of team leader. "Berni's going to be gone at least until late tomorrow, maybe even the day after," he told them. "From the relative distances, it'll probably take about the same amount of time to travel between here and Sylvanian as it does between here and Lakedon. I really hope we can get the working parts of the water system put together by then." "I need to have some pipe fabricated," Diane said. "That piece you cut for us is a model. Your builder must have somebody that makes it?"

Andrion considered. Several dozen feet of copper pipe were due to be installed between the bottom of the cistern and the house, coming up to valves in the kitchen and bathroom. Hegmar must know the provider. "I'll take the sample down to show him. Maybe Erik and I can go down together in a little while. Will you be able to get started assembling your components?" Now it was Diane who pondered.

425

"I'm hoping to work in close proximity to the Maiden's system, so I can make sure that I'm matching the model. But what about getting it up and out of the basement?"

"As long as it's small enough to fit through the trap door to the deck, that shouldn't be a problem. We can lift it up and push it out, or we can rig ropes to hoist it."

"Okay," Diane said. "That should work... Oh! I also need a flat sheet of dypalfar metal two by three feet, very thin, and perforated all over with a lot of tiny holes so that it's like a fine screen. I hope your fabricator can handle that, too. There'll be a few little levers and bars and so forth, but I can craft those myself – or you can, Erik."

The blond giant grinned at her. "I've been getting in a bit of practice at the smithy lately with some more finely-detailed work," he admitted. "I don't know about pipe or your screen plate, but I should be able to modify or create any levers you need."

"All right," Diane said with a smile. "I think we're ready to get started. Gentlemen, give me a hand taking things down to the basement?"

The three hefted their packs and carried them downstairs, then spread the contents on the crafting bench with more pieces occupying the chemia and enchanting tables. Andrion pointed out the supplies on the shelves to Diane, also noting that there seemed to be quite a bit of miscellaneous dypalfar scrap in the chest. "Berni's had that stuff for months," he told her. "I doubt she'd miss any of it if it turns out there's something here you can use." Diane gave him a businesslike smile, and handed him the cut section of dypalfar pipe.

"We need four straight lengths of this three feet long," she said, "and another four sections with a U bend. Plus some kind of collar that will let the pieces be joined."

Andrion took the piece and looked at her questioningly. "Would you mind jotting that down?" he asked hopefully. Realizing that memorizing her specifications and getting them all right after hearing them one time was not something she could reasonably expect even a bright mind like Andrion's to do, Diane extracted a piece of paper from the collection spread around the room and used her dypalfar pen to produce detailed drawings showing the sizes, shapes, and diameters of the pipes they needed. She passed it to Andrion and he pocketed it.

As they had no plans for questing through hostile regions, Erik changed into some more appropriate clothing before he and Andrion went back upstairs. He was completely casual about stripping down, but Diane found herself simultaneously wanting to look and wanting to look away. In a minute or so he was dressed again, and after the men had vanished up the ladder she headed for the Maiden's water system to refresh her memories and make some notes.

Chapter 59: The Project Advances

Upstairs, Drelos collared Erik. "Erik, Bernadette mentioned you ordered the new Owner's Table. Right?" Erik nodded. "Could you get your carpenter to make some chairs, too? We'll take as many as he can produce. And see if you can order us another four small tables." Erik looked at him questioningly, and he continued "It's for the wedding party on the 18th. And then we've got another one here next month, if you recall," He winked.

Erik grinned, saying "All right, I'll take care of it. With the way business around here is going, it might not just be parties you need the extra furniture for." Drelos nodded seriously.

"Too bad there's no room for any more beds. Next thing you know, she'll have us building another wing."

Meanwhile, Andrion continued up the stairs to the master bedroom and changed into trousers and shirt with soft boots. No need to be going around fully armored. As he came down again, carrying his pack with the pipe sample and various other needed items, Erik was concluding his discussion with Drelos. The two set off out the front doors of the Maiden and down the road a quarter mile to Coldburn Farm.

This late in the afternoon, the crew had been on the job for hours and work was proceeding at a blazing pace. They spotted Bjorn, and went over to talk with him. The powerfully-built Norseman smiled at them. "I've been wondering when you were going to turn up," he said. "Did you find what you were looking for?"

"Diane seems to think so," Andrion admitted. He'd been supposed to come up with their water systems by himself, but the task had been beyond him. At least he'd known whom to turn to for help.

Bjorn led them on a tour of the construction site. The addition's stone foundations, encompassing a full basement, had now been laid. A large gap on the downhill side was accessed by a stone staircase leading down from ground level. "The bottom landing is canted out slightly," Bjorn pointed out. "And that opening there in the cut feeds to a drainpipe leading off down the hillside so rainwater coming down the steps will drain away instead of into the basement."

As yet there were no doors, but the opening was a full six feet wide. Sturdy timber joists for the floor above had been laid, and thick boards on which the wall timbers would stand capped the stone all around the edges. When the addition had been enclosed and roofed, a hole would be cut through from the existing house giving on the long central hallway.

In the back yard, between the house and the walls of Waterdon, a lower stone foundation stood and a timber tower was rising on it. A trench ran from this to the house, where small gaps had been left in the new foundation. A single large pipe would deliver water from the cistern atop the tower to the house, where it would split into three smaller pipes feeding the kitchen, bathroom, and water privy.

After Bjorn had completed the rounds with them Andrion asked, "Is Hegmar around? I have something I need to discuss with him."

"He's actually up in town," Bjorn told him. "You know where his house is?" Andrion nodded. "He's sort of made me project overseer, though obviously I don't know as much about the construction details as the workers do," Bjorn explained. "But I'm here to keep an eye on things and make sure that the work matches the specs. He's even paying me!"

Erik smiled at him. He had the feeling Bjorn might be needing a career that kept him close to home after the wedding, and was glad his friend was picking up some new skills. "We need to go into town anyhow," he told him.

"Andrion, you want to look up Hegmar while I go talk to Arngeld, and then meet me back here later?" Erik asked.

"Sounds like a plan," Andrion replied. "We'll see you later, Bjorn. Thanks for the tour." The two continued up the road to the city.

They split up inside the gates, Erik to visit Arngeld at his carpentry workshop while Andrion sought out the builder at his home. Hegmar's wife directed Andrion to the Flying Horseman, where he found the little Norseman enjoying a pint of ale in company with some visiting businessmen. "Hegmar," Andrion greeted him. "Can I have a word with you?" The builder smiled ingratiatingly. Andrion was the biggest client he'd had in two years.

Hegmar excused himself and joined Andrion at an empty table where he could pull out his dypalfar pipe example and the plans that Diane had drawn up. Britta came over to ask if Andrion wanted anything, and he asked for an ale. Room temperature of course, here; but drinkable. "You're having pipe fabricated for bringing the water into the house from the cistern, right?" Hegmar, intrigued, nodded.

"Aye. It's due for delivery next week," he said. "I expect we'll have the walls up by then. I'm having the cistern made over in Forestville, out of that wood they've got down there that doesn't rot. And that'll be coming in on a wagon. We'll have to rig a temporary crane up on the platform to hoist it up."

Andrion took this information in with a certain amount of impatience. He was glad to learn that Hegmar had things well in hand; but he didn't need an entire rundown of the project's progress. "I need to get some pipe pieces made, but they need to be constructed from dypalfar metal. This piece of pipe is a sample of the construction technique, and the diagram shows the pieces we need. Can your fabricator produce these?"

Hegmar peered at the pipe section and drawings with an air of concentration. "Dypalfar metal, eh?" He trailed off for a bit, then recaptured his train of thought. "Makes sense, mind, good for anything to do with water. Those pipes down t' dypalfar ruins, run water through 'em for a thousand years, and they're still fine. But costly. This'll run you quite a bit above what I quoted."

"That's not a problem," Andrion told him, wincing internally as he wondered how much of a soaking he was letting himself in for. "We have quite a lot of dypalfar metal available, more than enough for these pipes if your fabricator doesn't have his own supply."

He half-expected Hegmar to recoil at the thought, eager to preserve the markup that his fabricator would add to the cost of the ingots, as well as that he would tack on for himself. Instead, the man's ugly yet somehow appealing face lit, and he replied "Oh! That's all right then. Looks like we might need around eleven ingots for this. If you can deliver it down t' the site tomorrow, I'll get the job ordered. There'll still be some cost for my man, mind…"

Well I'll be, Andrion thought. Was it possible that he and Erik, babes in the woods of house renovation, had managed to stumble onto a builder who was competent, swift, and (gasp) honest? It appeared so. Perhaps it was Berni's famous Fireblood luck rubbing off on them. He would have married Berni had he met her herding goats on the slopes of the Hochstein – it was she he loved, not her wealth or her status. But it certainly was nice, he thought, how her Fireblood heritage seemed to make everything they wanted fall into place.

They discussed the additional specifications for the thin dypalfar metal screen Diane had asked for, which should take no more than one additional ingot once hammered out. Andrion thanked Hegmar and shook his hand, passing the drawings and pipe sample over to him and promising to deliver a dozen dypalfar ingots first thing in the morning. Then he made his way out of the Flying Horseman whistling a happy tune, and headed down the main street toward the gates and Coldburn Farm.

Chapter 60: Arngeld

Across town, Erik was welcomed into the home/workshop of Arngeld, pretty much all Waterdon had to offer in the way of a professional carpenter. His family was large and growing larger, and he had a couple of young sons coming along in the trade. His wife and daughters contributed to the business by weaving and sewing seat cushions, bolsters, mattresses, and bedding.

The tall, sandy-haired Norseman's face split in a grin as Erik was ushered into the workshop in the rear of the residence by Arngeld's youngest daughter, a girl of seven. Like most people who met Erik, the carpenter had liked him on first meeting – and was pleased at the extra business Erik had been bringing him of late. "Erik! Are you here for the table?" he asked genially. Erik was a bit surprised. It had only been a few days since he'd ordered it.

"Nope, actually it's something else. But is the table ready? Can I see it?"

"Just waiting for the final coat of varnish to dry, then we should be able to deliver it tomorrow," Arngeld told him. He'd had some past experience with inn tables and knew that if they didn't have a good hard, shiny finish on them they'd either become filthy and unappetizing (not good for business, if the inn was selling food) or sanded down to nothing in a few months as the inn staff used Holystone on them to remove the inevitable stains.

Arngeld led Erik out into a side area of the yard, where the table Erik had ordered sat under a protective overhang. Waterdon weather being what it was, you had to be prepared to get everything under cover at a moment's notice. Following, Erik gasped as he beheld what Arngeld had wrought. In keeping with the style employed throughout Iscandia for home furnishings, the table had simple lines. It was made from solid oak and its legs were unadorned, sturdy and slightly tapered. But the top!

"By the gods," Erik exclaimed, studying the design that had been inlaid in the top. "This is beautiful!" The golden oak that composed the entire table was joined here with designs cut in a dark red hardwood and an even darker, almost black one. They formed stylized dragons embedded in the table surface, intricately fitted together and protected by multiple layers of a hard, shiny varnish. "I didn't realize you were such an artist, Arngeld."

The older man bowed his head slightly, but the smile on his face could not be suppressed. "It's not often I get the chance for any artistic expression," he said humbly. "But I think that The Fireblood deserves the thanks of the entire province for what she's done. I wanted something that would be a fitting tribute to her."

"I'm sure she'll love it," Erik replied whole-heartedly. He had a brief mental image of the Maiden's entire collection of tables (and chairs, no doubt) being refitted with the dragon motif.

"In any case," Erik went on, "I'm afraid the reason I'm here is not going to provide you with an outlet for artistic expression. I need a whole bunch of chairs and some basic tables, as many as you can provide in the next week or so." Arngeld smiled. The special "Owner's Table" for The Fireblood had been a rare opportunity for him to pour his soul into his work. But his bread and butter, the work that kept his growing family fed, was just such quick-and-dirty assignments as the one Erik described. All of the output of his shop was sturdy and well-made; but the vast majority of it was as plain as porridge.

Erik pulled out a coin purse, and handed Arngeld a fistful of gold. "This is for materials. We'll take as many chairs as you can deliver to the Maiden by the seventeenth. And we need four of the small basic tables, thirty inches square. The seventeenth was now eight days away, and Arngeld was calculating. "The boys are getting pretty good at tables, and they're starting to get the hang of chairs. I think we might be able to do twenty chairs by then. Is that too many?"

Erik cast his mind back to the Maiden. He'd been living there for more than two years, and could walk through it in his memories counting the chairs. They might need to stack some of these new ones up in a corner between parties, but he thought they'd certainly need that many at least a few times a year. He'd never really had a proprietary attitude toward anything in his life before – but as the wedding approached, he was beginning to feel as if he, Berni, and Andrion were not just life partners but business partners. And it was time for him to act like a grownup and look to the future.

"Twenty chairs and four tables will be fine, Arngeld," Erik said confidently. "Uh, how's the bed coming?" A puckish expression suffused his friend's features. With five kids and another on the way Arngeld clearly spent a fair amount of time in bed with his wife; but the circumstances of Erik's forthcoming marriage and the bed he was crafting to accommodate its participants could not help but provoke certain... fantasies. These fantasies might have been more to his taste if Erik were marrying two beautiful women; but he'd take what he could get.

"It's coming along," he said. "You still don't need it until early next month, right?" Erik nodded. He'd ordered well in advance. The room the bed was to be assembled in was as yet only a glimmer in the architect's eye. "Irmagard and the girls are nearly done with the mattress, but there's the issue of the bedding." Erik blinked. He'd ordered the bed and the mattress, but had not even considered the sheets, blankets, and coverlet.

"Take a look at this," Arngeld said, motioning to the other side of the yard. Erik surveyed the large wooden structure set up under a roof, lining one wall.

"Uh, I give up," he said after studying it for a moment, "what is it?" Arngeld grinned at him, pride shining in his face.

"It is," he said, "probably the largest loom in Iscandia. When you ordered your bed, I got to thinking. You usually can't get cloth wider than about six feet. But with three people working the loom, there's no reason we couldn't go wider. This will make a sheet of cloth ten feet wide by up to twenty feet long!"

"Wow," Erik said, at a loss for words. Weaving was not one of the crafts he'd ever paid much attention to. Arngeld went on, "We can make tablecloths fit for the eorl's table, sheets and blankets any size, really big sails, tents, almost anything." Considering the possibilities, Erik eyed his friend.

"You might be needing to pop out a few more daughters, Arngeld..." Arngeld laughed.

"Three is enough for this loom," he said. "I'd need to build another one and hire some help to take on any more work. But we'll have top and bottom sheets for your bed made from the finest cotton, and a good wool blanket too."

Chapter 61: Attraction

"Thank you for thinking of that," Erik said. "It looks like you've got more than enough to keep you busy, so I guess I'll leave you for now. See you soon." They shook hands and Erik took his leave, winding his way down to the main road and heading back toward Coldburn Farm. He spotted Andrion walking ahead of him, and jogged to catch up. "Hey!" he cried, pulling alongside.

Andrion grinned at him. "Everything go all right?" he asked.

"More than all right," Erik replied. He related the details of his visit to Arngeld's, and Andrion told him of the successful meeting with Hegmar. Both of them felt as though things were really beginning to come together. They returned to the farm as the sun was heading toward the western horizon, disappearing behind the walls of Waterdon.

They found Bjorn and conferred with him again. In the few hours since they'd last seen him the crews had finished laying the joists for the main floor above the sunken, stone-lined basement. A double line of vertical supports ran down the length of that basement, providing additional support for the floor above. They were now starting to lay floorboards atop those joists, but at the moment the workers were engaged in cleaning up the site and stowing their tools before quitting for the day. Waterdon guards patrolled the area overnight.

"We'll see you tomorrow," Andrion told Bjorn as he and Erik set their feet toward the Maiden and home. "We'll be by fairly early with some dypalfar ingots for Hegmar."

"All right, see you then," their friend said before turning his attention to the site and the departing crew. It was his responsibility to make sure everything was in order before he returned to Brightsgate Cottage and his little family.

The men rolled into the Maiden and greeted Lev, who was still behind the bar. "We're getting twenty chairs and four tables before the seventeenth," Erik reported. "And wait'll you see what Arngeld did with the Owner's Table I ordered! It should be here tomorrow." Lev passed them a couple of bottles of chilled ale and a bowl of fresh, hot potato chips. They carried them over to the existing Owner's Table and sat chatting, having a little Happy Hour after their busy day. It was hard to believe they'd awakened this morning in a robbers' den all those miles away from here.

It was getting on toward suppertime but there was no sign of Diane. "I think I'll go check on her," Andrion said, and headed for the trap door behind the bar. Erik waved him on as Hjaermond and Selden, ever together, came down the stairs and headed in the direction of their table to join them for supper. When Andrion entered the basement, it appeared to be deserted. There was evidence that work had been going on, and the piles of dypalfar artifacts that had been spread around had been rearranged or removed. But where was Diane?

He had a fairly good idea where to look, so he went into the Well's little chamber and followed the hidden corridor down to the "engine room" of the Maiden's water system. Sure enough, the Galise woman was kneeling on the stone floor, tinkering with a box a little smaller than a standard chest. This box, unlike the wooden ones so common throughout Iscandia, seemed to be crafted of dypalfar metal plate.

She was deep in concentration and didn't hear Andrion come in. "Diane?" he asked gently. She started, glancing up suddenly.

"Oh!" she exclaimed, pressing a hand that was clutching one of her dypalfar tools to her chest. "What's up?"

"It's getting close to suppertime," he told her. "Thought you might want to take a break and eat something." Diane considered, then set down her tools, got to her feet and gave herself a slight all-over shake.

"You're right," she said ruefully. "I've been so engrossed in this project that I might have stayed down here until I starved to death. Let's go!"

They climbed the ladder and took seats at the table with Erik and the two old fellows from Alfenstein. This was a bit of a squeeze, but they managed. Diane, at least, was not a large person. Lev, acting as innkeep through the dinner hour, soon brought them sizzling pork chops with steamed carrots and cabbage on the side, and some baked potatoes dripping with butter. The men all appreciated this hearty meal, but Diane found it far too much to eat at a sitting – and after consuming about half of it, she asked Lev for a covered dish so she could take the rest of it away to eat later.

The three conspirators (with Hjaermond and Selden by necessity admitted to the plot and sworn to secrecy, but taking no active role in it) discussed their progress over the meal. Diane had built the enclosure and configured the heating and sanitizing units, installing the power cells that would provide power to draw water through the system. The rest of the assembly would have to wait for the arrival of the pipes and the filtration screen. Next she would build the unit that would provide hot water on demand only (as opposed to the constant maintenance of hot water to be used in the bathing tub) for the house's kitchen sink.

"I should be able to complete that tomorrow, except for the hookups. Your kitchen is in the existing part of the house, right?" Andrion nodded. "If you can get the sink and have a small amount of pipe available, we might want to consider installing it and its hot water unit now, before the addition is completed. Even if it won't be hooked up to the water supply until your tower and cistern are completed – and filled. I'll need to be getting back to Daywatch soon, and I don't think I can wait for the pipes to arrive."

Andrion's brows knit. He hadn't considered that they could hardly keep Diane hanging around the Maiden for days or weeks with nothing to do while waiting for the pieces she had ordered to be fabricated and delivered. She wasn't the sort of person to sit idle, as Hjaermond and Selden seemed content to be. "If you can leave us some very explicit instructions, probably Erik and I between us can finish the assembly. And if not, I suppose that sometime between now and early next month I could come get you again."

Diane considered. "That ought to work fine," she said agreeably. "I can't leave for home in any case until after Bernadette returns from Sylvanian with her map. So I have another day or two to work on things." That problem dealt with, Andrion suggested to Diane she might like to try the bathing pool. All this while, she'd been working toward duplicating the pool's systems in smaller scale; but had not yet had the opportunity to enjoy it herself.

Erik volunteered to help Diane get settled in. They fetched her pack from the basement and a robe from the Maiden's collection, but on searching the sleeping lofts for a bed discovered that every one was occupied. They returned downstairs for a consultation. "It looks like we're out of beds, Andrion," Erik said. "How about if you and I bunk in together in the master bed tonight and I let Diane have my bed in the basement? I get the idea she's going to be spending a lot of time down there in any case," he added with a grin to Diane.

Andrion smiled. "That'll be fine, Erik. Diane, why don't you take your things back down and slip on a robe, then you can get into the pool. I'll join you in a bit." She smiled and thanked them both, the words "Oh no problem, Erik can bunk with *me* in his *own* bed" playing in her imagination. As she made her way to the trap door for the second time in the past few minutes, all that escaped her lips was a sigh. She'd scarcely given a thought to love or carnal urges in years, but something about being here and around these people, especially Erik, seemed to be triggering forgotten longings inside her.

In the basement, Diane stripped down and put on the robe. I wonder if Andrion was being polite when he suggested the bath, she thought, realizing how grubby she was. It was a part of her nature to get so caught up in her work, be it technical hands-on stuff or scholarly investigations, that little details like personal hygiene fell by the wayside. No doubt, she sighed, that's one of the reasons I have no love life.

Diane returned to the common room and found not only Andrion, but Erik and a couple of other men plus another woman she didn't know, all relaxing naked in the pool. Feeling a little ill-at-ease but determined not to show it, she dropped her robe at poolside and stepped gingerly into the water. It was hot, but perfectly so. She took a seat on one of the benches that ran along one side, beside Andrion and across from Erik. Shortly, one of the other men came over to sit on her other side.

Andrion introduced them. "Diane LeBois, this is Georges Baudin, one of my colleagues here at the Maiden. Georges, Diane..." Diane smiled shyly and extended her hand to Georges, who gave her a reassuring grin.

"Welcome to the Maiden, Diane," he said. Mmm, quite a hunk. As Diane had already observed, Erik without his clothes was a veritable god. But Andrion looked almost as good, and this Georges, with his light tan skin, fairly short wavy black hair and gray-green eyes, was even better looking than Andrion as far as her personal preferences were concerned. He seemed friendly, too, though glancing down through the crystalline water she observed he wasn't *that* friendly. At least not at the moment.

Trying to maintain her cool surrounded by hot water and hotter men, Diane leaned back until the water was up to her chin, running her hands over her limbs to wash away the grime of the past few days. She noticed the way in which any soil in the water quickly vanished, sucked down into the grate-covered holes at the bottom of the pool. Cleaned, reheated water came in via ports on the sides. After soaking for a while had relaxed her physically if not mentally or emotionally, she sat up again.

Well, Andrion and Erik were clearly off-limits. Diane shuddered to think what The Fireblood might be capable of doing to any woman who tried to poach on her preserve (which goes to show that she didn't know Bernadette all that well); so she turned her attention to Georges, who looked good enough to eat and appeared to be unattached.

Diane had spent too many years in the wilds by herself, pursuing her fascination with dypalfar technology. She had no idea that her lack of a love life had everything to with a lack of effort on her part, and not with any lack of personal appeal. At age 33 she had a figure that was lithe and trim, an active lifestyle and frequent missed meals (due to her tendency to get lost in her work) taking most of the credit.

Her face was pretty, deep blue-green eyes sparkling with intelligence, bobbed chestnut hair glossy and shimmering with auburn glints when she bothered to wash and comb it. She'd never been married, never even been in a serious relationship and had just about decided, by now, that such things would pass her by forever.

Diane was surprised, therefore, at the interest Georges was showing toward her in turn. "You're Galise, too?" he asked.

"Yes," she admitted. "I left Auverne around eight years ago, pursuing my dypalfar studies. Iscandia has so many fascinating sites! … Um, how about you?" she asked belatedly, trying to get into the swing of conversation with an attractive (she was attempting to ignore the fact, also naked) man. The etiquette associated with the Maiden's clothing-optional policy meant that you were supposed to deal with people as people, and not concern yourself with what they were, or were not, wearing.

Georges looked deep into Diane's eyes and poured out his life story. They talked about her work with dypalfar weaponry, about the recent quest to defeat Lord Karazin (some of which he'd already heard from Andrion, Erik, and Bernadette; but he was happy to get her perspective), about life in general. Andrion and Erik, beginning to get wrinkly, glanced at her and then back at each other and discreetly removed themselves from the pool, going back to their rooms to get dressed. Erik gathered a few things and brought them upstairs, so that he'd be prepared for spending the night in the master bed with Andrion.

Diane's fingertips were deeply wrinkled now, as were Georges'; but neither of them seemed to notice. Her complexion was flushed an attractive shade of light rose from the combination of the long soak in hot water and her stimulating conversation with Georges. Her eyes looked dark, dilated with pleasure and excitement. She hadn't had such an engrossing conversation in years.

Though Georges' interest in dypalfar technology could not match her own, it was a subject on which he had some knowledge. They were both from the same region of Auverne and he was only a year or so younger than her. They might well have passed on a city street and never known they were destined to meet, a decade later, in this pool of hot water in the middle of Iscandia.

Abruptly, Diane realized what her skin had been telling her for some time now. She had been soaking too long! Her eyes had been fixed on Georges' face for the longest time, as they spoke back and forth and reached into each other's souls. Now she wheeled her focus back a bit, taking him *all* in, from the top of his head to his wrinkling toes – and realized that his cock had risen to half-mast. Another look at his eyes confirmed that they were glowing with desire, and her nipples stood pink and rigid despite the heat of the water. She wanted him! But there were still a few people in and around the pool, and how did one go about broaching this subject anyway?

Georges watched Diane's thoughts passing over her face like an animated billboard would look if such things existed in Iscandia. She was a-dork-able! He had long held a secret passion for smart, shy women and this one was all of that and more. He was pretty sure she wanted him as much as he wanted her, and he also had a feeling they'd be sitting in here until they were as shriveled as old Selden, over there at the Owner's Table, unless he made the first move. "Diane?" he said, getting her attention. "Would you like a bed-warmer for the evening?"

Diane looked stricken with embarrassment. "A bed...?"

"It's part of the service we provide at the Maiden," he explained, though he didn't want to scare her away. "We're here to make the customers feel at home, and if there's a mutual attraction, we can join them in bed. Or go off questing with them, for that matter." He waved his amulet. "It's all safe, no risks." Except the risk of losing your heart, Diane thought. But then her second mind riposted, what the hell? I've spent the past several years alone, and I'm not getting any younger. Why shouldn't I have a little pleasure in life that doesn't involve dusty ruins?

Gathering her resolve, Diane replied "I would very much like to have a bed-warmer, Georges. Specifically, you. And if we don't get out of this water soon, I think we're both going to melt." Georges' face lit with delight, and he rose from the water – his member still elongated and stiffening but not *too* impudent for public view.

"My lady?" He offered her his hand and they proceeded up the steps, where he threw a towel around her shoulders before grabbing one for himself. The two of them dried off, then donned their robes and Diane led him toward the bar and the trap door to the basement.

Chapter 62: A Difference of Opinion

At the Owner's Table, Erik and Andrion watched them go with a certain amount of amused satisfaction. As the two disappeared behind the bar they slapped hands in a high-five. "Oh, I think she is going to *enjoy* Georges," Erik said with quiet amusement. They were trying not to involve Hjaermond and Selden, who as usual were watching the passing parade and had not yet retired, in their conversation. Andrion gave his friend a questioning look. "Back before Berni came here," Erik explained, "Georges and I sometimes, uh, did bed-warmer duty for the same customers. He's pretty skilled in that department, from what I heard."

Andrion looked at Erik with an expression of annoyance. He'd never had quite the right attitude for a Maiden guy. It had been all fun and games, for Erik and many of the other men who'd been hired to serve as resident hosts/greeters/bed-warmers/sellswords. And not just for the younger among them – Georges was his own age. For Andrion, sex was pointless unless love was involved, or at least the possibility of it. In a way, he had fallen in love with Berni at first sight – though it had probably taken him as much as 48 hours to realize it.

"What about love, Erik?" he asked, sounding a little wounded. Erik looked perplexed.

"Diane and Georges? Sure, I suppose it could happen. But aren't you getting a little ahead of yourself?" Andrion lightened up a little, though he knew Berni would feel the same way. She was in love, and she wanted the whole world to share the joy.

"Georges is Galise, just like me and Berni. And just like Diane, too. Did you see the way they were talking? They never took their eyes off each other. I'm just saying, it *could* happen. And maybe it *will* happen. So there." He crossed his arms and mugged a scowl, looking up at Erik from under glowering brows. Erik snorted.

"Okay, Mister Romantic. True Love has just blossomed before our eyes and we'll be heading off to another wedding in Daywatch this time next year. Right?" Andrion gave him a tight-lipped smile.

"Right!"

Waxing puckish, Erik continued, "Speaking of True Love, my dear, are you about ready to go to bed?" He gave Andrion a coquettish glance that was utterly incongruous on his powerfully masculine features. Andrion felt like slugging him and laughing at the same time.

"I'll be along in a while, 'my dear.' You go ahead and turn in, if you like."

Erik was looking forward to a busy day tomorrow, and the bath (along with several ales during the evening and half a bottle of wine with dinner) had relaxed him to the point where, barring the presence of his beloved, going to sleep seemed like a good idea. He stood, clapping his friend and soon-to-be co-husband on the shoulder. "See you in bed," he said.

Chapter 63: Breaking Through

Diane led the way down the ladder, to the bedroom that Erik had obligingly donated to her for the night. Georges had been down here quite a few times over the years he had worked at the Maiden, before Erik had claimed it as his personal purview. Erik and Andrion, in their special relationship with the owner, had gotten an edge over the other Maiden employees and were no longer entirely part of the brotherhood. Which, as he thought of it, he realized had now gone co-ed.

During most of Georges' tenure, at least, the Maiden had only employed men. They welcomed customers to the Maiden with camaraderie or flirtation, offered themselves as bed-warmers to those that took their fancy (and by no means had all the Maiden men been straight), and were available as questing companions for any who needed a sword, or a spell, to guard their backs. Sometimes these assignments turned into permanent arrangements and replacements had to be hired. Other times, after the quest was over the companion returned to the Maiden – ready to offer his services to the next customer in need.

These services drew customers to the Maiden like moths to a flame. And since Bernadette (the latest in a long line of fireblood owners) had come into possession, female employees had joined the ranks. Some of these were mages or swordmaidens, prepared to take service as questing companions as well as sharing the beds of customers who caught their eyes (again, male or female). Others did more mundane duty as serving maids, cleaning staff, cooks, and laundresses. Now, at 32, Georges was beginning to feel as if it might be time for him to consider a future beyond the Maiden. Most young men who came to work here saw it as a great opportunity, a chance to meet a wealthy patron or just to have some fun for a few years. But it was not something you did for life.

All these thoughts passed through his mind in an instant, on a parallel channel from the one that had been completely taken over by his libido. Diane was beautiful and entrancing, and the vulnerability he sensed from her only made him hunger for her more, even as it also filled him with a desire to shelter her from whatever she thought was threatening her. She was strong, intelligent, yet somehow unable to cope with certain aspects of the world.

Diane was very nearly trembling as her bare feet hit the floor at the foot of the ladder and she led Georges around the foot of the bed. I ought to have had more to drink with dinner, she thought. She had drunk a glass of wine or two washing down what little of that enormous meal she had been able to eat; but that was hours ago and she was now stone cold sober, aroused, confused, and fearful that she had somehow forgotten how to make love. It had been a long time.

Georges stepped to her at the foot of the bed and took her in his arms, gently. They were not that far apart in height, and kissing her was easy – and very pleasant. From their conversation he knew she had been a long time without, and he approached her as one might a wild fawn in the forest. Gently, carefully, no sudden moves. The kissing went from soft and tender to increasing passion in a few short moments, and he ran his hands over her body beneath the robe.

Diane broke away from the kiss with a gasp, her breast heaving. She looked up into his light eyes and saw them dilated with desire – and behind the desire, patience and concern and kindness. Oh, yes. More than a handsome man or one with a magnificent physique and a big stiff cock, what she needed was a man with a fund of patience and kindness. She reached for his shoulder and slipped the robe open, causing it to fall to the floor, then gazed at him. It looked like she might have hit the jackpot.

Georges resumed kissing her with increased fervor, pushing her own robe off her shoulders to fall on the floor. He put his hands on her breasts, which were a nice size – not too big, perfectly formed – and thumbed her nipples to attention as he continued to claim her mouth with his. Soon they were both gasping and panting. Diane reached down to him, a few things beginning to come back to her from encounters in the past, and gripped his rigid cock where it thrust up between them. It was hot to the touch, smooth-skinned, and pulsing slightly. Ooh. She could not actually remember the last time she'd had such a fine thing in her hand.

Georges moaned slightly when she grasped him, and gently pushed her back until her knees hit the end of the bed and she sat. Then he knelt before her, taking her breasts in both hands while he tongued and suckled her nipples, before continuing on down her body. Her legs were spread to allow him this close, and he now spread them further as he stroked her inner thighs, pushing them apart so he could get to her slit with his tongue.

Diane gasped as he applied his mouth to her sex, her fingers knotting in the somewhat stiff bush of slightly waving black hair atop his head as she urged him to dive deeper. She had almost forgotten what that sensation could be like. As he worked with his mouth and tongue, Georges stroked her thighs and belly, gentle teasing strokes that sent ripples of sensation across her skin. She had felt so anxious taking him to her bed, even after the connection they had made earlier. But she began to feel herself letting go, letting the feelings rise, letting… Oh, by the gods, yes!

Diane fell back on the bed and arched her back, the first orgasm she had had in months (well yeah, there had been some solo ventures…) surging over her. Georges was pleased, but slightly taken aback at the ferocity of her response. How long had it *been*? Diane remained quivering for a few moments, a flood of juices teasing Georges' tongue as her climax lingered on. Then finally she lay quiescent, breathing in gasps.

Georges wiped his mouth on his arm. Some women were more fastidious than others, and he didn't want to offend her by bringing her own cunt juices to her mouth on his as he moved up the bed to kiss her again. She didn't appear to notice one way or the other, as she attacked him hungrily. It seemed that the dam had burst, and there was no stopping the floodwaters now. "Georges!" she gasped between kisses, "Georges! I want you…" gasp… "inside me…" gasp… "*now!*"

Oh. All right, then. His cock was stiff as a sword, quivering with eagerness, and he eased it inside her. As wet as she was after his tonguing and her orgasm, there was no problem whatsoever getting in. She was still lying at the edge of the bed, but he could not both kneel on the floor to enter her and smother her with kisses as he very much wanted to do; so he grasped her around the hips and lifted her bodily, using his powerfully muscled arms to move her up the bed until he could kneel on it while pressing his upper body to hers, mouth to mouth.

Diane's mind blazed with passion as Georges moved inside her. Oh! All of the hunger that had gone unfulfilled these past few years, all of the lonely nights, that whole side of her nature that she had blithely ignored as she tried to make her intellectual pursuits the sum total of her being, rose up like a savage beast, demanding to be fed. And he answered her thrust for thrust, filling her up.

In a while they collapsed on Erik's coverlet, entwined and panting. Diane hugged him tight around the neck, her eyes closed, as his still-throbbing cock filled her. He kissed her eyelids, her neck, brought her hand up to kiss her fingertips. "Diane," he murmured, "that was amazing…" She'd second that, if she could speak. By the gods, what had come over her? And into her? She had not met a man who attracted her so strongly since once during her teen years in Auverne, and that had been only an adolescent crush.

As swept away as she was by emotion, Diane's mind would not rest and she soon found herself analyzing the encounter. Was this just a chance joining, a one-shot? The connection she'd felt while they were talking in the bathing pool said there was so much more they could do together. But had he felt it too? For the moment, she felt she was not ready to face knowing the answer to that question. Much better just to float in the moment, enjoying whatever it was while it lasted, however long – or short –that might be.

Chapter 64: Sylvanian Again

As she'd feared would be the case, Bernadette materialized inside the gates of Sylvanian in pitch darkness. A light rain was falling, and she made a dash for the Dancing Rabbit. Her first order of business was learning the time, so that she would know how much extra time to allow for trips here in the future. Severus Vinius was behind the bar, as usual. She had been here numerous times since first arriving in Iscandia, and he had only rarely been absent no matter what the time of day.

"Hello, Severus," she said with a wry grin.

"Fireblood! How kind of you to grace us with your presence," the Reman replied. From anyone else that would sound snarky, but Bernadette knew he really meant it.

"Do you happen to know the time?" she asked him. He checked for her. Palaces and inns were the two places in Iscandia you could usually find a clock – rarely elsewhere. "It's a bit past midnight," Severus informed her. "Say, 12:15." Almost exactly eleven hours, she thought, confirming her earlier guess. Not bad... and not good, either. A pity fast-traveling wasn't as instant as it seemed.

"I'd like a small bottle of wine and a wedge of cheddar cheese brought to my table," she said beckoning toward a small table over against the wall. "And I'll be needing a room in a while. But I'm not ready to go to bed yet." He nodded cheerfully and Bernadette made her way over to the table she'd indicated, sighing slightly. She missed Andrion, she missed Erik, and she wished to hell she could just conclude her business here right now and go home, already. She was sure the men and Diane must be back from their dypalfar expedition by now.

Severus hurried right over with the wine and cheese and she paid him. "Your usual room all right, Miss?" By this, she knew he meant the one where she and Erik had spent a remarkably exciting night on her first visit to this establishment several months before. It was large and comfortable, and she had often slept in it when visiting Sylvanian overnight.

Bernadette nodded to Severus, acknowledging that his choice of the room was satisfactory. Then she sat sipping her wine and nibbling at the excellent cheese, lost in her thoughts. When she'd visited this city for the first time with Andrion and Lifa, stepping aside from their quest to deliver the Staff of Zauber to the Old Ones, she'd been dazzled and excited by the size and splendor of the place. Now, familiarity had worn away much of the excitement and she realized she didn't really want to live here. Not now, and certainly not after she and her loves were married. But here was where the wedding would take place, and she had several chores to perform.

The inn was sparsely populated this late, most customers having gone home or retired to their beds here; but to discourage any unwanted attention she pulled out her journal and sat reading (perhaps "deciphering" would be a more accurate term) her past adventures. I ought to write this up and publish it as a book, she realized, remembering her concern that the deeds she and her companions had performed were already receding into legend. Of course she had absolutely no idea how to go about doing that. Perhaps a consultation with someone from Remus might shed light on the subject.

The wine and cheese finished, Bernadette arose feeling fairly well buzzed. She'd hoped that the snack and alcohol would work to make her sleepy, enabling her to drop off in her inn bed and catch a few hours' sleep at what felt like three or four in the afternoon, in terms of what time she'd arisen this morning. There was not much else she could do but sleep, until the stores opened in the morning. She swung by the bar to collect her key from Severus, then made her way up the stairs, yawning.

In the morning, Bernadette awoke feeling a bit the worse for wear. Maybe drinking half a bottle of wine on a nearly empty stomach wasn't the best sleep aid possible. Bleah. However, a few seconds with her healing spell soon put things to rights. Between potions and these spells, it was a wonder anybody in Iscandia ever endured a day's sickness or died of anything besides sudden trauma or extreme old age.

Shouldering her pack, Bernadette descended the stairs and sat at the bar eating a couple of delicious, warm pastries washed down with hot unsweetened tea. The astringent tea cut the sugariness of the pastries nicely. Then she thanked Severus, told him she'd see him next time, and sauntered across the road to The Golden Thread.

Senalie greeted her with what, in a member of the ljosalfar race, passed for extreme friendliness. Bernadette was, after all, a VIP as well as a client prepared to part with plenty of cash. By making high-profile clothing such as The Fireblood's wedding gown, Senalie had found herself besieged with requests from the high and mighty of Sylvanian for expensive clothing that was rapidly making her, and her sister, wealthy.

Bernadette was ushered right back into the rear of the shop, where a magnificent wedding gown in a traditional style stood displayed on an extremely buxom mannequin. The fabric shimmered, the cut was designed to flatter the goddess-like curves of the mannequin's hourglass figure, and accents of ribbon and lace were strategically placed to provide the gown with more modesty than it seemed at first glance to possess.

Bernadette's eyes lit. This could only be Lifa's wedding gown, and it was just what she had envisioned. Lifa was going to *love* this! It might well turn into an heirloom of her house, worn by daughters and granddaughters for generations to come on that one special day of their lives – provided the body shape bred true, of course... "Senalie, this is wonderful!" she said, her sincerity shining through and bringing a faint blush of pleasure to the elf woman's cheeks.

"I've prepared a muslin bag for you to carry it in, so that it won't get soiled or wrinkled," Senalie said, her usual cool, businesslike demeanor reasserting itself. "And now, for your own dress..." She pulled out the drawing that she had begun when Bernadette was here some time ago. It was now finished. The pencil lines had been replaced with ink, and the drawing was alive with color. There was Bernadette, looking remarkably radiant with her auburn hair piled atop her head, her blue-gray eyes seeming to glow with happiness, her skin pinkish where it showed – which was not all that much. The arms were mostly bare, but other than that the dress flowed in multi-colored streamers from her neck to the ground.

Bernadette was captivated by the image. To see one's imagination brought to life on the page was an amazing thing, a kind of magic they didn't teach at the Academy in Eisenstag. There was one thing that seemed a little off, though it enhanced the overall appearance and emphasized the gown's vertical flow... "I'm not that tall, am I?" she asked, perplexed. The rest of the drawing was so exact that it seemed odd for this exaggeration to have crept in.

Senalie smiled at her, an expression that made Bernadette realize for almost the first time that the elf woman could be lovely. "Ah, but you *will* be!" she said, and produced from under the counter the most curious-looking pair of shoes that Bernadette had ever seen. Throughout Bernadette's life shoes had been practical things. They protected your feet from dirt and rocks, ice and snow and sharp objects, perhaps supported your ankles to help prevent sprains and gave you extra traction on slippery surfaces. A nice pair of leather boots could be quite handsome, and a soft pair of velvet slippers was pretty enough below a gown, provided you weren't planning on leaving the house. But these!

They appeared to be made out of leather, but the leather was bright red. They were sandals of a sort, not a common style this far north, with soles of wood and laminated leather, and straps to hold the shoes to the foot. But the most amazing thing about them was their height. The part of the shoe that went around the ball of the foot was elevated on a wooden platform more than an inch tall, and the rest of the shoe curved up from there, with a wooden heel less than half an inch in diameter but four or more inches in height protruding downward like a spike. Red leather ankle straps helped to assure that the shoes would stay on your feet, but it would be like walking on tiptoe – permanently!

What an absurd concoction. Totally impractical. But… somehow, the shoes beckoned to her. Senalie was taking in her reaction. Bernadette wasn't the first pretty young adventuress she'd met, and she had an instinct for these things. "They're not for running or fighting in, yes? But I think you'll find that the extra height will make you look utterly magnificent in your wedding gown. And your husbands? They'll go crazy for these."

Bernadette blinked. Damn, they were impossible! But they were so sexy-looking. Andrion was 8 inches taller than she was, Erik nearly a foot. Raising her height by four inches wouldn't put her in danger of looking either of them in the eyes, even. "Go ahead," Senalie urged. "Try them on. Take off your skirt, so you can see what they do for your legs."

Somewhat reluctantly, Bernadette peeled off her skirt and the leather boots she was wearing underneath it. Now in her underdrawers, she sat on an upholstered chair and slipped her feet into the shoes. They were a good fit, as if Senalie had expertly measured her feet when she was not looking. Perhaps that was the case. Her toes slipped down into the web of strapping at the front of the shoes, her neatly trimmed and clean but quite plain-looking toenails peeping out. Her feet were bent into a remarkable curve as she fastened the ankle straps, which were held together by tiny brass buckles.

Now she had them on, Bernadette gazed down at her feet encased in these ridiculous fripperies of strappy red leather. Her feet were arched, her toes pointed, and she had to admit that they looked, if anything, even sexier on her feet than they had looked sitting on the counter. But what was it going to be like standing in them, let alone walking? Well, nothing for it but to try.

She drew herself up onto her feet, mostly just poised on her toes and not trying to put her full weight on the heels. They were possibly a little more comfortable than she'd expected, the footbeds deeply cushioned. The straps didn't cut into her feet as much as she'd feared, either. "Here," Senalie said, pulling aside a length of silken cloth that was hanging from the ceiling to reveal a full-length mirror. Ooh, Bernadette thought, I want one of those. The surface was of polished silver, probably a thin coating over a baser metal and varnished after polishing to prevent tarnishing.

Looking at her reflection, Bernadette twisted and turned in place. The posture her body was thrown into by the tip-toe posture the shoes forced on her did remarkable things to her silhouette. Her legs, which were lithe and muscular, seemed more curvy. Her butt protruded a bit more, her back slightly arched to compensate for the displacement of her weight. And she was so *tall*! The floor looked a *long* way down compared to what she was used to seeing.

This wasn't too painful, but what about walking? She took a few steps, putting her weight on the heels for the first time. There was a bit of wobble, and Bernadette could tell that twisting an ankle was a real hazard if you didn't pay attention to what you were doing. But she was an athlete, strong from head to toe, and it was easy enough to keep her balance. Those heels were broad enough to provide support if you kept your weight in a straight line from hip down the length of the leg to the floor, envisioning the shoe and its four-inch heel as only an extension of your leg bone.

After a few tentative steps Bernadette was strutting around the small fitting room, admiring herself in the mirror, and grinning from ear to ear. "*Yes*, Senalie! This is genius!" she exclaimed. "I don't think I'm going to be wearing these on my next expedition to kill dragons, but I am *definitely* wearing these to my wedding! And probably for the wedding night… at least the start of it, anyway." Senalie smiled back at her. She'd known it.

"Excellent," she said. "And the dress? You approve?"

"The dress looks just like I envisioned it," Bernadette said. "And the construction? It'll peel down without a lot of effort?" Senalie produced a handful of brightly colored, silken tongues of fabric. In a few moments she had draped several of these around Bernadette's body. She was still wearing a blouse above so the fit was not right, but she could see how they attached, and more importantly, detached. Still wearing the high-heeled sandals, Bernadette did a little pirouette and plucked a length of fabric off, waving it around her head in a hypnotic swirl of color before letting it fall to the floor. She was careful not to step on it.

"Perfect!" Bernadette declared, her delight shining for all to see. Then she reverted to a more serious mode. "Let's see, I guess I'm going to have to be here by mid-morning a month from today so you can build the dress onto my body. I can't imagine being able to put it on by myself. I'll show up with my hair done and soft shoes, and if you can provide one of those muslin bags for the, uh, 'take me' shoes, I can carry them down to the temple with me and put them on before the ceremony."

Senalie considered this request. "If you want me to match the dress to the extra height, you're going to need to wear the shoes or else part of the dress will be dragging on the ground," she pointed out. Bernadette thought about it. She had very specific plans for the dress, but could not be sure that she wouldn't find herself required to do walking that would not be wise in those shoes.

"Better take the dress up a little then," she said. "Make it hang to ankle length, and that way I can show off the shoes – when I'm wearing them. And if I'm not, it won't be a problem."

Pleased with her customer's sensible approach, Senalie nodded. She whipped out a tape measure and confirmed the distance between Bernadette's shoulder and her ankle. Then she produced the muslin bag she had mentioned, and slipped it over the top of Lifa's wedding gown after inserting a curious sort of metal contraption into the gown's neck. It seemed to support the shoulders and rise in a shallow triangle to a hook maybe two inches in diameter, situated at the dress's center line. A hole at the top of the bag allowed the hook to protrude, giving Bernadette something to carry it by. This was just the sort of thing she'd been thinking about, a few weeks back!

"I'll need to come by and pick this up on my way out of town," Bernadette told Senalie. "I have a few more errands to run, and this is far too bulky to be carrying around. But here's the additional payment I owe you." She slipped Senalie a substantial tip on top of the agreed-upon price. The work had been excellent. "I'll be back as soon as I conclude the rest of my business here," she promised, getting out of the sexy shoes and into her soft boots and skirt.

Leaving the shop, Bernadette forged up Sylvanian's main street with a will. Occasionally greeting familiar faces without stopping to talk, she cut to the left on the far side of the wall dividing the city's western section from the upper-class district beyond it. Shortly, she fetched up at the entrance to the famous Bards' Academy.

Throughout her time in Iscandia, Bernadette had heard this place mentioned over and over again – almost as much as the Mages' Academy in Eisenstag. She had visited both, but had no great ambitions toward a career as either a bard or a mage. Why would she need to spend years studying magic, with Andrion by her side? Well, there was that "instant hot bathing pool" notion; but she held out hopes that at some future date she might get *him* to take on the project, and save her the trouble.

But she now had specific business at the Bards' Academy that had nothing to do with enrolling as a student. Entering the spacious quarters, Bernadette sought out and soon found Augustin, the headmaster. They had met a few times previously, and he greeted her with respect. "How can I help you, Fireblood?" he asked. She smiled at him. "I have a commission for you," she replied, cutting to the heart of the matter with her usual directness.

He looked at her questioningly. "I'm in need of a small musical group," Bernadette explained. "I'm throwing a party near Waterdon on the eighteenth of this month, and another one on the eleventh of next month. There should be three or four musicians including some kind of percussion and a good singer, and they should be able to perform all the standards as well as music we can dance to. I'll pay for coach fare for them both ways each time, and put them up and feed them while they are at my inn, in addition to your fee."

Augustin's demeanor brightened at this news. Like most people in Iscandia who hadn't been living in a cave for the past six months, he was aware of The Fireblood's fame and assumed that she must be fabulously rich due to the services she had performed. Actually, Bernadette's wealth was almost entirely due to hard work, though of course there had been some treasure gathered during her various quests – most of them performed at the behest of one eorl or another, and of course aided by her valiant companions. Whatever the source, rich they were – and she was delighted to spend some of that wealth in the cause of throwing a couple of parties that people in the Waterdon area would not soon forget.

Bernadette respected Augustin's judgment as to the actual personnel, and left him with a large sum of money and instructions that the musicians should present themselves at the doors to the Bathing Maiden no later than five o'clock in the evening on the seventeenth. Likely she and the rest of Lifa and Bjorn's wedding party would not be there at that hour, caught in the interstices of time as they fast-traveled back from Lakedon; but Lev and Drelos would be there to take them in. She was beginning to think they might need to run off the triceratops and other local monsters and pitch a large tent in the field to north of the Maiden, to create sleeping arrangements for all the extra people.

Resuming her brisk pace, Bernadette surged up the road toward the eorl's palace, passing the palatial homes of Sylvanian's elite along the way. Climbing the stairs to Eorl Bergen's throne room, Bernadette found the ordinary-looking, middle-aged fellow on his throne and his faithful steward Rudiger standing by, as usual. The eorl's beautiful wife Odwyna, who looked young enough to be his daughter, sat in a smaller throne at his side. There was more to her than her looks, and she participated in the ruling of the march despite her youth.

Formal greetings were exchanged, after which Bernadette smiled at Bergen. "I bring good tidings," Bernadette said. Bergen's face took on a look of polite interest, mirrored on the face of Odwyna. "Engbard at the Pantheatos here in Sylvanian has agreed to perform the marriage ceremony for me and my two betrothed," Bernadette stated baldly. "It's to be at one in the afternoon on the tenth of Fevrous, and it would honor us greatly were you and your steward to attend." The eorl blinked. A written invitation was much more customary, and what was this about "two betrothed"?

Bernadette pulled a folded piece of paper out of her pouch, handing it to Bergen. "Here is the official invitation," she told him. In fact it was the only written invitation she'd produced. She and her fiancés wanted to have a big party with as many of their friends as possible in attendance on the eighteenth, but they'd be having only a few people at the actual ceremony. Had any of them had family they were in regular touch with, these would have come; but the three of them were orphans of circumstance.

Bernadette didn't care to stand there in front of Bergen's court trying to explain the details of her unorthodox marriage. The invitation laid out the details quite clearly, and she felt it was up to Bergen to decide whether he wished to give his unofficial blessing to the proceedings by standing by as the three were wed. He passed the invitation to Odwyna, who broke the seal and scanned the parchment. As she read, an expression of delighted disbelief came over her pretty face.

Bernadette stood there for perhaps a minute, her carriage erect and her head held high, as Odwyna read. It was just a courtesy, she was telling herself, because they were marrying in Sylvanian, to invite the ruler of that city and the march of which it was the capital. It didn't matter to her in the least whether the eorl approved of their arrangements. She was The Fireblood, and she and the men she loved could bloody well do whatever they wanted…

"Bernadette!" Odwyna interrupted her internal dialog. "Congratulations, this is wonderful news. Bergen and I, and Rudiger as well, will be honored to witness your vows. Will there, um, be some sort of party afterward?" Bernadette swallowed, schooling her face to avoid broadcasting the relief she felt to the entire court.

"We're having a gathering near Waterdon on the following day," she explained, "at my inn. The fastest we can return after the ceremony would put us there in the middle of the night, so the celebration will be from around two p.m. until whenever on the eighteenth."

"That sounds delightful!" Odwyna said, looking at Bernadette expectantly. Oh.

"If you would like to attend, I could include you in my group as we fast-travel back to the Bathing Maiden. I can't guarantee the quality of the overnight accommodations, but possibly you and your people could stay with Eorl Ormund at Wyrmshalla?"

Odwyna considered for a moment. "That's a good idea, actually," she said. "Could you deliver a letter to Ormund for us, if you're going back soon? But we won't need you to carry us to Waterdon. I have my own magic map." Not surprising, Bernadette thought. The high and mighty would need to get around without having to slog, on foot or by coach, through miles of bandit-and-bear-infested territory.

All of this caused Bernadette to realize that she had probably better run up another invitation and formally invite Ormund to her own nuptials. She'd already arranged his attendance at the wedding of Lifa and Bjorn, but he *was* the political boss of the entire march in which she'd decided to make her home. It would only be polite. Meanwhile, Bergen had called for parchment and a pen and had quickly written a note to which he affixed his official seal. "We look forward to seeing you on the seventeenth of Fevrous, Bernadette," he said, handing over the note. Bernadette bowed and smiled, and made her exit.

Bernadette realized as she descended the stairs that her heart was pounding. Was she *ever* going to get used to rubbing elbows with the powerful – and learn to converse with them without putting her foot in her mouth? Shrugging it off, she continued down the stairs and out into the courtyard that fronted the eorl's palace. She needed to pick up Lifa's dress, so she'd have to walk all the way back down to the gates. But there was one more thing she felt she ought to do while she was here.

So, Bernadette continued up the hill and through the stone gates of Castle Grey, the Reman military headquarters for all of Iscandia. She had not been here since her brief visit with Erik, the day before her infiltration of the Ljosalfar Consulate. At that time she'd declined the offer to join the Imperial Army, speaking briefly with General Vadrian, the commander.

Bernadette passed through the ranks of Reman guards, some few of whom recognized her, and entered General Vadrian's headquarters. Though outright civil war had not broken out with the Norse partisans, he and his troops were actively involved in strategy and espionage. She was not surprised to find him pacing around the room, in the center of which stood a strategic map of the province. Military minds didn't know any other way to act.

Vadrian recognized her as well. "Fireblood," he said shortly, according her a modicum of respect. Bernadette nodded curtly and murmured, "General Vadrian." She intended to match him cool for cool. She shortly broached the reason for her visit, and the general was not as hostile as she'd feared he might be. She hadn't had many expectations of this effort, but after a half-hour discussion the two of them had reached an agreement. She left him with a sincere smile and a firm handshake, surprised to get the same in return, and hurried on her way to The Golden Thread.

Bernadette collected the magnificent wedding gown and draped it, in its protective cover, over one arm as she pulled out her map and wished herself back to the Maiden. If wishing had been all it would take, she'd have been there hours ago.

Chapter 65: The Conspiracy Proceeds

Diane woke drowsily, wrapped in Georges' arms. Her eyes opened and she recalled where she was, and all that had happened here since last night. They'd made love a second time, with less ferocious heat but with glorious pleasure, before falling asleep. Evidently he was not asleep now; for as soon as she stirred he held her tighter and nuzzled into her shoulder, kissing her neck. She smiled, then stretched and rolled over in his arms so that she was facing him. "Good morning," she murmured.

Diane wrapped her arms around Georges' neck and locked her lips on his, closing her eyes. This felt so wonderful! She hadn't awakened with a man in her bed in so long, yet it somehow felt right. Her mind wanted to discuss the likelihood that he'd soon be up and on his way, never to share her bed again, but she drove those thoughts away with a will. Live for the moment!

His stiffened member was pressed against her belly as they embraced, warm and throbbing. She reached down with one hand and guided him inside her, then pushed the covers down and away so she could lift her leg up over his hip and let him thrust all the way in. Oh, yesss! Georges was delighted. Much as he was drawn to geeky girls, they were sometimes a bit repressed in the sack. But Diane was proving to be a veritable smilodon once she'd gotten past her early hesitation. How had this passionate woman managed to suppress her desires all those years?

Her passion inflamed his own, and they rolled and writhed, gasped and moaned their way to an explosive mutual climax. As they lay there breathing heavily, still entwined and slippery with sweat, Georges said softly, "How about a bath before breakfast?" Diane smiled, gazing into his eyes.

"That would be wonderful," she replied.

As they sat soaking, alone in the pool at this hour, they talked quietly. "Today I need to build the on-demand hot water system for Erik and Andrion's kitchen," Diane told him. Georges, along with most of the Maiden personnel, was in on the surprise they were plotting.

"Do you need any help?" he asked. Unless they'd been invited along on a quest, the men of the Maiden (excepting Lev and Drelos, who had innkeeper duties) rarely got to put their hands to anything useful.

Diane looked at him appraisingly. "Do you know anything about plumbing?" she asked. He nodded slightly.

"A bit. Before I came here I spent some time on a builder's crew, and there was some pipe work involved. I know the basics." She grinned at him.

"Excellent! And it's clear you're plenty strong enough," she added, squeezing his wet bicep. "I hope to get the basic assembly done and then take the unit over to the building site up the road. It needs to be out of sight before Bernadette gets back."

A shadow passed over Georges' handsome face at the mention of Bernadette's return. "You're going right back to Daywatch after she gets back?" he asked. Diane looked a little surprised.

"Well, yes... I have responsibilities there. Besides, I'm eager to start working out how to build a pool like this there. I think the Daywatch Brigade could really benefit from it – and it might help us get more recruits." She subsided, thinking how much *less* eager she was to return to Daywatch now that it meant leaving her new-found lover behind.

Feeling uncharacteristically unsure of himself, Georges ventured "Uh, I was hoping you might want me to share your bed again tonight..." The expression of pure joy on Diane's face relieved any fears he might have had of rejection. This expression passed in a moment, to be replaced by one of happy inspiration.

"Georges, did you tell me last night that Maiden guests can invite the employees out on quests?" Hoping but not quite willing to assume, he smiled and nodded. "How would you like to join the Daywatch Brigade?"

He turned to her and embraced her, planting a deep kiss on her lips. "I'll follow you wherever you want to go. I'm good with a bow, so I think I should be able to easily pick up using your Daywatch crossbows."

She returned his hug and kiss, her heart singing with elation though all she said was "It's settled then. When I go back to Daywatch tomorrow, you're coming along!"

They exited the pool and were sitting in their robes at the bar devouring smoked sausage and scrambled eggs when Erik and Andrion came down the stairs. "I do *not* snore," Andrion insisted, apparently continuing a discussion that had begun in the master bedroom. "You're the one who snores. You sound like a walrus in heat." Erik grinned at the mental imagery. He'd only been teasing, well a little. Andrion did snore, but it wasn't that hard to sleep through. The two of them had passed a somewhat uncomfortable night, each wishing the other were Berni.

The two men stopped by the bar, greeting Diane and Georges. They made note of the companionable way in which the pair sat eating their breakfast. "Hey, that looks good," Erik told Drelos. "How about you bring about three times that amount over to our table, and maybe some tea."

The elf nodded, saying "Be right with you." The increased business at the Maiden was keeping him and Lev on the jump, and he was hoping they would soon be able to hire some more staff. Finding local people was tough, and hiring travelers left you short another bed.

After finishing their breakfast Diane and Georges waved to the men at the table, then walked behind the bar and climbed down into the basement. When Erik and Andrion had finished eating, they joined them. They found Diane and Georges working together, pounding dypalfar metal into sheets. Andrion walked over and checked the shelves, and was pleased to see that there were two dozen dypalfar ingots on the shelf. Lev had a supplier who came through with a cart at intervals, restocking as needed.

A small stack of burlap sacks of the type used for potatoes or other produce was lying on a bottom shelf, and Erik grabbed a couple of these and handed them to Andrion. They loaded the requisite number of ingots into the sacks and then each hefted one and headed for the ladder to the rear deck. "We're dropping these off with Hegmar so he can get your pipes and screen made," Erik told Diane. "See you down at the site later?"

"Georges is helping me construct the kitchen water heater unit," Diane explained. "That should speed things up a bit. I hope to be hauling it down there by sometime after lunch. Don't want it to be sitting on the floor here when Bernadette gets home!"

"Right," Erik grinned. "See you guys later then. We'll probably be back for lunch, and maybe we can give you a hand carrying it."

Erik and Andrion strolled on down the road toward Coldburn Farm, lugging their metallic burdens. "I told you, Erik!" Andrion said, smiling in satisfaction. He seemed to have gone completely over into Bernadette's camp when it came to rooting for every worthy individual being paired with a love-mate. As he realized this, he only smiled more. Yes, everyone deserved love. And if he and his own beloved could further the cause of helping them to find it, was that not to be applauded?

Erik remained a bit more cynical. It had taken Bernadette herself to shake him out of his hedonistic attitude toward love, and he wasn't convinced that Georges had reached that point yet. Sure, sooner or later Love was probably going to get its teeth into you; but that didn't mean every strong attraction had the potential to develop into a lifelong relationship. "We'll see," he grinned back.

The two arrived at Coldburn Farm, and were astonished at the progress that had taken place just since they had last seen it, near closing time yesterday evening. Did these people get up at four in the morning and eat breakfast so they'd be ready to raise tools as soon as the sun made it light enough to see? In point of fact these two had been spoiled by their recent careers as "hospitality specialists" at the Maiden.

Erik's idea of an early morning was eating breakfast maybe an hour after sunrise, while Andrion would cheerfully have arisen sometime after ten. His recent earlier risings were entirely due to Bernadette's influence, and neither he nor Erik had ever held a job as a construction worker – where the hours of daylight were your most important resource.

In any case, they found the construction site aswarm with workers all busily building. The floor joists of the addition were all laid now, supported by beams running the length of it which were supported in their turn by uprights set onto the stone floor of the basement. Flat boards had now been laid above those joists, and sections of wall were being constructed by several teams before being nailed in place. Some of these wall sections had door and/or window openings framed into them. In addition, floorboards were swiftly providing a roof for the empty space below.

Andrion and Erik stood for a moment, taking in the project. For Andrion, it was almost like performing a magic spell more powerful than any he had ever learned. You wave a bag of money in the right direction, and a myriad of industrious, skilled workers spring up and turn your thoughts into reality. Magic, indeed. Erik, for his part, was studying the scene and trying to make sense of exactly what was going on. This was an activity that had enormous value, that spelled the future of Iscandia, and he wanted to master the skills involved. Or at least, understand them.

Their eyes wandering, they both spotted Hegmar at the same moment. He was standing in the upper yard, answering a question from a crew foreman who was working on the construction of the tower on which the house's cistern would sit. "There he is," Andrion said, pointing. He and Erik stepped around the house and made their way up the slope to the little Norse builder.

He saw them coming from a long way off, dealing with the discussion at hand and then standing, waiting, as they approached. "Got my dypalfar ingots, have you?" he asked, not one to mince words.

"Oh aye," Erik said, poking mild fun at Hegmar's on-again, off-again accent. He and Andrion unshouldered their sacks, spilling the ingots out onto the ground.

"That'll do," Hegmar said. He'd had no doubt they would come through. He stood and waved a hand to a worker mounted on horseback some distance away, who'd been waiting while other workers loaded his saddlebags.

The loading finished, the man spurred his horse in their direction. "I'm about ready to leave," he told Hegmar.

"One more thing, Samir," the builder told him. The rider was a burly, fairly light-skinned Afran with curiously light-colored eyes. He reminded Andrion of Malden somewhat, though younger of course. Andrion and Erik helped load the ingots into the horse's saddlebags, in which there was yet plenty of room. The horses of

Iscandia were large and sturdy beasts, capable of a surprising turn of speed considering their massive builds.

With the last ingot loaded and the detailed instructions handed over, Hegmar waved Samir away. "Off you go then," he said. "Bring back whatever he's got ready, and I'll expect to see you back here in a few hours." The trip to Forestville was no more than a couple of hours on horseback, provided you didn't have to stop to fight off bandits or kill smilodons. Hegmar turned to his two clients, as Samir galloped off into the distance heading south. "Should have your pipe in a few days, then," he said. "Are you here to help today, or just lookin'?"

"I'm ready to help," Erik rumbled. He wanted as much hands-on experience as he could get. Not only was he learning new skills, it made the project seem more real to him. It was a labor of love, creating the home where he and his beloved and his closest friend on Terris would make a life together. Without his personal involvement, it was all at a remove. So he relished the chance to make real contributions.

"Go report to Berthold over there, then" the builder said, pointing to a tall middle-aged Norseman who was clearly a foreman of some sort. Erik grinned at him and headed that way, ready to offer his services. What he lacked in experience he made up for with enormous physical strength and an aptitude for quickly learning mechanical tasks.

Hegmar now turned to Andrion. "How about you, then?" he asked bluntly. He didn't have a great deal of patience for kibitzers, even if they *were* paying the rent.

"Our associates are working on the kitchen hot water system now," Andrion told him. "I'd like to focus my efforts on that, since the kitchen is part of the existing house." He was anxious to tackle the bathing pool, but that long-anticipated key piece of the addition was still just lines on paper – suspended, as it were, in the air where the floor of the new annex would shortly be formed.

"Go to it," Hegmar responded shortly. He was glad to see Andrion occupied with something, and could only hope that he wouldn't be getting too much in the way of his crew. He frankly preferred jobs where the owners spent their time in banquets and debauchery and didn't bother to show up at the site until the final touches had been applied to the interior trim. Ah, well.

Work proceeded apace, and by lunchtime the floorboards of the annex had been completely laid across the joists. They would need sanding and polishing, but this would have to wait until the outer walls and roof had been put into place. Inner walls would come still later, but their locations were already marked.

An opening through the floor in the bathroom area had been framed in where the bathing tub would lie. Many sections of the outer walls had been constructed and nailed to the sill plates, so that the addition was beginning to take on a certain skeletal reality. Andrion had supervised the construction of the framework that would support the kitchen sink, strategically positioned near an opening in the outer wall where pipe from the cistern would run into the house, and drain water pass back out on its way to the septic tank.

Erik and Andrion broke from their work not long past noon, as the site workers mostly downed tools and produced lunches from sacks – bread and cheese, fruit, bottles of ale and so forth. They were luckier, able to stroll the quarter mile up the road and lunch on hot food at the Maiden. They walked in to find Diane and Georges seated at the Owner's Table, chowing down on plates of food that looked utterly fantastic.

Brushing dust from their clothes (an activity that might more appropriately have been performed before they entered the building), the two budding builders took seats at the table and motioned to Lev, who was running around like a chicken with its head cut off. A couple of the Maiden's new and lovely young female employees also appeared to be engaged in taking lunch orders. There must be more than the usual number of people back in the kitchen cooking!

Despite his harried aspect, Lev seemed elated. "The new special is selling like crazy!" he announced with manic enthusiasm as he came over to the table. "You want some?"

"Uh, what is it?" Andrion had to ask.

"Minced beef, cooked on a grill over the coals, slice of cheese and some lettuce and tomato, on one of these new round rolls we're making," Lev gasped, pointing to the sandwiches Diane and Georges were eating. "With potato fingers," he added.

"Sounds great," Erik told him, sensing it would be a good idea to keep discussion to a minimum.

They chatted with their table companions while waiting for the food to arrive. In less time than they might have expected, a couple of the sizzling-hot sandwiches appeared, each accompanied on its plate by similarly hot and crispy potato fingers. Erik, always ready to demolish mass quantities of food, sank his teeth into the meal as soon as it arrived. "This is *fantastic,* Lev!" he enthused around a hot, meaty bite. "What's this sauce? I can't quite identify it."

"Oh that," Lev said grinning. "I think we're going to call it our 'secret sauce.' Actually it's a mixture of beaten eggs with oil and vinegar, some tomatoes pureed with sugar and vinegar, and some finely minced pickled vegetables. Oh yeah, and I'm thinking of calling the potato fingers 'Dragon fries.' What d'you think?"

Andrion and Erik exchanged a brief glance. It would appear Lev had gone over the edge. "Sounds great, Lev," Andrion told him encouragingly. "Well, we'd better let you get back to work." He bit into his hot sandwich. It was, in fact, amazingly delicious. The slightly caramelized flavor of the fire-seared beef was a top note, juices running into his mouth, with the piquancy of the mostly vinegar-based sauce, and the creamy mouth feel of the melted cheese, all combined into a flavor that made him want another bite. And another. The crispy, slightly salty fried potatoes were also appealing, the whole of it accompanied by chilled ale.

His mouth half full of food, Erik enthused "Lev has really got something here. I think this is going to be huge. And the food came so fast!"

"Mgrmph," was all Andrion had to say in reply. They devoured their meals, washing them down with the frosty ale, then sat nearly gasping in satisfaction. There was something about the combination of flavors that had been so compelling, the experience was almost orgasmic.

Erik belched mightily, then leaned back in his chair and sighed. "Wow," he said quietly. The rest of the party agreed.

"How are you and Georges coming along?" Andrion asked.

Diane, who had not been able to finish her plate of food but had found Georges more than willing to take up her slack, said "We're close to being ready to take it down to the site. Can you guys give us a hand getting it up out of the basement?"

The group of four soon climbed down the ladder behind the bar, waddling slightly. This hearty midday fare felt like it called for a hearty midday nap, but they had work to do. The kitchen water heater assembly was considerably smaller than the system that would be used for the bathing tub; but it was still fairly heavy – being completely shrouded with dypalfar metal. Diane and Georges had assembled it on the floor in front of the workbench, and the bench had an array of small parts scattered across it.

Erik and Georges hefted the main unit over to the ladder and Erik climbed it, bending down from a kneeling position on the deck to haul it up as Georges pushed from below. Then Diane and Andrion gathered up the parts not yet installed, along with Diane's tools, and led the way down the road toward the farm as the two most muscular of their party brought up the rear with the unit carried between them.

They arrived to find the construction site a hive of activity once again, the workers having finished their midday break. They carried their burdens in through the front door of the cottage and Andrion pointed the way to the framework that would hold the sink. Erik and Georges laid the box down, and stood back trying to envision how it would look when everything was in place.

"This is amazing, what you guys are doing for Bernadette," Georges said. He was a bit envious of his colleagues, though Bernadette wasn't really his type and she had never shown any romantic interest in him either, for that matter. He liked and respected her as a friend and employer, but he didn't get why two guys like Erik and Andrion, especially fun-loving Erik, were so head-over-heels in love with the woman that they were willing to share her. To each his own, he supposed.

"I have some more assembly work to do yet," Diane said, "and it's kind of tight quarters in here. Any chance you guys could go back and get the bathing pool unit? I think we should take advantage of Bernadette's absence to get it out of the basement, and the rest of the work on it really needs to be done on-site anyhow. I notice the tub location's been framed in."

The three men looked at each other. Andrion had seen the device and knew it was not going to be an easy task getting it up that ladder. "I think we'd better borrow some ropes before we go back to the Maiden," he said. He, Erik, and Georges trooped off to find a foreman while Diane bent to her work, glad to have them out of her hair for the moment. She was pleased to see that a small opening had been made in the outer wall of the existing house, for the water supply pipe to pass through.

Andrion's apprehension of problems raising the bathing tub's water system unit through the trap door proved to be only too accurate. Diane had carefully made it smaller than the trap door, but not by a hell of a lot. And it was heavy. The three of them were able to carry it out of the room in which it had been assembled and over to the foot of the ladder. Then a long time was spent getting it wrapped up in a rope harness, after which Andrion and Georges climbed the ladder, each with a rope to pull, while Erik (the biggest and strongest among them) bent his knees and heaved from below.

By the time the thing (which seemed to have grown by several inches in every dimension and increased dramatically in weight since they first picked it up) was resting on the deck, the three men decided that chilled ale all around was called for. It did seem to be unseasonably warm this afternoon. After they'd drunk their ales and recovered their wind Erik had the bright idea of nipping across the road to borrow the cart from Stormstrife Farm once again. This time, instead of also borrowing the horse, he and Georges did duty as draft animals after the three of them had managed to lift the accursed contraption into the bed of the cart.

This proved far easier than attempting to carry it by hand over the quarter mile to the construction site. As they arrived with their cartload, another cart was just pulling in coming from the south. Oh, it was Samir, back from Forestville. But instead of riding, he was now driving his horse hitched to a good-sized wagon. The back was loaded with lengths of dull copper pipe and crates of nails.

Chapter 66: Building

Andrion flagged a nearby burly workman and got him to add his strength to the task of getting the unit off of the cart and down the stone steps to the basement. One man on each corner made the job almost easy. They gently lowered it to the floor off to one side of the roughed-in framework intended to hold the bathing tub. He hoped they wouldn't need to move it again, but if so it was at least possible.

They all went back up the stairs, thankful to have finished the task. The workman, dismissed, returned to what he'd been doing and Andrion, Erik, and Georges pitched in to help unload the wagon Samir had brought. That was a pretty fast trip, if it included loading all this onto the wagon and hitching up the horse. The animal looked relieved to be standing still, if a little resentful to be still in harness.

When all of the wagon's contents were on the ground Samir led his long-suffering mount around, parking the wagon up near the western end of the property. It would probably go back to its owner on the next trip. But for now the horse was unhitched, rubbed down, and tied to a fence rail with a feed bag strapped on. It sighed contentedly.

The Maiden crew returned inside to see how Diane was doing, and reported to her that a load of pipe had arrived. "Excellent!" she exclaimed. "I'm almost done with this. Let's see if we can get some of the pipe hooked up at this end."

"If you don't need my help here, Diane, I think I'll volunteer with the crew outside," Georges said. He'd become seized with enthusiasm for the project. It was so nice to be doing something besides lounging around, for a change.

She gave him a sweet smile. "Thanks, dear. I'll see you in a while." Diane and the two remaining men went out for a conference with Hegmar and Bjorn in the yard. "I see that you have the entire bottom floor of the water tower built and the trench dug for the pipe between the cistern and the house," Diane said. "While I'm here, I'd like to run the pipe through the trench and into the house, install the tee for the water going to the bathroom, and bring the pipe in through the house wall to the sink area so I can hook up the heater system. Then when you get your cistern up, you can just run the pipe down to connect with what's already in place."

469

She peered at Hegmar and Bjorn, to see whether they were in accordance with this plan. Bjorn hadn't yet done any pipe work and didn't have a lot to say, but Hegmar frowned. "Hmm, well really, I suppose there's no reason not to do that. It'll let us close up the trench, which'll make it less of a hazard in the yard. 'Course we'll have to cap the pipe at the tee and over at the tower. I had my man fabricate some fittings, but they didn't include any caps."

"Why not just tie a square of leather over the stub end with some wire?" Diane suggested.

"Yeah, that'll work. I've got the lead on site… Sure, let's go ahead and do it." They conferred with the crew member who was tasked with laying the pipe. Pipe sections were joined by fitting lengths into the swaged ends of other lengths, or by fitting two pipe sections into one of the special fittings the fabricator had run up. The ends were cleaned with an abrasive cloth and brushed with an acid flux, then a hand-pumped blow torch was applied to a length of soft lead which flowed into the joint – fusing the pieces together.

They all assisted as they could, while Georges was off with the crews that were raising sections of wall. After watching the procedure with the lead, Andrion had an idea and asked if he could try to make the next joint. Instead of using the blowtorch, however, he used only a fire spell – no dual wielding with lightning, this time – but focused and concentrated as he had done when cutting the pipe section deep in that dypalfar ruin. It melted the lead wire in a trice, as effectively as the blowtorch. While a helper held the pieces to be joined in place, he moved around the joint with fire spell and lead, creating the join in no time.

By quitting time pipe was laid from the water tower to the house and the trench covered over, the ends of the line had been stubbed off, and Diane's kitchen water heater was in place. She was unable to demonstrate its operation, unless they were going to pour enough water down the water tower end of the pipe to run to the kitchen (into a bucket, there being as yet no sink); but she'd showed Andrion the operation of the buttons that turned the heat on and off. Elsewhere on the project, the frame walls had been erected around the entire foundation, and roof beams had begun to appear. They were supported in the middle by uprights that would form part of load-bearing interior walls flanking the central corridor.

The four friends met as the crews were stowing their tools and preparing to return to their homes, and stood in the front yard admiring the project. Diane expected that this might be the last look she and Georges would get at it for some time, since likely Bernadette would be here either this evening or early tomorrow and they'd be traveling to Daywatch. This was very nearly the first time she'd applied her considerable knowledge of dypalfar technology to something nonviolent, though weapons were the least of what the ancient dypalfar had achieved. It gave her a good feeling, and it triggered in her a peculiar sort of itching, as if a part of her soul had just been bitten by a mosquito. She felt there was something missing in her life, something she wanted. And it wasn't just the plans for a new and improved crossbow.

They journeyed the short distance back to the Maiden in camaraderie and good spirits, and as soon as they were in the door they all made a beeline for robes and the bathing pool. They were all hungry as well, but a day of working construction had left them grubby and sweaty. In the pool, Diane was anxious to relay all of her thoughts on the project to Andrion and Erik, since she would not be here to assist them in putting all the pieces together.

"Andrion, have you ordered the kitchen sink yet?" she asked.

"Not yet," he admitted. "I hadn't decided what construction I want. But I'm afraid I'd better get going on it."

"I think," she suggested with as much tact as she could muster, "that you ought to have it crafted at a smithy and made out of dypalfar metal. It should only take a little more metal than a suit of armor with a shield would, and you've still got plenty of dypalfar scrap downstairs. That will last you a lifetime, and you can pass it on to your children. It'll look nice, too."

"You're right," he agreed. "I think Valkyrie should be able to produce it without much trouble. I was thinking a double sink, one side shallow for dishes and the other deep for soaking pots and doing laundry. I'll see if Bjorn can do me some drawings I can give to Alessia." Diane smiled at him, pleased that her suggestion had been so readily accepted. Beneath the water Georges, who was sitting

471

quite close beside her, gave her thigh an encouraging squeeze. She appreciated the gesture, but found that the encouragement was a bit of a distraction.

"When the dypalfar pipe gets here, you'll need to run it between the bathing tub and the water system. You can put the stuff together using the same technique you used on the pipes today. But what's the tub going to be made of?" Oh, what am I doing? Andrion thought. Details were getting away from him. Their wedding was only a few weeks away, and he had not even figured out how they were going to make the tub – an element of their new home as vital as the gigantic bed.

Most people in Iscandia did with a washtub set on the floor before the fire, water added by the bucketful. In the wealthier homes there were sometimes bathrooms with a handsome tub set on the floor, made of copper or possibly cast iron coated with a ceramic finish. Andrion's plan had been for their home's bathroom to have, in addition to the water privy and a basin for washing hands and faces, a tub set into the floor and kept permanently full of hot water – big enough for at least two, perhaps three adults to enjoy at one time. The hole in the floor had been roughed in to a size of four by six feet; but what would fill it?

Andrion's mind raced. He was supposed to be relaxing after a day well spent, but now found himself put on the spot. "I had been thinking masonry, like the pool here," he gestured to the water they were sitting in. "But I don't know. The distance from the main floor of the annex to the stone floor of the basement is 8 feet. The bathing tub doesn't want to be more than 4 feet deep. That would mean putting 4 feet of additional stone underneath it to support the weight of the tub floor, its walls, and the water inside it."

Diane, too, seemed caught out as she tried to work out the best solution to the problem. Georges gazed at her admiringly. There was something so *sexy* about watching a smart (and beautiful didn't hurt either, mind) woman applying her mind to something. He was getting half-hard just watching her in action, and that certainly wasn't appropriate under the circumstances. He put a lid on it.

After considering all the factors, Diane said "I think you're right, Andrion. No matter what the tub was made of the weight of the water will be so great that you'll need full bottom support. Better just get your masons to lay a four-foot-tall platform under there, wide enough for the water system to rest on it beside the tub. We can run the pipes in from the side, near the bottom of the tub. Probably you can use stone and face the inside with glazed tile. You want something that will hold the heat."

Andrion smiled at her. It was nice to have validation for his own thoughts. He didn't much like being put in the role of expert when his expertise was so wanting, but sometimes you just had to shoulder the load and push on through. "It's beginning to look like we'll be going to Daywatch in the morning," Diane said. "Let's be sure to drop by the site before we go and let Hegmar know the details. He'll need to leave circular openings in the side of the tub where the system is sitting, as close to the bottom as possible, to accommodate the pipes."

Erik and Georges, meanwhile, were just taking this all in. Neither of them had any magical ability to speak of so they were used to having to work to make things happen. But the details could be daunting. They were both happy not to have the burden of those details on their shoulders. "Is anybody besides me starving?" Erik asked hopefully. A day of physical labor had worked up a big appetite, and they'd skipped their early evening snack.

A general affirmative chorus went up, and they all got out. During the day the new Owner's Table had been delivered by Arngeld and his two strapping sons, the old one having been moved to fill some open space and provide more seating for Maiden guests. The party of conspirators had been so busy during the day they had completely missed it as it went past them; nor had they noticed it before getting into the bathing pool. Now, as they put on robes and made their way to the usual spot, all but Erik were astounded.

Erik grinned. "I told you it was amazing, didn't I?" He was as pleased as if he'd had more to do with its creation than simply walking down to Waterdon and ordering a table made. But its magnificence was entirely due to Arngeld's artistry. The four clustered around, exclaiming at the inlaid artwork. They were almost sorry to sit down and eat at it, possibly marring the beautiful surface.

Hjaermond and Selden were down for supper, as usual. The two spent much of each day wandering around the place, napping, reading, or chatting up the young and pretty women Lev had hired to help around the Maiden. But they never missed a meal, and they fully expected to take it at the Owner's Table. They'd been personally invited here by The Fireblood herself, after all. Now, however, there was plenty of room for all of them. And the old Norsemen joined the chorus of excited comments about the new table.

Tonight's menu included fresh chickens, sliced in half and marinated in a mixture of oil, wine, and herbs before being grilled. This was served with the traditional oblong bread rolls, halved and toasted with butter and garlic, and a collection of mixed greens that had been chopped and dressed with oil, wine vinegar, and more herbs. Apple pie was offered for dessert.

A light, chilled white wine accompanied the food, and gaiety reigned as the party at the new and magnificent table enjoyed the food and the evening. Diane and Georges were seated close together, and before the meal was over they were touching more and more, giving each other smoldering glances, and generally behaving in a manner more appropriate to people half their age. Nobody else at the table, even the old men, was surprised when they excused themselves right after dessert and disappeared down the ladder behind the bar.

Andrion exchanged a look with Erik as they disappeared once again. "Huh? Huh?" he said somewhat smugly, elbowing his friend in the ribs. Erik shook his head, smiling. Two nights of lust did not make a lifelong love affair. It had taken weeks before he'd realized how Berni had wrapped herself around his own heart. But the signs were positive; and it would have been mean, spiteful, and pointless to burst Andrion's bubble.

"Perhaps you're right," was all he said.

The night life of the Maiden came alive around them, and the men around the Owner's Table sat back to enjoy it. There was song and dance, and for a rare treat, a real minstrel was passing through and regaled everyone with a tale of Sigrandil and the Brave Company. It was enjoyed by all, but had special interest for Andrion and Erik – who had met the man himself in Valhaale in Asengard when they were there helping their beloved in the quest to defeat Tarragin.

After the story had concluded Hjaermond and Selden excused themselves and headed up the stairs to bed. The wine and food had dulled their senses, and they were struggling to stay awake. Though they'd worked hard today Erik and Andrion were still young enough to enjoy the evening, and they lingered at the table – nibbling on bites of apple pie and continuing to sip the wine, which had a sweet, fruity taste to it.

The minstrel had returned from a break and was now singing one of the familiar Iscandia standards, giving Lev a well-deserved rest, when the front doors of the Maiden opened and Bernadette strolled in.

Chapter 67: Homecoming

From late morning on a cloudy, somewhat breezy day in Sylvanian Bernadette found herself, after a few moments of complete darkness, looking at the near-darkness of nighttime outside the Maiden. It ought to be around ten in the evening, she thought. There was no reason to assume that the fast-travel trip between two locations would take any longer one way than it did the other. Oh, she was so glad to be home! And her men would be here, and likely still awake. She could hardly wait to get through the doors!

As soon as she stepped inside, Bernadette's gaze flew to the table that had now become known as the Owner's Table. It was situated on the mezzanine immediately beyond the bathing pool, and offered a great view of almost the entire common room. Yes! Erik and Andrion were there, and they were looking in her direction. An unfamiliar minstrel was standing in front of the bar strumming a lute, and he hesitated for a moment as she strode into the room. Then he continued, and she practically flew across the room and up the couple of steps to the mezzanine.

Bernadette was brought up short, staring at the table. Drelos had been by, clearing away the plates and polishing the surface with a rag, so that the inlays were revealed in all their new-made glory. She felt utterly confused. Coming in the door she'd had no thought but to be reunited with the men who were the loves of her life. But now she was looking at this unexpected wonder!

Love won. Erik was standing on the side closest to her and he stepped forward to enfold her in a bear hug. "Berni!" was all he got out, before lifting her up off the floor to claim her mouth with a deep kiss. Joy filled her heart as she pressed herself to him. In a moment, though, she pulled away to gasp for breath.

"Erik, love, set me down please?" He smiled at her, joy radiating from him as well. She continued on to embrace Andrion as well, and he gave her a long kiss that left her panting.

Whew! Breaking away from that as well, Bernadette plopped herself down on a chair. Lifa's dress, in its protective cover, was still draped over her arm and had narrowly averted being crushed and wrinkled. "Oh!" she said, looking around. A nearby support pillar offered a protruding peg, intended to hold a lantern. It was currently empty, and she popped back up to hang the dress on it before returning to her seat.

Head swiveling, looking from Erik to Andrion and back again, Bernadette gestured at the table and said "What...?" Erik grinned.

"Do you remember when you asked me to order us a bigger table?" She nodded. With all that had been going on, she'd completely forgotten. But she'd just been expecting a bigger version of the regular Maiden tables that were scattered throughout the room. This was... magnificent!

"I went to Arngeld," Erik was continuing, "and it turns out he's quite an artist. Also, apparently, a big fan of yours." He squeezed her hand, careful not to crush it. Realizing that he could not tell the whole story without blowing his cover, Erik added "He and his sons just showed up with this today. He decided to do the inlay as a tribute to you."

Bernadette was touched. Though she did enjoy a certain amount of respect and prestige as The Fireblood, it was rare for any of the people whose lives she'd theoretically saved to express much gratitude. "This is wonderful, Erik!" she exclaimed. "We should definitely give Arngeld some more work."

"Already doing it," he assured her. "Lev asked me to order up a bunch of extra chairs and tables for the parties. With the way business is going around here, I think we're going to need them even without any parties."

Bernadette ran her hands over the tabletop, admiring its smooth surface and the glowing grain of the woods forming the dragon motifs. In a moment, she said "It seems as if it's time for lunch. It was around eleven in the morning when I left Sylvanian, and breakfast was a long time ago." She suspected that fast-traveling somehow split the difference between the few seconds of apparent elapsed time and the several hours of actual time lost in the transition. She didn't feel as though it had been eleven hours since she left Sylvanian, but it certainly didn't feel like five minutes, either.

Andrion waved to Drelos, who was on the bar. He came over, greeting Bernadette with a mixture of friendliness and respect. "What's left in the kitchen?" Andrion asked him.

"There's a little cold chicken," he said. "And about half an apple pie. Not much this time of night." Bernadette's eyes lit.

"Cold chicken and apple pie sounds just fine, Drelos," she said smiling. "Bring it on! And something to drink, too, please."

In short order Bernadette was chowing down on a succulent chicken forequarter, washing it down with more of the fruity white wine, and looking forward to the slice of apple pie that awaited her on a plate to the side, demurely peeking out from beneath a dollop of clotted cream. As she shoveled food into her mouth with her usual un-self-conscious enthusiasm, Andrion and Erik regaled her with tales of their trip to the dypalfar ruin with Diane.

"She's confident she can duplicate the Maiden's system at Daywatch," Erik told her.

"*And*, I think she's got a romance going with Georges!" Andrion added gleefully. Her mouth full, Bernadette's eyebrows rose and her eyes gleamed with interest. She truly *did* want to see everyone she knew and liked enjoying a love affair. She'd known Georges for months, and he was a nice enough guy. Good-looking and a hunk too, but there'd never been any spark between him and her.

Her connection with Andrion had happened almost the minute she had walked in the door of the inn, and her love for Erik had grown exponentially since she'd first gotten into bed with him. There hadn't been room for anybody else. Diane had seemed a little abstracted, so absorbed in her fascination with dypalfar technology that love was not on her agenda. Bernadette was glad to hear it had crept in, after all.

When she'd finished eating, Bernadette filled the guys in on her trip to Sylvanian. Nothing she'd done there was being kept secret from them, so she was happy to share. "Wait'll you see the dress I got Lifa!" she said, gesturing to the garment hanging, in its muslin shroud, from the nearby peg. "I'm going to take it down and give it to her tomorrow, so we can make sure it fits before the wedding." She gathered her thoughts. "Oh! I guess you're going back to Daywatch with Diane tomorrow, Andrion?"

He nodded somewhat solemnly. Now that Berni was back, he was *not* anxious to absent himself from her for a minimum of 24 hours. But there was no getting around it. It was the price he'd agreed to for Diane's help. And that help had been invaluable. He'd never have been able to create their new home's water systems without her. Bernadette, too, looked sad at the realization. But she perked up shortly. "Erik, maybe *you* could come with me. I know you'd like to visit with Anja, and I think it's going to be priceless to see Lifa's face when I show her the dress. Is Bjorn still working every day up the road?"

Erik nodded. "They're coming right along with that, but it looks like a project that's going to take weeks." Bernadette smiled.

"Good. It's supposed to be bad luck for the groom to see the bride in her wedding dress before the ceremony. Well, technically of course since I have to bring us all to Lakedon together he's going to see her before the ceremony anyhow – unless he wears a blindfold! But at least it'll be a surprise for his wedding day..."

Bernadette told them about the attendance of Eorl Bergen and his wife, along with other members of their court, at their wedding in Sylvanian as well as at the party the next day. Which reminded her, she needed to drop the note off with Ormund in the morning. Then there were the musicians for the two parties, news she also needed to share with Lev and Drelos; and the arrangements she'd made with General Vadrian.

After all this, the three of them glanced around. The hour was getting late, though it was later for Erik and Andrion than it seemed for Bernadette. She'd gotten out of bed after a good night's sleep at the Rabbit not six hours ago, subjectively. The men looked at each other, both of them realizing there was an issue to be dealt with. "Uh, Berni..." Erik said, broaching the issue, "Diane and Georges are likely fucking like bunnies in my bed downstairs at the moment. Andrion and I have been sharing the master bed, because the Maiden is full up. I think we three are going to have to squeeze in together tonight."

Bernadette looked from one to the other of them. Her eyes lit, and a slow, lascivious smile spread across her pretty face. "Oh," she said. "What a terrible thing."

Chapter 68: Onward

Bernadette's internal clock woke her at what she hoped was sometime after dawn. Here on the Maiden's upper story, there was no natural light. She was pressed in between Erik and Andrion – and though it was a little crowded, it felt so wonderful to have them with her once again. The few days of separation had been far too long – but the passion of their reunion had been, perhaps, worth the trouble. Ooh. She lay there recalling the things they had done in bed last night. Taking them both on at once always left her feeling a bit overwhelmed.

Well, time for a bath before getting on with the day's activities. Getting out of the bed without waking the men might be a bit of a trick, though. She chose to climb over Andrion on the theory that he was harder to wake, but he still grabbed her as she made her way across. "Where do you think *you're* going?" he murmured softly, hugging her to him.

"Bath time," she whispered. His eyes popped open.

"I'll come with you," he said softly, and rolled out of bed. Erik slept on. Well, *this* was a turnabout...

The two slipped on robes and descended the stairs. Evidently it was pretty early, for almost no one was stirring around the Maiden. One early customer, dressed for traveling, sat eating a pastry and sipping tea while studying some papers propped on his table. Drelos was behind the bar. They waved to him and got into the tub, relaxing in the hot water. "The map's in my pack," Bernadette told Andrion. "I guess you're going to be needing it pretty soon."

Andrion's expression was not a happy one. "I wish I didn't have to leave again. I feel like I just got here. But I promised Diane I'd take her back. I'm going to miss you..." She turned from where she sat beside him in the hot water and threw her arms around his neck, kissing him deeply. She'd scarcely been with him for a few hours, much of that time asleep, in the past several days.

"You're going to just turn around and come right back, right?" Bernadette murmured.

He grinned at her ruefully. "Bloody well right!"

The two had climbed out of the pool and were sitting at the table deciding what to have for breakfast when Diane and Georges

480

emerged from behind the bar. They appeared to be dressed in their travel garb, and came swiftly over to the table. "Bernadette! When did you get in?" Diane asked.

"Oh around ten last night," she replied. "Looks like you're about ready to return to Daywatch?"

Diane nodded, gesturing toward Georges. "Georges is coming with us. I've sort of talked him into joining the Daywatch Brigade." Bernadette's eyebrows rose. Georges had always seemed to be one of the Maiden guys who, like Erik, really enjoyed the hospitality aspects of his job and had taken relatively few quests – let alone something as serious and open-ended as joining the Brigade. That would be like signing up with the Brave Company, or perhaps the Guardians. Maybe Andrion's belief that the connection between Diane and Georges was more than a brief fling was accurate.

Searching for something to say, Bernadette finally came out with "I'm sure they'll be glad to get you, Georges. You're pretty good with a bow, from what I hear." He nodded un-self-consciously, and smiled at Diane. "The next time I'm down there, Diane, I'll be expecting a hot bath inside the fortress mind you," Bernadette teased. "That might be sooner than you think," the older woman promised.

Unbidden, Drelos arrived at the table with a tray on which an array of breakfast goodies were presented. He set it down and passed them all plates, pouring mugs of tea for the four of them. Bernadette enjoyed a couple of the pastries, which were fresh from the oven and smelled too good to pass up, while Andrion had some scrambled eggs and a toasted bread roll with butter. The others ate with good appetite as well, and in short order they had finished their meal and all stood up.

Bernadette and Andrion returned to the master bedroom, and found Erik just finishing his dressing. Not expecting to go anywhere much today, he was wearing casual clothes. His friends soon donned their own garments, Andrion choosing to wear armor since the region around Daywatch could be hazardous. He hadn't forgotten that dragon attack.

They all went outside and Andrion enfolded Bernadette in a careful embrace, then squeezed Erik's hand. "See you in about 24 hours," he said. Then he, Diane, and Georges walked on down the road far enough to assure that Bernadette and Erik did not get included in their party, and soon shimmered out of sight. Bernadette stood gazing at the spot where they'd vanished and sighed. Erik took her little hand in his big one and gave it a gentle squeeze, then put his powerful arm around her.

"We'll all be back together pretty soon, love," he told her philosophically. She smiled at him, and they returned inside.

Chapter 69: Surprises Sprung

"I'm going in to Waterdon pretty soon," Bernadette told Erik. "Do you want to get some breakfast and come with me?"

"I don't need to eat right now," he replied, "if you want to leave right away…"

She gave him a conspiratorial grin, saying "Okay! Let's get Lifa's dress and a couple of other things and go up there." They returned inside the Maiden. The dress had come upstairs with them the night before to hang on a peg in the bedroom. Before leaving, Bernadette took a few minutes with pen and paper at the table. Then, her pack loaded and a good dagger at her side, she was ready to leave. "Could you bring along some kind of weapon too, Erik?" she asked as they got to the ground floor.

"Sure, just a minute," he replied.

Erik nipped down to the basement and returned in moments wearing a handsome leather breastplate, the axe he favored for close-in combat hanging at his belt. Any attacker suicidal enough to take on the combination of Erik and this deadly, oversized weapon generally did *not* live to regret it. Bernadette stood there admiring him as he bounded back into the room. His combination of golden good looks, sunny disposition and utter lethality in battle was just so appealing to her.

They set off down the road to Waterdon, the dress in its protective cover draped over Bernadette's left arm. "Are we expecting armed attack?" Erik asked casually, wondering why his beloved thought a weapon was necessary on this short local jaunt. One did occasionally encounter shria or more dangerous wildlife between the Maiden and town, but it hardly seemed likely they would need the kind of armament he was packing.

"I'm just being over-vigilant," Bernadette admitted with a wry grin. "This dress cost about the same as a skilled worker's wage for half a year, and getting it made took a lot of time and effort. In case some stray bandits are thinking we look like rich pickings, I'd like to discourage them *before* they attack." Erik nodded. Bandits were everywhere, at least two groups of them lurking within a ten-minute walk of the city gates.

The day was sunny and sparkling, remarkably beautiful weather for this early in the year, and the walk was enjoyable. They spotted Bjorn on the construction site and waved to him as they walked by – Bernadette making some effort to conceal what she was carrying. If Lifa wanted the dress to be a surprise for him, as it was Bernadette's surprise for Lifa, she wanted to facilitate that. Erik, meanwhile, was silently thanking the gods that they had come up with such a plausible, near-truthful explanation for the work and Bjorn's role in it.

"That place is growing like wildfire," Bernadette remarked as they continued up the road. "We ought to see about hiring the builder, whoever that is, when we find our land and are ready to build our new house." Erik nodded.

"Yeah, he really seems to know how to get things done." They continued walking in silence for a while, just enjoying the morning air. Blue butterflies fluttered here and there, gathering nectar from early-blooming wildflowers.

Bernadette's mind, as usual when she was simply enjoying a walk without fear of attack, was wandering. Sometimes it would go hither and yon like those butterflies, and with as little effect; but its instincts usually made it more like the dragonflies found near water throughout the province. These little but fearsome aerial predators flew with purpose, ready to seize any target of opportunity and demolish it. Likewise, her mind would seem to cruise aimlessly until it found a thought to pounce on. Then it would pursue it until it gave up its import to her relentless probing. Though there were many people who loved her, this trait was unsettling to some.

"Erik," Bernadette remarked casually, "have you noticed that the Maiden's business seems to be bursting at the seams, lately?"

"Hence our crowded bed," he replied with a smile.

"True," she mused. "I think there are a number of factors contributing to it, including my current fame. But I also get the sense that the whole Waterdon area is going through a sort of boom. I think that builder, whoever he is, may soon find himself busier than hell."

Erik considered, as they continued walking. The discussion didn't have long to reach its conclusion, as they had just passed the stables and were moving up past the outer ramparts toward the main gate. "There does seem to be a lot of activity around town," Erik admitted. "And there's almost no place for newcomers to the city to live. That was one of the problems we had when we were trying to find a house for us. No vacant properties."

This train of thought was sparking more ideas in Bernadette's mind, but she tabled it for the time being as they were welcomed through the gates by two of the faceless City guards (the one on the left, she knew, was named Gunther; she recognized the scar on his chin) and found themselves standing a few paces from Brightsgate Cottage.

Alessia Adelini was working at her forge, and looked up as they came in. "Ho, Bernadette!" she called. "Did you bring me any armaments today?"

"Sorry," Bernadette replied. "I just got back from Sylvanian. But I'll probably have a few more pieces for you tomorrow or early next week." She and Erik continued down the road a few paces and knocked at the door of Brightsgate Cottage.

Lifa answered the door. Of late her complexion seemed to be glowing slightly, as if her new life had been very good for her health. Certainly keeping house and enjoying the company of an adorable girl-child was less *hazardous* than guarding Bernadette's back had been, in the early days of their association. But healthy? She greeted them with a warm smile, and Anja was soon hugging Bernadette around the hips before demanding to be picked up by Uncle Erik. He held her at arms' length and proclaimed that she was getting prettier all the time – and would soon be looking her Aunt Berni in the eyes, at the rate she was growing. The little girl brushed off Erik's bullshit with a grin of her own, just glad to see them.

Lifa's eyes had fallen to the mysterious package draped over Bernadette's arm. Her eyes went from it to Bernadette's face, and seeing the glow of pleasure there, she anticipated that something marvelous was about to unfold. "Lifa," Bernadette said somewhat solemnly. "I know that when I asked you to take up a new chapter in your life you were somewhat unprepared. But you have stepped in beautifully, and I think that you deserve something beautiful in return. I had this made for you to wear at your wedding." She proffered the shrouded dress.

Lifa's dark blue eyes were enormous, luminous, and widened in surprise. She'd been thinking a few bows sewn onto the nicest of her small collection of dresses would do. She took it from Bernadette's hands but was almost afraid to remove the protective sacking. Bernadette grinned at her. "Well, go try it on! We need to see if it will need any alteration before next week!"

"Yes! Yes! Try it on, Mama!" Anja squealed, bouncing up and down. The thrill of an exotic surprise appearing on this ordinary morning had made her forget herself.

Anja remembered no other mama, and though she had known Lifa and Bjorn only a few weeks she had begun to think of them, not as "Aunt Lifa" and "Uncle Bjorn" but as "Mama" and "Papa." At some level of her tiny being, she sensed that this was probably a betrayal of the people who had given her birth, who had loved her as a baby. But those people were gone from the world and her memories, and these people were here. They *were* her parents, and she shrugged off the inner voice that told her they were not.

Certainly, nobody else objected. In fact, Lifa glanced down at her with a look of melting love. This would not be her only child, but Anja was her first. When she herself had been orphaned, many people had been kind to her and she had not grown up without love, or without care; but there had never been a real family for her again. Now, she had her own.

Anja and Lifa bounced up the steps to the cottage's loft, while Bernadette and Erik took seats before the fire, waiting for the presentation. They could hear oohs and aahs coming from the floor above, and Lifa asking Anja to assist her with the dress's rear fastenings. In a few minutes the two emerged and Lifa picked her way down the steps, holding onto the dress's full skirts lest she trip, to stand before them.

Oh, it was magnificent! And the fit was perfect. Bernadette's eye and her luck as well had stood her in good stead when she'd plucked that young woman from the street in Sylvanian to serve as Lifa's body double. At the time, she'd thought the girl might be a little too big around the middle; but it seemed Lifa had filled out some. Not surprising, she supposed, with fewer swordfights and more domestic chores on the body servant's agenda.

"Oh, Lifa!" Bernadette said softly. "If only I had a mirror for you to see yourself! You are a vision!" Lifa's beautiful dark eyes seemed to be on the verge of tears. What a change from the stern, impassive warrior she had been just a few months ago.

"She's right, Mama!" Anja assured the woman. "You are a... bision." Anja wasn't sure exactly what the word meant, or how to pronounce it, but she'd gotten the context spot on.

Heedless of any possible wrinkling, Lifa embraced Bernadette. "Thank you! This is magnificent!" Pulling away, she was lost in thought for a moment. "I'd really like for Bjorn not to know about this until the day of the wedding. Would it be all right if you take it back to the Maiden and store it for me? When we come on the sixteenth to fast-travel to Lakedon, I can put the dress on then and... maybe come down the stairs from the loft?" Bernadette grinned, liking the idea.

"I think that'll be great," she said. "I just needed to have you try it on to make sure we wouldn't need any alterations." She patted her friend's belly jokingly. "Have you been eating a bit more lately?"

To her surprise, Lifa blushed to her hair roots at this teasing comment.

"No offense meant!" Bernadette hurried to say. Lifa shook her head, then smiling, she stepped close and whispered in Bernadette's ear. Now it was Bernadette's turn to blush, though with her redhead's complexion the effect was more spectacular.

She threw her arms around Lifa and whispered, "I'm so happy for you! And I won't tell anyone until you say."

"Just let me go change!" Lifa said breathlessly, and swept up the stairs calling "Anja, I need your help again." Anja followed her, and in another couple of minutes the two returned down the stairs with the dress once more in its muslin sack, protected from the elements. Lifa handed it over to Bernadette and said "Thank you so much. I can't wait to see Bjorn's expression on the sixteenth!"

"Can I offer you anything?" Lifa asked next, unsure what else might be on their agenda. Bernadette, at least, didn't usually come to town for no other reason than a visit. "We've already eaten breakfast, of course – Bjorn leaves for his job so early these mornings! But there's some fresh bread and apple butter, and I can make a pot of tea."

Bernadette said "Tea would be fine," even as Erik said "Fresh bread?! Sure!" Clearly, getting him out the door without breakfast in him was a tactical blunder. As the rest of them sipped tea sweetened with honey, Erik devoured half a dozen bread rolls and a medium-sized ceramic pot of apple butter. At which point he looked around somewhat guiltily to see if there was anything more.

"I think we'd better feed you an early lunch, Erik," Bernadette said wryly. "I apologize for bringing this ravening beast to your door." Lifa shrugged, smiling.

"This ravening beast is welcome here at any time, I assure you," she said, patting Erik's massive arm. Most times, he came laden with far more food than he ate.

"Well," Bernadette said rising. "Andrion is off to Daywatch again for a day or so and Erik and I have a few more errands to run. We'll see you soon." Draping the dress over her arm once again, she and Erik took their leave.

They took the nearer set of stairs and walked through upper Waterdon to the series of soaring staircases that led to Wyrmshalla. As they walked into the palace, Bernadette spotted some of the ladies she'd schmoozed with on her recent visit, and stopped by briefly to say hello. Such women, living the lives of art objects, didn't have much in common with her – but she thought it paid to be nice to everyone, or at least everyone she could manage to. Her diplomacy skills were still a work in progress.

Their curiosity was aroused by the package draped over her arm – so of course, she had to show it to them. Erik stood to one side, amused and long-suffering, as the pampered wives and daughters of Waterdon's elite waxed ecstatic over the dress. It *was*, really, magnificent. Bernadette, trying on her society matron act to see if it was something she could tolerate for longer than a minute at a time, said "Yes, if you are ever in Sylvanian you must see Senalie at The Golden Thread. Her work is absolutely divine. Quite expensive, of course, but you know – you have to pay for top quality…"

When the ladies had subsided, Bernadette slipped the cover back over the dress and she and Erik continued to the dais for a brief consultation with Eorl Ormund. Behind them, the women were all atwitter. "Who was that lady I just saw?" Erik asked, nudging Bernadette in the ribs. She winced, then grinned at him.

"I think that might have been Lady Lamonte-Johannessohn, matron of the Bouchard-Lamonte-Johannessohn clan," she told him jokingly. "Bit of a snob, isn't she?" He grinned back at her and nodded.

Eorl Ormund was pleased to see them. He was coming to regard Bernadette and her friends as among his more valued citizens. After the usual pleasantries had been exchanged, Bernadette said respectfully "I have two missives for you, Ormund. This one" – she proffered the roll of paper she'd penned before leaving the Maiden this morning – "Is an invitation to my wedding in Sylvanian on the tenth of next month – and to the party we're having at the Maiden to celebrate the marriage, on the eleventh."

The elder man, his face careworn but eyes bright, accepted the parchment happily. After scanning it he said, "I should be delighted to attend. No doubt my party and I can travel by coach to Sylvanian, and Bergen can put us up at the palace. But how will we get back to Waterdon in time for your party?" Bernadette smiled and passed him a second piece of paper.

"Ah, that brings me to my second letter. Bergen plans to fast-travel here after the ceremony using his magic map, and he's hoping that you will accommodate him and his party here at Wyrmshalla. I'm sure he can include you and your party with those he brings along."

Reading the second note, Ormund smiled. "Well, that works out nicely," he said. "I look forward to seeing you in Sylvanian on the tenth of next month, and of course in Lakedon next week. Now if you'll excuse me, I have march business to attend to." Bernadette gave a slight bow, and she and Erik took their leave. They popped in briefly to say hi to Garimund, mostly at Erik's behest, then exited the palace's grand front doors and walked down the steps toward the lower part of town.

"That was it!" Bernadette said with relief. "I do believe there is nothing more I *have* to get done before it's time to leave for Lakedon, and Lifa and Bjorn's wedding next week. Well… I do need

to tell Lev and Drelos about the musicians that will be coming for the party, and now I think about it we probably ought to consider putting up a big tent to handle more sleeping accommodations, and…"
Before long her brain had kicked up another dozen concerns, and they were discussing them most of the way back to the Maiden.

As they passed Coldburn Farm Erik glanced at the progress of the construction and saw that more roof beams had been installed. Almost the entire length of the annex now had beams and support columns running across from wall to wall. Next angled rafters would arise from the beams to a central roof tree, supporting wooden sheathing over which slate tiles would be laid. He felt torn, wanting to be there helping and learning; but also wanting to be spending time with Berni. It was not often that the two of them were at loose ends together in the middle of the day, able to do whatever they wanted to. And he had a few ideas.

After they returned to the Maiden, Bernadette carried the dress upstairs and returned it to the peg. It would be safe enough there until Lifa came to claim it again. Now that she thought about it, she felt like getting into more comfortable clothing. She'd gotten increasingly used to going around dressed in skirts since they'd finished their campaign with the Daywatch Brigade; but she really enjoyed wearing trousers for ease of movement. She put on her snug-fitting, stretchy ones with a loose, full-sleeved shirt, gathered around the bodice with a laced corset that displayed her bust to best effect. A pair of nice leather high boots completed the look.

Meanwhile, Erik was downstairs talking with Lev and Drelos about the inn's accommodations. He'd be getting his bed back tonight, though he expected that either it or the master bed would go unoccupied since he fully intended to be sleeping with Berni. But the rest of the inn's beds were full most nights. Bernadette joined them, and gave the innkeepers the details of the musicians who'd be travelling from the Academy in Sylvanian. They would be needing beds, as would some of the party guests. They needed a way to expand the Maiden's capacity, and soon.

Lev volunteered, "I think I know where I can lay hands on a good-sized tent, about twenty by forty feet. Very elegant, actually. And if we can scare off the triceratops we could pitch it over on that flat stretch north of here. That land actually belongs to the Maiden, though it hasn't been used for anything in centuries."

"That'd be great," Bernadette said. "But what about beds? Erik, can your carpenter make us some more beds?"

Erik shook his head. "Arngeld and his sons have their hands full with the order for chairs and tables I put in with them. There's no way they could make enough bedsteads by next week. And then there's still the mattresses. Those things take time to sew." Bernadette nodded. Besides, how could they know if this upsurge in business was a trend and not just a temporary fluctuation? She didn't want to pay for another dozen beds and mattresses and then have them sitting there growing mold and bedbugs if the extra trade dried up again.

"Can we get some carpets and fur bedrolls?" she asked Lev. He seemed to have his fingers on all sorts of supply sources.

"Around twelve or fifteen of them?" he asked. When she nodded he said, "Sure. We can even fix up the inside of the tent so the accommodations come across as some kind of exotic 'fun experience.' Besides, the Maiden personnel can all bunk in the tent and that will free up more beds for guests. There are some beds out in the guardhouse, and we can put guests in there, too."

"That sounds good," Bernadette affirmed. "Oh, can we get somebody to scythe the field before the tent is pitched? I think that would help to make the interior more homey."

Lev nodded. "I'll get right on it. Drelos, can you take my lunch shift while I run some errands?" Drelos winced. He'd been on last night and again this morning, and wasn't looking forward to the insane rush that descended on the Maiden every day around midday. But with the new girls working the kitchen, he should be able to handle it.

"Okay. But don't be gone too long, eh?" Lev grinned at him. The two had been working together for years.

Chapter 70: A Pleasant Afternoon

"Well, that's settled then," Bernadette declared beaming. She felt as if a weight had been lifted off her shoulders. All she really needed to do for the next few days was maybe craft some arms and armor for Valkyrie to sell, and come up with an appropriate outfit to wear to the wedding next week. Oh, and she really ought to be sure Andrion and Erik had something decent to wear too, and… Cut that *out*! she rebuked herself sharply. The preparations for two weddings had her in a frenzy, and she just needed to take a breath and relax.

Erik touched her elbow. "Nice outfit," he remarked, giving her the sort of look with which a hungry smilodon might regard a wandering goat. "I was thinking, if all your chores are done for now, we might have a little picnic. It's an awfully nice day…" Bernadette smiled up at him, dimpling.

"Why Erik, that's a great idea. Drelos, do you think you could throw together some things for us before the rush gets started?" She gave the elf her best pretty-lady-asking-the-big-strong-man-for-a-teeny-tiny-favor look.

He eyed her coolly with his big, tip-tilted eyes. Then he cracked a wry smile and said, "Sure. I'll knock something together. Just give me about ten minutes." Bernadette rewarded him with a brilliant smile that could have melted the main square in Coldstein. While Drelos prepared the food, she and Erik gathered the other items they'd need.

"Where are we going?" Bernadette asked him sweetly.

"Down by the river, I think," he replied. "You'd better bring your bow."

"Oh, good point," she replied. It'd been ages since she'd killed anything, and she wouldn't mind a little exercise. There were usually crackclaws down along the Brightwater shore, and frequently ogres as well. Once you'd killed whatever attacked you immediately on arrival, you could usually count on at least a few hours of peace and quiet in the immediate area.

After some consideration Bernadette replaced her laced bodice with the top to her sablium armor, which still looked pretty sexy but offered a lot more protection. She left the snug trousers and boots as is, and slung her best bow along with a plentiful quiver of arrows across her back. For headgear, she wore a handsome jeweled circlet she'd enchanted to enhance her archery skills – though she scarcely needed it any more.

Erik was waiting for her at their table when she returned downstairs, and a covered basket with a long leather strap for a carrying handle was sitting on the table in front of him. Breakfast had been quite a while ago, and Bernadette found herself drawn to the basket. "Ooh, what's in there?" she asked eagerly. He waved her away.

"Wait and see. Let's be surprised. I've got a couple of bedrolls in my pack, so we'll have something to sit on," he added.

Giving him a mock glare for balking her, Bernadette took Erik's arm as he slung the strap of the basket over his shoulder, and the two of them strolled out the back doors of the Maiden onto the deck. What a glorious day it was, warm sunshine beating down out of a clear sky. Though the Waterdon area had a pleasant climate, days like this were rare at any season.

They went down the deck's rear steps and walked down a grassy slope toward the banks of the Brightwater. Erik touched her elbow and pointed, before unslinging his axe. Sure enough, an ogre was approaching them with hostile intent. These curiously lumpy creatures, considerably larger than Bernadette but smaller than Erik, were apparently sentient and usually wore armor – though how they came by it was anybody's guess. They were yet another not-quite-human denizen of Iscandia that always attacked humans on sight, making any kind of rapprochement impossible.

Bernadette had her bow drawn and an arrow flying toward the beastie before it had gotten within striking distance of them. It staggered, badly hurt, and as she readied another arrow Erik charged it and hacked off its head. That axe of his was downright scary. They left the ogre lying. Its valuables could be collected on their way back, but they didn't want to be lugging anything extra at the moment. Bernadette retrieved her arrow, though.

They moved along the riverbank for some distance to the north and east after reaching the shore, wanting to get well out of view of the Maiden's deck. They killed four crackclaws along the way, Bernadette easily picking off the enormous and aggressive crustaceans from a distance. Then, after a walk 'round to assure themselves that all of the hostile wildlife had been temporarily routed, they put their bedrolls down on a sandy beach beside a slight bend in the river wherein a shallow pool had formed. The water was sparkling, and myriad little brightly-colored fish swam in it. These were periodically chased by much-larger salmon. If they hadn't brought food with them, they could have made a fire and eaten lunch right out of the river.

The brief hike, coupled with the invigorating life-or-death fight with the ogre, had roused their appetites. All of their appetites; but first, what was in the basket? Erik set it on the end of his bedroll and took off the lid, then began removing items one at a time. On top was a smallish tablecloth, which he spread on the sand between the bedrolls. Next came a couple of plates and some cutlery. Then finally Erik burrowed down to the layer with food in it.

Drelos had made them a couple of fresh sandwiches, with cold sliced chicken, cheese and fresh spinach. There was a large paper packet of fresh potato chips, and a sort of salad made with shredded cabbage in a sauce somewhat similar to Lev's "special sauce," but apparently without any tomato or pickled vegetables in it. There was also a bunch of fresh grapes, slightly chilled, and a couple of roasted nut confections right down near the bottom – as well as a couple of napkins.

Bernadette's delight had increased as each item appeared. The idea of an elegant spread prepared just for them, to be eaten in this beautiful wilderness, had a strong appeal. As she reached for a sandwich, Erik put a hand on her wrist and held her gaze. His friendly, sky-blue eyes somehow contrived to be smoldering as he said softly, "You know, I only got you out here so I could have my way with you…"

Bernadette returned his look with interest. "What a coincidence," she said with a slight smile. "But first, food!" He sighed and removed his hand, letting her load her plate with food from the array on the tablecloth. They uncorked a couple of chilled bottles of mead, which had rested near the grapes, and tucked into the delicious repast.

Bernadette glanced at Erik's crotch and saw that his hard-on was subsiding as they ate. She sighed slightly, then sank her teeth into another bite of food. Erik was so tempting, but she knew he would be ready again before long. And freshly prepared picnics complete with perfectly chilled drinks would not keep. When they'd eaten their fill and drained the mead bottles they tucked everything back into the basket, leaving the grapes out to be nibbled at leisure.

Now that the picnic was concluded they pulled the bedrolls closer together and sat side by side, gazing out over the sparkling waters of the river and admiring the fish as they chased each other around the pool. The sating of their appetites for food and drink had temporarily blunted their appetites for each other. But it was so pleasant just to sit here quietly, alone together in the wilderness, with warm sunshine and gentle breezes caressing them.

In a while, after checking the area to make sure no new threats had cropped up, Bernadette removed her breastplate. Erik took his off, as well. He cupped her face in his hands and kissed her deeply. They sat necking for a few minutes, enjoying each other's touch, their desire growing hotter and hotter. Erik slipped a hand up under her loose shirt and cupped a breast, squeezing gently and brushing his thumb across the nipple. Bernadette murmured "Ooh!" and put her hand down to stroke his cock where it pressed hard against the leg of his trousers.

Next he sat and helped her pull off her boots, removing his own as well. Their toes dipped into the soft, cool sand. Erik began working at the waistband of her snug-fitting trousers and got them open, finding she was not wearing underdrawers beneath them. While kissing her, he slipped his hand down inside and inserted a couple of fingers into her vestibule. He found it hot, wet, and slippery. Mmm.

She returned the favor, opening his pants to set that eager cock free from its confinement. It leapt out, eager to be stroked, and she squeezed it firmly. By now they were reclining on the bedrolls, and Erik had pushed Bernadette's shirt all the way up to her collarbone, exposing her breasts. They writhed and rubbed together, building to a fever pitch of excitement.

Finally, panting, they broke apart long enough to pull the rest of their clothing off. Then, completely nude, they pressed their bodies together again. Bernadette bent her knees, spreading her thighs wide, and pulled Erik to her – not so much beckoning him inside as dragging him in the door. He entered her, his huge cock pressing into her tight wetness, going all the way in as she gave a faint shriek like a very small mouse getting stepped on by a very large draft horse.

The meal earlier had taken just enough of the edge off Erik's lust that he was able to prolong their lovemaking. They tried to stay on the bedrolls as much as possible, but despite their best efforts the sand was churned up for feet in every direction, the bedrolls rumpled and pushed out of position as they enjoyed the beautiful afternoon to the utmost. Bernadette had come half a dozen times before, as was often the case with them, they finished up with her kneeling while Erik thrust into her from behind.

Erik had come to find this position the one he was least able to resist, when trying to forestall his own climax. Whether it was Berni's liking for it, or his own association with making love to her in this way, the excitement almost always became too much to bear. With a groan he pumped his seed into her, musing that it was now likely live seed and not just seminal fluid. He'd had his amulet off for a while.

Bernadette's own latest climax was gripping him spasmodically as he shot his load, and the two of them collapsed to lie flat on the bedrolls before rolling over to lie, spooning, on their sides. "Oh, Erik," she breathed, panting. When they'd had time for their heartbeats to return to normal, they both realized that not only were they sticky in several places, but sand seemed to have gotten everywhere.

"Are you up for an icy dip, my love?" Bernadette asked playfully, standing and darting down to the pool. "I thought maybe we could bring back some salmon for Lev to cook," she suggested, standing there in water up to her waist. Erik lay back on the sandy bedroll, admiring her as she dunked to rinse off sand and body fluids, the cold water screwing her nipples up like fingertips. Then he admitted that she was right, and there was no help for it. They couldn't walk back to the Maiden naked, and he couldn't put his clothes back on over the top of the sand that was adhering to him in some rather tender places.

Shuddering a bit as he stepped into the chill water, Erik joined Berni in the pool. He sat to sluice off the sand and stickiness, then stood – his own nipples painfully erect and his genitals shriveled – and worked cooperatively with Berni to herd the pool's small complement of fish into her lightning-quick hands. She fetched the tablecloth out of the picnic basket and caught it by four corners to form a sack, into which she tossed each fish as she caught it. She took the little ones, used in chemia, as well as the large salmon.

When the pool was cleaned out Bernadette dipped her "sack" all the way into the water, tying the ends tight on its wriggling contents, and hung it on a bush at the riverside before stepping out. She picked up one of the bedrolls and carefully shook the sand off of it, then sat down on the now-clean surface and toweled herself off with a napkin before putting her clothing back on.

Erik followed her lead, and soon both of them were dressed and armored again and ready for the walk back to the Maiden. They stopped at the corpse of the ogre to relieve it of its armor and weapons, then walked up onto the deck and were shortly back inside the Maiden. Lev, who'd long since returned from his expedition, was delighted to receive the bundle of fish. He loosened the ends and dropped it, fish and all, into a washtub full of cold water to keep Bernadette's catch alive longer. The little ones would be plucked out and dried, later.

Bernadette and Erik went into the hot pool for a while, completing the bath they'd taken in the river and getting warmed up again. "I probably ought to do a little crafting," she said thoughtfully. "Do you want to help?"

"Sure," he replied with a grin. "I've been getting better and better lately. Since I have a smithy in my bedroom, it's pretty convenient." After a quick trip upstairs to change clothes, she joined him in the basement.

Chapter 71: What's In a Name?

Some time after Bernadette and Erik had left Wyrmshalla, Eorl Ormund sat musing. Then he seemed to make a decision of some kind, and beckoned to Paolo Adelini. The loyal steward approached, eager to obey his master's wishes. "Paolo," the old man said, "perhaps you can refresh my memory. You know the little stream that runs down out of the hillside we're sitting on, and flows along below the city walls on the east side, at the rear of Coldburn Farm?" Paolo nodded. "Does that water have a name?"

"Ah, yes, it does," the balding Reman replied. "It's called the Drakespring Water, because it flows from a spring within the hill Wyrmshalla is built on. Nothing very dragonish about it – it's just a rivulet, really." His master seemed lost in thought for a moment. "Hmm, Drakespring… yes, I think that will do. Do you recall some of the papers our young Fireblood had you draw up recently? The ones regarding the name?" "Certainly," said the Steward. If you needed any legal documents in Waterdon, Paolo was the only man to see. "I'll need you to do another set. Get your pen and paper, and I'll give you the details…"

Chapter 72: Back to Business

Bernadette and Erik spend the rest of the afternoon and on into the evening crafting. Erik made some pieces, surprising her with his fine touch on items like jewelry, and she enchanted them. She wanted to make some more daimonic pieces, especially given Alessia 's interest in them; but she had only a small quantity of daimon's blood available and it was not easy to come by. The sentient residents of the planes of the Netherworld found their way here only rarely, and when they did it was not that easy to kill them.

Neither Adele nor Bernard often had ingredients that exotic, and it wasn't as if you could just trot off to some stronghold with the expectation that you'd be able to find and kill daimons. The few vials of blood she'd accumulated over her months in Iscandia had all been the result of chance. Some of them, she'd found lying around in the stores of hostile mages.

Recalling that Drelos was on his own for providing the Maiden with ice for its chilled beverages and that she'd promised him some help, Bernadette enchanted some of Erik's jewelry with increased ease of casting battle spells, extra magical energy, and magical energy regeneration. Those three ought to help him, though as yet she'd been unable to locate a more powerful frost spellbook for him. When they knocked off for the evening and returned upstairs for supper Bernadette gave him the necklace, ring, and a jeweled silver circlet that made him look a bit exotic. The effect was not unattractive – it might possibly even be a draw to an elf woman, she thought.

Bernadette and Erik took supper with Hjaermond and Selden, as usual. There were not enough of the hyper-fresh salmon to go around the whole inn, but everyone at the Owner's Table got some. Lev cut the fish, scarcely minutes after they'd stopped wriggling, into steaks and brushed them with a mixture of oil, garlic, and fresh herbs before flash-grilling them over the coals. The fish was accompanied by some seasonal greens, lightly tossed with grated hard cheese and a mix of oil and vinegar with spices; and a dish Bernadette had never seen before.

She was inclined to believe that Iscandia had never seen it before, either. In her homeland of Auverne the cuisine leaned more toward elaborately prepared dishes in rich sauces, at least in the cities. Such of these dishes as filtered out into the towns and countryside tended to rely heavily on cream and butter. But she'd never tasted anything like this, and called Lev over for a discussion.

He had started with what was very nearly a bread dough, he explained, but with the addition of egg and without any leavening. The dough had been thoroughly kneaded and then rolled out very thin, before being cut into thin, even strips. These could be hung up to dry and cooked days or weeks later, or (as had been the case with these tonight) immediately dropped into boiling water for a short time to cook them. The strips were then drained and sauced, in this case with a sauce any Auverne denizen would have found delightful – consisting as it did of butter, cream, grated cheese, and a few spices.

According to Lev, this dough preparation was called "pasta" and it had come from Remus. Though there were rumors that it had come there from someplace still further afield. Whatever, it proved to be a huge hit with the Maiden customers and everybody was ordering it. Finishing her meal with enthusiasm, Bernadette made a note to herself to see if there was any compensation that Lev thought should be added to what he currently received. She was not at liberty to offer him part ownership in the Maiden, as it was held in trust for each generation of firebloods; but anything else he might want, she was determined to give him. The man was a treasure!

The evening wore on, and the elders from Alfenstein tottered off to their beds. Bernadette was looking forward to returning them to Sylvanian, though it would be a while yet. She and Erik entertained a few of the other Maiden guests at their table, people they knew and liked or just visiting dignitaries. They got up and danced to the music, sang and drank and laughed, and tiredly made their way down to the basement again fairly late.

They'd had a couple of mind-blowing sex sessions over the past 24 hours, including the one with Andrion the night before and today's prolonged affair in the breezes beside the river. So initially they just stripped and climbed into bed. But Bernadette and Erik were young; and that nearly magical sex connection of theirs soon reared its head when they were snuggled in together skin to skin. As did Erik's member. They made love quietly and with some concentration, building in time to an explosive climax that left them both gasping – and even closer to dropping off to sleep. In minutes they were both out like a light.

Chapter 73: The Dance of Deception

In the morning Bernadette slipped out of bed before Erik awoke and took a brief bath, then ate some breakfast and put on her smithing gear. He was barely stirring when she returned downstairs, ready to get in a good session of crafting with an eye to bringing pieces to Valkyrie for sale. "You got away," he remarked woefully. She smiled and stepped in to kiss and hug him.

"Inspiration calls!" she declared. "Sorry…"

Grinning ruefully, Erik completed getting dressed and headed up the ladder to get some breakfast. He was wondering if he might manage to slip away to the construction site today, and join one of the crews. He was particularly interested in the way they were setting the rafters to form the roof, and the attachment of the roof to the veranda that would run almost the full length of the annex's eastern side. He just needed to be sure Bernadette didn't spot him, as his presence there might be harder to explain than Bjorn's had been.

After eating Erik returned downstairs to consult with Berni. She was whaling away, hammer and tongs, at some smithing project. "Hey love," he said diffidently, interrupting her work with a kiss on her somewhat sweaty forehead. "I was thinking I might take a trip in to town, visit with Lifa and Anja and drop them off some supplies. Do you need anything?" Her brow furrowed.

"Rats," she said quietly. "I'm in the middle of crafting a bunch of stuff and I was hoping you'd help me carry it in later."

Erik's mind, as agile as any despite his lack of a scholarly bent, began crunching numbers. "Assuming Andrion just dropped Diane off at Daywatch and came right back here, he ought to be back by sometime this afternoon," he offered. "Maybe he could help you."

Bernadette grinned. "That's a good idea. Okay, see you later then…" She went back to her hammering.

Erik went up the ladder behind the bar again, needing to pick up some things to take to Lifa and her little family. He usually brought them supplies at least a couple of times a week, though now that Bjorn was earning a wage he supposed they were really able to buy what they needed for themselves. What the hell, it was an excuse to visit. He calculated he could stay at the construction site until perhaps an hour or two after lunch and still manage to have been at

Brightsgate Cottage for a while by the time Bernadette and Andrion might arrive there. So, he had Drelos give him some bread, cheese, apples, and a bottle or two of water to take along.

Erik got to the site and consulted with Bjorn, then joined one of the crews that was constructing roof trusses and raising them. The work went amazingly quickly with many hands (guided by heads that knew what they were about). Erik's prodigious strength and unusual height were assets in this enterprise. Around noontime he downed tools and ate his minimal lunch on site while chatting with the rest of the workers.

Few construction laborers were willing to spend the time or money to buy lunch down the road at the Maiden, so he hadn't met many of them before they had worked together today. When they got back to work after the break, their camaraderie was growing; and he was sorry to have to walk out in the middle of the afternoon shift in order to get to Brightsgate Cottage before Berni should come by. He explained what was going on to his coworkers, and they all grinned and slapped him on the back, happy to go along with the plot.

Andrion, tired of fast traveling already, lingered at Daywatch only long enough for Diane to give him several pages of detailed instructions for completing the water systems and their hookups, along with a verbal rundown of what they contained. He gave her a brief hug and his thanks, shook hands with Georges and wished him good hunting; then shimmered out of existence and reappeared outside the Maiden at around 2:30 in the afternoon. It had now been more than 24 hours since he'd departed the morning before, but it seemed like less than an hour of elapsed time. So why did he feel so tired… and hungry?

He went on in through the front doors and didn't see either Berni or Erik around. Stopping off at the bar, he greeted Lev. "You're back!" the innkeeper exclaimed, welcoming him home. "Can I get you anything?"

"In fact, I'm starving," Andrion admitted with a smile. In moments, Lev had slapped together a cold sandwich and some warm potato fingers, the last from the lunchtime rush that had recently ended. Between bites, Andrion asked "Are Berni and Erik around?"

"I think Erik went to town this morning," Lev replied. "But Bernadette's down in the basement working at the smithy. She popped up for lunch a while ago and then went right back down there." Wolfing the last of his food and washing it down with a quick drink of water, Andrion thanked him. Then, walking around the bar, he opened the trap door and descended the ladder.

Bernadette was working with her back to him, making so much noise with her hammer that she didn't hear him come down. Andrion crept lithely toward her, making little or no sound in his soft boots. Then he pounced. Bernadette squealed, rising nearly a foot in the air and almost hitting him with the hammer she was holding. She spun in his arms, her eyes wide, but her outrage turned to delight when she saw who it was. Dropping the hammer to the floor, she threw her arms around his neck and hopped up to lock her legs around his hips. Then she kissed him thoroughly.

Well that worked out okay, he thought. There was a moment there when he had begun to regret his impulse to surprise her. "I've missed you!" she said, kissing him again.

"But I've only been gone an hour," he teased. She considered that.

"You wouldn't believe how much I've gotten done in that hour," Bernadette told him. She dropped back down, somewhat to his regret, and after one more firm kiss gestured around at the arms and armor she'd created during her day-long session.

"I was just about to knock off for the day and take this all up to Valkyrie," she said. "Are you up for giving me a hand carrying it?" Andrion gave her a meaningful look.

"How about a quickie, first?" He'd made love with Berni (in a threesome with Erik, admittedly) only a few hours ago in subjective time. But, like his appetite for food, his libido seemed to think it had been much longer. He might have what Erik regarded as admirable self-control, but that didn't mean he wouldn't like to have sex with his darling every day.

His darling eyed him with amusement. Andrion could be quiet and reserved, sometimes, not as volatile as she or as unabashedly randy as Erik; but occasionally a side of him cropped up that reminded her why she found him not only lovable but deeply exciting. His brown eyes gazed into hers, hot with desire. "Right here and now?" Bernadette asked, looking around. She knew well the potential some of the room's furnishings offered, but wasn't sure whether he did.

He looked around. "The crafting bench is a little high (Andrion was three inches shorter than Erik, though still a tall man), but how about the enchanting table? Maybe I can enchant you…" he leered. A bolt of sexual excitement hit Bernadette at the thought. After a couple of experiences with Erik she'd developed a sort of kink for the things. The idea of doing it with Andrion on this same table where Erik had had her filled her with a slightly guilty excitement, and she began stripping off her enchanted smithing gear.

She turned it into a little bit of a striptease while disrobing, strolling around the area and slowly removing first one piece then another, all the way making eye contact with Andrion and writhing in a suggestive manner. He stood there devouring her with glowing eyes, enjoying the show. When she was finally completely nude she bent her legs, crouching with knees apart, and reached between her legs to fondle her crotch and finger herself.

Andrion was still wearing his armor from the trip to Daywatch, and from this angle Bernadette could look right up the skirt of it and see that his balls were tight, his cock erect. She'd have thought that would be painful – he'd complained it about it once before – but he seemed too distracted by watching her to notice. She got back onto her feet and strutted slowly over to him, putting her hands on his shoulders. Then she leaned close to him and murmured, "Are you planning to participate, or just watch?"

Right! Startled out of his lascivious reverie, Andrion hastened to unfasten the buckles and dropped the armor unceremoniously to the floor after only a few moments' effort. It was Bernadette's turn to watch, though he took far less time about it. Still, he looked magnificent when he'd finished disrobing. Firm muscles rippled beneath his smooth, light tan skin and his fine cock was standing up big and hard, ready to go.

Bernadette stepped close to press her body to his, kissing him deeply. Then she led him by the hand over to the enchanting table. He took her by the hips and boosted her up onto it. She perched with her buttocks on the table's front edge, knees bent and legs apart, poised to take him inside. The surface of the table was smooth and cool beneath her bare skin.

Smiling slightly, Andrion stepped close and guided his cock inside her. Oh yes, she was hot and slippery and ready for him, as usual. He pressed against her, sliding all the way in, and locked his mouth on hers. Then he stepped back slightly so that he could thrust in and out. Bernadette tipped her head back, resting the weight of her upper body on her hands as they were planted on the table's top, just soaking up the sensations as that powerful cock of his plowed her furrow.

Having promised Berni a quickie, and realizing they couldn't take all afternoon at it, Andrion gave himself permission for a change to lose himself in the sensations. He was watching Berni's face and chest, as her color rose and her breasts bobbed appealingly with each thrust. Her vocalizations went from little sighs and whimpers to moans, to screams as she seized him around the hips with her legs and began banging up against him, urging him all the way in on each stroke. He let it carry him away.

They climaxed together, very nearly their shortest sex session on record – but powerfully moving in spite of it. Still pressed all the way inside her, Andrion gathered Bernadette in his arms and squeezed her tight to him, kissing the top of her head. Her face pressed into his chest, she kissed him – and then mischievously tongued a nipple. He jumped a bit. "Whoo!" she said, her face pink. "That was fun!" As he slipped out she asked, "Could you hand me a towel please?" He fetched her one from a pile over near the bed, and she used it to keep from getting semen all down her legs as she hopped down from the table.

Cleaned up a bit, she approached her lover to give him a full-body hug. Then she said casually, "Um, where were we?" He had the grace to look a little guilty. She'd been all productive, and he'd spoked the smoothly turning wheel of her day's plans with his importunate lusts. Bernadette didn't seem to mind in the least, however. All work and no play... She pondered and said, "We both could probably use a bath. Why don't we just throw on some robes and take a quick dip, then go upstairs and put on some more appropriate clothing before we go into town?"

Andrion grinned at her. Hugging her once again he said, "Have I mentioned lately that I love you?" She nuzzled his neck.

"Love you more."

"No, love *you* more…" They both grinned at this nonsense game, then set about finding a couple of robes to put on. This area was regularly stocked with towels and spare robes as well as ores and ingots as part of the Maiden's housekeeping service.

After the bath and clothing change the two returned downstairs and loaded up the wares Bernadette wanted to take to sell. They went up through the trap door to the deck and, as Bernadette now had her map back, saved some effort in hauling by fast-traveling to just inside the gates of Waterdon. Valkyrie was only a few paces away, and in a short time they'd dropped off their load.

The pieces Bernadette brought, as well as all the other items the store bought and sold, were recorded in a ledger kept by Wolaf. He counted out a few thousand in gold and gave them to Bernadette, also making a note of the disbursement. She and Andrion shook hands with him and waved to Alessia, who was working at the bench, as they left to go next door.

By the time Andrion and Bernadette got to Brightsgate Cottage, Erik was starting to regret having run off so early from the job site. It was beginning to look as if he could have put in another couple of hours. But then they arrived, and it was just as well he'd gotten there in plenty of time to work out his cover story with Lifa and Anja. To explain why he was here so late when he'd left the Maiden hours ago, Erik said he'd run into a friend in town and had been hanging out with him and some others for a while. Much better to be thought an idle layabout than to admit one had been working!

Bernadette and Andrion visited with Lifa and Anja for a while, but they didn't want to impose on the little family at suppertime; so soon after Bjorn returned they made their goodbyes, Erik accompanying them. Before leaving though, Andrion asked Bjorn how the project was coming. "Another couple of days and we'll be putting on siding, I think," he said. "The cistern's due to be delivered next week, and that ought to be a real project getting it installed."

Bernadette and Erik were across the room talking with Lifa, and Andrion murmured in an undertone, "I need to get you to make a production drawing of the kitchen sink. The overall size needs to fit the frame that we built in the kitchen, and it wants to have two bowls – one about eight inches deep and the other two feet deep, each with a hole in the bottom for the drainpipe. Then once you've got the drawing done, I'm hoping you or Lifa can take it over and give it Alessia. We want it fabricated out of dypalfar metal."

Bjorn lifted an eyebrow. That was going to cost a pretty penny. But with his friends now in partnership with Valkyrie, he supposed that cost would be reduced. And clearly, Bernadette and her two fiancés had no shortage of coin. "I'll take care of it, don't worry," he told Andrion quietly. Then they joined the others and said goodbyes before the three friends returned to the Maiden for supper.

As they were leaving, Andrion said "It's a nice evening. Now that we're not burdened, why don't we walk back?" He was really anxious to see what progress had been made on the annex during the "hour" he'd been gone. With Andrion at her side, whether fully armored or stark naked, Bernadette knew that the road between Waterdon and the Maiden held no peril they couldn't defeat. A bolt of his battle magic could send a shri into the next march. So, walk they did.

The three were soon sharing another excellent supper at Bernadette's magnificent new table, in company with Hjaermond, Selden, and a visiting warden from Normarsh. Bernadette was feeling remarkably pleased with herself – after earning a bunch of money, having a jolly fuck with one of her two favorite men on the planet, enjoying a get-together with friends, and taking a pleasant walk in the fresh air. "Do you realize," she said to Erik and Andrion, "there is almost nowhere we have to go or anything we have to do before Bjorn and Lifa's wedding next week? It's going to be like a vacation!"

Chapter 74: The Home Stretch

That wasn't quite the case. While she was not strictly required, herself, to perform any of these tasks, there were a number that needed doing and Bernadette found herself involved in them. Two triceratops, slow and generally less aggressive than mammoths, had to be killed because they refused to remove themselves from the area north of the Maiden where the tent was to be erected. Lev opined that the meat was as good as beef, and since there was so much of it they should butcher the carcasses and preserve it for the party.

Bernadette and Erik found themselves working together out on the deck to produce an enormous chest, with inner and outer layers of wood stuffed with wool between them and thin sheets of dypalfar metal lining the inside. This had a drain hole at the bottom. Hunks of the meat were wrapped in waxed paper to prevent damage from freezing, then Andrion used his best frost spell on one layer of meat packages at a time as they filled the chest up to the top. The frozen meat helped to keep itself cold, and once or twice a day depending on the weather Andrion or Drelos would apply some additional frost.

Erik borrowed a small crew from Hegmar for a one-day job at the Maiden, extending the deck on the south side by some twenty feet and putting a ten-foot deep, open-fronted lean-to shed on it running the depth of the building, attached to the Maiden building across its southern end. A hole cut in the Maiden's kitchen area on one side of the fireplace gave access to the lean-to from within the building (with a door to close it, when not in use). They put their "cold storage chest" in there, protected from the elements and offering more counter space for kitchen operations.

The men took turns going down to the project site for a few hours at a time while Bernadette was busy with other things and not likely to notice. This gave them the opportunity to keep tabs on progress, supervise the job to make sure their intentions were being fulfilled (though both had to admit, Hegmar seemed to have it well in hand), and learn about house construction from watching and working with Hegmar's experienced crew.

Bernadette considered removing the tall grass from the intended tent site by having Andrion use a fire spell on it. His powerful battle magic should have been able to char the grass right down to the ground. But she feared a wildfire getting out of control, and the possibility existed that the smell of charred grass, contained by the tent, might make sleeping in it a nightmare. So, they did it the old-fashioned way. She hired a couple of farm laborers from Stormstrife Farm, across the road, and they scythed the grass down to the height of a nice lawn in few hours. The area was only about the size of a small wheat field, after all.

The people Lev had gotten the tent from were willing to provide a couple of crew to help get it up, but more including Bernadette herself (and, to her immense surprise, even Hjaermond) came out to assist with the effort. The thing was quite magnificent, a pavilion of some sort she guessed, and probably intended to house a traveling bazaar. Such things were rare sights in Iscandia, but more common in Zahar – or so she'd been told.

Arngeld's two young sons came by with a partial delivery of their order, two more of the small tables and eight chairs. These were almost immediately pressed into service, as the Maiden continued to fill up in the evenings and at lunchtime. Lev soon set up more cooking equipment in the lean-to, and requested that some removable panels be made for the front of it so that it could be used in foul weather. This also necessitated the installation of chimney pipe in the lean-to's simple sloped roof.

Carpets covered the shorn field, providing a floor for the tent, and bedrolls were distributed in it. Those Maiden employees who normally slept in beds, including Fenris (who acted as Security for the inn), began sleeping in the tent. This freed more beds for inn guests, and eased the congestion. Lower lodging rates were offered to those guests willing to bunk in the tent or in the guardhouse, which sat on the rear deck.

In the midst of all this Bernadette found time to finalize some sketches of clothing she wanted made for her, and fast-travelled into Waterdon (giving both Erik and Andrion a rare opportunity to spend a few hours at the project site together). She visited Gerde at the Snowhairs' main residence (though several of the clan were members of the Brave Company and resided at Ynglingar). Gerde was quite intrigued with the designs Bernadette had brought her, took all of her measurements, and let her choose from among several fabric samples. One dress, the one she wanted to wear to the wedding in Lakedon, would be ready on the fifteenth.

Chapter 75: For the Rest of My Life

And so it was, finally, that Beridtag the sixteenth of Fevrous arrived. Everything was in readiness. The new cooking table had been delivered, the food and drink for the party were on order and scheduled to be here early on the eighteenth. The last of the chairs and tables would be here by the time they returned. Bernadette had a splendid but sober (not wishing to compete with the bride) dress to wear for the occasion, and had seen to it that Erik, Andrion, and Bjorn all had suitable clothing as well. Now *that* had been like pulling teeth. Why would an activity so enjoyable for women be such a trial for men? She knew that once they were polished up and wearing their resplendent garb, they would feel good about it. Little Anja had a lovely dress made for the occasion too.

Bernadette had gotten Larissa, an exotically beautiful young elf woman Lev had hired a few weeks ago to help out at the Maiden, to pile her hair up on her head for her this morning, and she liked the effect. Not only did it look elegant, it kept the hair out of her eyes and away from anything she might be working on. She only hoped it would hold up for the several hours of travel ahead of them.

Bernadette had made a pair of simple gold rings and after enchanting them with the Blessing of Marmira (which she'd learned from the ring obtained from Daaralie), had given them to Erik to pass to Yusuf for the ceremony. He was acting in the role of head groomsman. Large bouquets of flowers had been picked from the surrounding countryside. She'd invited Lifa, Bjorn, and Anja to join them for supper at the Maiden this evening, as they didn't really need to leave for Lakedon until about eight.

Lev outdid himself, serving a perfectly seasoned and roasted haunch of venison with roasted potatoes and vegetables that had been sautéed with herbs. For dessert, he produced something he'd worked out with Andrion beforehand, but had not yet tried out on his customers. He'd mixed cream, milk, sugar, and pureed icefruit. Then Andrion had applied a frost spell to the bowl while Lev stirred the mixture constantly with a long-handled Galise whisk. The result was an icy but soon melting, rich and creamy treat. The general opinion was he was going to have to come up with a way to produce mass quantities of this delight in order to meet the demand he was sure to find – especially once summer came around.

After the meal Bernadette along with Erik, Andrion, and Lifa all went up the stairs to change. Anja was already wearing her wedding outfit, as was Bjorn his. The men, after stripping down to their underwear, quickly slipped into their finery. Then Bernadette and Lifa helped each other get into theirs. Once again, Bernadette was struck by how truly beautiful Lifa looked in that dress. You would never guess she had spent most of her adult life as a hard-bitten fighter wearing chain mail.

Erik and Andrion had returned to the lower level, and they were clustered with Bjorn, Anja, Hjaermond, and Selden at the Owner's Table watching as the ladies descended the stairs. Erik and Andrion had already seen the dress, of course, but this was the first time Bjorn had beheld his bride in her magnificent wedding gown. He was gaping at her in silent awe. He could scarcely believe his good fortune that this goddess was his. And she truly looked like a celestial vision in that dress!

Bernadette thought Bjorn looked pretty darn good himself in the fine clothing she'd induced him to wear. His face might be little scarred, but his body was superb and those clothes showed him off to good advantage while making him look wealthy and respectable in addition to studly. Bjorn stood as Lifa approached, all of his attention on her and her alone. His one eye glowing, he approached her almost hesitantly. He would have liked to crush her to him, but that was out of the question. He settled for taking her hands and looking into her eyes. Her look of love and joy filled his soul.

The rest of the party just watched the pair as they drank each other in. Awww… Hjaermond and Selden were beaming. Their lives had been awfully dull before they came to the Maiden, and now there seemed to be always something interesting going on, such as this touching love story unfolding before them. Both of them were delighted to see young Bjorn, who had given his oath of service to Hjaermond when he was little more than a boy, marrying such a lovely young woman – and with such an important patron as The Fireblood.

Last-minute good wishes were distributed to the couple from various Maiden employees, most of whom knew Lifa from her months as a resident here. Bernadette's checklist was produced and double-checked, then they all stepped out onto the front porch and she gathered them around her. Here goes! After a few seconds of blackness, they found themselves standing in bright morning sunshine just inside the gates of Lakedon. Bernadette was relieved to find the entire party here and accounted for.

Anja, who did not remember her only other fast-travelling experience (having been unconscious at the time), was riveted. "Ooh!" she exclaimed. "Where *are* we?" She clung to Lifa's skirts, her little hands fortunately having been cleaned after supper.

"This is Lakedon, Ani," Lifa told her. "We're here for the wedding!" Anja had thought of little else since the idea had first been explained to her, and she was so excited at the thought that she brushed aside her unease at their translocation in a moment.

They took a little while to orient themselves, then began walking down the street to their left, heading toward the Temple of Marmira. From the activity in the central marketplace ahead of them, it was just around 8 in the morning – as planned. They were pleased to encounter Eorl Ormund and his party as they approached the temple, coming in the other direction after having put up for the night with Eorl Trudwynne Lakeholm at her in-town keep. He'd brought along his two eldest children; and as his wife was long deceased, his body servant Miralis also accompanied him.

Greetings were exchanged at the entry to the temple, and Ormund smiled avuncularly at Lifa. By the gods, the girl had turned into a beauty! He remembered her as a half-starved orphan lurking around the kitchens at Wyrmshalla, then as a grim and doughty warrior seldom to be seen without full armor. But now! He felt quite pleased with the arrangements that he and Paolo had worked out with The Fireblood regarding this young woman's future. She surely deserved all the best.

The party, jostling a bit, climbed the steps of the temple and entered through the doors. It was now approaching 8:30, and the priests and priestesses were getting ready for the ceremony to begin. Lifa, Anja, and Bjorn took a bench at one side of the altar for now, while Bernadette, Erik, and Andrion sat on the other. The rest of the wedding guests, certainly not a large group, took seats on benches in rows behind them. The entire temple, fully packed, would not hold much more than two dozen people. Weddings in Iscandia were not usually large affairs.

They all sat talking quietly, waiting for Yusuf to arrive. He appeared in a few minutes and engaged in some consultation with the happy couple and their adopted daughter, then had a few words with Bernadette and her posse. A little while later he indicated it was time to begin. While he stood near the altar Anja, who'd been given a basket of flowers cut with short stems, walked up the aisle between the rows of benches. She was dropping the blossoms to either side of her in time with her steps, and grinning from ear to ear as all those assembled grinned back at her.

Behind her, Bjorn and Lifa walked hand in hand. For the moment, their attention was focused on the little gamin who had brought them together and was ushering them into a new life. As Anja approached the altar Erik, Bernadette, and Andrion stood to the right and Anja joined them – standing on Erik's left. He patted her shoulder and gave her a smile to let her know she'd done an excellent job. Her little face was shining like the sun, joy rendered solid.

Lifa and Bjorn reached the altar, standing before Yusuf with Anja and Erik on Bjorn's right hand. Then Yusuf began the ceremony. "Our father Aderos created the world and all its creatures. But it was from Marmira, the mother who loves and watches over us, that we first learned to love one another. And love shared is what makes life worth living. We are gathered here today to bear witness to the joining of two of Aderos' children in the holy bonds of matrimony. May they walk side by side in this life, sharing all it may bring. Do you agree to be united in love, for the rest of your lives?"

His question was initially directed to Lifa. She had been gazing at the young Afran priest, but now turned her shining eyes to Bjorn. "I do," she said proudly. "For the rest of my life."

Yusuf repeated the question to Bjorn, who also replied, his deep voice rumbling with emotion, "I do. For the rest of my life."

Erik handed the rings to Yusuf and he continued, "Under the auspices of our loving mother Marmira, I declare this couple to be wed. I present to the two of you these matching rings, blessed by Marmira's divine grace. May they protect each of you in your new life together."

So simple a ceremony, and so brief. The effort to bring all these people together had taken a hundred times as long, and more. But it was all worth it! Bjorn slipped one of the rings onto Lifa's finger, and she did the same for him. Then they kissed, a gesture that started out chaste and ended up with a little heat trail that suggested there would be fireworks back at Brightsgate Cottage tonight.

After that the happy couple thanked Yusuf and Bernadette gave him yet another "donation." The wedding guests clustered around to congratulate them, and Bernadette said "I think it's time. Eorl Ormund, might I get you to do the honors?" She passed him a sheaf of papers she'd been keeping in the bag she carried with her when she was dressed more formally and didn't want to lug a pack.

The old man, so often grim and careworn, grinned. Bernadette had a brief glimpse of the vigorous young Norseman he must have been back around the time her parents were starting to eye one another with interest. He drew himself up, aware of his own importance. "Lifa," he said, "it's my pleasure on behalf of the march of Waterdon to thank you for your years of faithful service. I am hereby releasing you from your oath, so that you can live your life as you wish. Should you desire to continue in service to the march, that will be your choice. But you are now freed from all prior obligations. And in recognition of the service you have already given, I present you with this token of our gratitude." He deposited a purse of gold in her hand, along with a parchment declaring her obligations to the march concluded.

Lifa was stunned. Her oath of service, given to Eorl Ormund when she was barely into womanhood, had given her a sense of purpose in life. But she now had a new purpose, and she'd been wondering how that purpose was going to conflict with her preexisting obligations. Now she found herself free, and incidentally quite a bit richer. "My eorl! Thank you!" she curtsied to him, liking the way the silken fabric of her dress rustled as she did so.

Ormund was not finished, however. "It has come to my attention that you and your new husband have been acting as parents toward a young orphan girl" – he nodded toward Anja, who was taking this all in goggle-eyed – "originally from Westmarch. Is that not right?" Lifa and Bjorn nodded a little uncertainly. Ormund smiled at them. "Have no fear! I have received confirmation from the Eorl of Westmarch that he has no claim on this child. Therefore, I am confirming you two as the official and legal parents of… Anja, is it?" He glanced at the girl again. My, she was cute.

Anja, Lifa, and Bjorn all nodded in unison. Eorl Ormund handed them another signed and sealed document. Then he went on, "You are now truly a family, but you do not have a family name. At the behest of The Fireblood, to whom you have given steadfast service, I am pleased to grant you this official patent establishing the Clan of Steadfast. Henceforth you will be known as Lifa Steadfast, Bjorn Steadfast, and Anja Steadfast, and this clan name will pass to your descendants."

Lifa and Bjorn were stunned. To be granted a name for their House was almost the same as being elevated to the nobility! But what of Bjorn's obligations to Westmarch? At this point Bernadette stepped in, trying hard to suppress a grin though delight was practically seeping out of her pores. Erik and Andrion, as surprised by all of this as anybody, were just watching her in love and admiration as she made things happen.

"Thank you, Eorl Ormund, for all you have done. I have my own contribution to add. Bjorn, I have made arrangements with Eorl Galdur Staerlin, who inherited your oath to Westmarch with his accession to the eorlship. He has happily agreed to release you from that oath." She handed a sealed document to Bjorn.

Hjaermond, who was standing close, patted Bjorn on the shoulder. "Congratulations, boy," he said quietly and with glee.

Bjorn took the paper with a smile of satisfaction. Since the change in eorlship, he had felt a little like a slave who's been sold down the river. "Thank you," he murmured.

"And there is one last thing," Bernadette said – the smile finally escaping her not-so-well-schooled face to glow like the sun on all assembled there. "I have in my hand the deed to Brightsgate Cottage.

It has duly been transferred to Bjorn and Lifa Steadfast, signed and sealed by Paolo Adelini." She passed it over to Lifa, knowing full well who'd be presiding over that little home.

Lifa's face lit up, and she whooped. They were free, Anja was theirs, and they owned their home outright! Life opened up before her like a vision of Asengard. Only without quite so many battle-axes. And with lots more adorable babies and little children. "Thank you, thank you, Bernadette!" she exclaimed. "Clan Steadfast owes you everything, and we will be eternally grateful." She gulped a little, and then her happiness spilled out of her and she decided not to try holding it back any longer.

"I have my own announcement to make," she said. "Before this year is out, Anja will have a baby brother or sister." This was not news to Bernadette, but certain other members of Lifa's audience were riveted by the announcement. Andrion and Erik were surprised and delighted, and Bjorn was well-nigh floored.

"Lifi!" he exclaimed, his one eye alight with love and joy. He drew her into his arms and kissed her thoroughly, never mind the damn dress. She didn't object in the slightest.

The party broke up at this point and they left the temple, allowing Yusuf and his coreligionists to prepare for the next wedding. As this was the only temple in Iscandia devoted exclusively to Marmira, it got the lion's share of the province's wedding business. They milled around on the sidewalk, and Bernadette suggested that they all repair to the nearby Smiling Salmon for some celebratory drinks before their return to Waterdon. It would likely be ten in the evening on this day, the seventeenth, before they were back.

Everyone liked this idea; and Zendna and Argani-Zhe, the saurion proprietors of the Smiling Salmon, were not displeased with it either. Bernadette passed a large quantity of gold across to the respectable-looking lizard matron, then slipped away in the hubbub and made her way across to Daaralie's jewelry stand in the marketplace. "Ah, Fireblood! You have returned as promised," she said in her melodious voice. Did you expect me not to, she wondered?

"The rings are ready?" Bernadette asked, skipping the bush-beating with her usual direct approach.

Daaralie looked pleased. "Ah, yes… I think that you will like them." She reached under the stall and produced a small velvet bag, spilling the rings out onto a velvet-lined tray atop the counter. The fabric set off the glimmer of the gold and gems that were her stock in trade.

They were locked into their joined forms, each consisting of sinuous bands of gold in colors of yellow, red, and bronze; but the jeweler took a ring in her graceful hands and demonstrated how it came apart to form three separate rings. It was exactly as Bernadette had conceived it, but had not had the skill herself to turn into reality. "Daaralie!" These are wonderful!" she exclaimed, then looked about her. She didn't have much time. Paying the elf woman the additional gold they'd agreed on – and a hefty tip besides – she tucked the rings in their velvet pouch into her bag. Then, thanking Daaralie again, she hastened back to the nearby inn.

No one appeared to have noticed her absence. The mood was jubilant, and everyone was toasting and chattering away, delighted with the wedding and all that had come after it. Mindful of the time, Bernadette called for everyone's attention. "It will be late when we get back to Waterdon," she pointed out. "I think that we should return now. Eorl Ormund, unless you've made other arrangements, I'd like to include you and your guests in our party for fast-traveling."

He smiled at her. "That should be fine," he said. "From my experience with those things you can take up to a couple of dozen people with you provided your mind is strong enough." They all looked at him questioningly. He looked mildly embarrassed. "In my youth," he added, "we used to use them for transporting raiding parties…"

Bernadette smiled radiantly. "I've had occasion to use mine in the same way," she admitted. "Shall we gather outside?" They all gathered around: Bernadette, Andrion, Erik, the newly made Steadfast clan, Hjaermond and Selden, Ormund and his small entourage. Bernadette enfolded them with her mind and wished them all back in the direction of Waterdon. Out of respect for the eorl, their first stop was at Wyrmshalla. "See you at the party tomorrow?" she asked. "

Wouldn't miss it," he promised. Addressing Bjorn he added, "Take care of those girls, young fellow. You're a lucky man."

Bjorn nodded, murmuring "I know."

They debated whether to fast-travel down to Brightsgate Cottage, and decided to walk instead as it was a pleasant night. Bernadette's only concern was for Selden, but he negotiated the many steps down to the lower city with a sprightly air, requiring only an arm from his nephew in the way of assistance. At the door of Brightsgate Cottage, Lifa, Bjorn, and Anja (who was beginning to wilt, it being well past her bedtime), thanked and hugged the rest of the party before bidding them good night. They'd all be walking down to the Maiden tomorrow after lunch for the party celebrating their marriage.

Bernadette then fast-traveled herself, Erik, Andrion, and the two old men from Alfenstein back to the Maiden. By now it was well past eleven p.m., and their elderly companions thanked her for the enjoyable experience before heading right upstairs to bed. The life of the Maiden at this late hour had mostly subsided, and no one was around the common room but Drelos, a couple of night-owl guests, and young Larissa. She greeted Bernadette saying "Oh, good! Your hairstyle has survived beautifully!"

Bernadette patted her 'do, realizing that is was in fact still perfectly arrayed atop her head. Of course, it had only been around four hours of subjective time since it was first arranged. Still… "Thank you, Larissa!" she said. "I really appreciate your help. You'll do it again for me next month?"

The elf woman smiled shyly. "I'd be delighted to, Fireblood," she said.

"Please, call me Bernadette." There were a few occasions where she valued her fame and was happy to be identified as The Fireblood; but not with people that she interacted with as friends. Larissa smiled, and went back to her duties. There was a lot of clearing-up to be done after a typical evening at the Maiden.

Though the hour was late and they had a busy day tomorrow, the three were not yet ready to turn in. They'd lost a full day in fast-travelling; but they needed time to decompress, and to savor the emotions that had been provoked by that day's momentous events. They decided to take a soak in the hot pool together, and since there was almost nobody around they stripped on the spot and hopped right in. Before disrobing completely, Bernadette had a thought and asked Drelos, "Did the chairs and tables get here?"

"All good," he replied. "Actually, they brought a couple more chairs than they'd promised. Oh, and the musicians from Sylvanian came in too. Lev put them out in the tent, and they were fine with it."

Bernadette smiled in relief. After weeks of planning and organizing, the culmination of some of those plans had driven others completely out of her mind. "Thank you, Drelos," she said sincerely. Then she dropped her drawers and stepped into the pool with (in her opinion, at least), the two finest men on Agena. Probably, all of Terris. She slipped in between and put an arm around each of them. Not that she could get her small, slender, but well-muscled arms very far around either of these exemplary hunks. Love welled up in her like a hot spring, bubbling to the surface and suffusing her with joy.

Her guys were less overcome. "Berni, that was sensational," Erik said. "I had no *idea* what you were up to. And then, when Ormund started in…" he lapsed into a happy grin, reaching down to squeeze her naked body.

"And Lifa's announcement," Andrion threw in. That had struck him to the core, watching Bjorn's reaction to the news that he would soon be the father of a new baby. He wanted that more than anything, wanted to hold his child – and Berni's – in his arms. "Did you know?..."

Bernadette smiled and squeezed his thigh. "She told me a couple of days ago," she admitted. "But I don't think anyone else knew. Certainly not Bjorn, and Anja wouldn't have a clue. But the signs were there, if you thought about it. I've got a couple of much younger siblings, so I watched my mom through two pregnancies. I hope everything goes all right." A silent prayer went up from all three of them to the gods, Marmira in particular, for the health of Lifa's unborn child.

They all sat there soaking and enjoying the hot water and warm feelings for a while. Then Bernadette sighed. "Well, we're up next. I hope you guys are ready for this." The two of them exchanged glances over her head, confirming that they were, indeed ready. Except for the fact that their home was little more than half finished. Then Bernadette added, "But first, a party!"

Chapter 76: The Gala Event

Bernadette woke early. She'd chosen to sleep with Andrion, but they'd been so tired they hadn't made love before going to sleep; and now she was too hyped up with excitement about the wedding celebration. She opted to wear comfortable trousers and a less than elegant shirt, with soft shoes – anticipating she'd be getting her clothes messed up. She could put on something nicer later on.

The Maiden was a hive of activity when she came downstairs, and Erik, too, was up and dressed. They breakfasted together, then reported to Lev for instructions on where they might best help. "We're in luck," he said, "the weather is beautiful and I don't think we're going to get any rain. So your plans to bring a lot of the party out onto the deck should work fine. I want to set up the new cooking table on the south side of the new deck section, and put up a counter at the open end of the lean-to so we can serve party guests across that."

Bernadette was checking these items off in her mind. She'd been heavily involved in the planning of this event, but had left most of the details up to Lev since he was so capable. A lot of the work fell on him in any case. She and Erik went out onto the deck and admired the view of the sun rising above the mountains, breathing in the cool air. By this afternoon it should be warm enough to make lounging out here downright pleasant.

They helped set out extra tables and chairs, then went around to the southern end and found Maiden staff trying to haul the cooking table out of the lean-to and over to the deck railing opposite. They laid sheets of steel under it to catch any drippings or hot coals escaping through the bottom vent holes, lest they set the deck on fire.

The thing was heavy, and they jumped to lend a hand. Erik could carry one end of it all by himself, with others arrayed around the other three sides, and it was soon in place. Bernadette went off and chopped a bunch of firewood, which Erik carried off for her to stack by the table. The fire would be laid and set ablaze after lunch, as party time approached.

Erik went off in search of any remaining heavy lifting, and Bernadette returned inside through the lean-to's connecting door to see if she could help with kitchen prep. There were a lot of chickens to be processed, and a lot of that wrapped triceratops meat had been defrosted. It would need cutting into suitable size chunks for the grill, and probably some tenderizing with a large hammer as well.

Inside, she found Andrion. He was dressed and was applying his freeze spell to pan after pan of water, building up a collection of ice for the chilling of drinks. "Hey!" he said pleasantly, on spotting her. "You got away…" She came over and gave him a hug, then waved her arms at everything that was going on around them.

"You know," she said. "Busy, busy…" He nodded.

Many hands make light work. Lev had hung a sign out front warning the usual lunch crowd that a private party was in progress, and that they would not be serving today. Instead, he piled sandwiches on a platter with fresh fruit, cold drinks, and a mountain of potato chips alongside, for the work crew to eat as they grew hungry. He found Larissa a big help in the kitchen especially, and was pleased that he'd hired her. If he could just find another four or five like her, they'd be doing well.

A little before two the Steadfast clan arrived on foot, dressed in their wedding clothes. Lifa and Anja oohed at the enormous Bride's Cake Lev had prepared. They'd pushed the Owner's Table up against a wall and arrayed the cake on it, flanked by vases of flowers. Guests bringing gifts would pile those around the table, to be opened by the bride and groom later in the festivities.

The musicians had arisen late and had not helped with the party preparations, other than to dress in their performing finery and tune up their instruments. They'd set up in a corner of the common room overlooking the bathing pool, and had begun playing some soft instrumental pieces as a soothing counterpart to the bustling atmosphere.

The coals on the cooking table were hot, chickens and other meats were sizzling on the grill, and barrels full of ice and bottled drinks were scattered here and there around the deck and the Maiden's interior. Bernadette and her men had cleaned up after eating and put on some party clothes, less formal and more fun than their garb at the wedding.

And gradually the guests began to arrive. Some brought children with them, and Larissa volunteered to take charge of them – bringing them out onto the deck for some games and keeping them out of the adults' hair. Anja joined the group. Lifa and Bjorn, holding hands, lingered near the table with the cake on it so they could greet guests as they arrived.

Eorl Ormund came, accompanied by Miralis and all three of his children. The two younger ones joined the group with Larissa. The eldest was practically a young woman, and she soon became very interested in the musicians – one of them in particular. While the sun shone the party guests spent much of their time on the decks. The musicians relocated to a corner of the deck near the stairs to the river, fortunately unmolested by any ogres. Even a beast like that would hesitate to approach a gathering of humans this large.

Lev had much earlier supervised the spitting and roasting of the ox, for which they'd dug an enormous fire pit beyond the new southern deck section. It cooked from mid-morning until almost sunset, before it was finally declared ready to eat. Sections were carved off and piled high on platters. As it grew dark outside, the happy couple (once again accompanied by their daughter) retired inside and most of the guests packed into the common room to present toasts. Wedding gifts were displayed and enthused over, thanks were given, and those who were not already stuffed to the gills with the food and drink that had been flowing all afternoon now had the chance to partake of a more serious supper.

After everyone had eaten, Lifa and Bjorn ceremoniously cut the cake – making sure there were enough pieces to go around. Bride's cake, rich with nuts and dried fruits, was a heavy and delicious concoction. And it would last for weeks, if wrapped up and kept in a cool place. Some pieces were carried off as souvenirs or to be eaten later.

Many of the older guests, as well as Ormund and his party, gave their congratulations to the happy couple and then left after the cake had been distributed. But some of the younger ones, and all the Maiden residents of course, stayed on. The musicians had had many breaks during the course of the day but in the evening they were back on the job and their playlist now strayed into moving ballads, sung in two-part harmony, and lively dance tunes that got the remaining guests up on their feet. Even Bjorn danced, with Anja standing on his boot tops!

Things finally began to wind down, and by around ten the last guest had departed. Anja had been laid down to sleep on the Maiden's master bed, and Bernadette volunteered to run the family back to Brightsgate Cottage using her map. That saved jostling the sleeping child any more than necessary. She fast-traveled back as well, and found the seemingly tireless Maiden crew well on their way to having everything cleaned up. Amazing!

Bernadette hugged Erik and Andrion on her return, then stood there beside them and rapped on the table for attention. "Everybody, thank you! You all did a tremendous job today, and I think nobody will argue with me that this was the greatest party the Waterdon area has seen in a generation at least. I really appreciate your efforts, and I want you all to have a bonus." She produced a sack of gold from her pack, which she'd carried with her on the quick trip to Waterdon. "Lev, here is 500 guilders. Please distribute this to the Maiden staff and everybody else who helped today."

Lev smiled somewhat tiredly and took the bag. "I suppose I should give some of it right back to you, then. You and the guys were a big help this morning." Bernadette waved him away.

"Thanks, Lev, but as the hosts we're expected to help. I just hope this will let everyone know how much we appreciate you and the things that you do." A round of spontaneous applause burst from the assembled crew. Bernadette, Erik, and Andrion nodded their heads in acknowledgement. Then she murmured to the guys, "This is where we do our disappearing act, I think. I'm exhausted."

They nodded. It had been a bloody long, tiring day. A hell of a lot more fun than some other long, tiring days they'd had together, but nobody was going to argue with her. They climbed the stairs to the master bedroom, where Erik and Andrion sat at the table while Bernadette stood at the foot of the bed and then over-dramatically jumped backwards to fall on it with a soft thump, arms and legs spread wide. "Ooofff…" she said. They grinned at her.

After a while Bernadette spoke more coherently. "There's no *way* we're doing this again in a little over three weeks," she moaned. "When we get back from Sylvanian it's going to be something like two or three in the morning of the same day the party is held. What can we do?"

"We're just going to have to get Lev and Drelos some more help," Andrion said. "I'll put out the word in town, and mention it to Britta at the Flying Horseman. Travelers are always asking her for news and gossip. And even if we can't take on that many permanent employees, we can hire a bunch of people just to help out on the day of the party."

"Do you think so?" she asked hopefully. After weeks of effort, she was ready for all of her headaches to be over with and her new life to start. Of course, there was still the issue of finding land and designing their house, then getting it built. That would probably take months, and until it was done she'd be keeping her amulet on. She didn't want to be trying to raise a baby in this hectic place.

Andrion came over and sat on the bed beside her. "Don't worry, love," he said, leaning down to kiss her sweetly. Erik came over too, kneeling at the end of the bed and reaching across to pull her soft dancing slippers off her feet. He began massaging first one foot, then the other. Ooh, that felt wonderful! "By the way," Andrion said, "did I tell you how sexy you look in that outfit?" She smiled at him. He continued to kiss her, but with more heat than sweet. His hand strayed to the soft fabric of her party dress, and he squeezed her breasts, cupping her head to pull her to him as he kissed her still more deeply. She was beginning to feel her fatigue burn off like fog on an autumn morning.

She sat up, and Erik leaned back so she could pull her feet beneath her and lift the dress off over her head. She'd worn no undershirt with this, but did have underdrawers on. Then they resumed where they'd left off, Andrion kissing her and rubbing her breasts while Erik began kissing and licking her feet. Then he reached up and pulled her drawers down and off, before crawling up to apply his mouth and tongue to her slit.

As Erik began eating her, Bernadette sat up and scooted down toward the foot of the bed and off toward one side of it. He now had full access to her while kneeling on the floor. Then she motioned to Andrion to remove his clothes, which he did with remarkable alacrity. He stood on the floor at the side of the bed, where she could reach him to suck his cock while Erik licked her cunt. Oh, yeah! If she'd been fading a bit earlier, the excitement of this situation had her wide awake and concentrating fully.

Having her mouth full of Andrion while Erik stimulated her with his mouth and hands soon had Bernadette climbing toward orgasm, bucking on the bed – which made it somewhat hard for her to keep a grip with her mouth. As she came, she gripped Andrion with her hands instead. Then she resumed using her mouth on Andrion, but less aggressively and with more tongue.

In a little while, still panting, she said "Erik, take your clothes off already!" He grinned, her juices glistening in his short beard, and stripped. Then she relocated herself. As exciting as it was for her to make love with the two of them at once sometimes, there were relatively few positions that would let her pleasure both of them at the same time. Unless she felt like getting fucked in the ass, which she didn't. She'd tried it a couple of times and had found it rather more painful than pleasurable.

So, she knelt crosswise on the bed and Erik stood behind her, entering her from behind. With Andrion standing on the other side of the bed before her, she now began sucking him vigorously, fully penetrated from both ends at once. The sense of brotherhood between the two men Bernadette loved had grown over recent months, especially since their pledge of marriage. They no longer found anything wrong or odd about fucking her together, each of them secure in her love and not worried that the other might be a better lover or something like that. Erik grinned at Andrion across Berni's heaving back, then focused on what he was doing.

Bernadette found herself overwhelmed by sensations: Erik's immense cock piercing her to her depths, the friction of it moving in and out, the hot, slightly salty taste of Andrion's cock in her mouth, the velvety smoothness of the head, his balls clenched tight as she tickled them with the fingers of one hand while supporting her weight with the other. Her lovers were familiar to her now. She knew every inch of their bodies, the triggers for their responses. But knowing them did not mute the passionate desire she felt for them, individually or in concert. A rush of excitement started where Erik filled her behind and hurtled through her core like a magical bolt, filling her mind with coruscations of hot red fire.

Both of them were attuned to her and knew she was about to come, and the anticipation brought them up to the tipping point. As her climax seized her and her vaginal walls clamped tight around Erik's cock, squeezing him in rhythmic waves, she went all the way down on Andrion, taking him part of the way down her throat. She managed to keep from choking as his hot cum shot inside her, even as Erik was filling her from the other end. For a moment, the three of them were suspended in an instant of sexual ecstasy.

Releasing Andrion from her mouth and pulling free from Erik as well, Bernadette collapsed on the bed as the two men who adored her stood on either side, dicks subsiding. They soon surged toward her and helped her get turned around, so that the two of them could join her lying on the bed. They were both weak in the knees. The three of them lay pressed together in the bed like the elements of a sandwich, gasping for air.

When Bernadette could speak again she said, "Funny. I thought I was tired a few minutes ago. Now I'm *really* tired…" She was not the only one. Despite the crowded conditions in the bed, the three of them soon dropped off to sleep.

Chapter 77: Bringing it All Together

Bernadette awoke around dawn, and wriggled out of bed. This left enough room for Andrion and Erik to get a little more sleep, and they did so. Slugabeds, she thought affectionately as she threw on a robe and went down to the common room for a quick bath. She was astounded at the almost total lack of evidence that a party had taken place here yesterday.

The tables and chairs were all in their places, the floor was clean, and Drelos was bustling around the bar while the smell of baking wafted from the kitchen. Bernadette soaked in the hot water, still a little sleepy (and with a warm sensation in her crotch as she remembered their lovemaking the previous night), reveling in the wonderfulness that is good help. She'd heard members of the upper classes she'd had occasion to hobnob with complain about the impossibility of obtaining it; yet she seemed to be surrounded by people who were willing to do whatever it took to make all her desires come true. She felt like the luckiest woman in the world.

Her enthusiasm for their wedding plans was now restored, somewhat. The immense amount of work involved in trying to make everything wonderful for Lifa, Bjorn, and Anja had left her momentarily burned out; but now, after a night's rest (and some other therapeutic activities) she felt ready to face the future. Today was only the nineteenth, after all. They didn't need to leave for Sylvanian until the ninth of next month. That was almost three weeks!

Those weeks flew by far faster than she expected. Bernadette applied the Blessing of Marmira enchantment to the rings Daaralie had made, and kept them in a pouch close to her heart. This was almost the only remaining item on her original pre-nuptial agenda, not counting the concerns of the Maiden, producing more arms and armor for Valkyrie to sell, and continuing to develop her skills. But other things kept cropping up.

For Andrion and Erik, the three weeks were a time of high anxiety. Erik brought Andrion in on the crafting project he had been working on, finally convinced that his skills were up to the task. What he had made was one ring that was two. They were shaped so that they locked together, in yellow gold and bronze-colored gold for contrast. Each was studded with diamonds and rubies. "When the priest talks about the rings, I'll give her the yellow gold one and you'll give her the bronze," Erik told Andrion. They'll lock together on her finger, one ring of two parts."

"I like the symbolism," Andrion assured him, "and your work is beautiful, Erik! No wonder you've been hiding down here all these evenings. But who's going to give her one first?" Erik hadn't considered that, or if he had he'd assumed that he, as the creator of the rings, would go first. But that wasn't necessarily fair, nor was it fair to automatically assign precedence to Andrion. Even if Andrion had been with Berni first, his relationship with her didn't predate Erik's by much more than a week or two. And now they were both in it for the long haul.

"How about we flip for it," Erik suggested.

"Best of three?" His friend grinned at him.

"Deal," he said briefly. Erik dug into a pocket and produced a guilder. The head of some recent emperor graced one side, while the other had a design they couldn't quite make out. "I'll let you pick," Erik said, "and then flip it and let it hit the ground."

Andrion nodded in agreement, and said "I'll take whatever that thing is on the back."

"Tails it is," Erik said, and flipped the coin up. The basement ceiling was only about a foot above his head, and he had calculated it beautifully. The glittering golden disk sparkled in the air and clinked on the stone floor, coming to rest with the emperor's head showing. "One for me," he said. Their unspoken understanding was that Andrion's pick would stand for the entire series, until one of them had won.

Erik flipped again, and it came up "tails." He grinned at his friend. Were they not now as brothers, Andrion might have flinched from that grin. "Third time for all," Erik said – though he was overplaying it for effect. It didn't matter to him at all which of them first placed a ring on Berni's finger. The coin spun in air, it hit the floor, it bounced and spun again – and came to rest, finally, with the emperor's head pressed against the floor. "You win!" Erik crowed, sounding as delighted as if the opposite had occurred. He clasped

Andrion around the shoulders, then slapped the coin into his hand. "Your good luck piece," he said facetiously.

Andrion returned a grin as wolfish as the one Erik had given him earlier. Intellectually he knew it didn't matter a whit, but somehow it had been important to him to come out the winner in this contest. He tucked the coin in his pocket. "The ring still needs to go up to Wyrmshalla so Garimund can enchant it," Erik reminded him. "I bribed him to learn the enchantment. I'll take care of it as soon as I can get away."

Getting away was an issue for both of them. They each had things they needed to do, many of them connected with the house project; but they were short on excuses for absenting themselves from the Maiden. They hit upon the scheme of luring Berni into a series of minor quests. She was anxious, she was restless, and until the wedding she had really not that much to do. So first Andrion, then Erik, would suggest a quick excursion to plunder a dypalfar ruin or clean out a bandit stronghold.

Bernadette loved such activities. There was, in the case of places they hadn't visited before, the thrill of discovery and the chance of unexpected lore. Plus with their skill levels there was little or no risk of actually being killed. It was good exercise, an opportunity for untold treasure, and the feeling of performing a public service. Given her issues with having them both along on a quest, she wasn't the least bit suspicious if one suggested the quest and the other declined to participate.

So, they traded her off and the project went forward. The kitchen sink arrived from Valkyrie and Andrion hooked it up to the drains (which Hegmar and his crews had laid, running from the west side of the annex around to the north and down slope toward the east, where the septic tank and leach field were located). The kitchen had a single water pipe, the valve delivering either hot or cold water depending on whether the dypalfar mechanism had been activated. It was simple and had its problems, but it was a big step beyond heating pots of water over the fire.

The cistern was delivered and installed atop its tower, a massive effort that Erik was on site for while Andrion quested with Berni in some far-off dypalfar ruin. A temporary crane erected atop the tower served to hoist it into place, after which it was secured to its base and the final connection made between the cistern's outflow (which sat some six inches above the bottom, postponing the time at which the cistern would need to be opened and cleaned of silt) and the pipes running to the house.

Once in place, the cistern was still empty. It had been an unusually dry winter so far, and it was beginning to look as if the project would be finished leaving the house without a supply of water. But Hegmar had other ideas. The little rivulet known as the Drakespring Water ran below the city walls to the west of the farm, at the rear of the property. It was narrow, but its supply was steady. Hegmar brought in a wagonload of woven coils that proved to be a long, long hose around two inches in diameter. As water saturated the interior of the hose, the fabric's threads swelled – tightening the weave so that only small droplets passed through.

Along with the hose came a hand pump, which was fitted into the hose a few paces from the end that was immersed in the stream. A series of strong-armed workers worked the crank, sucking up water from the stream and lifting it the thirty feet or so to the top of the cistern. This was hard work, and nobody could do it for long though Erik gave it his best shot.

They managed to get the cistern half-filled before the rains suddenly came. This restricted outdoor construction activity, but by now the annex was mostly enclosed with siding and slate roof tiles. As rainwater ran down the cistern's conical roof and passed through the screen that filtered out things like sticks, leaves, feathers, and the carcasses of rats, the workers moved inside to erect the interior walls, apply shutters to the window openings, and build the bathing pool in the bathroom.

Andrion returned from his quest with Berni, enriched with several additional dypalfar components. Now that his conferences with Diane had opened his eyes to the possibilities, he viewed dypalfar ruins as a treasure trove beyond any previous understanding of the term. He consulted with Erik, catching up on progress, and the situation with the hand pump gave him an idea.

After some tinkering in the basement, Andrion had come up with a small unit containing a robon power cell and a collection of gears, all plunder from his recent trip. Some modifications to the hand pump allowed it to be attached to this unit, and he found that it would produce a slow but steady flow of water up from the burn, with no human effort required at all. He arranged with Hegmar to purchase the hose and pump, and stowed it with his contraption in the cistern tower. Waterdon's climate should deliver enough rain to keep up with their household needs most of the time. But if it failed to do so, they now had a backup supply.

Erik inveigled Berni into an expedition to the north, moving through unmapped territory in search of a legendary weapon on behalf of the Eorl of Icemarch. While they were at it, they popped in at Norcove and visited Erik's parents. Erik's father Jurgen was a tall, gaunt man who had probably been magnificent in his youth. Silver-haired, he seemed shrunken by hard work and age. His mother Hildegard was tall for a woman and broad, her blonde hair streaked with gray. Neither of them seemed all that excited to greet their wayward son and his intended bride, and politely declined their invitation to attend either the wedding or the party that would follow it.

Meanwhile, the masonry for the bathing pool (including the massive support platform beneath it) had been put in place and the interior of the pool faced with polished stone. While it cured, Andrion applied himself to the task of attaching the water system to it using the pipes which had long since arrived from Hegmar's fabricator in Forestville.

He was beginning to have a good understanding of the system after studying Diane's drawings and talking with her; but his skills in metalcraft were lacking. In desperation, he pulled Alessia away from Waterdon and brought her to the site. With some drawings she'd produced in cooperation with Bjorn, she returned to her forge and crafted the connecting pieces needed to tie the pool in with the system that would heat and purify its waters.

When Bernadette and Erik got back from their northern excursion she foiled their plans by dragging them both up to Sylvanian, along with Hjaermond and Selden. The old men were sorry to be returning to their lives of boredom in the basement of the eorl's palace, but they realized they could hardly expect to impose on

Bernadette's hospitality for the rest of their lives. Thus they were taken by surprise when she accompanied them, not to the eorl's palace, but to Castle Grey.

The entire party trooped in through the door to General Vadrian's command headquarters, where as usual he was conferring with the Norsewoman who was his immediate subordinate. Bernadette got the most courteous reception she'd yet received from him. "Ah, Fireblood! You have returned. And I see that you have brought the two new members of my advisory council with you." Hjaermond and Selden looked around. Were Bernadette's fiancés taking up service with the Reman army?

Vadrian continued, this time clearly addressing the two elder men, "Eorl Hjaermond, Warden Selden, your quarters here in the castle have been prepared for you. Danske, will you please see these gentlemen to their apartment and explain to them the usual schedule of staff meetings?" Hjaermond was dumbfounded. After a lifetime of loyal service to the empire, he had felt as if he had been brushed aside into a corner and forgotten. Now, he was being offered an active role in Reman affairs?

Selden was still trying to make sense of the exchange. For somebody his age his mind was still sharp, but he was having trouble taking this in. Hjaermond turned to Bernadette, fixing her with a gimlet eye. "This is your doing?" he asked. Bernadette smiled at him, eyes sparkling.

"I felt it was wrong for the imperial government to treat you so unfairly," she admitted. "You and your uncle deserve better from the empire than to be summarily forced into retirement."

A bit of the spark of command he must have had before losing his position appeared in Hjaermond's eyes. "Indeed!" he said. Then added, with a twinkle of his own, "Excellent! Thank you, Fireblood. Say, I understand you and your young men are to be married here at the Pantheatos on the 10th of next month. Might we be allowed to attend?" In the end, Bernadette ended up extending invitations to the wedding ceremony to Hjaermond, Selden, Vadrian, and Danske as well. Fortunately, the courtyard at the temple offered much more seating than did the chapel in Lakedon.

They lingered in Sylvanian for days, getting Andrion and Erik fitted for the clothes Bernadette intended them to wear at their wedding – and crafting their vows. After seeing what the standard Iscandia version of a wedding ceremony was like, Bernadette had decided that they must rewrite it to suit their unique situation; and time was running short on the deadline Engbard had given her for special requests.

Bernadette had been expecting to put up in the Dancing Rabbit for the duration of this trip, but when she and the men paid a courtesy visit to Bergen at the eorl's palace after dropping Hjaermond and Selden off at Castle Grey, the eorl invited them to stay there. Bernadette got the idea that Odwyna, like some other people she'd met since their engagement was announced, was at least a little titillated by the unusual circumstances of their relationship.

With recent experience, Bernadette was expecting their twin errands to be met by Erik and Andrion with enthusiasm of the sort usually reserved for spending a few days hanging by shackles from a dungeon wall. Instead, she was pleasantly surprised. The two of them were excited by the options Senalie offered them, and each selected a style he thought would express his true essence on this most important formal occasion of their lives. These were stock designs, and Senalie promised both outfits would be ready for final fitting within two days; so they stayed in the eorl's palace and worked on their vows in the interim.

Bernadette had not mentioned the rings to them, nor had Erik or Andrion mentioned the ring Erik had crafted to her. Yet all of them knew some such thing was coming, and they carefully avoided discussing it as they worked out all the other details: what Engbard would say, what each of them would reply. At some point she was wondering why the hell they bothered with all this rigmarole. They loved each other, they were bonded together. Why were these words, this ceremony, so important? While she had no answers to those questions, she knew that, regardless, they were.

The men seemed to treat the whole affair with utmost seriousness. This was, after all, in all likelihood the only such ceremony either of them would ever go through in their lives. Unless something happened to Bernadette, or even if something did, they would probably never marry again. Their attitude helped to validate her feelings that this was not just some silly pursuit. They had hammered out the details and dropped them off with Engbard in time to pick up the men's outfits from The Golden Thread before returning to the Maiden.

It was getting too late to start any more quests, so Erik and Andrion now applied their diversion strategy closer to home. One or the other of them would engage Berni in a project at the Maiden, or perhaps a walk in the country, some salmon fishing in the river, whatever would occupy her attention for a while as the other hastened down to the farm to supervise last-minute details.

The kitchen system had been tested and proven successful. Water hot enough almost to scald your skin would flow from the swivel-mounted tap while the heating unit was activated, cooling to whatever temperature the cistern's supply had to offer, gradually, after the unit was turned off. In the bathroom, the bathing tub (around a third the size of the pool at the Maiden) had been filled with water. No leaks were detected, and over the course of a day during which the water had been circulating through Diane's dypalfar mechanism, it had reached the desired temperature.

The water privy was a whole other issue. Hegmar had ordered it from afar, and it had taken the better part of a month to arrive. Such things were nearly unheard-of in this backward province. It had a complex series of curving pipes designed to carry away wastes and prevent odors from the drain system coming back up. A tank mounted high on the wall provided enough water force to flush wastes away down the drain. It was certainly more comfortable to use than a chamber pot, and a lot less smelly.

While Andrion beguiled Berni with lessons in battle magic, Erik supervised the delivery of their amazing bed. Arngeld's entire family participated in the effort, arriving with a large wagon and bringing the bed inside through the doors leading out to the veranda, in sections. The mattress was cushy and exactly fitted the assembled bed frame, which had twelve legs in all supporting its platform. The girls made the mattress up with the sheets and blanket they'd woven, and even brought in three pillows stuffed with goose down.

The annex, and the entire house, was really beginning to take shape as a residence; but large areas remained unfurnished. Bram had moved out, gone to live with his daughter's family in Deepwald and glad of it. Staying here while the construction was going on had been a huge annoyance, but the farm was still a going concern and somebody had to look after the livestock and the crops. Andrion and Erik, with help from Maiden employees, had taken over since his departure.

As of now, the small bedroom that was part of the original house was furnished with a bed, end table and chest of drawers. The former main room of the house had been reconfigured with a dining table and chairs nicer than the ones that had been there originally, and the large fire pit had been replaced with a medium-sized wall-mounted fireplace, with some added features Erik had designed. The kitchen sink, with an attached counter, took up one wall and there was some additional counter space on the adjoining wall with storage beneath it.

A door through the north wall gave onto the large central hall of the annex, with the bathroom on the left. A bedroom stood opposite the bathroom, as yet completely unfurnished. Continuing north up the hall, the master bedroom was on the right and a crafting room (empty at this time) on the left. The master bedroom now contained their magnificent bed along with a small table and chairs, a couple of nightstands, a bookcase, some carpets, and a chest of drawers. A third bedroom on the right beyond the master bedroom was also bare, as was the intended nursery spanning the width of the annex's northern end.

Each of the three bedrooms along the annex's eastern side had a door out to the veranda – which was broad enough to sleep on, come warm summer nights. Erik had gotten Arngeld to let him have three more chairs, and had set them out there so it was obvious that the main purpose of the veranda was to give you a place from which to sit quietly and gaze out at the river, at the end of a busy day. Or perhaps watch the sun rise, first thing on a summer morning.

On the eighth of Fevrous, at four in the afternoon while Bernadette was busy down the road putting together a special order of steel plate armor for Alessia, Erik and Andrion met to survey what they'd wrought. A few workmen lingered on the site, tidying things up and attending to last-minute details like the hanging of lamps and placement of candle sconces; but Hegmar had already received his final payment.

They walked through, taking in all that they'd achieved with forethought, persistence, and huge sacks of money. Already, Andrion was thinking about improvements that he wished he'd thought to make in their original design; but he made an effort to stifle those thoughts. This was to be their home, probably for the rest of their lives. There would be plenty of time to make changes for the better. For one thing, he needed to do some studying and pursue the issue of plate glass for the windows. If he let himself, he'd think of a dozen more things before he'd walked the length of the building.

The two had brought some items from the Maiden with them. They dropped off a few towels in the kitchen, to be used for drying dishes or as potholders for removing hot items from the cooking fire. Additional pots and pans, plates, bowls and cutlery were arrayed on the shelves built there for the purpose. A tablecloth was draped over the dining table, brightening up the room. In addition to the bathroom, only their master bedroom as yet had any furnishings; but the other rooms were finished, the wooden floors polished, and they would soon be ready for occupation.

The rest of the towels were set into a cupboard in the bathroom. The water privy was in its own little enclosure with a door, the bathing tub and a washbasin (with cold water supply only) in a separate section of the room. The enclosed area, much smaller than the Maiden's common room, was a little steamy from the hot water in the tub.

Andrion bent and stuck his hand in the water. The temperature felt perfect, a few degrees above normal body temperature. "Want to take a bath?" he suggested to Erik.

Erik considered, then demurred. "Let's have Berni take the first one," he replied.

Andrion nodded. "I think we need to come up with some kind of a cover for the tub," he remarked. "This much steam in the air is going to cause damage to the walls and ceiling." Now it was Erik's turn to nod.

They moved on to the master bedroom, where they both stood admiring that bed. There was room in there for Berni, both of them, and two or three kids if the kids weren't very large. Perfect. It was a short distance down and across the hall from the bathroom, and there were connecting doors between it and the bedrooms on either side. Each of them would have space for themselves, as well as a room where they could all sleep together.

They stepped out the room's outside door to the veranda and sat on the chairs out there, admiring the play of the afternoon light on the mountains and river to the east. It was a stellar view. They sighed in unison as if choreographed, a sigh of contentment and relief. The job was finished, or at least finished enough. Lev and Drelos between them had managed to line up enough extra help that none of them would be required to do anything but party down and enjoy themselves, three days hence. With half of Waterdon as well as residents of several other cities having been invited, they were very glad of this fact.

"Well," Erik said, rising. "It's done." He reached across the small table between them and shook Andrion's hand. "And I'd say," he added in his agreeable rumble, "well done."

"I can't believe we pulled it off," Andrion responded, clasping Erik's hand. "Don't think we *could* have done it, without so many people helping." Erik nodded.

"I suppose we'd better be getting back to the Maiden," he said. The two descended the short flight of steps from the veranda to the yard, and began walking the short distance up the road to the place that would be their home for only a little while longer – though it would always be near to their hearts as well as to their residence.

Chapter 78: Drumroll

Erik and Bernadette awoke in the basement, fairly early in the morning on the ninth of Fevrous. Their plan was to get a few things done, burn off some energy (they'd already recouped the energy they'd burned off together at bedtime), then take a nap. The three of them, blessedly unencumbered by anyone else, needed to leave for Sylvanian at around nine or ten this evening, in order for Bernadette to get her dress built onto her at The Golden Thread and arrive at the Pantheatos by the specified hour for the ceremony.

After the ceremony they would probably be detained socializing with the guests for a while, and they didn't want to be creaking on the edge of exhaustion when all of that was finished. Never mind that the three of them had been lovers without benefit of matrimony for these many months – the wedding night was special, and not to be spoiled by its participants having gone too many hours without sleep.

They met Andrion in the common room, up as early as they. Bernadette stepped into his arms. She would like to sleep with both her men every night, but unless they were to be packed in like sardines, she would have to continue trading off with one or the other until their home was built. There was room in the basement for an enormous bed, but unless Andrion could come up with a spell for translocation there was no way to get one down there. Hmm, she mused. The bed that was already down there must have been brought in as lumber and assembled on the spot. Perhaps they could do the same with a much larger one?...

After they'd breakfasted on steak and eggs, the three put on some light armor and went hunting out across the fields to the north and east of the Maiden. Behind them, Lev's tent had been fully occupied since it was first erected almost a month before. He was now talking about hiring Bjorn's employer, Hegmar, to put up a more permanent structure. Tent canvas was sturdy but could not survive the elements indefinitely.

Evidently since Erik and Bernadette had killed that ogre on the way to their picnic a few weeks ago, another had taken up residence in the area. The three of them dispatched it in a flurry of battle magic and arrows, Erik having become a quite-decent archer over the time since Bernadette had first met him. He still preferred that axe of his for close quarters, and seemed to take a grisly delight in obliterating his enemies in a shower of blood; but there were times when a ranged weapon made more sense.

They were pleased to perform this service, as keeping ogres out of the area helped to prevent incidents. On one occasion a few months back, when Bernadette and her men had been away from the Maiden, an ogre had come right up onto the deck and seriously savaged a guest before Fenris had managed to kill it. It was good to know that it would be a few weeks at least before another moved in. The creatures were solitary and territorial.

Stripping the dead ogre of its valuables, they moved on quietly. Deer were often to be found drinking at the riverside, and even crackclaws had tasty flesh if you were willing to make the effort to extract it from their rock-like carapaces. The trio hiked for miles, moving stealthily, and returned to the Maiden shortly after lunchtime dusty, sweaty, and carrying the gutted carcass of a large deer along with a couple of crackclaws, some rabbits, and a small stringer of salmon (Bernadette had gotten those – she'd developed quite a talent for tickling them out of the water and was now the least sweaty and dusty of the three).

They dropped these items off at the kitchen, where Lev was busily preparing food for the late lunchtime crowd. He nodded to them in thanks, and asked one of his assistants to throw the crabs, rabbits, and salmon (which Bernadette had obligingly cleaned before delivering them) into clean muslin sacks. They were tucked into the cold storage chest, which still contained a small layer of frozen parcels of triceratops meat at the bottom. This meat acted as a chilling agent for anything else put in there, helping to preserve it until it could be dealt with.

He had Erik hang the deer carcass from a meat hook in the corner, on the far side of the chest and away from the fire. A metal pan on the floor caught any fluids dripping down. Game like this really needed to be hung in a cold place like a root cellar for a few days, to soften the tough fibers and reduce the strong gamey flavor. The Maiden didn't have a root cellar, and with Erik's bedroom and the hot forge in the basement it was too warm down there for hanging meat. They'd probably need to carry it across the road, and pay part of the meat as a fee for the use of Stormstrife Farm's cold room.

Lev added that to his mental checklist. Perhaps along with the new dormitory wing he wanted to build, they could excavate a stone-lined cold cellar for food storage. He was up to his eyeballs in to-do lists at the moment, and working like a fiend to keep up with the demand for the new dishes he'd invented in recent weeks. He loved every minute of it.

Bernadette, Erik, and Andrion peeled off to their rooms and stripped down, grabbing robes and meeting in the bathing pool. Bernadette wanted to be perfectly clean and serene for her wedding, but needed to bathe early enough so that her hair would be dry, and Larissa could arrange it for her after the nap. Erik and Andrion had achieved that state of consciousness which comes to some men as their wedding day approaches, a feeling that whatever the universe or their beloved wanted to hand them, they would accept it with grace. These are the men who survive to become *old* married men.

After their bath the three, still clad in robes, ate a light lunch. They planned to eat a similarly light supper before leaving. Bernadette went upstairs with Andrion, having spent the night with Erik, but no sex was in the offing. They'd get to that soon enough; but right now, the important thing was to get some sleep. It was fairly warm in the bedroom, here in the early part of the afternoon, and Bernadette found it incredibly difficult to drop off. It was even too warm for much snuggling, though she adored snuggling with either of her men. After embracing Andrion, she lay atop the coverlet in her underwear and put herself through a series of mental exercises intended to empty the mind of thoughts. It occurred to her as she did this that getting her brains fucked out would probably have been just as effective; but then she'd be all sweaty and sticky again, would have to bathe again, and so forth… Sigh.

The two of them eventually dropped off, as did Erik – downstairs alone in his basement bedroom. He at least had the luxury of lying flat on his back with his arms spread wide. Noises here and there in the Maiden brought Bernadette near the verge of consciousness several times. Napping in the middle of the day was no easy task. Finally, when she awakened to a heightened level of the kind of noise associated with supper being served, she sat up. As always, it seemed, Andrion had slept more deeply than she had and was dozing away on the bed beside her. She decided to let him sleep a little longer, sorry *she* hadn't, and slipped quietly out of bed to put on the clothes in which she intended to travel to Sylvanian.

Before she had left the bedroom Andrion stirred. He gazed up at her sleepily. "You look nice… what time is it?" he asked. Just occasionally, this man a decade older than she was seemed like a child whom she wanted to hold and protect. Bernadette came to his side and sat on the edge of the bed to kiss him, love for him welling up inside her. He immediately dispelled the "vulnerable little boy" image by seizing her in an embrace and delivering a kiss that was anything but childlike.

After enjoying it for a moment, Bernadette pulled away with a whoop. "All right, you!" she declared, panting slightly. "Time you were up and dressed!" Andrion and Erik had taken their wedding clothes with them from The Golden Thread, there being no need for assistance in putting them on. They'd been hung on hooks, protected from dust by more of the muslin bags furnished by Senalie. He got up, hair tousled, standing there in his underwear with a slight erection pushing out the fabric.

Bernadette couldn't resist – she stepped near him and kissed him sweetly, one hand wrapping around him to squeeze his muscular buttocks while the other stroked his cock beneath the thin fabric of his underdrawers. Ooh, she wanted him! And the timing was simply impossible. She went into Boss Mode, partly as a defense against her own feelings before they got her into trouble. "Comb your hair, first," she told Andrion firmly.

Realizing that his beloved was not going to be led down the primrose path to unscheduled fun and games (and also realizing why this was a good idea), Andrion sighed faintly and stood before the mirror above the chest of drawers to apply a comb to his recently washed, shoulder-length locks. Sleeping before his hair was dry had given him some unusual waves, and even after combing it looked a mess.

Bernadette regarded him critically. "Have you ever thought about tying it back in a ponytail?" she asked. This style was popular with many men in Iscandia, especially those who worked in occupations where keeping one's hair out of one's eyes was a good idea. She'd always liked the way Andrion's blond-streaked medium brown hair brushed his shoulders, but if he were to grow it a little longer, the ponytail might not be a bad look for him.

Bernadette dug out one of the many soft leather thongs she kept around for tying her own hair back. Long hair dangling in one's face when working at the forge was definitely a *bad* idea. Requesting Andrion to stoop a bit, so that she could reach the top of his head more easily, she dipped the comb in the basin of water at the bedside and smoothed it through his hair. Then she pulled the hair back and tied it with the thong. His hair was a bit short for this, but it worked; and with the hair pulled back tight the finely chiseled lines of his face were drawn more into prominence. It made him look a little older, perhaps, more sober… She concluded that it would do, for this day of days.

"What do *you* think?" she asked, standing behind his left shoulder as he looked at himself in the mirror. He put on an expression of command, then smiled.

"I feel more important already," he said.

Bernadette squeezed him from the side and murmured, "It's not possible for you to be more important than you already are…" He kissed her.

After all this Bernadette and Andrion went downstairs, Andrion dressed as he would be at his wedding and Bernadette in her travelling clothes. She intended to have Larissa put her hair up for her after they had had some supper, during the last hour before they embarked via the magic map for Sylvanian. They found Erik waiting for them, utterly resplendent in the clothes he'd selected for their nuptials.

Men the size of Erik, and there *were* a few if not many, often went around dressed in ill-fitting clothes that hung on them like tents or were too tight across the chest, too short in the legs and arms. Bernadette realized as she gazed admiringly at Erik in his finery what a huge difference it made, being able to afford clothing that was custom-tailored. Naked, Erik looked like a particularly well-endowed god. In these clothes, he looked like a god on his way to a formal ball. Wow.

They all seated themselves at the Owner's Table, Bernadette between her two bridegrooms. They'd finally grown accustomed to having it to themselves, now that Hjaermond and Selden were off in Sylvanian living in pleasantly appointed quarters at Castle Grey and making their contributions to Reman military policy. Bernadette guessed that Hjaermond, at least, might have more to offer than Vadrian had expected when he'd agreed to her plan.

"I feel like a sparrow among peacocks," Bernadette joked. Erik and Andrion smiled down at her. They felt pretty damn spiffy, in fact. Having clothes this well-tailored and fine-looking was a new experience for both of them. Part of the trick of spending enough money on your raiment was that you not only got an outfit that would inspire envy in all around you, it was fitted so exactly to your body that it was comfortable to wear.

Lev came up to them, nearing the end of his long shift. Drelos was already on the bar. "What's the time, please?" Bernadette asked.

"It's seven o'clock, approximately," he replied, anticipating the question and having checked the clock behind the bar before coming over. The Maiden's dinner rush was winding down. "I saved those crackclaws for you," Lev said. "Are you ready for a treat?" Bernadette grinned at him. After the exercise earlier followed by an undersized lunch, she was ready for some more substantial fare.

"Bring it on!" she said.

By the gods, Bernadette thought a few minutes later. The Maiden's dinner fare was beginning to approach a level of sophistication only seen in the palaces of major cities in Auverne (though for all she knew, imperial Remus might boast culinary arts still more fantastic). Lev had brought them good-sized bowls in which an assortment of chopped, chilled greens had been mixed with some kind of crunchy chopped nuts, and crumbled bits of a strong-flavored cheese. The whole had been tossed in a mixture of vinegar, oil, wine, and herbs.

The salad had been presented with bread rolls fresh from the oven and a small quantity of chilled butter. Then their plates of the main course arrived: thin "pasta" tossed with succulent chunks of mudcrab meat and mushrooms in a sauce that seemed to be composed of cream, butter, white wine, garlic, and herbs.

Andrion and Bernadette, Galise after all, found this food delicious and astonishing considering they were eating it here in the middle of Iscandia. Erik, a Norseman whose childhood favorite foods had generally involved potatoes and cabbage at every meal, regarded it with a bit of initial suspicion; but you don't reach that size by being a picky eater. He soon decided it tasted all right, and dug in with enthusiasm.

They had nearly finished eating, and Bernadette was already plotting her get-together with Larissa for the hairdressing session, when there was a commotion at the front doors of the Maiden. A party of people were coming in from the front porch, and her attention (along with that of most of the people in the common room) was riveted on them. Was that... Nerissa! And Diane, Georges, Malden, Brother Julianos, Grindmar, and could that be Marya?

Bernadette stood up, then left the table and went down the steps to greet them as they came down from the opposite side of the room. Erik and Andrion trailed in her wake. They'd invited as many of the Daywatch people as might want to come to the party, but hadn't held out much hope that any of them would make the trip. It was a long way even by fast-travelling, and twice as long on foot.

Bernadette hadn't seen Nerissa since she'd returned to Daywatch, and she was the first one Bernadette greeted. She felt a warm friendship for the former vampire woman, and was delighted to think she had come all this way to help them celebrate their wedding. "Nerissa!" she exclaimed. "You all came?..." Nerissa smiled at her, truly glad to see the woman who had been the first mortal friend she'd had since being turned vampire centuries before. It was largely due to Bernadette that she'd decided to seek the cure, and she was (so far, at least) very happy she'd made that decision.

"Bernadette!" Nerissa called in turn, hugging her friend. "You didn't think we'd miss a chance for a party at the Maiden, did you?"

"Oh!" Bernadette said. "I'm so glad you came! Actually, I was just getting ready to have my hair done and then we're leaving for Sylvanian in an hour or so. We won't be back until day after tomorrow, what with the fast-travel time lag... Will that be all right?" Nerissa gave her a frank gaze. She'd known what date it was, and that the party wasn't until a couple of days hence.

"Oh!" she said, feigning dismay. "Forced to spend two whole days hanging around this dreadful place? How shall we cope?"

Bernadette laughed. "Okay, you're right, never mind. Thing is, I can't promise you there will be beds. Though now I think of it, somebody could probably take the master bed and Erik's bed in the basement for tonight. Diane and Georges were down there a few weeks ago…" The party stood in the common room, engaged in a general discussion. The Daywatch contingent had walked to Norcove, a day's travel from the fortress, and caught a coach that had taken a couple of days to bring them here.

Bernadette was surprised and a little confused to learn that Nerissa and Malden were a couple now. But after talking with Malden a little, she concluded that the man had mellowed considerably since their time together in the Daywatch Brigade. Hmm, she thought. Maybe all that time he just needed to get laid? Nerissa was beautiful, simultaneously old enough to be his remote ancestor and young enough to be his daughter. She hoped he appreciated getting her. She got the sense that Nerissa had tackled Malden initially as a sort of "revenge fuck," proving that she could overcome his resistance to her and all she represented through her powers of attraction. Evidently, it had now turned into something else. Well, as long as everybody was happy…

Bernadette explained about the situation with the tent, and after some discussion it was agreed that Erik's bed in the basement would be available to Diane and Georges for tonight and tomorrow night as well. Bernadette expected she and her bridegrooms would return to the Maiden at some wee hour of the morning day after tomorrow and could spent the remainder of the night in the master bedroom, as they'd done on quite a few other occasions. Nerissa and Malden would have to take their chances, and might have to sleep in the tent – as would the others. These were the Brigade members Bernadette and Andrion had spent the most time with, and had begun to develop the bonds of friendship. Plus, they liked the idea of attending a gala party at a fancy inn. Who could blame them?

These arrangements concluded, Bernadette excused herself and ran to find Larissa, who'd actually been standing by looking a little concerned as time went by. They adjourned upstairs, the young elf woman working on Bernadette sitting at one of the chairs in the master suite. The updo was produced through a combination of cleverness, small metal clips, and a little bit of a solution that Larissa claimed was a secret formula passed down through her family for generations. Whatever it was, it seemed to encourage Bernadette's silken, often flyaway locks to cooperate and stay where they'd been put – without making the hair stiff.

In a while Bernadette descended the stairs again, pretending she was balancing a heavy book on her head. The outfit she was wearing didn't suit the look, but its main selling point was that it unbuttoned down the front and would not need to be taken off over her head. The Daywatch party had joined Erik and Andrion at the Owner's Table in her absence, and were chattering away. A hush fell as she came down the stairs, followed by Larissa.

To Bernadette's surprise, the party broke into soft applause. She went with it, beaming at them all and making motions that suggested curtsies without actually inclining her head from the vertical. "Oh, I wish we could see you in your wedding gown," Diane said.

"I'll put it on for the party," Bernadette promised, wondering as she said it whom she could get to help with that task. Larissa, perhaps. Might as well get a little more use out of the fabulous thing.

She was still amazed, on occasion, at how a young Galise woman without two guilders to rub together had been transformed, in a few months' time, into the wealthy and well-regarded Fireblood. All her girlish dreams had come true, and more joy was still ahead.

"I'm so glad you all were able to come," Bernadette said graciously – though truly meaning it. "But I think it's about time for us to leave." Slight hugs were exchanged, and she conferred with Lev one more time. He was now off-duty, relaxing on a barstool between sets as the Maiden's resident bard. "The musicians from Sylvanian should be here tomorrow," she told him. "I think you probably have everything else well in hand, right?" He smiled at her reassuringly. "Of course you do," she said, patting him on the arm. "See you the morning of the eleventh, then."

Bidding everyone goodbye, the trio bound for Sylvanian stepped out into the blackness of night. Bernadette was relieved that no rain was falling, as that would surely have ruined her hairdo. After a few moments of deeper blackness, they found themselves looking at the city of Sylvanian, spread out before them on a morning that showed some promise of eventually becoming sunny. At the moment, though, it was a bit overcast.

Chapter 79: The Rest of Our Lives

The Golden Thread was certainly convenient to the city's main gates. Looking from Andrion to Erik, Bernadette took their arms and the three of them stepped off jauntily toward the shop. All of the anxieties and concerns of the past few weeks had fallen from her shoulders, and joy was bubbling in her soul. This was it! They would be united in the sight of gods and men, and in a few months when they had found their land and built their home, their new life would really begin.

They entered the shop and found Senalie at the front counter. Her rather stern, naturally cold-looking face lit with welcome, improving her looks immensely. "You're right on time." Bernadette beamed at her.

Turning to Andrion, she said "You and Erik are going to be on your own for a while. If you like, you can wait here for me while I get into my dress." She turned to Senalie. "How long do you think it will take?..."

Senalie considered. The design Bernadette had presented her with was complex, and it would take a while to get it to hang just right. "I think perhaps twenty minutes should be sufficient," she said.

"Time enough for an ale, then," Bernadette said. "Why don't you go across the street to the Rabbit?" The two perked up. Few trials are harder for a man to bear than a long wait in a dress shop while the missus tries on clothing. Who could *not* love this woman? As the two made to leave she reminded them, "Don't be late getting back, please. I plan to dazzle you…"

Andrion and Erik made their retreat to the inn across the road and sat enjoying a couple of room-temperature ales while talking a bit nervously. They'd memorized the vows they'd written, but both were still experiencing a touch of stage fright. Kill a few dozen marauding bandits or a dragon, no problem. Stand up in front of an audience and tell the world how much you love your sweetheart? Something else entirely.

Senalie surveyed Bernadette critically. "I like the hair," she said in a moment. "Who did it for you?"

"It was an elf woman, one of the employees at my inn," Bernadette replied. Senalie nodded in satisfaction. Only the alfar were truly possessed of refinement and good taste, in her opinion. They stepped on through to the back, and Bernadette removed her clothing.

"The underwear too," the ljosalfar woman commanded. Bernadette obediently continued stripping until she was naked from head to toe. She'd made sure to have her toenails neatly trimmed and polished, in anticipation of the revealing high-heeled sandals.

"Such lovely feet," Senalie murmured approvingly as she positioned Bernadette in the center of the floor. Then, with her colored drawing to hand, she began plucking lengths of colored silk from a series of pegs that had been hammered into a board and hung on the wall. "I can't imagine how you're going to store this," she remarked, as she began draping the tongues of rainbow-hued fabric around Bernadette's body.

Some strips were longer, and wrapped about her in long swaths, covering a considerable stretch of her skin. These went on first, to be followed by smaller strips that covered some of the gaps while revealing small sections of skin in other areas. By the time Senalie was finished, Bernadette resembled an exotic bird of some kind. Her curves were still visible, but her overall shape was sometimes hidden, sometimes revealed as the cloth strips moved while she walked.

Senalie produced the outrageously sexy shoes and Bernadette sat, carefully, to put them on her feet. She got the full effect in the mirror, then strutted to the front of the shop. As she'd hoped, her bridegrooms had returned from their ale break just moments before. She smiled alluringly at them, eyes shining. "Well," she said, spinning around so the strips of fabric whirled out around her before falling down again to drape against her body. "What do you think?"

Erik and Andrion gaped at her. They'd expected their darling to be a vision of loveliness. To them, she was lovely wearing stained armor, her hair a mess, face dirty. But this dress was so... indescribable. And those shoes! Each of them was glad that their formal wedding garb was not particularly snug-fitting, as Berni in this outfit forged a path from the eyes straight to the crotch.

They seemed awfully inarticulate, these loves of hers. But the look on their faces was all Bernadette could have hoped for. "I feel pretty!" she trilled facetiously. Then added, "But I'm afraid these shoes are going to have to come off for the walk up to the temple." It was close to a quarter of a mile from here, up a fairly steep hill paved with stone.

The men recovered their presence of mind enough to focus on what she was saying, and looked a little disappointed. But they had to admit, they couldn't imagine wearing anything like those shoes and being able to stand up, let alone walk or spin around in circles. Dimpling at them, Bernadette retreated to the back room and emerged in another minute wearing her soft shoes, the high-heeled sandals in a bag Senalie had provided. Thanking Senalie and paying her the rest of the money due, Bernadette then exited the shop, flanked by her grooms.

The clouds were already breaking up into puffy white cumulonimbus, and it looked as though the day would be fine. They walked down the main street of Sylvanian toward the Pantheatos, drawing stares from all who beheld them. Who was this beautiful, outlandishly-dressed woman, accompanied by two tall and handsome men in formal garb?

They entered the temple and met with Frieda, Engbard's priestess wife. "Welcome, Fireblood," she said softly. "You will find my husband in the courtyard." She led them out through a door to the open-air space, which could have accommodated a hundred guests with ease. Their own little party would be dwarfed, but Bernadette didn't care. That they were having a real ceremony with a real priest and some important guests, however few, was so much more than she'd initially hoped for that she didn't really mind.

Engbard was strolling down the aisle as Frieda ushered them out to the courtyard. He smiled at them. "My lady, you look stunning," he said. "And these are your bridegrooms?" As happy and excited as she was, Bernadette's mind couldn't resist inserting a snarky comment. No, she thought, I ran into these guys on the way over here and thought they looked nice, so I just scooped them up and brought them along. She smiled at him.

Engbard was oblivious. "Now," he was saying, leading them back down the aisle toward the altar, "When the guests are all seated and the hour is at hand, you three will walk together down the aisle.

Not too fast, I think, you'll want to look dignified." He pulled the piece of paper from his pocket, the one they'd given him some days ago on their last visit to the city. "I'll read the ceremony as you requested, and you'll deliver your responses. Am I right, you want to hold the rings until they are presented?"

The three exchanged glances. The unspoken subject had come up at last, and at this late date there didn't seem to be any point in keeping it a secret any more. "I have a ring for each of them," Bernadette said.

"And Erik and I each have a ring that joins with its other half to become one," Andrion added. "I'll be presenting mine first." Bernadette eyed him. Had Erik and Andrion hit on the same symbolism she'd had in mind in designing the rings she was giving to them?

"Very well, then," Engbard said, "since you'll be presenting your ring first, we'll have you say your vows first. Then Bernadette, you'll say yours to him – Andrion, is it? Then Erik will say his, Bernadette will say hers to Erik, and then the rest of the ceremony. I think it'll all work out fine." He looked around, trying to recall if there was anything he'd forgotten. They didn't do that many weddings here, usually only fancy state weddings or those of the wealthy – or special cases like this one, thanks to the favor of Aderos.

Engbard slapped his forehead. "Oh!" he said, "one more thing – how do you want the flowers placed?" Bernadette looked at him blankly.

"Flowers?"

"Yes, there was a cartload of them delivered to the temple just a few minutes before you arrived. I assumed you had arranged for them." Huh, Bernadette thought. A secret benefactor?

"Would it be all right to put them on either side of the altar?" she asked.

"Certainly," Engbard replied. "And then perhaps we could hang a bouquet on the aisle side of each row of benches. There's one particular bouquet that I think is intended for you to carry as you walk down the aisle. I can take it for you when we get to the vows, if you need both hands for the rings…"

Bernadette smiled at him. "Thank you, that would be lovely. Do you need us to help with the set-up?"

"Not at all," he replied. "My wife and I can handle everything. In the meantime, would you like to come inside and take some refreshment?" She considered. They might as well have a bite to eat and something cool to drink while they were waiting to "go on." And she could slip into her outrageous shoes, too.

Engbard led them back into the temple and down to the modest living quarters, where he seated them at a small table and offered them some bread and cheese, along with cool water to drink. Andrion and Erik had had some ale to drink earlier, but Bernadette was feeling parched and eagerly downed a tankard of the water. It was probably from some underground spring, judging from the temperature and flavor.

They sat talking quietly together and enjoying their snack for the better part of an hour, tension simmering beneath the surface of their banter. Finally Frieda came to tell them, "It's time to get ready for your walk down the aisle, now." Bernadette had put the shoes on, leaving her other shoes and a bag with the clothes she'd worn from the Maiden on the table. They would come back for this before returning home. Now she stood, the men astounded at the added height, and stalked gracefully up the stairs. She was glad she'd had Senalie make the dress a little shorter.

Frieda directed them to the door leading out into the courtyard at the entrance to the aisle, handing a large bouquet as multi-colored as her gown to Bernadette, and they stepped outside. By the gods, where had all these people come from? It seemed as though Bergen and Ormund must have invited half their courts to come along as attendants. And it appeared that Hjaermond and Selden had more people than just Vadrian and Danske with them. They hadn't filled the courtyard, by any means, but it was a respectable crowd gathered here to see them wed.

Bernadette's heart skipped a beat, and a lump rose in her throat. She looked from Erik to Andrion, smiled slightly, and said very quietly "Let's do this." They smiled back at her nervously and the three of them stepped in unison down the long aisle toward the altar. It certainly did look festive, with large vases of the same multi-hued flowers standing on either side of the altar and smaller bouquets hung from each row of benches. It was almost, Bernadette thought, as though the sender of the flowers had known what her dress looked like.

After an endless, slow journey between the rows of benches, with many of those benches' occupants smiling encouragingly at them, Bernadette, Andrion, and Erik at last stood at the altar before Engbard. He'd changed clothes since last they saw him and was looking positively resplendent. He smiled on the three of them, then began the revised ceremony they'd written.

"Our father Aderos created the world and all its creatures. But it was from Marmira, the mother who loves and watches over us, that we first learned to love one another. And love shared is what makes life worth living. We are gathered here today to bear witness to the joining of Bernadette, Andrion, and Erik in the holy bonds of matrimony. These three will walk as one through their lives to come, and they have asked that each be allowed to pledge their love in their own words. Andrion, please begin."

Andrion stepped forward and turned, so that he was facing Bernadette and the assembled audience. He stood so tall, so proud, that Bernadette's heart melted at the sight of him and tears were shimmering in her eyes. "Bernadette," he said. He and Erik had both taken to calling her "Berni" since very early in their relationship. But this was a formal, public occasion.

He continued, "You are my love and the joy of my life. Your beauty and your courage are my inspiration. I am bound to you in love, for the rest of my life." He slipped the ring he held onto the third finger of her left hand. "This ring is a token of our joining, and it in turn will be joined."

Andrion stepped back and Bernadette now stepped forward to face him. This was going to be quite the dance before they had finished, but they'd agreed that those who'd come to do them honor at their wedding deserved to see their faces as they spoke their vows. She spoke clearly and firmly, head held high (as indeed was necessary, were she to look into the eyes of her beloved instead of gazing at his chin).

"Andrion, you are my love and my bastion. Your kind heart and your wise head are my inspiration. I am bound to you in love, for the rest of my life." Gazing into his melting brown eyes, which were shining with joy, she placed his ring on his finger. This one, she turned so that the bronze-colored gold was nearest to his hand. "This ring," she said, "represents the three of us united as one. We each are individuals, but together we make a whole – and a family."

Bernadette now returned to her place, and Erik stepped forward turning around. His inborn warmth was blazing like the sun, delight seeming to radiate from his summer blue eyes as he spoke. "Bernadette, you are my love and my creative spark. Your warmth and your beautiful mind are my inspiration. I am bound to you in love, for the rest of my life." He pulled forth his half of the dual ring, which sparkled in the sunlight with its bright gold and gems. Placing it on her finger he pressed gently but firmly, turning it slightly until it clicked together with its mate. "As the two halves of the ring are joined together, so Andrion and I are joined together with you."

He stepped back to his place, and his fire-haired beloved turned to face him, a brilliant smile on her face. "Erik, you are my love and the wellspring of my joy in life. Your strength and your gift for happiness are my inspiration. I am bound to you in love, for the rest of my life." This time the ring was turned the other way, so that the yellow gold band was at the bottom, pressed up against Erik's massive hand. She repeated the words she had said to Andrion: "This ring represents the three of us united as one. We each are individuals, but together we make a whole – and a family."

Now came the final and most controversial part of the ceremony they had crafted for themselves. Andrion and Erik turned now to face, not Bernadette or Engbard or the audience, but each other. "Erik," Andrion said firmly. "We are now brothers. We are bound to each other in love, for the rest of our lives, even as we are bound to Bernadette."

Erik smiled into Andrion's eyes. "Andrion," he rumbled, "we are now brothers. We are bound to each other in love, for the rest of our lives, even as we are bound to Bernadette."

They clasped hands firmly – not the right hand, as in the ancient gesture that said "I'm not armed," but with the hands on which they each bore a ring Bernadette had given them. The rings touched, and Bernadette would have liked to imagine that a spark of some supernatural power flowed through the connection. But it was probably just the sun, glinting off the polished gold.

Bernadette returned now to stand between her husbands, facing the priest. "These three are now bound together as one," he told them and the assembled guests. "May they walk side by side throughout their lives, sharing all that those lives may bring. In the sight of gods and men, I declare that you three are now wed."

It was done! Tears of joy were streaming down Bernadette's cheeks now, unnoticed. Her heart felt so full of happiness it might burst. The three of them joined in a fierce group hug, then Erik stepped back and let Andrion get first crack at kissing their bride. Next, Andrion moved aside to let Erik do the same. Tongues were involved, and Bernadette's bliss turned a little pink around the edges.

They shook hands with Engbard and thanked him. A purse of gold would be passed to Frieda when they collected the items they'd left inside. Then they turned around and walked down the aisle a little way – whereupon they were surrounded with smiling faces, wishing them well. Some of these people they hardly knew, others were old friends; though for the most part, because of the logistics, most of the people they truly regarded as close friends had not attended the ceremony. They'd be at the party, though!

Eorl Ormund, once again dressed in splendid clothing and looking very pleased with himself, approached to offer them congratulations. He took Andrion's hand, and Erik's, and then squeezed Bernadette's in a somewhat avuncular fashion. After which he drew himself up, produced a piece of parchment from inside his robe, and said in ringing tones, "I have an announcement to make."

"Inasmuch as Warden Bernadette, known to all in Iscandia as The Fireblood, has provided great service to everyone on Terris by defeating the Soul-Devourer – and with the aid of these two fine men who are now her husbands, I might add – the march of Waterdon owes her a great debt. She and hers have chosen to make my march their permanent home, and I believe that this new family deserves to have a family name. Therefore, I am presenting you with this patent establishing Clan Drakespring in the march of Waterdon's list of

House names. Long may you and your descendants wear it with pride."

Andrion and Erik were as surprised as Bernadette, but all were pleased. The three of them were sundered from the families that gave them birth, and had no great sentimental attachment to their current surnames. This scheme of Ormund's seemed like a wonderful solution. Now all three of them and their children to come would be Drakesprings, not Bouchard-Lamonte-Johannessohns or some such. So much tidier!

Spontaneously, Bernadette jumped up and hugged Ormund around the neck, planting a kiss on his cheek. "Thank you, Eorl Ormund! This is such an honor!" The dignified old man seemed a little flustered, but not entirely displeased.

"I trust you and your husbands, and your children to follow, will bring still more honor on the name of Drakespring," he said, his ears looking pink.

They were milling about in the courtyard, accepting congratulations and thanking people for coming, for the better part of an hour. If you invite the powerful and wealthy to attend your nuptials, it won't do to be rude to them and run off too soon – no matter how eager you are for the next part of the day. Finally they broke away, telling many of those assembled that they'd see them tomorrow at the party. Bergen had been prevailed upon to use his magic map to carry Ormund and his entourage as well as his own – and a small contingent from Castle Grey, including Hjaermond and Selden – to and from Waterdon for the festivities. Fortunately, they were all going to be put up at Wyrmshalla.

Bidding them all farewell, Bernadette and her husbands went back inside the temple to collect the things they'd left behind. Bernadette asked Frieda to keep the flowers for the temple (she never had learned who had provided them, but suspected Odwyna), and gave her a large honorarium for Engbard's services and the use of the courtyard. She sat down and was about to change back into her more sensible shoes, when Erik stopped her with a hand on her arm. "Why don't you leave those on for a little while longer, dear?" he murmured.

"Yes," Andrion chimed in. "We think you might want them in a few minutes."

Still seated, Bernadette put both feet on the floor and sat looking at her men questioningly. What were they up to *now*? Andrion bent closer to kiss her neck. "These, uh, pennants… look like they're intended to come off?" He reached to the attachment for one and removed it, exposing a small amount of cleavage. "Perfect," he said, and in moments had tied the strip of fabric around her head as a blindfold. Bernadette began to get the feeling she was in for a delicious surprise of some sort.

Andrion was holding the map, as there was nowhere Bernadette could carry it about her person dressed as she was. Lifting her to a standing position with an arm beneath her elbow, he and Erik guided her out through the Temple to one of its side doors. When they had reached the street, now bathed in mid-afternoon sunshine, he wished them away from Sylvanian. But not to the Bathing Maiden.

Chapter 80: Home

Bernadette was disoriented and wondering what was going on, out there on the other side of her blindfold. From the cool temperature of the air against her bare arms, she knew that it was night and assumed they had returned to the Waterdon area. Which ought to make it somewhere around 1:30 in the morning. Perhaps that accounted for the lack of any noise. The only sounds she could hear were a few insects chirping, and the occasional call of some night bird.

But instead of stepping up onto the front porch of the Maiden, her men, each of them gently guiding her by an elbow, led her up a slight incline. It felt as if a gravel path were underfoot, definitely *not* good footing for these shoes. But in only a few paces they reached a door, which was opened. She was led into a wood-floored room, and Erik removed her blindfold.

Oh! Where *were* they?! The room was good-sized, and appeared to be a combination kitchen/dining area. The place felt old and new at the same time, as if an ancestral residence had undergone a recent makeover. Despite some outré-looking fixtures over on the far side of the room, it had a warm, homey look to it. A low fire burned on a cooking hearth across the room, lamps were lit (some of them, she was astounded to note, seemed to be those ever-glowing dypalfar lamps!), and the table was set with a fine linen cloth and three place settings.

The suspense was killing her, and Bernadette gave up. She had to know. "Erik? Andrion? Where are we?" Andrion looked into her eyes, his own glowing with love and satisfaction.

"We're home," he told her.

"Home? I thought you said you hadn't been able to find a place…" The wheels were turning, and she felt as if she'd just been smacked by a realization that was so blatantly obvious she couldn't believe she hadn't figured it out before. "Coldburn Farm!"

Erik smiled at her. "Nope," he said. "Not anymore. This is Drakespring Farm." Tumultuous emotions surged through Bernadette. She'd been reconciled to living in the Maiden for months yet to come, was even looking forward to the task, however arduous, of finding land and getting a house built on it. But from what she'd seen of this place from the outside, it was now every bit as big as that dream home she'd envisioned months ago, when she'd first decided that marriage wouldn't be so bad. Love and gratitude toward her men, for preparing this surprise for her, warred with pique that they'd done something this major without letting her consult with them on it.

Well, she reasoned. The location is perfect. I love the view from up here. If Andrion's and Erik's notions of the perfect house don't coincide with mine, we'll just get that builder back here to make changes. She gave them both a happy smile, showing that she loved them for it even if this wasn't necessarily the way she'd have chosen to acquire her home. Then she put on an imperious air, pulling herself up to her current far-beyond-full height, and said "As the matron of Clan Drakespring, I would like to be given the official tour."

The guys grinned back at her like boys with a new toy. They couldn't wait to show her the fruits of their labors. Thinking back on all the times in recent weeks when one or the other one was inexplicably absent from the Maiden, she was sure that they'd done a lot more than just turn their builder loose on the place. Andrion assumed the role of tour guide, leading her first across the room to peer into the small bedroom. Its floor had been refinished and its furnishings upgraded. "Here is a small bedroom, perhaps for a housekeeper... or a nanny?" He wiggled his eyebrows at her, and she laughed.

The kitchen cooking area took her by surprise. As well as the usual roasting spit, the fireplace's firebox had a couple of finned brackets lining the walls on either side. An upper and a lower cooking grate had been installed, so that one could have 3 or 4 pots on the fire at once, and at different heats. The grates could be moved around to suit what you were doing, and the chimney was vented and supplied with a damper so that you could close two steel doors hinged on either side of the fireplace and use the cookfire as an oven.

The kitchen also had a considerable stretch of polished stone counter, with shelves underneath for the storing of pots and pans, dishes, etc. Some shallow drawers were suspended below the counter offering handy storage for cutlery. And the sink! In all her life,

Bernadette had never seen a sink like this one. It was beautiful, resembling dypalfar armor on the half shell. But what was that pipe protruding above it, with a valve mounted at the end of a swiveling arm?

Grinning like a proud papa, Andrion placed a stopper in the drain hole on the bottom of the shallow sink bowl. Then he swiveled the arm toward that side and opened the valve. Clear, cool water came running out, collecting in the bottom of the sink. Then he turned the valve off and reached below the counter to where a pair of buttons sat side by side on a small panel. When he pressed the left one, a little blue light glowed on the wall behind the sink.

Andrion gave it a few moments, then turned the valve on again. Cool water ran out as before, but in a few moments it was coming out hot. Very hot! Not hot enough to cause burns, but hot enough to make you pull your hand away in a hurry. Bernadette's eyes were as round as saucers. As Andrion pressed the right button, shutting down the water heater, she said "Andrion! You did this?"

"I had a lot of help from Diane," he admitted. "Couldn't have done it without her, really."

"By the gods, this is marvelous! I'll never scrub dishes with cold water and sand again!" In another moment Bernadette added, "I suppose this means that thing about Diane building a hot bathing pool at Daywatch was just a made-up excuse, then?"

"Oh, I think she really means to do that," Andrion replied. "But I needed her to help us with this project, or we'd never have gotten it done in time."

Erik opened the door to the annex's long, fairly broad central hallway, lit by oil lamps for warmth and a few dypalfar glow bulbs for safety and reliability. After seeing what Diane had done with the ones she'd brought back from their original expedition, Andrion had been loading up his pack with these endlessly useful objects whenever the opportunity arose. An iron crowbar isn't as delicate as the dypalfar tools Diane used, but it gets the job done.

There were two doors leading off the corridor to their left and three to their right, with a pair of double doors visible at the far end. Bernadette took it in with a certain amount of hesitation. Confronted with such an arrangement while questing, it would inevitably turn out that the first one held shria, the second a few dead bodies, the rest a collection of hostile aptrgangr and the one at the far end a boss aptrgangr plus a chest full of fabulous riches. But in this instance, she had every reason to expect she could skip the nasties and go straight to the treasure. Frankly, this roof over their heads and the two men at her side were all the treasure she could ever want.

Andrion insisted on leading her to first door on the left, immediately. As he opened it, warm steamy air wafted out into the corridor, putting all of Bernadette's senses on alert. Constrained by her shoes, she hurried inside and gasped in amazement at the big, deep, tiled hot pool sitting off to one side of the good-sized room. She bent as gracefully as she could in this outfit to feel the water, finding it a perfect temperature.

She stood up and seized Andrion around the middle, planting a big kiss on him. "Andrion! You did it! Oh, I love you!" He knew that. She was almost tempted to peel down and take a bath right here and now. The tub was easily big enough for the three of them. It had been designed with overflow drains around the outside, so that if multiple bathers displaced too much water it would run back into the system, rather than all over the floor.

Bernadette noticed that a corner of the room was walled off behind a door, and assumed that must be the privy. But when she opened the door for a look at it, she stood dumfounded. It appeared to be a privy stool, all right, but unlike anything she'd ever seen before. Instead of an opening down to a cesspit it had a contained bowl that was partly full of clean water. And what was that tank on the wall above it?

Still bursting with pride and delight at the opportunity to blow his darling's mind, Andrion pulled a piece of scrap paper from his tunic. He'd had his vows notes on that, but it was no longer needed. He ripped a small strip from the edge, wadded it into a ball, and dropped it into the water privy's bowl. Then he reached up and pulled the handle on the tank, releasing its several gallons of water with a whoosh that pushed the paper, and the bowl water in which it was floating, down the pipes and out into the drain system Hegmar had crafted for them.

As soon as Andrion released the pull chain the valve at the bottom of the tank closed. Meanwhile, gravity-fed water from the cistern atop the tower was filling the tank again, until a float valve inside it shut off the supply. This took a couple of minutes, so clearly they couldn't stand here playing with it for the rest of the evening. Andrion explained how the system worked, and Bernadette was deeply impressed at the effort and planning that had gone into it. He and Erik hadn't just added some rooms to an old farm house. They had created what was probably the most high-tech residence in Waterdon, if not in the whole province of Iscandia – dypalfar ruins excepted.

On leaving the bathroom, Bernadette stepping smartly on her heels, they turned to the left and continued down the hall. Bernadette was somewhat surprised to find the large room inside the next door completely empty. It had a series of large windows, currently shuttered, looking out on what would be a view of the cistern tower and the walls of Waterdon to the west. The wooden floors were polished and gleaming, and it had a collection of lamps and dypalfar glow bulbs similar to that in the hallway and bathroom.

Bernadette looked questioningly at Andrion. He in turn glanced at Erik, who said "This is the extra bedroom space for after we have our tenth child." She raised an eyebrow at him. He grinned. "Actually, I thought it would be for whatever we want to do. Enchanting, chemia, sewing, weaving… maybe turn it into a library or a sitting room? I'm assuming you'll want to continue to use the smelter and forge facilities at the Maiden, at least until we can build something here. Not a good idea to have a forge inside a wooden building, I'm thinking…" Bernadette grinned at him. She was pleased, actually, that they had not totally prepared the place for her. She would get her chance at making decisions and designing some of the uses to which the house would be put.

At the far end of the hall, the largest room in the house ran the width of the annex and had windows looking out on 3 sides. It extended slightly wider than the width of the annex, in fact, protruding another 4 feet toward the east to make room for a door giving onto the northern end of the veranda.

"This is the room we actually intended for a nursery," Andrion said. "I'm hoping we'll have at least a couple of kids, and this will give them plenty of indoor space for play." In their world, with panacea potions available from any chemia shop and healing spells widely known, large families like Arngeld's were the exception. People living in towns could count on raising all their babies to adulthood, and unless you needed a pack of farm hands or a bunch of helpers for your business, there was no need to have more than two.

They stepped through the doors onto the veranda. Bernadette had noticed this while walking past, but had not really understood its details or purpose. In the wee hours of the morning in late winter, it was not at its best; but her imagination could easily assure her this would be her second favorite spot in the house – after the bathroom of course. Erik locked the doors behind him, and they continued along the veranda to the next door. Erik opened it. They'd paid extra for a locksmith to produce five exterior locksets all keyed the same, and a bit harder to pick than the usual residential lock.

"This is going to be my personal space and sleeping quarters, in case my snoring gets too bad," Andrion said. He gestured at the wall shared with the nursery, which was lined with simple but nicely crafted built-in bookshelves. "I plan to fill those up with books. I suppose I can't just steal them from din-Tzrek up at the Academy, but I hope I can find my own copies."

There was plenty of space for a double bed and some clothing storage, plus a work table where he might possibly craft designs for new mechanisms. His collaboration with Diane had filled him with the desire to learn more about the dypalfar, and to try to understand their technology. He didn't care about their weaponry, but saw a huge potential for their machines in making everyday life more convenient.

Set in the room's southern wall, there was a door. "That door connects to the master bedroom," Andrion told Bernadette. The three went out through the door to the veranda again, Erik locking it behind them. They skipped the next door and went to the one beyond it. The veranda stopped short before reaching the main house, with a railing preventing anyone walking on it from falling down the stone steps that, on the other side, led down into the basement.

Bernadette peered over the railing. There was some starlight, but the moons were not up and it was pretty dark out here. "Those stairs go down to a lower floor?" She asked. "There's a full stone basement," Andrion explained. "Some of it up at this end is taken up with the water system for the pool, but I suppose you could put a smelter and forge down there if you wanted. Or use some of the space for a root cellar. I suppose we'll have a lot of farm produce to store..."

Bernadette blinked. This place was huge, bigger than her "dream house" of a few months before. And it did have a view of the river... Lifa and Bjorn, and Anja with them, were not going to be resident body servants taking care of the place while she and Andrion and Erik went on adventures, of course. They had their own house, and their own lives to live. But she had the feeling their families would remain close in the years to come.

Meanwhile, Erik had turned the lock and opened the last door. It gave onto another essentially empty room. "And this," he said, gesturing at the empty space with its polished, gleaming floors and a few small lamps providing dim illumination, "is *my* personal space and sleeping quarters in case Andrion's snoring gets too bad yet you still mysteriously want him in our communal bed instead of me. Probably won't get to use it much..."

Andrion favored him with a mock glare, and Bernadette grinned. She *liked* this idea. Each of them would have a room that was theirs alone, to pursue their own interests, and she would not necessarily have to share her own bed with both of them – or either of them – every night for the rest of their lives. She loved them both, more than words could express, but sometimes, she knew, she would want time alone – or with just one of them so she could concentrate all her attention on him.

Once again, the three went out through the veranda door and Erik locked it behind them. Then he turned the key on the door in the middle, which was actually a pair of doors that appeared to have been salvaged from a dypalfar ruin. They were handsome, but a bit out of place on this homely Norse farmhouse. It had been no easy chore getting the locksmith to fit *those* with the same locks used in the wooden doors elsewhere throughout the place.

Bernadette walked in on a vision. Unlike almost every other room in the new section of the house, this one had been furnished completely. It was larger than the flanking rooms by a considerable amount, but made slightly smaller by a bank of built-in closets along the northern wall, running from just past the door that connected this room with Andrion's, all the way to the eastern wall. Each of these had double doors, with a rod inside on which one might hang garments. There were even a few garments hanging in them, on hangers similar to the one on which Senalie had supplied Lifa's wedding dress.

Bernadette guessed that the compartments on either side were intended for Andrion and Erik to store their clothing. The central closet was larger by half and one of the double doors was covered with a floor-to ceiling mirror, similar to the one that she'd used at The Golden Thread. She was nearly speechless. The room was lined with lamps and candles in sconces, but none of the dypalfar glow lamps here. One might prefer darkness for sleeping.

The south wall had three racks for displaying armor, and some wall mounts for holding weapons, in addition to a door leading to Erik's room. On either side of the doors leading out to the veranda, large windows would give a fine view of the river and mountains when the shutters were opened. A decent-sized table stood in a corner, with four chairs around it. But the most amazing thing of all was the bed!

Erik, who'd been enjoying watching her expression as she took in all these delights, grinned at her as she looked at him in surmise. "*You* had something to do with this, didn't you?" she asked accusingly. She walked over to the bed and threw herself into the middle of it, which required a considerable jump. The thing was *huge*.

"Arngeld made it," he confessed, "from my specifications. His wife and daughters made the mattress and wove the bedding. That guy is going places."

"I believe he is," Bernadette agreed, struggling into a sitting position. The new mattress was maybe a little softer and cushier than she was used to, but the fabric of the blanket was soft and she could not *believe* how big it was. All one piece of fabric, amazing!

Bernadette scooted her way across the sea of bedding to the shore, and sat on the end of the bed looking at Erik and Andrion.

Bernadette took a breath, then expelled it. "Wow," she said. "I may have just fallen off the turnip wagon," she added, looking at Andrion, "but all I have to say is 'wow.'" Her face split into a huge grin. "This is the most amazing, fantastic thing I could ever imagine!" she burst out. "I can't believe it! We're married, the eorls of two marches and a representative of the Reman government blessed our marriage, and we get to live *here*!"

Erik and Andrion grinned right back at her. After all their work, they could hardly have hoped for a better reaction. The thought had crossed their minds, separately and together, that their strong-willed Fireblood darling might take exception to their commandeering the project of finding them a home, without bringing her in on the plans.

Bernadette got back onto her feet, not as easy a project as you might think. Reestablishing her balance on those sexy, treacherous shoes, she told her men "I had a little surprise in mind for you two, and I was expecting to have to do it in the confines of the master bedroom at the Maiden. But this is much, much better. Gentlemen, please sit." She gestured toward the huge bed, and they obediently sat down on the end of it, their feet on the floor.

Andrion was not one for singing and regrettably recorded music had not yet been invented in this universe; but Erik had a good ear and an acceptable singing voice ranging from bass to baritone. "Erik, you know the tune to 'Lay of the Fireblood ', I believe?" He nodded. "Could you please just sing it without the words – 'dum de dah dum dum dah dum de dah dum' and so forth?" Erik broke into the opening bars, as requested. "Perfect!" Bernadette said, her eyes wide with excitement. "Continue, if you will."

Aside from wanting a dress that was unique and colorful, Bernadette had planned this dress with a purpose; and that purpose was upon them. She started by reaching up to unpin her auburn locks, letting them fall down around her shoulders. As Erik continued to provide musical accompaniment, she went into a sinuous dance. Dancing in those heels was a bit of a trick, but she was quite sober and her excitement had erased any tiredness she might be feeling. Every couple of bars she plucked another of the tongues of vibrantly-colored fabric from the curious concoction that was her wedding gown, twirled it around in the air to catch the lamplight, then flung it to the side.

Andrion and Erik watched in fascination. Erik thought it was fortunate that he was not required to remember the words, just repeating the song's melodic line over and over in nonsense syllables as the woman who had drawn him like a moth to the flame since they had first met whirled before them, gradually becoming more and more... and more, naked.

Sure, they had both seen her completely unclothed times beyond number. Not that either of them had grown tired of the sight; far from it. But the exotic nature of Berni's dance, the visual dazzlement as a tiny strip of her beautiful flesh was revealed bit by bit with a flourish of vivid color each time, seemed a hundred times more exciting than simple nudity.

They glanced at each other briefly at one point, these now-official brothers, and began pulling off some of their formal clothing as Erik continued to sing his "dum de dah dums" and Berni continued to move gracefully about the room in those astonishing shoes, gradually peeling away layers. By the time she had stripped to a couple of strategically-placed tongues of brightly colored fabric, they were sitting there on the bed in their underdrawers, their fine clothing tossed aside without a second thought. Each set of drawers sported a "tent pole."

Bernadette, her eyes bright, was getting as excited looking at them sitting there as they were getting, looking at her. This was it, the culmination of her dreams, but with a huge and unexpected bonus. They had their private home at last. She glanced over to a chest of drawers standing against the wall on the south side of the bed. Still wearing her two bare snippets of fabric she stood on one leg and, lifting the other in a balletic gesture, removed one shoe. She flung the shoe to Erik and he caught it, not missing a beat.

Dancing with one shoe on and one off wasn't going to work, so the very next thing Bernadette took off was the other shoe. She threw it to Andrion. Now she was standing barefoot on the nice carpet they'd bought for the room, dancing a little more slowly as Erik began to wind down, his anticipation of the finale beginning to distract him from his task.

Spinning, Bernadette removed the last bit of cloth that covered her nipples, and her generous breasts fell free, bouncing in a way sure to draw the gaze of Erik and Andrion. Erik almost ground to a halt, forgetting to continue the "music." The last piece of cloth, having nothing to attach to but itself, was not held on very well. It was soon to go.

Now Bernadette stood nude before them, clad in nothing but the amulet she had worn since she was a girl of fifteen. The amulet neither of them had ever seen her without. She looked them in the eyes, her own full of promise, and walked to the chest of drawers. Then carefully, reverently, she removed the amulet.

The End

(For Now…)

www.ingramcontent.com/pod-product-compliance
Lightning Source LLC
Chambersburg PA
CBHW071332020726
47502CB00001B/74